# BRIDGERTON

## THE DUKE AND I

AND

## THE VISCOUNT WHO LOVED ME

By Julia Quinn

THE BRIDGERTON PREQUELS

*Because of Miss Bridgerton*
*The Girl with the Make-Believe Husband*
*The Other Miss Bridgerton*
*First Comes Scandal*

THE BRIDGERTON SERIES

*The Duke and I*
*The Viscount Who Loved Me*
*An Offer from a Gentleman*
*Romancing Mister Bridgerton*
*To Sir Phillip, With Love*
*When He Was Wicked*
*It's in His Kiss*
*On the Way to the Wedding*
*The Bridgertons: Happily Ever After*

ANTHOLOGIES

*The Further Observations of Lady Whistledown*
*Lady Whistledown Strikes Back*

THE SMYTHE-SMITH QUARTET

*Just Like Heaven*
*A Night Like This*
*The Sum of All Kisses*
*The Secrets of Sir Richard Kenworthy*

## The Bevelstoke Series

*The Secret Diaries of Miss Miranda Cheever*
*What Happens in London*
*Ten Things I Love About You*

## The Two Dukes of Wyndham

*The Lost Duke of Wyndham*
*Mr. Cavendish, I Presume*

## Agents of the Crown

*To Catch an Heiress*
*How to Marry a Marquis*

## The Lyndon Sisters

*Everything and the Moon*
*Brighter Than the Sun*

## The Splendid Trilogy

*Splendid*
*Dancing at Midnight*
*Minx*

# BRIDGERTON

## THE DUKE AND I

AND

## THE VISCOUNT WHO LOVED ME

JULIA QUINN

AVON
*An Imprint of* Harper Collins*Publishers*

"The Duke and I: The 2nd Epilogue" was originally published in *The Bridgertons: Happily Ever After* in April 2013.



"The Viscount Who Loved Me: The 2nd Epilogue" was originally published as an ebook.



Originally published separately as *The Duke and I* and *The Viscount Who Loved Me* in the United States by Avon Books in 2000.

*Bridgerton Family Tree designed by Emily Cotler, Waxcreative Design*

Library of Congress Cataloging-in-Publication Data has been applied for.

ISBN 978-0-06-338360-9

2 SKY 24

# Table of Contents

# *Bridgerton* FAMILY TREE

## Violet Ledger *m.* EDMUND
1766- | 1764-1803

**ANTHONY**
1784-
*The Viscount Who Loved Me*
BOOK 2
*featuring*
Kate Sheffield
1793-

**BENEDICT**
1786-
*An Offer From a Gentleman*
BOOK 3
*featuring*
Sophie Beckett
1794-

**COLIN**
1791-
*Romancing Mister Bridgerton*
BOOK 4
*featuring*
Penelope Featherington
1796-

**DAPHNE**
1792-
*The Duke and I*
BOOK 1
*featuring*
Simon Basset
*Duke of Hastings*
1784-

**ELOISE**
1796-
*To Sir Phillip, With Love*
BOOK 5
*featuring*
Sir Phillip Crane
1794-

**FRANCESCA**
1797-
*When He Was Wicked*
BOOK 6
*featuring*
Michael Stirling
*9th Earl of Kilmartin*
1791-

**GREGORY**
1801-
*On the Way to the Wedding*
BOOK 8
*featuring*
Lucy Abernathy
1807-

**HYACINTH**
1803-
*It's in His Kiss*
BOOK 7
*featuring*
Gareth St. Clair
1797-

FOR MORE INFORMATION
PLEASE VISIT JULIAQUINN.COM

# BRIDGERTON

## THE DUKE & I

*For Danelle Harmon and Sabrina Jeffries,*
*without whom I never would have*
*turned this book in on time.*

*And for Martha*
*of* The Romance Journal *electronic bulletin board,*
*for suggesting I call it* Daphne's Bad Heir Day.

*And also for Paul,*
*even though his idea of dancing*
*is standing still while*
*he holds my hand and watches me twirl.*

# Prologue

The birth of Simon Arthur Henry Fitzranulph Basset, Earl Clyvedon, was met with great celebration. Church bells rang for hours, champagne flowed freely through the gargantuan castle that the newborn would call home, and the entire village of Clyvedon quit work to partake of the feast and holiday ordered by the young earl's father.

"This," the baker said to the blacksmith, "is no ordinary baby."

For Simon Arthur Henry Fitzranulph Basset would not spend his life as Earl Clyvedon. That was a mere courtesy title. Simon Arthur Henry Fitzranulph Basset—the baby who possessed more names than any baby could possibly need—was the heir to one of England's oldest and richest dukedoms. And his father, the ninth Duke of Hastings, had waited years for this moment.

As he stood in the hall outside his wife's confinement room, cradling the squalling infant, the duke's heart near burst with pride. Already several years past forty, he had watched his cronies—dukes and earls, all—beget heir after heir. Some had had to suffer through a few daughters before siring a precious son, but in the end, they'd all been assured that their lines would continue, that their blood would pass forward into the next generation of England's elite.

But not the Duke of Hastings. Though his wife had managed to conceive five times in the fifteen years of their marriage, only twice had she carried to full term, and both of those infants had been stillborn. After the fifth pregnancy, which had ended with a bloody miscarriage in the fifth month, surgeons and physicians alike had warned their graces that they absolutely must not make another attempt to have a child. The duchess's very life was in danger. She was too frail, too weak, and perhaps, they said gently, too old. The duke was simply going to have to reconcile himself to the fact that the dukedom would pass out of the Basset family.

But the duchess, God bless her, knew her role in life, and after a six-month recuperative period, she opened the connecting door between their bedrooms, and the duke once again commenced his quest for a son.

Five months later, the duchess informed the duke that she had conceived. The duke's immediate elation was tempered by his grim determination that nothing—absolutely nothing—would cause this pregnancy to go awry. The duchess was confined to her bed the minute it was realized that she'd missed her monthly courses. A physician was brought in to visit her every day, and halfway through the pregnancy, the duke located the most respected doctor in London and paid him a king's ransom to abandon his practice and take up residence at Clyvedon Castle temporarily.

The duke was taking no chances this time. He *would* have a son, and the dukedom *would* remain in Basset hands.

The duchess experienced pains a month early, and pillows were tucked under her hips. Gravity might keep the babe inside, Dr. Stubbs explained. The duke thought that a sound argument, and, once the doctor had retired for the evening, placed yet another pillow under his wife, raising her to a twenty-degree angle. She remained that way for a month.

And then finally, the moment of truth arrived. The household prayed for the duke, who so wanted an heir, and a few remembered to pray for the duchess, who had grown thin and frail even as her belly had grown round and wide. They tried not to be too hopeful—after all, the duchess had already delivered and buried two babes. And even if she did manage to safely deliver a child, it could be, well, a girl.

As the duchess's screams grew louder and more frequent, the duke shoved his way into her chamber, ignoring the protests of the doctor, the midwife, and her grace's maid. It was a bloody mess, but the duke was determined to be present when the babe's sex was revealed.

The head appeared, then the shoulders. All leaned forward to watch as the duchess strained and pushed, and then . . .

And then the duke knew that there was a God, and He still smiled on the Bassets. He allowed the midwife one minute to clean the babe, then took the little boy into his arms and marched into the great hall to show him off.

"I have a son!" he boomed. "A perfect little son!"

And while the servants cheered and wept with relief, the duke looked down upon the tiny little earl, and said, "You are perfect. You are a Basset. You are mine."

The duke wanted to take the boy outside to prove to everyone that he had finally sired a healthy male child, but there was a slight chill in the early April air, so he allowed the midwife to take the babe back to his mother. The duke mounted one of his prized geldings and rode off to celebrate, shouting his good fortune to all who would listen.

Meanwhile, the duchess, who had been bleeding steadily since the birth, slipped into unconsciousness, and then finally just slipped away.

The duke mourned his wife. He truly did. He hadn't loved her, of course, and she hadn't loved him, but they'd been friends in an oddly distant sort of way. The duke hadn't expected anything more from marriage than a son and an heir, and in that regard, his wife had proven herself an exemplary spouse. He arranged for fresh flowers to be laid at the base of her funereal monument every week, no matter the season, and her portrait was moved from the sitting room to the hall, in a position of great honor over the staircase.

And then the duke got on with the business of raising his son.

There wasn't much he could do in the first year, of course. The babe was too young for lectures on land management and responsibility, so the duke left Simon in the care of his nurse and went to London, where his life continued much as it had before he'd been blessed by parenthood, except that he forced everyone—even the king—to gaze upon the miniature he'd had painted of his son shortly after his birth.

The duke visited Clyvedon from time to time, then returned for good on Simon's second birthday, ready to take the young lad's education in hand. A pony had been purchased, a small gun had been selected for future use at the fox hunt, and tutors were engaged in every subject known to man.

"He's too young for all that!" Nurse Hopkins exclaimed.

"Nonsense," Hastings replied condescendingly. "Clearly, I don't expect him to master any of this anytime soon, but it is never too early to begin a duke's education."

"He's not a duke," Nurse muttered.

"He will be." Hastings turned his back on her and crouched beside his son, who was building an asymmetrical castle with a set of blocks on the floor. The duke hadn't been down to Clyvedon in several months, and was pleased with Simon's growth. He was a sturdy, healthy young boy, with glossy brown hair and clear blue eyes.

"What are you building there, son?"

Simon smiled and pointed.

Hastings looked up at Nurse Hopkins. "Doesn't he speak?"

She shook her head. "Not yet, your grace."

The duke frowned. "He's two. Shouldn't he be speaking?"

"Some children take longer than others, your grace. He's clearly a bright young boy."

"Of course he's bright. He's a Basset."

Nurse nodded. She always nodded when the duke talked about the superiority of the Basset blood. "Maybe," she suggested, "he just doesn't have anything he wants to say."

The duke didn't look convinced, but he handed Simon a toy soldier, patted him on the head, and left the house to go exercise the new mare he'd purchased from Lord Worth.

Two years later, however, he wasn't so sanguine.

"*Why isn't he talking?*" he boomed.

"I don't know," Nurse answered, wringing her hands.

"What have you done to him?"

"I haven't done anything!"

"If you'd been doing your job correctly, *he*"—the duke jabbed an angry finger in Simon's direction—"would be speaking."

Simon, who was practicing his letters at his miniature desk, watched the exchange with interest.

"He's four years old, God damn it," the duke roared. "He should be able to speak."

"He can write," Nurse said quickly. "Five children I've raised, and not a one of them took to letters the way Master Simon has."

"A fat lot of good writing is going to do him if he can't talk." Hastings turned to Simon, rage burning in his eyes. "Talk to me, damn you!"

Simon shrank back, his lower lip quivering.

"Your grace!" Nurse exclaimed. "You're scaring the child."

Hastings whipped around to face her. "Maybe he needs scaring. Maybe what he needs is a good dose of discipline. A good paddling might help him find his voice."

The duke grabbed the silver-backed brush Nurse used on Simon's hair and advanced on his son. "I'll make you talk, you stupid little—"

"*No!*"

Nurse gasped. The duke dropped the brush. It was the first time they'd ever heard Simon's voice.

"What did you say?" the duke whispered, tears forming in his eyes.

Simon's fists balled at his sides, and his little chin jutted out as he said, "Don't you h-h-h-h-h-h-h—"

The duke's face turned deathly pale. "What is he saying?"

Simon attempted the sentence again. "D-d-d-d-d-d-d—"

"My God," the duke breathed, horrified. "He's a moron."

"He's not a moron!" Nurse cried out, throwing her arms around the boy.

"D-d-d-d-d-d-don't you h-h-h-h-h-h-hit"—Simon took a deep breath—"*me*."

Hastings sank onto the window seat, his head dropping into his hands. "What have I done to deserve this? What could I have possibly done . . ."

"You should be giving the boy praise!" Nurse Hopkins admonished. "Four years you've been waiting for him to speak, and—"

"And he's an idiot!" Hastings roared. "A goddamned, bloody little idiot!"

Simon began to cry.

"Hastings is going to go to a half-wit," the duke moaned. "All those years of praying for an heir, and now it's all for ruin. I should have let the title go to my cousin." He turned back to his son, who was sniffling and wiping his eyes, trying to appear strong for his father. "I can't even look at him," he gasped. "I can't even bear to look at him."

And with that, the duke stalked out of the room.

Nurse Hopkins hugged the boy close. "You're not an idiot," she whispered fiercely. "You're the smartest little boy I know. And if anyone can learn to talk properly, I know it's you."

Simon turned into her warm embrace and sobbed.

"We'll show him," Nurse vowed. "He'll eat his words if it's the last thing I do."

Nurse Hopkins proved true to her word. While the Duke of Hastings removed himself to London and tried to pretend he had no son, she spent every waking minute with Simon, sounding out words and syllables, praising him lavishly when he got something right, and giving him encouraging words when he didn't.

The progress was slow, but Simon's speech did improve. By the time he was six, "d-d-d-d-d-d-don't" had turned into "d-d-don't," and by the time he was eight, he was managing entire sentences without faltering. He still ran into trouble when he was upset, and Nurse had to remind him often that he needed to remain calm and collected if he wanted to get the words out in one piece.

But Simon was determined, and Simon was smart, and perhaps most importantly, he was damned stubborn. He learned to take breaths before each sentence, and to think about his words before he attempted to say them. He studied the feel of his mouth when he spoke correctly, and tried to analyze what went wrong when he didn't.

And finally, at the age of eleven, he turned to Nurse Hopkins, paused to collect his thoughts, and said, "I think it is time we went to see my father."

Nurse looked up sharply. The duke had not laid eyes on the boy in seven years. And he had not answered a single one of the letters Simon had sent him.

Simon had sent nearly a hundred.

"Are you certain?" she asked.

Simon nodded.

"Very well, then. I'll order the carriage. We'll leave for London on the morrow."

The trip took a day and a half, and it was late afternoon by the time their carriage rolled up to Basset House. Simon gazed at the busy London streetscape with wonder as Nurse Hopkins led him up the steps. Neither had ever visited Basset House before, and so Nurse didn't know what to do when she reached the front door other than knock.

The door swung open within seconds, and they found themselves being looked down upon by a rather imposing butler.

"Deliveries," he intoned, reaching to close the door, "are made in the rear."

"Hold there!" Nurse said quickly, jamming her foot in the door. "We are not servants."

The butler looked disdainfully at her garments.

"Well, I am, but he's not." She grabbed Simon's arm and yanked him forward. "This is Earl Clyvedon, and you'd do well to treat him with respect."

The butler's mouth actually dropped open, and he blinked several times before saying, "It is my understanding that Earl Clyvedon is dead."

"What?" Nurse screeched.

"I most certainly am not!" Simon exclaimed, with all the righteous indignation of an eleven-year-old.

The butler examined Simon, recognized immediately that he had the look of the Bassets, and ushered them in.

"Why did you think I was d-dead?" Simon asked, cursing himself for misspeaking, but not surprised. He was always most likely to stutter when he was angry.

"It is not for me to say," the butler replied.

"It most certainly is," Nurse shot back. "You can't say something like that to a boy of his years and not explain it."

The butler was silent for a moment, then finally said, "His grace has not mentioned you in years. The last I heard, he said he had no son. He looked quite pained as he said it, so no one pursued the conversation. We—the servants, that is—assumed you'd passed on."

Simon felt his jaw clench, felt his throat working wildly.

"Wouldn't he have gone into mourning?" Nurse demanded. "Did you think about that? How could you have assumed the boy was dead if his father was not in mourning?"

The butler shrugged. "His grace frequently wears black. Mourning wouldn't have altered his costume."

"This is an outrage," Nurse Hopkins said. "I demand you summon his grace at once."

Simon said nothing. He was trying too hard to get his emotions under control. He had to. There was no way he'd be able to talk with his father while his blood was racing so.

The butler nodded. "He is upstairs. I'll alert him immediately to your arrival."

Nurse started pacing wildly, muttering under her breath and referring to his grace with every vile word in her surprisingly extensive vocabulary. Simon remained in the center of the room, his arms angry sticks at his sides as he took deep breaths.

*You can do this*, he shouted in his mind. *You can do this.*

Nurse turned to him, saw him trying to control his temper, and immediately gasped. "Yes, that's it," she said quickly, dropping to her knees and taking his hands in hers. She knew better than anyone what would happen if Simon tried to face his father before he calmed down. "Take deep breaths. And make sure to think about your words before you speak. If you can control—"

"I see you're still mollycoddling the boy," came an imperious voice from the doorway.

Nurse Hopkins straightened and turned slowly around. She tried to think of something respectful to say. She tried to think of anything that would smooth over this awful situation. But when she looked at the duke, she saw Simon in him, and her rage began anew. The duke might look just like his son, but he was certainly no father to him.

"You, sir," she spat out, "are despicable."

"And you, madam, are fired."

Nurse lurched back.

"No one speaks to the Duke of Hastings that way," he roared. "No one!"

"Not even the king?" Simon taunted.

Hastings whirled around, not even noticing that his son had spoken clearly. "You," he said in a low voice.

Simon nodded curtly. He'd managed one sentence properly, but it had been a short one, and he didn't want to push his luck. Not when he was this upset. Normally, he could go days without a stutter, but now . . .

The way his father stared at him made him feel like an infant. An idiot infant.

And his tongue suddenly felt awkward and thick.

The duke smiled cruelly. "What do you have to say for yourself, boy? Eh? What do you have to *say*?"

"It's all right, Simon," Nurse Hopkins whispered, throwing a furious glance at the duke. "Don't let him upset you. You can do it, sweetling."

And somehow her encouraging tone made it all the worse. Simon had come here to prove himself to his father, and now his nurse was treating him like a baby.

"What's the matter?" the duke taunted. "Cat got your tongue?"

Simon's muscles clenched so hard he started to shake.

Father and son stared at each other for what felt like an eternity, until finally the duke swore and stalked toward the door. "You are my worst failure," he hissed at his son. "I don't know what I did to deserve you, but God help me if I ever lay eyes on you again."

"Your grace!" Nurse Hopkins said indignantly. This was no way to speak to a child.

"Get him out of my sight," he spat at her. "You can keep your job just so long as you keep him away from me."

"Wait!"

The duke turned slowly around at the sound of Simon's voice. "Did you say something?" he drawled.

Simon took three long breaths in through his nose, his mouth still clamped together in anger. He forced his jaw to relax and rubbed his tongue against the roof of his mouth, trying to remind himself of how it felt to speak properly. Finally, just as the duke was about to dismiss him again, he opened his mouth and said, "I am your son."

Simon heard Nurse Hopkins breathe a sigh of relief, and something he'd never seen before blossomed in his father's eyes. Pride. Not much of it, but there was something there, lurking in the depths; something that gave Simon a whisper of hope.

"I am your son," he said again, this time a little louder, "and I am not d—"

Suddenly his throat closed up. And Simon panicked.

*You can do this. You can do this.*

But his throat felt tight, and his tongue felt thick, and his father's eyes started to narrow . . .

"I am not d-d-d—"

"Go home," the duke said in a low voice. "There is no place for you here."

Simon felt the duke's rejection in his very bones, felt a peculiar kind of pain enter his body and creep around his heart. And, as hatred flooded his body and poured from his eyes, he made a solemn vow.

If he couldn't be the son his father wanted, then by God, he'd be the *exact opposite* . . .

# Chapter 1

*The Bridgertons are by far the most prolific family in the upper echelons of society. Such industriousness on the part of the viscountess and the late viscount is commendable, although one can find only banality in their choice of names for their children. Anthony, Benedict, Colin, Daphne, Eloise, Francesca, Gregory, and Hyacinth—orderliness is, of course, beneficial in all things, but one would think that intelligent parents would be able to keep their children straight without needing to alphabetize their names.*

*Furthermore, the sight of the viscountess and all eight of her children in one room is enough to make one fear one is seeing double—or triple—or worse. Never has This Author seen a collection of siblings so ludicrously alike in their physical regard. Although This Author has never taken the time to record eye color, all eight possess similar bone structure and the same thick, chestnut hair. One must pity the viscountess as she seeks advantageous marriages for her brood that she did not produce a single child of more fashionable coloring. Still, there are advantages to a family of such consistent looks—there can be no doubt that all eight are of legitimate parentage.*

*Ah, Gentle Reader, your devoted Author wishes that that were the case amid all large families . . .*

LADY WHISTLEDOWN'S SOCIETY PAPERS,
26 APRIL 1813

"Ooooooooohhhhhhhhh!" Violet Bridgerton crumpled the single-page newspaper into a ball and hurled it across the elegant drawing room.

Her daughter Daphne wisely made no comment and pretended to be engrossed in her embroidery.

"Did you read what she said?" Violet demanded. "Did you?"

Daphne eyed the ball of paper, which now rested under a mahogany end table. "I didn't have the opportunity before you, er, finished with it."

"Read it, then," Violet wailed, her arm slicing dramatically through the air. "Read how *that woman* has maligned us."

Daphne calmly set down her embroidery and reached under the end table. She smoothed the sheet of paper out on her lap and read the paragraph about her family. Blinking, she looked up. "This isn't so bad, Mother. In fact, it's a veritable benediction compared to what she wrote about the Featheringtons last week."

"How am I supposed to find you a husband while *that woman* is slandering your name?"

Daphne forced herself to exhale. After nearly two seasons in London, the mere mention of the word *husband* was enough to set her temples pounding. She wanted to marry, truly she did, and she wasn't even holding out for a true love match. But was it really too much to hope for a husband for whom one had at least some affection?

Thus far, four men had asked for her hand, but when Daphne had thought about living the rest of her days in the company of any of them, she just couldn't do it. There were a number of men she thought might make reasonably good husbands, but the problem was—none of them was interested. Oh, they all *liked* her. Everyone liked her. Everyone thought she was funny and kind and a quick wit, and no one thought her the least bit unattractive, but at the same time, no one was dazzled by her beauty, stunned into speechlessness by her presence, or moved to write poetry in her honor.

Men, she thought with disgust, were interested only in those women who terrified them. No one seemed inclined to court someone like her. They all adored her, or so they said, because she was so easy to talk to, and she always seemed to understand how a man felt. As one of the men Daphne had thought might make a reasonably good husband had said, "Deuce take it, Daff, you're just not like regular females. You're positively normal."

Which she might have managed to consider a compliment if he hadn't proceeded to wander off in search of the latest blond beauty.

Daphne looked down and noticed that her hand was clenched into a fist. Then she looked up and realized her mother was staring at her, clearly waiting for her to say something. Since she had already exhaled, Daphne cleared her throat, and said, "I'm sure Lady Whistledown's little column is not going to hurt my chances for a husband."

"Daphne, it's been two years!"

"And Lady Whistledown has only been publishing for three months, so I hardly see how we can lay the blame at her door."

"I'll lay the blame wherever I choose," Violet muttered.

Daphne's fingernails bit her palms as she willed herself not to make a retort. She knew her mother had only her best interests at heart, she knew her mother loved her. And she loved her mother, too. In fact, until Daphne had reached marriageable age, Violet had been positively the best of mothers. She still was, when she wasn't despairing over the fact that after Daphne she had three more daughters to marry off.

Violet pressed a delicate hand to her chest. "She cast aspersions on your parentage."

"No," Daphne said slowly. It was always wise to proceed with caution when contradicting her mother. "Actually, what she said was that there could be no doubt that we are all legitimate. Which is more than one can say for most large families of the *ton*."

"She shouldn't have even brought it up," Violet sniffed.

"Mother, she's the author of a scandal sheet. It's her job to bring such things up."

"She isn't even a real person," Violet added angrily. She planted her hands on her slim hips, then changed her mind and shook her finger in the air. "Whistledown, ha! I've never heard of any Whistledowns. Whoever this depraved woman is, I doubt she's one of *us*. As if anyone of breeding would write such wicked lies."

"Of course she's one of us," Daphne said, her brown eyes filling with amusement. "If she weren't a member of the *ton*, there is no way she'd be privy to the sort of news she reports. Did you think she was some sort of impostor, peeking in windows and listening at doors?"

"I don't like your tone, Daphne Bridgerton," Violet said, her eyes narrowing.

Daphne bit back another smile. "I don't like your tone" was Violet's standard answer when one of her children was winning an argument.

But it was too much fun to tease her mother. "I wouldn't be surprised," she said, cocking her head to the side, "if Lady Whistledown was one of your friends."

"Bite your tongue, Daphne. No friend of mine would ever stoop so low."

"Very well," Daphne allowed, "it's probably not one of your friends. But I'm certain it's someone we know. No interloper could ever obtain the information she reports."

Violet crossed her arms. "I should like to put her out of business once and for all."

"If you wish to put her out of business," Daphne could not resist pointing out, "you shouldn't support her by buying her newspaper."

"And what good would that do?" Violet demanded. "Everyone else is reading it. My puny little embargo would do nothing except make me look ignorant when everyone else is chuckling over her latest gossip."

That much was true, Daphne silently agreed. Fashionable London was positively addicted to *Lady Whistledown's Society Papers*. The mysterious newspaper had arrived on the doorstep of every member of the *ton* three months earlier. For two weeks it was delivered unbidden every Monday, Wednesday, and Friday. And then, on the third Monday, butlers across London waited in vain for the pack of paperboys who normally delivered *Whistledown*, only to discover that instead of free delivery, they were selling the gossip sheet for the outrageous price of five pennies a paper.

Daphne had to admire the fictitious Lady Whistledown's savvy. By the time she started forcing people to pay for their gossip, all the *ton* was addicted. Everyone forked over their pennies, and somewhere some meddlesome woman was getting very rich.

While Violet paced the room and huffed about this "hideous slight" against her family, Daphne looked up to make certain her mother wasn't paying her any attention, then let her eyes drop to peruse the rest of the scandal sheet. *Whistledown*—as it was now called—was a curious mix of commentary, social news, scathing insult, and the occasional compliment. What set it apart from any previous society news sheets was that the author actually listed her subjects' names in full. There was no hiding behind abbreviations such as Lord S—— and Lady G——. If Lady Whistledown wanted to write about someone, she used his full name. The *ton* declared themselves scandalized, but they were secretly fascinated.

This most recent edition was typical *Whistledown.* Aside from the short piece on the Bridgertons—which was really no more than a description of the family—Lady Whistledown had recounted the events at the previous night's ball. Daphne hadn't attended, as it had been her younger sister's birthday, and the Bridgertons always made a big fuss about birthdays. And with eight children, there were a lot of birthdays to celebrate.

"You're reading that rubbish," Violet accused.

Daphne looked up, refusing to feel the least bit guilty. "It's a rather good column today. Apparently Cecil Tumbley knocked over an entire tower of champagne glasses last night."

"Really?" Violet asked, trying not to look interested.

"Mmm-hmm," Daphne replied. "She gives quite a good account of the Middlethorpe ball. Mentions who was talking to whom, what everyone was wearing—"

"And I suppose she felt the need to offer her opinions on that point," Violet cut in.

Daphne smiled wickedly. "Oh, come now, Mother. You know that Mrs. Featherington has always looked dreadful in purple."

Violet tried not to smile. Daphne could see the corners of her mouth twitching as she tried to maintain the composure she deemed appropriate for a viscountess and mother. But within two seconds, she was grinning and sitting next to her daughter on the sofa. "Let me see that," she said, snatching up the paper. "What else happened? Did we miss anything important?"

Daphne said, "Really, Mother, with Lady Whistledown as a reporter, one needn't actually *attend* any events." She waved toward the paper. "This is almost as good as actually being there. Better, probably. I'm certain we had better food last night than they did at the ball. And give that back." She yanked the paper back, leaving a torn corner in Violet's hands.

"Daphne!"

Daphne affected mock righteousness. "I was reading it."

"Well!"

"Listen to this."

Violet leaned in.

Daphne read: " 'The rake formerly known as Earl Clyvedon has finally seen fit to grace London with his presence. Although he has not yet deigned to make an appearance at a respectable evening function, the new Duke of Hastings has been spotted several times at White's and once at Tattersall's.' " She paused to take a breath. " 'His grace has resided abroad for six years. Can it be any coincidence that he has returned only now that the old duke is dead?' "

Daphne looked up. "My goodness, she *is* blunt, isn't she? Isn't Clyvedon one of Anthony's friends?"

"He's Hastings now," Violet said automatically, "and yes, I do believe he and Anthony were friendly at Oxford. And Eton as well, I think." Her brow scrunched and her blue eyes narrowed with thought. "He was something of a hellion, if my memory serves. Always at odds with his father. But reputed to be quite brilliant. I'm fairly sure that Anthony said he took a first in mathematics. Which," she added with a maternal roll of her eyes, "is more than I can say for any of *my* children."

"Now, now, Mother," Daphne teased. "I'm sure I would take a first if Oxford would only see fit to admit women."

Violet snorted. "I corrected your arithmetic papers when your governess was ill, Daphne."

"Well, maybe in history, then," Daphne said with a grin. She looked back down at the paper in her hands, her eyes straying to the new duke's name. "He sounds quite interesting," she murmured.

Violet looked at her sharply. "He's quite unsuitable for a young lady of your years is what he is."

"Funny how my 'years,' as you put it, volley back and forth between being so young that I cannot even meet Anthony's friends and being so old that you despair of my ever contracting a good marriage."

"Daphne Bridgerton, I don't—"

"—like my tone, I know." Daphne grinned. "But you love me."

Violet smiled warmly and wrapped an arm around Daphne's shoulder. "Heaven help me, I do."

Daphne gave her mother a quick peck on the cheek. "It's the curse of motherhood. You're required to love us even when we vex you."

Violet just sighed. "I hope that someday you have children—"

"—just like me, I know." Daphne smiled nostalgically and rested her head on her mother's shoulder. Her mother could be overly inquisitive, and her father had been more interested in hounds and hunting than he'd been in society affairs, but theirs had been a warm marriage, filled with love, laughter, and children. "I could do a great deal worse than follow your example, Mother," she murmured.

"Why, Daphne," Violet said, her eyes growing watery, "what a lovely thing to say."

Daphne twirled a lock of her chestnut hair around her finger, and grinned, letting the sentimental moment melt into a more teasing one. "I'm happy to follow in your footsteps when it comes to marriage and children, Mother, just so long as I don't have to have *eight*."

At that exact moment, Simon Basset, the new Duke of Hastings and the erstwhile topic of the Bridgerton ladies' conversation, was sitting at White's. His companion was none other than Anthony Bridgerton, Daphne's eldest brother. The two cut a striking pair, both tall and athletic, with thick dark hair. But where Anthony's eyes were the same deep chocolate brown as his sister's, Simon's were icy blue, with an oddly penetrating gaze.

It was those eyes as much as anything that had earned him his reputation as a man to be reckoned with. When he stared at a person, clear and unwavering, men grew uncomfortable. Women positively shivered.

But not Anthony. The two men had known each other for years, and Anthony just laughed when Simon raised a brow and turned his icy gaze upon him. "You forget, I've seen you with your head being lowered into a chamber pot," Anthony had once told him. "It's been difficult to take you seriously ever since."

To which Simon had replied, "Yes, but if I recall, you were the one holding me over that fragrant receptacle."

"One of my proudest moments, to be sure. But you had your revenge the next night in the form of a dozen eels in my bed."

Simon allowed himself a smile as he remembered both the incident and their subsequent conversation about it. Anthony was a good friend, just the sort a man would want by his side in a pinch. He'd been the first person Simon had looked up upon returning to England.

"It's damned fine to have you back, Clyvedon," Anthony said, once they'd settled in at their table at White's. "Oh, but I suppose you'll insist I call you Hastings now."

"No," Simon said rather emphatically. "Hastings will always be my father. He never answered to anything else." He paused. "I'll assume his title if I must, but I won't be called by his name."

"If you must?" Anthony's eyes widened slightly. "Most men would not sound quite so resigned about the prospect of a dukedom."

Simon raked a hand through his dark hair. He knew he was supposed to cherish his birthright and display unwavering pride in the Basset family's illustrious history, but the truth was it all made him sick inside. He'd spent his entire life not living up to his father's expectations; it seemed ridiculous now to try to live up to his name. "It's a damned burden is what it is," he finally grumbled.

"You'd best get used to it," Anthony said pragmatically, "because that's what everyone will call you."

Simon knew it was true, but he doubted if the title would ever sit well upon his shoulders.

"Well, whatever the case," Anthony added, respecting his friend's privacy by not delving further into what was obviously an uncomfortable topic, "I'm glad to have you back. I might finally get some peace next time I escort my sister to a ball."

Simon leaned back, crossing his long, muscular legs at the ankles. "An intriguing remark."

Anthony raised a brow. "One that you're certain I'll explain?"

"But of course."

"I ought to let you learn for yourself, but then, I've never been a cruel man."

Simon chuckled. "This coming from the man who dunked my head in a chamber pot?"

Anthony waved his hand dismissively. "I was young."

"And now you're a model of mature decorum and respectability?"

Anthony grinned. "Absolutely."

"So tell me," Simon drawled, "how, exactly, am I meant to make your existence that much more peaceful?"

"I assume you plan to take your place in society?"

"You assume incorrectly."

"But you *are* planning to attend Lady Danbury's ball this week," Anthony said.

"Only because I am inexplicably fond of the old woman. She says what she means, and—" Simon's eyes grew somewhat shuttered.

"And?" Anthony prompted.

Simon gave his head a little shake. "It's nothing. Just that she was rather kind to me as a child. I spent a few school holidays at her house with Riverdale. Her nephew, you know."

Anthony nodded once. "I see. So you have no intention of entering society. I'm impressed by your resolve. But allow me to warn you—even if you do not choose to attend the *ton*'s events, *they* will find you."

Simon, who had chosen that moment to take a sip of his brandy, choked on the spirit at the look on Anthony's face when he said, "they." After a few moments of coughing and sputtering, he finally managed to say, "Who, pray tell, are 'they'?"

Anthony shuddered. "Mothers."

"Not having had one myself, I can't say I grasp your point."

"Society mothers, you dolt. Those fire-breathing dragons with daughters of—God help us—marriageable age. You can run, but you'll never manage to hide from them. And I should warn you, my own is the worst of the lot."

"Good God. And here I thought Africa was dangerous."

Anthony shot his friend a faintly pitying look. "They will hunt you down. And when they find you, you will find yourself trapped in conversation with a pale young lady all dressed in white who cannot converse on topics other than the weather, who received vouchers to Almack's, and hair ribbons."

A look of amusement crossed Simon's features. "I take it, then, that during my time abroad you have become something of an eligible gentleman?"

"Not out of any aspirations to the role on my part, I assure you. If it were up to me, I'd avoid society functions like the plague. But my sister made her bow last year, and I'm forced to escort her from time to time."

"Daphne, you mean?"

Anthony looked up in surprise. "Did the two of you ever meet?"

"No," Simon admitted, "but I remember her letters to you at school, and I recalled that she was fourth in the family, so she had to start with D, and—"

"Ah, yes," Anthony said with a slight roll of his eyes, "the Bridgerton method of naming children. Guaranteed to make certain no one forgets who you are."

Simon laughed. "It worked, didn't it?"

"Say, Simon," Anthony suddenly said, leaning forward, "I've promised my mother I'll have dinner at Bridgerton House later this week with the family. Why don't you join me?"

Simon raised a dark brow. "Didn't you just warn me about society mothers and debutante daughters?"

Anthony laughed. "I'll put my mother on her best behavior, and don't worry about Daff. She's the exception that proves the rule. You'll like her immensely."

Simon narrowed his eyes. Was Anthony playing matchmaker? He couldn't tell.

As if Anthony were reading his thoughts, he laughed. "Good God, you don't think I'm trying to pair you off with Daphne, do you?"

Simon said nothing.

"You would never suit. You're a bit too brooding for her tastes."

Simon thought that an odd comment, but instead chose to ask, "Has she had any offers, then?"

"A few." Anthony kicked back the rest of his brandy, then let out a satisfied exhale. "I've allowed her to refuse them all."

"That's rather indulgent of you."

Anthony shrugged. "Love is probably too much to hope for in a marriage these days, but I don't see why she shouldn't be happy with her husband. We've had offers from one man old enough to be her father, another old enough to be her father's younger brother, one who was rather too high in the instep for our often boisterous clan, and then this week, dear God, that was the worst!"

"What happened?" Simon asked curiously.

Anthony gave his temples a weary rub. "This last one was perfectly amiable, but a rather bit dim in the head. You'd think, after our rakish days, I'd be completely without feelings—"

"Really?" Simon asked with a devilish grin. "You'd think that?"

Anthony scowled at him. "I didn't particularly enjoy breaking this poor fool's heart."

"Er, wasn't Daphne the one to do that?"

"Yes, but I had to *tell* him."

"Not many brothers would allow their sister such latitude with their marriage proposals," Simon said quietly.

Anthony just shrugged again, as if he couldn't imagine treating his sister in any other way. "She's been a good sister to me. It's the least I can do."

"Even if it means escorting her to Almack's?" Simon said wickedly.

Anthony groaned. "Even then."

"I'd console you by pointing out that this will all be over soon, but you've what, three other sisters waiting in the wings?"

Anthony positively slumped in his seat. "Eloise is due out in two years, and Francesca the year after that, but then I've a bit of a reprieve before Hyacinth comes of age."

Simon chuckled. "I don't envy you your responsibilities in that quarter." But even as he said the words, he felt a strange longing, and he wondered what it would be like to be not quite so alone in this world. He had no plans to start a family of his own, but maybe if he'd had one to begin with, his life would have turned out a bit differently.

"So you'll come for supper, then?" Anthony stood. "Informal, of course. We never take meals formally when it's just family."

Simon had a dozen things to do in the next few days, but before he could remind himself that he needed to get his affairs in order, he heard himself saying, "I'd be delighted."

"Excellent. And I'll see you at the Danbury bash first?"

Simon shuddered. "Not if I can help it. My aim is to be in and out in under thirty minutes."

"You really think," Anthony said, raising a doubtful brow, "that you're going to be able to go to the party, pay your respects to Lady Danbury, and leave?"

Simon's nod was forceful and direct.

But Anthony's snort of laughter was not terribly reassuring.

## Chapter 2

*The new Duke of Hastings is a most interesting character. While it is common knowledge that he was not on favorable terms with his father, even This Author is unable to learn the reason for the estrangement.*

*LADY WHISTLEDOWN'S SOCIETY PAPERS,*
26 APRIL 1813

Later that week, Daphne found herself standing on the fringes of Lady Danbury's ballroom, far away from the fashionable crowd. She was quite content with her position.

Normally she would have enjoyed the festivities; she liked a good party as well as the next young lady, but earlier that evening, Anthony had informed her that Nigel Berbrooke had sought him out two days earlier and asked for her hand. Again. Anthony had, of course, refused (again!), but Daphne had the sinking feeling that Nigel was going to prove uncomfortably persistent. After all, two marriage proposals in two weeks did not paint a picture of a man who accepted defeat easily.

Across the ballroom she could see him looking this way and that, and she shrank further into the shadows.

She had no idea how to deal with the poor man. He wasn't very bright, but he also wasn't unkind, and though she knew she had to somehow put an end to his infatuation, she was finding it far easier to take the coward's way out and simply avoid him.

She was considering slinking into the ladies' retiring room when a familiar voice stopped her in her tracks.

"I say, Daphne, what are you doing all the way over here?"

Daphne looked up to see her eldest brother making his way toward her. "Anthony," she said, trying to decide if she was pleased to see him or annoyed that he might be coming over to meddle in her affairs. "I hadn't realized you would be in attendance."

"Mother," he said grimly. No other words were necessary.

"Ah," Daphne said with a sympathetic nod. "Say no more. I understand completely."

"She made a list of potential brides." He shot his sister a beleaguered look. "We do love her, don't we?"

Daphne choked on a laugh. "Yes, Anthony, we do."

"It's temporary insanity," he grumbled. "It has to be. There is no other explanation. She was a perfectly reasonable mother until you reached marriageable age."

"Me?" Daphne squeaked. "Then this is all my fault? You're a full eight years older than I am!"

"Yes, but she wasn't gripped by this matrimonial fervor until you came along."

Daphne snorted. "Forgive me if I lack sympathy. I received a list last year."

"Did you?"

"Of course. And lately she's been threatening to deliver them to me on a weekly basis. She badgers me on the issue of marriage far more than you could ever imagine. After all, bachelors are a challenge. Spinsters are merely pathetic. And in case you hadn't noticed, I'm female."

Anthony let out a low chuckle. "I'm your brother. I don't notice those things." He gave her a sly, sideways look. "Did you bring it?"

"My list? Heavens, no. What can you be thinking?"

His smile widened. "I brought mine."

Daphne gasped. "You didn't!"

"I did. Just to torture Mother. I'm going to peruse it right in front of her, pull out my quizzing glass—"

"You don't have a quizzing glass."

He grinned—the slow, devastatingly wicked smile that all Bridgerton males seemed to possess. "I bought one just for this occasion."

"Anthony, you absolutely cannot. She will *kill* you. And then, somehow, she'll find a way to blame *me*."

"I'm counting on it."

Daphne swatted him in the shoulder, eliciting a loud enough grunt to cause a half dozen partygoers to send curious looks in their direction.

"A solid punch," Anthony said, rubbing his arm.

"A girl can't live long with four brothers without learning how to throw one." She crossed her arms. "Let me see your list."

"After you just assaulted me?"

Daphne rolled her brown eyes and cocked her head in a decidedly impatient gesture.

"Oh, very well." He reached into his waistcoat, pulled out a folded slip of paper, and handed it to her. "Tell me what you think. I'm sure you'll have no end of cutting remarks."

Daphne unfolded the paper and stared down at her mother's neat, elegant handwriting. The Viscountess Bridgerton had listed the names of eight women. Eight very eligible, very wealthy young women.

"Precisely what I expected," Daphne murmured.

"Is it as dreadful as I think?"

"Worse. Philipa Featherington is as dumb as a post."

"And the rest of them?"

Daphne looked up at him under raised brows. "You didn't really want to get married this year, anyway, did you?"

Anthony winced. "And how was your list?"

"Blessedly out-of-date, now. Three of the five married last season. Mother is still berating me for letting them slip through my fingers."

The two Bridgertons let out identical sighs as they slumped against the wall. Violet Bridgerton was undeterred in her mission to marry off her children. Anthony, her eldest son, and Daphne, her eldest daughter, had borne the brunt of the pressure, although Daphne suspected that the viscountess might have cheerfully married off ten-year-old Hyacinth if she'd received a suitable offer.

"Good God, you look a pair of sad sorts. What are you doing so far off in the corner?"

Another instantly recognizable voice. "Benedict," Daphne said, glancing sideways at him without moving her head. "Don't tell me Mother managed to get you to attend tonight's festivities."

He nodded grimly. "She has completely bypassed cajoling and moved on to guilt. Three times this week she has reminded me I may have to provide the next viscount, if Anthony here doesn't get busy."

Anthony groaned.

"I assume that explains your flight as well to the darkest corners of the ballroom?" Benedict continued. "Avoiding Mother?"

"Actually," Anthony replied, "I saw Daff skulking in the corner and—"

"Skulking?" Benedict said with mock horror.

She shot them both an irritated scowl. "I came over to hide from Nigel Berbrooke," she explained. "I left Mother in the company of Lady Jersey, so she's not likely to pester me anytime soon, but Nigel—"

"Is more monkey than man," Benedict quipped.

"Well, I wouldn't have put it *that* way precisely," Daphne said, trying to be kind, "but he isn't terribly bright, and it's so much easier to stay out of his way than to hurt his feelings. Of course now that you lot have found me, I shan't be able to avoid him for long."

Anthony voiced a simple, "Oh?"

Daphne looked at her two older brothers, both an inch above six feet with broad shoulders and melting brown eyes. They each sported thick chestnut hair—much the same color as her own—and more to the point, they could not go anywhere in polite society without a small gaggle of twittering young ladies following them about.

And where a gaggle of twittering young ladies went, Nigel Berbrooke was sure to follow.

Already Daphne could see heads turning in their direction. Ambitious mamas were nudging their daughters and pointing to the two Bridgerton brothers, off by themselves with no company save for their sister.

"I knew I should have made for the retiring room," Daphne muttered.

"I say, what's that piece of paper in your hand, Daff?" Benedict inquired.

Somewhat absentmindedly, she handed him the list of Anthony's supposed brides.

At Benedict's loud chortle, Anthony crossed his arms, and said, "Try not to have too much fun at my expense. I predict you'll be receiving a similar list next week."

"No doubt," Benedict agreed. "It's a wonder Colin—" His eyes snapped up. "Colin!"

Yet another Bridgerton brother joined the crowd.

"Oh, Colin!" Daphne exclaimed, throwing her arms around him. "It's so *good* to see you."

"Note that we didn't receive similarly enthusiastic greetings," Anthony said to Benedict.

"You I see all the time," Daphne retorted. "Colin's been away a full year." After giving him one last squeeze, she stepped back, and scolded, "We didn't expect you until next week."

Colin's one-shoulder shrug matched his lopsided smile to perfection. "Amsterdam grew dull."

"Ah," Daphne said with a shrewd look in her eye. "Then you ran out of money."

Colin laughed and held up his hands in surrender. "Guilty as charged."

Anthony hugged his brother, and said gruffly, "It's damned fine to have you home, brother. Although the funds I sent you should have lasted you at least until—"

"Stop," Colin said helplessly, laughter still tinging his voice. "I promise you may scold me all you want tomorrow. Tonight I merely wish to enjoy the company of my beloved family."

Benedict let out a snort. "You must be completely broke if you're calling us 'beloved.' " But he leaned forward to give his brother a hearty hug all the same. "Welcome home."

Colin, always the most devil-may-care of the family, grinned, his green eyes twinkling. "Good to be back. Although I must say the weather is not nearly so fine as on the Continent, and as for the women, well, England would be hard-pressed to compete with the signorina I—"

Daphne punched him in the arm. "Kindly recall that there is a lady present, churl." But there was little ire in her voice. Of all her siblings, Colin was the closest to her in age—only eighteen months her elder. As children, they had been inseparable—and always in trouble. Colin was a natural prankster, and Daphne had never needed much convincing to go along with his schemes. "Does Mother know you're home?" she asked.

Colin shook his head. "I arrived to an empty house, and—"

"Yes, Mother put the younger ones to bed early tonight," Daphne interrupted.

"I didn't want to wait about and twiddle my thumbs, so Humboldt gave me your direction and I came here."

Daphne beamed, her wide smile lending warmth to her dark eyes. "I'm glad you did."

"Where *is* Mother?" Colin asked, craning his neck to peer over the crowd. Like all Bridgerton males, he was tall, so he didn't have to stretch very far.

"Over in the corner with Lady Jersey," Daphne replied.

Colin shuddered. "I'll wait until she's extricated herself. I have no wish to be flayed alive by that dragon."

"Speaking of dragons," Benedict said pointedly. His head didn't move, but his eyes flicked off to the left.

Daphne followed his line of vision to see Lady Danbury marching slowly toward them. She carried a cane, but Daphne swallowed nervously and steeled her shoulders. Lady Danbury's often cutting wit was legendary among the *ton*. Daphne had always suspected that a sentimental heart beat under her acerbic exterior, but still, it was always terrifying when Lady Danbury pressed one into conversation.

"No escape," Daphne heard one of her brothers groan.

Daphne shushed him and offered the old lady a hesitant smile.

Lady Danbury's brows rose, and when she was but four feet away from the group of Bridgertons, she stopped, and barked, "Don't pretend you don't see me!"

This was followed by a thump of the cane so loud that Daphne jumped back just enough to trample Benedict's toe.

"Euf," said Benedict.

Since her brothers appeared to have gone temporarily mute (except for Benedict, of course, but Daphne didn't think that grunts of pain counted as intelligible speech) Daphne swallowed, and said, "I hope I did not give that impression, Lady Danbury, for—"

"Not you," Lady Danbury said imperiously. She jabbed her cane into the air, making a perfectly horizontal line that ended perilously close to Colin's stomach. "Them."

A chorus of mumbled greetings emerged as a response.

Lady Danbury flicked the men the briefest of glances before turning back to Daphne, and saying, "Mr. Berbrooke was asking after you."

Daphne actually felt her skin turn green. "He was?"

Lady Danbury gave her a curt nod. "I'd nip that one in the bud, were I you, Miss Bridgerton."

"Did you tell him where I was?"

Lady Danbury's mouth slid into a sly, conspiratorial smile. "I always knew I liked you. And no, I did not tell him where you were."

"Thank you," Daphne said gratefully.

"It'd be a waste of a good mind if you were shackled to that nitwit," Lady Danbury said, "and the good Lord knows that the *ton* can't afford to waste the few good minds we've got."

"Er, thank you," Daphne said.

"As for you lot"—Lady Danbury waved her cane at Daphne's

brothers—"I still reserve judgment. You"—she pointed the cane at Anthony—"I'm inclined to be favorable toward, since you refused Berbrooke's suit on your sister's behalf, but the rest of you . . . Hmmph."

And with that she walked away.

" 'Hmmph?' " Benedict echoed. " 'Hmmph?' She purports to quantify my intelligence and all she comes up with is 'Hmmph?' "

Daphne smirked. "She *likes* me."

"You're welcome to her," Benedict grumbled.

"Rather sporting of her to warn you about Berbrooke," Anthony admitted.

Daphne nodded. "I believe that was my cue to take my leave." She turned to Anthony with a beseeching look. "If he comes looking for me—"

"I'll take care of it," he said gently. "Don't worry."

"Thank you." And then, with a smile to her brothers, she slipped out of the ballroom.

As Simon walked quietly through the halls of Lady Danbury's London home, it occurred to him that he was in a singularly good mood. This, he thought with a chuckle, was truly remarkable, considering the fact that he was about to attend a society ball and thus subject himself to all the horrors Anthony Bridgerton had laid out before him earlier that afternoon.

But he could console himself with the knowledge that after today, he needn't bother with such functions again; as he had told Anthony earlier that afternoon, he was only attending this particular ball out of loyalty to Lady Danbury, who, despite her curmudgeonly ways, had always been quite nice to him as a child.

His good mood, he was coming to realize, derived from the simple fact that he was pleased to be back in England.

Not that he hadn't enjoyed his journeys across the globe. He'd traveled the length and breadth of Europe, sailed the exquisitely blue seas of the Mediterranean, and delved into the mysteries of North Africa. From there he'd gone on to the Holy Land, and then, when inquiries revealed that it was not yet time to return home, he crossed the Atlantic and explored the West Indies. At that point he considered moving on to the United States of America, but the new nation had seen fit to enter into conflict with Britain, so Simon had stayed away.

Besides, that was when he'd learned that his father, ill for several years, had finally died.

It was ironic, really. Simon wouldn't have traded his years of exploration for anything. Six years gave a man a lot of time to think, a lot of time to learn what it meant to be a man. And yet the only reason the then-twenty-two-year-old Simon had left England was because his father had suddenly decided that he was finally willing to accept his son.

Simon hadn't been willing to accept his father, though, and so he'd simply packed his bags and left the country, preferring exile to the old duke's hypocritical overtures of affection.

It had all started when Simon had finished at Oxford. The duke hadn't originally wanted to pay for his son's schooling; Simon had once seen a letter written to a tutor stating that he refused to let his idiot son make a fool of the family at Eton. But Simon had had a hungry mind as well as a stubborn heart, and so he'd ordered a carriage to take him to Eton, knocked on the headmaster's door, and announced his presence.

It had been the most terrifying thing he'd ever done, but he'd somehow managed to convince the headmaster that the mix-up was the school's fault, that somehow Eton must have lost his enrollment papers and fees. He'd copied all of his father's mannerisms, raising an arrogant brow, lifting his chin, and looking down his nose, and generally appearing as if he thought he owned the world.

And the entire time, he'd been quaking in his shoes, terrified that at any moment his words would grow garbled and land on top of each other, that "I am Earl Clyvedon, and I am here to begin classes," would instead come out as, "I am Earl Clyvedon, and I am h-h-h-h-h-h—"

But it hadn't, and the headmaster, who'd spent enough years educating England's elite to immediately recognize Simon as a member of the Basset family, had enrolled him posthaste and without question. It had taken several months for the duke (who was always quite busy with his own pursuits) to learn of his son's new status and change in residence. By that point, Simon was well ensconced at Eton, and it would have looked very bad if the duke had pulled the boy out of school for no reason.

And the duke didn't like to look bad.

Simon had often wondered why his father hadn't chosen to make an overture at that time. Clearly Simon wasn't tripping over his every word at Eton; the duke would have heard from the headmaster if his son weren't able to keep up with his studies. Simon's speech still occasionally slipped, but by then he'd grown remarkably proficient in covering up his mistakes with a cough or, if he was lucky enough to be taking a meal at the time, a well-timed sip of tea or milk.

But the duke never even wrote him a letter. Simon supposed his father had grown so used to ignoring his son that it didn't even matter that he wasn't proving to be an embarrassment to the Basset name.

After Eton, Simon followed the natural progression to Oxford, where he earned the reputations of both scholar and rake. Truth be told, he hadn't deserved the label of rake any more than most of the young bucks at university, but Simon's somewhat aloof demeanor somehow fed the persona.

Simon wasn't exactly certain how it had happened, but gradually he became aware that his peers craved his approval. He was intelligent and athletic, but it seemed his elevated status had more to do with his manner than anything else. Because Simon didn't speak when words were not necessary, people judged him to be arrogant, just as a future duke should be. Because he preferred to surround himself with only those friends with whom he truly felt comfortable, people decided he was exceptionally discriminating in his choice of companions, just as a future duke should be.

He wasn't very talkative, but when he did say something, he had a quick and often ironic wit—just the sort of humor that guaranteed that people would hang on his every word. And again, because he didn't constantly run off at the mouth, as did so many of the *ton*, people were even *more* obsessed with what he had to say.

He was called "supremely confident," "heartstoppingly handsome," and "the perfect specimen of English manhood." Men wanted his opinion on any number of topics.

The women swooned at his feet.

Simon never could quite believe it all, but he enjoyed his status nonetheless, taking what was offered him, running wild with his friends, and enjoying the company of all the young widows and opera singers who sought his attention—and every escapade was all the more delicious for knowing that his father must disapprove.

But, as it turned out, his father didn't *entirely* disapprove. Unbeknownst to Simon, the Duke of Hastings had already begun to grow interested in the progress of his only son. He requested academic reports from the university and hired a Bow Street Runner to keep him apprised of Simon's extracurricular activities. And eventually, the duke stopped expecting every missive to contain tales of his son's idiocy.

It would have been impossible to pinpoint exactly when his change of heart occurred, but one day the duke realized that his son had turned out rather nicely, after all.

The duke puffed out with pride. As always, good breeding had proven true in the end. He should have known that Basset blood could not produce an imbecile.

Upon finishing Oxford with a first in mathematics, Simon came to London with his friends. He had, of course, taken bachelor's lodgings, having no wish to reside with his father. And as Simon went out in society, more and more people misinterpreted his pregnant pauses for arrogance and his small circle of friends for exclusivity.

His reputation was sealed when Beau Brummel—the then recognized leader of society—had asked a rather involved question about some trivial new fashion. Brummel's tone had been condescending and he had clearly hoped to embarrass the young lord. As all London knew, Brummel loved nothing better than to reduce England's elite into blithering idiots. And so he had pretended to care about Simon's opinion, ending his question with a drawled, "Don't you think?"

As an audience of gossips watched with baited breath, Simon, who couldn't have cared less about the specific arrangement of the Prince's cravat, simply turned his icy blue eyes on Brummel, and answered, "No."

No explanation, no elaboration, just, "No."

And then he walked away.

By the next afternoon, Simon might as well have been the king of society. The irony was unnerving. Simon didn't care for Brummel or his tone, and he would probably have delivered a more loquacious set-down if he'd been sure he could do so without stumbling over his words. And yet in this particular instance, less had most definitely proven to be more, and Simon's terse sentence had turned out to be far more deadly than any long-winded speech he might have uttered.

Word of the brilliant and devastatingly handsome Hastings heir naturally reached the duke's ears. And although he did not immediately seek Simon out, Simon began to hear bits and pieces of gossip that warned him that his relationship with his father might soon see a change. The duke had laughed when he'd heard of the Brummel incident, and said, "Naturally. He's a Basset." An acquaintance mentioned that the duke had been heard crowing about Simon's first at Oxford.

And then the two came face-to-face at a London ball.

The duke would not allow Simon to give him the cut direct.

Simon tried. Oh, how he tried. But no one had the ability to crush his confidence like his father, and as he stared at the duke, who might as well have been a mirror image, albeit slightly older version, of himself, he couldn't move, couldn't even try to speak.

His tongue felt thick, his mouth felt odd, and it almost seemed as if his stutters had spread from his mouth to his body, for he suddenly didn't even feel right in his own skin.

The duke had taken advantage of Simon's momentary lapse of reason by embracing him with a heartfelt, "Son."

Simon had left the country the very next day.

He'd known that it would be impossible to avoid his father completely if he remained in England. And he refused to act the part of his son after having been denied a father for so many years.

Besides, lately he'd been growing bored of London's wild life. Rake's reputation aside, Simon didn't really have the temperament of a true debauché. He had enjoyed his nights on the town as much as any of his dissolute cronies, but after three years in Oxford and one in London, the endless round of parties and prostitutes was growing, well, old.

And so he left.

Now, however, he was glad to be back. There was something soothing about being home, something peaceful and serene about an English springtime. And after six years of solitary travel, it was damned good to find his friends again.

He moved silently through the halls, making his way to the ballroom. He hadn't wanted to be announced; the last thing he desired was a declaration of his presence. The afternoon's conversation with Anthony Bridgerton had reaffirmed his decision not to take an active role in London society.

He had no plans to marry. Ever. And there wasn't much point in attending *ton* parties if one wasn't looking for a wife.

Still, he felt he owed some loyalty to Lady Danbury after her many kindnesses during his childhood, and truth be told, he held a great deal of affection for the forthright old lady. It would have been the height of rudeness to spurn her invitation, especially since it had come accompanied by a personal note welcoming him back to the country.

Since Simon knew his way around this house, he'd entered through a side door. If all went well, he could slip unobtrusively into the ballroom, give his regards to Lady Danbury, and leave.

But as he turned a corner, he heard voices, and he froze.

Simon suppressed a groan. He'd interrupted a lovers' tryst. Bloody hell. How to extricate himself without notice? If his presence was discovered, the ensuing scene was sure to be replete with histrionics, embarrassment, and no end of tedious emotion. Better just to melt into the shadows and let the lovers go on their merry way.

But as Simon started backing quietly up, he heard something that caught his attention.

"No."

No? Had some young lady been forced into the deserted hallway against her will? Simon had no great desire to be anyone's hero, but even he could not let such an insult pass. He craned his neck slightly, pressing his ear forward so that he might hear better. After all, he might have heard incorrectly. If no one needed saving, he certainly wasn't going to charge forward like some bullish fool.

"Nigel," the girl was saying, "you really shouldn't have followed me out here."

"But I love you!" the young man cried out in a passionate voice. "All I want is to make you my wife."

Simon nearly groaned. Poor besotted fool. It was painful to listen to.

"Nigel," she said again, her voice surprisingly kind and patient, "my brother has already told you that I cannot marry you. I hope that we may continue on as friends."

"But your brother doesn't understand!"

"Yes," she said firmly, "he does."

"Dash it all! If you don't marry me, who will?"

Simon blinked in surprise. As proposals went, this one was decidedly *un*romantic.

The girl apparently thought so, too. "Well," she said, sounding a bit disgruntled, "it's not as if there aren't dozens of other young ladies in Lady Danbury's ballroom right now. I'm sure one of them would be thrilled to marry you."

Simon leaned forward slightly so that he could get a glimpse of the scene. The girl was in shadows, but he could see the man quite clearly. His face held a hangdog expression, and his shoulders were slumped forward in defeat. Slowly, he shook his head. "No," he said forlornly, "they don't. Don't you see? They . . . they . . ."

Simon winced as the man fought for words. He didn't appear to be stuttering so much as emotionally overcome, but it was never pleasant when one couldn't get a sentence out.

"No one's as nice as you," the man finally said. "You're the only one who ever smiles at me."

"Oh, Nigel," the girl said, sighing deeply. "I'm sure that's not true."

But Simon could tell she was just trying to be kind. And as she sighed again, it became apparent to him that she would not need any rescuing. She seemed to have the situation well in hand, and while Simon felt vague pangs of sympathy for the hapless Nigel, there wasn't anything he could do to help.

Besides, he was beginning to feel like the worst sort of voyeur.

He started inching backward, keeping his eye focused on a door that he knew led to the library. There was another door on the other side of that room, one that led to the conservatory. From there he could enter the main hall and make his way to the ballroom. It wouldn't be as discreet as cutting through the back corridors, but at least poor Nigel wouldn't know that his humiliation had had a witness.

But then, just a footstep away from a clean getaway, he heard the girl squeal.

"You have to marry me!" Nigel cried out. "You have to! I'll never find anyone else—"

"Nigel, stop!"

Simon turned around, groaning. It looked like he was going to have to rescue the chit, after all. He strode back into the hall, putting his sternest, most dukish expression on his face. The words, "I believe the lady asked you to stop," rested on the tip of his tongue, but it seemed that he wasn't fated to play the hero tonight, after all, because before he could make a sound, the young lady pulled back her right arm and landed a surprisingly effective punch squarely on Nigel's jaw.

Nigel went down, his arms comically flailing in the air as his legs slid out from under him. Simon just stood there, watching in disbelief as the girl dropped to her knees.

"Oh dear," she said, her voice squeaking slightly. "Nigel, are you all right? I didn't mean to hit you so hard."

Simon laughed. He couldn't help it.

The girl looked up, startled.

Simon caught his breath. She had been in shadows until now, and all he'd been able to discern of her appearance was a wealth of thick, dark hair. But now, as she lifted her head to face him, he saw that she had large, equally dark eyes, and the widest, lushest mouth he'd ever seen. Her heart-shaped face wasn't beautiful by society standards, but something about her quite simply sucked the breath from his body.

Her brows, thick but delicately winged, drew together. "Who," she asked, not sounding at all pleased to see him, "are you?"

# *Chapter 3*

*It has been whispered to This Author that Nigel Berbrooke was seen at Moreton's Jewelry Shop purchasing a diamond solitaire ring. Can a new Mrs. Berbrooke be very far behind?*

*LADY WHISTLEDOWN'S SOCIETY PAPERS,*
28 April 1813

The night, Daphne decided, couldn't possibly get much worse. First she'd been forced to spend the evening in the darkest corner of the ballroom (which wasn't such an easy task, since Lady Danbury clearly appreciated both the aesthetic and illuminating qualities of candles), then she'd managed to trip over Philipa Featherington's foot as she tried to make her escape, which had led Philipa, never the quietest girl in the room, to squeal, "Daphne Bridgerton! Are you hurt?" Which must have captured Nigel's attention, for his head had snapped up like a startled bird, and he'd immediately started hurrying across the ballroom. Daphne had hoped, no *prayed* that she could outrun him and make it to the ladies' retiring room before he caught up with her, but no, Nigel had cornered her in the hall and started wailing out his love for her.

It was all embarrassing enough, but now it appeared this man—this shockingly handsome and almost disturbingly poised stranger—had witnessed the entire thing. And worse, he was laughing!

Daphne glared at him as he chuckled at her expense. She'd never seen him before, so he had to be new to London. Her mother had made certain that Daphne had been introduced to, or at least been made aware of, all eligible gentlemen. Of course, this man could be married and therefore not on Violet's list of potential victims, but Daphne instinctively knew that he could not have been long in London without all the world whispering about it.

His face was quite simply perfection. It took only a moment to realize that he put all of Michelangelo's statues to shame. His eyes were oddly intense—so blue they practically glowed. His hair was thick and dark, and he was tall—as tall as her brothers, which was a rare thing.

This was a man, Daphne thought wryly, who could quite possibly steal the gaggle of twittering young ladies away from the Bridgerton men for good.

Why that annoyed her so much, she didn't know. Maybe it was because she knew a man like him would never be interested in a woman like her. Maybe it was because she felt like the veriest frump sitting there on the floor in his splendid presence. Maybe it was simply because he was standing there laughing as if she were some sort of circus amusement.

But whatever the case, an uncharacteristic peevishness rose within her, and her brows drew together as she asked, "Who are you?"

Simon didn't know why he didn't answer her question in a straightforward manner, but some devil within caused him to reply, "My intention had been to be your rescuer, but you clearly had no need of my services."

"Oh," the girl said, sounding slightly mollified. She clamped her lips together, twisting them slightly as she considered his words. "Well, thank you, then, I suppose. Pity you didn't reveal yourself ten seconds earlier. I'd rather not have had to hit him."

Simon looked down at the man on the ground. A bruise was already darkening on his chin, and he was moaning, "Laffy, oh Laffy. I love you, Laffy."

"You're Laffy, I presume?" Simon murmured, sliding his gaze up to her face. Really, she was quite an attractive little thing, and from this angle the bodice of her gown seemed almost decadently low.

She scowled at him, clearly not appreciating his attempt at subtle humor—and also clearly not realizing that his heavy-lidded gaze had rested on portions of her anatomy that were not her face. "What are we to do with him?" she asked.

" 'We?' " Simon echoed.

Her scowl deepened. "You did say you aspired to be my rescuer, didn't you?"

"So I did." Simon planted his hands on his hips and assessed the situation. "Shall I drag him out into the street?"

"Of course not!" she exclaimed. "For goodness' sake, isn't it still raining outside?"

"My dear Miss Laffy," Simon said, not particularly concerned about the condescending tone of his voice, "don't you think your concern is slightly misplaced? This man tried to attack you."

"He didn't try to attack me," she replied. "He just . . . He just . . . Oh, very well, he tried to attack me. But he would never have done me any real harm."

Simon raised a brow. Truly, women were the most contrary creatures. "And you can be sure of that?"

He watched as she carefully chose her words. "Nigel isn't capable of malice," she said slowly. "All he is guilty of is misjudgment."

"You're a more generous soul than I, then," Simon said quietly.

The girl let out another sigh, a soft, breathy sound that Simon somehow felt across his entire body. "Nigel's not a bad person," she said with quiet dignity. "It's just that he isn't always terribly bright, and perhaps he mistook kindness on my part for something more."

Simon felt a strange sort of admiration for this girl. Most women of his acquaintance would have been in hysterics at this point, but she—whoever she was—had taken the situation firmly in hand, and was now displaying a generosity of spirit that was astounding. That she could even think to defend this Nigel person was quite beyond him.

She rose to her feet, dusting her hands off on the sage green silk of her skirts. Her hair had been styled so that one thick lock fell over her shoulder, curling seductively at the top of her breast. Simon knew he should be listening to her—she was prattling on about something, as women were wont to do—but he couldn't seem to take his eyes off that single dark lock of hair. It fell like a silky ribbon across her swanlike neck, and Simon had the most appalling urge to close the distance between them and trace the line of her hair with his lips.

He'd never dallied with an innocent before, but all the world had already painted him a rake. What could be the harm? It wasn't as if he were going to ravish her. Just a kiss. Just one little kiss.

It was tempting, so deliciously, maddeningly tempting.

"Sir! Sir!"

With great reluctance, he dragged his eyes up to her face. Which was, of course, delightful in and of itself, but it was difficult to picture her seduction when she was scowling at him.

"Were you listening to me?"

"Of course," he lied.

"You weren't."

"No," he admitted.

A sound came from the back of her throat that sounded suspiciously like a growl. "Then why," she ground out, "did you say you were?"

He shrugged. "I thought it was what you wanted to hear."

Simon watched with fascinated interest as she took a deep breath and muttered something to herself. He couldn't hear her words, but he doubted any of them could be construed as complimentary. Finally, her voice almost comically even, she said, "If you don't wish to aid me, I'd prefer it if you would just leave."

Simon decided it was time to stop acting like such a boor, so he said, "My apologies. Of course I'll help you."

She exhaled, and then looked back to Nigel, who was still lying on the floor, moaning incoherently. Simon looked down, too, and for several seconds they just stood there, staring at the unconscious man, until the girl said, "I really didn't hit him very hard."

"Maybe he's drunk."

She looked dubious. "Do you think? I smelled spirits on his breath, but I've never seen him drunk before."

Simon had nothing to add to that line of thought, so he just asked, "Well, what do you want to do?"

"I suppose we could just leave him here," she said, the expression in her dark eyes hesitant.

Simon thought that was an excellent idea, but it was obvious she wanted the idiot cared for in a more tender manner. And heaven help him, but he felt the strangest compulsion to make her happy. "Here is what we're going to do," he said crisply, glad that his tone belied any of the odd tenderness he was feeling. "I am going to summon my carriage—"

"Oh, good," she interrupted. "I really didn't want to leave him here. It seemed rather cruel."

Simon thought it seemed rather generous considering the big oaf had nearly attacked her, but he kept that opinion to himself and instead continued on with his plan. "You will wait in the library while I'm gone."

"In the library? But—"

"In the library," he repeated firmly. "With the door shut. Do you really want to be discovered with Nigel's body should anyone happen to wander down this hallway?"

"His body? Good gracious, sir, you needn't make it sound as if he were dead."

"As I was saying," he continued, ignoring her comment completely, "you will remain in the library. When I return, we will relocate Nigel here to my carriage."

"And how will we do that?"

He gave her a disarmingly lopsided grin. "I haven't the faintest idea."

For a moment Daphne forgot to breathe. Just when she'd decided that her would-be rescuer was irredeemingly arrogant, he had to go and smile at her like that. It was one of those boyish grins, the kind that melted female hearts within a ten-mile radius.

And, much to Daphne's dismay, it was awfully hard to remain thoroughly irritated with a man under the influence of such a smile. After growing up with four brothers, all of whom had seemed to know how to charm ladies from birth, Daphne had thought she was immune.

But apparently not. Her chest was tingling, her stomach was turning cartwheels, and her knees felt like melted butter.

"Nigel," she muttered, desperately trying to force her attention away from the nameless man standing across from her, "I must see to Nigel." She crouched down and shook him none too gently by the shoulder. "Nigel? Nigel? You have to wake up now, Nigel."

"Daphne," Nigel moaned. "Oh, Daphne."

The dark-haired stranger's head snapped around. "Daphne? Did he say Daphne?"

She drew back, unnerved by his direct question and the rather intense look in his eyes. "Yes."

"Your name is Daphne?"

Now she was beginning to wonder if he was an idiot. "Yes."

He groaned. "Not Daphne Bridgerton."

Her face slid into a puzzled frown. "The very one."

Simon staggered back a step. He suddenly felt physically ill, as his brain finally processed the fact that she had thick, chestnut hair. The famous Bridgerton hair. Not to mention the Bridgerton nose, and cheekbones, and—Bugger it all, this was Anthony's *sister*!

Bloody hell.

There were rules among friends, commandments, really, and the most important one was Thou Shalt Not Lust After Thy Friend's Sister.

While he stood there, probably staring at her like a complete idiot, she planted her hands on her hips, and demanded, "And who are *you*?"

"Simon Basset," he muttered.

"The duke?" she squeaked.

He nodded grimly.

"Oh, dear."

Simon watched with growing horror as the blood drained from her face. "Good God, woman, you're not going to swoon, are you?" He couldn't imagine why she would, but Anthony—her brother, he reminded himself—had spent half the afternoon warning him about the effects of a young, unmarried duke on the young, unmarried female population. Anthony had specifically singled out Daphne as the exception to the rule, but still, she looked deucedly pale. "Are you?" he demanded, when she said nothing. "Going to swoon?"

She looked offended that he'd even considered the notion. "Of course not!"

"Good."

"It's just that—"

"What?" Simon asked suspiciously.

"Well," she said with a rather dainty shrug of her shoulders, "I've been warned about you."

This was really too much. "By whom?" he demanded.

She stared at him as if he were an imbecile. "By everyone."

"That, my d—" He felt something suspiciously like a stammer coming on, and so he took a deep breath to steady his tongue. He'd become a master at this kind of control. All she would see was a man who looked as if he were trying to keep his temper in check. And considering the direction of their conversation, that image could not seem terribly far-fetched.

"My dear Miss Bridgerton," Simon said, starting anew in a more even and controlled tone, "I find that difficult to believe."

She shrugged again, and he had the most irritating sensation that she was enjoying his distress. "Believe what you will," she said blithely, "but it was in the paper today."

"*What?*"

"In *Whistledown*," she replied, as if that explained anything.

"Whistle-which?"

Daphne stared at him blankly for a moment until she remembered that he was newly returned to London. "Oh, you must not know about it," she said softly, a wicked little smile crossing her lips. "Fancy that."

The duke took a step forward, his stance positively menacing.

"Miss Bridgerton, I feel I should warn you that I am within an inch of strangling the information out of you."

"It's a gossip sheet," she said, hastily backing up a step. "That's all. It's rather silly, actually, but everyone reads it."

He said nothing, just arched one arrogant brow.

Daphne quickly added, "There was a report of your return in Monday's edition."

"And what"—his eyes narrowed dangerously—"precisely"—now they turned to ice—"did it say?"

"Not very much, ah, precisely," Daphne hedged. She tried to back up a step, but her heels were already pressing against the wall. Any further and she'd be up on her tiptoes. The duke looked beyond furious, and she was beginning to think that she should try for a quick escape and just leave him here with Nigel. The two were perfect for each other—madmen, the both of them!

"Miss Bridgerton." There was a wealth of warning in his voice.

Daphne decided to take pity on him since, after all, he was new to town and hadn't had time to adjust to the new world according to *Whistledown*. She supposed she couldn't really blame him for being so upset that he'd been written about in the paper. It had been rather startling for Daphne the first time as well, and she'd at least had the warning of a month's previous *Whistledown* columns. By the time Lady Whistledown got around to writing about Daphne, it had been almost anticlimactic.

"You needn't upset yourself over it," Daphne said, attempting to lend a little compassion to her voice but probably not succeeding. "She merely wrote that you were a terrible rake, a fact which I'm sure you won't deny, since I have long since learned that men positively *yearn* to be considered rakes."

She paused and gave him the opportunity to prove her wrong and deny it. He didn't.

She continued, "And then my mother, whose acquaintance I gather you must have made at some point or another before you left to travel the world, confirmed it all."

"Did she?"

Daphne nodded. "She then forbade me ever to be seen in your company."

"Really?" he drawled.

Something about the tone of his voice—and the way his eyes seemed to have grown almost smoky as they focused on her face—made her extremely uneasy, and it was all she could do not to shut her eyes.

She refused—absolutely refused—to let him see how he'd affected her.

His lips curved into a slow smile. "Let me make certain I have this correctly. Your mother told you I am a very bad man and that you are under no circumstances to be seen with me."

Confused, she nodded.

"Then what," he asked, pausing for dramatic effect, "do you think your mother would say about *this* little scenario?"

She blinked. "I beg your pardon?"

"Well, unless you count Nigel here"—he waved his hand toward the unconscious man on the floor—"no one has actually *seen* you in my presence. And yet . . ." He let his words trail off, having far too much fun watching the play of emotions on her face to do anything but drag this moment out to its lengthiest extreme.

Of course most of the emotions on her face were varying shades of irritation and dismay, but that made the moment all the sweeter.

"And yet?" she ground out.

He leaned forward, narrowing the distance between them to only a few inches. "And yet," he said softly, knowing that she'd feel his breath on her face, "here we are, completely alone."

"Except for Nigel," she retorted.

Simon spared the man on the floor the briefest of glances before returning his wolfish gaze to Miss Bridgerton. "I'm not terribly concerned about Nigel," he murmured. "Are you?"

Simon watched as she looked down at Nigel in dismay. It had to be clear to her that her spurned suitor wasn't going to save her should Simon decide to make an amorous advance. Not that he would, of course. After all, this was Anthony's younger sister. He might have to remind himself of this at frequent intervals, but it wasn't a fact that was likely to slip his mind on a permanent basis.

Simon knew that it was past time to end this little game. Not that he thought she would report the interlude to Anthony; somehow he knew that she would prefer to keep this to herself, stewing over it in privately righteous fury, and, dare he hope it—just a touch of excitement?

But even as he knew it was time to stop this flirtation and get back to the business of hauling Daphne's idiotic suitor out of the building, he couldn't resist one last comment. Maybe it was the way her lips pursed when she was annoyed. Or maybe it was the way they parted when she was shocked. All he knew was that he was helpless against his own devilish nature when it came to this girl.

And so he leaned forward, his eyes heavy-lidded and seductive as he said, "I think I know what your mother would say."

She looked a little befuddled by his onslaught, but still she managed a rather defiant, "Oh?"

Simon nodded slowly, and he touched one finger to her chin. "She'd tell you to be very, very afraid."

There was a moment of utter silence, and then Daphne's eyes grew very wide. Her lips tightened, as if she were keeping something inside, and then her shoulders rose slightly, and then . . .

And then she laughed. Right in his face.

"Oh, my goodness," she gasped. "Oh, that was funny."

Simon was not amused.

"I'm sorry." This was said between laughs. "Oh, I'm sorry, but really, you shouldn't be so melodramatic. It doesn't suit you."

Simon paused, rather irritated that this slip of a girl had shown such disrespect for his authority. There were advantages to being considered a dangerous man, and being able to cow young maidens was supposed to be one of them.

"Well, actually, it does suit you, I ought to admit," she added, still grinning at his expense. "You looked quite dangerous. And very handsome, of course." When he made no comment, her face took on a bemused expression, and she asked, "That was your intention, was it not?"

He still said nothing, so she said, "Of course it was. And I would be remiss if I did not tell you that you would have been successful with any other woman besides me."

A comment he couldn't resist. "And why is that?"

"Four brothers." She shrugged as if that should explain everything. "I'm quite immune to your games."

"Oh?"

She gave his arm a reassuring pat. "But yours was a most admirable attempt. And truly, I'm quite flattered you thought me worthy of such a magnificent display of dukish rakishness." She grinned, her smile wide and unfeigned. "Or do you prefer rakish dukishness?"

Simon stroked his jaw thoughtfully, trying to regain his mood of menacing predator. "You're a most annoying little chit, did you know that, Miss Bridgerton?"

She gave him her sickliest of smiles. "Most people find me the soul of kindness and amiability."

"Most people," Simon said bluntly, "are fools."

Daphne cocked her head to the side, obviously pondering his words. Then she looked over at Nigel and sighed. "I'm afraid I have to agree with you, much as it pains me."

Simon bit back a smile. "It pains you to agree with me, or that most people are fools?"

"Both." She grinned again—a wide, enchanting smile that did odd things to his brain. "But mostly the former."

Simon let out a loud laugh, then was startled to realize how foreign the sound was to his ears. He was a man who frequently smiled; occasionally chuckled, but it had been a very long time since he'd felt such a spontaneous burst of joy. "My dear Miss Bridgerton," he said, wiping his eyes, "if you are the soul of kindness and amiability, then the world must be a very dangerous place."

"Oh, for certain," she replied. "At least to hear my mother tell it."

"I can't imagine why I do not recall your mother," Simon murmured, "because she certainly sounds a memorable character."

Daphne raised a brow. "You don't remember her?"

He shook his head.

"Then you don't know her."

"Does she look like you?"

"That's an odd question."

"Not so very odd," Simon replied, thinking that Daphne was exactly right. It *was* an odd question, and he had no idea why he'd voiced it. But since he had, and since she had questioned it, he added, "After all, I'm told that all of you Bridgertons look alike."

A tiny, and to Simon mysterious, frown touched her face. "We do. Look alike, that is. Except for my mother. She's rather fair, actually, with blue eyes. We all get our dark hair from our father. I'm told I have her smile, though."

An awkward pause fell across the conversation. Daphne was shifting from foot to foot, not at all certain what to say to the duke, when Nigel exhibited stellar timing for the first time in his life, and sat up. "Daphne?" he said, blinking as if he couldn't see straight. "Daphne, is that you?"

"Good God, Miss Bridgerton," the duke swore, "how hard did you hit him?"

"Hard enough to knock him down, but no worse than that, I swear!" Her brow furrowed. "Maybe he *is* drunk."

"Oh, Daphne," Nigel moaned.

The duke crouched next to him, then reeled back, coughing.

"Is he drunk?" Daphne asked.

The duke staggered back. "He must have drunk an entire bottle of whiskey just to get up the nerve to propose."

"Who would have thought I could be so terrifying?" Daphne murmured, thinking of all the men who thought of her as a jolly good friend and nothing more. "How wonderful."

Simon stared at her as if she were insane, then muttered, "I'm not even going to question that statement."

Daphne ignored his comment. "Should we set our plan into action?"

Simon planted his hands on his hips and reassessed the scene. Nigel was trying to rise to his feet, but it didn't appear, to Simon's eye at least, that he was going to find success anytime in the near future. Still, he was probably lucid enough to make trouble, and certainly lucid enough to make noise, which he was doing. Quite well, actually.

"Oh, Daphne. I luff you so much, Daffery." Nigel managed to raise himself to his knees, weaving around as he shuffled toward Daphne, looking rather like a sotted churchgoer attempting to pray. "Please marry me, Duffne. You have to."

"Buck up, man," Simon grunted, grabbing him by the collar. "This is getting embarrassing." He turned to Daphne. "I'm going to have to take him outside now. We can't leave him here in the hall. He's liable to start moaning like a sickened cow—"

"I rather thought he'd already started," Daphne said.

Simon felt one corner of his mouth twist up in a reluctant smile. Daphne Bridgerton might be a marriageable female and thus a disaster waiting to happen for any man in his position, but she was certainly a good sport.

She was, it occurred to him in a rather bizarre moment of clarity, the sort of person he'd probably call friend if she were a man.

But since it was abundantly obvious—to both his eyes and his body—that she wasn't a man, Simon decided it was in both of their best interests to wrap up this "situation" as soon as possible. Aside from the fact that Daphne's reputation would suffer a deadly blow if they were discovered, Simon wasn't positive that he could trust himself to keep his hands off of her for very much longer.

It was an unsettling feeling, that. Especially for a man who so valued his self-control. Control was everything. Without it he'd never have stood up to his father or taken a first at university. Without it, he'd—

Without it, he thought grimly, he'd still be speaking like an idiot.

"I'll haul him out of here," he said suddenly. "You go back to the ballroom."

Daphne frowned, glancing over her shoulder to the hall that led back to the party. "Are you certain? I thought you wanted me to go to the library."

"That was when we were going to leave him here while I summoned the carriage. But we can't do that if he's awake."

She nodded her agreement, and asked, "Are you sure you can do it? Nigel's a rather large man."

"I'm larger."

She cocked her head. The duke, although lean, was powerfully built, with broad shoulders and firmly muscled thighs. (Daphne knew she wasn't supposed to notice such things, but, really, was it *her* fault that current fashions dictated such snug breeches?) More to the point, he had a certain air about him, something almost predatory, something that hinted of tightly controlled strength and power.

Daphne decided she had no doubt that he'd be able to move Nigel.

"Very well," she said, giving him a nod. "And thank you. It's very kind of you to help me in this way."

"I'm rarely kind," he muttered.

"Really?" she murmured, allowing herself a tiny smile. "How odd. I couldn't possibly think of anything else to call it. But then again, I've learned that men—"

"You do seem to be the expert on men," he said, somewhat acerbically, then grunted as he hauled Nigel to his feet.

Nigel promptly reached for Daphne, practically sobbing her name. Simon had to brace his legs to keep him from lunging at her.

Daphne darted back a step. "Yes, well, I do have four brothers. A better education I cannot imagine."

There was no way of knowing if the duke had intended to answer her, because Nigel chose that moment to regain his energy (although clearly not his equilibrium) and yanked himself free of Simon's grip. He threw himself onto Daphne, making incoherent, drunken noises all the way.

If Daphne hadn't had her back to the wall, she would have been knocked to the ground. As it was, she hit the wall with a bone-jarring thud, knocking all the breath from her body.

"Oh, for the love of Christ," the duke swore, sounding supremely disgusted. He hauled Nigel off Daphne, then turned to her, and asked, "Can I hit him?"

"Oh, please do go ahead," she replied, still gasping for breath. She'd tried to be kind and generous toward her erstwhile suitor, but really, enough was enough.

The duke muttered something that sounded like "good" and landed a stunningly powerful blow on Nigel's chin.

Nigel went down like a stone.

Daphne regarded the man on the floor with equanimity. "I don't think he's going to wake up this time."

Simon shook out his fist. "No."

Daphne blinked and looked back up. "Thank you."

"It was my pleasure," he said, scowling at Nigel.

"What shall we do now?" Her gaze joined his on the man on the floor—now well and truly unconscious.

"Back to the original plan," he said crisply. "We leave him here while you wait in the library. I'd rather not have to drag him out until I've a carriage waiting."

Daphne gave him a sensible nod. "Do you need help righting him, or should I proceed directly to the library?"

The duke was silent for a moment. His head tilted this way and that as he analyzed Nigel's position on the floor. "Actually, a bit of help would be greatly appreciated."

"Really?" Daphne asked, surprised. "I was sure you'd say no."

That earned her a faintly amused and superior look from the duke. "And is that why you asked?"

"No, of course not," Daphne replied, slightly offended. "I'm not so stupid as to offer help if I have no intention of giving it. I was merely going to point out that men, in my experience—"

"You have too much experience," the duke muttered under his breath.

"What?!"

"I beg your pardon," he amended. "You *think* you have too much experience."

Daphne glared at him, her dark eyes smoldering nearly to black. "That is not true, and who are you to say, anyway?"

"No, that's not quite right, either," the duke mused, completely ignoring her furious question. "I think it's more that *I* think you think you have too much experience."

"Why you—You—" As retorts went, it wasn't especially effective, but it was all Daphne could manage to get out. Her powers of speech tended to fail her when she was angry.

And she was really angry.

Simon shrugged, apparently unmoved by her furious visage. "My dear Miss Bridgerton—"

"If you call me that one more time, I swear I shall scream."

"No, you won't," he said with a rakish smile. "That would draw a crowd, and if you recall, you don't want to be seen with me."

"I am considering risking it," Daphne said, each word squeezed out between her teeth.

Simon crossed his arms and leaned lazily against the wall. "Really?" he drawled. "This I should like to see."

Daphne nearly threw up her arms in frustration. "Forget it. Forget me. Forget this entire evening. I'm leaving."

She turned around, but before she could even take a step, her movement was arrested by the sound of the duke's voice.

"I thought you were going to help me."

Drat. He had her there. She turned slowly around. "Why, yes," she said, her voice patently false, "I'd be delighted."

"You know," he said innocently, "if you didn't want to help you shouldn't have—"

"I said I'd help," she snapped.

Simon smiled to himself. She was such an easy mark. "Here is what we are going to do," he said. "I'm going to haul him to his feet and drape his right arm over my shoulders. You will go around to the other side and shore him up."

Daphne did as she was bid, grumbling to herself about his autocratic attitude. But she didn't voice a single complaint. After all, for all his annoying ways, the Duke of Hastings was helping her out of a possibly embarrassing scandal.

Of course if anyone found her in this position, she'd find herself in even worse straits.

"I have a better idea," she said suddenly. "Let's just leave him here."

The duke's head swung around to face her, and he looked as if he'd dearly like to toss her through a window—preferably one that was still closed. "I thought," he said, clearly working hard to keep his voice even, "that you didn't want to leave him on the floor."

"That was before he knocked me into the wall."

"Could you possibly have notified me of your change of heart before I expended my energy to lift him?"

Daphne blushed. She hated that men thought that women were fickle, changeable creatures, and she hated even more that she was living up to that image right then.

"Very well," he said simply, and dropped Nigel.

The sudden weight of him nearly took Daphne down to the floor as well. She let out a surprised squeal as she ducked out of the way.

"Now may we leave?" the duke asked, sounding insufferably patient.

She nodded hesitantly, glancing down at Nigel. "He looks rather uncomfortable, don't you think?"

Simon stared at her. Just stared at her. "You're concerned for his comfort?" he finally asked.

She gave her head a nervous shake, then a nod, then went back to the shake. "Maybe I should—That is to say—Here, just wait a moment." She crouched and untwisted Nigel's legs so he lay flat on his back. "I didn't think he deserved a trip home in your carriage," she explained as she rearranged his coat, "but it seemed rather cruel to leave him here in this position. There, now I'm done." She stood and looked up.

And just managed to catch sight of the duke as he walked away, muttering something about Daphne and something about women in general and something else entirely that Daphne didn't quite catch.

But maybe that was for the best. She rather doubted it had been a compliment.

# Chapter 4

*London is awash these days with Ambitious Mamas. At Lady Worth's ball last week This Author saw no fewer than eleven Determined Bachelors, cowering in corners and eventually fleeing the premises with those Ambitious Mamas hot on their heels.*

*It is difficult to determine who, precisely, is the worst of the lot, although This Author suspects the contest may come down to a near draw between Lady Bridgerton and Mrs. Featherington, with Mrs. F edging Lady B out by a nose. There are three Featherington misses on the market right now, after all, whereas Lady Bridgerton need only worry about one.*

*It is recommended, however, that all safety-minded people stay far, far away from the latest crop of unmarried men when Bridgerton daughters E, F, and H come of age. Lady B is not likely to look both ways when she barrels across a ballroom with three daughters in tow, and the Lord help us all should she decide to don metal-toed boots.*

*Lady Whistledown's Society Papers,*
28 April 1813

The night, Simon decided, couldn't possibly get much worse. He wouldn't have believed it at the time, but his bizarre encounter with Daphne Bridgerton was definitely turning out to be the evening's high point. Yes, he'd been horrified to discover that he'd been lusting—even briefly—after his best friend's younger sister. Yes, Nigel Berbrooke's oafish attempts at seduction had offended every one of his rakish sensibilities. And yes, Daphne had finally exasperated him beyond endurance with her indecision over whether to treat Nigel like a criminal or care for him as she would her dearest friend.

But none of that—not one bit—compared to the torture that he'd been about to endure.

His oh-so-clever plan of slipping into the ballroom, giving his regards to Lady Danbury, and leaving unnoticed had fallen into instant ruin. He'd taken no more than two steps into the ballroom when he'd been recognized by an old friend from Oxford, who, much to Simon's dismay, had recently married. The wife was a perfectly charming young woman, but unfortunately one with rather high social aspirations, and she had quickly determined that her road to happiness lay in her position as the one to introduce the new duke to society. And Simon, even though he fancied himself a world-weary, cynical sort, discovered that he wasn't quite rude enough to directly insult the wife of his old university friend.

And so, two hours later, he'd been introduced to every unmarried lady at the ball, every *mother* of every unmarried lady at the ball, and, of course, every older married sister of every unmarried lady at the ball. Simon couldn't decide which set of women was the worst. The unmarried ladies were decidedly boring, the mothers were annoyingly ambitious, and the *sisters*—well, the sisters were so forward Simon began to wonder if he'd stumbled into a brothel. Six of them had made extremely suggestive remarks, two had slipped him notes inviting him to their boudoirs, and one had actually run her hand down his thigh.

In retrospect, Daphne Bridgerton was starting to look very good, indeed.

And speaking of Daphne, where the hell was she? He'd thought he'd caught a glimpse of her about an hour earlier, surrounded by her rather large and forbidding brothers. (Not that Simon found them individually forbidding, but he'd quickly decided that any man would have to be an imbecile to provoke them as a group.)

But since then she seemed to have disappeared. Indeed, he thought she might have been the only unmarried female at the party to whom he *hadn't* been introduced.

Simon wasn't particularly worried about her being bothered by Berbrooke after he'd left them in the hall. He'd delivered a solid punch to the man's jaw and had no doubt that he'd be out for several minutes. Probably longer, considering the vast quantities of alcohol Berbrooke had consumed earlier in the evening. And even if Daphne had been foolishly tenderhearted when it came to her clumsy suitor, she wasn't stupid enough to remain in the hallway with him until he woke up.

Simon glanced back over to the corner where the Bridgerton brothers were gathered, looking as if they were having a grand old time. They had been accosted by almost as many young women and old mothers as Simon, but at least there seemed to be some safety in numbers. Simon noticed that the young debutantes didn't seem to spend half as much time in the Bridgertons' company as they did in his.

Simon sent an irritated scowl in their direction.

Anthony, who was leaning lazily against a wall, caught the expression and smirked, raising a glass of red wine in his direction. Then he cocked his head slightly, motioning to Simon's left. Simon turned, just in time to be detained by yet another mother, this one with a trio of daughters, all of whom were dressed in monstrously fussy frocks, replete with tucks and flounces, and of course, heaps and heaps of lace.

He thought of Daphne, with her simple sage green gown. Daphne, with her direct brown eyes and wide smile . . .

"Your grace!" the mother shrilled. "Your grace!"

Simon blinked to clear his vision. The lace-covered family had managed to surround him with such efficiency that he wasn't even able to shoot a glare in Anthony's direction.

"Your grace," the mother repeated, "it is such an honor to make your acquaintance."

Simon managed a frosty nod. Words were quite beyond him. The family of females had pressed in so close he feared he might suffocate.

"Georgiana Huxley sent us over," the woman persisted. "She said I simply must introduce my daughters to you."

Simon didn't remember who Georgiana Huxley was, but he thought he might like to strangle her.

"Normally I should not be so bold," the woman went on, "but your dear, dear papa was such a friend of mine."

Simon stiffened.

"He was truly a marvelous man," she continued, her voice like nails to Simon's skull, "so conscious of his duties to the title. He must have been a marvelous father."

"I wouldn't know," Simon bit off.

"Oh!" The woman had to clear her throat several times before managing to say, "I see. Well. My goodness."

Simon said nothing, hoping an aloof demeanor would prompt her to take her leave. Damn it, where was Anthony? It was bad enough having these women acting as if he were some prize horse to be bred, but to have to stand here and listen to this woman tell him what a *good* father the old duke had been . . .

Simon couldn't possibly bear it.

"Your grace! Your grace!"

Simon forced his icy eyes back to the lady in front of him and told himself to be more patient with her. After all, she was probably only complimenting his father because she thought it was what he wanted to hear.

"I merely wanted to remind you," she said, "that we were introduced several years ago, back when you were still Clyvedon."

"Yes," Simon murmured, looking for any break in the barricade of ladies through which he might make his escape.

"These are my daughters," the woman said, motioning to the three young ladies. Two were pleasant-looking, but the third was still cloaked in baby fat and an orangey gown which did nothing for her complexion. She didn't appear to be enjoying the evening.

"Aren't they lovely?" the lady continued. "My pride and joy. And so even-tempered."

Simon had the queasy feeling that he'd heard the same words once when shopping for a dog.

"Your grace, may I present Prudence, Philipa, and Penelope."

The girls made their curtsies, not a one of them daring to meet his eye.

"I have another daughter at home," the lady continued. "Felicity. But she's a mere ten years of age, so I do not bring her to such events."

Simon could not imagine why she felt the need to share this information with him, but he just kept his tone carefully bored (this, he'd long since learned, was the best way not to show anger) and prompted, "And you are . . . ? "

"Oh, beg pardon! I am Mrs. Featherington, of course. My husband passed on three years ago, but he was your papa's, er, dearest friend." Her voice trailed off at the end of her sentence, as she remembered Simon's last reaction to mention of his father.

Simon nodded curtly.

"Prudence is quite accomplished on the pianoforte," Mrs. Featherington said, with forced brightness.

Simon noted the oldest girl's pained expression and quickly decided never to attend a musicale chez Featherington.

"And my darling Philipa is an expert watercolorist."

Philipa beamed.

"And Penelope?" some devil inside Simon forced him to ask.

Mrs. Featherington shot a panicked look at her youngest daughter, who looked quite miserable. Penelope was not terribly attractive, and her somewhat pudgy figure was not improved by her mother's choice of attire for her. But she seemed to have kind eyes.

"Penelope?" Mrs. Featherington echoed, her voice a touch shrill. "Penelope is . . . ah . . . well, she's Penelope!" Her mouth wobbled into a patently false grin.

Penelope looked as if she wanted to dive under a rug. Simon decided that if he was forced to dance, he'd ask Penelope.

"Mrs. Featherington," came a sharp and imperious voice that could only belong to Lady Danbury, "are you pestering the duke?"

Simon wanted to answer in the affirmative, but the memory of Penelope Featherington's mortified face led him to murmur, "Of course not."

Lady Danbury raised a brow as she moved her head slowly toward him. "Liar."

She turned back to Mrs. Featherington, who had gone quite green. Mrs. Featherington said nothing. Lady Danbury said nothing. Mrs. Featherington finally mumbled something about seeing her cousin, grabbed her three daughters, and scurried off.

Simon crossed his arms, but he wasn't able to keep his face completely free of amusement. "That wasn't very well done of you," he said.

"Bah. She's feathers for brains, and so do her girls, except maybe that unattractive young one." Lady Danbury shook her head. "If they'd only put her in a different color . . ."

Simon fought a chuckle and lost. "You never did learn to mind your own business, did you?"

"Never. And what fun would that be?" She smiled. Simon could tell she didn't want to, but she smiled. "And as for you," she continued. "You are a monstrous guest. One would have thought you'd possess the manners to greet your hostess by now."

"You were always too well surrounded by your admirers for me to dare even approach."

"So glib," she commented.

Simon said nothing, not entirely certain how to interpret her words. He'd always had the suspicion that she knew his secret, but he'd never been quite sure.

"Your friend Bridgerton approaches," she said.

Simon's eyes followed the direction of her nod. Anthony ambled over, and was only half a second in their presence before Lady Danbury called him a coward.

Anthony blinked. "I beg your pardon?"

"You could have come over and saved your friend from the Featherington quartet ages ago."

"But I was so enjoying his distress."

"Hmmph." And without another word (or another grunt) she walked away.

"Strangest old woman," Anthony said. "I wouldn't be surprised if she's that cursed Whistledown woman."

"You mean the gossip columnist?"

Anthony nodded as he led Simon around a potted plant to the corner where his brothers were waiting. As they walked, Anthony grinned, and said, "I noticed you speaking with a number of very proper young ladies."

Simon muttered something rather obscene and unflattering under his breath.

But Anthony only laughed. "You can't say I didn't warn you, can you?"

"It is galling to admit that you might be right about anything, so please do not ask me to do so."

Anthony laughed some more. "For that comment I shall start introducing you to the debutantes myself."

"If you do," Simon warned, "you shall soon find yourself dying a very slow and painful death."

Anthony grinned. "Swords or pistols?"

"Oh, poison. Very definitely poison."

"Ouch." Anthony stopped his stroll across the ballroom in front of two other Bridgerton men, both clearly marked by their chestnut hair, tall height, and excellent bone structure. Simon noted that one had green eyes and the other brown like Anthony, but other than that, the dim evening light made the three men practically interchangeable.

"You do remember my brothers?" Anthony queried politely. "Benedict and Colin. Benedict I'm sure you recall from Eton. He was the one who dogged our footsteps for three months when he first arrived."

"Not true!" Benedict said with a laugh.

"I don't know if you've met Colin, actually," Anthony continued. "He was probably too young to have crossed your path."

"Pleased to meet you," Colin said jovially.

Simon noted the rascally glint in the young man's green eyes and couldn't help but smile in return.

"Anthony here has said such insulting things about you," Colin continued, his grin growing quite wicked, "that I know we're sure to be great friends."

Anthony rolled his eyes. "I'm certain you can understand why my mother is convinced that Colin will be the first of her children to drive her to insanity."

Colin said, "I pride myself on it, actually."

"Mother, thankfully, has had a brief respite from Colin's tender charms," Anthony continued. "He is actually just returned from a grand tour of the Continent."

"Just this evening," Colin said with a boyish grin. He had a devil-may-care youthful look about him. Simon decided he couldn't be much older than Daphne.

"I have just returned from travels as well," Simon said.

"Yes, except yours spanned the globe, I hear," Colin said. "I should love to hear about them someday."

Simon nodded politely. "Certainly."

"Have you met Daphne?" Benedict inquired. "She's the only Bridgerton in attendance who's unaccounted for."

Simon was pondering how best to answer that question when Colin let out a snort, and said, "Oh, Daphne's accounted for. Miserable, but accounted for."

Simon followed his gaze across the ballroom, where Daphne was standing next to what had to be her mother, looking, just as Colin had promised, as miserable as could be.

And then it occurred to him—Daphne was one of those dreaded unmarried young ladies being paraded about by her mother. She'd seemed far too sensible and forthright to be such a creature, and yet of course that was what she had to be. She couldn't have been more than twenty, and as her name was still Bridgerton she was clearly a maiden. And since she had a mother—well, of course she'd be trapped into an endless round of introductions.

She looked every bit as pained by the experience as Simon had been. Somehow that made him feel a good deal better.

"One of us should save her," Benedict mused.

"Nah," Colin said, grinning. "Mother's only had her over there with Macclesfield for ten minutes."

"Macclesfield?" Simon asked.

"The earl," Benedict replied. "Castleford's son."

"Ten minutes?" Anthony asked. "Poor Macclesfield."

Simon shot him a curious look.

"Not that Daphne is such a chore," Anthony quickly added, "but when Mother gets it in her head to, ah . . ."

"Pursue," Benedict filled in helpfully.

"—a gentleman," Anthony continued with a nod of thanks toward his brother, "she can be, ah . . ."

"Relentless," Colin said.

Anthony smiled weakly. "Yes. Exactly."

Simon looked back over toward the trio in question. Sure enough, Daphne looked miserable, Macclesfield was scanning the room, presumably looking for the nearest exit, and Lady Bridgerton's eyes held a gleam so ambitious that Simon cringed in sympathy for the young earl.

"We should save Daphne," Anthony said.

"We really should," Benedict added.

"And Macclesfield," Anthony said.

"Oh, certainly," Benedict added.

But Simon noticed that no one was leaping into action.

"All talk, aren't you?" Colin chortled.

"I don't see *you* marching over there to save her," Anthony shot back.

"Hell no. But I never said we should. *You*, on the other hand . . ."

"What the devil is going on?" Simon finally asked.

The three Bridgerton brothers looked at him with identical guilty expressions.

"We *should* save Daff," Benedict said.

"We really should," Anthony added.

"What my brothers are too lily-livered to tell you," Colin said derisively, "is that they are terrified of my mother."

"It's true," Anthony said with a helpless shrug.

Benedict nodded. "I freely admit it."

Simon thought he'd never seen a more ludicrous sight. These were the Bridgerton brothers, after all. Tall, handsome, athletic, with every miss in the nation setting her cap after them, and here they were, completely cowed by a mere slip of a woman.

Of course, it *was* their mother. Simon supposed one had to make allowances for that.

"If I save Daff," Anthony explained, "Mother might get me into her clutches, and then I'm done for."

Simon choked on laughter as his mind filled with a vision of Anthony being led around by his mother, moving from unmarried lady to unmarried lady.

"Now you see why I avoid these functions like the plague," Anthony said grimly. "I'm attacked from both directions. If the debutantes and their mothers don't find me, *my* mother makes certain I find *them*."

"Say!" Benedict exclaimed. "Why don't *you* save her, Hastings?"

Simon took one look at Lady Bridgerton (who at that point had her hand firmly wrapped around Macclesfield's forearm) and decided he'd rather be branded an eternal coward. "Since we haven't been introduced, I'm sure it would be most improper," he improvised.

"I'm sure it wouldn't," Anthony returned. "You're a duke."

"So?"

"So?" Anthony echoed. "Mother would forgive any impropriety if it meant gaining an audience for Daphne with a duke."

"Now look here," Simon said hotly, "I'm not some sacrificial lamb to be slaughtered on the altar of your mother."

"You *have* spent a lot of time in Africa, haven't you?" Colin quipped.

Simon ignored him. "Besides, your sister said—"

All three Bridgerton heads swung around in his direction. Simon immediately realized he'd blundered. Badly.

"You've met Daphne?" Anthony queried, his voice just a touch too polite for Simon's comfort.

Before Simon could even reply, Benedict leaned in ever-so-slightly closer, and asked, "Why didn't you mention this?"

"Yes," Colin said, his mouth utterly serious for the first time that evening. "Why?"

Simon glanced from brother to brother and it became perfectly clear why Daphne must still be unmarried. This belligerent trio would scare off all but the most determined—or stupid—of suitors.

Which would probably explain Nigel Berbrooke.

"Actually," Simon said, "I bumped into her in the hall as I was making my way into the ballroom. It was"—he glanced rather pointedly at the Bridgertons—"rather obvious that she was a member of your family, so I introduced myself."

Anthony turned to Benedict. "Must have been when she was fleeing Berbrooke."

Benedict turned to Colin. "What did happen to Berbrooke? Do you know?"

Colin shrugged. "Haven't the faintest. Probably left to nurse his broken heart."

*Or broken head*, Simon thought acerbically.

"Well, that explains everything, I'm sure," Anthony said, losing his overbearing big-brother expression and looking once again like a fellow rake and best friend.

"Except," Benedict said suspiciously, "why he didn't mention it."

"Because I didn't have the chance," Simon bit off, about ready to throw his arms up in exasperation. "In case you hadn't noticed, Anthony, you have a ridiculous number of siblings, and it takes a ridiculous amount of time to be introduced to all of them."

"There are only two of us present," Colin pointed out.

"I'm going home," Simon announced. "The three of you are mad."

Benedict, who had seemed to be the most protective of the brothers, suddenly grinned. "You don't have a sister, do you?"

"No, thank God."

"If you ever have a daughter, you'll understand."

Simon was rather certain he would never have a daughter, but he kept his mouth shut.

"It can be a trial," Anthony said.

"Although Daff is better than most," Benedict put in. "She doesn't have that many suitors, actually."

Simon couldn't imagine why not.

"I'm not really sure why," Anthony mused. "I think she's a perfectly nice girl."

Simon decided this wasn't the time to mention that he'd been one inch away from easing her up against the wall, pressing his hips against hers, and kissing her senseless. If he hadn't discovered that she was a Bridgerton, frankly, he might have done exactly that.

"Daff's the best," Benedict agreed.

Colin nodded. "Capital girl. Really good sport."

There was an awkward pause, and then Simon said, "Well, good sport or not, I'm not going over there to save her, because she told me quite specifically that your mother forbade her ever to be seen in my presence."

"Mother said *that*?" Colin asked. "You must really have a black reputation."

"A good portion of it undeserved," Simon muttered, not entirely certain why he was defending himself.

"That's too bad," Colin murmured. "I'd thought to ask you to take me 'round."

Simon foresaw a long and terrifyingly roguish future for the boy.

Anthony's fist found its way to the small of Simon's back, and he started to propel him forward. "I'm sure Mother will change her mind given the proper encouragement. Let's go."

Simon had no choice but to walk toward Daphne. The alternative required making a really big scene, and Simon had long since learned that he didn't do well with scenes. Besides, if he'd been in Anthony's position, he probably would have done the exact same thing.

And after an evening with the Featherington sisters and the like, Daphne didn't sound half-bad.

"Mother!" Anthony called out in a jovial voice as they approached the viscountess. "I haven't seen you all evening."

Simon noticed that Lady Bridgerton's blue eyes lit up when she saw her son approaching. Ambitious Mama or not, Lady Bridgerton clearly loved her children.

"Anthony!" she said in return. "How nice to see you. Daphne and I were just chatting with Lord Macclesfield."

Anthony sent Lord Macclesfield a commiserating look. "Yes, I see."

Simon caught Daphne's eye for a moment and gave his head the tiniest shake. She responded with an even tinier nod, sensible girl that she was.

"And who is this?" Lady Bridgerton inquired, her eyes lighting upon Simon's face.

"The new Duke of Hastings," Anthony replied. "Surely you remember him from my days at Eton and Oxford."

"Of course," Lady Bridgerton said politely.

Macclesfield, who had been keeping scrupulously quiet, quickly located the first lull in the conversation, and burst in with, "I think I see my father."

Anthony shot the young earl an amused and knowing glance. "Then by all means, go to him."

The young earl did, with alacrity.

"I thought he detested his father," Lady Bridgerton said with a confused expression.

"He does," Daphne said baldly.

Simon choked down a laugh. Daphne raised her brows, silently daring him to comment.

"Well, he had a terrible reputation, anyway," Lady Bridgerton said.

"There seems to be quite a bit of that in the air these days," Simon murmured.

Daphne's eyes widened, and this time Simon got to raise *his* brows, silently daring *her* to comment.

She didn't, of course, but her mother gave him a sharp look, and Simon had the distinct impression that she was trying to decide whether his newly acquired dukedom made up for his bad reputation.

"I don't believe I had the chance to make your acquaintance before I left the country, Lady Bridgerton," Simon said smoothly, "but I am very pleased to do so now."

"As am I." She motioned to Daphne. "My daughter Daphne."

Simon took Daphne's gloved hand and laid a scrupulously polite kiss on her knuckles. "I am honored to officially make your acquaintance, Miss Bridgerton."

"Officially?" Lady Bridgerton queried.

Daphne opened her mouth, but Simon cut in before she could say anything. "I already told your brother about our *brief* meeting earlier this evening."

Lady Bridgerton's head turned rather sharply in Daphne's direction. "You were introduced to the duke earlier this evening? Why did you not say anything?"

Daphne smiled tightly. "We were rather occupied with the earl. And before that, with Lord Westborough. And before that, with—"

"I see your point, Daphne," Lady Bridgerton ground out.

Simon wondered how unforgivably rude it would be if he laughed.

Then Lady Bridgerton turned the full force of her smile on him—and Simon quickly learned where Daphne got that wide, wide smile from—and Simon realized that Lady Bridgerton had decided that his bad reputation could be overlooked.

A strange light appeared in her eye, and her head bobbed back and forth between Daphne and Simon.

Then she smiled again.

Simon fought the urge to flee.

Anthony leaned over slightly, and whispered in his ear, "I am *so* sorry."

Simon said between clenched teeth, "I may have to kill you."

Daphne's icicle glare said that she'd heard both of them and was not amused.

But Lady Bridgerton was blissfully oblivious, her head presumably already filling with images of a grand wedding.

Then her eyes narrowed as she focused on something behind the men. She looked so overwhelmingly annoyed that Simon, Anthony, and Daphne all twisted their necks to see what was afoot.

Mrs. Featherington was marching purposefully in their direction, Prudence and Philipa right behind. Simon noticed that Penelope was nowhere to be seen.

Desperate times, Simon quickly realized, called for desperate measures. "Miss Bridgerton," he said, whipping his head around to face Daphne, "would you care to dance?"

# Chapter 5

*Were you at Lady Danbury's ball last night? If not, shame on you. You missed witnessing quite the most remarkable coup of the season. It was clear to all partygoers, and especially to This Author, that Miss Daphne Bridgerton has captured the interest of the newly returned to England Duke of Hastings.*

*One can only imagine the relief of Lady Bridgerton. How mortifying it will be if Daphne remains on the shelf for yet another season! And Lady B—with three more daughters to marry off. Oh, the horror.*

*Lady Whistledown's Society Papers,*
30 April 1813

There was no way Daphne could refuse. First of all, her mother was impaling her with her deadly I-Am-Your-Mother-Don't-You-Dare-Defy-Me gaze.

Secondly, the duke had clearly not given Anthony the entire story of their meeting in the dimly lit hallway; to make a show of refusing to dance with him would certainly raise undue speculation.

Not to mention that Daphne really didn't particularly relish getting drawn into a conversation with the Featheringtons, which was sure to happen if she didn't make immediate haste for the dance floor.

And finally, she kind of sort of just a little teeny bit actually *wanted* to dance with the duke.

Of course the arrogant boor didn't even give her the chance to accept. Before Daphne could manage an "I'd be delighted," or even a mere, "Yes," he had her halfway across the room.

The orchestra was still producing those awful noises it makes while the musicians were getting ready to begin, so they were forced to wait a moment before they actually danced.

"Thank God you didn't refuse," the duke said with great feeling.

"When would I have had the opportunity?"

He grinned at her.

Daphne answered that with a scowl. "I wasn't given the opportunity to accept, either, if you recall."

He raised a brow. "Does that mean I must ask you again?"

"No, of course not," Daphne replied, rolling her eyes. "That would be rather childish of me, don't you think? And besides, it would cause a terrible scene, which I don't think either of us desires."

He cocked his head and gave her a rather assessing glance, as if he had analyzed her personality in an instant and decided she might just be acceptable. Daphne found the experience somewhat unnerving.

Just then the orchestra ceased its discordant warm-up and struck the first notes of a waltz.

Simon groaned. "Do young ladies still need permission to waltz?"

Daphne found herself smiling at his discomfort. "How long have you been away?"

"Five years. Do they?"

"Yes."

"Do you have it?" He looked almost pained at the prospect of his escape plan falling apart.

"Of course."

He swept her into his arms and whirled her into the throng of elegantly clad couples. "Good."

They had made a full circle of the ballroom before Daphne asked, "How much of our meeting did you reveal to my brothers? I saw you with them, you know."

Simon only smiled.

"What are you grinning about?" she asked suspiciously.

"I was merely marveling at your restraint."

"I beg your pardon?"

He shrugged slightly, his shoulders rising as his head tilted to the right. "I hadn't thought you the most patient of ladies," he said, "and here it took you a full three and a half minutes before asking me about my conversation with your brothers."

Daphne fought a blush. The truth was, the duke was a most accomplished dancer, and she'd been enjoying the waltz too much even to think of conversation.

"But since you asked," he said, mercifully sparing her from having to make a comment, "all I told them was that I ran into you in the hall and that, given your coloring, I instantly recognized you as a Bridgerton and introduced myself."

"Do you think they believed you?"

"Yes," he said softly, "I rather think they did."

"Not that we have anything to hide," she added quickly.

"Of course not."

"If there is any villain in this piece it is most certainly Nigel."

"Of course."

She chewed on her lower lip. "Do you think he's still out in the hall?"

"I certainly have no intention of finding out."

There was an awkward moment of silence, and then Daphne said, "It has been some time since you have attended a London ball, has it not? Nigel and I must have been quite a welcome."

"You were a welcome sight. He was not."

She smiled slightly at the compliment. "Aside from our little escapade, have you been enjoying your evening?"

Simon's answer was so unequivocally in the negative that he actually snorted a laugh before saying it.

"Really?" Daphne replied, her brows arching with curiosity. "Now *that* is interesting."

"You find my agony interesting? Remind me never to turn to you should I ever fall ill."

"Oh, please," she scoffed. "It can't have been that bad."

"Oh, it can."

"Certainly not as bad as *my* evening."

"You did look rather miserable with your mother and Macclesfield," he allowed.

"How kind of you to point it out," she muttered.

"But I still think my evening was worse."

Daphne laughed, a light musical sound that warmed Simon's bones. "What a sad pair we are," she said. "Surely we can manage a conversation on a topic other than our respective terrible evenings."

Simon said nothing.

Daphne said nothing.

"Well, I can't think of anything," he said.

Daphne laughed again, this time with more gaiety, and Simon once again found himself mesmerized by her smile.

"I give in," she gasped. "What has turned your evening into such a dreadful affair?"

"What or *whom*?"

" 'Whom'?" she echoed, tilting her head as she looked at him. "This grows even more interesting."

"I can think of any number of adjectives to describe all of the 'whoms' I have had the pleasure of meeting this evening, but 'interesting' is not one of them."

"Now, now," she chided, "don't be rude. I did see you chatting with my brothers, after all."

He nodded gallantly, tightening his hand slightly at her waist as they swung around in a graceful arc. "My apologies. The Bridgertons are, of course, excluded from my insults."

"We are all relieved, I'm sure."

Simon cracked a smile at her deadpan wit. "I live to make Bridgertons happy."

"Now *that* is a statement that may come back to haunt you," she chided. "But in all seriousness, what has you in such a dither? If your evening has gone that far downhill since our interlude with Nigel, you're in sad straits, indeed."

"How shall I put this," he mused, "so that I do not completely offend you?"

"Oh, go right ahead," she said blithely. "I promise not to be offended."

Simon grinned wickedly. "A statement that may come back to haunt *you*."

She blushed slightly. The color was barely noticeable in the shadowy candlelight, but Simon had been watching her closely. She didn't say anything, however, so he added, "Very well, if you must know, I have been introduced to every single unmarried lady in the ballroom."

A strange snorting sound came from the vicinity of her mouth. Simon had the sneaking suspicion that she was laughing at him.

"I have also," he continued, "been introduced to all of their mothers."

She gurgled. She actually gurgled.

"Bad show," he scolded. "Laughing at your dance partner."

"I'm sorry," she said, her lips tight from trying not to smile.

"No, you're not."

"All right," she admitted, "I'm not. But only because I have had to suffer the same torture for two years. It's difficult to summon too much pity for a mere evening's worth."

"Why don't you just find someone to marry and put yourself out of your misery?"

She shot him a sharp look. "Are you asking?"

Simon felt the blood leave his face.

"I thought not." She took one look at him and let out an impatient exhale. "Oh, for goodness' sake. You can start breathing now, your grace. I was only teasing."

Simon wanted to make some sort of dry, cutting, and utterly ironic comment, but the truth was, she had so startled him that he couldn't utter a word.

"To answer your question," she continued, her voice a touch more brittle than he was accustomed to hearing from her, "a lady must consider her options. There is Nigel, of course, but I think we must agree he is not a suitable candidate."

Simon shook his head.

"Earlier this year there was Lord Chalmers."

"Chalmers?" He frowned. "Isn't he—"

"On the darker side of sixty? Yes. And since I would someday like to have children, it seemed—"

"Some men that age can still sire brats," Simon pointed out.

"It wasn't a risk I was prepared to take," she returned. "Besides—" She shuddered slightly, a look of revulsion passing over her features. "I didn't particularly care to have children with *him*."

Much to his annoyance, Simon found himself picturing Daphne in bed with the elderly Chalmers. It was a disgusting image, and it left him feeling faintly furious. At whom, he didn't know; maybe at himself for even bothering to imagine the damned thing, but—

"Before Lord Chalmers," Daphne continued, thankfully interrupting his rather unpleasant thought process, "there were two others, both just as repulsive."

Simon looked at her thoughtfully. "Do you want to marry?"

"Well, of course." Her face registered her surprise. "Doesn't everyone?"

"I don't."

She smiled condescendingly. "You think you don't. All men think they don't. But you will."

"No," he said emphatically. "I will never marry."

She gaped at him. Something in the duke's tone of voice told her that he truly meant what he said. "What about your title?"

Simon shrugged. "What about it?"

"If you don't marry and sire an heir, it will expire. Or go to some beastly cousin."

That caused him to raise an amused brow. "And how do you know that my cousins are beastly?"

"All cousins who are next in line for a title are beastly." She cocked her head in a mischievous manner. "Or at least they are according to the men who actually *possess* the title."

"And this is information you've gleaned from your extensive knowledge of men?" he teased.

She shot him a devastatingly superior grin. "Of course."

Simon was silent for a moment, and then he asked, "Is it worth it?"

She looked bemused by his sudden change of subject. "Is what worth it?"

He let go of her hand just long enough to wave at the crowd. "This. This endless parade of parties. Your mother nipping at your heels."

Daphne let out a surprised chuckle. "I doubt she'd appreciate the metaphor." She fell silent for a moment, her eyes taking on a faraway look as she said, "But yes, I suppose it is worth it. It has to be worth it."

She snapped back to attention and looked back to his face, her dark eyes meltingly honest. "I want a husband. I want a family. It's not so silly when you think about it. I'm fourth of eight children. All I know are large families. I shouldn't know how to exist outside of one."

Simon caught her gaze, his eyes burning hot and intense into hers. A warning bell sounded in his mind. He wanted her. He wanted her so desperately he was straining against his clothing, but he could never, ever so much as touch her. Because to do so would be to shatter every last one of her dreams, and rake or not, Simon wasn't certain he could live with himself if he did that.

He would never marry, never sire a child, and that was all she wanted out of life.

He might enjoy her company; he wasn't certain he could deny himself that. But he had to leave her untouched for another man.

"Your grace?" she asked quietly. When he blinked, she smiled and said, "You were woolgathering."

He inclined his head graciously. "Merely pondering your words."

"And did they meet with your approval?"

"Actually, I can't remember the last time I conversed with someone with such obvious good sense." He added in a slow voice, "It's good to know what you want out of life."

"Do you know what you want?"

Ah, how to answer that. There were some things he knew he could not say. But it was so easy to talk to this girl. Something about her put his mind at ease, even as his body tingled with desire. By all rights they should not have been having such a frank conversation so soon into an acquaintance, but somehow it just felt natural.

Finally, he just said, "I made some decisions when I was younger. I try to live my life according to those vows."

She looked ravenously curious, but good manners prevented her from questioning him further. "My goodness," she said with a slightly forced smile, "we've grown serious. And here I thought all we meant to debate was whose evening was less pleasant."

They were both trapped, Simon realized. Trapped by their society's conventions and expectations.

And that's when an idea popped into his mind. A strange, wild, and appallingly wonderful idea. It was probably also a dangerous idea, since it would put him in her company for long periods of time, which would certainly leave him in a perpetual state of unfulfilled desire, but Simon valued his self-control above all else, and he was certain he could control his baser urges.

"Wouldn't you like a respite?" he asked suddenly.

"A respite?" she echoed bemusedly. Even as they twirled across the floor, she looked from side to side. "From this?"

"Not precisely. This, you'd still have to endure. What I envision is more of a respite from your mother."

Daphne choked on her surprise. "You're going to remove my mother from the social whirl? Doesn't that seem a touch extreme?"

"I'm not talking about removing your mother. Rather, I want to remove you."

Daphne tripped over her feet, and then, just as soon as she'd regained her balance, she tripped over his. "I beg your pardon?"

"I had hoped to ignore London society altogether," he explained, "but I'm finding that may prove to be impossible."

"Because you've suddenly developed a taste for ratafia and weak lemonade?" she quipped.

"No," he said, ignoring her sarcasm, "because I've discovered that half of my university friends married in my absence, and their wives seem to be obsessed with throwing the perfect party—"

"And you've been invited?"

He nodded grimly.

Daphne leaned in close, as if she were about to tell him a grave secret. "You're a duke," she whispered. "You can say no."

She watched with fascination as his jaw tightened. "These men," he said, "their husbands—they are my friends."

Daphne felt her lips moving into an unbidden grin. "And you don't want to hurt their wives' feelings."

Simon scowled, clearly uncomfortable with the compliment.

"Well, I'll be," she said mischievously. "You might just be a nice person after all."

"I'm hardly nice," he scoffed.

"Perhaps, but you're hardly cruel, either."

The music drew to a close, and Simon took her arm and guided her to the perimeter of the ballroom. Their dance had deposited them on the opposite side of the room from Daphne's family, so they had time to continue their conversation as they walked slowly back to the Bridgertons.

"What I was trying to say," he said, "before you so skillfully diverted me, was that it appears I must attend a certain number of London events."

"Hardly a fate worse than death."

He ignored her editorial. "You, I gather, must attend them as well."

She gave him a single regal nod.

"Perhaps there is a way that I might be spared the attentions of the Featheringtons and the like, and at the same time, you might be spared the matchmaking efforts of your mother."

She looked at him intently. "Go on."

"We"—he leaned forward, his eyes mesmerizing hers—"will form an attachment."

Daphne said nothing. Absolutely nothing. She just stared at him as if she were trying to decide if he were the rudest man on the face of the earth or simply mad in the head.

"Not a true attachment," Simon said impatiently. "Good God, what sort of man do you think I am?"

"Well, I *was* warned about your reputation," she pointed out. "And you yourself tried to terrify me with your rakish ways earlier this evening."

"I did no such thing."

"Of course you did." She patted his arm. "But I forgive you. I'm sure you couldn't help it."

Simon gave her a startled look. "I don't believe I have ever been condescended to by a woman before."

She shrugged. "It was probably past time."

"Do you know, I'd thought that you were unmarried because your brothers had scared off all your suitors, but now I wonder if you did it all on your own."

Much to his surprise, she just laughed. "No," she said, "I'm unmarried because everyone sees me as a friend. No one ever has any romantic interest in me." She grimaced. "Except Nigel."

Simon pondered her words for a few moments, then realized that his plan could work to her benefit even more than he'd originally imagined. "Listen," he said, "and listen quickly because we're almost back to your family, and Anthony looks as if he's about to bolt in our direction any minute now."

They both glanced quickly to the right. Anthony was still trapped in conversation with the Featheringtons. He did not look happy.

"Here is my plan," Simon continued, his voice low and intense. "We shall pretend to have developed a tendre for each other. I won't have quite so many debutantes thrown in my direction because it will be perceived that I am no longer available."

"No it won't," Daphne replied. "They won't believe you're unavailable until you're standing up before the bishop, taking your vows."

The very thought made his stomach churn. "Nonsense," he said. "It may take a bit of time, but I'm sure I will eventually be able to convince society that I am not anyone's candidate for marriage."

"Except mine," Daphne pointed out.

"Except yours," he agreed, "but we will know that isn't true."

"Of course," she murmured. "Frankly, I do not believe that this will work, but if you're convinced . . ."

"I am."

"Well, then, what do I gain?"

"For one thing, your mother will stop dragging you from man to man if she thinks you have secured my interest."

"Rather conceited of you," Daphne mused, "but true."

Simon ignored her gibe. "Secondly," he continued, "men are always more interested in a woman if they think other men are interested."

"Meaning?"

"Meaning, quite simply, and pardon my *conceit*"—he shot her a sardonic look to show that he hadn't missed her earlier sarcasm—

"but if all the world thinks I intend to make you my duchess, all of those men who see you as nothing more than an affable friend will begin to view you in a new light."

Her lips pursed. "Meaning that once you throw me over, I shall have hordes of suitors at my beck and call?"

"Oh, I shall allow you to be the one to cry off," he said gallantly.

He noticed she didn't bother to thank him.

"I still think I'm gaining much more from this arrangement than you," she said.

He squeezed her arm slightly. "Then you'll do it?"

Daphne looked at Mrs. Featherington, who looked like a bird of prey, and then at her brother, who looked as if he had swallowed a chicken bone. She'd seen those expressions dozens of times before—except on the faces of her own mother and some hapless potential suitor.

"Yes," she said, her voice firm. "Yes, I'll do it."

"What do you suppose is taking them so long?"

Violet Bridgerton tugged on her eldest son's sleeve, unable to take her eyes off of her daughter—who appeared to have thoroughly captured the attention of the Duke of Hastings—only one week in London and already the catch of the season.

"I don't know," Anthony replied, looking gratefully at the backs of the Featheringtons as they moved on to their next victim, "but it feels as if it's been hours."

"Do you think he likes her?" Violet asked excitedly. "Do you think our Daphne truly has a chance to be a duchess?"

Anthony's eyes filled with a mixture of impatience and disbelief. "Mother, you told Daphne she wasn't even to be *seen* with him, and now you're thinking of marriage?"

"I spoke prematurely," Violet said with a blithe wave of her hand. "Clearly he is a man of great refinement and taste. And how, may I ask, do you know what I said to Daphne?"

"Daff told me, of course," Anthony lied.

"Hmmph. Well, I am certain that Portia Featherington won't be forgetting this evening anytime soon."

Anthony's eyes widened. "Are you trying to marry Daphne off so that she might be happy as a wife and a mother, or are you just trying to beat Mrs. Featherington to the altar?"

"The former, of course," Violet replied in a huff, "and I am offended you would even imply otherwise." Her eyes strayed off of Daphne and the duke for just long enough to locate Portia Featherington and her daughters. "But I certainly shan't mind seeing the look on her face when she realizes that *Daphne* will make the season's greatest match."

"Mother, you are hopeless."

"Certainly not. Shameless, perhaps, but never hopeless."

Anthony just shook his head and muttered something under his breath.

"It's impolite to mumble," Violet said, mostly just to annoy him. Then she spotted Daphne and the duke. "Ah, here they come. Anthony, behave yourself. Daphne! Your grace!" She paused as the couple made their way to her side. "I trust you enjoyed your dance."

"Very much," Simon murmured. "Your daughter is as graceful as she is lovely."

Anthony let out a snort.

Simon ignored him. "I hope we may have the pleasure of dancing together again very soon."

Violet positively glowed. "Oh, I'm *sure* Daphne would *adore* that." When Daphne didn't answer with all possible haste, she added, quite pointedly, "Wouldn't you, Daphne?"

"Of course," Daphne said demurely.

"I'm certain your mother would never be so lax as to allow me a second waltz," Simon said, looking every inch the debonair duke, "but I do hope she will permit us to take a stroll around the ballroom."

"You just took a stroll around the ballroom," Anthony pointed out.

Simon ignored him again. He said to Violet, "We shall, of course, remain in your sight at all times."

The lavender silk fan in Violet's hand began to flutter rapidly. "I should be delighted. I mean, Daphne should be delighted. Shouldn't you, Daphne?"

Daphne was all innocence. "Oh, I should."

"And I," Anthony snapped, "should take a dose of laudanum, for clearly I am fevered. What the devil is going on?"

"Anthony!" Violet exclaimed. She turned hastily to Simon. "Don't mind him."

"Oh, I never do," Simon said affably.

"Daphne," Anthony said pointedly, "I should be delighted to act as your chaperon."

"Really, Anthony," Violet cut in, "they hardly need one if they are to remain here in the ballroom."

"Oh, I *insist*."

"You two run along," Violet said to Daphne and Simon, waving her hand at them. "Anthony will be with you in just a moment."

Anthony tried to follow immediately, but Violet grabbed onto his wrist. Hard. "What the devil do you think you're doing?" she hissed.

"Protecting my sister!"

"From the duke? He can't be that wicked. Actually, he reminds me of you."

Anthony groaned. "Then she definitely needs my protection."

Violet patted him on the arm. "Don't be so overprotective. If he attempts to spirit her out onto the balcony, I promise you may dash out to rescue her. But until that unlikely event occurs, please allow your sister her moment of glory."

Anthony glared at Simon's back. "Tomorrow I will kill him."

"Dear me," Violet said, shaking her head, "I had no idea you could be so high-strung. One would think, as your mother, I would know these things, especially since you are my firstborn, and thus I have known you for the longest of any of my children, but—"

"Is that Colin?" Anthony interrupted, his voice strangled.

Violet blinked, then squinted her eyes. "Why, yes, it is. Isn't it lovely that he returned early? I could hardly believe my eyes when I saw him an hour ago. In fact, I—"

"I'd better go to him," Anthony said quickly. "He looks lonely. Good-bye, Mother."

Violet watched as Anthony ran off, presumably to escape her chattering lecture. "Silly boy," she murmured to herself. None of her children seemed to be on to any of her tricks. Just blather on about nothing in particular, and she could be rid of any of them in a trice.

She let out a satisfied sigh and resumed her watch of her daughter, now on the other side of the ballroom, her hand nestled comfortably in the crook of the duke's elbow. They made a most handsome couple.

Yes, Violet thought, her eyes growing misty, her daughter would make an excellent duchess.

Then she let her gaze wander briefly over to Anthony, who was now right where she wanted him—out of her hair. She allowed herself a secret smile. Children were so easy to manage.

Then her smile turned to a frown as she noticed Daphne walking back toward her—on the arm of another man. Violet's eyes immediately scanned the ballroom until she found the duke.

Dash it all, what the devil was he doing dancing with Penelope Featherington?

# Chapter 6

*It has been reported to This Author that the Duke of Hastings mentioned no fewer than six times yestereve that he has no plans to marry. If his intention was to discourage the Ambitious Mamas, he made a grave error in judgment. They will simply view his remarks as the greatest of challenges.*

*And in an interesting side note, his half dozen anti-matrimony remarks were all uttered before he made the acquaintance of the lovely and sensible Miss (Daphne) Bridgerton.*

LADY WHISTLEDOWN'S SOCIETY PAPERS,
30 April 1813

The following afternoon found Simon standing on the front steps of Daphne's home, one hand rapping the brass knocker on the door, the other wrapped around a large bouquet of fiendishly expensive tulips. It hadn't occurred to him that his little charade might require his attention during the daylight hours, but during their stroll about the ballroom the previous night, Daphne had sagely pointed out that if he did not call upon her the next day, no one—least of all her mother—would truly believe he was interested.

Simon accepted her words as truth, allowing that Daphne almost certainly had more knowledge in this area of etiquette than he did. He'd dutifully found some flowers and trudged across Grosvenor Square to Bridgerton House. He'd never courted a respectable woman before, so the ritual was foreign to him.

The door was opened almost immediately by the Bridgertons' butler. Simon gave him his card. The butler, a tall thin man with a hawkish nose, looked at it for barely a quarter second before nodding, and murmuring, "Right this way, your grace."

Clearly, Simon thought wryly, he had been expected.

What was unexpected, however, was the sight that awaited him when he was shown into the Bridgertons' drawing room.

Daphne, a vision in ice-blue silk, perched on the edge of Lady Bridgerton's green damask sofa, her face decorated with another one of those wide wide smiles.

It would have been a lovely sight, had she not been surrounded by at least a half dozen men, one of whom had actually descended to one knee, gales of poetry spewing from his mouth.

Judging from the florid nature of the prose, Simon fully expected a rosebush to sprout from the nitwit's mouth at any moment.

The entire scene, Simon decided, was most disagreeable.

He fixed his gaze on Daphne, who was directing her magnificent smile at the buffoon reciting poetry, and waited for her to acknowledge him.

She didn't.

Simon looked down at his free hand and noticed that it was curled into a tight fist. He scanned the room slowly, trying to decide on which man's face to use it.

Daphne smiled again, and again not at him.

The idiot poet. Definitely the idiot poet. Simon tilted his head slightly to the side as he analyzed the young swain's face. Would his fist fit best in the right eye socket or the left? Or maybe that was too violent. Maybe a light clip to the chin would be more appropriate. At the very least, it might actually shut the man up.

"This one," the poet announced grandly, "I wrote in your honor last night."

Simon groaned. The last poem he had recognized as a rather grandiose rendition of a Shakespearean sonnet, but an original work was more than he could bear.

"Your grace!"

Simon looked up to realize that Daphne had finally noticed that he had entered the room.

He nodded regally, his cool look very much at odds with the puppy-dog faces of her other suitors. "Miss Bridgerton."

"How lovely to see you," she said, a delighted smile crossing her face.

Ah, that was more like it. Simon straightened the flowers and started to walk toward her, only to realize that there were three young suitors in his path, and none appeared inclined to move. Simon pierced the first one with his haughtiest stare, which caused the boy—really, he looked all of twenty, hardly old enough to be called a *man*—to cough in a most unattractive manner and scurry off to an unoccupied window seat.

Simon moved forward, ready to repeat the procedure with the next annoying young man, when the viscountess suddenly stepped into his path, wearing a dark blue frock and a smile that might possibly rival Daphne's in its brightness.

"Your grace!" she said excitedly. "What a pleasure to see you. You honor us with your presence."

"I could hardly imagine myself anywhere else," Simon murmured as he took her gloved hand and kissed it. "Your daughter is an exceptional young lady."

The viscountess sighed contentedly. "And such lovely, lovely flowers," she said, once she was finished with her little revel of maternal pride. "Are they from Holland? They must have been terribly dear."

"Mother!" Daphne said sharply. She extricated her hand from the grasp of a particularly energetic suitor and made her way over. "What can the duke possibly say to that?"

"I could tell her how much I paid for them," he said with a devilish half-smile.

"You wouldn't."

He leaned forward, lowering his voice so that only Daphne could hear. "Didn't you remind me last night that I'm a duke?" he murmured. "I thought you told me I could do anything I wanted."

"Yes, but not that," Daphne said with a dismissive wave of her hand. "You would never be so crass."

"Of course the duke would not be crass!" her mother exclaimed, clearly horrified that Daphne would even mention the word in his presence. "What are you talking about? Why would he be crass?"

"The flowers," Simon said. "The cost. Daphne thinks I shouldn't tell you."

"Tell me later," the viscountess whispered out of the side of her mouth, "when she's not listening." Then she moved back over to the green damask sofa where Daphne had been sitting with her suitors and cleared it out in under three seconds. Simon had to admire the military precision with which she managed the maneuver.

"There now," the viscountess said. "Isn't that convenient? Daphne, why don't you and the duke sit right there?"

"You mean where Lord Railmont and Mr. Crane were sitting just moments ago?" Daphne asked innocently.

"Precisely," her mother replied, with what Simon considered to be an admirable lack of obvious sarcasm. "Besides, Mr. Crane said that he has to meet his mother at Gunter's at three."

Daphne glanced at the clock. "It's only two, Mother."

"The traffic," Violet said with a sniff, "is nothing short of dreadful these days. Far too many horses on the road."

"It ill becomes a man," Simon said, getting into the spirit of the conversation, "to keep his mother waiting."

"Well said, your grace." Violet beamed. "You can be sure that I have expressed that very same sentiment to my own children."

"And in case you're not sure," Daphne said with a smile, "I'd be happy to vouch for her."

Violet merely smiled. "If anyone should know, it would be you, Daphne. Now, if you will excuse me, I have business to attend to. Oh, Mr. Crane! Mr. Crane! Your mother would never forgive me if I did not shoo you out in time." She bustled off, taking the hapless Mr. Crane by the arm and leading him toward the door, barely giving him time to say farewell.

Daphne turned to Simon with an amused expression. "I can't quite decide if she is being terribly polite or exquisitely rude."

"Exquisitely polite, perhaps?" Simon asked mildly.

She shook her head. "Oh, definitely not that."

"The alternative, of course, is—"

"Terribly rude?" Daphne grinned and watched as her mother looped her arm through Lord Railmont's, pointed him toward Daphne so that he could nod his good-bye, and led him from the room. And then, as if by magic, the remaining beaux murmured their hasty farewells and followed suit.

"Remarkably efficient, isn't she?" Daphne murmured.

"Your mother? She's a marvel."

"She'll be back, of course."

"Pity. And here I thought I had you well and truly in my clutches."

Daphne laughed. "I don't know how anyone considered you a rake. Your sense of humor is far too superb."

"And here we rakes thought we were so wickedly droll."

"A rake's humor," Daphne stated, "is essentially cruel."

Her comment surprised him. He stared at her intently, searching her brown eyes, and yet not really knowing what it was he was looking for. There was a narrow ring of green just outside her pupils, the color as deep and rich as moss. He'd never seen her in the daylight before, he realized.

"Your grace?" Daphne's quiet voice snapped him out of his daze.

Simon blinked. "I beg your pardon."

"You looked a thousand miles away," she said, her brow wrinkling.

"I've been a thousand miles away." He fought the urge to return his gaze to her eyes. "This is entirely different."

Daphne let out a little laugh, the sound positively musical. "You have, haven't you? And here I've never even been past Lancashire. What a provincial I must seem."

He brushed aside her remark. "You must forgive my woolgathering. We were discussing my lack of humor, I believe?"

"We were not, and you well know it." Her hands found their way to her hips. "I specifically told you that you were in possession of a sense of humor far superior to that of the average rake."

One of his brows lifted in a rather superior manner. "And you wouldn't classify your brothers as rakes?"

"They only *think* they are rakes," she corrected. "There is a considerable difference."

Simon snorted. "If Anthony isn't a rake, I pity the woman who meets the man who is."

"There is more to being a rake than seducing legions of women," Daphne said blithely. "If a man can't do more than poke his tongue into a woman's mouth and kiss—"

Simon felt his throat close up, but somehow he managed to sputter, "You should not be speaking of such things."

She shrugged.

"You shouldn't even *know* about them," he grunted.

"Four brothers," she said by way of an explanation. "Well, three, I suppose. Gregory is too young to count."

"Someone ought to tell them to hold their tongues around you."

She shrugged again, this time with only one shoulder. "Half the time they don't even notice I'm there."

Simon couldn't imagine *that*.

"But we seem to have veered away from the original subject," she said. "All I meant to say is that a rake's humor has its basis in cruelty. He needs a victim, for he cannot imagine ever laughing at himself. You, your grace, are rather clever with the self-deprecating remark."

"I just don't know whether to thank you or throttle you."

"Throttle me? Good heavens, why?" She laughed again, a rich, throaty sound that Simon felt deep in his gut.

He exhaled slowly, the long whoosh of air just barely steadying his pulse. If she continued laughing, he wasn't going to be able to answer to the consequences.

But she just kept looking at him, her wide mouth curved into one of those smiles that looked as if it were perpetually on the verge of laughter.

"I am going to throttle you," he growled, "on general principle."

"And what principle is that?"

"The general principle of *man*," he blustered.

Her brows lifted dubiously. "As opposed to the general principle of woman?"

Simon looked around. "Where is your brother? You're far too cheeky. Surely someone needs to take you in hand."

"Oh, I'm sure you'll be seeing more of Anthony. In fact I'm rather surprised he hasn't made an appearance yet. He was quite irate last night. I was forced to listen to a full hour's lecture on your many faults and sins."

"The sins are almost certainly exaggerated."

"And the faults?"

"Probably true," Simon admitted sheepishly.

That remark earned him another smile from Daphne. "Well, true or not," she said, "he thinks you're up to something."

"I *am* up to something."

Her head tilted sarcastically as her eyes rolled upward. "He thinks you're up to something nefarious."

"I'd like to be up to something nefarious," he muttered.

"What was that?"

"Nothing."

She frowned. "I think we should tell Anthony about our plan."

"And what could possibly be the benefit to that?"

Daphne remembered the full-hour grilling she'd endured the previous night, and just said, "Oh, I think I'll let you figure that out for yourself."

Simon merely raised his brows. "My dear Daphne . . ."

Her lips parted slightly in surprise.

"Surely you're not going to force me to call you Miss Bridgerton." He sighed dramatically. "After all that we've been through."

"We've been through nothing, you ridiculous man, but I suppose you may call me Daphne nonetheless."

"Excellent." He nodded in a condescending manner. "You may call me 'your grace.' "

She swatted him.

"Very well," he replied, his lips twitching at the corners. "Simon, if you must."

"Oh I must," Daphne said, rolling her eyes, "clearly, I must."

He leaned toward her, something odd and slightly hot sparking in the depths of his pale eyes. "Must you?" he murmured. "I should be very excited to hear it."

Daphne had the sudden sense that he was talking about something far more intimate than the mere mention of his given name. A strange, tingling sort of heat shot down her arms, and without thinking, she jumped back a step. "Those flowers are quite lovely," she blurted out.

He regarded them lazily, rotating the bouquet with his wrist. "Yes, they are, aren't they?"

"I adore them."

"They're not for you."

Daphne choked on air.

Simon grinned. "They're for your mother."

Her mouth slowly opened in surprise, a short little gasp of air passing through her lips before she said, "Oh, you clever clever man. She will positively melt at your feet. But this will come back to haunt you, you know."

He gave her an arch look. "Oh really?"

"Really. She will be more determined than ever to drag you to the altar. You shall be just as beleaguered at parties as if we hadn't concocted this scheme."

"Nonsense," he scoffed. "Before I would have had to endure the attentions of dozens of Ambitious Mamas. Now I must deal with only one."

"Her tenacity might surprise you," Daphne muttered. Then she twisted her head to look out the partially open door. "She must truly like you," she added. "She's left us alone far longer than is proper."

Simon pondered that and leaned forward to whisper, "Could she be listening at the door?"

Daphne shook her head. "No, we would have heard her shoes clicking down the hall."

Something about that statement made him smile, and Daphne found herself smiling right along with him. "I really should thank you, though," she said, "before she returns."

"Oh? Why is that?"

"Your plan is a brilliant success. At least for me. Did you notice how many suitors came to call this morning?"

He crossed his arms, the tulips dangling upside down. "I noticed."

"It's brilliant, really. I've never had so many callers in a single afternoon before. Mother was beside herself with pride. Even Humboldt—he's our butler—was beaming, and I've never seen him so much as smile before. Ooops! Look, you're dripping." She leaned down and righted the flowers, her forearm grazing the front of his coat. She immediately jumped back, startled by both the heat and power of him.

Good God, if she could sense all that through his shirt and coat, what must he be like—

Daphne colored red. Deep, dark red.

"I should give my entire fortune for those thoughts," Simon said, his brows rising in question.

Thankfully, Violet chose that moment to sail into the room. "I'm terribly sorry for abandoning you for so long," she said, "but Mr. Crane's horse threw a shoe, so naturally I had to accompany him to the stables and find a groom to repair the damage."

In all their years together—which, Daphne thought acerbically, naturally constituted her entire life—Daphne had never known her mother to step foot in the stables.

"You are truly an exceptional hostess," Simon said, holding out the flowers. "Here, these are for you."

"For me?" Violet's mouth fell open in surprise, and a strange little breathy sound escaped her lips. "Are you certain? Because I—" She looked over at Daphne, and then at Simon, and then finally back at her daughter. "Are you certain?"

"Absolutely."

Violet blinked rapidly, and Daphne noticed that there were actually tears in her mother's eyes. No one ever gave her flowers, she realized. At least not since her father had died ten years earlier. Violet was such a mother—Daphne had forgotten that she was a woman as well.

"I don't know what to say," Violet sniffled.

"Try 'thank you,' " Daphne whispered in her ear, her grin lending warmth to her voice.

"Oh, Daff, you are the *worst*." Violet swatted her in the arm, looking more like a young woman than Daphne had ever seen her. "But thank you, your grace. These are beautiful blooms, but more importantly, it was a most thoughtful gesture. I shall treasure this moment always."

Simon looked as if he were about to say something, but in the end he just smiled and inclined his head.

Daphne looked at her mother, saw the unmistakable joy in her cornflower blue eyes, and realized with a touch of shame that none of her own children had ever acted in such a thoughtful manner as this man standing beside her.

The Duke of Hastings. Daphne decided then and there that she'd be a fool if she didn't fall in love with him.

Of course it would be nice if he returned the sentiment.

"Mother," Daphne said, "would you like me to fetch you a vase?"

"What?" Violet was still too busy sniffing blissfully at her flowers to pay attention to her daughter's words. "Oh. Yes, of course. Ask Humboldt for the cut crystal from my grandmother."

Daphne flashed a grateful smile at Simon and headed for the door, but before she could take more than two steps, the large and forbidding form of her eldest brother materialized in the doorway.

"Daphne," Anthony growled. "Just the person I needed to see."

Daphne decided the best strategy was simply to ignore his churlish mood. "In just a moment, Anthony," she said sweetly. "Mother has asked me to fetch a vase. Hastings has brought her flowers."

"Hastings is here?" Anthony looked past her to the duo further in the room. "What are you doing here, Hastings?"

"Calling on your sister."

Anthony pushed past Daphne and strode into the room, looking rather like a thundercloud on legs. "I did not give you leave to court my sister," he bellowed.

"I did," Violet said. She shoved the flowers in Anthony's face, wiggling them so as to deposit the greatest amount of pollen on his nose. "Aren't these lovely?"

Anthony sneezed and pushed them aside. "Mother, I am trying to have a conversation with the duke."

Violet looked at Simon. "Do you want to have this conversation with my son?"

"Not particularly."

"Fine, then. Anthony, be quiet."

Daphne clapped her hand over her mouth, but a snuffly-giggly sound escaped nonetheless.

"You!" Anthony jabbed a finger in her direction. "Be quiet."

"Perhaps I should fetch that vase," Daphne mused.

"And leave me to the tender mercies of your brother?" Simon said in a mild voice. "I think not."

Daphne raised a brow. "Do you imply that you are not man enough to deal with him?"

"Nothing of the sort. Merely that he ought to be your problem, not mine, and—"

"What the *hell* is going on here?" Anthony roared.

"Anthony!" Violet exclaimed. "I will not tolerate such unbecoming language in my drawing room."

Daphne smirked.

Simon did nothing more than cock his head, regarding Anthony with a curious stare.

Anthony threw a dark scowl at both of them before turning his attention to his mother. "He is not to be trusted. Do you have any idea what is happening here?" he demanded.

"Of course I do," Violet replied. "The duke is paying a call upon your sister."

"And I brought flowers for your mother," Simon said helpfully.

Anthony gazed longingly at Simon's nose. Simon had the distinct impression that Anthony was imagining smashing it in.

Anthony whipped his head around to face his mother. "Do you understand the extent of his reputation?"

"Reformed rakes make the best husbands," Violet said.

"Rubbish and you know it."

"He's not a true rake, anyway," Daphne added.

The look Anthony shot at his sister was so comically malevolent Simon nearly laughed. He managed to restrain himself, but mostly just because he was fairly certain that any show of humor would cause Anthony's fist to lose its battle with his brain, with Simon's face emerging as the conflict's primary casualty.

"You don't know," Anthony said, his voice low and nearly shaking with rage. "You don't know what he has done."

"No more than what you have done, I'm sure," Violet said slyly.

"Precisely!" Anthony roared. "Good God, I know *exactly* what is going on in his brain right now, and it has nothing to do with poetry and roses."

Simon pictured laying Daphne down on a bed of rose petals. "Well, maybe roses," he murmured.

"I'm going to kill him," Anthony announced.

"These are tulips, anyway," Violet said primly, "from Holland. And Anthony, you really must summon control of your emotions. This is most unseemly."

"He is not fit to lick Daphne's boots."

Simon's head filled with more erotic images, this time of himself licking her toes. He decided not to comment.

Besides, he had already decided that he wasn't going to allow his thoughts to wander in such directions. Daphne was Anthony's sister, for God's sake. He couldn't seduce her.

"I refuse to listen to another disparaging word about his grace," Violet stated emphatically, "and that is the end of the subject."

"But—"

"I don't like your tone, Anthony Bridgerton!"

Simon thought he heard Daphne choke on a chuckle, and he wondered what that was all about.

"If it would please Your Motherhood," Anthony said in excruciatingly even tones, "I would like a private word with his grace."

"This time I'm really going to get that vase," Daphne announced, and dashed from the room.

Violet crossed her arms, and said to Anthony, "I will not have you mistreat a guest in my home."

"I shan't lay so much as a hand on him," Anthony replied. "I give you my word."

Having never had a mother, Simon was finding this exchange fascinating. Bridgerton House was, after all, technically Anthony's house, not his mother's, and Simon was impressed that Anthony had refrained from pointing this out. "It's quite all right, Lady Bridgerton," he interjected. "I'm sure Anthony and I have much to discuss."

Anthony's eyes narrowed. "Much."

"Very well," Violet said. "You're going to do what you want no matter what I say, anyway. But I'm not leaving." She plopped down onto the sofa. "This is my drawing room, and I'm comfortable here. If the two of you want to engage in that asinine interchange that passes for conversation among the males of our species, you may do so elsewhere."

Simon blinked in surprise. Clearly there was more to Daphne's mother than met the eye.

Anthony jerked his head toward the door, and Simon followed him into the hall.

"My study is this way," Anthony said.

"You have a study here?"

"I *am* the head of the family."

"Of course," Simon allowed, "but you do reside elsewhere."

Anthony paused and turned an assessing stare on Simon. "It cannot have escaped your notice that my position as head of the Bridgerton family carries with it serious responsibilities."

Simon looked him evenly in the eye. "Meaning Daphne?"

"Precisely."

"If I recall," Simon said, "earlier this week you told me you wanted to introduce us."

"That was before I thought you'd be interested in her!"

Simon held his tongue as he preceded Anthony into his study, remaining silent until Anthony shut the door. "Why," he asked softly, "would you assume I would not be interested in your sister?"

"Besides the fact that you have sworn to me that you will never marry?" Anthony drawled.

He had a good point. Simon hated that he had such a good point. "Besides that," he snapped.

Anthony blinked a couple of times, then said, "No one is interested in Daphne. At least no one we'd have her marry."

Simon crossed his arms and leaned back against the wall. "You don't hold her in terribly high regard, do y—?"

Before he could even finish the query, Anthony had him by the throat. "Don't you dare insult my sister."

But Simon had learned quite a bit about self-defense on his travels, and it took him only two seconds to reverse their positions. "I wasn't insulting your sister," he said in a malevolent voice. "I was insulting you."

Strange gurgling sounds were coming from Anthony's throat, so Simon let him go. "As it happens," he said, brushing his hands against each other, "Daphne explained to me why she has not attracted any suitable suitors."

"Oh?" Anthony asked derisively.

"Personally, I think it has everything to do with your and your brothers' apelike ways, but she tells me it is because all London views her as a friend, and none sees her as a romantic heroine."

Anthony was silent for a long moment before saying, "I see." Then, after another pause, he added thoughtfully, "She's probably right."

Simon said nothing, just watched his friend as he sorted all of this out. Finally, Anthony said, "I still don't like your sniffing about her."

"Good God, you make me sound positively canine."

Anthony crossed his arms. "Don't forget, we ran in the same pack after we left Oxford. I know exactly what you've done."

"Oh, for the love of Christ, Bridgerton, we were twenty! All men are idiots at that age. Besides, you know damn well that h—h—"

Simon felt his tongue grow awkward, and faked a coughing fit to cover his stammer. Damn. This happened so infrequently these days, but when it did, it was always when he was upset or angry. If he lost control over his emotions, he lost control over his speech. It was as simple as that.

And unfortunately, episodes such as this only served to make him upset and angry with himself, which in turn exacerbated the stammer. It was the worst sort of vicious circle.

Anthony looked at him quizzically. "Are you all right?"

Simon nodded. "Just a bit of dust in my throat," he lied.

"Shall I ring for tea?"

Simon nodded again. He didn't particularly want tea, but it seemed the sort of thing one would ask for if one truly did have dust in one's throat.

Anthony tugged at the bellpull, then turned back to Simon and asked, "You were saying?"

Simon swallowed, hoping the gesture would help him to regain control over his ire. "I merely meant to point out that you know better than anyone that at least half of my reputation is undeserved."

"Yes, but I was there for the half that *was* deserved, and while I don't mind your occasionally socializing with Daphne, I don't want you courting her."

Simon stared at his friend—or at least the man he thought was his friend—in disbelief. "Do you really think I'd seduce your sister?"

"I don't know what to think. I know you plan never to marry. I know that Daphne *does*." Anthony shrugged. "Frankly, that's enough for me to keep you two on opposite sides of the dance floor."

Simon let out a long breath. While Anthony's attitude was irritating as hell, he supposed it was understandable, and in fact even laudable. After all, the man was only acting in the best interests of his sister. Simon had difficulty imagining being responsible for anyone save himself, but he supposed that if he had a sister, he'd be damned picky about who courted her as well.

Just then, a knock sounded at the door.

"Enter!" Anthony called out.

Instead of the maid with tea, Daphne slipped into the room. "Mother told me that the two of you are in beastly moods, and I should leave you alone, but I thought I ought to make certain neither of you had killed the other."

"No," Anthony said with a grim smile, "just a light strangle."

To Daphne's credit, she didn't bat an eyelash. "Who strangled whom?"

"I strangled him," her brother replied, "then he returned the favor."

"I see," she said slowly. "I'm sorry to have missed the entertainment."

Simon couldn't suppress a smile at her remark. "Daff," he began.

Anthony whirled around. "You call her Daff?" His head snapped back to Daphne. "Did you give him permission to use your given name?"

"Of course."

"But—"

"I think," Simon interrupted, "that we are going to have to come clean."

Daphne nodded somberly. "I think you're right. If you recall, I told you so."

"How genteel of you to mention it," Simon murmured.

She smiled gamely. "I could not resist. With four brothers, after all, one must always seize the moment when one may say, 'I told you so.' "

Simon looked from sibling to sibling. "I don't know which one of you I pity more."

"What the devil is going on?" Anthony demanded, and then added as an aside, "And as for your remark, pity me. I am a far more amiable brother than she is a sister."

"Not true!"

Simon ignored the squabble and focused his attention on Anthony. "You want to know what the devil is going on? It's like this . . ."

# Chapter 7

*Men are sheep. Where one goes, the rest will soon follow.*
LADY WHISTLEDOWN'S SOCIETY PAPERS,
30 April 1813

All in all, Daphne thought, Anthony was taking this rather well. By the time Simon had finished explaining their little plan (with, she had to admit, frequent interruptions on her part), Anthony had raised his voice only seven times.

That was about seven fewer than Daphne would have predicted.

Finally, after Daphne begged him to hold his tongue until she and Simon were done with their story, Anthony gave a curt nod, crossed his arms, and clamped his mouth shut for the duration of the explanation. His frown was enough to shake the plaster off the walls, but true to his word, he remained utterly silent.

Until Simon finished with, "And that's that."

There was silence. Dead silence. For a full ten seconds, nothing but silence, although Daphne would have sworn she could hear her eyes moving in their sockets as they darted back from Anthony to Simon.

And then finally, from Anthony: "Are you *mad*?"

"I thought this might be his reaction," Daphne murmured.

"Are you both completely, irrevocably, abominably *insane*?" Anthony's voice rose to a roar. "I don't know which of you is more clearly the idiot."

"Will you hush!" Daphne hissed. "Mother will hear you."

"*Mother* would perish of heart failure if she knew what you were about," Anthony retorted, but he did use a softer tone.

"But *Mother* is not going to hear of it, is she?" Daphne shot back.

"No, she's not," Anthony replied, his chin jutting forward, "because your little scheme is finished as of this very moment."

Daphne crossed her arms. "You can't do anything to stop me."

Anthony jerked his head toward Simon. "I can kill *him*."

"Don't be ridiculous."

"Duels have been fought for less."

"By idiots!"

"I'm not disputing the title as regards to *him*."

"If I might interrupt," Simon said quietly.

"He's your best friend!" Daphne protested.

"Not," Anthony said, the single syllable brimming with barely contained violence, "anymore."

Daphne turned to Simon with a huff. "Aren't you going to *say* anything?"

His lips quirked into an amused half-smile. "And when would I have had the chance?"

Anthony turned to Simon. "I want you out of this house."

"Before I may defend myself?"

"It's my house, too," Daphne said hotly, "and I want him to stay."

Anthony glared at his sister, exasperation evident in every inch of his posture. "Very well," he said, "I'll give you two minutes to state your case. No more."

Daphne glanced hesitantly at Simon, wondering if he'd want to use the two minutes himself. But all he did was shrug, and say, "Go right ahead. He's *your* brother."

She took a fortifying breath, planted her hands on her hips without even realizing it, and said, "First of all, I must point out that I have far more to gain from this alliance than his grace. He says he wishes to use me to keep the other women—"

"And their mothers," Simon interrupted.

"—and their mothers at bay. But frankly"—Daphne glanced at Simon as she said this—"I think he's wrong. The women aren't going to stop pursuing him just because they think he might have formed an attachment with another young lady—especially when that young lady is *me*."

"And what is wrong with you?" Anthony demanded.

Daphne started to explain, but then she caught a strange glance pass between the two men. "What was that all about?"

"Nothing," Anthony muttered, looking a trifle sheepish.

"I explained to your brother your theory on why you have not had more suitors," Simon said gently.

"I see." Daphne pursed her lips as she tried to decide whether that was something she ought to be irritated about. "Hmmph. Well, he should have figured that out on his own."

Simon made an odd snorting sound that might have been a laugh.

Daphne leveled a sharp look at both men. "I do hope my two minutes do not include all of these interruptions."

Simon shrugged. "He's the timekeeper."

Anthony clutched at the edge of the desk, probably, Daphne thought, to keep himself from going for Simon's throat. "And *he*," he said menacingly, "is going to find himself headfirst through the goddamned window if he doesn't shut up."

"Did you know I have always suspected that men were idiots," Daphne ground out, "but I was never positive until today."

Simon grinned.

"Allowing for interruptions," Anthony bit off, shooting yet another deadly glare in Simon's direction even as he spoke to Daphne, "you have a minute and a half left."

"Fine," she snapped. "Then I'll reduce this conversation to one single fact. Today I had six callers. Six! Can you recall the last time I had six callers?"

Anthony just stared at her blankly.

"I can't," Daphne continued, in fine form now. "Because it *has never happened*. Six men marched up our steps, knocked on our door, and gave Humboldt their cards. Six men brought me flowers, engaged me in conversation, and one even recited poetry."

Simon winced.

"And do you know *why*?" she demanded, her voice rising dangerously. "Do you?"

Anthony, in his somewhat belatedly arrived wisdom, held his tongue.

"It is all because *he*"—she jabbed her forefinger toward Simon—"was kind enough to feign interest in me last night at Lady Danbury's ball."

Simon, who had been leaning casually against the edge of the desk, suddenly straightened. "Well, now," he said quickly, "I wouldn't quite put it that way."

She turned to him, her eyes remarkably steady. "And how would you put it?"

He didn't get much past, "I—" before she added, "Because I can assure you those men have never seen fit to call on me before."

"If they are so myopic," Simon said quietly, "why do you care for their regard?"

She fell silent, drawing back slightly. Simon had the sinking suspicion that he might have said something very, very wrong, but he wasn't positive until he saw her blinking rapidly.

Oh, damn.

Then she wiped one of her eyes. She coughed as she did it, trying to hide the maneuver by pretending to cover her mouth, but Simon still felt like the worst sort of heel.

"Now look what you've done," Anthony snapped. He placed a comforting hand on his sister's arm, all the while glaring at Simon. "Pay him no mind, Daphne. He's an ass."

"Maybe," she sniffled. "But he's an intelligent ass."

Anthony's mouth fell open.

She shot him a testy look. "Well, if you didn't want me to repeat it, you shouldn't have said it."

Anthony let out a weary sigh. "Were there really six men here this afternoon?"

She nodded. "Seven including Hastings."

"And," he asked carefully, "were any of them men you might be interested in marrying?"

Simon realized that his fingers were gouging small holes in his thigh and forced himself to move his hand to the desk.

Daphne nodded again. "They are all men with whom I have enjoyed a previous friendship. It is only that they never viewed me as a candidate for romance before Hastings led the way. I might, if given the opportunity, develop an attachment for one of them."

"But—" Simon quickly shut his mouth.

"But what?" Daphne asked, turning to him with curious eyes.

It occurred to him that what he wanted to say was that if those men had only noticed Daphne's charms because a duke had shown interest in her, then they were idiots, and thus she shouldn't even contemplate marrying them. But considering that *he* had been the one to originally point out that his interest would gain her more suitors—well, frankly, it seemed a bit self-defeating to mention it.

"Nothing," he finally said, raising a hand in a don't-mind-me motion. "It doesn't signify."

Daphne looked at him for a few moments, as if waiting for him to change his mind, and then turned back to her brother. "Do you admit the wisdom of our plan, then?"

" 'Wisdom' might be a bit of a stretch, but"—Anthony looked pained to say it—"I can see where you might think it might benefit you."

"Anthony, I have to find a husband. Besides the fact that Mother is pestering me to death, I *want* a husband. I want to marry and have a family of my own. I want it more than you could ever know. And thus far, no one acceptable has asked."

Simon had no idea how Anthony could possibly hold out against the warm pleading in her dark eyes. And sure enough, Anthony sagged against the desk and let out a weary groan. "Very well," he said, closing his eyes as if he couldn't believe what he was saying, "I shall agree to this if I must."

Daphne jumped up and threw her arms around him. "Oh, Anthony, I knew you were the very best of brothers." She gave him a kiss on the cheek. "You're just occasionally misguided."

Anthony's eyes floated heavenward before focusing on Simon. "Do you see what I have to put up with?" he asked with a shake of his head. His tone was that particular timbre used only from one beleaguered male to another.

Simon chuckled to himself as he wondered when he'd turned from evil seducer back into good friend.

"But," Anthony said loudly, causing Daphne to back up, "I am placing some conditions on this."

Daphne didn't say anything, just blinked as she waited for her brother to continue.

"First of all, this goes no further than this room."

"Agreed," she said quickly.

Anthony looked pointedly at Simon.

"Of course," he replied.

"Mother would be devastated if she learned the truth."

"Actually," Simon murmured, "I rather think your mother would applaud our ingenuity, but since you have quite obviously known her longer, I bow to your discretion."

Anthony shot him a frosty look. "Second, under no circumstances are the two of you to be alone together. Ever."

"Well, that should be easy," Daphne said, "as we wouldn't be allowed to be alone if we were courting in truth, anyway."

Simon recalled their brief interlude in the hall at Lady Danbury's house, and found it a pity that he wasn't to be allowed any more private time with Daphne, but he recognized a brick wall when he saw one, especially when said wall happened to be named Anthony Bridgerton. So he just nodded and murmured his assent.

"Third—"

"There is a *third*?" Daphne asked.

"There would be thirty if I could think of them," Anthony growled.

"Very well," she acceded, looking most aggrieved. "If you must."

For a split second Simon thought Anthony might strangle her.

"What are you laughing about?" Anthony demanded.

It was only then that Simon realized that he had snorted a laugh. "Nothing," he said quickly.

"Good," Anthony grunted, "because the third condition is this: If I ever, even once, catch you in any behavior that compromises her . . . If I ever even catch you kissing her bloody hand without a chaperon, I shall tear your head off."

Daphne blinked. "Don't you think that's a bit excessive?"

Anthony leveled a hard stare in her direction. "No."

"Oh."

"Hastings?"

Simon had no choice but to nod.

"Good," Anthony replied gruffly. "And now that we're done with that, you"—he cocked his head rather abruptly toward Simon—"can leave."

"Anthony!" Daphne exclaimed.

"I assume this means I am disinvited for supper this evening?" Simon asked.

"Yes."

"No!" Daphne jabbed her brother in the arm. "Is Hastings invited for supper? Why did you not say something?"

"It was days ago," Anthony grumbled. "Years."

"It was Monday," Simon said.

"Well, then you must join us," Daphne said firmly. "Mother will be so delighted. And you"—she poked her brother in the arm—"stop thinking about how you may poison him."

Before Anthony could reply, Simon waved off her words with a chuckle. "Do not worry on my behalf, Daphne. You forget that I attended school with him for nearly a decade. He never did understand the principles of chemistry."

"I shall kill him," Anthony said to himself. "Before the week is out, I shall kill him."

"No you won't," Daphne said blithely. "By tomorrow you will have forgotten all of this and will be smoking cheroots at White's."

"I don't think so," Anthony said ominously.

"Of course you will. Don't you agree, Simon?"

Simon studied his best friend's face and realized he was seeing something new. Something in his eyes. Something serious.

Six years ago, when Simon had left England, he and Anthony had been boys. Oh, they'd thought they were men. They'd gambled and whored and strutted about society, consumed with their own importance, but now they were different.

Now they were men in truth.

Simon had felt the change within himself during his travels. It had been a slow transformation, wrought over time as he faced new challenges. But now he realized that he'd returned to England still picturing Anthony as that twenty-two-year-old boy he'd left behind.

He'd done his friend a great disservice, he'd realized, in failing to realize that he, too, had grown up. Anthony had responsibilities Simon had never even dreamed of. He had brothers to guide, sisters to protect. Simon had a dukedom, but Anthony had a *family.*

There was a grave difference, and Simon found that he couldn't fault his friend for his overprotective and indeed somewhat mulish behavior.

"I think," Simon said slowly, finally answering Daphne's question, "that your brother and I are both different people than we were when we ran wild six years ago. And I think that might not be such a bad thing."

Several hours later, the Bridgerton household was in chaos.

Daphne had changed into an evening dress of dark green velvet that someone had once said almost made her eyes look not quite brown, and was presently idling about in the great hall, trying to find a way to calm her mother's racing nerves.

"I cannot *believe,*" Violet said, one hand fluttering on her chest, "that Anthony forgot to tell me he invited the duke to dinner. I had no time to prepare. None at all."

Daphne eyed the menu in her hand, which began with turtle soup and marched through three more courses before finishing with lamb à la bechamel (followed, of course, by a choice of four desserts). She tried to keep her voice free of sarcasm as she said, "I do not think the duke will have cause to complain."

"I pray that he won't," Violet replied. "But if I had known he was coming, I would have made sure we had a beef dish as well. One cannot entertain without a beef dish."

"He knows this is an informal meal."

Violet shot her an acerbic look. "No meal is informal when a duke is calling."

Daphne regarded her mother thoughtfully. Violet was wringing her hands and gnashing her teeth. "Mother," Daphne said, "I don't think the duke is the sort to expect us to dramatically alter our family supper plans on his behalf."

"He might not expect it," Violet said, "but I do. Daphne, there are certain rules in society. Expectations. And frankly, I do not understand how you can be quite so calm and disinterested."

"I'm not disinterested!"

"You certainly don't look nervous." Violet eyed her suspiciously. "How can you not be nervous? For goodness' sake, Daphne, this man is thinking of marrying you."

Daphne caught herself just before she groaned. "He has never said as much, Mother."

"He didn't have to. Why else would he have danced with you last night? The only other lady he so honored was Penelope Featherington, and we both know that that had to be out of pity."

"I *like* Penelope," Daphne said.

"I like Penelope, too," Violet returned, "and I long for the day her mother realizes that a girl of her complexion cannot be dressed in tangerine satin, but that is beside the point."

"What *is* the point?"

"I don't know!" Violet very nearly wailed.

Daphne shook her head. "I'm going to find Eloise."

"Yes, do that," Violet said distractedly, "and make sure Gregory is clean. He never washes behind his ears. And Hyacinth—Good God, what are we to do about Hyacinth? Hastings will not expect a ten-year-old at the table."

"Yes, he will," Daphne replied patiently. "Anthony told him we were dining as a family."

"Most families do not allow their younger children to dine with them," Violet pointed out.

"Then that is their problem." Daphne finally gave in to her exasperation and let out a loud sigh. "Mother, I spoke to the duke. He understands that this is not a formal meal. And he specifically told me that he was looking forward to a change of pace. He has no family himself, so he has never experienced anything like a Bridgerton family dinner."

"God help us." Violet's face went utterly pale.

"Now, Mother," Daphne said quickly, "I know what you're thinking, and I assure you that you don't have to worry about Gregory putting creamed potatoes on Francesca's chair again. I'm certain he has outgrown such childish behavior."

"He did it last week!"

"Well, then," Daphne said briskly, not missing a beat, "then I'm sure he's learned his lesson."

The look Violet gave her daughter was dubious in the extreme.

"Very well, then," Daphne said, her tone considerably less businesslike, "then I will simply threaten him with death if he does anything to upset you."

"Death won't scare him," Violet mused, "but perhaps I can threaten to sell his horse."

"He'll never believe you."

"No, you're right. I'm far too softhearted." Violet frowned. "But he might believe me if I told him he would be forbidden to go on his daily ride."

"That might work," Daphne agreed.

"Good. I shall go off and scare some sense into him." Violet took two steps then turned around. "Having children is such a challenge."

Daphne just smiled. She knew it was a challenge her mother adored.

Violet cleared her throat softly, signaling a more serious turn of conversation. "I do hope this supper goes well, Daphne. I think Hastings might be an excellent match for you."

" 'Might'?" Daphne teased. "I thought dukes were good matches even if they had two heads and spit while they talked." She laughed. "Out of both mouths!"

Violet smiled benignly. "You might find this difficult to believe, Daphne, but I don't want to see you married off to just anyone. I may introduce you to no end of eligible men, but that is only because I would like you to have as many suitors as possible from which to choose a husband." Violet smiled wistfully. "It is my fondest dream to see you as happy as I was with your father."

And then, before Daphne could reply, Violet disappeared down the hall.

Leaving Daphne with second thoughts.

Maybe this plan with Hastings wasn't such a good idea, after all. Violet was going to be crushed when they broke off their faux alliance. Simon had said that Daphne might be the one to do the jilting, but she was beginning to wonder if perhaps it wouldn't be better the other way around. It would be mortifying for Daphne to be thrown over by Simon, but at least that way she wouldn't have to endure Violet's bewildered chorus of "Why?"

Violet was going to think she was insane for letting him get away.

And Daphne would be left wondering if maybe her mother was right.

Simon had not been prepared for supper with the Bridgertons. It was a loud, raucous affair, with plenty of laughter and thankfully, only one incident involving a flying pea.

(It had looked as if the pea in question had originated at Hyacinth's end of the table, but the littlest Bridgerton had looked so innocent and angelic that Simon had difficulty believing she had actually aimed the legume at her brother.)

Thankfully, Violet had not noticed the flying pea, even though it sailed right over her head in a perfect arc.

But Daphne, who was sitting directly across from him, most certainly had, because her napkin flew up to cover her mouth with remarkable alacrity. Judging from the way her eyes were crinkling at the corners, she was definitely laughing under the square of linen.

Simon spoke little throughout the meal. Truth be told, it was far easier to listen to the Bridgertons than actually try to converse with them, especially considering the number of malevolent stares he was receiving from Anthony and Benedict.

But Simon had been seated clear at the opposite end of the table from the two eldest Bridgertons (no accident on Violet's part, he was sure) so it was relatively simple to ignore them and instead enjoy Daphne's interactions with the rest of her family. Every now and then one of them would ask him a direct question, and he would answer, and then he would return to his demeanor of quiet observation.

Finally, Hyacinth, who was seated to Daphne's right, looked him straight in the eye, and said, "You don't talk much, do you?"

Violet choked on her wine.

"The duke," Daphne said to Hyacinth, "is being far more polite than we are, constantly jumping into the conversation and interrupting one another as if we're afraid we might not be heard."

"I'm not afraid I might not be heard," Gregory said.

"I'm not afraid of that, either," Violet commented dryly. "Gregory, eat your peas."

"But Hyacinth—"

"Lady Bridgerton," Simon said loudly, "may I trouble you for another helping of those delicious peas?"

"Why certainly." Violet shot an arch look at Gregory. "Notice how the duke is eating his peas."

Gregory ate his peas.

Simon smiled to himself as he spooned another portion of peas onto his plate, thankful that Lady Bridgerton had not decided to serve dinner *à la russe*. It would have been difficult to stave off Gregory's certain accusation of Hyacinth as a pea-tosser if he'd had to summon a footman to serve him.

Simon busied himself with his peas, since he really had no choice but to finish off every last one. He stole a glance at Daphne, however, who was wearing a secret little smile. Her eyes were brimming with infectious good humor, and Simon soon felt the corners of his mouth turning up as well.

"Anthony, why are you scowling?" asked one of the other Bridgerton girls—Simon thought it might be Francesca, but it was hard to say. The two middle ones looked amazingly alike, right down to their light eyes, so like their mother's.

"I'm not scowling," Anthony snapped, but Simon, having been on the receiving end of those scowls for the better part of an hour, rather thought he was lying.

"You are, too," either Francesca or Eloise said.

Anthony's tone of reply was condescending in the extreme. "If you think I am going to say, 'Am not,' you are sadly mistaken."

Daphne laughed into her napkin again.

Simon decided life was more amusing than it had been in ages.

"Do you know," Violet suddenly announced, "that I think this might be one of the most pleasant evenings of the year. Even"—she sent a knowing glance down the table at Hyacinth—"if my youngest is tossing peas down the table."

Simon looked up just as Hyacinth cried out, "How did you know?"

Violet shook her head as she rolled her eyes. "My dear children," she said, "when will you learn that I know everything?"

Simon decided he had a great deal of respect for Violet Bridgerton.

But even still, she managed to completely confuse him with a question and a smile. "Tell me, your grace," she said, "are you busy tomorrow?"

Despite her blond and blue-eyed coloring, she looked so like Daphne as she asked him this question that he was momentarily befuddled. Which had to be the only reason he didn't bother to think before he stammered, "N-no. Not that I recall."

"Excellent!" Violet exclaimed, beaming. "Then you must join us on our outing to Greenwich."

"Greenwich?" Simon echoed.

"Yes, we've been planning a family outing for several weeks now. We thought we'd take a boat, then perhaps have a picnic on the shores of the Thames." Violet smiled at him confidently. "You'll come, won't you?"

"Mother," Daphne interjected, "I'm certain the duke has any number of commitments."

Violet gave Daphne a look so frigid Simon was surprised that neither one of them turned to ice. "Nonsense," Violet replied. "He just said himself that he wasn't busy." She turned back to Simon. "And we shall be visiting the Royal Observatory as well, so you needn't worry that this will be a mindless jaunt. It's not open to the public, of course, but my late husband was a great patron, so we are assured entry."

Simon looked at Daphne. She just shrugged and apologized with her eyes.

He turned back to Violet. "I'd be delighted."

Violet beamed and patted him on the arm.

And Simon had the sinking sensation that his fate had just been sealed.

# Chapter 8

*It has reached This Author's ears that the entire Bridgerton family (plus one duke!) embarked upon a journey to Greenwich on Saturday.*

*It has also reached This Author's ears that the aforementioned duke, along with a certain member of the Bridgerton family, returned to London very wet indeed.*

LADY WHISTLEDOWN'S SOCIETY PAPERS, 3 May 1813

"If you apologize to me one more time," Simon said, leaning his head back against his hands, "I may have to kill you."

Daphne shot him an irritated look from her position in her deck chair on the small yacht her mother had commissioned to take the entire family—and the duke, of course—to Greenwich. "Pardon me," she said, "if I am polite enough to apologize for my mother's quite obvious manipulations. I thought that the purpose of our little charade was to shield you from the tender mercies of match-making mothers."

Simon waved off her comment, as he settled deeper into his own chair. "It would only be a problem if I were not enjoying myself."

Daphne's chin lurched backward slightly in surprise. "Oh," she said (stupidly, in her opinion). "That's nice."

He laughed. "I am inordinately fond of boat travel, even if it is just down to Greenwich, and besides, after spending so much time at sea, I rather fancy a visit to the Royal Observatory to see the Greenwich Meridian." He cocked his head in her direction. "Do you know much about navigation and longitude?"

She shook her head. "Very little, I'm afraid. I must confess I'm not even certain what this meridian here at Greenwich *is*."

"It's the point from which all longitude is measured. It used to be that sailors and navigators measured longitudinal distance from their point of departure, but in the last century, the astronomer royal decided to make Greenwich the starting point."

Daphne raised her brows. "That seems rather self-important of us, don't you think, positioning ourselves at the center of the world?"

"Actually, it's quite convenient to have a universal reference point when one is attempting to navigate the high seas."

She still looked doubtful. "So everyone simply agreed on Greenwich? I find it difficult to believe that the French wouldn't have insisted upon Paris, and the Pope, I'm sure, would have preferred Rome . . ."

"Well, it wasn't an agreement, precisely," he allowed with a laugh. "There was no official treaty, if that is what you mean. But the Royal Observatory publishes an excellent set of charts and tables each year—it's called the *Nautical Almanac*. And a sailor would have to be insane to attempt to navigate the ocean without one on board. And since the *Nautical Almanac* measures longitude with Greenwich as zero . . . well, everyone else has adopted it as well."

"You seem to know quite a bit about this."

He shrugged. "If you spend enough time on a ship, you learn."

"Well, I'm afraid it wasn't the sort of thing one learned in the Bridgerton nursery." She cocked her head to the side in a somewhat self-deprecating manner. "Most of my learning was restricted to what my governess knew."

"Pity," he murmured. Then he asked, "Only most?"

"If there was something that interested me, I could usually find several books to read on the topic in our library."

"I would wager then, that your interests did not lie in abstract mathematics."

Daphne laughed. "Like you, you mean? Hardly, I'm afraid. My mother always said that it was a wonder I could add high enough to put shoes on my feet."

Simon winced.

"I know, I know," she said, still smiling. "You sorts who excel at arithmetic simply don't understand how we lesser mortals can look at a page of numbers and not know the answer—or at least how to *get* to the answer—instantly. Colin is the same way."

He smiled, because she was exactly right. "What, then, were your favorite subjects?"

"Hmm? Oh, history and literature. Which was fortunate, since we had no end of books on those topics."

He took another sip of his lemonade. "I've never had any great passion for history."

"Really? Why not, do you think?"

Simon pondered that for a moment, wondering if perhaps his lack of enthusiasm for history was due to his distaste for his dukedom and all the tradition that wrapped around it. His father had been so passionate about the title . . .

But of course all he said was, "Don't know, really. Just didn't like it, I suppose."

They fell into a few moments of companionable silence, the

gentle river wind ruffling their hair. Then Daphne smiled, and said, "Well, I won't apologize again, since I'm too fond of my life to sacrifice it needlessly at your hands, but I am glad that you're not miserable after my mother browbeat you into accompanying us."

The look he gave her was vaguely sardonic. "If I hadn't wanted to join you, there is nothing your mother could have said that would have secured my presence."

She snorted. "And this from a man who is feigning a courtship to *me*, of all people, all because he's too polite to refuse invitations from his friends' new wives."

A rather irritable scowl immediately darkened his features. "What do you mean, *you* of all people?"

"Well, I . . ." She blinked in surprise. She had no idea *what* she meant. "I don't know," she finally said.

"Well, stop saying it," he grumbled, then settled back into his chair.

Daphne's eyes inexplicably focused on a wet spot on the railing as she fought to keep an absurd smile off her face. Simon was so sweet when he was grumpy.

"What are you looking at?" he asked.

Her lips twitched. "Nothing."

"Then what are you smiling about?"

*That* she most certainly was not going to reveal. "I'm not smiling."

"If you're not smiling," he muttered, "then you're either about to suffer a seizure or sneeze."

"Neither," she said in a breezy voice. "Just enjoying the excellent weather."

Simon was leaning his head against the back of the chair, so he just rolled it to the side so he could look at her. "And the company's not that bad," he teased.

Daphne shot a pointed look at Anthony, who was leaning against the rail on the opposite side of the deck, glowering at them both. "*All* of the company?" she asked.

"If you mean your belligerent brother," Simon replied, "I'm actually finding his distress most amusing."

Daphne fought a smile and didn't win. "That's not very kind-hearted of you."

"I never said I was kind. And look—" Simon tipped his head ever so slightly in Anthony's direction. Anthony's scowl had, unbelievably, turned even blacker. "He knows we're talking about him. It's killing him."

"I thought you were friends."

"We *are* friends. This is what friends do to one another."

"Men are mad."

"Generally speaking," he agreed.

She rolled her eyes. "I thought the primary rule of friendship was that one was not supposed to dally with one's friend's sister."

"Ah, but I'm not dallying. I'm merely *pretending* to dally."

Daphne nodded thoughtfully and glanced at Anthony. "And it's still killing him—even though he knows the truth of the matter."

"I know." Simon grinned. "Isn't it brilliant?"

Just then Violet came sailing across the deck. "Children!" she called out. "Children! Oh, pardon me, your grace," she added when she spied him. "It's certainly not fair for me to lump you with my children."

Simon just smiled and waved off her apology.

"The captain tells me we're nearly there," Violet explained. "We should gather up our things."

Simon rose to his feet and extended a helpful hand to Daphne, who took it gratefully, wobbling as she stood.

"I haven't my sea legs yet," she laughed, clutching his arm to steady herself.

"And here we're merely on the river," he murmured.

"Beast. You're not supposed to point out my lack of grace and balance."

As she spoke, she turned her face toward his, and in that instant, with the wind catching her hair and painting her cheeks pink, she looked so enchantingly lovely that Simon nearly forgot to breathe.

Her lush mouth was caught somewhere between a laugh and a smile, and the sun glinted almost red on her hair. Here on the water, away from stuffy ballrooms, with the fresh air swirling about them, she looked natural and beautiful and just being in her presence made Simon want to grin like an idiot.

If they hadn't been about to pull into dock, with her entire family running around them, he would have kissed her. He knew he couldn't dally with her, and he knew he would never marry her, and still he found himself leaning toward her. He didn't even realize what he was doing until he suddenly felt off-balance and lurched back upright.

Anthony, unfortunately, caught the entire episode, and he rather brusquely insinuated himself between Simon and Daphne, grasping her arm with far more strength than grace. "As your eldest brother," he growled, "I believe it is my honor to escort you ashore."

Simon just bowed and let Anthony have his way, too shaken and angered by his momentary loss of control to argue.

The boat settled next to the dock, and a gangplank was put into place. Simon watched as the entire Bridgerton family disembarked, then he brought up the rear, following them onto the grassy banks of the Thames.

At the top of the hill stood the Royal Observatory, a stately old building of rich red brick. Its towers were topped with gray domes, and Simon had the sense that he was, as Daphne had put it, at the very center of the world. Everything, he realized, was measured from this point.

After having crossed a good portion of the globe, the thought was rather humbling.

"Do we have everyone?" the viscountess called out. "Hold still, everyone, so I may be sure we are all present and accounted for." She started counting heads, finally ending on herself with a triumphant, "Ten! Good, we're all here."

"Just be glad she doesn't make us line up by age any longer."

Simon looked to the left to see Colin grinning at him.

"As a method of keeping order, age worked when it still corresponded with height. But then Benedict gained an inch on Anthony, and then Gregory outgrew Francesca—" Colin shrugged. "Mother simply gave up."

Simon scanned the crowd and lifted one shoulder in a shrug. "I'm just trying to figure out where I'd fit in."

"Somewhere near Anthony, if I had to hazard a guess," Colin replied.

"God forbid," Simon muttered.

Colin glanced at him with a mix of amusement and curiosity.

"Anthony!" Violet called out. "Where's Anthony?"

Anthony indicated his location with a rather ill-tempered grunt.

"Oh, there you are, Anthony. Come and escort me in."

Anthony reluctantly let go of Daphne's arm and walked to his mother's side.

"She's shameless, isn't she?" Colin whispered.

Simon thought it best not to comment.

"Well, don't disappoint her," Colin said. "After all her machinations, the least you can do is go and take Daphne's arm."

Simon turned to Colin with a quirked eyebrow. "You might be just as bad as your mother."

Colin just laughed. "Yes, except that at least I don't *pretend* to be subtle."

Daphne chose that moment to walk over. "I find myself without an escort," she said.

"Imagine that," Colin returned. "Now, if the two of you will excuse me, I'm off to find Hyacinth. If I'm forced to escort Eloise, I may have to swim back to London. She's been a wretch ever since she attained the age of fourteen."

Simon blinked in confusion. "Didn't you just return from the Continent last week?"

Colin nodded. "Yes, but Eloise's fourteenth birthday was a year and a half ago."

Daphne swatted him on the elbow. "If you're lucky, I won't tell her you said that."

Colin just rolled his eyes and disappeared into the small crowd, bellowing Hyacinth's name.

Daphne laid her hand in the crook of Simon's elbow as he offered her his arm, then asked, "Have we scared you off yet?"

"I beg your pardon?"

She offered him a rueful smile. "There is nothing quite as exhausting as a Bridgerton family outing."

"Oh, that." Simon stepped quickly to the right to avoid Gregory, who was racing after Hyacinth, yelling something about mud and revenge. "It's, ah, a new experience."

"Very politely put, your grace," Daphne said admiringly. "I'm impressed."

"Yes, well—" He jumped back as Hyacinth barreled by, squealing at such a pitch that Simon was certain that dogs would start howling from there to London. "I have no siblings, after all."

Daphne let out a dreamy sigh. "No siblings," she mused. "Right now it sounds like heaven." The faraway look remained in her eyes for a few more seconds, then she straightened and shook off her reverie. "Be that as it may, however—" Her hand shot out just as Gregory ran past, catching the boy firmly by the upper arm. "Gregory Bridgerton," she scolded, "you should know better than to run thus through a crowd. You're liable to knock someone over."

"How did you do that?" Simon asked.

"What, catch him?"

"Yes."

She shrugged. "I have years of practice."

"Daphne!" Gregory whined. His arm, after all, was still attached to her hand.

She let go. "Now, slow down."

He took two exaggerated steps then broke into a trot.

"No scolding for Hyacinth?" Simon asked.

Daphne motioned over her shoulder. "It appears my mother has Hyacinth in hand."

Simon saw that Violet was shaking her finger quite vehemently at Hyacinth. He turned back to Daphne. "What were you about to say before Gregory appeared on the scene?"

She blinked. "I have no idea."

"I believe you were about to go into raptures at the thought of having no siblings."

"Oh, of course." She let out a little laugh as they followed the rest of the Bridgertons up the hill toward the observatory. "Actually, believe it or not, I was going to say that while the concept of eternal solitude is, at times, tempting, I think I would be quite lonely without family."

Simon said nothing.

"I cannot imagine having only one child myself," she added.

"Sometimes," Simon said in a dry voice, "one has little choice in the matter."

Daphne's cheeks turned an immediate red. "Oh, I'm so sorry," she stammered, her feet absolutely refusing to take a step. "I'd forgotten. Your mother . . ."

Simon paused beside her. "I didn't know her," he said with a shrug. "I didn't mourn her."

But his blue eyes were strangely hollow and shuttered, and Daphne somehow knew that his words were false.

And at the same time, she knew that he believed them one hundred percent.

And she wondered—what could have happened to this man to make him lie to himself for so many years?

She studied his face, her head tilting slightly as she took in his features. The wind had brought color to his cheeks and ruffled his dark hair. He looked rather uncomfortable under her scrutiny, and finally he just grunted, and said, "We're falling behind."

Daphne looked up the hill. Her family was a good distance ahead of them. "Yes, of course," she said, straightening her shoulders. "We should get going."

But as she trudged up the hill, she wasn't thinking of her family, or of the observatory, or even of longitude. Instead, she was wondering why she had the most bizarre urge to throw her arms around the duke and never let go.

Several hours later, they were all back on the grassy banks of the Thames, enjoying the last bites of an elegant yet simple luncheon that had been prepared by the Bridgertons' cook. As he had the night before, Simon spoke little, instead observing the often boisterous interactions of Daphne's family.

But Hyacinth apparently had other ideas.

"Good day, your grace," she said, seating herself next to him on the blanket one of the footmen had laid out for their picnic. "Did you enjoy your tour of the observatory?"

Simon couldn't quite suppress a smile as he answered, "Indeed I did, Miss Hyacinth. And you?"

"Oh, very much so. I especially appreciated your lecture on longitude and latitude."

"Well, I don't know that I'd call it a *lecture*," Simon said, the word making him feel just the slightest bit old and stodgy.

Across the blanket, Daphne was grinning at his distress.

Hyacinth just smiled flirtatiously—*flirtatiously*?—and said, "Did you know that Greenwich also has a most romantic history?"

Daphne started to shake with laughter, the little traitor.

"Really?" Simon managed to get out.

"Indeed," Hyacinth replied, using such cultured tones that Simon briefly wondered if there were actually a forty-year-old matron inside her ten-year-old body. "It was here that Sir Walter Raleigh laid his cloak upon the ground so that Queen Elizabeth would not have to dirty her slippers in a puddle."

"Is that so?" Simon stood and scanned the area.

"Your grace!" Hyacinth's face reverted to ten-year-old impatience as she jumped to her feet. "What are you doing?"

"Examining the terrain," he replied. He cast a secret glance at Daphne. She was looking up at him with mirth and humor and something else that made him feel about ten feet tall.

"But what are you looking for?" Hyacinth persisted.

"Puddles."

"Puddles?" Her face slowly transformed into one of utter delight as she grasped his meaning. "Puddles?"

"Indeed. If I'm going to have to ruin a cloak to save your slippers, Miss Hyacinth, I'd like to know about it in advance."

"But you're not wearing a cloak."

"Heavens above," Simon replied, in such a voice that Daphne burst into laughter below him. "You do not mean that I will be forced to remove my *shirt*?"

"No!" Hyacinth squealed. "You don't have to remove anything! There aren't any puddles."

"Thank heavens," Simon breathed, clasping one hand to his chest for added effect. He was having far more fun with this than he would have ever dreamed possible. "You Bridgerton ladies are very demanding, did you know that?"

Hyacinth viewed him with a mixture of suspicion and glee. Suspicion finally won out. Her hands found their way to her little hips as she narrowed her eyes and asked, "Are you funning me?"

He smiled right at her. "What do you think?"

"I think you are."

"I think I'm lucky there aren't any puddles about."

Hyacinth pondered that for a moment. "If you decide to marry my sister—" she said.

Daphne choked on a biscuit.

"—then you have my approval."

Simon choked on air.

"But if you don't," Hyacinth continued, smiling shyly, "then I'd be much obliged if you'd wait for me."

Luckily for Simon, who had little experience with young girls and not a clue how to respond, Gregory came dashing by and yanked on Hyacinth's hair. She immediately took off after him, her eyes narrowed with the single-minded determination to get even.

"I never thought I'd say this," Daphne said, laughter in her voice, "but I believe you have just been saved by my younger brother."

"How old is your sister?" Simon asked.

"Ten, why?"

He shook his head in bewilderment. "Because for a moment, I could have sworn she was forty."

Daphne smiled. "Sometimes she is so like my mother it's frightening."

At that moment, the woman in question stood and began to summon her children back to the boat. "Come along!" Violet called out. "It's growing late!"

Simon looked at his pocket watch. "It's three."

Daphne shrugged as she rose to her feet. "To her that's late. According to Mother, a lady should always be home at five o'clock."

"Why?"

She reached down to pick up the blanket. "I have no idea. To get ready for the evening, I suppose. It's one of those rules I've grown up with and deemed best not to question." She straightened, holding the soft blue blanket to her chest, and smiled. "Are we ready to go?"

Simon held out his arm. "Certainly."

They took a few steps toward the boat, and then Daphne said, "You were very good with Hyacinth. You must have spent a great deal of time with children."

"None," he said tersely.

"Oh," she said, a puzzled frown decorating her face. "I knew you had no siblings, but I had assumed you must have met some children on your travels."

"No."

Daphne held silent for a moment, wondering if she should pursue the conversation. Simon's voice had grown hard and forbidding, and his face . . .

He didn't look like the same man who had teased Hyacinth mere minutes earlier.

But for some reason—maybe because it had been such a lovely afternoon, maybe it was just because the weather was fine—she faked a sunny smile and said, "Well, experience or no, you clearly have the touch. Some adults don't know how to talk to children, you know."

He said nothing.

She patted his arm. "You'll make some lucky child an excellent father someday."

His head whipped around to face her, and the look in his eyes nearly froze her heart. "I believe I told you I have no intention of marrying," he bit off. "Ever."

"But surely you—"

"Therefore it is unlikely that I shall ever have children."

"I . . . I see." Daphne swallowed and attempted a shaky smile, but she had a feeling she didn't manage anything more than a slight quivering of her lips. And even though she knew that their courtship was nothing more than a charade, she felt a vague sense of disappointment.

They reached the edge of the dock, where most of the rest of the Bridgertons were milling about. A few had already boarded, and Gregory was dancing on the gangplank.

"Gregory!" Violet called out, her voice sharp. "Stop that at once!"

He stilled, but didn't move from his position.

"Either get on the boat or come back to the dock."

Simon slipped his arm from Daphne's, muttering, "That gangplank looks wet." He started moving forward.

"You heard Mother!" Hyacinth called out.

"Oh, Hyacinth," Daphne sighed to herself. "Can't you just keep out of it?"

Gregory stuck out his tongue.

Daphne groaned, then noticed that Simon was still walking toward the gangplank. She hurried to his side, whispering, "Simon, I'm sure he'll be fine."

"Not if he slips and gets caught in the ropes." He motioned with his chin to a tangled mess of ropes that were hanging off the boat.

Simon reached the end of the gangplank, walking casually, as if he hadn't a worry in the world. "Are you going to get moving?" he called out, stepping out onto the narrow piece of wood. "So that I might cross?"

Gregory blinked. "Don't you have to escort Daphne?"

Simon groaned and moved forward, but just then, Anthony, who had already boarded the small yacht, appeared at the top of the gangplank.

"Gregory!" he called out sharply. "Get on this boat at once!"

From down on the dock, Daphne watched with horror as Gregory spun around in surprise, losing his footing on the slippery wood. Anthony leapt forward, making a frantic grab with his arms, but Gregory had already slid to his bottom, and Anthony caught only air.

Anthony fought for balance as Gregory slid down the gangplank, clipping Simon rather neatly in the shins.

"Simon!" Daphne croaked, running forward.

Simon went tumbling into the murky water of the Thames, just as Gregory wailed a heartfelt, "I'm sorry!" He scooted up the gangplank backwards on his behind—rather like a crab, actually—not at all looking where he was going.

Which probably explained why he had no idea that Anthony—who had almost managed to regain his balance—was only a few short feet behind him.

Gregory rammed into Anthony with a thud on his part and a

grunt on Anthony's, and before anyone knew it, Anthony was sputtering in the water, right next to Simon.

Daphne clapped a hand to her mouth, her eyes wide as saucers.

Violet yanked on her arm. "I highly suggest you don't laugh."

Daphne pinched her lips together in an effort to comply, but it was difficult. "*You're* laughing," she pointed out.

"I'm not," Violet lied. Her entire neck was quivering with the exertion required to keep her laughter inside. "And besides, I'm a *mother.* They wouldn't dare do anything to *me.*"

Anthony and Simon came stalking out of the water, dripping and glaring at each other.

Gregory crawled the rest of the way up the gangplank and disappeared over the edge.

"Maybe you should intercede," Violet suggested.

"Me?" Daphne squeaked.

"It looks as if they might come to blows."

"But why? It was all Gregory's fault."

"Of course," Violet said impatiently, "but they're *men*, and they're both furious and embarrassed, and they can't very well take it out on a boy of twelve."

Sure enough, Anthony was muttering, "I could have taken care of him," just as Simon growled, "If you hadn't surprised him . . ."

Violet rolled her eyes, and said to Daphne, "Any man, you'll soon learn, has an insurmountable need to blame someone else when he is made to look a fool."

Daphne rushed forward, fully intending to attempt to reason with the two men, but one close look at their faces told her that nothing she could possibly say could imbue them with as much intelligence and sensibility as a woman would have in such a situation, so she simply pasted on a bright smile, grabbed Simon's arm, and said, "Escort me up?"

Simon glared at Anthony.

Anthony glared at Simon.

Daphne yanked.

"This isn't over, Hastings," Anthony hissed.

"Far from it," Simon hissed back.

Daphne realized that they were simply looking for an excuse to come to blows. She yanked harder, prepared to dislocate Simon's shoulder if need be.

After one last burning glare, he acquiesced and followed her up into the boat.

It was a very long trip home.

Later that night, as Daphne prepared for bed, she found herself oddly restless. Sleep, she could already tell, would prove impossible, so she pulled on a robe and wandered downstairs in search of warm milk and some company. With so many siblings, she thought wryly, surely *someone* had to be up and about.

On her way to the kitchen, however, she heard rustlings in Anthony's study, so she poked her head in. Her eldest brother was hunched over his desk, ink spots on his fingers from the correspondence he was answering. It was uncommon to find him here so late into the evening. He'd preferred to keep his study at Bridgerton House even after he'd moved into his bachelor's lodgings, but he usually took care of his business matters during the day.

"Don't you have a secretary to do that?" Daphne asked with a smile.

Anthony looked up. "Damned fool got married and moved to Bristol," he muttered.

"Ah." She walked into the room and perched on a chair opposite the desk. "That would explain your presence here in the wee hours of the morning."

Anthony glanced up at the clock. "Midnight is hardly wee. And besides, it took me all afternoon just to get the Thames out of my hair."

Daphne tried not to smile.

"But you're right," Anthony said with a sigh, setting down his quill. "It's late, and there's nothing here that won't keep until the morning." He leaned back and stretched out his neck. "What are you doing up and about?"

"Couldn't sleep," Daphne explained with a shrug. "I came downstairs for some hot milk and heard you cursing."

Anthony let out a grunt. "It's this bloody quill. I swear I—" He smiled sheepishly. "I suppose 'I swear' pretty much takes care of it, eh?"

Daphne smiled in return. Her brothers had never minded their language around her. "So you'll be heading home soon, then?"

He nodded. "Although that warm milk you mentioned sounds rather nice. Why don't you ring for it?"

Daphne stood. "I've a better idea. Why don't we get it ourselves? We're not complete idiots. We should be able to warm some milk. And besides, the servants are probably in bed."

Anthony followed her out the door. "Very well, but you shall have to do all the work. I haven't the faintest idea how to boil milk."

"I don't think one is supposed to let it boil," Daphne said with a frown. She rounded the last corner on the way to the kitchen and pushed open the door. The room was dark, save for moonlight glowing through the windows. "Find a lamp while I find some milk," she said to Anthony. Her face took on a slight smirk. "You *can* light a lamp, can't you?"

"Oh, I believe I can manage that," he said good-naturedly.

Daphne smiled to herself as she fumbled about in the dark, pulling a small pot from the hanging rack above her. She and Anthony usually had an easy, joking relationship, and it was nice to see him back to his normal self again. He'd been in such a beastly mood for the past week, with most of his sour temper directed squarely at her.

And Simon, of course, but Simon was rarely present to receive Anthony's scowls.

A light flickered to life behind her, and Daphne turned to see Anthony smiling triumphantly. "Have you found the milk," he asked, "or must I venture out in search of a cow?"

She laughed and held up a bottle. "Found it!" She wandered over to the enclosed range, a rather modern-looking contraption that Cook had purchased earlier in the year. "Do you know how to work this?" she asked.

"No idea. You?"

Daphne shook her head. "None." She reached forward and gingerly touched the surface of the stove top. "It's not hot."

"Not even a little bit?"

She shook her head. "It's rather cold, actually."

Brother and sister were silent for a few seconds.

"You know," Anthony finally said, "cold milk might be quite refreshing."

"I was just thinking that very thing!"

Anthony grinned and found two mugs. "Here, you pour."

Daphne did, and soon they were seated on stools, gulping down the fresh milk. Anthony drained his mug in short order, and poured another. "You need some more?" he asked, wiping off his milk mustache.

"No, I'm barely halfway to the bottom," Daphne said, taking another sip. She licked at her lips, fidgeting in her chair. Now that she was alone with Anthony, and he seemed like he was back in his usual good humor, it seemed like a good time to . . . Well, the truth was . . .

*Oh, blast*, she thought to herself, *just go ahead and ask him.*

"Anthony?" she said, a touch hesitantly. "Could I ask you a question?"

"Of course."

"It's about the duke."

Anthony's mug hit the table with a loud thunk. "What about the duke?"

"I know you don't like him . . ." she began, her words trailing off.

"It's not that I don't like him," Anthony said with a weary sigh. "He's one of my closest friends."

Daphne's brows rose. "One would be hard-pressed to deduce that based on your recent behavior."

"I just don't trust him around women. Around you in particular."

"Anthony, you must know that that is one of the silliest things you have ever said. The duke might have been a rake—I suppose he might still be a rake for all I know—but he would never seduce me, if only because I'm your sister."

Anthony looked unconvinced.

"Even if there weren't some male code of honor about such things," Daphne persisted, barely resisting the urge to roll her eyes, "he knows you'd kill him if he touched me. The man isn't stupid."

Anthony refrained from commenting, instead saying, "What was it you wanted to ask me?"

"Actually," Daphne said slowly, "I was wondering if you knew why the duke was so opposed to marriage."

Anthony spit his milk halfway across the table. "For Christ's sake, Daphne! I thought we agreed that this was just a charade! Why are you even thinking about marrying him?"

"I'm not!" she insisted, thinking that she might be lying but unwilling to examine her feelings closely enough to be sure. "I'm just curious," she muttered defensively.

"You had better not be thinking about trying to get him to marry you," Anthony said with a grunt, "because I'll tell you right now he'll never do it. Never. Do you understand me, Daphne? He won't marry you."

"I would have to be a half-wit not to understand you," she grumbled.

"Good. Then that's the end of it."

"No, it's not!" she returned. "You still haven't answered my question."

Anthony leveled a stony stare at her across the table.

"About why he won't get married," she prodded.

"Why are you so interested?" he asked wearily.

The truth, Daphne feared, lay a little too close to Anthony's accusations, but she just said, "I'm curious, and besides, I think I have a right to know, since, if I don't find an acceptable suitor soon, I may become a pariah after the duke drops me."

"I thought *you* were supposed to jilt *him*," Anthony said suspiciously.

Daphne snorted. "Who is going to believe *that*?"

Anthony didn't immediately jump to her defense, which Daphne found vaguely annoying. But he did say, "I don't know why Hastings refuses to marry. All I know is that he has maintained this opinion for as long as I've known him."

Daphne opened her mouth to speak, but Anthony cut her off by adding, "*And* he's stated it in such a way so that I do not believe his is the weak vow of the beleaguered bachelor."

"Meaning?"

"Meaning that unlike most men, when he says he will never marry, he means it."

"I see."

Anthony let out a long, tired breath, and Daphne noticed tiny lines of concern around his eyes that she'd never seen before. "Choose a man from your new crowd of suitors," he said, "and forget Hastings. He's a good man, but he's not for you."

Daphne latched on to the first part of his sentence. "But you think he's a good—"

"He's not for you," Anthony repeated.

But Daphne couldn't help thinking that maybe, just maybe, Anthony might be wrong.

# Chapter 9

*The Duke of Hastings was espied yet again with Miss Bridgerton. (That is Miss Daphne Bridgerton, for those of you who, like This Author, find it difficult to differentiate between the multitudes of Bridgerton offspring.) It has been some time since This Author has seen a couple so obviously devoted to one another.*

*It does seem odd, however, that, with the exception of the Bridgerton family outing to Greenwich, which was reported in this newspaper ten days earlier, they are seen together only at evening functions. This Author has it on the best authority that while the duke called upon Miss Bridgerton at her home a fortnight ago, this courtesy has not been repeated, and indeed, they have not been seen riding together in Hyde Park even once!*

*Lady Whistledown's Society Papers,*
14 May 1813

Two weeks later, Daphne found herself in Hampstead Heath, standing on the fringes of Lady Trowbridge's ballroom, far away from the fashionable crowd. She was quite content with her position.

She didn't want to be at the center of the party. She didn't want to be found by the dozens of suitors now clamoring to claim her in a dance. In all truth, she didn't want to be in Lady Trowbridge's ballroom at all.

Because Simon was not there.

This did not mean that she was destined to spend the evening as a wallflower. All of Simon's predictions in regard to her burgeoning popularity had proven correct, and Daphne, who had always been the girl everyone liked but no one adored, was suddenly proclaimed the season's Incomparable. Everyone who cared to air an opinion on the subject (and this being the *ton*, that meant everyone) declared that they always knew that Daphne was special and were just waiting for everyone else to notice. Lady Jersey told everyone who would listen that she had been predicting Daphne's success for months, and the only mystery was why no one had listened to her sooner.

Which was, of course, hogwash. While Daphne had certainly never been the object of Lady Jersey's scorn, not one Bridgerton could recall ever hearing Lady Jersey refer to her (as she was presently doing) as "Tomorrow's Treasure."

But even though Daphne's dance card was now full within minutes of her arrival at any ball, and even though men fought for the privilege of fetching her a glass of lemonade (Daphne had almost laughed out loud the first time *that* had happened), she found that no evening was truly memorable unless Simon was at her side.

It didn't matter that he seemed to find it necessary to mention at least once every evening that he was adamantly opposed to the institution of marriage. (Although, to his credit, he usually mentioned this in conjunction with his thankfulness to Daphne for saving him from the multitudes of Ambitious Mamas.) And it didn't matter that he occasionally fell silent and was even almost rude to certain members of society.

All that seemed to matter were those moments when they were not quite alone (they were never alone), but still somehow left to their own devices. A laughing conversation in a corner, a waltz around a ballroom. Daphne could look into his pale blue eyes and almost forget that she was surrounded by five hundred onlookers, all of whom were inordinately interested in the state of her courtship.

And she could almost forget that her courtship was a complete sham.

Daphne hadn't tried to talk to Anthony about Simon again. Her brother's hostility was apparent every time the duke's name was brought up in conversation. And when he and Simon actually met—well, Anthony usually managed a certain level of cordiality, but that was all he seemed able to muster.

And yet even amidst all this anger, Daphne could see faint glimmers of the old friendship between them. She could only hope that when all this was over—and she was married off to some boring but affable earl who never quite managed to make her heart sing—that the two men would be friends again.

At Anthony's somewhat forceful request, Simon had elected not to attend every social event to which Violet and Daphne had RSVPed in the affirmative. Anthony said that the only reason he had agreed to this ridiculous scheme was so that Daphne might find a husband among all her new suitors. Unfortunately, in Anthony's opinion (and fortunately in Daphne's) none of these eager young gentlemen dared to approach her in Simon's presence.

"A fat lot of good this is doing," were Anthony's exact words.

Actually, those exact words had been appended a fair amount of cursing and invective, but Daphne had seen no reason to dwell on this. Ever since the incident at—or rather *in*—the Thames, Anthony had spent a great deal of time applying expletives to Simon's name.

But Simon had seen Anthony's point, and Simon had told Daphne that he wanted her to find a suitable husband.

And so Simon stayed away.

And Daphne was miserable.

She supposed she should have known that this was going to happen. She should have realized the dangers of being courted—even falsely—by the man society had recently dubbed The Devastating Duke.

The moniker had begun when Philipa Featherington had pronounced him "devastatingly handsome," and since Philipa didn't know the meaning of the word "whisper," all the *ton* bore witness to her statement. Within minutes some droll young buck just down from Oxford had shortened and alliterated, and The Devastating Duke was born.

Daphne found the name woefully ironic. For The Devastating Duke was devastating her heart.

Not that he meant to. Simon treated her with nothing but respect and honor and good humor. Even Anthony was forced to admit that he'd been given no cause to complain in that quarter. Simon never tried to get Daphne alone, never did anything more than kiss her gloved hand (and much to Daphne's dismay, that had only happened twice).

They had become the best of companions, their conversations ranging from comfortable silences to the wittiest of repartée. At every party, they danced together twice—the maximum permitted without scandalizing society.

And Daphne knew, without a shadow of a doubt, that she was falling in love.

The irony was exquisite. She had, of course, begun spending so much time in Simon's company specifically so that she might attract other men. For his part, Simon had begun spending time in *her* company so that he might avoid marriage.

Come to think of it, Daphne thought, sagging against the wall, the irony was exquisitely painful.

Although Simon was still quite vocal on the subject of marriage and his determination never to enter that blessed state, she did on occasion catch him looking at her in ways that made her think he might desire her. He never repeated any of the risqué comments he'd made before he'd learned she was a Bridgerton, but sometimes she caught him looking at her in the same hungry, feral way he'd done that first evening. He turned away, of course, as soon as she noticed, but it was always enough to set her skin tingling and shorten her breath with desire.

And his eyes! Everyone likened their color to ice, and when Daphne watched him converse with other members of society, she could see why. Simon wasn't as loquacious with others as he was with her. His words were more clipped, his tone more brusque, and his eyes echoed the hardness in his demeanor.

But when they were laughing together, just the two of them poking fun at some silly society rule, his eyes changed. They grew softer, gentler, more at ease. In her more fanciful moments, she almost thought they looked as if they were melting.

She sighed, leaning even more heavily against the wall. It seemed her fanciful moments were coming closer and closer together these days.

"Ho, there, Daff, why are you skulking in the corner?"

Daphne looked up to see Colin approaching, his usual cocky smile firmly in place on his handsome face. Since his return to London, he had taken the town by storm, and Daphne could easily name a dozen young ladies who were *positive* they were in love with him and *desperate* for his attention. She wasn't worried about her brother's returning any of their affections, however; Colin obviously had many more wild oats to sow before he settled down.

"I'm not skulking," she corrected. "I'm avoiding."

"Avoiding whom? Hastings?"

"No, of course not. He's not here tonight, anyway."

"Yes, he is."

Since this was Colin, whose primary purpose in life (after chasing loose women and betting on horses, of course) was to torment his sister, Daphne meant to act blasé, but still she lurched to attention as she asked, "He is?"

Colin nodded slyly and motioned with his head toward the ballroom entrance. "I saw him enter not fifteen minutes ago."

Daphne narrowed her eyes. "Are you bamming me? He told me quite specifically that he wasn't planning to attend tonight."

"And you still came?" Colin laid both his hands on his cheeks and faked surprise.

"Of course I did," she retorted. "My life does not revolve around Hastings."

"Doesn't it?"

Daphne had the sinking feeling that he was not being facetious. "No, it doesn't," she replied, lying through her teeth. Her life might not revolve around Simon, but her thoughts certainly did.

Colin's emerald eyes grew uncharacteristically serious. "You've got it bad, don't you?"

"I have no idea what you mean."

He smiled knowingly. "You will."

"Colin!"

"In the meantime"—he motioned back toward the ballroom's entrance—"why don't you go and locate him? Clearly my scintillating company pales in comparison. I can see that your feet are already inching away from me."

Horrified that her body would betray her in such a way, Daphne looked down.

"Ha! Made you look."

"Colin Bridgerton," Daphne ground out, "sometimes I swear I think you're no more than three years old."

"An interesting concept," he mused, "and one that would place you at the tender age of one and a half, little sister."

Lacking a suitably cutting retort, Daphne just fixed upon him her blackest scowl.

But Colin only laughed. "An attractive expression to be sure, sis, but one you might want to remove from your cheeks. His Devastatingness is heading this way."

Daphne refused to fall for his bait this time. He wasn't going to Make Her Look.

Colin leaned forward and whispered conspiratorially, "This time I'm not kidding, Daff."

Daphne held her scowl.

Colin chuckled.

"Daphne!" Simon's voice. Right at her ear.

She whirled around.

Colin's chuckles grew more heartfelt. "You really ought to have more faith in your favorite brother, dear sis."

"*He's* your favorite brother?" Simon asked, one dark brow raised in disbelief.

"Only because Gregory put a toad in my bed last night," Daphne bit off, "and Benedict's standing has never recovered from the time he beheaded my favorite doll."

"Makes me wonder what Anthony's done to deny him even an honorable mention," Colin murmured.

"Don't you have somewhere else to be?" Daphne asked pointedly.

Colin shrugged. "Not really."

"Didn't," she asked through clenched teeth, "you just tell me you promised a dance to Prudence Featherington?"

"Gads, no. You must have misheard."

"Perhaps Mother is looking for you, then. In fact, I'm certain I hear her calling your name."

Colin grinned at her discomfort. "You're not supposed to be so obvious," he said in a stage whisper, purposely loud enough for Simon to hear. "He'll figure out that you like him."

Simon's entire body jerked with barely contained mirth.

"It's not his company I'm trying to secure," Daphne said acidly. "It's yours I'm trying to avoid."

Colin clapped a hand over his heart. "You wound me, Daff." He turned to Simon. "Oh, how she wounds me."

"You missed your calling, Bridgerton," Simon said genially. "You should have been on the stage."

"An interesting idea," Colin replied, "but one that would surely give my mother the vapors." His eyes lit up. "Now that's an idea. And just when the party was growing tedious. Good eve to you both." He executed a smart bow and walked off.

Daphne and Simon remained silent as they watched Colin disappear into the crowd. "The next shriek you hear," Daphne said blandly, "will surely be my mother's."

"And the thud will be her body hitting the floor in a dead faint?"

Daphne nodded, a reluctant smile playing across her lips. "But of course." She waited a moment before saying, "I wasn't expecting you this evening."

He shrugged, the black cloth of his evening jacket wrinkling slightly with the movement. "I was bored."

"You were bored so you decided to come all the way out to Hampstead Heath to attend Lady Trowbridge's annual ball?" Her eyebrows arched up. Hampstead Heath was a good seven miles from Mayfair, at least an hour's drive in the best of conditions, more on nights like tonight, when all the *ton* was clogging the roads. "Forgive me if I start to question your sanity."

"I'm starting to question it myself," he muttered.

"Well, whatever the case," she said with a happy sigh, "I'm glad you're here. It's been a ghastly evening."

"Really?"

She nodded. "I have been plagued by questions about you."

"Well, now, this grows interesting."

"Think again. The first person to interrogate me was my mother. She wants to know why you never call upon me in the afternoon."

Simon frowned. "Do you think it's necessary? I rather thought my undivided attention at these evening affairs would be enough to perpetrate the ruse."

Daphne surprised herself by managing not to growl in frustration. He didn't need to make this sound like such a chore. "Your undivided attention," she said, "would have been enough to fool anyone but my mother. And she probably wouldn't have said anything except that your lack of calls was reported in *Whistledown*."

"Really?" Simon asked with great interest.

"Really. So now you'd better call tomorrow or everyone will start to wonder."

"I'd like to know who that woman's spies are," Simon murmured, "and then I'd like to hire them for myself."

"What do you need spies for?"

"Nothing. But it seems a shame to let such stellar talent go to waste."

Daphne rather doubted that the fictitious Lady Whistledown would agree that any talents were being wasted, but she didn't particularly want to get into a discussion of the merits and evils of that newspaper, so she just shrugged off his comment. "And then," she continued, "once my mother was through with me, everyone else set in, and they were even worse."

"Heaven forfend."

She turned an acerbic look on him. "All but one of the questioners were female, and although they all vehemently professed their happiness on my behalf, they were clearly trying to deduce the probability of our not becoming betrothed."

"You told them all I was desperately in love with you, I assume?"

Daphne felt something lurch in her chest. "Yes," she lied, offering him a too-sweet smile. "I have a reputation to maintain, after all."

Simon laughed. "So then, who was the lone male doing the questioning?"

Daphne pulled a face. "It was another duke, actually. A bizarre old man who claimed to have been friends with your father."

Simon's face went suddenly tight.

She just shrugged, not having seen the change in his expression. "He went on and on about what a *good duke* your father was." She let out a little laugh as she tried to imitate the old man's voice. "I had no idea you dukes had to look out for one another so much. We don't want an incompetent duke making the title look bad, after all."

Simon said nothing.

Daphne tapped her finger against her cheek in thought. "Do you know, I've never heard you mention your father, actually."

"That is because I don't choose to discuss him," Simon said curtly.

She blinked with concern. "Is something wrong?"

"Not at all," he said, his voice clipped.

"Oh." She caught herself chewing on her lower lip and forced herself to stop. "I won't mention it then."

"I said there is *nothing wrong*."

Daphne kept her expression impassive. "Of course."

There was a long, uncomfortable silence. Daphne picked awkwardly at the fabric of her skirts before finally saying, "Lovely flowers Lady Trowbridge used for decoration, don't you think?"

Simon followed the motion of her hand toward a large arrangement of pink and white roses. "Yes."

"I wonder if she grew them."

"I haven't the faintest."

Another awkward silence.

"Roses are so difficult to grow."

This time his reply was just a grunt.

Daphne cleared her throat, and then, when he didn't even so much as look at her, asked, "Have you tried the lemonade?"

"I don't drink lemonade."

"Well, I do," she snapped, deciding she'd had enough. "And I'm thirsty. So if you will excuse me, I'm going to fetch myself a glass and leave you to your black mood. I'm certain you can find someone more entertaining than I."

She turned to leave, but before she could take a step, she felt a heavy hand on her arm. She looked down, momentarily mesmerized by the sight of his white-gloved hand resting against the peach silk of her gown. She stared at it, almost waiting for it to move, to travel down the length of her arm until it reached the bare skin of her elbow.

But of course he wouldn't do that. He only did such things in her dreams.

"Daphne, please," he said, "turn around."

His voice was low, and there was an intensity to it that made her shiver.

She turned, and as soon as her eyes met his, he said, "Please accept my apologies."

She nodded.

But he clearly felt the need to explain further. "I did not . . ." He stopped and coughed quietly into his hand. "I was not on good terms with my father. I—I don't like to talk about him."

Daphne stared at him in fascination. She'd never seen him at such a loss for words.

Simon let out an irritated exhale. It was strange, Daphne thought, because it seemed as if he were irritated with himself.

"When you brought him up . . ." He shook his head, as if deciding to try a different avenue of conversation. "It grabs at my mind. I can't stop thinking about him. It—it—it makes me extremely angry."

"I'm sorry," she said, knowing her confusion must show on her face. She thought she should say more, but she didn't know what words to use.

"Not at you," he said quickly, and as his pale blue eyes focused on hers, something seemed to clear in them. His face seemed to relax as well, especially the tight lines that had formed around his mouth. He swallowed uncomfortably. "I'm angry at myself."

"And apparently at your father as well," she said softly.

He said nothing. She hadn't expected him to, she realized. His hand was still on her arm, and she covered it with her own. "Would you like to get a bit of air?" she asked gently. "You look as if you might need it."

He nodded. "You stay. Anthony will have my head if I take you out onto the terrace."

"Anthony can hang for all I care." Daphne's mouth tightened with irritation. "I'm sick of his constant hovering, anyway."

"He is only trying to be a good brother to you."

Her lips parted in consternation. "Whose side are you on, anyway?"

Deftly ignoring her question, he said, "Very well. But just a short walk. Anthony I can take on, but if he enlists the aid of your brothers, I'm a dead man."

There was a door leading out to the terrace a few yards away. Daphne nodded toward it, and Simon's hand slid down her arm and around the crook of her elbow.

"There are probably dozens of couples out on the terrace, anyway," she said. "He'll have nothing about which to complain."

But before they could make their way outside, a loud male voice sounded from behind them. "Hastings!"

Simon halted and turned around, grimly realizing that he had grown used to the name. In no time, he'd be thinking of it as his own.

Somehow that concept made him ill.

An older man leaning on a cane hobbled his way toward them. "That's the duke I told you about," Daphne said. "Of Middlethorpe, I believe."

Simon nodded curtly, having no desire to speak.

"Hastings!" the old man said, patting him on the arm. "I have wanted to make your acquaintance for so very long. I am Middlethorpe. Your father was a good friend of mine."

Simon just nodded again, the motion almost military in its precision.

"He missed you, you know. While you were off traveling."

A rage began to build in his mouth, a rage that rendered his tongue swollen and his cheeks tight and rigid. He knew, beyond a shadow of a doubt, that if he tried to speak, he would sound just as he'd done when he was a lad of eight.

And there was no way he'd shame himself in such a way in front of Daphne.

Somehow—he'd never know how, maybe it was because he'd never had much trouble with vowels aside from "I"—he managed to say, "Oh?" He was pleased that his voice came out sharp and condescending.

But if the old man heard the rancor in his tone, he made no reaction to it. "I was with him when he died," Middlethorpe said.

Simon said nothing.

Daphne—bless her—leapt into the fray with a sympathetic, "My goodness."

"He asked me to pass along some messages to you. I have several letters in my house."

"Burn them."

Daphne gasped and grabbed Middlethorpe by the arm. "Oh, no, don't do that. He might not want to see them now, but surely he will change his mind in the future."

Simon blasted her with an icy glare before turning back to Middlethorpe. "I said burn them."

"I—ah—" Middlethorpe looked hopelessly confused. He must have been aware that the Basset father and son were not on good terms, but clearly the late duke had not revealed to him the true depth of the estrangement. He looked to Daphne, sensing a possible ally, and said to her, "In addition to the letters, there were things he asked me to tell him. I could tell them to him now."

But Simon had already dropped Daphne's arm and stalked outside.

"I'm so sorry," Daphne said to Middlethorpe, feeling the need to apologize for Simon's atrocious behavior. "I'm sure he doesn't mean to be rude."

Middlethorpe's expression told her that he *knew* Simon meant to be rude.

But Daphne still said, "He's a bit sensitive about his father."

Middlethorpe nodded. "The duke warned me he'd react this way. But he laughed as he said it, then made a joke about the Basset pride. I must confess I didn't think he was completely serious."

Daphne looked nervously through the open door to the terrace. "Apparently he was," she murmured. "I had best see to him."

Middlethorpe nodded.

"Please don't burn those letters," she said.

"I would never dream of it. But—"

Daphne had already taken a step toward the terrace door and turned around at the halting tone of the old man's voice. "What is it?" she asked.

"I'm not a well man," Middlethorpe said. "I—The doctor says it could be anytime now. May I trust the letters into your safekeeping?"

Daphne stared at the duke with a mix of shock and horror. Shock because she could not believe he would trust such personal correspondence to a young woman he'd known for barely an hour. Horror because she knew that if she accepted them, Simon might never forgive her.

"I don't know," she said in a strained voice. "I'm not sure I'm the right person."

Middlethorpe's ancient eyes crinkled with wisdom. "I think you might be exactly the right person," he said softly. "And I believe you'll know when the time is right to give him the letters. May I have them delivered to you?"

Mutely, she nodded. She didn't know what else to do.

Middlethorpe lifted his cane and pointed it out toward the terrace. "You'd best go to him."

Daphne caught his gaze, nodded, and scurried outside. The terrace was lit by only a few wall sconces, so the night air was dim, and it was only with the aid of the moon that she saw Simon off in the corner. His stance was wide and angry, and his arms were crossed across his chest. He was facing the endless lawn that stretched out past the terrace, but Daphne sincerely doubted he saw anything aside from his own raging emotions.

She moved silently toward him, the cool breeze a welcome change from the stagnant air in the overcrowded ballroom. Light murmurs of voices drifted through the night, indicating that they were not alone on the terrace, but Daphne saw no one else in the dim light. Clearly the other guests had elected to sequester themselves in dark corners. Or maybe they had descended the steps to the garden and were sitting on the benches below.

As she walked to him, she thought about saying something like, "You were very rude to the duke," or "Why are you so angry at your father?" but in the end she decided this was not the time to probe into Simon's feelings, and so when she reached his side, she just leaned against the balustrade, and said, "I wish I could see the stars."

Simon looked at her, first with surprise, then with curiosity.

"You can never see them in London," she continued, keeping her voice purposefully light. "Either the lights are too bright, or the fog has rolled in. Or sometimes the air is just too filthy to see through it." She shrugged and glanced back up at the sky, which was overcast. "I'd hoped that I'd be able to see them here in Hampstead Heath. But alas, the clouds do not cooperate."

There was a very long moment of silence. Then Simon cleared his throat, and asked, "Did you know that the stars are completely different in the southern hemisphere?"

Daphne hadn't realized how tense she was until she felt her entire body relax at his query. Clearly, he was trying to force their evening back into normal patterns, and she was happy to let him. She looked at him quizzically, and said, "You're joking."

"I'm not. Look it up in any astronomy book."

"Hmmm."

"The interesting thing," Simon continued, his voice sounding less strained as he moved further into the conversation, "is that even if you're not a scholar of astronomy—and I'm not—"

"And obviously," Daphne interrupted with a self-deprecating smile, "neither am I."

He patted her hand, and smiled, and Daphne noticed with relief that his happiness reached his eyes. Then her relief turned into something a little more precious—joy. Because she had been the one to chase the shadows from his eyes. She wanted to banish them forever, she realized.

If only he would let her . . .

"You'd notice the difference anyway," he said. "That's what's so strange. I never cared to learn the constellations and yet when I was in Africa, I looked up into the sky—and the night was so clear. You've never seen a night like that."

Daphne stared at him, fascinated.

"I looked up into the sky," he said with a bewildered shake of his head, "and it looked wrong."

"How can a sky look wrong?"

He shrugged, lifting one of his hands in an unknowing gesture. "It just did. All the stars were in the wrong place."

"I suppose I should want to see the southern sky," Daphne mused. "If I were exotic and dashing, and the sort of female men write poetry about, I suppose I should want to travel."

"You *are* the sort of female men write poetry about," Simon reminded her with a slightly sarcastic tilt to his head. "It was just bad poetry."

Daphne laughed. “Oh, don’t tease. It was exciting. My first day with six callers and Neville Binsby actually wrote poetry.”

“Seven callers,” Simon corrected, “including me.”

“Seven including you. But you don’t really count.”

“You wound me,” he teased, doing a fair imitation of Colin. “Oh, how you wound me.”

“Perhaps you should consider a career in the theater as well.”

“Perhaps not,” he replied.

She smiled gently. “Perhaps not. But what I was going to say is that, boring English girl that I am, I have no desire to go anywhere else. I’m happy here.”

Simon shook his head, a strange, almost electric light appearing in his eyes. “You’re not boring. And”—his voice dropped down to an emotional whisper—“I’m glad you’re happy. I haven’t known many truly happy people.”

Daphne looked up at him, and it slowly dawned on her that he had moved closer. Somehow she doubted he even realized it, but his body was swaying toward hers, and she was finding it nigh near impossible to pull her eyes from his.

“Simon?” she whispered.

“There are people here,” he said, his voice oddly strangled.

Daphne turned her head to the corners of the terrace. The murmuring voices she’d heard earlier were gone, but that just might mean that their erstwhile neighbors were eavesdropping.

In front of her the garden beckoned. If this were a London ball, there would have been no place to go past the terrace, but Lady Trowbridge prided herself on being different, and thus always hosted her annual ball at her second residence in Hampstead Heath. It was less than ten miles from Mayfair, but it might as well have been in another world. Elegant homes dotted wide patches of green, and in Lady Trowbridge’s garden, there were trees and flowers, shrubs and hedges—dark corners where a couple could lose themselves.

Daphne felt something wild and wicked take hold. "Let's walk in the garden," she said softly.

"We can't."

"We must."

*"We can't."*

The desperation in Simon's voice told her everything she needed to know. He wanted her. He desired her. He was *mad* for her.

Daphne felt as if her heart was singing the aria from *The Magic Flute*, somersaulting wildly as it tripped past high C.

And she thought—what if she kissed him? What if she pulled him into the garden and tilted her head up and felt his lips touch hers? Would he realize how much she loved him? How much he could grow to love her? And maybe—just maybe he'd realize how happy she made him.

Then maybe he'd stop talking about how determined he was to avoid marriage.

"I'm going for a walk in the garden," she announced. "You may come if you wish."

As she walked away—slowly, so that he might catch up with her—she heard him mutter a heartfelt curse, then she heard his footsteps shortening the distance between them.

"Daphne, this is insanity," Simon said, but the hoarseness in his voice told her he was trying harder to convince himself of that than he was her.

She said nothing, just slipped farther into the depths of the garden.

"For the love of God, woman, will you listen to me?" His hand closed hard around her wrist, whirling her around. "I promised your brother," he said wildly. "I made a vow."

She smiled the smile of a woman who knows she is wanted. "Then leave."

"You know I can't. I can't leave you out in the garden unprotected. Someone could try to take advantage of you."

Daphne gave her shoulders a dainty little shrug and tried to wiggle her hand free of his grasp.

But his fingers only tightened.

And so, although she knew it was not his intention, she let herself be drawn to him, slowly moving closer until they were but a foot apart.

Simon's breathing grew shallow. "Don't do this, Daphne."

She tried to say something witty; she tried to say something seductive. But her bravado failed her at the last moment. She'd never been kissed before, and now that she had all but invited him to be the first, she didn't know what to do.

His fingers loosened slightly around her wrist, but then they tugged, pulling her along with him as he stepped behind a tall, elaborately carved hedge.

He whispered her name, touched her cheek.

Her eyes widened, lips parted.

And in the end, it was inevitable.

# *Chapter 10*

*Many a woman has been ruined by a single kiss.*
LADY WHISTLEDOWN'S SOCIETY PAPERS,
14 May 1813

Simon wasn't sure at what moment he knew he was going to kiss her. It was probably something he never knew, just something he felt.

Up until that very last minute he'd been able to convince himself that he was only pulling her behind the hedge to scold her, upbraid her for careless behavior that would only land both of them in serious trouble.

But then something had happened—or maybe it had been happening all along, and he'd just been trying too hard not to notice it. Her eyes changed; they almost glowed. And she opened her mouth—just the tiniest bit, barely enough for a breath, but it was enough that he couldn't take his eyes off of her.

His hand snaked up her arm, over the pale satin fabric of her glove, across bare skin, and then finally past the wispy silk of her sleeve. It stole around to her back, pulling her closer, squeezing out the distance between them. He wanted her closer. He wanted her around him, atop him, beneath him. He wanted her so much it terrified him.

He molded her to him, his arms wrapping around her like a vise. He could feel the length of her now, every last inch. She was considerably shorter than he was, so her breasts flattened against the bottom of his ribs, and his thigh—

He shuddered with desire.

His thigh wedged between her legs, his firm muscles feeling the heat that was pouring from her skin.

Simon groaned, a primitive sound that mixed need with frustration. He wasn't going to be able to have her this night—he wasn't able to have her ever, and he needed to make this touch last him a lifetime.

The silk of her dress was soft and flimsy beneath his fingers, and as his hands roved along her back, he could feel every elegant line of her.

And then somehow—to his dying day he would never know how—he stepped away from her. Just an inch, but it was enough for the cool night air to slide between their bodies.

"No!" she cried out, and he wondered if she had any idea the invitation she made with that simple word.

His hands cupped her cheeks, holding her steady so that he might drink in the sight of her. It was too dark to see the exact colors that made her unforgettable face, but Simon knew that her lips were soft and pink, with just a tinge of peach at the corners. He knew that her eyes were made up of dozens of shades of brown, with that one enchanting circle of green constantly daring him to take a closer look, to see if it was really there or just a figment of his imagination.

But the rest—how she would feel, how she would taste—he could only imagine.

And Lord, how he'd been imagining it. Despite his composed demeanor, despite all of his promises to Anthony, he burned for her. When he saw her across a crowded room, his skin grew hot, and when he saw her in his dreams, he went up in flames.

Now—now that he had her in his arms, her breath fast and uneven with desire, her eyes glazed with need she couldn't possibly comprehend—now he thought he might explode.

And so kissing her became a matter of self-preservation. It was simple. If he did not kiss her now, if he did not *consume* her, he would die. It sounded melodramatic, but at the moment he would have sworn it to be true. The hand of desire twisting around his gut would burst into flame and take him along with it.

He needed her that much.

When his lips finally covered hers, he was not gentle. He was not cruel, but the pulse of his blood was too ragged, too urgent, and his kiss was that of a starving lover, not that of a gentle suitor.

He would have forced her mouth open, but she, too, was caught up in the passion of the moment, and when his tongue sought entry, he found no resistance.

"Oh, my God, Daphne," he moaned, his hands biting into the soft curve of her buttocks, pulling her closer, needing her to feel the pulse of desire that had pooled in his groin. "I never knew . . . I never dreamed . . ."

But that was a lie. He had dreamed. He'd dreamed in vivid detail. But it was nothing next to the real thing.

Every touch, every movement made him want her even more, and as each second passed, he felt his body wresting control from his mind. It no longer mattered what was right, what was proper. All that mattered was that she was here, in his arms, and he wanted her.

And, his body realized, she wanted him, too.

His hands clutched at her, his mouth devoured her. He couldn't get enough.

He felt her gloved hand slide hesitantly over his upper back, lightly resting at the nape of his neck. His skin prickled where she touched him, then burned.

And it wasn't enough. His lips left her mouth, trailing down her neck to the soft hollow above her collarbone. She moaned at each touch, the soft mewling sounds firing his passion even more.

With shaking hands, he reached for the delicately scalloped neckline of her gown. It was a gentle fit, and he knew it would take no more than the lightest push to ease the delicate silk down over the swell of her breast.

It was a sight he had no right to see, a kiss he did not deserve to make, but he couldn't help himself.

He gave her the opportunity to stop him. He moved with agonizing slowness, stopping before he bared her to give her one last chance to say no. But instead of maidenly dismay, she arched her back and let out the softest, most arousing rush of breath.

Simon was undone.

He let the fabric of her dress fall away, and in a staggering, shuddering moment of desire, just gazed at her. And then, as his mouth descended to claim her as his prize, he heard—

"You bastard!"

Daphne, recognizing the voice before he did, shrieked and jerked away. "Oh, my God," she gasped. "Anthony!"

Her brother was only ten feet away, and closing the distance fast. His brows were knit together into a mask of utter fury, and as he launched himself at Simon, he let out a primeval warrior cry unlike anything Daphne had ever heard in her life. It barely sounded human.

She just had time to cover herself before Anthony's body crashed into Simon's with such force that she, too, was knocked to the ground by someone's flailing arm.

"I'll kill you, you bloody—" The rest of Anthony's rather violent curse was lost as Simon flipped him over, knocking the breath from him.

"Anthony, no! Stop!" Daphne cried, still clutching at the bodice of her gown, even though she'd already yanked it up and it was in no danger of falling down.

But Anthony was a man possessed. He pummeled Simon, his rage showing on his face, in his fists, in the primitive grunts of fury that emanated from his mouth.

And as for Simon—he was defending himself, but he wasn't really fighting back.

Daphne, who had been standing aside, feeling like a helpless idiot, suddenly realized that she had to intervene. Otherwise, Anthony was going to kill Simon, right there in Lady Trowbridge's garden. She reached down to try to wrest her brother away from the man she loved, but at that moment they suddenly rolled over in a quick flipping motion, clipping Daphne in the knees and sending her sprawling into the hedge.

"Yaaaaaaaahhhhhhh!" she howled, pain stabbing her in more parts of her body than she would have thought possible.

Her cry must have contained a sharper note of agony than she'd thought she'd let slip, because both men immediately stilled.

"Oh, my God!" Simon, who had been at the top of the altercation when Daphne fell over, rushed to her aid. "Daphne! Are you all right?"

She just whimpered, trying not to move. The brambles were cutting into her skin, and every movement just elongated the scratches.

"I think she's hurt," Simon said to Anthony, his voice sharp with worry. "We need to lift her straight out. If we twist, she's likely to become even more entangled."

Anthony gave a curt, businesslike nod, his fury at Simon temporarily put aside. Daphne was in pain, and she had to come first.

"Just hold still, Daff," Simon crooned, his voice soft and soothing. "I'm going to put my arms around you. Then I'm going to lift you forward and pull you out. Do you understand?"

She shook her head. "You'll scratch yourself."

"I have long sleeves. Don't worry about me."

"Let me do it," Anthony said.

But Simon ignored him. While Anthony stood by helplessly, Simon reached into the tangled bramble of the hedge, and slowly pushed his gloved hands through the mess, trying to wedge his coat-covered arms between the prickly branches and Daphne's bare, tortured skin. When he reached her sleeves, however, he had to stop to disentangle the razor-sharp points from the silk of her dress. Several branches had poked straight through the fabric and were biting her skin.

"I can't get you completely loose," he said. "Your dress will tear."

She nodded, the movement jerky. "I don't care," she gasped. "It's already ruined."

"But—" Even though Simon had just been in the process of pulling that very same dress down to her waist, he still felt uncomfortable pointing out that the fabric was likely to fall right off her body once the branches were done tearing through the silk. Instead, he turned to Anthony, and said, "She'll need your coat."

Anthony was already shrugging out of it.

Simon turned back to Daphne and locked his eyes on hers. "Are you ready?" he asked softly.

She nodded, and maybe it was his imagination, but he thought she seemed a little calmer now that her eyes were focused on his face.

After making sure that no branches were still stuck to her skin, he pushed his arms farther back into the bramble, and then around her body until his hands met and locked together behind her back.

"On the count of three," he murmured.

She nodded again. "One . . . Two . . ."

He yanked her up and out, the force sending them both sprawling.

"You said three!" Daphne yelled.

"I lied. I didn't want you to tense up."

Daphne might have wanted to pursue the argument, but it was at that moment that she realized that her dress was in tatters, and she squealed as her arms flew up to cover herself.

"Take this," Anthony said, thrusting his coat at her. Daphne gratefully accepted and wrapped herself in Anthony's superfine coat. It fit him to perfection, but on her it hung so loose that she could easily wrap herself up.

"Are you all right?" he asked gruffly.

She nodded.

"Good." Anthony turned to Simon. "Thank you for pulling her out."

Simon said nothing, but his chin dipped in acknowledgment of Anthony's remark.

Anthony's eyes darted back to Daphne. "Are you certain you're all right?"

"It stings a little," she admitted, "and I'll surely need to apply a salve when I get home, but it's nothing I can't bear."

"Good," Anthony said again. Then he drew back his fist and slammed it into Simon's face, easily knocking his unsuspecting friend to the ground.

"That," Anthony spat out, "is for defiling my sister."

"Anthony!" Daphne shrieked. "Stop this nonsense right now! He didn't defile me."

Anthony swung around and glared at her, his eyes burning. "I saw your—"

Daphne's stomach churned, and for a moment she feared she'd actually cast up her accounts. Good God, Anthony had seen her breast! Her brother! It was unnatural.

"Stand up," Anthony grunted, "so I can hit you again."

"Are you mad?" Daphne cried out, jumping between him and Simon, who was still on the ground, his hand clutching his injured eye. "Anthony, I swear if you hit him again, I shall not forgive you."

Anthony pushed her aside, and not gently. "The next one," he spit, "is for betraying our friendship."

Slowly, and to Daphne's horror, Simon rose to his feet.

"No!" she yelled, jumping back between them.

"Get out of the way, Daphne," Simon ordered softly. "This is between us."

"It most certainly is not! In case no one recalls, I'm the one who—" She stopped herself in mid-sentence. There was no point in speaking. Neither man was listening to her.

"Get out of the way, Daphne," Anthony said, his voice frighteningly still. He didn't even look at her; his gaze remained focused over her head, straight into Simon's eyes.

"This is ridiculous! Can we not all discuss this like adults?" She looked from Simon to her brother, then whipped her head back to Simon. "Merciful heavens! Simon! Look at your eye!"

She hurried to him, reaching up to his eye, which was already swelling shut.

Simon remained impassive, not moving even a muscle under her concerned touch. Her fingers skimmed lightly over his swollen skin, oddly soothing. He ached for her still, although this time not with desire. She felt so good next to him, good and honorable and pure.

And he was about to do the most dishonorable thing he'd ever done in his life.

When Anthony finished with his violence, finished with his fury, and finally demanded that Simon marry his sister, Simon was going to say no.

"Move out of the way, Daphne," he said, his voice strange in his own ears.

"No, I—"

"*Move!*" he roared.

She fled, pressing her back up against the very hedge in which she'd been caught, staring in horror at the two men.

Simon nodded grimly at Anthony. "Hit me."

Anthony looked stunned by the request.

"Do it," Simon said. "Get it over with."

Anthony's fist fell slack. He didn't move his head, but his eyes flitted to Daphne. "I can't," he blurted out. "Not when he's just standing there asking for it."

Simon took a step forward, bringing his face mockingly close. "Do it now. Make me pay."

"You'll pay at the altar," Anthony replied.

Daphne gasped, the sound drawing Simon's attention. Why was she surprised? Surely she understood the consequences of, if not their actions, their stupidity in getting caught?

"I won't force him," Daphne said.

"I will," Anthony bit out.

Simon shook his head. "By tomorrow I'll be on the Continent."

"You're leaving?" Daphne asked. The stricken sound of her voice sliced a guilty knife through Simon's heart.

"If I stay, you'll forever be tainted by my presence. It's best if I'm gone."

Her lower lip was trembling. It killed him that it was trembling. A single word fell from her lips. It was his name, and it was filled with a longing that squeezed his heart in two.

It took Simon a moment to summon the words: "I can't marry you, Daff."

"Can't or won't?" Anthony demanded.

"Both."

Anthony punched him again.

Simon hit the ground, stunned by the force of the blow to his chin. But he deserved every sting, every shot of pain. He didn't want to look at Daphne, didn't want to catch even the barest of glances at her face, but she knelt beside him, her gentle hand sliding behind his shoulder to help him right himself.

"I'm sorry, Daff," he said, forcing himself to look at her. He felt odd and off-balance, and he could see out of only one eye, but she'd come to his aid, even after he'd rejected her, and he owed her that much. "I'm so sorry."

"Save your pathetic words," Anthony spat. "I'll see you at dawn."

"No!" Daphne cried out.

Simon looked up at Anthony and gave him the briefest of nods. Then he turned back to Daphne, and said, "If it c-could be anybody, Daff, it would be you. I p-promise you that."

"What are you talking about?" she asked, bewilderment turning her dark eyes to frantic orbs. "What do you mean?"

Simon just closed his eye and sighed. By this time tomorrow he'd be dead, because he sure as hell wasn't going to raise a pistol at Anthony, and he rather doubted that Anthony's temper would have cooled enough for him to shoot into the air.

And yet—in a bizarre, pathetic sort of way, he would be getting what he'd always wanted out of life. He'd have his final revenge against his father.

Strange, but even so, this wasn't how he'd thought it would end. He'd thought—Well, he didn't know what he'd thought—most men avoided trying to predict their own deaths—but it wasn't this. Not with his best friend's eyes burning with hatred. Not on a deserted field at dawn.

Not with dishonor.

Daphne's hands, which had been stroking him so gently, wrapped around his shoulders and shook. The motion jolted his watery eye open, and he saw that her face was very close to his—close and furious.

"What is the matter with you?" she demanded. Her face was like he'd never seen it before, eyes flashing with anger, and anguish, and even a little desperation. "He's going to kill you! He's going to meet you on some godforsaken field tomorrow and shoot you dead. And you're acting like you want him to."

"I d-don't w-w-want to d-die," he said, too exhausted in mind and body to even care that he'd stammered. "B-but I can't marry you."

Her hands fell off his shoulders, and she lurched away. The look of pain and rejection in her eyes was almost impossible to bear. She looked so forlorn, wrapped up in her brother's too-big coat, pieces of twigs and brambles still caught in her dark hair. When she opened her mouth to speak, it looked as if her words were ripped from her very soul. "I-I've always known that I wasn't the sort of woman men dream of, but I never thought anyone would prefer death to marriage with me."

"No!" Simon cried out, scrambling to his feet despite the dull aches and stinging pains that jolted his body. "Daphne, it's not like that."

"You've said enough," Anthony said in a curt voice, stepping between them. He placed his hands on his sister's shoulders, steering her away from the man who had broken her heart and possibly damaged her reputation for eternity.

"Just one more thing," Simon said, hating the pleading, pathetic look he knew must be in his eyes. But he had to talk to Daphne. He had to make sure she understood.

But Anthony just shook his head.

"Wait." Simon laid a hand on the sleeve of the man who had once been his closest friend. "I can't fix this. I've made—" He let out a ragged breath, trying to collect his thoughts. "I've made vows, Anthony. I can't marry her. I can't fix this. But I can tell her—"

"Tell her what?" Anthony asked with a complete lack of emotion.

Simon lifted his hand from Anthony's sleeve and raked it through his hair. He couldn't tell Daphne. She wouldn't understand. Or worse, she would, and then all he'd have was her pity. Finally, aware that Anthony was looking at him with an impatient expression, he said, "Maybe I can make it just a little bit better."

Anthony didn't move.

"Please." And Simon wondered if he'd ever put such depth of meaning behind that word before.

Anthony was still for several seconds, and then he stepped aside.

"Thank you," Simon said in a solemn voice, sparing Anthony the briefest of glances before focusing on Daphne.

He'd thought perhaps that she'd refuse to look at him, insulting him with her scorn, but instead he found her chin up, eyes defiant and daring. Never had he admired her more.

"Daff," he began, not at all sure what to say but hoping that the words somehow came out right and in one piece. "It—it isn't you. If it could be anyone it would be you. But marriage to me would destroy you. I could never give you what you want. You'd die a little every day, and it would kill me to watch."

"You could never hurt me," she whispered.

He shook his head. "You have to trust me."

Her eyes were warm and true as she said softly, "I do trust you. But I wonder if you trust me."

Her words were like a punch to the gut, and Simon felt impotent and hollow as he said, "Please know that I never meant to hurt you."

She remained motionless for so long that Simon wondered if she'd stopped breathing. But then, without even looking at her brother, she said, "I'd like to go home now."

Anthony put his arms around her and turned her away, as if he could protect her simply by shielding her from the sight of him. "We'll get you home," he said in soothing tones, "tuck you into bed, give you some brandy."

"I don't want brandy," Daphne said sharply, "I want to think."

Simon thought Anthony looked a bit bewildered by the statement, but to his credit, all he did was give her upper arm an affectionate squeeze, and say, "Very well, then."

And Simon just stood there, battered and bloodied, until they disappeared into the night.

# *Chapter 11*

*Lady Trowbridge's annual ball at Hampstead Heath on Saturday evening was, as always, a highlight of the gossip season. This Author spied Colin Bridgerton dance with all three of the Featherington sisters (not at once, of course) although it must be said that this most dashing Bridgerton did not appear to be charmed by his fate. Additionally, Nigel Berbrooke was seen courting a woman who was not Miss Daphne Bridgerton—perhaps Mr. Berbrooke has finally realized the futility of his pursuit.*

*And speaking of Miss Daphne Bridgerton, she made an early departure. Benedict Bridgerton informed the curious that she had the headache, but This Author spied her earlier in the evening, while she was talking to the elderly Duke of Middlethorpe, and she appeared to be in perfect health.*

*LADY WHISTLEDOWN'S SOCIETY PAPERS,*
17 May 1813

It was, of course, impossible to sleep.

Daphne paced the length of her room, her feet wearing treads in the blue-and-white carpet that had lain in her room since childhood. Her mind was spinning in a dozen different directions, but one thing was clear.

She had to stop this duel.

She did not, however, underestimate the difficulties involved in carrying out that task. For one thing, men tended to be mulish idiots when it came to things like honor and duels, and she rather doubted that either Anthony or Simon would appreciate her interference. Secondly, she didn't even know where the duel was to take place. The men hadn't discussed that out in Lady Trowbridge's garden. Daphne assumed that Anthony would send word to Simon by a servant. Or maybe Simon got to choose the location since he was the one who'd been challenged. Daphne was certain there had to be some sort of etiquette surrounding duels, but she certainly didn't know what it was.

Daphne paused by the window and pushed the curtain aside to peer out. The night was still young by the standards of the *ton*; she and Anthony had left the party prematurely. As far as she knew, Benedict, Colin, and her mother were all still at Lady Trowbridge's house. The fact that they had not yet returned (Daphne and Anthony had been home for nearly two hours) Daphne took as a good sign. If the scene with Simon had been witnessed, surely the gossip would have raged across the ballroom in seconds, causing her mother to rush home in disgrace.

And maybe Daphne would make it through the night with only her dress in shreds—and *not* her reputation.

But concern for her good name was the least of her worries. She needed her family home for another reason. There was no way she'd be able to stop this duel on her own. Only an idiot would ride through London in the wee hours of the morning and try to reason with two belligerent men by herself. She was going to need help.

Benedict, she feared, would immediately take Anthony's side of the whole thing; in fact, she'd be surprised if Benedict didn't act as Anthony's second.

But Colin—Colin might come around to her way of thinking. Colin would grumble, and Colin would probably say that Simon deserved to be shot at dawn, but if Daphne begged, he would help her.

And the duel had to be stopped. Daphne didn't understand what was going on in Simon's head, but he was clearly anguished about something, probably something having to do with his father. It had long been obvious to her that he was tortured by some inner demon. He hid it well, of course, especially when he was with her, but too often she'd seen a desperate bleak look in his eyes. And there had to be a reason why he fell silent with such frequency. Sometimes it seemed to Daphne that she was the only person with whom he was ever truly relaxed enough to laugh and joke and make small talk.

And maybe Anthony. Well, maybe Anthony before all of *this*.

But despite it all, despite Simon's rather fatalistic attitude in Lady Trowbridge's garden, she didn't think he wanted to die.

Daphne heard the sound of wheels on cobbles and rushed back to the open window just in time to see the Bridgerton carriage rolling past the house on its way to the mews.

Wringing her hands, she hurried across the room and pressed her ear to the door. It wouldn't do for her to go downstairs; Anthony thought she was asleep, or at least tucked into her bed and contemplating her actions of the evening.

He'd said he wasn't going to say anything to their mother. Or at least he wasn't until he could determine what she knew. Violet's delayed return home led Daphne to believe that there hadn't been any huge or dreadful rumors circulating about her, but that didn't mean that she was off scot-free. There would be whispers. There were always whispers. And whispers, if left unchecked, could quickly grow into roars.

Daphne knew that she would have to face her mother eventually. Sooner or later Violet would hear something. The *ton* would make certain she heard something. Daphne just hoped that by the time Violet was assaulted by rumors—most of them regrettably true—her daughter would already be safely betrothed to a duke.

People would forgive anything if one was connected to a duke.

And that would be the crux of Daphne's strategy to save Simon's life. He wouldn't save himself, but he might save *her*.

Colin Bridgerton tiptoed down the hall, his boots moving silently over the runner carpet that stretched across the floor. His mother had gone off to bed, and Benedict was ensconced with Anthony in the latter's study. But he wasn't interested in any of them. It was Daphne he wanted to see.

He knocked softly on her door, encouraged by the pale shaft of light that glowed at the bottom. Clearly she'd left several candles burning. Since she was far too sensible ever to fall asleep without snuffing her candles, she was still awake.

And if she were still awake, then she'd have to talk to him.

He raised his hand to knock again, but the door swung open on well-oiled hinges, and Daphne silently motioned for him to enter.

"I need to talk to you," she whispered, her words coming out in a single, urgent rush of air.

"I need to talk to you, too."

Daphne ushered him in, and then, after a quick glance up and down the hall, shut the door. "I'm in big trouble," she said.

"I know."

The blood drained from her face. "You do?"

Colin nodded, his green eyes for once deadly serious. "Do you remember my friend Macclesfield?"

She nodded. Macclesfield was the young earl her mother had

insisted upon introducing her to a fortnight ago. The very night she'd met Simon.

"Well, he saw you disappear into the gardens tonight with Hastings."

Daphne's throat felt suddenly scratchy and swollen, but she managed to get out, "He did?"

Colin nodded grimly. "He won't say anything. I'm sure of it. We've been friends for nearly a decade. But if he saw you, someone else might have as well. Lady Danbury was looking at us rather queerly when he was telling me what he'd seen."

"Lady Danbury saw?" Daphne asked sharply.

"I don't know if she did or if she didn't. All I know is that"—Colin shuddered slightly—"she was looking at me as if she knew my every transgression."

Daphne gave her head a little shake. "That's just her way. And if she did see anything, she won't say a word."

"Lady Danbury?" Colin asked doubtfully.

"She's a dragon, and she can be rather cutting, but she isn't the sort to ruin someone just for the fun of it. If she saw something, she'll confront me directly."

Colin looked unconvinced.

Daphne cleared her throat several times as she tried to figure out how to phrase her next question. "What exactly did he see?"

Colin eyed her suspiciously. "What do you mean?"

"Exactly what I said," Daphne very nearly snapped, her nerves stretched taut by the long and stressful evening. "What did he see?"

Colin's back straightened and his chin jolted back in a defensive manner. "Exactly what I said," he retorted. "He saw you disappear into the gardens with Hastings."

"But that's all?"

"That's all?" he echoed. His eyes widened, then narrowed. "What the hell happened out there?"

Daphne sank onto an ottoman and buried her face in her hands. "Oh, Colin, I'm in such a tangle."

He didn't say anything, so she finally wiped her eyes, which weren't exactly crying but did feel suspiciously wet, and looked up. Her brother looked older—and harder—than she'd ever before seen him. His arms were crossed, his legs spread in a wide and implacable stance, and his eyes, normally so merry and mischievous, were as hard as emeralds. He'd clearly been waiting for her to look up before speaking.

"Now that you're done with your display of self-pity," he said sharply, "suppose you tell me what you and Hastings did tonight in Lady Trowbridge's garden."

"Don't use that tone of voice with me," Daphne snapped back, "and don't accuse me of indulging in self-pity. For the love of God, a man is going to die tomorrow. I'm entitled to be a little upset."

Colin sat down on a chair opposite her, his face immediately softening into an expression of extreme concern. "You'd better tell me everything."

Daphne nodded and proceeded to relate the events of the evening. She didn't, however, explain the precise extent of her disgrace. Colin didn't need to know exactly what Anthony had seen; the fact that she'd been caught in a compromising position ought to be enough.

She finished with, "And now there is going to be a duel, and Simon is going to die!"

"You don't know that, Daphne."

She shook her head miserably. "He won't shoot Anthony. I'd bet my life on it. And Anthony—" Her voice caught, and she had to swallow before continuing. "Anthony is so furious. I don't think he'll delope."

"What do you want to do?"

"I don't know. I don't even know where the duel is to be held. All I know is that I have to stop it!"

Colin swore under his breath, then said softly, "I don't know if you can, Daphne."

"I must!" she cried out. "Colin, I can't sit here and stare at the ceiling while Simon dies." Her voice broke, and she added, "I love him."

He blanched. "Even after he rejected you?"

She nodded dejectedly. "I don't care if that makes me a pathetic imbecile, but I can't help it. I still love him. He needs me."

Colin said quietly, "If that were true, don't you think he would have agreed to marry you when Anthony demanded it?"

Daphne shook her head. "No. There's something else I don't know about. I can't really explain it, but it was almost as if a part of him wanted to marry me." She could feel herself growing agitated, feel her breath starting to come in jerky gasps, but still she continued. "I don't know, Colin. But if you could have seen his face, you'd understand. He was trying to protect me from something. I'm sure of it."

"I don't know Hastings nearly as well as Anthony," Colin said, "or even as well as you, but I've never even heard the barest hint of a whisper about some deep, dark secret. Are you certain—" He broke off in the middle of his sentence, and let his head fall into his hands for a moment before looking back up. When he spoke again, his voice was achingly gentle. "Are you certain you might not be imagining his feelings for you?"

Daphne took no offense. She knew her story sounded a fantasy. But she knew in her heart that she was right. "I don't want him to die," she said in a low voice. "In the end, that's all that's important."

Colin nodded, but then asked one last question. "You don't want him to die, or you don't want him to die on your account?"

Daphne stood on shaky feet. "I think you'd better leave," she said, using every last bit of her energy to keep her voice steady. "I can't believe you just asked that of me."

But Colin didn't leave. He just reached over and squeezed his sister's hand. "I'll help you, Daff. You know I'd do anything for you."

And Daphne just fell into his arms and let out all the tears she'd been keeping so valiantly inside.

Thirty minutes later, her eyes were dried and her mind was clear. She'd needed to cry; she realized that. There'd been too much trapped inside her—too much feeling, too much confusion, hurt, and anger. She'd had to let it out. But now there was no more time for emotion. She needed to keep a cool head and remain focused on her goal.

Colin had gone off to question Anthony and Benedict, whom he'd said were talking in low and intense voices in Anthony's study. He'd agreed with her that Anthony had most probably asked Benedict to act as his second. It was Colin's job to get them to tell him where the duel was to take place. Daphne had no doubt that Colin would succeed. He'd always been able to get anybody to tell him anything.

Daphne had dressed in her oldest, most comfortable riding habit. She had no idea how the morning would play out, but the last thing she wanted was to be tripping over lace and petticoats.

A swift knock on her door brought her to attention, and before she could even reach for the knob, Colin entered the room. He, too, had changed out of his evening clothes.

"Did you find out everything?" Daphne asked urgently.

His nod was sharp and brief. "We don't have much time to lose. I assume you want to try to get there before anyone else arrives?"

"If Simon gets there before Anthony, maybe I can convince him to marry me before anyone even pulls out a gun."

Colin let out a tense breath. "Daff," he began, "have you considered the possibility that you might not succeed?"

She swallowed, her throat feeling like it had a cannonball lodged in it. "I'm trying not to think about that."

"But—"

Daphne cut him off. "If I think about it," she replied in a strained voice, "I might lose my focus. I might lose my nerve. And I can't do that. For Simon's sake, I can't do that."

"I hope he knows what he has in you," Colin said quietly. "Because if he doesn't, I may have to shoot him myself."

Daphne just said, "We'd better go."

Colin nodded, and they were off.

Simon guided his horse along Broad Walk, making his way to the farthest, most remote corner in the new Regent's Park. Anthony had suggested, and he had agreed, that they carry out their business far from Mayfair. It was dawn, of course, and no one was likely to be out, but there was no reason to be flaunting a duel in Hyde Park.

Not that Simon much cared that dueling was illegal. After all, he wouldn't be around to suffer the legal consequences.

It was, however, a damned distasteful way to die. But Simon didn't see any alternatives. He had disgraced a gently bred lady whom he could not marry, and now he must suffer the consequences. It was nothing Simon had not known before he'd kissed her.

As he made his way to the designated field, he saw that Anthony and Benedict had already dismounted and were waiting for him. Their chestnut hair ruffled in the breeze, and their faces looked grim.

Almost as grim as Simon's heart.

He brought his horse to a halt a few yards away from the Bridgerton brothers and dismounted.

"Where is your second?" Benedict called out.

"Didn't bother with it," Simon replied.

"But you have to have a second! A duel isn't a duel without one."

Simon just shrugged. "There didn't seem a point. You brought the guns. I trust you."

Anthony walked toward him. "I don't want to do this," he said.

"You don't have a choice."

"But you do," Anthony said urgently. "You could marry her. Maybe you don't love her, but I know you like her well enough. Why won't you marry her?"

Simon thought about telling them everything, all the reasons he'd sworn never to take a wife and perpetuate his line. But they wouldn't understand. Not the Bridgertons, who only knew that family was good and kind and true. They didn't know anything about cruel words and shattered dreams. They didn't know the impossible feeling of rejection.

Simon then thought about saying something cruel, something that would make Anthony and Benedict despise him and get this mockery of a duel over with more quickly. But that would require him to malign Daphne, and he just couldn't do that.

And so, in the end, all he did was look up into the face of Anthony Bridgerton, the man who had been his friend since his earliest days at Eton, and said, "Just know it isn't Daphne. Your sister is the finest woman I've ever had the privilege to know."

And then, with a nod to both Anthony and Benedict, he picked up one of the two pistols in the case Benedict had laid on the ground, and began his long walk to the north side of the field.

"Waaaaaaaaaaaiiiiiiittttttttt!"

Simon gasped and whirled around. Dear God, it was Daphne!

She was bent low over her mare, in full gallop as she raced across the field, and for one stunned moment Simon forgot to be absolutely furious with her for interfering with the duel and instead just marveled at how utterly magnificent she looked in the saddle.

By the time she yanked on the reins and brought the horse to a halt right in front of him, however, his rage was back in full force.

"What the *hell* do you think you're doing?" he demanded.

"Saving your miserable life!" Her eyes flashed fire at him, and he realized he'd never seen her so angry.

Almost as angry as he was. "Daphne, you little idiot. Do you realize how dangerous this little stunt was?" Without realizing what he was doing, his hands wrapped around her shoulders and started to shake. "One of us could have shot you."

"Oh, please," she scoffed. "You hadn't even reached your end of the field."

She had a point, but he was far too furious to acknowledge it. "And riding here in the dead of night by yourself," he yelled. "You should know better."

"I do know better," she shot back. "Colin escorted me."

"Colin?" Simon's head whipped back and forth as he looked for the youngest of her older brothers. "I'm going to kill him!"

"Would that be before or after Anthony shoots you through the heart?"

"Oh, definitely before," Simon growled. "Where is he? Bridgerton!" he bellowed.

Three chestnut heads swiveled in his direction.

Simon stomped across the grass, murder in his eyes. "I meant the idiot Bridgerton."

"That, I believe," Anthony said mildly, tilting his chin toward Colin, "would refer to you."

Colin turned a deadly stare in his direction. "And I was supposed to let her stay at home and cry her eyes out?"

"Yes!" This came from three different sources.

"Simon!" Daphne yelled, tripping across the grass after him. "Get back here!"

Simon turned to Benedict. "Get her out of here."

Benedict looked undecided.

"Do it," Anthony ordered.

Benedict held still, his eyes darting back and forth between his brothers, his sister, and the man who'd shamed her.

"For the love of Christ," Anthony swore.

"She deserves to have her say," Benedict said, and crossed his arms.

"What the hell is wrong with you two?" Anthony roared, glaring at his two younger brothers.

"Simon," Daphne said, gasping for breath after her race across the field, "you must listen to me."

Simon tried to ignore her tugs on his sleeve. "Daphne, leave it. There's nothing you can do."

Daphne looked pleadingly at her brothers. Colin and Benedict were obviously sympathetic, but there was little they could do to help her. Anthony still looked like an angry god.

Finally she did the only thing she could think of to delay the duel. She punched Simon.

In his good eye.

Simon howled in pain as he staggered back. "What the hell was that for?"

"Fall down, you idiot," she hissed. If he was prostrate on the ground, Anthony couldn't very well shoot him.

"I am certainly not going to fall down!" He clutched his eye as he muttered, "Good God, being felled by a woman. Intolerable."

"Men," Daphne grunted. "Idiots, all." She turned to her brothers, who were staring at her with identical expressions of open-mouthed shock. "What are you looking at?" she snapped.

Colin started to clap.

Anthony smacked him in the shoulder.

"Might I have one, single, tiny, ever-so-brief moment with his grace?" she asked, half the words mere hisses.

Colin and Benedict nodded and walked away. Anthony didn't move.

Daphne glared at him. "I'll hit you, too."

And she might have done it too, except that Benedict returned and nearly yanked Anthony's arm out of the socket as he pulled him away.

She stared at Simon, who was pressing his fingers against his eyebrow, as if that might lessen the pain in his eye.

"I can't believe you punched me," he said.

She glanced back at her brothers to make sure they'd moved out of earshot. "It seemed like a good idea at the time."

"I don't know what you hoped to accomplish here," he said.

"I should think that would be abundantly obvious."

He sighed, and in that moment he looked weary and sad and infinitely old. "I've already told you I cannot marry you."

*"You have to."*

Her words emerged with such urgency and force that he looked up, his eyes on sharp alert. "What do you mean?" he asked, his voice a study in control.

"I mean that we were seen."

"By whom?"

"Macclesfield."

Simon relaxed visibly. "He won't talk."

"But there were others!" Daphne bit her lip. It wasn't necessarily a lie. There might have been others. In fact, there probably *were* others.

"Whom?"

"I don't know," she admitted. "But I've heard rumblings. By tomorrow it will be all over London."

Simon swore so viciously that Daphne actually took a step back.

"If you don't marry me," she said in a low voice, "I will be ruined."

"That's not true." But his voice lacked conviction.

"It is true, and you know it." She forced her eyes to meet his. Her entire future—and his life!—was riding on this moment. She couldn't afford to falter. "No one will have me. I shall be packed away to some godforsaken corner of the country—"

"You know your mother would never send you away."

"But I will never marry. You know that." She took a step forward, forcing him to acknowledge her nearness. "I will be forever branded as used goods. I'll never have a husband, never bear children—"

"Stop!" Simon fairly yelled. "For the love of God, just stop."

Anthony, Benedict, and Colin all started at his shout, but Daphne's frantic shake of her head kept them in their places.

"Why can't you marry me?" she asked in a low voice. "I know you care for me. What is it?"

Simon wrapped his hand across his face, his thumb and forefinger pressing mercilessly into his temples. Christ, he had a headache.

And Daphne—dear God, she kept moving closer. She reached out and touched his shoulder, then his cheek. He wasn't strong enough. Dear God, he wasn't going to be strong enough.

"Simon," she pleaded, "save me."

And he was lost.

# Chapter 12

*A duel, a duel, a duel. Is there anything more exciting, more romantic . . . or more utterly moronic?*

*It has reached This Author's ears that a duel took place earlier this week in Regent's Park. Because dueling is illegal, This Author shall not reveal the names of the perpetrators, but let it be known that This Author frowns heavily upon such violence.*

*Of course, as this issue goes to press, it appears that the two dueling idiots (I am loath to call them gentlemen; that would imply a certain degree of intelligence, a quality which, if they ever possessed it, clearly eluded them that morning) are both unharmed.*

*One wonders if perhaps an angel of sensibility and rationality smiled down upon them that fateful morn.*

*If so, it is the belief of This Author that This Angel ought to shed her influence on a great many more men of the ton. Such an action could only make for a more peaceful and amiable environment, leading to a vast improvement of our world.*

*Lady Whistledown's Society Papers,*
19 May 1813

Simon raised ravaged eyes to meet hers. "I'll marry you," he said in a low voice, "but you need to know—"

His sentence was rendered incomplete by her exultant shout and fierce hug. "Oh, Simon, you won't be sorry," she said, her words coming out in a relieved rush. Her eyes sparkled with unshed tears, but they glowed with joy. "I'll make you happy. I promise you. I'll make you so happy. You won't regret this."

"Stop!" Simon ground out, pushing her away. Her unfeigned joy was too much to bear. "You have to listen to me."

She stilled, and her face grew apprehensive.

"You listen to what I have to say," he said in a harsh voice, "and then decide if you want to marry me."

Her bottom lip caught between her teeth, and she gave the barest of nods.

Simon took in a shaky breath. How to tell her? *What* to tell her? He couldn't tell her the truth. Not all of it, at least. But she had to understand . . . If she married him . . .

She'd be giving up more than she'd ever dreamed.

He had to give her the opportunity to refuse him. She deserved that much. Simon swallowed, guilt sliding uncomfortably down his throat. She deserved much more than that, but that was all he could give her.

"Daphne," he said, her name as always soothing his frazzled mouth, "if you marry me . . ."

She stepped toward him and reached out her hand, only to pull it back at his burning glare of caution. "What is it?" she whispered. "Surely nothing could be so awful that—"

"I can't have children."

There. He'd done it. And it was almost the truth.

Daphne's lips parted, but other than that, there was no indication that she'd even heard him.

He knew his words would be brutal, but he saw no other way to force her understanding. "If you marry me, you will never have children. You will never hold a baby in your arms and know it is yours, that you created it in love. You will never—"

"How do you know?" she interrupted, her voice flat and unnaturally loud.

"I just do."

"But—"

"I cannot have children," he repeated cruelly. "You need to understand that."

"I see." Her mouth was quivering slightly, as if she wasn't quite sure if she had anything to say, and her eyelids seemed to be blinking a bit more than normal.

Simon searched her face, but he couldn't read her emotions the way he usually could. Normally her expressions were so open, her eyes startlingly honest—it was as if he could see to her very soul and back. But right now she looked shuttered and frozen.

She was upset—that much was clear. But he had no idea what she was going to say. No idea how she would react.

And Simon had the strangest feeling that Daphne didn't know, either.

He became aware of a presence to his right, and he turned to see Anthony, his face torn between anger and concern.

"Is there a problem?" Anthony asked softly, his eyes straying to his sister's tortured face.

Before Simon could reply, Daphne said, "No."

All eyes turned to her.

"There will be no duel," she said. "His grace and I will be getting married."

"I see." Anthony looked as if he wanted to react with considerably more relief, but his sister's solemn face forced a strange quietude on the scene. "I'll tell the others," he said, and walked off.

Simon felt a rush of something utterly foreign fill his lungs. It was air, he realized dumbly. He'd been holding his breath. He hadn't even realized he'd been holding his breath.

And something else filled him as well. Something hot and terrible, something triumphant and wonderful. It was emotion, pure and undiluted, a bizarre mix of relief and joy and desire and dread. And Simon, who'd spent most of his life avoiding such messy feelings, had no idea what to do about it.

His eyes found Daphne's. "Are you certain?" he asked, his voice whisper soft.

She nodded, her face strangely devoid of emotion. "You're worth it." Then she walked slowly back to her horse.

And Simon was left wondering if he had just been snatched up into heaven—or perhaps led to the darkest corner of hell.

Daphne spent the rest of the day surrounded by her family. Everyone was, of course, thrilled by the news of her engagement. Everyone, that was, except her older brothers, who while happy for her, were somewhat subdued. Daphne didn't blame them. She felt rather subdued herself. The events of the day had left them all exhausted.

It was decided that the wedding must take place with all possible haste. (Violet had been informed that Daphne *might* have been seen kissing Simon in Lady Trowbridge's garden, and that was enough for her to immediately send a request to the archbishop for a special license.) Violet had then immersed herself in a whirlwind of party details; just because the wedding was to be small, she'd announced, it didn't have to be shabby.

Eloise, Francesca, and Hyacinth, all vastly excited at the prospect of dressing up as bridesmaids, kept up a steady stream of questions. How had Simon proposed? Did he get down on one knee? What color would Daphne wear and when would he give her a ring?

Daphne did her best to answer their questions, but she could barely concentrate on her sisters, and by the time afternoon slipped into the eve, she was reduced to monosyllables. Finally, after Hyacinth asked her what color roses she wanted for her bouquet, and Daphne answered, "Three," her sisters gave up talking to her and left her alone.

The enormity of her actions had left Daphne nearly speechless. She had saved a man's life. She had secured a promise of marriage from the man she adored. And she had committed herself to a life without children.

All in one day.

She laughed, somewhat desperately. It made one wonder what she could do tomorrow as an encore.

She wished she knew what had gone through her head in those last moments before she'd turned to Anthony, and said, "There will be no duel," but in all truth, she wasn't sure it was anything she could possibly remember. Whatever had been racing through her mind—it hadn't been made up of words or sentences or conscious thought. It had been as if she was enveloped by color. Reds and yellows, and a swirling mishmash of orange where they met. Pure feeling and instinct. That's all there had been. No reason, no logic, nothing even remotely rational or sane.

And somehow, as all of that churned violently within her, she'd known what she had to do. She might be able to live without the children she hadn't yet borne, but she couldn't live without Simon. The children were amorphous, unknown beings she couldn't picture or touch.

But Simon—Simon was real and he was *here*. She knew how it felt to touch his cheek, to laugh in his presence. She knew the sweet taste of his kiss, and the wry quirk of his smile.

And she loved him.

And although she barely dared think it, maybe he was wrong. Maybe he *could* have children. Maybe he'd been misled by an incompetent surgeon, or maybe God was just waiting for the right time to bestow a miracle. She'd be unlikely to mother a brood the size of the Bridgertons, but if she could have even one child she knew she'd feel complete.

She wouldn't mention these thoughts to Simon, though. If he thought she was holding out even the tiniest hope for a child, he wouldn't marry her. She was sure of it. He'd gone to such lengths to be brutally honest. He wouldn't allow her to make a decision if he didn't think she had the facts absolutely straight.

"Daphne?"

Daphne, who had been sitting listlessly on the sofa in the Bridgertons' drawing room, looked up to see her mother gazing at her with an expression of deep concern.

"Are you all right?" Violet asked.

Daphne forced a weary smile. "I'm just tired," she replied. And she was. It hadn't even occurred to her until that very moment that she hadn't slept in over thirty-six hours.

Violet sat beside her. "I thought you'd be more excited. I know how much you love Simon."

Daphne turned surprised eyes to her mother's face.

"It's not hard to see," Violet said gently. She patted her on the hand. "He's a good man. You've chosen well."

Daphne felt a wobbly smile coming on. She *had* chosen well. And she would make the best of her marriage. If they weren't blessed with children—well, she reasoned, she might have turned out to be barren, anyway. She knew of several couples who had never had children, and she doubted any of them had known of their deficiencies prior to their marriage vows. And with seven brothers and sisters, she was sure to have plenty of nieces and nephews to hug and spoil.

Better to live with the man she loved than to have children with one she didn't.

"Why don't you take a nap?" Violet suggested. "You look terribly tired. I hate seeing such dark smudges below your eyes."

Daphne nodded and stumbled to her feet. Her mother knew best. Sleep was what she needed. "I'm sure I'll feel much better in an hour or two," she said, a wide yawn escaping her mouth.

Violet stood and offered her daughter her arm. "I don't think you're going to be able to make it up the stairs on your own," she said, smiling as she led Daphne out of the room and up the stairs. "And I sincerely doubt we'll see you in an hour or two. I shall give everyone explicit instructions that you are not to be disturbed until morning."

Daphne nodded sleepily. "Thaz good," she mumbled, stumbling into her room. "Morningsh good."

Violet steered Daphne to the bed and helped her into it. The shoes she pulled off, but that was all. "You might as well sleep in your clothes," she said softly, then bent to kiss her daughter on the forehead. "I can't imagine I'll be able to move you enough to get you out of them."

Daphne's only reply was a snore.

Simon, too, was exhausted. It wasn't every day that a man resigned himself to death. And then to be saved by—and betrothed to!—the woman who had occupied his every dream for the past two weeks.

If he weren't sporting two black eyes and a sizable bruise on his chin, he'd have thought he'd dreamed the whole thing.

Did Daphne realize what she'd done? What she was denying herself? She was a levelheaded girl, not given to foolish dreams and flights of fancy; he didn't think she would have agreed to marry him without sorting through all the consequences.

But then again, she'd reached her decision in under a minute. How could she have thought everything through in under a minute?

Unless she fancied herself in love with him. Would she give up her dream of a family because she loved him?

Or maybe she did it out of guilt. If he'd died in that duel, he was sure Daphne could come up with some line of reasoning that would make it seem her fault. Hell, he *liked* Daphne. She was one of the finest people he knew. He didn't think he could live with her death on his conscience. Perhaps she felt the same way about him.

But whatever her motives, the simple truth was that come this Saturday (Lady Bridgerton had already sent him a note informing him that the engagement would not be an extended one) he would be bound to Daphne for life.

And she to him.

There was no stopping it now, he realized. Daphne would never back out of the marriage at this point, and neither would he. And to his utter surprise, this almost fatalistic certainty felt . . .

Good.

Daphne would be his. She knew of his shortcomings, she knew what he could not give her, and she had still chosen him.

It warmed his heart more than he would ever have thought possible.

"Your grace?"

Simon looked up from his slouchy position in his study's leather chair. Not that he needed to; the low, even voice was obviously that of his butler. "Yes, Jeffries?"

"Lord Bridgerton is here to see you. Shall I inform him that you are not at home?"

Simon pulled himself to his feet. Damn, but he was tired. "He won't believe you."

Jeffries nodded. "Very well, sir." He took three steps, then turned around. "Are you certain you wish to receive a guest? You do seem to be a trifle, er, indisposed."

Simon let out a single humorless chuckle. "If you are referring to my eyes, Lord Bridgerton would be the one responsible for the larger of the two bruises."

Jeffries blinked like an owl. "The larger, your grace?"

Simon managed a half-smile. It wasn't easy. His entire face hurt. "I realize it's difficult to discern, but my right eye is actually a touch worse off than the left."

Jeffries swayed closer, clearly intrigued.

"Trust me."

The butler straightened. "Of course. Shall I show Lord Bridgerton to the drawing room?"

"No, bring him here." At Jeffries's nervous swallow, Simon added, "And you needn't worry for my safety. Lord Bridgerton isn't likely to add to my injuries at this juncture. Not," he added in a mutter, "that he'd find it easy to find a spot he hasn't already injured."

Jeffries's eyes widened, and he scurried out of the room.

A moment later Anthony Bridgerton strode in. He took one look at Simon, and said, "You look like hell."

Simon stood and raised a brow—not an easy feat in his current condition. "This surprises you?"

Anthony laughed. The sound was a little mirthless, a little

hollow, but Simon heard a shadow of his old friend. A shadow of their old friendship. He was surprised by how grateful he was for that.

Anthony motioned to Simon's eyes. "Which one is mine?"

"The right," Simon replied, gingerly touching his abused skin. "Daphne packs quite a punch for a girl, but she lacks your size and strength."

"Still," Anthony said, leaning forward to inspect his sister's handiwork, "she did quite a nice job."

"You should be proud of her," Simon grunted. "Hurts like the devil."

"Good."

And then they were silent, with so much to say and no idea how to say it.

"I never wanted it to be like this," Anthony finally said.

"Nor I."

Anthony leaned against the edge of Simon's desk, but he shifted uncomfortably, looking oddly ill at ease in his own body. "It wasn't easy for me to let you court her."

"You knew it wasn't real."

"You *made* it real last night."

What was he to say? That Daphne had been the seducer, not he? That she'd been the one to lead him off the terrace and dance into the darkness of the night? None of that mattered. He was far more experienced than Daphne. He should have been able to stop.

He said nothing.

"I hope we may put this behind us," Anthony said.

"I'm certain that would be Daphne's fondest wish."

Anthony's eyes narrowed. "And is it now your aim in life to grant her fondest wishes?"

*All but one*, Simon thought. *All but the one that really matters.* "You know that I will do everything in my capabilities to keep her happy," he said quietly.

Anthony nodded. "If you hurt her—"

"I will never hurt her," Simon vowed, his eyes blazing.

Anthony regarded him with a long and even stare. "I was prepared to kill you for dishonoring her. If you damage her soul, I guarantee you will never find peace as long as you live. Which," he added, his eyes turning slightly harder, "would not be long."

"Just long enough to put me in excruciating pain?" Simon asked mildly.

"Exactly."

Simon nodded. Even though Anthony was threatening torture and death, Simon could not help but respect him for it. Devotion to one's sister was an honorable thing.

Simon wondered if Anthony perhaps saw something in him that no one else did. They had known each other for over half of their lives. Did Anthony somehow see the darkest corners of his soul? The anguish and fury he tried so hard to keep hidden?

And if so, was that why he worried for his sister's happiness?

"I give you my word," Simon said. "I will do everything in my power to keep Daphne safe and content."

Anthony nodded curtly. "See that you do." He pushed himself away from the desk and walked to the door. "Or you'll be seeing me."

He left.

Simon groaned and sank back into the leather chair. When had his life grown so damned complicated? When had friends become enemies and flirtations grown to lust?

And what the hell was he going to do with Daphne? He didn't want to hurt her, couldn't bear to hurt her, actually, and yet he was doomed to do so simply by marrying her. He burned for her, ached for the day when he could lay her down and cover her body with his, slowly entering her until she moaned his name—

He shuddered. Such thoughts could not possibly be advantageous to his health.

"Your grace?"

Jeffries again. Simon was too tired to look up, so he just made an acknowledging motion with his hand.

"Perhaps you would like to retire for the evening, your grace."

Simon managed to look at the clock, but that was only because he didn't have to move his head to do it. It was barely seven in the evening. Hardly his usual bedtime. "It's early yet," he mumbled.

"Still," the butler said pointedly, "perhaps you'd like to retire."

Simon closed his eyes. Jeffries had a point. Maybe what he needed was a long engagement with his feather mattress and fine linen sheets. He could escape to his bedroom, where he might manage to avoid seeing a Bridgerton for an entire night.

Hell, the way he felt, he might hole up there for days.

# Chapter 13

*It's marriage for the Duke of Hastings and Miss Bridgerton!*

*This Author must take this opportunity to remind you, dear reader, that the forthcoming nuptials were predicted in this very column. It has not escaped the note of This Author that when this newspaper reports a new attachment between an eligible gentleman and an unmarried lady, the odds in the betting books at gentleman's clubs change within hours, and always in favor of marriage.*

*Although This Author is not allowed in White's, she has reason to believe that the official odds concerning the marriage of the duke and Miss Bridgerton were 2–1 for.*

LADY WHISTLEDOWN'S SOCIETY PAPERS,
21 May 1813

The rest of the week flew by in a rush. Daphne didn't see Simon for several days. She might have thought he'd left town, except that Anthony told her he'd been over to Hastings House to settle the details of the marriage contract.

Much to Anthony's surprise, Simon had refused to accept even a penny as dowry. Finally, the two men had decided that Anthony would put the money his father had put aside for Daphne's marriage in a separate estate with himself as the trustee. It would be hers to spend or save as she liked.

"You can pass it along to your children," Anthony suggested.

Daphne only smiled. It was either that or cry.

A few days after that, Simon called upon Bridgerton House in the afternoon. It was two days before the wedding.

Daphne waited in the drawing room after Humboldt announced his arrival. She sat primly on the edge of the damask sofa, her back straight and her hands clasped together in her lap. She looked, she was sure, the very model of genteel English womanhood.

She felt a bundle of nerves.

Correction, she thought, as her stomach turned itself inside out, a bundle of nerves with frayed edges.

She looked down at her hands and realized that her fingernails were leaving red, crescent-shaped indentations on her palms.

Second correction, a bundle of nerves with frayed edges with an arrow stuck through them. Maybe a flaming arrow at that.

The urge to laugh was almost as overwhelming as it was inappropriate. She had never felt nervous at seeing Simon before. In fact, that had been possibly the most remarkable aspect of their friendship. Even when she caught him gazing at her with smoldering heat, and she was sure that her eyes reflected the same need, she had felt utterly comfortable with him. Yes, her stomach flipped and her skin tingled, but those were symptoms of desire, not of unease. First and foremost, Simon had been her friend, and Daphne knew that the easy, happy feeling she'd experienced whenever he was near was not something to be taken for granted.

She was confident that they would find their way back to that sense of comfort and companionship, but after the scene in Regent's Park, she very much feared that this would occur later rather than sooner.

"Good day, Daphne."

Simon appeared in the doorway, filling it with his marvelous presence. Well, perhaps his presence wasn't quite as marvelous as usual. His eyes still sported matching purple bruises, and the one on his chin was starting to turn an impressive shade of green.

Still, it was better than a bullet in the heart.

"Simon," Daphne replied. "How nice to see you. What brings you to Bridgerton House?"

He gave her a surprised look. "Aren't we betrothed?"

She blushed. "Yes, of course."

"It was my impression that men were supposed to visit their betrothed." He sat down across from her. "Didn't Lady Whistledown say something to that effect?"

"I don't think so," Daphne murmured, "but I'm certain my mother must have done."

They both smiled, and for a moment Daphne thought that all would be well again, but as soon as the smiles faded, an uncomfortable silence fell across the room.

"Are your eyes feeling any better?" she finally asked. "They don't look quite as swollen."

"Do you think?" Simon turned so that he was facing a large gilt mirror. "I rather think the bruises have turned a spectacular shade of blue."

"Purple."

He leaned forward, not that that brought him appreciably closer to the mirror. "Purple then, but I suppose it might be a debatable fact."

"Do they hurt?"

He smiled humorlessly. "Only when someone pokes at them."

"I shall refrain from doing so, then," she murmured, her lips quirking in a telltale twitch. "It shall be difficult, of course, but I shall persevere."

"Yes," he said, with a perfectly deadpan expression, "I've often been told I make women want to poke me in the eye."

Daphne's smile was one of relief. Surely if they could joke about such things, everything would go back to the way it was.

Simon cleared his throat. "I did have a specific reason for coming to see you."

Daphne gazed at him expectantly, waiting for him to continue.

He held out a jeweler's box. "This is for you."

Her breath caught in her throat as she reached for the small, velvet-covered box. "Are you certain?" she asked.

"I believe betrothal rings are considered quite *de rigueur*," he said quietly.

"Oh. How stupid of me. I didn't realize . . ."

"That it was a betrothal ring? What did you think it was?"

"I *wasn't* thinking," she admitted sheepishly. He'd never given her a gift before. She'd been so taken aback by the gesture she'd completely forgotten that he owed her a betrothal ring.

"Owed." She didn't like that word, didn't like that she'd even thought it. But she was fairly certain that that was what Simon must have been thinking when he'd picked out the ring.

This depressed her.

Daphne forced a smile. "Is this a family heirloom?"

"No!" he said, with enough vehemence to make her blink.

"Oh."

Yet another awkward silence.

He coughed, then said, "I thought you might like something of your own. All of the Hastings jewelry was chosen for someone else. This I chose for you."

Daphne thought it a wonder she didn't melt on the spot. "That's so sweet," she said, just barely managing to stifle a sentimental sniffle.

Simon squirmed in his seat, which didn't surprise her. Men did so hate to be called sweet.

"Aren't you going to open it?" he grunted.

"Oh, yes, of course." Daphne shook her head slightly as she snapped back to attention. "How silly of me." Her eyes had glazed over slightly as she stared at the jeweler's box. Blinking a few times to clear her vision, she carefully released the box's clasp and opened it.

And couldn't possibly say anything besides, "Oh, my goodness," and even that came out with more breath than voice.

Nestled in the box was a stunning band of white gold, adorned with a large marquis-cut emerald, flanked on either side by a single, perfect diamond. It was the most beautiful piece of jewelry Daphne had ever seen, brilliant but elegant, obviously precious but not overly showy.

"It's beautiful," she whispered. "I love it."

"Are you certain?" Simon removed his gloves, then leaned forward and took the ring out of the box. "Because it is your ring. You shall be the one to wear it, and it should reflect your tastes, not mine."

Daphne's voice shook slightly as she said, "Clearly, our tastes coincide."

Simon breathed a small sigh of relief and picked up her hand. He hadn't realized how much it meant to him that she liked the ring until that very moment. He hated that he felt so nervous around her when they'd been such easy friends for the past few weeks. He hated that there were silences in their conversations, when before she'd been the only person with whom he never felt the need to pause and take stock of his words.

Not that he was having any trouble speaking now. It was just that he didn't seem to know what to say.

"May I put it on?" he asked softly.

She nodded and started to remove her glove.

But Simon stilled her fingers with his own, then took over the task. He gave the tip of each finger a tug, then slowly slid the glove from her hand. The motion was unabashedly erotic, clearly an abbreviated version of what he wanted to do: remove every stitch from her body.

Daphne gasped as the edge of the glove trailed past the tips of her fingers. The sound of her breath rushing across her lips made him want her all the more.

With tremulous hands, he slid the ring on her finger, easing it over her knuckle until it rested in place.

"It fits perfectly," she said, moving her hand this way and that so that she could see how it reflected the light.

Simon, however, didn't let go of her hand. As she moved, her skin slid along his, creating a warmth that was oddly soothing. Then he lifted her hand to his mouth and dropped a gentle kiss on her knuckles. "I'm glad," he murmured. "It suits you."

Her lips curved—a hint of that wide smile he'd come to adore. Maybe a hint that all would be well between them.

"How did you know I like emeralds?" she asked.

"I didn't," he admitted. "They reminded me of your eyes."

"Of my—" Her head cocked slightly as her mouth twisted into what could only be described as a scolding grin. "Simon, my eyes are brown."

"They're mostly brown," he corrected.

She twisted until she was facing the gilt mirror he'd used earlier to inspect his bruises and blinked a few times. "No," she said slowly, as if she were speaking to a person of considerably small intellect, "they're brown."

He reached out and brushed one gentle finger along the bottom edge of her eye, her delicate lashes tickling his skin like a butterfly kiss. "Not around the edge."

She gave him a look that was mostly dubious, but a little bit hopeful, then let out a funny little breath and stood. "I'm going to look for myself."

Simon watched with amusement as she stood and marched over to the mirror and put her face close to the glass. She blinked several times, then held her eyes open wide, then blinked some more.

"Oh, my goodness!" she exclaimed. "I've never seen that!"

Simon stood and moved to her side, leaning with her against the mahogany table that stood in front of the mirror. "You'll soon learn that I am always right."

She shot him a sarcastic look. "But how did you notice that?"

He shrugged. "I looked very closely."

"You . . ." She seemed to decide against finishing her statement, and leaned back against the table, opening her eyes wide to inspect them again. "Fancy that," she murmured. "I have green eyes."

"Well, I wouldn't go so far as to say—"

"For today," she interrupted, "I refuse to believe they are anything but green."

Simon grinned. "As you wish."

She sighed. "I was always so jealous of Colin. Such beautiful eyes wasted on a man."

"I'm sure the young ladies who fancy themselves in love with him would disagree."

Daphne gave him a smirky glance. "Yes, but they don't signify, do they?"

Simon caught himself wanting to laugh. "Not if you say so."

"You'll soon learn," she said archly, "that I am always right."

This time he did laugh. There was no way he could have held it in. He finally stopped, realizing that Daphne was silent. She was regarding him warmly, though, her lips curved into a nostalgic smile.

"This was nice," she said, placing her hand on his. "Almost like it used to be, don't you think?"

He nodded, turning his hand palm up so that he could clasp hers.

"It will be like this again, won't it?" Her eyes showed a flicker of trepidation. "We'll go back to the way it was, won't we? Everything will be exactly the same."

"Yes," he said, even though he knew it could not be true. They might find contentment, but it would never be just as it was.

She smiled, closed her eyes, and rested her head against his shoulder. "Good."

Simon watched their reflection for several minutes. And he almost believed he would be able to make her happy.

The next evening—Daphne's last night as Miss Bridgerton—Violet knocked on her bedroom door.

Daphne was sitting on her bed, mementos of her childhood spread out before her, when she heard the rap. "Come in!" she called out.

Violet poked her head in, an awkward smile pasted on her face. "Daphne," she said, sounding queasy, "do you have a moment?"

Daphne looked at her mother with concern. "Of course." She stood as Violet edged into the room. Her mother's skin was a remarkable match with her yellow dress.

"Are you quite all right, Mother?" Daphne inquired. "You look a little green."

"I'm fine. I just—" Violet cleared her throat and steeled her shoulders. "It's time we had a talk."

"Ohhhhhh," Daphne breathed, her heart racing with anticipation. She'd been waiting for this. All her friends had told her that the night before one's wedding, one's mother delivered all the secrets of marriage. At the last possible moment, one was admitted into the company of womanhood, and told all those wicked and delicious facts that were kept so scrupulously from the ears of unmarried girls. Some of the young ladies of her set had, of course, already married, and Daphne and her friends had tried to get them to reveal what no one else would, but the young matrons had just giggled and smiled, saying, "You'll find out soon."

"Soon" had become "now," and Daphne couldn't wait.

Violet, on the other hand, looked as if she might lose the contents of her stomach at any moment.

Daphne patted a spot on her bed. "Would you like to sit here, Mother?"

Violet blinked in a rather distracted manner. "Yes, yes, that would be fine." She sat down, half-on and half-off the bed. She didn't look very comfortable.

Daphne decided to take pity on her and begin the conversation. "Is this about marriage?" she asked gently.

Violet's nod was barely perceptible.

Daphne fought to keep the fascinated glee out of her voice. "The wedding night?"

This time Violet managed to bob her chin up and down an entire inch. "I really don't know how to tell this to you. It's highly indelicate."

Daphne tried to wait patiently. Eventually her mother would get to the point.

"You see," Violet said haltingly, "there are things you need to know. Things that will occur tomorrow night. Things"—she coughed—"that involve your husband."

Daphne leaned forward, her eyes widening.

Violet scooted back, clearly uncomfortable with Daphne's obvious interest. "You see, your husband . . . that is to say, Simon, of course, since he will be your husband . . ."

Since Violet showed no sign of finishing that thought, Daphne murmured, "Yes, Simon will be my husband."

Violet groaned, her cornflower blue eyes glancing everywhere but Daphne's face. "This is very difficult for me."

"Apparently so," Daphne muttered.

Violet took a deep breath and sat up straight, her narrow shoulders thrown back as if she were steeling herself for the most unpleasant task. "On your wedding night," she began, "your husband will expect you to do your marital duty."

This was nothing Daphne didn't already know.

"Your marriage must be consummated."

"Of course," Daphne murmured.

"He will join you in your bed."

Daphne nodded. She knew this as well.

"And he will perform certain"—Violet groped for a word, her hands actually waving through the air—"*intimacies* upon your person."

Daphne's lips parted slightly, her short indrawn breath the room's only sound. This was finally getting interesting.

"I am here to tell you," Violet said, her voice turning quite brisk, "that your marital duty need not be unpleasant."

But what *was* it?

Violet's cheeks blazed. "I know that some women find the, er, act distasteful, but—"

"They do?" Daphne asked curiously. "Then why do I see so many maids sneaking off with the footmen?"

Violet instantly went into outraged employer mode. "Which maid was that?" she demanded.

"Don't try to change the subject," Daphne warned. "I've been waiting for this all week."

Some of the steam went out of her mother. "You have?"

Daphne's look was pure what-did-you-expect. "Well, of course."

Violet sighed and mumbled, "Where was I?"

"You were telling me that some women find their marital duty unpleasant."

"Right. Well. Hmmm."

Daphne looked down at her mother's hands and noticed that she'd practically shredded a handkerchief.

"All I really want you to know," Violet said, the words tumbling out as if she could not wait to be rid of them, "is that it needn't be unpleasant at all. If two people care for one another—and I believe that the duke cares for you very much—"

"And I for him," Daphne interrupted softly.

"Of course. Right. Well, you see, given that you do care for each other, it will probably be a very lovely and special moment." Violet started scooting to the foot of the bed, the pale yellow silk of her skirts spreading along the quilts as she moved. "And you shouldn't be nervous. I'm sure the duke will be very gentle."

Daphne thought of Simon's scorching kiss. "Gentle" didn't seem to apply. "But—"

Violet stood up like a shot. "Very well. Have a good night. That's what I came here to say."

*"That's all?"*

Violet dashed for the door. "Er, yes." Her eyes shifted guiltily. "Were you expecting something else?"

"Yes!" Daphne ran after her mother and threw herself against the door so she couldn't escape. "You can't leave telling me only that!"

Violet glanced longingly at the window. Daphne gave thanks that her room was on the second floor; otherwise, she wouldn't have put it past her mother to try to make a getaway that way.

"Daphne," Violet said, her voice sounding rather strangled.

"But what do I *do*?"

"Your husband will know," Violet said primly.

"I don't want to make a fool of myself, Mother."

Violet groaned. "You won't. Trust me. Men are . . ."

Daphne seized upon the half-finished thought. "Men are what? What, Mother? What were you going to say?"

By now Violet's entire face had turned bright red, and her neck and ears had progressed well into the pinks. "Men are easily pleased," she mumbled. "He won't be disappointed."

"But—"

"But enough!" Violet finally said firmly. "I have told you everything my mother told me. Don't be a nervous ninny, and do it enough so you'll have a baby."

Daphne's jaw dropped. "*What?*"

Violet chuckled nervously. "Did I forget to mention the bit about the baby?"

"Mother!"

"Very well. Your marital duty—the, er, consummation, that is—is how you have a baby."

Daphne sank against the wall. "So you did this eight times?" she whispered.

"No!"

Daphne blinked in confusion. Her mother's explanations had been impossibly vague, and she still didn't know what marital duty was, precisely, but something wasn't adding up. "But wouldn't you have had to do it eight times?"

Violet began to fan herself furiously. "Yes. No! Daphne, this is very personal."

"But how could you have had eight children if you—"

"I did it more than eight times," Violet ground out, looking as if she wanted to melt right into the walls.

Daphne stared at her mother in disbelief. "You did?"

"Sometimes," Violet said, barely even moving her lips, and certainly not moving her eyes off a single spot on the floor, "people just do it because they like to."

Daphne's eyes grew very wide. "They do?" she breathed.

"Er, yes."

"Like when men and women kiss?"

"Yes, exactly," Violet said, sighing with relief. "Very much like—" Her eyes narrowed. "Daphne," she said, her voice suddenly shrill, "have you kissed the duke?"

Daphne felt her skin turning a shade that rivaled her mother's. "I might have done," she mumbled.

Violet shook her finger at her daughter. "Daphne Bridgerton, I cannot believe you would do such a thing. You know very well I warned you about allowing men such liberties!"

"It hardly signifies now that we're to be married!"

"But still—" Violet gave a deflating sigh. "Never mind. You're right. It doesn't signify. You're to be married, and to a duke no less, and if he kissed you, well, then, that was to be expected."

Daphne just stared at her mother in disbelief. Violet's nervous, halting chatter was very much out of character.

"Now then," Violet announced, "as long as you don't have any more questions, I'll just leave you to your, er,"—she glanced distractedly at the mementos Daphne had been shuffling through—"whatever it is that you're doing."

"But I do have more questions!"

Violet, however, had already made her escape.

And Daphne, no matter how desperately she wanted to learn the secrets of the marital act, wasn't about to chase her mother down the hall—in full view of all the family and servants—to find out.

Besides, her mother's talk had raised a new set of worries. Violet had said that the marital act was a requirement for the creation of children. If Simon couldn't have children, did that mean he couldn't perform those intimacies her mother had mentioned?

And dash it all, what *were* those intimacies? Daphne suspected they had something to do with kissing, since society seemed so determined to make sure that young ladies keep their lips pure and chaste. And, she thought, a blush stealing over her cheeks as she remembered her time in the gardens with Simon, they might have something to do with a woman's breasts as well.

Daphne groaned. Her mother had practically ordered her not to be nervous, but she didn't see how she could be otherwise—not when she was expected to enter into this contract without the slightest idea of how to perform her duties.

And what of Simon? If he could not consummate the marriage, would it even *be* a marriage?

It was enough to make a new bride very apprehensive, indeed.

In the end, it was the little details of the wedding that Daphne remembered. There were tears in her mother's eyes (and then eventually on her face), and Anthony's voice had been oddly hoarse when he stepped forward to give her away. Hyacinth had strewn her rose petals too quickly, and there were none left by the time she reached the altar. Gregory sneezed three times before they even got to their vows.

And she remembered the look of concentration on Simon's face as he repeated his vows. Each syllable was uttered slowly and carefully. His eyes burned with intent, and his voice was low but true. To Daphne, it sounded as if nothing in the world could possibly be as important as the words he spoke as they stood before the archbishop.

Her heart found comfort in this; no man who spoke his vows with such intensity could possibly view marriage as a mere convenience.

*Those whom God hath joined together, let no man put asunder.*

A shiver raced down Daphne's spine, causing her to sway. In just a moment, she would belong to this man forever.

Simon's head turned slightly, his eyes darting to her face. *Are you all right?* his eyes asked.

She nodded, a tiny little jog of her chin that only he could see. Something blazed in his eyes—could it be relief?

*I now pronounce you—*

Gregory sneezed for a fourth time, then a fifth and sixth, completely obliterating the archbishop's "man and wife." Daphne felt a horrifying bubble of mirth pushing up her throat. She pressed her lips together, determined to maintain an appropriately serious facade. Marriage, after all, was a solemn institution, and not one to be treating as a joke.

She shot a glance at Simon, only to find that he was looking at her with a queer expression. His pale eyes were focused on her mouth, and the corners of his lips began to twitch.

Daphne felt that bubble of mirth rising ever higher.

*You may kiss the bride.*

Simon grabbed her with almost desperate arms, his mouth crashing down on hers with a force that drew a collective gasp from the small assemblage of guests.

And then both sets of lips—bride and groom—burst into laughter, even as they remained entwined.

Violet Bridgerton later said it was the oddest kiss she'd ever been privileged to view.

Gregory Bridgerton—when he finished sneezing—said it was disgusting.

The archbishop, who was getting on in years, looked perplexed.

But Hyacinth Bridgerton, who at ten should have known the least about kisses of anyone, just blinked thoughtfully, and said, "I think it's nice. If they're laughing now, they'll probably be laughing forever." She turned to her mother. "Isn't that a good thing?"

Violet took her youngest daughter's hand and squeezed it. "Laughter is always a good thing, Hyacinth. And thank you for reminding us of that."

And so it was that the rumor was started that the new Duke and Duchess of Hastings were the most blissfully happy and devoted couple to be married in decades. After all, who could remember another wedding with so much laughter?

# Chapter 14

*We are told that the wedding of the Duke of Hastings and the former Miss Bridgerton, while small, was most eventful. Miss Hyacinth Bridgerton (ten years of age) whispered to Miss Felicity Featherington (also aged ten) that the bride and groom actually laughed aloud during the ceremony. Miss Felicity then repeated this information to her mother, Mrs. Featherington, who then repeated it to the world.*

*This Author shall have to trust Miss Hyacinth's account, since This Author was not invited to view the ceremony.*

*Lady Whistledown's Society Papers,*
24 May 1813

There was to be no wedding trip. There hadn't, after all, been any time to plan one. Instead, Simon had made arrangements for them to spend several weeks at Clyvedon Castle, the Bassets' ancestral seat. Daphne thought this a fine idea; she was eager to get away from London and the inquiring eyes and ears of the *ton*.

Besides, she was oddly eager to see the place where Simon had grown up.

She found herself imagining him as a young boy. Had he been as irrepressible as he now was with her? Or had he been a quiet child, with the reserved demeanor he showed to most of society?

The new couple left Bridgerton House amidst cheers and hugs, and Simon quickly bundled Daphne into his finest carriage. Although it was summer, there was a chill in the air, and he carefully tucked a blanket over her lap. Daphne laughed. "Isn't that a bit much?" she teased. "I'm unlikely to catch a chill on the few short blocks to your home."

He regarded her quizzically. "We travel to Clyvedon."

"Tonight?" She could not disguise her surprise. She had assumed they would embark on their journey the following day. The village of Clyvedon was located near Hastings, all the way down on England's southeastern coast. It was already late afternoon; by the time they reached the castle, it would be the middle of the night.

This was not the wedding night Daphne had envisioned.

"Wouldn't it make more sense to rest here in London for one night, and then travel on to Clyvedon?" she asked.

"The arrangements have already been made," he grunted.

"I . . . see." Daphne made a valiant attempt to hide her disappointment. She was silent for a full minute as the carriage lurched into motion, the well-sprung wheels unable to disguise the bumps from the uneven cobbles beneath them. As they swung around the corner to Park Lane, she asked, "Will we be stopping at an inn?"

"Of course," Simon replied. "We need to eat supper. It wouldn't do for me to starve you on our first day of our marriage, would it?"

"Will we be spending the night at this inn?" Daphne persisted.

"No, we—" Simon's mouth clamped shut into a firm line, then inexplicably softened. He turned to her with an expression of heartmelting tenderness. "I've been a bear, haven't I?"

She blushed. She always blushed when he looked at her like that. "No, no, it's just that I was surprised that—"

"No, you're right. We will rest the night at an inn. I know of a good one halfway down to the coast. The Hare and Hounds. The food is hot, and the beds are clean." He touched her on the chin. "I shan't abuse you by forcing you to make the entire trip to Clyvedon in one day."

"It's not that I'm not hardy enough for the trip," she said, her face coloring even further as she considered her next words. "It's just that we did get married today, and if we don't stop at an inn, we'll be here in the carriage when night falls, and—"

"Say no more," he said, placing a finger to her lips.

Daphne nodded gratefully. She didn't really wish to discuss their wedding night like this. Besides, it seemed the sort of topic that the husband ought to bring up, not the wife. After all, Simon was certainly the more knowledgeable of the two on that subject.

He couldn't possibly be any *less* knowledgeable, she thought with a disgruntled grimace. Her mother, despite all her hemming and hawing, had managed to tell her absolutely nothing. Well, except for the bit about the creation of children, not that Daphne understood any of the particulars. But on the other hand, maybe—

Daphne's breath caught in her throat. What if Simon couldn't— Or what if he didn't want to—

No, she decided firmly, he definitely wanted to. Moreover, he definitely wanted *her*. She hadn't imagined the fire in his eyes or the fierce pounding of his heart that night in the gardens.

She glanced out the window, watching as London melted into the countryside. A woman could go mad obsessing over such things. She was going to put this from her mind. She was absolutely, positively, forever going to put this from her mind.

Well, at least until that night.

Her wedding night.

The thought made her shiver.

Simon glanced over at Daphne—his wife, he reminded himself, although it was still a bit difficult to believe. He'd never planned to have a wife. In fact, he'd planned quite specifically *not* to have one. And yet here he was, with Daphne Bridgerton—no, Daphne *Basset*. Hell, she was the Duchess of Hastings, that's what she was.

That was probably the strangest of all. His dukedom hadn't had a duchess in his lifetime. The title sounded odd, rusty.

Simon let out a long, calming exhale, letting his eyes rest on Daphne's profile. Then he frowned. "Are you cold?" he asked. She'd been shivering.

Her lips were slightly parted, so he saw her tongue press up against the roof of her mouth to make an N sound, then she moved ever so slightly and said, "Yes. Yes, but just a touch. You needn't—"

Simon tucked the blanket a bit more closely around her, wondering why on earth she would lie about such an innocuous fact. "It's been a long day," he murmured, not because he felt it—although, when he did stop to think about it, it *had* been a long day—but because it seemed like the right type of soothing remark for the moment.

He'd been thinking a lot about soothing remarks and gentle consideration. He was going to try to be a good husband to her. She deserved at least that much. There were a lot of things he wasn't going to be able to give Daphne, true and complete happiness unfortunately among them, but he could do his best to keep her safe and protected and relatively content.

She had chosen him, he reminded himself. Even knowing that

she would never have children, she had chosen him. Being a good and faithful husband seemed the least he could do in return.

"I enjoyed it," Daphne said softly.

He blinked and turned to her with a blank expression. "I beg your pardon?"

A shadow of a smile touched her lips. It was a sight to behold, something warm and teasing and just a little bit mischievous. It sent jolts of desire straight to his midsection, and it was all he could do to concentrate on her words as she said, "You said it had been a long day. I said I enjoyed it."

He looked at her blankly.

Her face screwed up with such enchanting frustration that Simon felt a smile tugging at his lips. "*You* said it had been a long day," she said yet again. "*I* said I enjoyed it." When he still didn't speak, she let out a little snort and added, "Perhaps this will all seem more clear if I point out that I implied the words 'yes' and 'but' as in 'Yeeeessss, but I enjoyed it.'"

"I see," he murmured, with all the solemnity he could muster.

"I suspect you see a great deal," she muttered, "and ignore at least half of it."

He quirked a brow, which caused her to grumble to herself, which of course caused him to want to kiss her.

Everything made him want to kiss her.

It was starting to grow quite painful, that.

"We should be at the inn by nightfall," he said crisply, as if a businesslike mien would relieve his tension.

It didn't, of course. All it did was remind him that he'd put off his wedding night by a full day. A full day of wanting, needing, of his body screaming for release. But he was damned if he was going to take her in some roadside inn, no matter how clean and tidy it might be.

Daphne deserved better. This was her one and only wedding night, and he *would* make it perfect for her.

She shot him a slightly startled look at the sudden change of subject. "That will be nice."

"The roads really aren't safe these days after dark," he added, trying not to remind himself that he'd originally planned on pushing straight through to Clyvedon.

"No," she agreed.

"And we'll be hungry."

"Yes," she said, starting to look puzzled at his current obsession with their newly scheduled stop at the inn. Simon couldn't blame her, but it was either discuss the travel plans to death or grab her and take her right there in the carriage.

Which was *not* an option.

So he said, "They have good food."

She blinked, once, before pointing out, "You said that."

"So I did." He coughed. "I believe I'll take a nap."

Her dark eyes widened, and her entire face actually bobbed forward as she asked, "Right now?"

Simon gave a brisk nod. "I do seem to be repeating myself, but I did, as you so thoughtfully reminded me, say it had been a long day."

"Indeed." She watched him curiously as he shifted in his seat, looking for the most comfortable position. Finally, she asked, "Are you truly going to be able to fall asleep here in the moving carriage? Don't you find the ride a bit bumpy?"

He shrugged. "I'm quite good at falling asleep whenever I wish to. Learned how on my travels."

"It's a talent," she murmured.

"Jolly good one," he agreed. Then he closed his eyes and faked sleep for the better part of three hours.

---

Daphne stared at him. Hard. He was faking it. With seven siblings, she knew every trick in the book, and Simon was definitely *not* asleep.

His chest was rising and falling in an admirably even manner, and his breath contained just the right amount of whoosh and wheeze to sound like he was almost but not quite snoring.

But Daphne knew better.

Every time she moved, made a rustling sound, or breathed just a little too loudly, his chin moved. It was barely perceptible, but it was there. And when she yawned, making a low, sleepy, moaning noise, she saw his eyes move under his closed lids.

There was something to admire, however, in the fact that he'd managed to keep up the charade for over two hours.

She'd never lasted past twenty minutes herself.

If he wanted to feign sleep, she decided in a rare fit of magnanimity, she might as well let him. Far be it from her to ruin such a marvelous performance.

With one last yawn—a loud one, just to watch his eyes snap to attention under his eyelids—she turned to the carriage window, drawing the heavy velvet curtain back so she could peer outside. The sun sat orange and fat on the western horizon, about one-third of it already resting below the edge of the earth.

If Simon had been correct in his estimation of their traveling time—and she had the feeling that he was frequently correct about such things; people who liked mathematics usually were—then they should be almost at the halfway point of their journey. Almost to The Hare and Hounds.

Almost to her wedding night.

Good God, she was going to *have* to stop thinking in such melodramatic terms. This was getting ridiculous.

"Simon?"

He didn't move. This irritated her.

"Simon?" A little louder this time.

The corner of his mouth twitched slightly, pulling down into a tiny frown. Daphne was positive he was trying to decide if she'd spoken too loudly for him to continue to feign sleep.

"Simon!" She poked him. Hard, right where his arm joined with his chest. There was no way he could possibly think a person could sleep through that.

His eyelids fluttered open, and he made a funny little breathy sound—the sort people made when they woke up.

He was *good*, Daphne thought with reluctant admiration.

He yawned. "Daff?"

She didn't mince words. "Are we there yet?"

He rubbed nonexistent sleep from his eyes. "I beg your pardon?"

"Are we *there* yet?"

"Uhhh . . ." He glanced around the inside of the carriage, not that that would tell him anything. "Aren't we still moving?"

"Yes, but we could be close."

Simon let out a little sigh and peered out the window. He was facing east, so the sky looked considerably darker than it had through Daphne's window. "Oh," he said, sounding surprised. "Actually, it's just up ahead."

Daphne did her best not to smirk.

The carriage rolled to a halt, and Simon hopped down. He exchanged some words with the driver, presumably informing him that they had changed their plans and now intended to spend the night. Then he reached up for Daphne's hand and helped her down.

"Does this meet with your approval?" he asked, with a nod and a wave toward the inn.

Daphne didn't see how she could render judgment without

seeing the interior, but she said yes, anyway. Simon led her inside, then deposited her by the door when he went to deal with the innkeeper.

Daphne watched the comings and goings with great interest. Right now a young couple—they looked to be landed gentry—were being escorted into a private dining room, and a mother was ushering her brood of four up the stairs. Simon was arguing with the innkeeper, and a tall, lanky gentleman was leaning against a—

Daphne swung her head back toward her husband. Simon was arguing with the innkeeper? Why on earth would he do that? She craned her neck. The two men were speaking in low tones, but it was clear that Simon was most displeased. The innkeeper looked as if he might die of shame at his inability to please the Duke of Hastings.

Daphne frowned. This didn't look right.

Should she intervene?

She watched them argue a few moments longer. Clearly, she should intervene.

Taking steps that weren't hesitant yet could never be called determined, she made her way over to her husband's side. "Is anything amiss?" she inquired politely.

Simon spared her a brief glance. "I thought you were waiting by the door."

"I was." She smiled brightly. "I moved."

Simon scowled and turned back to the innkeeper.

Daphne let out a little cough, just to see if he would turn around. He didn't. She frowned. She didn't like being ignored. "Simon?" She poked him in the back. "Simon?"

He turned slowly around, his face pure thundercloud.

Daphne smiled again, all innocence. "What is the problem?"

The innkeeper held his hands up in supplication and spoke

before Simon could make any explanations. "I have but one room left," he said, his voice a study in abject apology. "I had no idea his grace planned to honor us with his presence this eve. Had I known, I would never have let that last room out to Mrs. Weatherby and her brood. I assure you"—the innkeeper leaned forward and gave Daphne a commiserating look—"I would have sent them right on their way!"

The last sentence was accompanied by a dramatic whooshing wave of both hands that made Daphne a touch seasick. "Is Mrs. Weatherby the woman who just walked by here with four children?"

The innkeeper nodded. "If it weren't for the children, I'd—"

Daphne cut him off, not wanting to hear the remainder of a sentence that would obviously involve booting an innocent woman out into the night. "I see no reason why we cannot make do with one room. We are certainly not as high in the instep as that."

Beside her, Simon's jaw clenched until she would swear she could hear his teeth grinding.

He wanted separate rooms, did he? It was enough to make a new bride feel extremely unappreciated.

The innkeeper turned to Simon and waited for his approval. Simon gave a curt nod, and the innkeeper clapped his hands together in delight (and presumably relief; there was little worse for business than an irate duke on one's premises). He grabbed the key and scurried out from behind his desk. "If you'll follow me . . ."

Simon motioned for Daphne to go first, so she swept past him and climbed the stairs behind the innkeeper. After only a couple of twists and turns, they were deposited in a large, comfortably furnished room with a view of the village.

"Well, now," Daphne said, once the innkeeper had seen himself out, "this seems nice enough."

Simon's reply was a grunt.

"How articulate of you," she murmured, then disappeared behind the dressing screen.

Simon watched her for several seconds before it occurred to him where she'd gone. "Daphne?" he called out, his voice strangling on itself. "Are you changing your clothing?"

She poked her head out. "No. I was just looking around."

His heart continued to thud, although perhaps not at quite as rapid a pace. "Good," he grunted. "We'll be wanting to go down for supper soon."

"Of course." She smiled—a rather annoyingly winning and confident smile, in his opinion. "Are you hungry?" she asked.

"Extremely."

Her smile wobbled just a touch at his curt tone. Simon gave himself a mental scolding. Just because he was irate with himself didn't mean he had to extend the anger toward her. She'd done nothing wrong. "And you?" he asked, keeping his voice gentle.

She emerged fully from behind the screen and perched at the end of the bed. "A bit," she admitted. She swallowed nervously. "But I'm not certain I could eat anything."

"The food was excellent the last time I ate here. I assure you—"

"It's not the quality of the food that worries me," she interrupted. "It's my nerves."

He stared at her blankly.

"Simon," she said, obviously trying to hide the impatience in her voice (but not, in Simon's opinion, succeeding), "we were married this morning."

Realization finally dawned. "Daphne," he said gently, "you needn't worry."

She blinked. "I needn't?"

He drew a ragged breath. Being a gentle, caring husband was

not as easy as it sounded. "We will wait until we reach Clyvedon to consummate the marriage."

"We will?"

Simon felt his eyes widen in surprise. Surely she didn't sound disappointed? "I'm not going to take you in some roadside inn," he said. "I have more respect for you than that."

"You're not? You do?"

His breath stopped. She *did* sound disappointed.

"Uh, no."

She inched forward. "Why not?"

Simon stared at her face for several moments, just sat there on the bed and stared at her. Her dark eyes were huge as they returned his regard, filled with tenderness and curiosity and a touch of hesitation. She licked her lips—surely just another sign of nerves, but Simon's frustrated body reacted to the seductive movement with an instant quickening.

She smiled tremulously but didn't quite meet his eye. "I wouldn't mind."

Simon remained frozen, curiously rooted to the spot as his body screamed, *Tackle her! Haul her onto the bed! Do anything, just get her under you!*

And then, just when his urges began to outweigh his honor, she let out a small, tortured cry and jumped to her feet, turning her back on him as she covered her mouth with her hand.

Simon, who had just swiped one arm through the air to yank her to him, found himself off-balance and facedown on the bed. "Daphne?" he mumbled into the mattress.

"I should have known," she whimpered. "I'm so sorry."

She was sorry? Simon pushed himself back up. She was whimpering? What the hell was going on? Daphne never whimpered.

She turned back around, regarding him with stricken eyes.

Simon would have been more concerned, except that he couldn't even begin to imagine what had so suddenly upset her. And if he couldn't imagine it, he tended to believe it wasn't serious.

Arrogant of him, but there you had it.

"Daphne," he said with controlled gentleness, "what is wrong?"

She sat down opposite him and placed a hand on his cheek. "I'm so insensitive," she whispered. "I should have known. I should never have said anything."

"Should have known what?" he ground out.

Her hand fell away. "That you can't—that you couldn't—"

"Can't *what*?"

She looked down at her lap, where her hands were attempting to wring each other to shreds. "Please don't make me say it," she said.

"This," Simon muttered, "has got to be why men avoid marriage."

His words were meant more for his ears than hers, but she heard them and, unfortunately, reacted to them with another pathetic moan.

"What the hell is going on?" he finally demanded.

"You're unable to consummate the marriage," she whispered.

It was a wonder his erection didn't die off in that instant. Frankly, it was a wonder he was even able to strangle out the words: "I beg your pardon?"

She hung her head. "I'll still be a good wife to you. I'll never tell a soul, I promise."

Not since childhood, when his stuttering and stammering had attacked his every word, had Simon been so at a loss for speech.

She thought he was *impotent*?

"Why—why—why—?" A stutter? Or plain old shock? Simon thought shock. His brain didn't seem able to focus on anything other than that single word.

"I know that men are very sensitive about such things," Daphne said quietly.

"Especially when it's not true!" Simon burst out.

Her head jerked up. "It's not?"

His eyes narrowed to slits. "Did your brother tell you this?"

"No!" She slid her gaze away from his face. "My mother."

"Your mother?" Simon choked out. Surely no man had ever suffered so on his wedding night. "Your mother told you I'm *impotent*?"

"Is that the word for it?" Daphne asked curiously. And then, at his thunderous glare, she hastily added, "No, no, she didn't say it in so many words."

"What," Simon asked, his voice clipped, "did she say, exactly?"

"Well, not much," Daphne admitted. "It was rather annoying, actually, but she did explain to me that the marital act—"

"She called it an act?"

"Isn't that what everyone calls it?"

He waved off her question. "What else did she say?"

"She told me that the, ah, whatever it is *you* wish to call it—"

Simon found her sarcasm oddly admirable under the circumstances.

"—is related in some manner to the procreation of children, and—"

Simon thought he might choke on his tongue. "In some manner?"

"Well, yes." Daphne frowned. "She really didn't provide me with any specifics."

"Clearly."

"She did try her best," Daphne pointed out, thinking she ought at least to try to come to her mother's defense. "It was very embarrassing for her."

"After eight children," he muttered, "you'd think she'd be over that by now."

"I don't think so," Daphne said, shaking her head. "And then when I asked her if she'd participated in this"—she looked up at him with an exasperated expression. "I really don't know what else to call it but an act."

"Go right ahead," he said with a wave, his voice sounding awfully strained.

Daphne blinked with concern. "Are you all right?"

"Just fine," he choked.

"You don't sound fine."

He waved his hand some more, giving Daphne the odd impression that he couldn't speak.

"Well," she said slowly, going back to her earlier story, "I asked her if that meant she'd participated in this act eight times, and she became very embarrassed, and—"

"You asked her that?" Simon burst out, the words escaping his mouth like an explosion.

"Well, yes." Her eyes narrowed. "Are you laughing?"

"No," he gasped.

Her lips twisted into a small scowl. "You certainly look as if you're laughing."

Simon just shook his head in a decidedly frantic manner.

"Well," Daphne said, clearly disgruntled. "I thought my question made perfect sense, seeing as she has eight children. But then she told me that—"

He shook his head and held up a hand, and now he looked like he didn't know whether to laugh or cry. "Don't tell me. I beg of you."

"Oh." Daphne didn't know what to say to that, so she just clamped her hands together in her lap and shut her mouth.

Finally, she heard Simon take a long, ragged breath, and say, "I know I'm going to regret asking you this. In fact, I regret it already, but *why* exactly did you assume I was"—he shuddered—"unable to perform?"

"Well, you said you couldn't have children."

"Daphne, there are many, many other reasons why a couple might be unable to have children."

Daphne had to force herself to stop grinding her teeth. "I really *hate* how stupid I feel right now," she muttered.

He leaned forward and pried her hands apart. "Daphne," he said softly, massaging her fingers with his, "do you have any idea what happens between a man and a woman?"

"I haven't a clue," she said frankly. "You'd think I would, with three older brothers, and I thought I'd finally learn the truth last night when my mother—"

"Don't say anything more," he said in the oddest voice. "Not another word. I couldn't bear it."

"But—"

His head fell into his hands, and for a moment Daphne thought he might be crying. But then, as she sat there castigating herself for making her husband weep on his wedding day, she realized that his shoulders were shaking with laughter.

The fiend.

"Are you laughing at me?" she growled.

He shook his head, not looking up.

"Then what are you laughing about?"

"Oh, Daphne," he gasped, "you have a lot to learn."

"Well, I never disputed *that*," she grumbled. Really, if people weren't so intent on keeping young women completely ignorant of the realities of marriage, scenes like this could be avoided.

He leaned forward, his elbows resting on his knees. His eyes grew positively electric. "I can teach you," he whispered.

Daphne's stomach did a little flip.

Never once taking his eyes off of hers, Simon took her hand and raised it to his lips. "I assure you," he murmured, flicking his tongue down the line of her middle finger, "I am perfectly able to satisfy you in bed."

Daphne suddenly found it difficult to breathe. And when had the room grown so hot? "I-I'm not sure I know what you mean."

He yanked her into his arms. "You will."

# Chapter 15

*London seems terribly quiet this week, now that society's favorite duke and that duke's favorite duchess have departed for the country. This Author could report that Mr. Nigel Berbrooke was seen asking Miss Penelope Featherington to dance, or that Miss Penelope, despite her mother's gleeful urging and her eventual acceptance of his offer, did not seem terribly enamored with the notion.*

*But really, who wants to read about Mr. Berbrooke or Miss Penelope? Let us not fool ourselves. We are all still ravenously curious about the duke and duchess.*

*LADY WHISTLEDOWN'S SOCIETY PAPERS,*
28 May 1813

It was like being in Lady Trowbridge's garden all over again, Daphne thought wildly, except that this time there would be no interruptions—no furious older brothers, no fear of discovery, nothing but a husband, a wife, and the promise of passion.

Simon's lips found hers, gentle but demanding. With each touch, each flick of his tongue, she felt flutterings within her, tiny spasms of need that were building in pitch and frequency.

"Have I told you," he whispered, "how enamored I am of the corner of your mouth?"

"N-no," Daphne said tremulously, amazed that he'd ever even once examined it.

"I adore it," he murmured, and then went to show her how. His teeth scraped along her lower lip until his tongue darted out and traced the curve of the corner of her mouth.

It tickled, and Daphne felt her lips spreading into a wide, open-mouthed smile. "Stop," she giggled.

"Never," he vowed. He pulled back, cradling her face in his hands. "You have the most beautiful smile I've ever seen."

Daphne's initial reaction was to say, "Don't be silly," but then she thought—*Why ruin such a moment*?—and so she just said, "Really?"

"Really." He dropped a kiss on her nose. "When you smile it takes up half your face."

"Simon!" she exclaimed. "That sounds horrible."

"It's enchanting."

"Distorted."

"Desirable."

She grimaced, but somehow she laughed at the same time. "Clearly, you have no knowledge of the standards of female beauty."

He arched a brow. "As pertains to you, my standards are the only ones that count any longer."

For a moment she was speechless, then she collapsed against him, a torrent of laughter shaking both of their bodies. "Oh, Simon," she gasped, "you sounded so fierce. So wonderfully, perfectly, absurdly fierce."

"Absurd?" he echoed. "Are you calling me absurd?"

Her lips tightened to prevent another giggle, but they weren't entirely successful.

"It's almost as bad as being called impotent," he grumbled.

Daphne was instantly serious. "Oh, Simon. You know I didn't . . ."

She gave up trying to explain, and instead just said, "I'm so sorry about that."

"Don't be." He waved off her apology. "Your mother I may have to kill, but you have nothing to apologize for."

A horrified giggle escaped her lips. "Mother did try her best, and if I hadn't been confused because you said—"

"Oh, so now it's all my fault?" he said with mock outrage. But then his expression grew sly, seductive. He moved closer, angling his body so that she had to arch backwards. "I suppose I'll just have to work doubly hard to prove my capabilities."

One of his hands slid to the small of her back, supporting her as he lowered her onto the bed. Daphne felt the breath leave her body as she looked up into his intensely blue eyes. The world seemed somehow different when one was lying down. Darker, more dangerous. And all the more thrilling because Simon was looming above her, filling her vision.

And in that moment, as he slowly closed the distance between them, he became her entire world.

This time his kiss wasn't light. He didn't tickle; he devoured. He didn't tease; he possessed.

His hands slipped under her, cradling her derrière, pressing it up against his arousal. "Tonight," he whispered, his voice hoarse and hot in her ear, "I will make you mine."

Daphne's breath started coming faster and faster, each little gasp of air impossibly loud to her ears. Simon was so close, every inch of him covering her intimately. She'd imagined this night a thousand times since that moment in Regent's Park when he'd said he would marry her, but it had never occurred to her that the sheer weight of his body on hers would be so thrilling. He was large and hard and exquisitely muscled; there was no way she could escape his seductive onslaught, even if she'd wanted to.

How strange it was to feel such titillating joy at being so powerless. He could do with her whatever he desired—and she wanted to let him.

But when his body shuddered, and his lips tried to say her name but didn't get beyond "D-D-Daph—" she realized that she possessed her own kind of control. He wanted her so much he couldn't breathe, needed her so badly he couldn't speak.

And somehow, as she reveled in her newfound strength, she found that her body seemed to know what to do. Her hips arched up to meet his, and as his hands pushed her skirts up over her waist, her legs snaked around his, pulling him ever closer to the cradle of her femininity.

"My God, Daphne," Simon gasped, hauling his shaking body up on his elbows. "I want to—I can't—"

Daphne grabbed at his back, trying to pull him back down to her. The air felt cool where his body had just been.

"I can't go slow," he grunted.

"I don't care."

"I do." His eyes burned with wicked intention. "We seem to be getting ahead of ourselves."

Daphne just stared at him, trying to catch her breath. He'd sat up, and his eyes were raking across her body as one of his hands slid up the length of her leg to her knee.

"First of all," he murmured, "we need to do something about all of your clothes."

Daphne gasped with shock as he stood, pulling her to her feet along with him. Her legs were weak, her balance nonexistent, but he held her upright, his hands bunching her skirts around her waist. He whispered in her ear, "It's difficult to strip you naked when you're lying down."

One of his hands found the curve of her buttocks, and started massaging her in a circular motion. "The question," he mused, "is do I push the dress up, or pull it down?"

Daphne prayed that he wasn't expecting her to actually answer his question, because she couldn't make a sound.

"Or," he said slowly, one finger slipping under the ribboned bodice of her dress, "both?"

And then, before she had even a moment to react, he'd pushed her dress down so that the entire garment encircled her waist. Her legs were bare, and were it not for her thin silk chemise, she would have been completely naked.

"Now this is a surprise," Simon murmured, palming one of her breasts through the silk. "Not an entirely unwelcome one, of course. Silk is never as soft as skin, but it does have its advantages."

Daphne's breath fled as she watched him slide the silk slowly from side to side, the sweet friction causing her nipples to pucker and harden.

"I had no idea," Daphne whispered, her every breath sliding hot and moist across her lips.

Simon went to work on her other breast. "No idea of what?"

"That you were so wicked."

He smiled, slow and full of the devil. His lips moved to her ear, whispering, "You were my best friend's sister. Utterly forbidden. What was I to do?"

Daphne shivered with desire. His breath touched only her ear, but her skin prickled across her entire body.

"I could do nothing," he continued, edging one strap of her chemise off her shoulder, "except imagine."

"You thought about me?" Daphne whispered, her body thrilling at the notion. "You thought about this?"

His hand at her hip grew tight. "Every night. Every moment before I fell asleep, until my skin burned and my body begged for release."

Daphne felt her legs wobble, but he held her up.

"And then when I was asleep . . ." He moved to her neck, his hot breath as much of a kiss as the touch of his lips. "That's when I was truly naughty."

A moan escaped her lips, strangled and incoherent and full of desire.

The second chemise strap fell off her shoulder just as Simon's lips found the tantalizing hollow between her breasts. "But tonight—" he whispered, pushing the silk down until one breast was bared, and then the other. "Tonight all of my dreams come true."

Daphne had time only to gasp before his mouth found her breast and fastened on her hardened nipple.

"This is what I wanted to do in Lady Trowbridge's garden," he said. "Did you know that?"

She shook her head wildly, grabbing on to his shoulders for support. She was swaying from side to side, barely able to hold her head straight. Spasms of pure feeling were shooting through her body, robbing her of breath, of balance, even of thought.

"Of course you didn't," he murmured. "You're such an innocent."

With deft and knowing fingers, Simon slid the rest of her clothes from her body, until she was nude in his arms. Gently, because he knew she had to be almost as nervous as she was excited, he lowered her onto the bed.

His motions were uncontrolled and jerky as he yanked at his own clothing. His skin was on fire, his entire body burning with need. Never once, however, did he take his eyes off of her. She lay sprawled on the bed, a temptation like none he'd ever seen. Her skin glowed peachy smooth in the flickering candlelight, and her hair, long since released from its coiffure, fell around her face in wild abandon.

His fingers, which had removed her clothing with such finesse and speed, now felt awkward and clumsy as he tried to make sense of his own buttons and knots.

As his hands moved to his trousers, he saw that she was pulling the bedsheets over her. "Don't," he said, barely recognizing his own voice.

Her eyes met his, and he said, "I'll be your blanket."

He peeled the rest of his clothing off, and before she could utter a word, he moved to the bed, covering her body with his. He felt her gasp with surprise at the feel of him, and then her body stiffened slightly.

"Shhh," he crooned, nuzzling her neck while one of his hands made soothing circles on the side of her thigh. "Trust me."

"I do trust you," she said in a shaky voice. "It's just that—"

His hand moved up to her hip. "Just that what?"

He could hear the grimace in her voice as she said, "Just that I wish I weren't so utterly ignorant."

A low rumble of a laugh shook his chest.

"Stop that," she griped, swatting him on the shoulder.

"I'm not laughing at you," Simon insisted.

"You're certainly laughing," she muttered, "and don't tell me you're laughing *with* me, because that excuse *never* works."

"I was laughing," he said softly, lifting himself up on his elbows so that he could look into her face, "because I was thinking how very glad *I* am of your ignorance." He lowered his face down until his lips brushed hers in a feather-light caress. "I am honored to be the only man to touch you thus."

Her eyes shone with such purity of feeling that Simon was nearly undone. "Truly?" she whispered.

"Truly," he said, surprised by how gruff his voice sounded. "Although honor is most likely only the half of it."

She said nothing, but her eyes were enchantingly curious.

"I might have to kill the next man who so much as looks at you sideways," he grumbled.

To his great surprise, she burst out laughing. "Oh, Simon," she gasped, "it is so perfectly splendidly *wonderful* to be the object of such irrational jealousy. Thank you."

"You'll thank me later," he vowed.

"And perhaps," she murmured, her dark eyes suddenly far more seductive than they had any right to be, "you'll thank me as well."

Simon felt her thighs slide apart as he settled his body against hers, his manhood hot against her belly. "I already do," he said, his words melting into her skin as he kissed the hollow of her shoulder. "Believe me, I already do."

Never had he been so thankful for the hard-won control he had learned to exert over himself. His entire body ached to plunge into her and finally make her his in truth, but he knew that this night—their wedding night—was for Daphne, not for him.

This was her first time. He was her first lover—her *only* lover, he thought with uncharacteristic savagery—and it was his responsibility to make certain that this night brought her nothing but exquisite pleasure.

He knew she wanted him. Her breath was erratic, her eyes glazed with need. He could hardly bear to look at her face, for every time he saw her lips, half-open and panting with desire, the urge to slam into her nearly overwhelmed him.

So instead he kissed her. He kissed her everywhere, and ignored the fierce pounding of his blood every time he heard her gasp or mewl with desire. And then finally, when she was writhing and moaning beneath him, and he knew she was mad for him, he slipped his hand between her legs and touched her.

The only sound he could make was her name, and even that came out as a half-groan. She was more than ready for him, hotter and wetter than he'd ever dreamed. But still, just to be sure—or maybe it was because he couldn't resist the perverse impulse to torture himself—he slid one long finger inside her, testing her warmth, tickling her sheath.

"Simon!" she gasped, bucking beneath him. Already her muscles were tightening, and he knew that she was nearly to completion. Abruptly, he removed his hand, ignoring her whimper of protest.

He used his thighs to nudge hers further apart, and with a shuddering groan, positioned himself to enter her. "This m-may hurt a little," he whispered hoarsely, "but I p-promise you—"

"Just *do* it," she groaned, her head tossing wildly from side to side.

And so he did. With one powerful thrust, he entered her fully. He felt her maidenhead give way, but she didn't seem to flinch from pain. "Are you all right?" he groaned, his every muscle tensing just to keep himself from moving within her.

She nodded, her breath coming in shallow gasps. "It feels very odd," she admitted.

"But not bad?" he asked, almost ashamed by the desperate note in his voice.

She shook her head, a tiny, feminine smile touching her lips. "Not bad at all," she whispered. "But before . . . when you . . . with your fingers . . ."

Even in the dull candlelight he could see that her cheeks burned with embarrassment. "Is this what you want?" he whispered, pulling out until he was only halfway within her.

"No!" she cried out.

"Then perhaps *this* is what you want." He plunged back in.

She gasped. "Yes. No. Both."

He began to move within her, his rhythm deliberately slow and even. With each thrust, he pushed a gasp from her lips, each little moan the perfect pitch to drive him wild.

And then her moans grew into squeals and her gasps into pants, and he knew that she was near her peak. He moved ever faster, his teeth gritted as he fought to maintain his control as she spiralled toward completion.

She moaned his name, and then she screamed it, and then her entire body went rigid beneath him. She clutched at his shoulders, her hips rising off the bed with a strength he could barely believe. Finally, with one last, powerful shudder, she collapsed beneath him, oblivious to everything but the power of her own release.

Against his better judgment, Simon allowed himself one last thrust, burying himself to the hilt, savoring the sweet warmth of her body.

Then, taking her mouth in a searingly passionate kiss, he pulled out and spent himself on the sheets next to her.

It was to be only the first of many nights of passion. The newlyweds traveled down to Clyvedon, and then, much to Daphne's extreme embarrassment, sequestered themselves in the master suite for more than a week.

(Of course Daphne was not so embarrassed that she made anything more than a halfhearted attempt to actually *leave* the suite.)

Once they emerged from their honeymoonish seclusion, Daphne was given a tour of Clyvedon—which was much needed, since all she'd seen upon arrival was the route from the front door to the duke's bedroom. She then spent several hours introducing herself to the upper servants. She had, of course, been formally introduced to the staff upon her arrival, but Daphne thought it best to meet the more important members of the staff in a more individual manner.

Since Simon had not resided at Clyvedon for so many years, many of the newer servants did not know him, but those who had been at Clyvedon during his childhood seemed—to Daphne—to be almost ferociously devoted to her husband. She laughed about it to Simon as they privately toured the garden, and had been startled to find herself on the receiving end of a decidedly shuttered stare.

"I lived here until I went to Eton," was all he said, as if that ought to be explanation enough.

Daphne was made instantly uncomfortable by the flatness in his voice. "Did you never travel to London? When we were small, we often—"

"I lived here exclusively."

His tone signaled that he desired—no, *required*—an end to the conversation, but Daphne threw caution to the winds, and decided to pursue the topic, anyway. "You must have been a darling child," she said in a deliberately blithe voice, "or perhaps an extremely mischievous one, to have inspired such long-standing devotion."

He said nothing.

Daphne plodded on. "My brother—Colin, you know—is much the same way. He was the very devil when he was small, but so insufferably charming that all servants adored him. Why, one time—"

Her mouth froze, half-open. There didn't seem much point in continuing. Simon had turned on his heel and walked away.

He wasn't interested in roses. And he'd never pondered the existence of violets one way or another, but now Simon found himself leaning on a wooden fence, gazing out over Clyvedon's famed flower garden as if he were seriously considering a career in horticulture.

All because he couldn't face Daphne's questions about his childhood.

But the truth was, he hated the memories. He despised the reminders. Even staying here at Clyvedon was uncomfortable. The only reason he'd brought Daphne down to his childhood home was because it was the only one of his residences within a two-day drive from London that was ready for immediate occupancy.

The memories brought back the feelings. And Simon didn't want to feel like that young boy again. He didn't want to remember the number of times he'd sent letters to his father, only to wait in vain for a response. He didn't want to remember the kind smiles of the servants—kind smiles that were always accompanied by pitying eyes. They'd loved him, yes, but they'd also felt sorry for him.

And the fact that they'd hated his father on his behalf—well, somehow that had never made him feel better. He hadn't been—and, to be honest, still wasn't—so noble-minded that he didn't take a certain satisfaction in his father's lack of popularity, but that never took away the embarrassment or the discomfort.

Or the shame.

He'd wanted to be admired, not pitied. And it hadn't been until he'd struck out on his own by traveling unheralded to Eton that he'd had his first taste of success.

He'd come so far; he'd travel to hell before he went back to the way he'd been.

None of this, of course, was *Daphne's* fault. He knew she had no ulterior motives when she asked about his childhood. How could she? She knew nothing of his occasional difficulties with speech. He'd worked damned hard to hide it from her.

No, he thought with a weary sigh, he'd rarely had to work hard at all to hide it from Daphne. She'd always set him at ease, made him feel free. His stammer rarely surfaced these days, but when it did it was always during times of stress and anger.

And whatever life was about when he was with Daphne, it wasn't stress and anger.

He leaned more heavily against the fence, guilt forcing his posture into a slouch. He'd treated her abominably. It seemed he was fated to do that time and again.

"Simon?"

He'd felt her presence before she'd spoken. She'd approached from behind, her booted feet soft and silent on the grass. But he knew she was there. He could smell her gentle fragrance and hear the wind whispering through her hair.

"These are beautiful roses," she said. It was, he knew, her way of soothing his peevish mood. He knew she was dying to ask more. But she was wise beyond her years, and much as he liked to tease her about it, she did know a lot about men and their idiot tempers. She wouldn't say anything more. At least not today.

"I'm told my mother planted them," he replied. His words came out more gruffly than he would have liked, but he hoped she saw them as the olive branch he'd meant them to be. When she didn't say anything, he added by way of an explanation, "She died at my birth."

Daphne nodded. "I'd heard. I'm sorry."

Simon shrugged. "I didn't know her."

"That doesn't mean it wasn't a loss."

Simon considered his childhood. He had no way of knowing if his mother would have been more sympathetic to his difficulties than his father had been, but he figured there was no way she could have made it worse. "Yes," he murmured, "I suppose it was."

---

Later that day, while Simon was going over some estate accounts, Daphne decided it was as good a time as any to get to know Mrs. Colson, the housekeeper. Although she and Simon had not yet discussed where they would reside, Daphne couldn't imagine that they wouldn't spend some time there at Clyvedon, Simon's ancestral home, and if there was one thing she'd learned from her mother, it was that a lady simply *had* to have a good working relationship with her housekeeper.

Not that Daphne was terribly worried about getting along with Mrs. Colson. She had met the housekeeper briefly when Simon had introduced her to the staff, and it had been quickly apparent that she was a friendly, talkative sort.

She stopped by Mrs. Colson's office—a tiny little room just off the kitchen—a bit before teatime. The housekeeper, a handsome woman in her fifties, was bent over her small desk, working on the week's menus.

Daphne gave the open door a knock. "Mrs. Colson?"

The housekeeper looked up and immediately stood. "Your grace," she said, bobbing into a small curtsy. "You should have called for me."

Daphne smiled awkwardly, still unused to her elevation from the ranks of mere misses. "I was already up and about," she said, explaining her unorthodox appearance in the servants' domain. "But if you have a moment, Mrs. Colson, I was hoping we might get to know one another better, since you have lived here for many years, and I hope to do so for many to come."

Mrs. Colson smiled at Daphne's warm tone. "Of course, your grace. Was there anything in particular about which you cared to inquire?"

"Not at all. But I still have much to learn about Clyvedon if I am to manage it properly. Perhaps we could take tea in the yellow room? I do so enjoy the décor. It's so warm and sunny. I had been hoping to make that my personal parlor."

Mrs. Colson gave her an odd look. "The last duchess felt the same way."

"Oh," Daphne replied, not certain whether that ought to make her feel uncomfortable.

"I've given special care to that room over the years," Mrs. Colson continued. "It does get quite a bit of sun, being on the south side. I had all of the furniture reupholstered three years ago." Her chin rose in a slightly proud manner. "Went all the way to London to get the same fabric."

"I see," Daphne replied, leading the way out of the office. "The late duke must have loved his wife very much, to order such a painstaking conservation of her favorite room."

Mrs. Colson didn't quite meet her eyes. "It was my decision," she said quietly. "The duke always gave me a certain budget for the upkeep of the house. I thought it the most fitting use of the money."

Daphne waited while the housekeeper summoned a maid and gave her instructions for the tea. "It's a lovely room," she announced once they had exited the kitchen, "and although the current duke never had the opportunity to know his mother, I'm sure he'll be quite touched that you have seen fit to preserve her favorite room."

"It was the least I could do," Mrs. Colson said as they strolled across the hall. "I have not always served the Basset family, after all."

"Oh?" Daphne asked curiously. Upper servants were notoriously loyal, often serving a single family for generations.

"Yes, I was the duchess's personal maid." Mrs. Colson waited outside the doorway of the yellow room to allow Daphne to precede her. "And before that her companion. My mother was her nurse.

Her grace's family was kind enough to allow me to share her lessons."

"You must have been quite close," Daphne murmured.

Mrs. Colson nodded. "After she died I occupied a number of different positions here at Clyvedon until I finally became housekeeper."

"I see." Daphne smiled at her and then took a seat on the sofa. "Please sit," she said, motioning to the chair across from her.

Mrs. Colson seemed hesitant with such familiarity, but eventually sat. "It broke my heart when she died," she said. She gave Daphne a slightly apprehensive look. "I hope you don't mind my telling you so."

"Of course not," Daphne said quickly. She was ravenously curious about Simon's childhood. He said so little, and yet she sensed that it all meant so much. "Please, tell me more. I would love to hear about her."

Mrs. Colson's eyes grew misty. "She was the kindest, gentlest soul this earth has ever known. She and the duke—well, it wasn't a love match, but they got on well enough. They were friends in their own way." She looked up. "They were both very much aware of their duties as duke and duchess. Took their responsibilities quite seriously."

Daphne nodded understandingly.

"She was so determined to give him a son. She kept trying even after the doctors all told her she mustn't. She used to cry in my arms every month when her courses came."

Daphne nodded again, hoping the motion would hide her suddenly strained expression. It was difficult to listen to stories about not being able to have children. But she supposed she was going to have to get used to it. It was going to be even more strenuous to answer questions about it.

And there *would* be questions. Painfully tactful and hideously pitying questions.

But Mrs. Colson thankfully didn't notice Daphne's distress. She sniffled as she continued her story. "She was always saying things like how was she to be a proper duchess if she couldn't give him a son. It broke my heart. Every month it broke my heart."

Daphne wondered if her own heart would shatter every month. Probably not. She, at least, knew for a fact that she wouldn't have children. Simon's mother had her hopes crushed every four weeks.

"And of course," the housekeeper continued, "everyone talked as if it were *her* fault there was no baby. How could they know that, I ask you? It's not always the woman who is barren. Sometimes it's the man's fault, you know."

Daphne said nothing.

"I told her this time and again, but still she felt guilty. I said to her—" The housekeeper's face turned pink. "Do you mind if I speak frankly?"

"Please do."

She nodded. "Well, I said to her what my mother said to me. A womb won't quicken without strong, healthy seed."

Daphne held her face in an expressionless mask. It was all she could manage.

"But then she finally had Master Simon." Mrs. Colson let out a maternal sigh, then looked to Daphne with an apprehensive expression. "I beg your pardon," she said hastily. "I shouldn't be calling him that. He's the duke now."

"Don't stop on my account," Daphne said, happy to have something to smile about.

"It's hard to change one's ways at my age," Mrs. Colson said with a sigh. "And I'm afraid a part of me will always remember him as that poor little boy." She looked up at Daphne and shook her head. "He would have had a much easier time of it if the duchess had lived."

"An easier time of it?" Daphne murmured, hoping that would be all the encouragement Mrs. Colson would need to explain further.

"The duke just never understood that poor boy," the housekeeper said forcefully. "He stormed about and called him stupid, and—"

Daphne's head snapped up. "The duke thought Simon was stupid?" she interrupted. That was preposterous. Simon was one of the smartest people she knew. She'd once asked him a bit about his studies at Oxford and had been stunned to learn that his brand of mathematics didn't even use *numbers*.

"The duke never could see the world beyond his own nose," Mrs. Colson said with a snort. "He never gave that boy a chance."

Daphne felt her body leaning forward, her ears straining for the housekeeper's words. What had the duke done to Simon? And was this the reason he turned to ice every time his father's name was mentioned?

Mrs. Colson pulled out a handkerchief and dabbed at her eyes. "You should have seen the way that boy worked to improve himself. It broke my heart. It simply broke my heart."

Daphne's hands clawed at the sofa. Mrs. Colson was *never* going to get to the point.

"But nothing he ever did was good enough for the duke. This is just my opinion of course, but—"

Just then a maid entered with tea. Daphne nearly screamed with frustration. It took a good two minutes for the tea to be set up and poured, and all the while Mrs. Colson chitchatted about the biscuits, and did Daphne prefer them plain or with coarse sugar on top.

Daphne had to pry her hands off the sofa, lest she puncture holes in the upholstery Mrs. Colson had worked so hard to preserve. Finally, the maid left, and Mrs. Colson took a sip of her tea, and said, "Now then, where were we?"

"You were talking about the duke," Daphne said quickly. "The late duke. That nothing my husband did was ever good enough for him and in your opinion—"

"My goodness, you *were* listening." Mrs. Colson beamed. "I'm so flattered."

"But you were saying . . ." Daphne prompted.

"Oh yes, of course. I was simply going to say that I have long held the opinion that the late duke never forgave his son for not being perfect."

"But Mrs. Colson," Daphne said quietly, "none of us is perfect."

"Of course not, but—" The housekeeper's eyes floated up for a brief second in an expression of disdain toward the late duke. "If you'd known his grace, you would understand. He'd waited so long for a son. And in his mind, the Basset name was synonymous with perfection."

"And my husband wasn't the son he wanted?" Daphne asked.

"He didn't want a son. He wanted a perfect little replica of himself."

Daphne could no longer contain her curiosity. "But what did Simon do that was so repugnant to the duke?"

Mrs. Colson's eyes widened in surprise, and one of her hands floated to her chest. "Why, you don't know," she said softly. "Of course you wouldn't know."

"*What?*"

"He couldn't speak."

Daphne's lips parted in shock. "I beg your pardon?"

"He couldn't speak. Not a word until he was four, and then it was all stutters and stammers. It broke my heart every time he opened his mouth. I could see that there was a bright little boy inside. He just couldn't get the words out right."

"But he speaks so well now," Daphne said, surprised by the defensiveness in her voice. "I've never heard him stammer. Or if I have, I-I-I didn't notice it. See! Look, I just did it myself. Everyone stammers a bit when they're flustered."

"He worked very hard to improve himself. It was seven years, I recall. For seven years he did nothing but practice his speech with his nurse." Mrs. Colson's face wrinkled with thought. "Let's see, what was her name? Oh yes, Nurse Hopkins. She was a saint, she was. As devoted to that boy as if he'd been her own. I was the housekeeper's assistant at the time, but she often let me come up and help him practice his speech."

"Was it difficult for him?" Daphne whispered.

"Some days I thought he'd surely shatter from the frustration of it. But he was so stubborn. Heavens, but he was a stubborn boy. I've never seen a person so single-minded." Mrs. Colson shook her head sadly. "And his father still rejected him. It—"

"Broke your heart," Daphne finished for her. "It would have broken mine, as well."

Mrs. Colson took a sip of her tea during the long, uncomfortable silence that followed. "Thank you very much for allowing me to take tea with you, your grace," she said, misinterpreting Daphne's quietude for displeasure. "It was highly irregular of you to do so, but very . . ."

Daphne looked up as Mrs. Colson searched for the correct word.

"Kind," the housekeeper finally finished. "It was very kind of you."

"Thank you," Daphne murmured distractedly.

"Oh, but I haven't answered any of your questions about Clyvedon," Mrs. Colson said suddenly.

Daphne gave her head a little shake. "Another time, perhaps," she said softly. She had too much to think on just then.

Mrs. Colson, sensing her employer desired privacy, stood, bobbed a curtsy, and silently left the room.

# Chapter 16

*The stifling heat in London this week has certainly put a crimp in society functions. This Author saw Miss Prudence Featherington swoon at the Huxley ball, but it is impossible to discern whether this temporary lack of verticality was due to the heat or the presence of Mr. Colin Bridgerton, who has been cutting quite a swash through society since his return from the Continent.*

*The unseasonable heat has also made a casualty of Lady Danbury, who quit London several days ago, claiming that her cat (a long-haired, bushy beast) could not tolerate the weather. It is believed that she has retired to her country home in Surrey.*

*One would guess that the Duke and Duchess of Hastings are unaffected by these rising temperatures; they are down on the coast, where the sea wind is always a pleasure. But This Author cannot be certain of their comfort; contrary to popular belief, This Author does not have spies in all the important households, and certainly not outside of London!*

*Lady Whistledown's Society Papers*, 2 June 1813

It was odd, Simon reflected, how they'd not been married even a fortnight and yet had already fallen into comfortable patterns and routines. Just now, he stood barefoot in the doorway of his dressing room, loosening his cravat as he watched his wife brush her hair.

And he'd done the exact same thing yesterday. There was something oddly comforting in that.

And both times, he thought with a hint of a leer, he'd been planning how to seduce her into bed. Yesterday, of course, he'd been successful.

His once expertly tied cravat lying limp and forgotten on the floor, he took a step forward.

Today he'd be successful, too.

He stopped when he reached Daphne's side, perching on the edge of her vanity table. She looked up and blinked owlishly.

He touched his hand to hers, both of their fingers wrapped around the handle of the hairbrush. "I like to watch you brush your hair," he said, "but I like to do it myself better."

She stared at him in an oddly intent fashion. Slowly, she relinquished the brush. "Did you get everything done with your accounts? You were tucked away with your estate manager for quite a long time."

"Yes, it was rather tedious but necessary, and—" His face froze. "What are you looking at?"

Her eyes slid from his face. "Nothing," she said, her voice unnaturally staccato.

He gave his head a tiny shake, the motion directed more at himself than at her, then he began to brush her hair. For a moment it had seemed as if she were staring at his mouth.

He fought the urge to shudder. All through his childhood, people had stared at his mouth. They'd gazed in horrified fascination, occasionally forcing their eyes up to his, but always returning to his mouth, as if unable to believe that such a normal-looking feature could produce such gibberish.

But he had to be imagining things. Why would Daphne be looking at his mouth?

He pulled the brush gently through her hair, allowing his fingers to trail through the silky strands as well. "Did you have a nice chat with Mrs. Colson?" he asked.

She flinched. It was a tiny movement, and she hid it quite well, but he noticed it nonetheless. "Yes," she said, "she's very knowledgeable."

"She should be. She's been here forev—*what* are you looking at?"

Daphne practically jumped in her chair. "I'm looking at the mirror," she insisted.

Which was true, but Simon was still suspicious. Her eyes had been fixed and intent, focused on a single spot.

"As I was saying," Daphne said hastily, "I'm certain Mrs. Colson will prove invaluable as I adjust to the management of Clyvedon. It's a large estate, and I have much to learn."

"Don't make too much of an effort," he said. "We won't spend much time here."

"We won't?"

"I thought we would make London our primary residence." At her look of surprise, he added, "You'll be closer to your family, even when they retire to the country. I thought you'd like that."

"Yes, of course," she said. "I do miss them. I've never been away from them for so long before. Of course I've always known that when I married I would be starting my own family, and—"

There was an awful silence.

"Well, you're my family now," she said, her voice sounding just a bit forlorn.

Simon sighed, the silver-backed hairbrush halting its path through her dark hair. "Daphne," he said, "your family will always be your family. I can never take their place."

"No," she agreed. She twisted around to face him, her eyes like warm chocolate as she whispered, "But you can be something more."

And Simon realized that all his plans to seduce his wife were moot, because clearly *she* was planning to seduce *him*.

She stood, her silk robe slipping from her shoulders. Underneath she wore a matching negligee, one that revealed almost as much as it hid.

One of Simon's large hands found its way to the side of her breast, his fingers in stark contrast with the sage green fabric of her nightgown. "You like this color, don't you?" he said in a husky voice.

She smiled, and he forgot to breathe.

"It's to match my eyes," she teased. "Remember?"

Simon managed a returning smile, although how he didn't know. He'd never before thought it possible to smile when one was about to expire from lack of oxygen. Sometimes the need to touch her was so great it hurt just to look at her.

He pulled her closer. He *had* to pull her closer. He would have gone insane if he hadn't. "Are you telling me," he murmured against her neck, "that you purchased this just for me?"

"Of course," she replied, her voice catching as his tongue traced her earlobe. "Who else is going to see me in it?"

"No one," he vowed, reaching around to the small of her back and pressing her firmly against his arousal. "No one. Not ever."

She looked slightly bemused by his sudden burst of possessiveness. "Besides," she added, "it's part of my trousseau."

Simon groaned. "I love your trousseau. I adore it. Have I told you that?"

"Not in so many words," she gasped, "but it hasn't been too difficult to figure it out."

"Mostly," he said, nudging her toward the bed as he tore off his shirt, "I like you out of your trousseau."

Whatever Daphne had meant to say—and he was certain she'd meant to say something, because her mouth opened in a most delightful manner—was lost as she toppled onto the bed.

Simon covered her in an instant. He put his hands on either side of her hips, then slid them up, pushing her arms over her head. He paused on the bare skin of her upper arms, giving them a gentle squeeze.

"You're very strong," he said. "Stronger than most women."

The look Daphne gave him was just a bit arch. "I don't want to hear about most women."

Despite himself, Simon chuckled. Then, with movements quick as lightning, his hands flew to her wrists and pinned them above her head. "But not," he drawled, "as strong as I."

She gasped with surprise, a sound he found particularly thrilling, and he quickly circled both her wrists with one of his hands, leaving the other free to roam her body.

And roam he did.

"If you aren't the perfect woman," he groaned, sliding the hem of her nightgown up over her hips, "then the world is—"

"Stop," she said shakily. "You know I'm not perfect."

"I do?" His smile was dark and wicked as he slid his hand under one of her buttocks. "You must be misinformed, because this"—he gave her a squeeze—"is perfect."

"Simon!"

"And as for these—" He reached up and covered one of her breasts with his hand, tickling the nipple through the silk. "Well, I don't need to tell you how I feel about these."

"You're mad."

"Quite possibly," he agreed, "but I have excellent taste. And you"—he leaned down quite suddenly and nipped at her mouth—"taste quite good."

Daphne giggled, quite unable to help herself.

Simon wiggled his brows. "Dare you mock me?"

"Normally I would," she replied, "but not when you've got both my arms pinned over my head."

Simon's free hand went to work on the fastenings of his trousers. "Clearly I married a woman of great sense."

Daphne gazed at him with pride and love as she watched his words trip effortlessly from his lips. To hear him speak now, one could never guess that he'd stammered as a child.

What a remarkable man she'd married. To take such a hindrance and beat it with sheer force of will—he had to be the strongest, most disciplined man she knew.

"I am so glad I married you," she said in a rush of tenderness. "So very proud you're mine."

Simon stilled, obviously surprised by her sudden gravity. His voice grew low and husky. "I'm proud you're mine as well." He yanked at his trousers. "And I'd show you how proud," he grunted, "if I could get these damned things off."

Daphne felt another bubble of laughter welling up in her throat. "Perhaps if you used two hands . . ." she suggested.

He gave her an I'm-not-as-stupid-as-*that* sort of look. "But that would require my letting you go."

She cocked her head coyly. "What if I promised not to move my arms?"

"I wouldn't even begin to believe you."

Her smile turned wickedly suggestive. "What if I promised I *would* move them?"

"Now, *that* sounds interesting." He leapt off the bed with an odd combination of grace and frantic energy and managed to get himself naked in under three seconds. Hopping back on, he stretched out on his side, all along the length of her. "Now then, where were we?"

Daphne giggled again. "Right about here, I believe."

"A-ha," he said with a comically accusing expression. "You haven't been paying attention. We were right"—he slid atop her, his weight pressing her into the mattress—"here."

Her giggles exploded into full-throated laughter.

"Didn't anyone tell you not to laugh at a man when he's trying to seduce you?"

If she'd had any chance of stopping her laughter before, it was gone now. "Oh, Simon," she gasped, "I do love you."

He went utterly still. "What?"

Daphne just smiled and touched his cheek. She understood him so much better now. After facing such rejection as a child, he probably didn't realize he was worthy of love. And he probably wasn't certain how to give it in return. But she could wait. She could wait forever for this man.

"You don't have to say anything," she whispered. "Just know that I love you."

The look in Simon's eyes was somehow both overjoyed and stricken. Daphne wondered if anyone had ever said the words "I love you" to him before. He'd grown up without a family, without the cocoon of love and warmth she'd taken for granted.

His voice, when he found it, was hoarse and nearly broken, "D-Daphne, I—"

"Shhh," she crooned, placing a finger to his lips. "Don't say anything now. Wait until it feels right."

And then she wondered if perhaps she had said the most hurtful words imaginable—for Simon, did speaking *ever* feel right?

"Just kiss me," she whispered hurriedly, eager to move past what she was afraid might be an awkward moment. "Please, kiss me."

And he did.

He kissed her with ferocious intensity, burning with all the passion and desire that flowed between them. His lips and hands left no spot untouched, kissing, squeezing, and caressing until her nightgown lay tossed on the floor and the sheets and blankets were twisted into coils at the foot of the bed.

But unlike every other night, he never did quite render her senseless. She'd been given too much to think about that day—nothing, not even the fiercest cravings of her body, could stop the frantic pace of her thoughts. She was swimming in desire, every nerve expertly brought to a fever pitch of need, and yet still her mind whirred and analyzed.

When his eyes, so blue they glowed even in the candlelight, burned into hers, she wondered if that intensity were due to emotions he didn't know how to express through words. When he gasped her name, she couldn't help but listen for another tiny stammer. And when he sank into her, his head thrown back until the cords of his neck stood out in harsh relief, she wondered why he looked like he was in so much pain.

Pain?

"Simon?" she asked tentatively, worry putting a very slight damper on her desire. "Are you all right?"

He nodded, his teeth gritted together. He fell against her, his hips still moving in their ancient rhythm, and whispered against her ear, "I'll take you there."

It wouldn't be that difficult, Daphne thought, her breath catching as he captured the tip of her breast in his mouth. It was never that difficult. He seemed to know exactly how to touch her, when to move, and when to tease by remaining tauntingly in place. His fingers slipped between their bodies, tickling her hot skin until her hips were moving and grinding with the same force as his.

She felt herself sliding toward that familiar oblivion. And it felt so good . . .

"Please," he pleaded, sliding his other hand underneath her so that he might press her even more tightly against him. "I need you to—Now, Daphne, now!"

And she did. The world exploded around her, her eyes squeezing so tightly shut that she saw spots, and stars, and brilliant streaming bursts of light. She heard music—or maybe that was just her own high-pitched moan as she reached completion, providing a melody over the powerful pounding of her heart.

Simon, with a groan that sounded as if it were ripped from his very soul, yanked himself out of her with barely a second to spare before he spilled himself—as he always did—on the sheets at the edge of the bed.

In a moment he would turn to her and pull her into his arms. It was a ritual she'd come to cherish. He would hold her tightly against him, her back to his front, and nuzzle his face in her hair. And then, after their breathing had settled down to an even sigh, they would sleep.

Except tonight was different. Tonight Daphne felt oddly restless. Her body was blissfully weary and sated, but something felt wrong. Something niggled at the back of her mind, teasing her subconscious.

Simon rolled over and scooted his body next to hers, pushing her toward the clean side of the bed. He always did that, using his body as a barrier so that she would never roll into the mess he made. It was a thoughtful gesture, actually, and—

Daphne's eyes flew open. She almost gasped.

*A womb won't quicken without strong, healthy seed.*

Daphne hadn't given a thought to Mrs. Colson's words when the housekeeper had uttered the saying that afternoon. She'd been too consumed with the tale of Simon's painful childhood, too concerned with how she could bring enough love into his life to banish the bad memories forever.

Daphne sat up abruptly, the blankets falling to her waist. With shaking fingers she lit the candle that sat on her bedside table.

Simon opened a sleepy eye. "What's wrong?"

She said nothing, just stared at the wet spot on the other side of the bed.

His seed.

"Daff?"

He'd told her he couldn't have children. He'd *lied* to her.

"Daphne, what's wrong?" He sat up. His face showed his concern.

Was that, too, a lie?

She pointed. "What is that?" she asked, her voice so low it was barely audible.

"What is what?" His eyes followed the line of her finger and saw only the bed. "What are you talking about?"

"Why can't you have children, Simon?"

His eyes grew shuttered. He said nothing.

"*Why*, Simon?" She practically shouted the words.

"The details aren't important, Daphne."

His tone was soft, placating, with just a hint of condescension. Daphne felt something inside of her snap.

"Get out," she ordered.

His mouth fell open. "This is my bedroom."

"Then I'll get out." She stormed out of the bed, whipping one of the bedsheets around her.

Simon was on her heels in a heartbeat. "Don't you *dare* leave this room," he hissed.

"You lied to me."

"I never—"

"You lied to me," she screamed. "You lied to me, and I will never forgive you for that!"

"Daphne—"

"You took advantage of my stupidity." She let out a disbelieving breath, the kind that came from the back of one's throat, right before it closed up in shock. "You must have been so delighted when you realized how little I knew about marital relations."

"It's called making love, Daphne," he said.

"Not between us, it's not."

Simon nearly flinched at the rancor in her voice. He stood, utterly naked, in the middle of the room, desperately trying to come up with some way to salvage the situation. He still wasn't even certain what she knew, or what she *thought* she knew. "Daphne," he said, very slowly so that he would not let his emotions trip up his words, "perhaps you should tell me exactly what this is about."

"Oh, we're going to play *that* game, are we?" She snorted derisively. "Very well, let me tell you a story. Once upon a time, there was—"

The scathing anger in her voice was like a dagger in his gut. "Daphne," he said, closing his eyes and shaking his head, "don't do it like this."

"Once upon a time," she said, louder this time, "there was a young lady. We'll call her Daphne."

Simon strode to his dressing room and yanked on a robe. There were some things a man didn't want to deal with naked.

"Daphne was very, very stupid."

"Daphne!"

"Oh, very well." She flipped her hand through the air dismissively. "Ignorant, then. She was very, very ignorant."

Simon crossed his arms.

"Daphne knew nothing about what happened between a man and a woman. She didn't know what they did, except that they did it in a bed, and that at some point, the result would be a baby."

"This is enough, Daphne."

The only sign that she heard him was the dark, flashing fury in her eyes. "But you see, she didn't really *know* how that baby was made, and so when her husband told her he couldn't have children—"

"I told you that before we married. I gave you every option to back out. Don't you forget that," he said hotly. "Don't you *dare* forget it."

"You made me feel sorry for you!"

"Oh now, *that's* what a man wants to hear," he sneered.

"For the love of God, Simon," she snapped, "you know I didn't marry you *because* I felt sorry for you."

"Then why?"

"Because I loved you," she replied, but the acid in her voice made the declaration rather brittle. "And because I didn't want to see you die, which you seemed stupidly bent upon doing."

He had no ready comment, so he just snorted and glared at her.

"But don't try to make this about *me*," she continued hotly. "I'm not the one who lied. You said you can't have children, but the truth is you just *won't* have them."

He said nothing, but he knew the answer was in his eyes.

She took a step toward him, advancing with barely controlled fury. "If you truly couldn't have children, it wouldn't matter where your seed landed, would it? You wouldn't be so frantic every night to make certain it ended up anywhere but inside me."

"You don't know anything ab-bout this, Daphne." His words were low and furious, and only slightly damaged.

She crossed her arms. "Then tell me."

"I will never have children," he hissed. "*Never.* Do you understand?"

"No."

He felt rage rising within him, roiling in his stomach, pressing against his skin until he thought he would burst. It wasn't rage against her, it wasn't even against himself. It was, as always, directed at the man whose presence—or lack thereof—had always managed to rule his life.

"My father," Simon said, desperately fighting for control, "was not a loving man."

Daphne's eyes held his. "I know about your father," she said.

That caught him by surprise. "What do you know?"

"I know that he hurt you. That he rejected you." Something flickered in her dark eyes—not quite pity, but close to it. "I know that he thought you were stupid."

Simon's heart slammed in his chest. He wasn't certain how he was able to speak—he wasn't certain how he was able to breathe—but he somehow managed to say, "Then you know about—"

"Your stammer?" she finished for him.

He thanked her silently for that. Ironically, "stutter" and "stammer" were two words he'd never been able to master.

She shrugged. "He was an idiot."

Simon gaped at her, unable to comprehend how she could dismiss decades of rage with one blithe statement. "You don't understand," he said, shaking his head. "You couldn't possibly. Not with a family like yours. The only thing that mattered to him was blood. Blood and the title. And when I didn't turn out to be perfect—Daphne, he told people I was dead!"

The blood drained from her face. "I didn't know it was like that," she whispered.

"It was worse," he bit off. "I sent him letters. Hundreds of letters, begging him to come visit me. He didn't answer one."

"Simon—"

"D-did you know I didn't speak until I was four? No? Well, I didn't. And when he visited, he shook me, and threatened to beat my voice out of me. *That* was my f-father."

Daphne tried not to notice that he was beginning to stumble over his words. She tried to ignore the sick feeling in her stomach, the anger that rose within her at the hideous way Simon had been treated. "But he's gone now," she said in a shaky voice. "He's gone, and you're here."

"He said he couldn't even b-bear to look at me. He'd spent years praying for an heir. Not a *son*," he said, his voice rising dangerously, "an heir. And f-for what? Hastings would go to a half-wit. His precious dukedom would b-be ruled by an idiot!"

"But he was wrong," Daphne whispered.

"I don't care if he was wrong!" Simon roared. "All he cared about was the title. He never gave a single thought to me, about how I must feel, trapped with a m-mouth that didn't w-work!"

Daphne stumbled back a step, unsteady in the presence of such anger. This was the fury of decades-old resentment.

Simon very suddenly stepped forward and pressed his face very close to hers. "But do you know what?" he asked in an awful voice. "I shall have the last laugh. He thought that there could be nothing worse than Hastings going to a half-wit—"

"Simon, you're not—"

"Are you even listening to me?" he thundered.

Daphne, frightened now, scurried back, her hand reaching for the doorknob in case she needed to escape.

"Of course I know I'm not an idiot," he spat out, "and in the end,

I think h-he knew it, too. And I'm sure that brought him g-great comfort. Hastings was safe. N-never mind that I was not suffering as I once had. Hastings—*that's* what mattered."

Daphne felt sick. She knew what was coming next.

Simon suddenly smiled. It was a cruel, hard expression, one she'd never seen on his face before. "But Hastings dies with me," he said. "All those cousins he was so worried about inheriting . . ." He shrugged and let out a brittle laugh. "They all had girls. Isn't that something?"

Simon shrugged. "Maybe that was why my f-father suddenly decided I wasn't such an idiot. He knew I was his only hope."

"He knew he'd been wrong," Daphne said with quiet determination. She suddenly remembered the letters she'd been given by the Duke of Middlethorpe. The ones written to him by his father. She'd left them at Bridgerton House, in London. Which was just as well, since that meant she didn't have to decide what to do with them yet.

"It doesn't matter," Simon said flippantly. "After I die, the title becomes extinct. And I for one couldn't be h-happier."

With that, he stalked out of the room, exiting through his dressing room, since Daphne was blocking the door.

Daphne sank down onto a chair, still wrapped in the soft linen sheet she'd yanked from the bed. What was she going to do?

She felt tremors spread through her body, a strange shaking over which she had no control. And then she realized she was crying. Without a sound, without even a caught breath, she was crying.

Dear God, *what* was she going to do?

# Chapter 17

*To say that men can be bullheaded would be insulting to the bull.*

LADY WHISTLEDOWN'S SOCIETY PAPERS, 2 June 1813

In the end, Daphne did the only thing she knew how to do. The Bridgertons had always been a loud and boisterous family, not a one of them prone to keeping secrets or holding grudges.

So she tried to talk to Simon. To reason with him.

The following morning (she had no idea where he had spent the night; wherever it was, it hadn't been their bed) she found him in his study. It was a dark, overbearingly masculine room, probably decorated by Simon's father. Daphne was frankly surprised that Simon would feel comfortable in such surroundings; he hated reminders of the old duke.

But Simon, clearly, was not uncomfortable. He was sitting behind his desk, his feet insolently propped up on the leather blotter that protected the rich cherry wood of the desktop. In his hand he was holding a smoothly polished stone, turning it over and over in his hands. There was a bottle of whiskey on the desk next to him; she had a feeling it had been there all night.

He hadn't, however, drunk much of it. Daphne was thankful for small favors.

The door was ajar, so she didn't knock. But she wasn't quite so brave as to stride boldly in. "Simon?" she asked, standing back near the door.

He looked up at her and quirked a brow.

"Are you busy?"

He set down the stone. "Obviously not."

She motioned to it. "Is that from your travels?"

"The Caribbean. A memento of my time on the beach."

Daphne noticed that he was speaking with perfect elocution. There was no hint of the stammer that had become apparent the night before. He was calm now. Almost annoyingly so. "Is the beach very different there than it is here?" she asked.

He raised an arrogant brow. "It's warmer."

"Oh. Well, I'd assumed as much."

He looked at her with piercing, unwavering eyes. "Daphne, I know you didn't seek me out to discuss the tropics."

He was right, of course, but this wasn't going to be an easy conversation, and Daphne didn't think she was so much of a coward for wanting to put it off by a few moments.

She took a deep breath. "We need to discuss what happened last night."

"I'm sure you think we do."

She fought the urge to lean forward and smack the bland expression from his face. "I don't *think* we do. I *know* we do."

He was silent for a moment before saying, "I'm sorry if you feel that I have betrayed—"

"It's not that, exactly."

"—but you must remember that I *tried* to avoid marrying you."

"That's certainly a nice way of putting it," she muttered.

He spoke as if delivering a lecture. "You know that I had intended never to marry."

"That's not the point, Simon."

"It's exactly the point." He dropped his feet to the floor, and his chair, which had been balancing on its two back legs, hit the ground with a loud thunk. "Why do you think I avoided marriage with such determination? It was because I didn't want to take a wife and then hurt her by denying her children."

"You were never thinking of your potential wife," she shot back. "You were thinking of yourself."

"Perhaps," he allowed, "but when that potential wife became *you*, Daphne, everything changed."

"Obviously not," she said bitterly.

He shrugged. "You know I hold you in the highest esteem. I never wanted to hurt you."

"You're hurting me right now," she whispered.

A flicker of remorse crossed his eyes, but it was quickly replaced with steely determination. "If you recall, I refused to offer for you even when your brother demanded it. Even," he added pointedly, "when it meant my own death."

Daphne didn't contradict him. They both knew he would have died on that dueling field. No matter what she thought of him now, how much she despised the hatred that was eating him up, Simon had too much honor ever to have shot at Anthony.

And Anthony placed too much value on his sister's honor to have aimed anywhere but at Simon's heart.

"I did that," Simon said, "because I knew I could never be a good husband to you. I knew you wanted children. You'd told me so on a number of occasions, and I certainly don't blame you. *You* come from a large and loving family."

"You could have a family like that, too."

He continued as if he hadn't heard her. "Then, when you interrupted the duel, and begged me to marry you, I warned you. I told you I wouldn't have children—"

"You told me you *couldn't* have children," she interrupted, her eyes flashing with anger. "There's a very big difference."

"Not," Simon said coldly, "to me. I *can't* have children. My soul won't allow it."

"I see." Something shriveled inside Daphne at that moment, and she was very much afraid it was her heart. She didn't know how she was meant to argue with such a statement. Simon's hatred of his father was clearly far stronger than any love he might learn to feel for her.

"Very well," she said in a clipped voice. "This is obviously not a subject upon which you are open to discussion."

He gave her one curt nod.

She gave him one in return. "Good day, then."

And she left.

Simon kept to himself for most of the day. He didn't particularly want to see Daphne; that did nothing but make him feel guilty. Not, he assured himself, that he had anything to feel guilty about. He had told her before their marriage that he could not have children. He had given her every opportunity to back out, and she had chosen to marry him, anyway. He had not forced her into anything. It was not *his* fault if she had misinterpreted his words and thought that he was *physically* unable to sire brats.

Still, even though he was plagued by this nagging sense of guilt every time he thought of her (which pretty much meant all day), and even though his gut twisted every time he saw her stricken face in his mind (which pretty much meant he spent the day with an upset stomach), he felt as if a great weight had been lifted from his shoulders now that everything was out in the open.

Secrets could be deadly, and now there were no more between them. Surely that had to be a good thing.

By the time night fell, he had almost convinced himself that he had done nothing wrong. Almost, but not quite. He had entered this marriage convinced that he would break Daphne's heart, and that had never sat well with him. He liked Daphne. Hell, he probably liked her better than any human being he'd ever known, and that was why he'd been so reluctant to marry her. He hadn't wanted to shatter her dreams. He hadn't wanted to deprive her of the family she so desperately wanted. He'd been quite prepared to step aside and watch her marry someone else, someone who would give her a whole houseful of children.

Simon suddenly shuddered. The image of Daphne with another man was not nearly as tolerable as it had been just a month earlier.

Of course not, he thought, trying to use the rational side of his brain. She was his wife now. She was *his*.

Everything was different now.

He had known how desperately she had wanted children, and he had married her, knowing full well that he would not give her any.

*But*, he told himself, *you warned her*. She'd known exactly what she was getting into.

Simon, who had been sitting in his study, tossing that stupid rock back and forth between his hands since supper, suddenly straightened. He had not deceived her. Not truly. He had told her that they wouldn't have children, and she had agreed to marry him, anyway. He could see where she would feel a bit upset upon learning his reasons, but she could not say that she had entered this marriage with any foolish hopes or expectations.

He stood. It was time they had another talk, this one at his behest. Daphne hadn't attended dinner, leaving him to dine alone, the silence of the night broken only by the metallic clink of his fork against his plate. He hadn't seen his wife since that morning; it was high time he did.

She was his *wife*, he reminded himself. He ought to be able to see her whenever he damn well pleased.

He marched down the hall and swung open the door to the duke's bedroom, fully prepared to lecture her about *some*thing (the topic, he was sure, would come to him when necessary), but she wasn't there.

Simon blinked, unable to believe his eyes. Where the hell was she? It was nearly midnight. She should be in bed.

The dressing room. She had to be in the dressing room. The silly chit insisted upon donning her nightrobe every night, even though Simon wiggled her out of it mere minutes later.

"Daphne?" he barked, crossing to the dressing-room door. "Daphne?"

No answer. And no light shining in the crack between the door and the floor. Surely she wouldn't dress in the dark.

He pulled the door open. She most definitely wasn't present.

Simon yanked on the bellpull. Hard. Then he strode out into the hall to await whichever servant was unfortunate enough to have answered his summons.

It was one of the upstairs maids, a little blond thing whose name he could not recall. She took one look at his face and blanched.

"Where is my wife?" he barked.

"Your wife, your grace?"

"Yes," he said impatiently, "my wife."

She stared at him blankly.

"I assume you know about whom I am speaking. She's about

your height, long dark hair . . ." Simon would have said more, but the maid's terrified expression made him rather ashamed of his sarcasm. He let out a long, tense breath. "Do you know where she is?" he asked, his tone softer, although not what anyone would describe as gentle.

"Isn't she in bed, your grace?"

Simon jerked his head toward his empty room. "Obviously not."

"But that's not where she sleeps, your grace."

His eyebrows snapped together. "I beg your pardon."

"Doesn't she—" The maid's eyes widened in horror, then shot frantically around the hall. Simon had no doubt that she was looking for an escape route. Either that or someone who might possibly save her from his thunderous temper.

"Spit it out," he barked.

The maid's voice was very small. "Doesn't she inhabit the duchess's bedchamber?"

"The duchess's . . ." He pushed down an unfamiliar bolt of rage. "Since when?"

"Since today, I suppose, your grace. We had all assumed that you would occupy separate rooms at the end of your honeymoon."

"You did, did you?" he growled.

The maid started to tremble. "Your parents did, your grace, and—"

"*We are not my parents!*" he roared.

The maid jumped back a step.

"And," Simon added in a deadly voice, "I am not my father."

"Of- of course, your grace."

"Would you mind telling me which room my wife has chosen to designate as the duchess's bedchamber?"

The maid pointed one shaking finger at a door down the hall.

"Thank you." He took four steps away, then whirled around.

"You are dismissed." The servants would have plenty to gossip about on the morrow, what with Daphne moving out of their bedroom; he didn't need to give them any more by allowing this maid to witness what was sure to be a colossal argument.

Simon waited until she had scurried down the stairs, then he moved on angry feet down the hall to Daphne's new bedroom. He stopped outside her door, thought about what he'd say, realized he had no idea, and then went ahead and knocked.

No response.

He pounded.

No response.

He raised his fist to pound again, when it occurred to him that maybe she hadn't even locked the door. Wouldn't he feel like a fool if—

He twisted the knob.

She *had* locked it. Simon swore swiftly and fluently under his breath. Funny how he'd never once in his life stuttered on a curse.

"Daphne! Daphne!" His voice was somewhere between a call and a yell. "Daphne!"

Finally, he heard footsteps moving in her room. "Yes?" came her voice.

"Let me in."

A beat of silence, and then, "No."

Simon stared at the sturdy wooden door in shock. It had never occurred to him that she would disobey a direct order. She was his wife, damn it. Hadn't she promised to obey him?

"Daphne," he said angrily, "open this door this instant."

She must have been very close to the door, because he actually heard her sigh before saying, "Simon, the only reason to let you into this room would be if I were planning to let you into my bed, which I'm not, so I would appreciate it—indeed I believe the entire household would appreciate it—if you would take yourself off and go to sleep."

Simon's mouth actually fell open. He began to mentally weigh the door and compute how many foot-pounds per second would be required to bash the bloody thing in.

"Daphne," he said, his voice so calm it frightened even him, "if you do not open the door this instant I shall break it down."

"You wouldn't."

He said nothing, just crossed his arms and glared, confident that she would know *exactly* what sort of expression he wore on his face.

"Wouldn't you?"

Again, he decided that silence was the most effective answer.

"I *wish* you wouldn't," she added in a vaguely pleading voice.

He stared at the door in disbelief.

"You'll hurt yourself," she added.

"Then open the damned door," he ground out.

Silence, followed by a key slowly turning in the lock. Simon had just enough presence of mind not to throw the door violently open; Daphne was almost certainly directly on the other side. He shoved his way in and found her about five paces away from him, her arms crossed, her legs in a wide, militant stance.

"Don't you ever lock a door against me again," he spat out.

She shrugged. She actually shrugged! "I desired privacy."

Simon advanced several steps. "I want your things moved back into our bedroom by morning. And *you* will be moving back tonight."

"No."

"What the hell do you mean, no?"

"What the hell do you think I mean?" she countered.

Simon wasn't sure what shocked and angered him more—that she was defying him or that she was cursing aloud.

"No," she continued in a louder voice, "means no."

"You are my wife!" he roared. "You will sleep with me. In *my* bed."

"No."

"Daphne, I'm warning you . . ."

Her eyes narrowed to slits. "You have chosen to withhold something from me. Well, I have chosen to withhold something from you. Me."

He was speechless. Utterly speechless.

She, however, was not. She marched to the door and motioned rather rudely for him to go through it. "Get out of my room."

Simon started to shake with rage. "I own this room," he growled. "I own *you*."

"You own nothing but your father's title," she shot back. "You don't even own yourself."

A low roar filled his ears—the roar of red-hot fury. Simon staggered back a step, fearing that if he did not he might actually do something to hurt her. "What the *hell* do you m-mean?" he demanded.

She shrugged again, damn her. "You figure it out," she said.

All of Simon's good intentions fled the room, and he charged forward, grabbing her by her upper arms. He knew his grip was too tight, but he was helpless against the searing rage that flooded his veins. "Explain yourself," he said—between his teeth because he couldn't unclench his jaw. "Now."

Her eyes met his with such a level, knowing gaze that he was nearly undone. "You are not your own man," she said simply. "Your father is still ruling you from the grave."

Simon shook with untold fury, with unspoken words.

"Your actions, your choices—" she continued, her eyes growing very sad, "They have nothing to do with you, with what you want, or what you need. Everything you do, Simon, every move you make, every word you speak—it's all just to thwart him." Her voice broke as she finished with, "And he's not even *alive*."

Simon moved forward with a strange, predatory grace. "Not every move," he said in a low voice. "Not every word."

Daphne backed up, unnerved by the feral expression in his eyes. "Simon?" she asked hesitantly, suddenly devoid of the courage and bravado that had enabled her to stand up to him, a man twice her size and possibly thrice her strength.

The tip of his index finger trailed down her upper arm. She was wearing a silk robe, but the heat and power of him burned through the fabric. He came closer, and one of his hands stole around her until it cupped her buttock and squeezed. "When I touch you like this," he whispered, his voice perilously close to her ear, "it has nothing to do with him."

Daphne shuddered, hating herself for wanting him. Hating him for making her want him.

"When my lips touch your ear," he murmured, catching her lobe between his teeth, "it has nothing to do with him."

She tried to push him away, but when her hands found his shoulders, all they could do was clutch.

He started to push her, slowly, inexorably, toward the bed. "And when I take you to bed," he added, his words hot against the skin of her neck, "and we are skin to skin, it is just the two of—"

"No!" she cried out, shoving against him with all her might. He stumbled back, caught by surprise.

"When you take me to bed," she choked out, "it is never just the two of us. Your father is *always* there."

His fingers, which had crept up under the wide sleeve of her dressing gown, dug into her flesh. He said nothing, but he didn't have to. The icy anger in his pale blue eyes said everything.

"Can you look me in the eye," she whispered, "and tell me that when you pull from my body and give yourself instead to the bed you're thinking about *me*?"

His face was drawn and tight, and his eyes were focused on her mouth.

She shook her head and shook herself from his grasp, which had gone slack. "I didn't think so," she said in a small voice.

She moved away from him, but also away from the bed. She had no doubt that he could seduce her if he so chose. He could kiss her and caress her and bring her to dizzying heights of ecstasy, and she would hate him in the morning.

She would hate herself even more.

The room was deadly silent as they stood across from each other. Simon was standing with his arms at his sides, his face a heart-breaking mixture of shock and hurt and fury. But mostly, Daphne thought, her heart cracking a little as she met his eyes, he looked confused.

"I think," she said softly, "that you had better leave."

He looked up, his eyes haunted. "You're my wife."

She said nothing.

"Legally, I own you."

Daphne just stared at him as she said, "That's true."

He closed the space between them in a heartbeat, his hands finding her shoulders. "I can make you want me," he whispered.

"I know."

His voice dropped even lower, hoarse and urgent. "And even if I couldn't, you're mine. You belong to me. I could force you to let me stay."

Daphne felt about a hundred years old as she said, "You would never do that."

And he knew she was right, so all he did was wrench himself away from her and storm out of the room.

# Chapter 18

*Is This Author the only one who has noticed, or have the (gentle)men of the ton been imbibing more than usual these days?*

LADY WHISTLEDOWN'S SOCIETY PAPERS, 4 June 1813

Simon went out and got drunk. It wasn't something he did often. It wasn't even something he particularly enjoyed, but he did it anyway.

There were plenty of pubs down near the water, only a few miles from Clyvedon. And there were plenty of sailors there, too, looking for fights. Two of them found Simon.

He thrashed them both.

There was an anger in him, a fury that had simmered deep in his soul for years. It had finally found its way to the surface, and it had taken very little provocation to set him to fighting.

He was drunk enough by then so that when he punched, he saw not the sailors with their sun-reddened skin but his father. Every fist was slammed into that constant sneer of rejection. And it felt good. He'd never considered himself a particularly violent man, but damn, it felt good.

By the time Simon was through with the two sailors, no one else dared approach him. The local folk recognized strength, but more importantly they recognized rage. And they all knew that of the two, the latter was the more deadly.

Simon remained in the pub until the first lights of dawn streaked the sky. He drank steadily from the bottle he'd paid for, and then, when it was time to go, rose on unsteady legs, tucked the bottle into his pocket, and made his way back home.

He drank as he rode, the bad whiskey burning straight to his gut. And as he got drunker and drunker, only one thought managed to burst through his haze.

He wanted Daphne back.

She was his wife, damn her. He'd gotten used to having her around. She couldn't just up and move out of their bedroom.

He'd get her back. He'd woo her and he'd win her, and—

Simon let out a loud, unattractive belch. Well, it was going to have to be enough to woo her and win her. He was far too intoxicated to think of anything else.

By the time he reached Castle Clyvedon, he had worked himself into a fine state of drunken self-righteousness. And by the time he stumbled up to Daphne's door, he was making enough noise to raise the dead.

"Daphneeeeeeeeeeee!" he yelled, trying to hide the slight note of desperation in his voice. He didn't need to sound pathetic.

He frowned thoughtfully. On the other hand, maybe if he sounded desperate, she'd be more likely to open the door. He sniffled loudly a few times, then yelled again, "Daphneeeeeeeee!"

When she didn't respond in under two seconds, he leaned against the heavy door (mostly because his sense of balance was swimming in whiskey). "Oh, Daphne," he sighed, his forehead coming to rest against the wood, "If you—"

The door opened and Simon went tumbling to the ground.

"Didja . . . didja hafta open it so . . . so *fast*?" he mumbled.

Daphne, who was still yanking on her dressing gown, looked at the human heap on the floor and just barely recognized it as her husband. "Good God, Simon," she said, "What did you—" She leaned down to help him, then lurched back when he opened his mouth and breathed on her. "You're drunk!" she accused.

He nodded solemnly. "'Fraid so."

"Where have you been?" she demanded.

He blinked and looked at her as if he'd never heard such a stupid question. "Out getting foxed," he replied, then burped.

"Simon, you should be in bed."

He nodded again, this time with considerably more vigor and enthusiasm. "Yesh, yesh I should." He tried to rise to his feet, but only made it as far as his knees before he tripped and fell back down onto the carpet. "Hmmm," he said, peering down at the lower half of his body. "Hmmm, that's strange." He lifted his face back to Daphne's and looked at her in utter confusion. "I could have sworn those were my legs."

Daphne rolled her eyes.

Simon tried out his legs again, with the same results. "My limbs don't sheem to be working properly," he commented.

"Your *brain* isn't working properly!" Daphne returned. "What am I to do with you?"

He looked her way and grinned. "Love me? You said you loved me, you know." He frowned. "I don't think you can take that back."

Daphne let out a long sigh. She should be furious with him—blast it all, she *was* furious with him!—but it was difficult to maintain appropriate levels of anger when he looked so pathetic.

Besides, with three brothers, she'd had some experience with drunken nitwits. He was going to have to sleep it off, that's all there was to it. He'd wake up with a blistering headache, which would probably serve him right, and then he would insist upon drinking some noxious concoction that he was absolutely positive would eliminate his hangover completely.

"Simon?" she asked patiently. "How drunk are you?"

He gave her a loopy grin. "Very."

"I thought as much," she muttered under her breath. She bent down and shoved her hands under his arms. "Up with you now, we've got to get you to bed."

But he didn't move, just sat there on his fanny and looked up at her with an extremely foolish expression. "Whydul need t'get up?" he slurred. "Can't you sit wi' me?" He threw his arms around her in a sloppy hug. "Come'n sit wi' me, Daphne."

"Simon!"

He patted the carpet next to him. "It's nice down here."

"Simon, no, I cannot sit with you," she ground out, struggling out of his heavy embrace. "You have to go to bed." She tried to move him again, with the same, dismal outcome. "Heavens above," she said under her breath, "why did you have to go out and get so drunk?"

He wasn't supposed to hear her words, but he must have done, because he cocked his head, and said, "I wanted you back."

Her lips parted in shock. They both knew what he had to do to win her back, but Daphne thought he was far too intoxicated for her to conduct any kind of conversation on the topic. So she just tugged at his arm and said, "We'll talk about it tomorrow, Simon."

He blinked several times in rapid succession. "Think it already is tomorrow." He craned his neck this way and that, peering toward the windows. The curtains were drawn, but the light of the new day was already filtering through. "Iz day all right," he mumbled. "See?" He waved his arm toward the window. "Tomorrow already."

"Then we'll talk about it in the evening," she said, a touch desperately. She already felt as if her heart had been pushed through a windmill; she didn't think she could bear any more just then. "Please, Simon, let's just leave it be for now."

"The thing is, Daphrey—" He shook his head in much the same manner a dog shakes off water. "DaphNe," he said carefully. "DaphNe DaphNe."

Daphne couldn't quite stop a smile at that. "What, Simon?"

"The problem, y'see"—he scratched his head—"you just don't understand."

"What don't I understand?" she said softly.

"Why I can't do it," he said. He raised his face until it was level with hers, and she nearly flinched at the haunted misery in his eyes.

"I never wanted to hurt you, Daff," he said hoarsely. "You know that, don't you?"

She nodded. "I know that, Simon."

"Good, because the thing is—" He drew a long breath that seemed to shake his entire body. "I can't do what you want."

She said nothing.

"All my life," Simon said sadly, "all my life he won. Didjou know that? He always won. This time I get to win." In a long, awkward movement he swung his arm in a horizontal arc and jabbed his thumb against his chest. "Me. I want to win for once."

"Oh, Simon," she whispered. "You won long ago. The moment you exceeded his expectations you won. Every time you beat the odds, made a friend, or traveled to a new land you won. You did all the things he never wanted for you." Her breath caught, and she gave his shoulders a squeeze. "You beat him. You won. Why can't you see that?"

He shook his head. "I don't want to become what he wanted," he said. "Even though—" He hiccuped. "Even though he never expected it of m-me, what he w-wanted was a perfect son, someone who'd be the perfect d-duke, who'd then m-marry the perfect duchess, and have p-perfect children."

Daphne's lower lip caught between her teeth. He was stuttering again. He must be truly upset. She felt her heart breaking for him, for the little boy who'd wanted nothing other than his father's approval.

Simon cocked his head to the side and regarded her with a surprisingly steady gaze. "He would have approved of you."

"Oh," Daphne said, not sure how to interpret that.

"But"—he shrugged and gave her a secret, mischievous smile—"I married you anyway."

He looked so earnest, so boyishly serious, that it was a hard battle not to throw her arms around him and attempt to comfort him. But no matter how deep his pain, or how wounded his soul, he was going about this all wrong. The best revenge against his father would simply be to live a full and happy life, to achieve all those heights and glories his father had been so determined to deny him.

Daphne swallowed a heavy sob of frustration. She didn't see how he could possibly lead a happy life if all of his choices were based on thwarting the wishes of a dead man.

But she didn't want to get into all of that just then. She was tired and he was drunk and this just wasn't the right time. "Let's get you to bed," she finally said.

He stared at her for a long moment, his eyes filling with an ages-old need for comfort. "Don't leave me," he whispered.

"Simon," she choked out.

"Please don't. He left. Everyone left. Then I left." He squeezed her hand. "You stay."

She nodded shakily and rose to her feet. "You can sleep it off in my bed," she said. "I'm sure you'll feel better in the morning."

"But you'll stay with me?"

It was a mistake. She knew it was a mistake, but still she said, "I'll stay with you."

"Good." He wobbled himself upright. "Because I couldn't—I really—" He sighed and turned anguished eyes to her. "I need you."

She led him to her bed, nearly falling over with him when he tumbled onto the mattress. "Hold still," she ordered, kneeling to pull off his boots. She'd done this for her brothers before, so she knew to grab the heel, not the toe, but they were a snug fit, and she went sprawling on the ground when his foot finally slipped out.

"Good gracious," she muttered, getting up to repeat the aggravating procedure. "And they say women are slaves to fashion."

Simon made a noise that sounded suspiciously like a snore.

"Are you asleep?" Daphne asked incredulously. She yanked at the other boot, which came off with a bit more ease, then lifted his legs—which felt like deadweights—up onto the bed.

He looked young and peaceful with his dark lashes resting against his cheeks. Daphne reached out and brushed his hair off his forehead. "Sleep well, my sweet," she whispered.

But when she started to move, one of his arms shot out and wrapped around her. "You said you would stay," he said accusingly.

"I thought you were asleep!"

"Doesn't give you the right to break your promise." He tugged her at her arm, and Daphne finally gave up resisting and settled down next to him. He was warm, and he was hers, and even if she had grave fears for their future, at that moment she couldn't resist his gentle embrace.

Daphne awoke an hour or so later, surprised that she'd fallen asleep at all. Simon still lay next to her, snoring softly. They were both dressed, he in his whiskey-scented clothes, and she in her night-robe.

Gently, she touched his cheek. "What am I to do with you?" she whispered. "I love you, you know. I love you, but I hate what you're doing to yourself." She drew a shaky breath. "And to me. I hate what you're doing to me."

He shifted sleepily, and for one horrified moment, she was afraid that he'd woken up. "Simon?" she whispered, then let out a relieved exhale when he didn't answer. She knew she shouldn't have spoken words aloud that she wasn't quite ready for him to hear, but he'd looked so innocent against the snowy white pillows. It was far too easy to spill her innermost thoughts when he looked like that.

"Oh, Simon," she sighed, closing her eyes against the tears that were pooling in her eyes. She should get up. She should absolutely positively get up now and leave him to his rest. She understood why he was so dead set against bringing a child into this world, but she hadn't forgiven him, and she certainly didn't agree with him. If he woke up with her still in his arms, he might think she was willing to settle for his version of a family.

Slowly, reluctantly, she tried to pull away. But his arms tightened around her, and his sleepy voice mumbled, "No."

"Simon, I—"

He pulled her closer, and Daphne realized that he was thoroughly aroused.

"Simon?" she whispered, her eyes flying open. "Are you even awake?"

His response was another sleepy mumble, and he made no attempts at seduction, just snuggled her closer.

Daphne blinked in surprise. She hadn't realized that a man could want a woman in his sleep.

She pulled her head back so she could see his face, then reached out and touched the line of his jaw. He let out a little groan. The sound was hoarse and deep, and it made her reckless. With slow, tantalizing fingers, she undid the buttons of his shirt, pausing just once to trace the outline of his navel.

He shifted restlessly, and Daphne felt the strangest, most intoxicating surge of power. He was in her control, she realized. He was asleep, and probably still more than a little bit drunk, and she could do whatever she wanted with him.

She could *have* whatever she wanted.

A quick glance at his face told her that he was still sleeping, and she quickly undid his trousers. Underneath, he was hard and needy, and she wrapped her hand around him, feeling his blood leap beneath her fingers.

"Daphne," he gasped. His eyes fluttered open, and he let out a ragged groan. "Oh, God. That feels so damned good."

"Shhhh," she crooned, slipping out of her silken robe. "Let me do everything."

He lay on his back, his hands fisted at his sides as she stroked him. He'd taught her much during their two short weeks of marriage, and soon he was squirming with desire, his breath coming in short pants.

And God help her, but she wanted him, too. She felt so powerful looming over him. She was in control, and that was the most stunning aphrodisiac she could imagine. She felt a fluttering in her stomach, then a strange sort of quickening, and she knew that she needed him.

She wanted him inside her, filling her, giving her everything a man was meant to give to a woman.

"Oh, Daphne," he moaned, his head tossing from side to side. "I need you. I need you *now*."

She moved atop him, pressing her hands against his shoulders as she straddled him. Using her hand, she guided him to her entrance, already wet with need.

Simon arched beneath her, and she slowly slid down his shaft, until he was almost fully within her.

"More," he gasped. "Now."

Daphne's head fell back as she moved down that last inch. Her hands clutched at his shoulders as she gasped for breath. Then he was completely within her, and she thought she would die from the pleasure. Never had she felt so full, nor so completely a woman.

She keened as she moved above him, her body arching and writhing with delight. Her hands splayed flat against her stomach as she twisted and turned, then slid upward toward her breasts.

Simon let out a guttural moan as he watched her, his eyes glazing over as his breath came hot and heavy over his parted lips. "Oh, my God," he said in a hoarse, raspy voice. "What are you doing to me? What have you—" Then she touched one of her nipples, and his entire body bucked upwards. "Where did you learn that?"

She looked down and gave him a bewildered smile. "I don't know."

"More," he groaned. "I want to watch you."

Daphne wasn't entirely certain what to do, so she just let instinct take over. She ground her hips against his in a circular motion as she arched her back, causing her breasts to jut out proudly. She cupped both in her hands, squeezing them softly, rolling the nipples between her fingers, never once taking her eyes off Simon's face.

His hips started to buck in a frantic, jerky motion, and he grasped desperately at the sheets with his large hands. And Daphne realized that he was almost there. He was always so careful to please her, to make certain that she reached her climax before he allowed himself the same privilege, but this time, he was going to explode first.

She was close, but not as close as he was.

"Oh, Christ!" he suddenly burst out, his voice harsh and primitive with need. "I'm going to—I can't—" His eyes pinned upon her with a strange, pleading sort of look, and he made a feeble attempt to pull away.

Daphne bore down on him with all her might.

He exploded within her, the force of his climax lifting his hips off the bed, pushing her up along with him. She planted her hands underneath him, using all of her strength to hold him against her. She would not lose him this time. She would not lose this chance.

Simon's eyes flew open as he came, as he realized too late what he had done. But his body was too far gone; there was no stopping the power of his climax. If he'd been on top, he might have found the strength to pull away, but lying there under her, watching her tease her own body into a mass of desire, he was helpless against the raging force of his own need.

As his teeth clenched and his body bucked, he felt her small hands slip underneath him, pressing him more tightly against the cradle of her womb. He saw the expression of pure ecstasy on her face, and then he suddenly realized—she had done this on purpose. She had planned this.

Daphne had aroused him in his sleep, taken advantage of him while he was still slightly intoxicated, and held him to her while he poured his seed into her.

His eyes widened and fixed on hers. "How could you?" he whispered.

She said nothing, but he saw her face change, and he knew she'd heard him.

Simon pushed her from his body just as he felt her begin to tighten around him, savagely denying her the ecstasy he'd just had for himself. "How could you?" he repeated. "You knew. You *knew* th-that that I-I-I—"

But she had just curled up in a little ball, her knees tucked against her chest, obviously determined not to lose a single drop of him.

Simon swore viciously as he yanked himself to his feet. He opened his mouth to pour invective over her, to castigate her for betraying him, for taking advantage of him, but his throat tightened, and his tongue swelled, and he couldn't even begin a word, much less finish one.

"Y-y-you—" he finally managed.

Daphne stared at him in horror. "Simon?" she whispered.

He didn't want this. He didn't want her looking at him like he was some sort of freak. Oh God, oh God, he felt seven years old again. He couldn't speak. He couldn't make his mouth work. He was lost.

Daphne's face filled with concern. Unwanted, pitying concern. "Are you all right?" she whispered. "Can you breathe?"

"D-d-d-d-d—" It was a far cry from *don't pity me*, but it was all he could do. He could feel his father's mocking presence, squeezing at his throat, choking his tongue.

"Simon?" Daphne said, hurrying to his side. Her voice grew panicked. "Simon, say something!"

She reached out to touch his arm, but he threw her off. "Don't touch me!" he exploded.

She shrank back. "I guess there are still some things you can say," she said in a small, sad voice.

Simon hated himself, hated the voice that had forsaken him, and hated his wife because she had the power to reduce his control to rubble. This complete loss of speech, this choking, strangling feeling—he had worked his entire life to escape it, and now *she* had brought it all back with a vengeance.

He couldn't let her do this. He couldn't let her make him like he'd once been.

He tried to say her name, couldn't get anything out.

He had to leave. He couldn't look at her. He couldn't be with her. He didn't even want to be with himself, but that, unfortunately, was beyond his meager control.

"D-don't c-come n-near me," he gasped, jabbing his finger at her as he yanked on his trousers. "Y-y-y-you did this!"

"Did what?" Daphne cried, pulling a sheet around her. "Simon, stop this. What did I do that was so wrong? You wanted me. You know you wanted me."

"Th-th-this!" he burst out, pointing at his throat. Then he pointed toward her abdomen. "Th-th-that."

Then, unable to bear the sight of her any longer, he stormed from the room.

If only he could escape himself with the same ease.

Ten hours later Daphne found the following note:

> *Pressing business at another of my estates requires my attention. I trust you will notify me if your attempts at conception were successful.*
>
> *My steward will give you my direction, should you need it.*
>
> *Simon*

The single sheet of paper slipped from Daphne's fingers and floated slowly to the floor. A harsh sob escaped her throat, and she pressed her fingers to her mouth, as if that might possibly stem the tide of emotion that was churning within her.

He'd left her. He'd actually left her. She'd known he was angry, known he might not even forgive her, but she hadn't thought he would actually leave.

She'd thought—oh, even when he'd stormed out the door she'd thought that they might be able to resolve their differences, but now she wasn't so sure.

Maybe she'd been too idealistic. She'd egotistically thought that she could heal him, make his heart whole. Now she realized that she'd imbued herself with far more power than she actually possessed. She'd thought her love was so good, so shining, so pure that Simon would immediately abandon the years of resentment and pain that had fueled his very existence.

How self-important she'd been. How stupid she felt now.

Some things were beyond her reach. In her sheltered life, she'd never realized that until now. She hadn't expected the world to be handed to her upon a golden platter, but she'd always assumed that if she worked hard enough for something, treated everyone the way she would like to be treated, then she would be rewarded.

But not this time. Simon was beyond her reach.

The house seemed preternaturally quiet as Daphne made her way down to the yellow room. She wondered if all the servants had learned of her husband's departure and were now studiously avoiding her. They had to have heard bits and pieces of the argument the night before.

Daphne sighed. Grief was even more difficult when one had a small army of onlookers.

Or invisible onlookers, as the case may be, she thought as she gave the bellpull a tug. She couldn't see them, but she knew they were there, whispering behind her back and pitying her.

Funny how she'd never given much thought to servants' gossip before. But now—she plopped down on the sofa with a pained little moan—now she felt so wretchedly alone. What else was she supposed to think about?

"Your grace?"

Daphne looked up to see a young maid standing hesitantly in the doorway. She bobbed a little curtsy and gave Daphne an expectant look.

"Tea, please," Daphne said quietly. "No biscuits, just tea."

The young girl nodded and ran off.

As she waited for the maid to return, Daphne touched her abdomen, gazing down at herself with gentle reverence. Closing her eyes, she sent up a prayer. *Please God please*, she begged, *let there be a child.*

She might not get another chance.

She wasn't ashamed of her actions. She supposed she should be, but she wasn't.

She hadn't planned it. She hadn't looked at him while he was sleeping and thought—*he's probably still drunk. I can make love to him and capture his seed and he'll never know.*

It hadn't happened that way.

Daphne wasn't quite sure how it had happened, but one moment she was above him, and the next she'd realized that he wasn't going to withdraw in time, and she'd made certain he *couldn't* . . .

Or maybe— She closed her eyes. Tight. Maybe it had happened the other way. Maybe she *had* taken advantage of more than the moment, maybe she had taken advantage of *him*.

She just didn't know. It had all melted together. Simon's stutter, her desperate wish for a baby, his hatred of his father—it had all swirled and mixed in her mind, and she couldn't tell where one ended and the other began.

And she felt so alone.

She heard a sound at the door and turned, expecting the timid young maid back with tea, but in her stead was Mrs. Colson. Her face was drawn and her eyes were concerned.

Daphne smiled wanly at the housekeeper. "I was expecting the maid," she murmured.

"I had things to attend to in the next room, so I thought I'd bring the tea myself," Mrs. Colson replied.

Daphne knew she was lying, but she nodded anyway.

"The maid said no biscuits," Mrs. Colson added, "but I knew you'd skipped breakfast, so I put some on the tray, anyway."

"That's very thoughtful of you." Daphne didn't recognize the timbre of her own voice. It sounded rather flat to her, almost as if it belonged to someone else.

"It was no trouble, I assure you." The housekeeper looked as if she wanted to say more, but eventually she just straightened and asked, "Will that be all?"

Daphne nodded.

Mrs. Colson made her way to the door, and for one brief moment Daphne almost called out to her. She almost said her name, and asked her to sit with her, and share her tea. And she would have spilled her secrets and her shame, and then she would have spilled her tears.

And not because she was particularly close to the housekeeper, just because she had no one else.

But she didn't call out, and Mrs. Colson left the room.

Daphne picked up a biscuit and bit into it. Maybe, she thought, it was time to go home.

# Chapter 19

*The new Duchess of Hastings was spotted in Mayfair today. Philipa Featherington saw the former Miss Daphne Bridgerton taking a bit of air as she walked briskly around the block. Miss Featherington called out to her, but the duchess pretended not to hear.*

*And we know the duchess must have been pretending, for after all, one would have to be deaf to let one of Miss Featherington's shouts go unnoticed.*

*Lady Whistledown's Society Papers*, 9 June 1813

Heartache, Daphne eventually learned, never really went away; it just dulled. The sharp, stabbing pain that one felt with each breath eventually gave way to a blunter, lower ache—the kind that one could almost—but never quite—ignore.

She left Castle Clyvedon the day after Simon's departure, heading to London with every intention of returning to Bridgerton House. But going back to her family's house somehow seemed like an admission of failure, and so at the last minute, she instructed the driver to take her to Hastings House instead. She would be near her family if she felt the need for their support and companionship, but she was a married woman now; she should reside in her own home.

And so she introduced herself to her new staff, who accepted her without question (but not without a considerable amount of curiosity), and set about her new life as an abandoned wife.

Her mother was the first to come calling. Daphne hadn't bothered to notify anyone else of her return to London, so this was not terribly surprising.

"Where is he?" Violet demanded without preamble.

"My husband, I presume?"

"No, your great-uncle Edmund," Violet practically snapped. "Of course I mean your husband."

Daphne didn't quite meet her mother's eyes as she said, "I believe that he is tending to affairs at one of his country estates."

"You *believe*?"

"Well, I know," Daphne amended.

"And do you *know* why you are not with him?"

Daphne considered lying. She considered brazening it out and telling her mother some nonsense about an emergency involving tenants and maybe some livestock or disease or *anything*. But in the end, her lip quivered, and her eyes started to prick with tears, and her voice was terribly small, as she said, "Because he did not choose to take me with him."

Violet took her hands. "Oh, Daff," she sighed, "what happened?"

Daphne sank onto a sofa, pulling her mother along with her. "More than I could ever explain."

"Do you want to try?"

Daphne shook her head. She'd never, not even once in her life, kept a secret from her mother. There had never been anything she didn't feel she could discuss with her.

But there had never been this.

She patted her mother's hand. "I'll be all right."

Violet looked unconvinced. "Are you certain?"

"No." Daphne stared at the floor for a moment. "But I have to believe it, anyway."

Violet left, and Daphne placed her hand on her abdomen and prayed.

Colin was the next to visit. About a week later, Daphne returned from a quick walk in the park to find him standing in her drawing room, arms crossed, expression furious.

"Ah," Daphne said, pulling off her gloves, "I see you've learned of my return."

"What the hell is going on?" he demanded.

Colin, Daphne reflected wryly, had clearly not inherited their mother's talent for subtlety in speech.

"Speak!" he barked.

She closed her eyes for a moment. Just a moment to try to relieve the headache that had been plaguing her for days. She didn't want to tell her woes to Colin. She didn't even want to tell him as much as she told her mother, although she supposed he already knew. News always traveled fast at Bridgerton House.

She wasn't really sure where she got the energy, but there was a certain fortifying benefit to putting up a good front, so she squared her shoulders, raised a brow, and said, "And by that you mean . . . ?"

"I mean," Colin growled, "where is your husband?"

"He is otherwise occupied," Daphne replied. It sounded so much better than, "He left me."

"Daphne . . ." Colin's voice held no end of warning.

"Are you here alone?" she asked, ignoring his tone.

"Anthony and Benedict are in the country for the month, if that's what you mean," Colin said.

Daphne very nearly sighed with relief. The last thing she needed just then was to face her eldest brother. She'd already prevented him from killing Simon once; she wasn't sure if she'd be able to manage the feat a second time. Before she could say anything, however, Colin added, "Daphne, I am ordering you right now to tell me where the bastard is hiding."

Daphne felt her spine stiffening. She might have the right to call her errant husband nasty names, but her brother certainly didn't. "I assume," she said icily, "that by 'that bastard' you refer to my husband."

"You're damned right I—"

"I'm going to have to ask you to leave."

Colin looked at her as if she'd suddenly sprouted horns. "I beg your pardon?"

"I don't care to discuss my marriage with you, so if you cannot refrain from offering your unsolicited opinions, you're going to have to leave."

"You can't ask me to leave," he said in disbelief.

She crossed her arms. "This is my house."

Colin stared at her, then looked around the room—the drawing room of the Duchess of Hastings—then looked back at Daphne, as if just realizing that his little sister, whom he'd always viewed as a rather jolly extension of himself, had become her own woman.

He reached out and took her hand. "Daff," he said quietly, "I'll let you handle this as you see fit."

"Thank you."

"*For now*," he warned. "Don't think I'll let this situation continue indefinitely."

But it wouldn't, Daphne thought a half hour later as Colin left the house. It couldn't continue indefinitely. Within a fortnight, she would know.

---

Every morning Daphne woke to find she was holding her breath. Even before her courses were due to arrive, she bit her lip, said a little prayer, and gingerly peeled back the covers of her bed and looked for blood.

And every morning she saw nothing but snowy white linen.

A week after her courses were due, she allowed herself the first glimmerings of hope. Her courses had never been perfectly punctual; they could, she reasoned, still arrive at any time. But still, she had never been quite *this* late . . .

After another week, though, she found herself smiling each morning, holding on to her secret as she would a treasure. She wasn't ready to share this with anyone yet. Not her mother, not her brothers, and certainly not Simon.

She didn't feel terribly guilty about withholding the news from him. After all, he had withheld his seed from her. But more importantly, she feared that his reaction would be explosively negative, and she just wasn't ready to let his displeasure ruin her perfect moment of joy. She did, however, jot off a note to his steward, asking that he forward Simon's new address to her.

But then finally, after the third week, her conscience got the better of her, and she sat down at her desk to write him a letter.

Unfortunately for Daphne, the sealing wax hadn't even dried on her missive when her brother Anthony, obviously returned from his sojourn in the country, came crashing into the room. Since Daphne was upstairs, in her private chamber, where she was *not* supposed to receive visitors, she didn't even want to think about how many servants he had injured on his way up.

He looked furious, and she knew she probably shouldn't provoke him, but he always made her slightly sarcastic, so she asked, "And how did you get up here? Don't I have a butler?"

"You *had* a butler," he growled.

"Oh, dear."

"Where is he?"

"Not here, obviously." There didn't seem any point in pretending she didn't know exactly who he was talking about.

"I'm going to kill him."

Daphne stood, eyes flashing. "No, you're not!"

Anthony, who had been standing with his hands on his hips, leaned forward and speared her with a stare. "I made a vow to Hastings before he married you, did you know that?"

She shook her head.

"I reminded him that I had been prepared to kill him for damaging your reputation. Heaven help him if he damages your soul."

"He hasn't damaged my soul, Anthony." Her hand strayed to her abdomen. "Quite the opposite, actually."

But if Anthony found her words odd, she would never know, because his eyes strayed to her writing table, then narrowed. "What is that?" he asked.

Daphne followed his line of vision to the small pile of paper that constituted her discarded attempts at a letter to Simon. "It's nothing," she said, reaching forward to grab the evidence.

"You're writing him a letter, aren't you?" Anthony's already stormy expression grew positively thunderous. "Oh, for the love of God, don't try to lie about it. I saw his name at the top of the paper."

Daphne crumpled the wasted papers and dropped them into a basket under the desk. "It's none of your business."

Anthony eyed the basket as if he were about to lunge under the desk and retrieve the half-written notes. Finally, he just looked back at Daphne, and said, "I'm not going to let him get away with this."

"Anthony, this isn't your affair."

He didn't dignify that with a reply. "I'll find him, you know. I'll find him, and I'll kill—"

"Oh, for goodness' sake," Daphne finally exploded. "This is *my* marriage, Anthony, not yours. And if you interfere in my affairs, so help me God, I swear I will never speak to you again."

Her eyes were steady, and her tone was forceful, and Anthony looked slightly shaken by her words. "Very well," he muttered, "I won't kill him."

"Thank you," Daphne said, rather sarcastically.

"But I will find him," Anthony vowed. "And I will make my disapproval clear."

Daphne took one look at his face and knew that he meant it. "Very well," she said, reaching for the completed letter that she'd tucked away in a drawer. "I'll let you deliver this."

"Good." He reached for the envelope.

Daphne moved it out of his reach. "But only if you make me two promises."

"Which are . . . ? "

"First, you must promise that you won't read this."

He looked mortally affronted that she'd even suggested he would.

"Don't try that 'I'm so honorable' expression with me," Daphne said with a snort. "I know you, Anthony Bridgerton, and I know that you would read this in a second if you thought you could get away with it."

Anthony glared at her.

"But I also know," she continued, "that you would never break an explicit promise made to me. So I'll need your promise, Anthony."

"This is hardly necessary, Daff."

"Promise!" she ordered.

"Oh, all right," he grumbled, "I promise."

"Good." She handed him the letter. He looked at it longingly.

"Secondly," Daphne said loudly, forcing his attention back to her, "you must promise not to hurt him."

"Oh, now, wait one second, Daphne," Anthony burst out. "You ask for too much."

She held out her hand. "I'll be taking that letter back."

He shoved it behind his back. "You already gave it to me."

She smirked. "I didn't give you his address."

"I can get his address," he returned.

"No, you can't, and you know it," Daphne shot back. "He has no end of estates. It'd take you weeks to figure out which one he's visiting."

"A-ha!" Anthony said triumphantly. "So he's at one of his estates. You, my dear, let slip a vital clue."

"Is this a *game*?" Daphne asked in amazement.

"Just tell me where he is."

"Not unless you promise—no violence, Anthony." She crossed her arms. "I mean it."

"All right," he mumbled.

"Say it."

"You're a hard woman, Daphne Bridgerton."

"It's Daphne Basset, and I've had good teachers."

"I promise," he said—barely. His words weren't precisely crisp.

"I need a bit more than that," Daphne said. She uncrossed her arms and twisted her right hand in a rolling manner, as if to draw forth the words from his lips. "I promise not to . . ."

"I promise not to hurt your bloody idiot of a husband," Anthony spat out. "There. Is that good enough?"

"Certainly," Daphne said congenially. She reached into a drawer and pulled out the letter she'd received earlier that week from Simon's steward, giving his address. "Here you are."

Anthony took it with a decidedly ungraceful—and ungrateful—swipe of his hand. He glanced down, scanned the lines, then said, "I'll be back in four days."

"You're leaving today?" Daphne asked, surprised.

"I don't know how long I can keep my violent impulses in check," he drawled.

"Then by all means, go today," Daphne said.

He did.

"Give me one good reason why I shouldn't pull your lungs out through your mouth."

Simon looked up from his desk to see a travel-dusty Anthony Bridgerton, fuming in the doorway to his study. "It's nice to see you, too, Anthony," he murmured.

Anthony entered the room with all the grace of a thunderstorm, planted his hands on Simon's desk and leaned forward menacingly. "Would you mind telling me why my sister is in London, crying herself to sleep every night, while you're in—" He looked around the office and scowled. "Where the hell are we?"

"Wiltshire," Simon supplied.

"While you're in Wiltshire, puttering around an inconsequential estate?"

"Daphne's in London?"

"You'd think," Anthony growled, "that as her husband you'd know that."

"You'd think a lot of things," Simon muttered, "but most of the time, you'd be wrong." It had been two months since he'd left Clyvedon. Two months since he'd looked at Daphne and not been able to utter a word. Two months of utter emptiness.

In all honesty, Simon was surprised it had taken Daphne this long to get in touch with him, even if she had elected to do so through her somewhat belligerent older brother. Simon wasn't exactly certain why, but he'd thought she would have contacted him sooner, if only to blister his ears. Daphne wasn't the sort to stew in silence when she was upset; he'd half expected her to track him down and explain in six different ways why he was an utter fool.

And truth be told, after about a month, he'd half wished she would.

"I would tear your bloody head off," Anthony growled, breaking into Simon's thoughts with considerable force, "if I hadn't promised Daphne I wouldn't do you bodily harm."

"I'm sure that wasn't a promise easily made," Simon said.

Anthony crossed his arms and settled a heavy stare on Simon's face. "Nor easily kept."

Simon cleared his throat as he tried to figure out some way to ask about Daphne without seeming too obvious. He missed her. He felt like an idiot, he felt like a fool, but he missed her. He missed her laugh and her scent and the way, sometimes in the middle of the night, she always managed to tangle her legs with his.

Simon was used to being alone, but he wasn't used to being this lonely.

"Did Daphne send you to fetch me back?" he finally asked.

"No." Anthony reached into his pocket, pulled out a small, ivory envelope, and slapped it down on the desk. "I caught her summoning a messenger to send you this."

Simon stared at the envelope with growing horror. It could only mean one thing. He tried to say something neutral, such as "I see," but his throat closed up.

"I told her I'd be happy to conduct the letter to you," Anthony said, with considerable sarcasm.

Simon ignored him. He reached for the envelope, hoping that Anthony would not see how his fingers were shaking.

But Anthony did see. "What the devil is wrong with you?" he asked in an abrupt voice. "You look like hell."

Simon snatched the envelope and pulled it to him. "Always a pleasure to see you, too," he managed to quip.

Anthony gazed steadily at him, the battle between anger and concern showing clearly on his face. Clearing his throat a few times, Anthony finally asked, in a surprisingly gentle tone, "Are you ill?"

"Of course not."

Anthony went pale. "Is Daphne ill?"

Simon's head snapped up. "Not that she's told me. Why? Does she look ill? Has she—"

"No, she looks fine." Anthony's eyes filled with curiosity. "Simon," he finally asked, shaking his head, "what are you doing here? It's obvious you love her. And much as I can't comprehend it, she seems to love you as well."

Simon pressed his fingers to his temples, trying to stave off the pounding headache he never seemed to be without these days. "There are things you don't know," he said wearily, shutting his eyes against the pain. "Things you could never understand."

Anthony was silent for a full minute. Finally, just when Simon opened his eyes, Anthony pushed away from the desk and walked back to the door. "I won't drag you back to London," he said in a low voice. "I should but I won't. Daphne needs to know you came for her, not because her older brother had a pistol at your back."

Simon almost pointed out that that was why he'd married her, but he bit his tongue. That wasn't the truth. Not all of it, at least. In another lifetime, he'd have been on bended knee, begging for her hand.

"You should know, however," Anthony continued, "that people

are starting to talk. Daphne returned to London alone, barely a fortnight after your rather hasty marriage. She's keeping a good face about it, but it's got to hurt. No one has actually come out and insulted her, but there's only so much well-meaning pity a body can take. And that damned Whistledown woman has been writing about her."

Simon winced. He'd not been back in England long, but it was long enough to know that the fictitious Lady Whistledown could inflict a great deal of damage and pain.

Anthony swore in disgust. "Get yourself to a doctor, Hastings. And then get yourself back to your wife." With that, he strode out the door.

Simon stared at the envelope in his hands for many minutes before opening it. Seeing Anthony had been a shock. Knowing he'd just been with Daphne made Simon's heart ache.

Bloody hell. He hadn't expected to miss her.

This was not to say, however, that he wasn't still furious with her. She'd taken something from him that he quite frankly hadn't wanted to give. He didn't want children. He'd told her that. She'd married him knowing that. And she'd tricked him.

Or had she? He rubbed his hands wearily against his eyes and forehead as he tried to remember the exact details of that fateful morning. Daphne had definitely been the leader in their lovemaking, but he distinctly recalled his own voice, urging her on. He should not have encouraged what he knew he could not stop.

She probably wasn't pregnant, anyway, he reasoned. Hadn't it taken his own mother over a decade to produce a single living child?

But when he was alone, lying in bed at night, he knew the truth. He hadn't fled just because Daphne had disobeyed him, or because there was a chance he'd sired a child.

He'd fled because he couldn't bear the way he'd been with her. She'd reduced him to the stuttering, stammering fool of his childhood. She'd rendered him mute, brought back that awful, choking feeling, the horror of not being able to say what he felt.

He just didn't know if he could live with her if it meant going back to being the boy who could barely speak. He tried to remind himself of their courtship—their mock-courtship, he thought with a smile—and to remember how easy it had been to be with her, to talk with her. But every memory was tainted by where it had all led—to Daphne's bedroom that hideous morning, with him tripping over his tongue and choking on his own throat.

And he hated himself like that.

So he'd fled to another of his country estates—as a duke, he had a number of them. This particular house was in Wiltshire, which, he had reasoned, wasn't too terribly far from Clyvedon. He could get back in a day and a half if he rode hard enough. It wasn't so much like he'd run away, if he could go back so easily.

And now it looked like he was going to have to go back.

Taking a deep breath, Simon picked up his letter opener and slit the envelope. He pulled out a single sheet of paper and looked down.

*Simon,*

*My efforts, as you termed them, were met with success. I have removed myself to London, so that I might be near my family, and await your directive there.*

*Yours,*<br>
*Daphne*

Simon didn't know how long he sat there behind his desk, barely breathing, the cream-colored slip of paper hanging from his fingers. Then finally, a breeze washed over him, or perhaps the light changed, or the house creaked—but something broke him out of his reverie and he jumped to his feet, strode into the hall, and bellowed for his butler.

"Have my carriage hitched," he barked when the butler appeared. "I'm going to London."

# Chapter 20

*The marriage of the season seems to have gone sour. The Duchess of Hastings (formerly Miss Bridgerton) returned to London nearly two months ago, and This Author has seen neither hide nor hair of her new husband, the duke.*

*Rumor has it that he is not at Clyvedon, where the once happy couple took their honeymoon. Indeed, This Author cannot find anyone who professes to know his whereabouts. (If her grace knows, she is not telling, and furthermore, one rarely has the opportunity to ask, as she has shunned the company of all except her rather large and extensive family.)*

*It is, of course, This Author's place and indeed duty to speculate on the source of such rifts, but This Author must confess that even she is baffled. They seemed so very much in love . . .*

LADY WHISTLEDOWN'S SOCIETY PAPERS,
2 August 1813

The trip took two days, which was two days longer than Simon would have liked to be alone with his thoughts. He'd brought a few books to read, hoping to keep himself distracted during the tedious journey, but whenever he managed to open one it sat unread in his lap.

It was difficult to keep his mind off Daphne.

It was even more difficult to keep his mind off the prospect of fatherhood.

Once he reached London, he gave his driver instructions to take him directly to Bridgerton House. He was travel-weary, and probably could use a change of clothing, but he'd done nothing for the past two days but play out his upcoming confrontation with Daphne—it seemed foolish to put it off any longer than he had to.

Once admitted to Bridgerton House, however, he discovered that Daphne wasn't there.

"What do you mean," Simon asked in a deadly voice, not particularly caring that the butler had done little to earn his ire, "the duchess isn't here?"

The butler took his deadly voice and raised him one curled upper lip. "I mean, your grace"—this was not said with particular graciousness—"that she is not in residence."

"I have a letter from my wife—" Simon thrust his hand into his pocket, but—damn it—didn't come up with the paper. "Well, I have a letter from her somewhere," he grumbled. "And it specifically states that she has removed herself to London."

"And she has, your grace."

"Then where the hell is she?" Simon ground out.

The butler merely raised a brow. "At Hastings House, your grace."

Simon clamped his mouth shut. There was little more humiliating than being bested by a butler.

"After all," the butler continued, clearly enjoying himself now, "she is married to *you*, is she not?"

Simon glared at him. "You must be quite secure in your position."

"Quite."

Simon gave him a brief nod (since he couldn't quite bring himself to thank the man) and stalked off, feeling very much like a fool. Of course Daphne would have gone to Hastings House. She hadn't *left* him, after all; she just wanted to be near her family.

If he could have kicked himself on the way back to the carriage, he would have done so.

Once inside, however, he did kick himself. He lived just across Grosvenor Square from the Bridgertons. He could have walked across the blasted green in half the time.

Time, however, proved not to be particularly of the essence, because when he swung open the door to Hastings House and stomped into the hall, he discovered that his wife was not at home.

"She's riding," Jeffries said.

Simon stared at his butler in patent disbelief. "She's riding?" he echoed.

"Yes, your grace," Jeffries replied. "Riding. On a horse."

Simon wondered what the penalty was for strangling a butler. "Where," he bit off, "did she go?"

"Hyde Park, I believe."

Simon's blood began to pound, and his breath grew uneven. Riding? Was she bloody insane? She was pregnant, for God's sake. Even *he* knew that pregnant women weren't supposed to ride.

"Have a horse saddled for me," Simon ordered. "Immediately."

"Any particular horse?" Jeffries inquired.

"A fast one," Simon snapped. "And do it now. Or better yet, I'll do it." With that, he turned on his heel and marched out of the house.

But about halfway to the stables, his panic seeped from his blood to his very bones, and Simon's determined stride turned into a run.

It wasn't the same as riding astride, Daphne thought, but at least she was going *fast*.

In the country, when she'd been growing up, she'd always borrowed Colin's breeches and joined her brothers on their hell-for-leather rides. Her mother usually suffered an attack of the vapors every time she saw her eldest daughter return covered with mud, and quite frequently sporting a new and startling bruise, but Daphne hadn't cared. She hadn't cared where they were riding to or what they were riding from. It had all been about speed.

In the city, of course, she couldn't don breeches and thus was relegated to the sidesaddle, but if she took her horse out early enough, when fashionable society was still abed, and if she made certain to limit herself to the more remote areas of Hyde Park, she could bend over her saddle and urge her horse to a gallop. The wind whipped her hair out of its bun and stung her eyes to tears, but at least it made her forget.

Atop her favorite mare, tearing across the fields, she felt free. There was no better medicine for a broken heart.

She'd long since ditched her groom, pretending she hadn't heard him when he'd yelled, "Wait! Your grace! Wait!"

She'd apologize to him later. The grooms at Bridgerton House were used to her antics and well aware of her skill atop a horse. This new man—one of her husband's servants—would probably worry.

Daphne felt a twinge of guilt—but only a twinge. She needed to be alone. She needed to move fast.

She slowed down as she reached a slightly wooded area and took a deep breath of the crisp autumn air. She closed her eyes for a moment, letting the sounds and smells of the park fill her senses. She thought of a blind man she'd once met, who'd told her that the rest of his senses had grown sharper since he'd lost his sight. As she sat there and inhaled the scents of the forest, she thought he might be right.

She listened hard, first identifying the high-pitched chirp of the birds, then the soft, scurrying feet of the squirrels as they hoarded nuts for the winter. Then—

She frowned and opened her eyes. Damn. That was definitely the sound of another rider approaching.

Daphne didn't want company. She wanted to be alone with her thoughts and her pain, and she certainly didn't want to have to explain to some well-meaning society member why she was alone in the park. She listened again, identified the location of the oncoming rider, and took off in the other direction.

She kept her horse to a steady trot, thinking that if she just got out of the other rider's way, he'd pass her by. But whichever way she went, he seemed to follow.

She picked up speed, more speed than she should have in this lightly wooded area. There were too many low branches and protruding tree roots. But now Daphne was starting to get scared. Her pulse pounded in her ears as a thousand horrifying questions rocked through her head.

What if this rider wasn't, as she'd originally supposed, a member of the *ton*? What if he was a criminal? Or a drunk? It was early; there was no one about. If Daphne screamed, who would hear her? Was she close enough to her groom? Had he stayed put where she'd left him or had he tried to follow? And if he had, had he even gone in the right direction?

Her groom! She nearly cried out in relief. It had to be her groom. She swung her mare around to see if she could catch a glimpse of the rider. The Hastings livery was quite distinctly red; surely she'd be able to see if—

Smack!

Every bit of air was violently forced from her body as a branch caught her squarely in the chest. A strangled grunt escaped her lips, and she felt her mare moving forward without her. And then she was falling . . . falling . . .

She landed with a bone-jarring thud, the autumn brown leaves on the ground providing scant cushioning. Her body immediately curled into a fetal position, as if by making herself as small as possible, she could make the hurt as small as possible.

And, oh God, she hurt. Damn it, she hurt everywhere. She squeezed her eyes shut and concentrated on breathing. Her mind flooded with curses she'd never dared speak aloud. But it hurt. Bloody hell, it hurt to breathe.

But she had to. Breathe. *Breathe, Daphne*, she ordered. *Breathe. Breathe. You can do it.*

"Daphne!"

Daphne made no response. The only sounds she seemed able to make were whimpers. Even groans were beyond her capability.

"Daphne! Christ above, Daphne!"

She heard someone jump off a horse, then felt movement in the leaves around her.

"Daphne?"

"Simon?" she whispered in disbelief. It made no sense that he was here, but it was his voice. And even though she still hadn't pried her eyes open, it *felt* like him. The air changed when he was near.

His hands touched her lightly, checking for broken bones. "Tell me where it hurts," he said.

"Everywhere," she gasped.

He swore under his breath, but his touch remained achingly gentle and soothing. "Open your eyes," he ordered softly. "Look at me. Focus on my face."

She shook her head. "I can't."

"You *can.*"

She heard him strip off his gloves, and then his warm fingers were on her temples, smoothing away the tension. He moved to her eyebrows, then the bridge of her nose. "Shhhh," he crooned. "Let it go. Just let the pain go. Open your eyes, Daphne."

Slowly, and with great difficulty, she did so. Simon's face filled her vision, and for the moment she forgot everything that had happened between them, everything but the fact that she loved him, and he was here, and he was making the hurt go away.

"Look at me," he said again, his voice low and insistent. "Look at me and don't take your eyes off of mine."

She managed the tiniest of nods. She focused her eyes on his, letting the intensity of his gaze hold her still.

"Now, I want you to relax," he said. His voice was soft but commanding, and it was exactly what she needed. As he spoke, his hands moved across her body, checking for breaks or sprains.

His eyes never once left hers.

Simon kept speaking to her in low, soothing tones as he examined her body for injuries. She didn't appear to have suffered anything worse than a few bad bruises and having the wind knocked out of her, but one could never be too careful, and with the baby . . .

The blood drained from his face. In his panic for Daphne, he'd forgotten all about the child she was carrying. His child.

Their child.

"Daphne," he said slowly. Carefully. "Do you think you're all right?"

She nodded.

"Are you still in pain?"

"Some," she admitted, swallowing awkwardly as she blinked. "But it's getting better."

"Are you certain?"

She nodded again.

"Good," he said calmly. He was silent for several seconds and then he fairly yelled, "*What in God's name did you think you were doing?*"

Daphne's jaw dropped, and her eyelids started opening and closing with great rapidity. She made a strangled sort of sound that might have metamorphosed into an actual word, but Simon cut her off with more bellows.

"What the hell were you doing out here with no groom? And why were you galloping here, where the terrain clearly does not allow it?" His eyebrows slammed together. "And for the love of God, woman, what were you doing on a horse?"

"Riding?" Daphne answered weakly.

"Don't you even care about our child? Didn't you give even a moment's thought to its safety?"

"Simon," Daphne said, her voice very small.

"A pregnant woman shouldn't even get within ten feet of a horse! You should know better."

When she looked at him her eyes looked old. "Why do you care?" she asked flatly. "You didn't want this baby."

"No, I didn't, but now that it's here I don't want you to *kill* it."

"Well, don't worry." She bit her lip. "It's not here."

Simon's breath caught. "What do you mean?"

Her eyes flitted to the side of his face. "I'm not pregnant."

"You're—" He couldn't finish the sentence. The strangest feeling sank into his body. He didn't think it was disappointment, but he wasn't quite sure. "You lied to me?" he whispered.

She shook her head fiercely as she sat up to face him. "No!" she cried. "No, I never lied. I swear. I thought I'd conceived. I truly thought I had. But—" She choked on a sob, and squeezed her eyes shut against an onslaught of tears. She hugged her legs to her body and pressed her face against her knees.

Simon had never seen her like this, so utterly stricken with grief. He stared at her, feeling agonizingly helpless. All he wanted was to make her feel better, and it didn't much help to know that *he* was the cause of her pain. "But what, Daff?" he asked.

When she finally looked up at him, her eyes were huge, and full of grief. "I don't know. Maybe I wanted a child so badly that I somehow willed my courses away. I was so happy last month." She let out a shaky breath, one that teetered precariously on the edge of a sob. "I waited and waited, even got my woman's padding ready, and nothing happened."

"Nothing?" Simon had never heard of such a thing.

"Nothing." Her lips trembled into a faintly self-mocking smile. "I've never been so happy in my life to have nothing happen."

"Did you feel queasy?"

She shook her head. "I felt no different. Except that I didn't bleed. But then two days ago . . ."

Simon laid his hand on hers. "I'm sorry, Daphne."

"No you're not," she said bitterly, yanking her hand away. "Don't pretend something you don't feel. And for God's sake, don't lie to me again. You never wanted this baby." She let out a hollow, brittle laugh. "*This* baby? Good God, I talk as if it ever actually existed. As if it were ever more than a product of my imagination." She looked down, and when she spoke again, her voice was achingly sad. "And my dreams."

Simon's lips moved several times before he managed to say, "I don't like to see you so upset."

She looked at him with a combination of disbelief and regret. "I don't see how you could expect anything else."

"I—I—I—" He swallowed, trying to relax his throat, and finally he just said the only thing in his heart. "I want you back."

She didn't say anything. Simon silently begged her to say something, but she didn't. And he cursed at the gods for her silence, because it meant that he would have to say more.

"When we argued," he said slowly, "I lost control. I—I couldn't speak." He closed his eyes in agony as he felt his jaw tighten. Finally, after a long and shaky exhale, he said, "I hate myself like that."

Daphne's head tilted slightly as furrows formed in her brow. "Is that why you left?"

He nodded once.

"It wasn't about—what I did?"

His eyes met hers evenly. "I didn't like what you did."

"But that wasn't why you left?" she persisted.

There was a beat of silence, and then he said, "It wasn't why I left."

Daphne hugged her knees to her chest, pondering his words. All this time she'd thought he'd abandoned her because he hated her, hated what she'd done, but in truth, the only thing he hated was himself.

She said softly, "You know I don't think less of you when you stammer."

"I think less of myself."

She nodded slowly. Of course he would. He was proud and stubborn, and all the *ton* looked up to him. Men curried his favor, women flirted like mad. And all the while he'd been terrified every time he'd opened his mouth.

Well, maybe not every time, Daphne thought as she gazed into his face. When they were together, he usually spoke so freely, answered her so quickly that she knew he couldn't possibly be concentrating on every word.

She put her hand on his. "You're not the boy your father thought you were."

"I know that," he said, but his eyes didn't meet hers.

"Simon, look at me," she gently ordered. When he did, she repeated her words."You're not the boy your father thought you were."

"I know that," he said again, looking puzzled and maybe just a bit annoyed.

"Are you sure?" she asked softly.

"Damn it, Daphne, I know—" His words tumbled into silence as his body began to shake. For one startling moment, Daphne thought he was going to cry. But the tears that pooled in his eyes never fell, and when he looked up at her, his body shuddering, all he said was, "I hate him, Daphne. I h-h-h—"

She moved her hands to his cheeks and turned his face to hers, forcing him to meet her steady gaze. "That's all right," she said. "It sounds as if he was a horrid man. But you have to let it go."

"I can't."

"You *can*. It's all right to have anger, but you can't let that be the ruling factor in your life. Even now, you're letting him dictate your choices."

Simon looked away.

Daphne's hands dropped from his face, but she made sure they rested on his knees. She needed this connection. In a strange way she feared that if she let go of him right now she'd lose him forever. "Did you ever stop to wonder if *you* wanted a family? If you wanted a child of your own? You'd be such a wonderful father, Simon, and yet you won't even let yourself consider the notion. You think you're getting your revenge, but you're really just letting him control you from the grave."

"If I give him a child, he wins," Simon whispered.

"No, if you give *yourself* a child, *you* win." She swallowed convulsively. "We all win."

Simon said nothing, but she could see his body shaking.

"If you don't want a child because *you* don't want one, that's one thing. But if you deny yourself the joy of fatherhood because of a dead man, then you're a coward."

Daphne winced as the insult crossed her lips, but it had to be said. "At some point you've got to leave him behind and live your own life. You've got to let go of the anger and—"

Simon shook his head, and his eyes looked lost and hopeless. "Don't ask me to do that. It's all I had. Don't you see, it's *all I had*?"

"I don't understand."

His voice rose in volume. "Why do you think I learned to speak properly? What do you think drove me? It was anger. It was always anger, always to show him."

"Simon—"

A bubble of mocking laughter erupted from his throat. "Isn't that just too amusing? I hate him. I hate him so much, and yet he's the one reason I've managed to succeed."

Daphne shook her head. "That's not true," she said fervently, "you would have succeeded no matter what. You're stubborn and brilliant, and *I know you*. You learned to speak because of *you*, not because of him." When he said nothing, she added in a soft voice, "If he'd shown you love, it would have made it all the easier."

Simon started to shake his head, but she cut him off by taking his hand and squeezing it. "I was shown love," she whispered. "I knew nothing but love and devotion when I was growing up. Trust me, it makes everything easier."

Simon sat very still for several minutes, the only sound the low whoosh of his breath as he fought to control his emotions. Finally, just when Daphne was beginning to fear she'd lost him, he looked up at her with shattered eyes.

"I want to be happy," he whispered.

"You will be," she vowed, wrapping her arms around him. "You will be."

# Chapter 21

*The Duke of Hastings is back!*
*LADY WHISTLEDOWN'S SOCIETY PAPERS,*
6 August 1813

Simon didn't speak as they slowly rode home. Daphne's mare had been found munching contentedly on a patch of grass about twenty yards away, and even though Daphne had insisted that she was fit to ride, Simon had insisted that he didn't care. After tying the mare's reins to his own gelding, he had boosted Daphne into his saddle, hopped up behind her, and headed back to Grosvenor Square.

Besides, he needed to hold her.

He was coming to realize that he needed to hold on to something in life, and maybe she was right—maybe anger wasn't the solution. Maybe—just maybe he could learn to hold on to love instead.

When they reached Hastings House, a groom ran out to take care of the horses, and so Simon and Daphne trudged up the front steps and entered the hall.

And found themselves being stared down by the three older Bridgerton brothers.

"What the hell are you doing in my house?" Simon demanded. All he wanted to do was scoot up the stairs and make love to his wife, and instead he was greeted by this belligerent trio. They were standing with identical postures—legs spread, hands on hips, chins jutted out. If Simon hadn't been so damned irritated with the lot of them, he probably would have had the presence of mind to have been slightly alarmed.

Simon had no doubt that he could hold his own against one of them—*maybe* two—but against all three he was a dead man.

"We heard you were back," Anthony said.

"So I am," Simon replied. "Now leave."

"Not so fast," Benedict said, crossing his arms.

Simon turned to Daphne. "Which one of them may I shoot first?"

She threw a scowl at her brothers. "I have no preference."

"We have a few demands before we'll let you keep Daphne," Colin said.

"What?" Daphne howled.

"*She is my wife!*" Simon roared, effectively obliterating Daphne's angry query.

"She was our sister first," Anthony growled, "and you've made her miserable."

"This isn't any of your business," Daphne insisted.

"*You're* our business," Benedict said.

"She's *my* business," Simon snapped, "so now get the hell out of my house."

"When the three of you have marriages of your own, then you can presume to offer me advice," Daphne said angrily, "but in the meantime, keep your meddling impulses to yourselves."

"I'm sorry, Daff," Anthony said, "but we're not budging on this."

"On what?" she snapped. "You have no place to budge one way or the other. This isn't your affair!"

Colin stepped forward. "We're not leaving until we're convinced he loves you."

The blood drained from Daphne's face. Simon had never once told her that he loved her. He'd shown it, in a thousand different little ways, but he'd never said the words. When they came, she didn't want them at the hands of her overbearing brothers; she wanted them free and felt, from Simon's heart.

"Don't do this, Colin," she whispered, hating the pathetic, pleading note of her voice. "You have to let me fight my own battles."

"Daff—"

"Please," she pleaded.

Simon marched between them. "If you will excuse us," he said to Colin, and by extension, to Anthony and Benedict. He ushered Daphne to the other end of the hall, where they might talk privately. He would have liked to have moved to another room altogether, but he had no confidence that her idiot brothers wouldn't follow.

"I'm so sorry about my brothers," Daphne whispered, her words coming out in a heated rush. "They're boorish idiots, and they had no business invading your house. If I could disown them I would. After this display I wouldn't be surprised if you *never* want children—"

Simon silenced her with a finger to her lips. "First of all, it's our house, not my house. And as for your brothers—they annoy the hell out of me, but they're acting out of love." He leaned down, just an inch, but it brought him close enough so that she could feel his breath on her skin. "And who can blame them?" he murmured.

Daphne's heart stopped.

Simon moved ever closer, until his nose rested on hers. "I love you, Daff," he whispered.

Her heart started again, with a vengeance. "You do?"

He nodded, his nose rubbing against hers. "I couldn't help it."

Her lips wobbled into a hesitant smile. "That's not terribly romantic."

"It's the truth," he said, with a helpless shrug. "You know better than anyone that I didn't want any of this. I didn't want a wife, I didn't want a family, and I *definitely* didn't want to fall in love." He brushed his mouth softly against hers, sending shivers down both of their bodies. "But what I found"—his lips touched hers again—"much to my dismay"—and again—"was that it's quite impossible *not* to love you."

Daphne melted into his arms. "Oh, Simon," she sighed.

His mouth captured hers, trying to show her with his kiss what he was still learning to express in words. He loved her. He worshipped her. He'd walk across fire for her. He—

—still had the audience of her three brothers.

Slowly breaking the kiss, he turned his face to the side. Anthony, Benedict, and Colin were still standing in the foyer. Anthony was studying the ceiling, Benedict was pretending to inspect his fingernails, and Colin was staring quite shamelessly.

Simon tightened his hold on Daphne, even as he shot a glare down the hall. "What the hell are the three of you still doing in my house?"

Not surprisingly, none of them had a ready answer.

"Get *out*," Simon growled.

"Please." Daphne's tone didn't exactly suggest politeness.

"Right," Anthony replied, smacking Colin on the back of the head. "I believe our work here is done, boys."

Simon started steering Daphne toward the stairs. "I'm sure you can show yourselves out," he said over his shoulder.

Anthony nodded and nudged his brothers toward the door.

"Good," Simon said tersely. "We'll be going upstairs."

"Simon!" Daphne squealed.

"It's not as if they don't know what we're going to do," he whispered in her ear.

"But still—They're my *brothers*!"

"God help us," he muttered.

But before Simon and Daphne could even reach the landing, the front door burst open, followed by a stream of decidedly feminine invective.

"Mother?" Daphne said, the word croaking in her throat.

But Violet only had eyes for her sons. "I knew I'd find you here," she accused. "Of all the stupid, bullheaded—"

Daphne didn't hear the rest of her mother's speech. Simon was laughing too hard in her ear.

"He made her miserable!" Benedict protested. "As her brothers, it's our duty to—"

"Respect her intelligence enough to let her solve her own problems," Violet snapped. "And she doesn't look particularly unhappy right now."

"That's because—"

"And if you say that's because you lot barged into her home like a herd of mentally deficient sheep, I'm disowning all three of you."

All three men shut their mouths.

"Now then," Violet continued briskly, "I believe it's time we left, don't you?" When her sons didn't move quickly enough to suit her, she reached out and—

"Please, Mother!" Colin yelped. "Not the—"

She grabbed him by his ear.

"Ear," he finished glumly.

Daphne grabbed Simon's arm. He was laughing so hard now, she was afraid he'd tumble down the steps.

Violet herded her sons out the door with a loud, "March!" and then turned back to Simon and Daphne on the stairs.

"Glad to see you in London, Hastings," she called, gifting him with a wide, brilliant smile. "Another week and I would have dragged you here myself."

Then she stepped outside and shut the door behind her.

Simon turned to Daphne, his body still shaking with laughter. "Was that your mother?" he asked, smiling.

"She has hidden depths."

"Clearly."

Daphne's face grew serious. "I'm sorry if my brothers forced—"

"Nonsense," he said cutting her off. "Your brothers could never force me to say something I don't feel." He cocked his head and pondered that for a moment. "Well, not without a pistol."

Daphne smacked him in the shoulder.

Simon ignored her and pulled her body against his. "I meant what I said," he murmured, wrapping his arms around her waist. "I love you. I've known it for some time now, but—"

"It's all right," Daphne said, laying her cheek against his chest. "You don't need to explain."

"Yes, I do," he insisted. "I—" But the words wouldn't come. There was too much emotion inside, too many feelings rocking within him. "Let me show you," he said hoarsely. "Let me show you how much I love you."

Daphne answered by tilting her face up to receive his kiss. And as their lips touched, she sighed, "I love you, too."

Simon's mouth took hers with hungry devotion, his hands clutching at her back as if he were afraid she might disappear at any moment. "Come upstairs," he whispered. "Come with me now."

She nodded, but before she could take a step, he swept her into the cradle of his arms and carried her up the stairs.

By the time Simon reached the second floor, his body was rock hard and straining for release. "Which room have you been using?" he gasped.

"Yours," she replied, sounding surprised that he'd even asked.

He grunted his approval and moved swiftly into his—no, *their*—room, kicking the door shut behind him. "I love you," he said as they tumbled onto the bed. Now that he'd said the words once, they were bursting within him, demanding a voice. He needed to tell her, make sure she knew, make sure she understood what she meant to him.

And if it took a thousand sayings, he didn't care.

"I love you," he said again, his fingers frantically working on the fastenings of her dress.

"I know," she said tremulously. She cupped his face in her hands and caught his eyes with hers. "I love you, too."

Then she pulled his mouth down to hers, kissing him with a sweet innocence that set him afire.

"If I ever, ever hurt you again," he said fervently, his mouth moving to the corner of hers, "I want you to kill me."

"Never," she answered, smiling.

His lips moved to the sensitive spot where her jaw met her earlobe. "Then maim me," he murmured. "Twist my arm, sprain my ankle."

"Don't be silly," she said, touching his chin and turning his face back to hers. "You won't hurt me."

Love for this woman filled him. It flooded his chest, made his fingers tingle, and stole his very breath. "Sometimes," he whispered, "I love you so much it scares me. If I could give you the world, you know I would do it, don't you?"

"All I want is you," she whispered. "I don't need the world, just your love. And maybe," she added with a wry smile, "for you to take off your boots."

Simon felt his face erupt into a grin. Somehow his wife always seemed to know exactly what he needed. Just when his emotions were choking him, bringing him dangerously close to tears, she lightened the mood, made him smile. "Your wish is my command," he said, and rolled to her side to yank the offending footwear off.

One boot tumbled to the floor, the other skittered across the room.

"Anything else, your grace?" he asked.

She cocked her head coyly. "Your shirt could go, too, I suppose."

He complied, and the linen garment landed on the nightstand.

"Will that be all?"

"These," she said, hooking her finger around the waistband of his breeches, "are definitely in the way."

"I agree," he murmured, shrugging them off. He crawled over her, on his hands and knees, his body a hot prison around her. "Now what?"

Her breath caught. "Well, you're quite naked."

"That is true," he concurred, his eyes burning down on hers.

"And I'm not."

"That is also true." He smiled like a cat. "And a pity it is."

Daphne nodded, completely without words.

"Sit up," he said softly.

She did, and seconds later her dress was whipped over her head.

"Now that," he said hoarsely, staring hungrily at her breasts, "is an improvement."

They were now kneeling across from each other on the massive four-poster bed. Daphne stared at her husband, her pulse quickening at the sight of his broad chest, rising and falling with each heavy breath. With a trembling hand, she reached out and touched him, her fingers lightly skimming over his warm skin.

Simon stopped breathing until her forefinger touched his nipple, and then his hand shot up to cover hers. "I want you," he said.

Her eyes flicked downward, and her lips curved ever so slightly. "I know."

"No," he groaned, pulling her closer. "I want to be in your heart. I want—" His entire body shuddered when their skin touched. "I want to be in your soul."

"Oh, Simon," she sighed, sinking her fingers in his thick, dark hair. "You're already there."

And then there were no more words, only lips and hands and flesh against flesh.

Simon worshipped her in every way he knew how. He ran his hands along her legs and kissed the back of her knees. He squeezed her hips and tickled her navel. And when he was poised to enter her, his entire body straining against the most all-consuming desire he'd ever felt, he gazed down upon her with a reverence that brought tears to her eyes.

"I love you," he whispered. "In all my life, it's been only you."

Daphne nodded and although she made no sound, her mouth formed the words, "I love you, too."

He pushed forward, slowly, inexorably. And when he was settled fully within her body, he knew he was home.

He looked down at her face. Her head was thrown back, her lips parted as she struggled for breath. He grazed her flushed cheeks with his lips. "You're the most beautiful thing I've ever seen," he whispered. "I've never—I don't know how—"

She arched her back in response. "Just love me," she gasped. "Please, love me."

Simon began to move, his hips rising and falling in time's most ancient rhythm. Daphne's fingers pressed into his back, her nails digging into his skin every time he thrust further into her body.

She moaned and mewled, and his body burned at the sounds of her passion. He was spiraling out of control, his movements growing jerky, more frenetic. "I can't hold on much longer," he gasped. He wanted to wait for her, needed to know that he'd brought her bliss before he allowed himself his own release.

But then, just when he thought his body would shatter from the effort of his restraint, Daphne shook beneath him, her most intimate muscles squeezing around him as she cried out his name.

Simon's breath stopped in his throat as he watched her face. He'd always been so busy making sure he didn't spill his seed inside of her that he'd never seen her face as she climaxed. Her head was thrown back, the elegant lines of her throat straining as her mouth opened in a silent scream.

He was awestruck.

"I love you," he said. "Oh, God, how I love you." Then he plunged deeper.

Daphne's eyes fluttered open as he resumed his rhythm. "Simon?" she asked, her voice tinged with a touch of urgency. "Are you sure?"

They both knew what she meant.

Simon nodded.

"I don't want you to do this just for me," she said. "It has to be for you, too."

The strangest lump formed in his throat—it was nothing like his stutters, nothing like his stammers. It was, he realized, nothing but love. Tears stabbed at his eyes, and he nodded, utterly unable to speak.

He plunged forward, exploding within her. It felt good. Oh God, it felt good. Nothing in life had ever felt that good before.

His arms finally gave out, and he collapsed atop her, the only sound in the room the rasp of his ragged breathing.

And then Daphne smoothed his hair from his forehead and kissed his brow. "I love you," she whispered. "I will always love you."

Simon buried his face into her neck, breathing in the scent of her. She surrounded him, enveloped him, and he was complete.

Many hours later, Daphne's eyelids fluttered open. She stretched her arms above her as she noticed that the curtains had all been pulled shut. Simon must have done that, she thought with a yawn. Light filtered around the edges, bathing the room with a soft glow.

She twisted her neck, working the kinks out, then slid out of bed and padded to the dressing room to fetch her robe. How unlike her to sleep in the middle of the day. But, she supposed, this hadn't been an ordinary day.

She pulled on her robe, tying the silken sash around her waist. Where had Simon gone off to? She didn't think he'd left the bed too long before she had; she had a sleepy memory of lying in his arms that somehow seemed too fresh.

The master suite consisted of five rooms altogether: two bedrooms, each with its own dressing room off to the side, connected by a large sitting room. The door to the sitting room was ajar, and bright sunlight streamed through the aperture, suggesting that the curtains inside had been pulled open. Moving on deliberately quiet feet, Daphne walked to the open doorway and peered inside.

Simon was standing by the window, staring out over the city. He'd donned a lush burgundy dressing gown, but his feet were still bare. His pale blue eyes held a reflective look, unfocused and just the slightest bit bleak.

Daphne's brow wrinkled with concern. She crossed the room

toward him, quietly saying, "Good afternoon," when she was but a foot away.

Simon turned at the sound of her voice, and his haggard face softened at the sight of her. "Good afternoon to you, too," he murmured, pulling her into his arms. Somehow she ended up with her back pressed up against his broad chest, gazing out over Grosvenor Square as Simon rested his chin on the top of her head.

It took Daphne several moments before she worked up the courage to ask, "Any regrets?"

She couldn't see him, but she felt his chin rub against her scalp as he shook his head.

"No regrets," he said softly. "Just . . . thoughts."

Something about his voice didn't sound quite right, and so Daphne twisted in his arms until she could see his face. "Simon, what's wrong?" she whispered.

"Nothing." But his eyes didn't meet hers.

Daphne led him to a love seat, and sat, tugging on his arm until he settled in beside her. "If you're not ready to be a father yet," she whispered, "that's all right."

"It's not that."

But she didn't believe him. He'd answered too quickly, and there'd been a choked sound to his voice that made her uneasy. "I don't mind waiting," she said. "Truth be told," she added shyly, "I wouldn't mind having a little time just for the two of us."

Simon didn't say anything, but his eyes grew pained, and then he closed them as he brought his hand to his brow and rubbed.

A ripple of panic washed over Daphne, and she started talking faster. "It wasn't so much that I wanted a baby right away," she said. "I just . . . would like one eventually, that's all, and I think you might, too, if you let yourself consider it. I was upset because

I hated that you were denying us a family just to spite your father. It's not—"

Simon laid a heavy hand on her thigh. "Daphne, stop," he said. "Please."

His voice held just enough agonized emotion to silence her immediately. She caught her lower lip between her teeth and chewed nervously. It was his turn to speak. There was obviously something big and difficult squeezing at his heart, and if it took all day for him to find the words to explain it, she could wait.

She could wait forever for this man.

"I can't say I'm excited about having a child," Simon said slowly.

Daphne noticed his breathing was slightly labored, and she placed her hand on his forearm to offer comfort.

He turned to her with eyes that pleaded for understanding. "I've spent so long intending never to have one, you see." He swallowed. "I d-don't know even how to begin to think about it."

Daphne offered him a reassuring smile that in retrospect, she realized was meant for both of them. "You'll learn," she whispered. "And I'll learn with you."

"I-it's not that," he said, shaking his head. He let out an impatient breath. "I don't . . . want . . . to live my life j-just to spite my father."

He turned to her, and Daphne was nearly undone by the sheer emotion burning on his face. His jaw was trembling, and a muscle worked frantically in his cheek. There was incredible tension in his neck, as if every ounce of his energy was devoted to the task of delivering this speech.

Daphne wanted to hold him, to comfort the little boy inside. She wanted to smooth his brow, and squeeze his hand. She wanted to do a thousand things, but instead she just held silent, encouraging him with her eyes to continue.

"You were right," he said, the words tumbling from his mouth. "All along, you've been right. About my father. Th-that I was letting him win."

"Oh, Simon," she murmured.

"B-but what—" His face—his strong, handsome face, which was always so firm, always so in control—crumpled. "What if . . . if we have a child, a-a-and it comes out like me?"

For a moment Daphne couldn't speak. Her eyes tingled with unshed tears, and her hand moved unbidden to her mouth, covering lips that had parted in shock.

Simon turned away from her, but not before she saw the utter torment in his eyes. Not before she heard his breath catch, or the shaky exhale he finally expelled in an attempt to hold himself together.

"If we have a child who stutters," Daphne said carefully, "then I shall love him. And help him. And—" She swallowed convulsively, praying that she was doing the right thing. "And I shall turn to you for advice, because obviously you have learned how to overcome it."

He turned to face her with surprising swiftness. "I don't want my child to suffer as I have suffered."

A strange little smile moved across Daphne's face without her even realizing it, as if her body had realized before her mind that she knew exactly what to say. "But he wouldn't suffer," she said, "because you'll be his father."

Simon's face did not change expression, but his eyes shone with an odd, new, almost hopeful light.

"Would you reject a child who stuttered?" Daphne asked quietly.

Simon's negative reply was strong, swift, and accompanied by just a touch of blasphemy.

She smiled softly. "Then I have no fears for our children."

Simon held still for one moment more, and then in a rush of movement pulled her into his arms, burying his face in the crook of her neck. "I love you," he choked out. "I love you so much."

And Daphne was finally certain that everything was going to be all right.

Several hours later, Daphne and Simon were still sitting on the love seat in the sitting room. It had been an afternoon for holding hands, for resting one's head on the other's shoulder. Words hadn't been necessary; for both it had been enough simply to be next to the other. The sun was shining, the birds were chirping, and they were together.

It was all they needed.

But something was niggling at the back of Daphne's brain, and it wasn't until her eyes fell on a writing set on the desk that she remembered.

The letters from Simon's father.

She closed her eyes and exhaled, summoning the courage she knew she'd need to hand them over to Simon. The Duke of Middlethorpe had told her, when he'd asked her to take the packet of letters, that she'd know when the time was right to give them to him.

She disentangled herself from Simon's heavy arms and padded over to the duchess's chamber.

"Where are you going?" Simon asked sleepily. He'd been dozing in the warm afternoon sun.

"I—I have to get something."

He must have heard the hesitation in her voice, because he opened his eyes and craned his body around to look at her. "What are you getting?" he asked curiously.

Daphne avoided answering his question by scurrying into the next room. "I'll just be a moment," she called out.

She'd kept the letters, tied together by a red-and-gold ribbon—the ancestral colors of Hastings—in the bottom drawer of her desk. She'd actually forgotten about them for her first few weeks back in London, and they'd lain untouched in her old bedroom at Bridgerton House. But she'd stumbled across them on a visit to see her mother. Violet had suggested she go upstairs to gather a few of her things, and while Daphne was collecting old perfume bottles and the pillowcase she'd stitched at age ten, she found them again.

Many a time she'd been tempted to open one up, if only to better understand her husband. And truth be told, if the envelopes hadn't been closed with sealing wax, she probably would have tossed her scruples over her shoulder and read them.

She picked up the bundle and walked slowly back to the sitting room. Simon was still on the couch, but he was up and alert, and watching her curiously.

"These are for you," she said, holding up the bundle as she walked to his side.

"What are they?" he asked.

But from the tone of his voice, she was fairly certain he already knew.

"Letters from your father," she said. "Middlethorpe gave them to me. Do you remember?"

He nodded. "I also remember giving him orders to burn them."

Daphne smiled weakly. "He apparently disagreed."

Simon stared at the bundle. Anywhere but at her face. "And so, apparently, did you," he said in a very quiet voice.

She nodded and sat next to him. "Do you want to read them?"

Simon thought about his answer for several seconds and finally settled on complete honesty. "I don't know."

"It might help you to finally put him behind you."

"Or it might make it worse."

"It might," she agreed.

He stared at the letters, bundled up by a ribbon, resting innocently in her hands. He expected to feel animosity. He expected to feel rage. But instead, all he felt was . . .

Nothing.

It was the strangest sensation. There before him was a collection of letters, all written in his father's hand. And yet he felt no urge to toss them in the fire, or tear them to bits.

And at the same time no urge to read them.

"I think I'll wait," Simon said with a smile.

Daphne blinked several times, as if her eyes could not believe her ears. "You don't want to read them?" she asked.

He shook his head.

"And you don't want to burn them?"

He shrugged. "Not particularly."

She looked down at the letters, then back at his face. "What do you want to do with them?"

"Nothing."

"Nothing?"

He grinned. "That's what I said."

"Oh." She looked quite adorably befuddled. "Do you want me to put them back in my desk?"

"If you like."

"And they'll just sit there?"

He caught hold of the sash on her dressing robe and started pulling her toward him. "Mmm-hmm."

"But—" she spluttered. "But—but—"

"One more 'but,' " he teased, "and you're going to start to sound like me."

Daphne's mouth fell open. Simon wasn't surprised by her reaction. It was the first time in his life he'd ever been able to make a joke out of his difficulties.

"The letters can wait," he said, just as they fell off her lap onto the floor. "I've just finally managed—thanks to you—to boot my father from my life." He shook his head, smiling as he did so. "Reading those now would just invite him back in."

"But don't you want to see what he had to say?" she persisted. "Maybe he apologized. Maybe he even groveled at your feet!" She bent down for the bundle, but Simon pulled her tightly against him so she couldn't reach.

"Simon!" she yelped.

He arched one brow. "Yes?"

"What are you doing?"

"Trying to seduce you. Am I succeeding?"

Her face colored. "Probably," she mumbled.

"Only probably? Damn. I must be losing my touch."

His hand slid under her bottom, which prompted a little squeal. "I think your touch is just fine," she said hastily.

"Only fine?" He pretended to wince. " 'Fine' is so pale a word, don't you think? Almost wan."

"Well," she allowed, "I might have misspoken."

Simon felt a smile forming in his heart. By the time it spread to his lips, he was on his feet, and tugging his wife in the general direction of his four-poster bed.

"Daphne," he said, trying to sound businesslike, "I have a proposition."

"A proposition?" she queried, raising her brows.

"A request," he amended. "I have a request."

She cocked her head and smiled. "What kind of request?"

He nudged her through the doorway and into the bedroom. "It's actually a request in two parts."

"How intriguing."

"The first part involves you, me, and"—he picked her up and tossed her onto the bed amidst a fit of giggles—"this sturdy antique of a bed."

"Sturdy?"

He growled as he crawled up beside her. "It had better be sturdy."

She laughed and squealed as she scooted out of his grasp. "I think it's sturdy. What's the second part of your request?"

"That, I'm afraid involves a certain commitment of time on your part."

Her eyes narrowed, but she was still smiling. "What sort of commitment of time?"

In one stunningly swift move, he pinned her to the mattress. "About nine months."

Her lips softened with surprise. "Are you sure?"

"That it takes nine months?" He grinned. "That's what I've always been told."

But the levity had left her eyes. "You know that's not what I mean," she said softly.

"I know," he replied, meeting her serious gaze with one of his own. "But yes, I'm sure. And I'm scared to death. And thrilled to the marrow. And a hundred other emotions I never let myself feel before you came along."

Tears pricked her eyes. "That's the sweetest thing you've ever said to me."

"It's the truth," he vowed. "Before I met you I was only half-alive."

"And now?" she whispered.

"And now?" he echoed. " 'Now' suddenly means happiness, and joy, and a wife I adore. But do you know what?"

She shook her head, too overcome to speak.

He leaned down and kissed her. " 'Now' doesn't even compare to tomorrow. And tomorrow couldn't possibly compete with the next day. As perfect as I feel this very moment, tomorrow is going to be even better. Ah, Daff," he murmured, moving his lips to hers, "every day I'm going to love you more. I promise you that. Every day . . ."

# *Epilogue*

*It's a boy for the Duke and Duchess of Hastings!*

*After three girls, society's most besotted couple has finally produced an heir. This Author can only imagine the level of relief in the Hastings household; after all, it is a truth universally acknowledged that a married man in possession of a good fortune must be in want of an heir.*

*The name of the new babe has yet to be made public, although This Author feels herself uniquely qualified to speculate. After all, with sisters named Amelia, Belinda, and Caroline, could the new Earl Clyvedon be called anything but David?*

*LADY WHISTLEDOWN'S SOCIETY PAPERS,*
15 December 1817

Simon threw up his arms in amazement, the single-sheet newspaper flying across the room. "How does she know this?" he demanded. "We've told no one of our decision to name him David."

Daphne tried not to smile as she watched her husband sputter and storm about the room. "It's just a lucky guess, I'm sure," she said, turning her attention back to the newborn in her arms. It was far too early to know if his eyes would remain blue or turn brown like his older sisters', but already he looked so like his father; Daphne couldn't imagine that his eyes would spoil the effect by darkening.

"She must have a spy in our household," he said, planting his hands on his hips. "She must."

"I'm sure she doesn't have a spy in our household," Daphne said without looking up at him. She was too interested in the way David's tiny hand was gripping her finger.

"But—"

Daphne finally lifted her head. "Simon, you're being ridiculous. It's just a gossip column."

"Whistledown—ha!" he grumbled. "I've never heard of any Whistledowns. I'd like to know who this blasted woman is."

"You and the rest of London," Daphne said under her breath.

"Someone should put her out of business once and for all."

"If you wish to put her out of business," Daphne could not resist pointing out, "you shouldn't support her by buying her newspaper."

"I—"

"And don't even try to say that you buy *Whistledown* for me."

"You read it," Simon muttered.

"And so do you." Daphne dropped a kiss on the top of David's head. "Usually well before I can get my hands on it. Besides, I'm rather fond of Lady Whistledown these days."

Simon looked suspicious. "Why?"

"Did you read what she wrote about us? She called us London's most besotted couple." Daphne smiled wickedly. "I rather like that."

Simon groaned. "That's only because Philipa Featherington—"

"She's Philipa Berbrooke now," Daphne reminded him.

"Well, whatever her name, she has the bloodiest big mouth in London, and ever since she heard me calling you 'Dear Heart' at the theater last month, I have not been able to show my face at my clubs."

"Is it so very unfashionable to love one's wife, then?" Daphne teased.

Simon pulled a face, looking rather like a disgruntled young boy.

"Never mind," Daphne said. "I don't want to hear your answer."

Simon's smile was an endearing cross between sheepish and sly.

"Here," she said, holding David up. "Do you want to hold him?"

"Of course." Simon crossed the room and took the baby into his arms. He cuddled him for several moments, then glanced over at Daphne and grinned. "I think he looks like me."

"I know he does."

Simon kissed him on the nose, and whispered, "Don't you worry, my little man. I shall love you always. I'll teach you your letters and your numbers, and how to sit on a horse. And I shall protect you from all the awful people in this world, especially that Whistle-down woman . . ."

And in a small, elegantly furnished chamber, not so very far from Hastings House, a young woman sat at her desk with a quill and a pot of ink and pulled out a piece of paper.

With a smile on her face, she set her quill to paper and wrote:

Lady Whistledown's Society Papers
*19 December 1817*

*Ah Gentle Reader, This Author is pleased to report . . .*

*Dear Reader,*

*Have you ever wondered what happened to your favorite characters after you closed the final page? Wanted just a little bit more of a favorite novel? I have, and if the questions from my readers are any indication, I'm not the only one. So after countless requests from Bridgerton fans, I decided to try something a little different, and I wrote a "2nd Epilogue" for each of the novels. These are the stories that come after the stories.*

*At first, the Bridgerton 2nd Epilogues were available exclusively online; later they were published (along with a novella about Violet Bridgerton) in a collection called* The Bridgertons: Happily Ever After. *I'm delighted that each is now included with the novel it follows. I hope you enjoy Daphne and Simon as they continue their journey.*

*Warmly,*
*Julia Quinn*

# *The Duke and I: The Second Epilogue*

Mathematics had never been Daphne Basset's best subject, but she could certainly count to thirty, and as thirty was the maximum number of days that usually elapsed between her monthly courses, the fact that she was currently looking at her desk calendar and counting to forty-three was cause for some concern.

"It can't be possible," she said to the calendar, half expecting it to reply. She sat down slowly, trying to recall the events of the past six weeks. Maybe she'd counted wrong. She'd bled while she was visiting her mother, and that had been on March twenty-fifth and twenty-sixth, which meant that . . . She counted again, physically this time, poking each square on the calendar with her index finger.

Forty-three days.

She was pregnant.

"Good God."

Once again, the calendar had little to say on the matter.

No. No, it couldn't be. She was forty-one years old. Which wasn't to say that no woman in the history of the world had given birth at forty-two, but it had been seventeen years since she'd last conceived. Seventeen years of rather delightful relations with her husband during which time they had done nothing—absolutely nothing—to block conception.

Daphne had assumed she was simply done being fertile. She'd had her four children in rapid succession, one a year for the first four years of her marriage. Then . . . nothing.

She had been surprised when she realized that her youngest had reached his first birthday, and she was not pregnant again. And then he was two, then three, and her belly remained flat, and Daphne looked at her brood—Amelia, Belinda, Caroline, and David—and decided she had been blessed beyond measure. Four children, healthy and strong, with a strapping little boy who would one day take his father's place as the Duke of Hastings.

Besides, Daphne did not particularly enjoy being pregnant. Her ankles swelled and her cheeks got puffy, and her digestive tract did things that she absolutely did not wish to experience again. She thought of her sister-in-law Lucy, who positively glowed throughout pregnancy—which was a good thing, as Lucy was currently fourteen months pregnant with her fifth child.

Or nine months, as the case might be. But Daphne had seen her just a few days earlier, and she *looked* as if she were fourteen months along.

Huge. Staggeringly huge. But still glowing, and with astonishingly dainty ankles.

"I can't be pregnant," Daphne said, placing a hand on her flat belly. Maybe she was going through the change. Forty-one did seem a bit young, but then again, it wasn't one of those things anyone ever talked about. Maybe lots of women stopped their monthly courses at forty-one.

She should be happy. Grateful. Really, bleeding was such a bother.

She heard footsteps coming toward her in the hallway, and she quickly slid a book on top of the calendar, although what she thought she might be hiding she had no idea. It was just a calendar. There was no big red X, followed by the notation, "Bled this day."

Her husband strode into the room. "Oh good, there you are. Amelia has been looking for you."

"For me?"

"If there is a merciful God, she is not looking for *me*," Simon returned.

"Oh, dear," Daphne murmured. Normally she'd have a more quick-witted response, but her mind was still in the possibly-pregnant-possibly-growing-very-old fog.

"Something about a dress."

"The pink one or the green one?"

Simon stared at her. "Really?"

"No, of course you wouldn't know," she said distractedly.

He pressed his fingers to his temples and sank into a nearby chair. "When will she be married?"

"Not until she's engaged."

"And when will that be?"

Daphne smiled. "She had five proposals last year. You were the one who insisted that she hold out for a love match."

"I did not hear you disagreeing."

"I did not disagree."

He sighed. "How is it we have managed to have three girls out in society at the same time?"

"Procreative industriousness at the outset of our marriage," Daphne answered pertly, then remembered the calendar on her desk. The one with the red X that no one could see but her.

"Industriousness, hmmm?" He glanced over at the open door. "An interesting choice of words."

She took one look at his expression and felt herself turn pink. "Simon, it's the middle of the day!"

His lips slid into a slow grin. "I don't recall that stopping us when we were at the height of our industriousness."

"If the girls come upstairs . . ."

He bound to his feet. "I'll lock the door."

"Oh, good heavens, they'll *know*."

He gave the lock a decisive click and turned back to her with an arched brow. "And whose fault is that?"

Daphne drew back. Just a tiny bit. "There is no way I am sending any of my daughters into marriage as hopelessly ignorant as I was."

"Charmingly ignorant," he murmured, crossing the room to take her hand.

She allowed him to tug her to her feet. "You didn't think it was so charming when I assumed you were impotent."

He winced. "Many things in life are more charming in retrospect."

"Simon . . ."

He nuzzled her ear. "Daphne . . ."

His mouth moved along the line of her throat, and she felt herself melting. Twenty-one years of marriage and still . . .

"At least draw the curtains," she murmured. Not that anyone could possibly see in with the sun shining so brightly, but she would feel more comfortable. They were in the middle of Mayfair, after all, with her entire circle of acquaintances quite possibly strolling outside the window.

He positively dashed over to the window but pulled shut only the sheer scrim. "I like to see you," he said with a boyish smile.

And then, with remarkable speed and agility, he adjusted the situation so that he was seeing *all* of her, and she was on the bed, moaning softly as he kissed the inside of her knee.

"Oh, Simon," she sighed. She knew exactly what he was going to do next. He'd move up, kissing and licking his way along her thigh.

And he did it *so* well.

"What are you thinking about?" he murmured.

"Right now?" she asked, trying to blink her way out of her daze. He had his tongue at the crease between her leg and her abdomen and he thought she could *think*?

"Do you know what I'm thinking?" he asked.

"If it's not about me, I'm going to be terribly disappointed."

He chuckled, moved his head so that he could drop a light kiss on her belly button, then scooted up to brush his lips softly against hers. "I was thinking how marvelous it is to know another person so completely."

She reached out and hugged him. She couldn't help it. She buried her face in the warm crook of his neck, inhaled the familiar scent of him, and said, "I love you."

"I adore you."

Oh, so he was going to make a competition of it, was he? She pulled away, just far enough to say, "I fancy you."

He quirked a brow. "You *fancy* me?"

"It was the best I could summon on such short notice." She gave a tiny shrug. "And besides, I do."

"Very well." His eyes darkened. "I *worship* you."

Daphne's lips parted. Her heart thumped, then flipped, and any facility she might have possessed for synonym retrieval flew right out of her. "I think you've won," she said, her voice so husky she barely recognized it.

He kissed her again, long, hot, and achingly sweet. "Oh, I know I have."

Her head fell back as he made his way down to her belly. "You still have to worship me," she said.

He moved lower. "In that, your grace, I am ever your servant."

And that was the last thing either of them said for quite some time.

Several days later Daphne found herself staring at her calendar once more. It had been forty-six days now since she'd last bled, and she still had not said anything to Simon. She knew that she should, but it felt somewhat premature. There could be another explanation for the lack of her courses—one had only to recall her last visit with her mother. Violet Bridgerton had been constantly fanning herself, insisting that the air was stifling even though Daphne had found it to be perfectly pleasant.

The one time Daphne had asked someone to light a fire, Violet had countermanded her with such ferocity that Daphne had half expected her to guard the grate with a poker.

"Do not so much as strike a match," Violet had growled.

To which Daphne had wisely replied, "I do believe I shall fetch a shawl." She looked at her mother's housemaid, shivering next to the fireplace. "Er, and perhaps you should, too."

But she did not feel hot *now*. She felt . . .

She did not know what she felt. Perfectly normal, really. Which was suspicious, as she had never felt the least bit normal while pregnant before.

"Mama!"

Daphne flipped over her calendar and looked up from her writing desk just in time to see her second daughter, Belinda, pause at the entrance of the room.

"Come in," Daphne said, welcoming the distraction. "Please."

Belinda sat down in a nearby comfortable chair, her bright blue eyes meeting her mother's with her usual directness. "You must do something about Caroline."

"*I* must?" Daphne queried, her voice lingering ever-so-slightly longer on the "I."

Belinda ignored the sarcasm. "If she does not stop talking about Frederick Snowe-Mann-Formsby, I shall go mad."

"Can't you simply ignore her?"

"His *name* is Frederick Snowe . . . Mann . . . *Formsby*!"

Daphne blinked.

"Snowman, Mama! Snowman!"

"It *is* unfortunate," Daphne allowed. "But, Lady Belinda Basset, do not forget that you could be likened to a rather droopy hound."

Belinda's gaze grew very jaded, and it became instantly clear that someone had indeed likened her to a basset hound.

"Oh," Daphne said, somewhat surprised that Belinda had never told her about it. "I'm so sorry."

"It was long ago," Belinda said with a sniff. "And I assure you, it was not said more than once."

Daphne pressed her lips together, trying not to smile. It was definitely not good form to encourage fisticuffs, but as she had fought her way to adulthood with seven siblings, four of them brothers, she could not help but utter a quiet "Well-done."

Belinda gave her a regal nod, then said, "Will you have a talk with Caroline?"

"What is it you wish for me to say?"

"I don't know. Whatever it is you usually say. It always seems to work."

There was a compliment in there somewhere, Daphne was fairly certain, but before she could dissect the sentence, her stomach did a nasty flip, followed by the oddest sort of squeeze, and then—

"Excuse me!" she yelped, and she made it to the washroom just in time to reach the chamber pot.

Oh dear God. This wasn't the change. She was pregnant.

"Mama?"

Daphne flicked her hand back at Belinda, trying to dismiss her.

"Mama? Are you all right?"

Daphne retched again.

"I'm getting Father," Belinda announced.

"No!" Daphne fairly howled.

"Was it the fish? Because I thought the fish tasted a bit dodgy."

Daphne nodded, hoping that would be the end of it.

"Oh, wait a moment, you didn't have the fish. I remember it quite distinctly."

Oh, bugger Belinda and her bloody attention to detail.

It was not the most maternal of sentiments, Daphne thought as she once again heaved her innards, but she was not feeling particularly charitable at the moment.

"You had the squab. I had the fish, and so did David, but you and Caroline ate only squab, and I think Father and Amelia had both, and we all had the soup, although—"

"Stop!" Daphne begged. She didn't want to talk about food. Even the mere mention . . .

"I think I had better get Father," Belinda said again.

"No, I'm fine," Daphne gasped, still jerking her hand behind her in a shushing motion. She didn't want Simon to see her like this. He would know instantly what was about.

Or perhaps more to the point, what was about to happen. In seven and a half months, give or take a few weeks.

"Very well," Belinda conceded, "but at least let me fetch your maid. You should be in bed."

Daphne threw up again.

"After you're through," Belinda corrected. "You should be in bed once you're through with . . . ah . . . *that*."

"My maid," Daphne finally agreed. Maria would deduce the

truth instantly, but she would not say a word to anyone, servants or family. And perhaps more pressing, Maria would know exactly what to bring as a remedy. It would taste vile and smell worse, but it would settle her stomach.

Belinda dashed off, and Daphne—once she was convinced there could be nothing left in her stomach—staggered to her bed. She held herself extremely still; even the slightest rocking motion made her feel as if she were at sea. "I'm too old for this," she moaned, because she was. Surely, she was. If she remained true to form—and really, why should this confinement be any different from the previous four—she would be gripped by nausea for at least two more months. The lack of food would keep her slender, but that would last only until mid-summer, when she would double in size, practically overnight. Her fingers would swell to the point that she could not wear her rings, she would not fit into any of her shoes, and even a single flight of stairs would leave her gasping for breath.

She would be an elephant. A two-legged, chestnut-haired elephant.

"Your grace!"

Daphne could not lift her head, so she lifted her hand instead, a pathetic silent greeting to Maria, who was by now standing by the bed, staring down at her with an expression of horror . . .

. . . that was quickly sliding into one of suspicion.

"Your grace," Maria said again, this time with unmistakable inflection. She smiled.

"I know," Daphne said. "I know."

"Does the duke know?"

"Not yet."

"Well, you won't be able to hide it for long."

"He leaves this afternoon for a few nights at Clyvedon," Daphne said. "I will tell him when he returns."

"You should tell him now," Maria said. Twenty years of employment did give a maid some license to speak freely.

Daphne carefully edged herself up into a reclining position, stopping once to calm a wave of nausea. "It might not take," she said. "At my age, they very often don't."

"Oh, I think it's taken," Maria said. "Have you looked in the mirror yet?"

Daphne shook her head.

"You're green."

"It might not—"

"You're not going to throw the baby up."

"Maria!"

Maria crossed her arms and speared Daphne with a stare. "You know the truth, your grace. You just don't want to admit it."

Daphne opened her mouth to speak, but she had nothing to say. She knew Maria was right.

"If the baby hadn't taken," Maria said, a bit more gently, "you wouldn't be feeling so sickly. My mum had eight babies after me, and four losses early on. She never was sick, not even once, with the ones that didn't take."

Daphne sighed and then nodded, conceding the point. "I'm still going to wait, though," she said. "Just a bit longer." She wasn't sure why she wanted to keep this to herself for a few more days, but she did. And as she was the one whose body was currently trying to turn itself inside out, she rather thought it was her decision to make.

"Oh, I almost forgot," Maria said. "We received word from your brother. He's coming to town next week."

"Colin?" Daphne asked.

Maria nodded. "With his family."

"They must stay with us," Daphne said. Colin and Penelope did not own a home in town, and to economize they tended to stay with either Daphne or their oldest brother, Anthony, who had inherited the title and all that went with it. "Please ask Belinda to pen a letter on my behalf, insisting that they come to Hastings House."

Maria gave a nod and departed.

Daphne moaned and went to sleep.

By the time Colin and Penelope arrived, with their four darling children in tow, Daphne was throwing up several times a day. Simon still didn't know about her condition; he'd been delayed in the country—something about a flooded field—and now he wasn't due back until the end of the week.

But Daphne wasn't going to let a queasy belly get in the way of greeting her favorite brother. "Colin!" she exclaimed, her smile growing positively giddy at the familiar sight of his sparkling green eyes. "It has been much too long."

"I fully agree," he said, giving her a quick hug while Penelope attempted to shoo their children into the house.

"No, you may not chase that pigeon!" she said sternly. "So sorry, Daphne, but—" She dashed back out onto the front steps, neatly nabbing seven-year-old Thomas by the collar.

"Be grateful your urchins are grown," Colin said with a chuckle as he took a step back. "We can't keep—Good God, Daff, what's wrong with you?"

Trust a brother to dispense with tact.

"You look awful," he said, as if he hadn't made that clear with his first statement.

"Just a bit under the weather," she mumbled. "I think it was the fish."

"Uncle Colin!"

Colin's attention was thankfully distracted by Belinda and Caroline, who were racing down the stairs with a decided lack of ladylike grace.

"You!" he said with a grin, pulling one into a hug. "And you!" He looked up. "Where's the other you?"

"Amelia's off shopping," Belinda said, before turning her attention to her little cousins. Agatha had just turned nine, Thomas was seven, and Jane was six. Little Georgie would be three the following month.

"You're getting so big!" Belinda said to Jane, beaming down at her.

"I grew two inches in the last month!" she announced.

"In the last year," Penelope corrected gently. She couldn't quite reach Daphne for a hug, so she leaned over and squeezed her hand. "I know your girls were quite grown-up last time I saw them, but I swear, I am still surprised by it every time."

"So am I," Daphne admitted. She still woke some mornings half expecting her girls to be in pinafores. The fact that they were ladies, fully grown . . .

It was baffling.

"Well, you know what they say about motherhood," Penelope said.

" 'They'?" Daphne murmured.

Penelope paused just long enough to shoot her a wry grin. "The years fly by, and the days are endless."

"That's impossible," Thomas announced.

Agatha let out an aggrieved sigh. "He's so literal."

Daphne reached out to ruffle Agatha's light brown hair. "Are you really only nine?" She adored Agatha, always had. There was something about that little girl, so serious and determined, that had always touched her heart.

Agatha, being Agatha, immediately recognized the question as rhetorical and popped up to her tiptoes to give her aunt a kiss.

Daphne returned the gesture with a peck on the cheek, then turned to the young family's nurse, standing near the doorway holding little Georgie. "And how are you, you darling thing?" she cooed, reaching out to take the boy into her arms. He was plump and blond with pink cheeks and a heavenly baby smell despite the fact that he wasn't really a baby any longer. "You look scrumptious," she said, pretending to take a nibble of his neck. She tested the weight of him, rocking slightly back and forth in that instinctive motherly way.

"You don't need to be rocked anymore, do you?" she murmured, kissing him again. His skin was so soft, and it took her back to her days as a young mother. She'd had nurses and nannies, of course, but she couldn't even count the number of times she'd crept into the children's rooms to sneak a kiss on the cheek and watch them sleep.

Ah well. She was sentimental. This was nothing new.

"How old are you now, Georgie?" she asked, thinking that maybe she *could* do this again. Not that she had much choice, but still, she felt reassured, standing here with this little boy in her arms.

Agatha tugged on her sleeve and whispered, "He doesn't talk."

Daphne blinked. "I beg your pardon?"

Agatha glanced over at her parents, as if she wasn't sure she should be saying anything. They were busy chatting with Belinda and Caroline and took no notice. "He doesn't talk," she said again. "Not a word."

Daphne pulled back slightly so that she could look at Georgie's face again. He smiled at her, his eyes crinkling at the corners exactly the same way Colin's did.

Daphne looked back at Agatha. "Does he understand what people say?"

Agatha nodded. "Every word. I'm sure of it." Her voice dropped to a whisper. "I think my mother and father are concerned."

A child nearing his third birthday without a word? Daphne was *sure* they were concerned. Suddenly the reason for Colin and Penelope's unexpected trip to town became clear. They were looking for guidance. Simon had been just the same way as a child. He hadn't spoken a word until he was four. And then he'd suffered a debilitating stutter for years. Even now, when he was particularly upset about something, it would creep back over him, and she'd hear it in his voice. A strange pause, a repeated sound, a halting catch. He was still self-conscious about it, although not nearly so much as he had been when they'd first met.

But she could see it in his eyes. A flash of pain. Or maybe anger. At himself, at his own weakness. Daphne supposed that there were some things people never got past, not completely.

Reluctantly, Daphne handed Georgie back to his nurse and urged Agatha toward the stairs. "Come along, darling," she said. "The nursery is waiting. We took out all of the girls' old toys."

She watched with pride as Belinda took Agatha by the hand. "You may play with my favorite doll," Belinda said with great gravity.

Agatha looked up at her cousin with an expression that could only be described as reverence and then followed her up the stairs.

Daphne waited until all the children were gone and then turned back to her brother and his wife. "Tea?" she asked. "Or do you wish to change out of your traveling clothes?"

"Tea," Penelope said with the sigh of an exhausted mother. "Please."

Colin nodded his agreement, and together they went into the drawing room. Once they were seated Daphne decided there was no point in being anything but direct. This was her brother, after all, and he knew he could talk to her about anything.

"You're worried about Georgie," she said. It was a statement, not a question.

"He hasn't said a word," Penelope said quietly. Her voice was even, but her throat caught in an uncomfortable swallow.

"He understands us," Colin said. "I'm sure of it. Just the other day I asked him to pick up his toys, and he did so. Immediately."

"Simon was the same way," Daphne said. She looked from Colin to Penelope and back. "I assume that is why you came? To speak with Simon?"

"We hoped he might offer some insight," Penelope said.

Daphne nodded slowly. "I'm sure he will. He was detained in the country, I'm afraid, but he is expected back before the week's end."

"There is no rush," Colin said.

Out of the corner of her eye, Daphne saw Penelope's shoulders slump. It was a tiny motion but one any mother would recognize. Penelope knew there was no rush. They had waited nearly three years for Georgie to talk; a few more days wouldn't make a difference. And yet she wanted so desperately to do *some*thing. To take an action, to make her child whole.

To have come this far only to find that Simon was gone . . . It had to be discouraging.

"I think it is a very good sign that he understands you," Daphne said. "I would be much more concerned if he did not."

"Everything else about him is completely normal," Penelope said passionately. "He runs, he jumps, he eats. He even reads, I think."

Colin turned to her in surprise. "He does?"

"I believe so," Penelope said. "I saw him with William's primer last week."

"He was probably just looking at the illustrations," Colin said gently.

"That's what I thought, but then I watched his eyes! They were moving back and forth, following the words."

They both turned to Daphne, as if she might have all the answers.

"I suppose he might be reading," Daphne said, feeling rather inadequate. She wanted to have all the answers. She wanted to say something to them other than *I suppose* or *Perhaps*. "He's rather young, but there's no reason he couldn't be reading."

"He's very bright," Penelope said.

Colin gave a look that was mostly indulgent. "Darling . . ."

"He is! And William read when he was four. Agatha, too."

"Actually," Colin admitted thoughtfully, "Agatha did start to read at three. Nothing terribly involved, but I know she was reading short words. I remember it quite well."

"Georgie is reading," Penelope said firmly. "I am sure of it."

"Well, then, that means we have even less to be concerned about," Daphne said with determined good cheer. "Any child who is reading before his third birthday will have no trouble speaking when he is ready to do so."

She had no idea if this was actually the case. But she rather thought it ought to be. And it *seemed* reasonable. And if Georgie turned out to have a stutter, just like Simon, his family would still love him and adore him and give him all the support he needed to grow into the wonderful person she knew he would be.

He'd have everything Simon hadn't had as a child.

"It will be all right," Daphne said, leaning forward to take Penelope's hand in hers. "You'll see."

Penelope's lips pressed together, and Daphne saw her throat tighten. She turned away, wanting to give her sister-in-law a moment to compose herself. Colin was munching on his third biscuit and reaching for a cup of tea, so Daphne decided to direct her next question to him.

"Is everything well with the rest of the children?" she asked.

He swallowed his tea. "Quite well. And yours?"

"David has got into a bit of mischief at school, but he seems to be settling down."

Colin picked up another biscuit. "And the girls aren't giving you fits?"

Daphne blinked with surprise. "No, of course not. Why do you ask?"

"You look terrible," he said.

"Colin!" Penelope interjected.

He shrugged. "She does. I asked about it when we first arrived."

"But still," his wife admonished, "you shouldn't—"

"If I can't say something to her, who can?" he said plainly. "Or more to the point, who *will*?"

Penelope dropped her voice to an urgent whisper. "It's not the sort of thing one talks about."

He stared at her for a moment. Then he looked at Daphne. Then he turned back to his wife. "I have no idea what you're talking about," he said.

Penelope's lips parted, and her cheeks went a bit pink. She looked over at Daphne, as if to say, *Well?*

Daphne just sighed. Was her condition *that* obvious?

Penelope gave Colin an impatient look. "She's—" She turned back to Daphne. "You are, aren't you?"

Daphne gave a tiny nod of confirmation.

Penelope looked at her husband with a certain degree of smugness. "She's pregnant."

Colin froze for about one half a second before continuing on in his usual unflappable manner. "No, she's not."

"She is," Penelope replied.

Daphne decided not to speak. She was feeling queasy, anyway.

"Her youngest is seventeen," Colin pointed out. He glanced over at Daphne. "He is, isn't he?"

"Sixteen," Daphne murmured.

"Sixteen," he repeated, directing this at Penelope. "Still."

"Still?"

"Still."

Daphne yawned. She couldn't help it. She was just *exhausted* these days.

"Colin," Penelope said, in that patient yet vaguely condescending tone that Daphne *loved* to hear directed at her brother, "David's age hardly has anything to do with—"

"I realize that," he cut in, giving her a vaguely annoyed look. "But don't you think, if she were going to . . ." He waved a hand in Daphne's general direction, leaving her to wonder if he could not bring himself to utter the word *pregnant* in relation to his own sister.

He cleared his throat. "Well, there wouldn't have been a sixteen-year gap."

Daphne closed her eyes for a moment, then let her head settle against the back of the sofa. She really *should* feel embarrassed. This was her brother. And even if he was using rather vague terms, he was talking about the most intimate aspects of her marriage.

She let out a tired little noise, something between a sigh and a hum. She was too sleepy to be embarrassed. And maybe too old, too. Women ought to be able to dispense with maidenly fits of modesty when they passed forty.

Besides, Colin and Penelope were bickering, and that was a good thing. It took their minds off Georgie.

Daphne found it rather entertaining, really. It was lovely to watch any of her brothers stuck in a stalemate with his wife.

Forty-one definitely wasn't too old to feel just a little bit of pleasure at the discomfort of one's brothers. Although—she yawned again—it would be more entertaining if she were a bit more alert to enjoy it. Still . . .

---

"Did she fall asleep?"

Colin stared at his sister in disbelief.

"I think she did," Penelope replied.

He stretched toward her, craning his neck for a better view. "There are so many things I could do to her right now," he mused. "Frogs, locusts, rivers turning to blood."

"Colin!"

"It's so tempting."

"It's also proof," Penelope said with a hint of a smirk.

"Proof?"

"She's pregnant! Just like I said." When he did not agree with her quickly enough, she added, "Have you ever known her to fall asleep in the middle of a conversation?"

"Not since—" He cut himself off.

Penelope's smirk grew significantly less subtle. "Exactly."

"I hate when you're right," he grumbled.

"I know. Pity for you I so often am."

He glanced back over at Daphne, who was starting to snore. "I suppose we should stay with her," he said, somewhat reluctantly.

"I'll ring for her maid," Penelope said.

"Do you think Simon knows?"

Penelope glanced over her shoulder once she reached the bell-pull. "I have no idea."

Colin just shook his head. "Poor bloke is in for the surprise of his life."

When Simon finally returned to London, fully one week delayed, he was exhausted. He had always been a more involved landowner than most of his peers—even as he found himself approaching the age of fifty. And so when several of his fields flooded, including one that provided the sole income for a tenant family, he rolled up his sleeves and got to work alongside his men.

Figuratively, of course. All sleeves had most definitely been down. It had been bloody cold in Sussex. Worse when one was wet. Which of course they all had been, what with the flood and all.

So he was tired, and he was still cold—he wasn't sure his fingers would ever regain their previous temperature—and he missed his family. He would have asked them to join him in the country, but the girls were preparing for the season, and Daphne had looked a bit peaked when he left.

He hoped she wasn't coming down with a cold. When she got sick, the entire household felt it.

She thought she was a stoic. He had once tried to point out that a true stoic wouldn't go about the house repeatedly saying, "No, no, I'm fine," as she sagged into a chair.

Actually, he had tried to point this out twice. The first time he said something she had not responded. At the time, he'd thought she hadn't heard him. In retrospect, however, it was far more likely that she had *chosen* not to hear him, because the second time he said something about the true nature of a stoic, her response had been such that . . .

Well, let it be said that when it came to his wife and the common cold, his lips would never again form words other than "You poor, poor dear" and "May I fetch you some tea?"

There were some things a man learned after two decades of marriage.

When he stepped into the front hall, the butler was waiting, his face in its usual mode—that is to say, completely devoid of expression.

"Thank you, Jeffries," Simon murmured, handing him his hat.

"Your brother-in-law is here," Jeffries told him.

Simon paused. "Which one?" He had seven.

"Mr. Colin Bridgerton, Your Grace. With his family."

Simon cocked his head. "Really?" He didn't hear chaos and commotion.

"They are out, your grace."

"And the duchess?"

"She is resting."

Simon could not suppress a groan. "She's not ill, is she?"

Jeffries, in a most un-Jeffries-like manner, blushed. "I could not say, your grace."

Simon regarded Jeffries with a curious eye. "Is she ill, or isn't she?"

Jeffries swallowed, cleared his throat, and then said, "I believe she is tired, your grace."

"Tired," Simon repeated, mostly to himself since it was clear that Jeffries would expire of inexplicable embarrassment if he pursued the conversation further. Shaking his head, he headed upstairs, adding, "Of course, she's tired. Colin's got four children under the age of ten, and she probably thinks she's got to mother the lot while they're here."

Maybe he'd have a lie-down next to her. He was exhausted, too, and he always slept better when she was near.

The door to their room was shut when he got to it, and he almost knocked—it was a habit to do so at a closed door, even if it did lead to his own bedchamber—but at the last moment he instead gripped the doorknob and gave a soft push. She could be sleeping. If she truly was tired, he ought to let her rest.

Stepping lightly, he entered the room. The curtains were partway drawn, and he could see Daphne lying in bed, still as a bone. He tiptoed closer. She *did* look pale, although it was hard to tell in the dim light.

He yawned and sat on the opposite side of the bed, leaning forward to pull off his boots. He loosened his cravat and then slid it off entirely, scooting himself toward her. He wasn't going to wake her, just snuggle up for a bit of warmth.

He'd missed her.

Settling in with a contented sigh, he put his arm around her, resting its weight just below her rib cage, and—

"Grughargh!"

Daphne shot up like a bullet and practically hurled herself from the bed.

"Daphne?" Simon sat up, too, just in time to see her race for the chamber pot.

The chamber pot????

"Oh dear," he said, wincing as she retched. "Fish?"

"Don't say that word," she gasped.

Must have been fish. They really needed to find a new fishmonger here in town.

He crawled out of bed to find a towel. "Can I get you anything?"

She didn't answer. He hadn't really expected her to. Still, he held out the towel, trying not to flinch when she threw up for what had to be the fourth time.

"You poor, poor dear," he murmured. "I'm so sorry this happened to you. You haven't been like this since—"

Since . . .

Oh, dear God.

"*Daphne?*" His voice shook. Hell, his whole body shook.

She nodded.

"But . . . how . . . ? "

"The usual way, I imagine," she said, gratefully taking the towel.

"But it's been— It's been—" He tried to think. He couldn't think. His brain had completely ceased working.

"I think I'm done," she said. She sounded exhausted. "Could you get me a bit of water?"

"Are you certain?" If he recalled correctly, the water would pop right back up and into the chamber pot.

"It's over there," she said, motioning weakly to a pitcher on a table. "I'm not going to swallow it."

He poured her a glass and waited while she swished out her mouth.

"Well," he said, clearing his throat several times, "I . . . ah . . ." He coughed again. He could not get a word out to save his life. And he couldn't blame his stutter this time.

"Everyone knows," Daphne said, placing her hand on his arm for support as she moved back to bed.

"Everyone?" he echoed.

"I hadn't planned to say anything until you returned, but they guessed."

He nodded slowly, still trying to absorb it all. A baby. At his age. At *her* age.

It was . . .

It was . . .

It was *amazing.*

Strange how it came over him so suddenly. But now, after the initial shock wore off, all he could feel was pure joy.

"This is wonderful news!" he exclaimed. He reached out to hug her, then thought better of it when he saw her pasty complexion. "You never cease to delight me," he said, instead giving her an awkward pat on the shoulder.

She winced and closed her eyes. "Don't rock the bed," she moaned. "You're making me seasick."

"You don't get seasick," he reminded her.

"I do when I'm expecting."

"You're an odd duck, Daphne Basset," he murmured, and then stepped back to A) stop rocking the bed and B) remove himself from her immediate vicinity should she take exception to the duck comparison.

(There was a certain history to this. While heavily pregnant with Amelia, she had asked him if she was radiant or if she just looked like a waddling duck. He told her she'd looked like a radiant duck. This had not been the correct answer.)

He cleared his throat and said, "You poor, poor dear."

Then he fled.

Several hours later Simon was seated at his massive oak desk, his elbows resting atop the smooth wood, his right index finger ringing the top of the brandy snifter that he had already refilled twice.

It had been a momentous day.

An hour or so after he'd left Daphne to her nap, Colin and Penelope had returned with their progeny, and they'd all had tea and biscuits in the breakfast room. Simon had started for the drawing room, but Penelope had requested an alternative, someplace without "expensive fabrics and upholstery."

Little Georgie had grinned up at him at that, his face still smeared with a substance Simon hoped was chocolate.

As Simon regarded the blanket of crumbs spilling from the table to the floor, along with the wet napkin they'd used to sop up Agatha's overturned tea, he remembered that he and Daphne had always taken their tea here when the children were small.

Funny how one forgot such details.

Once the tea party had dispersed, however, Colin had asked for a private word. They had repaired to Simon's study, and it was there that Colin confided in him about Georgie.

He wasn't talking.

His eyes were sharp. Colin thought he was reading.

But he wasn't talking.

Colin had asked for his advice, and Simon realized he had none. He'd thought about this, of course. It had haunted him every time Daphne had been pregnant, straight through until each of his children had begun to form sentences.

He supposed it would haunt him now. There would be another baby, another soul to love desperately . . . and worry over.

All he'd known to tell Colin was to love the boy. To talk to him, and praise him, and take him riding and fishing and all those things a father ought to do with a son.

All those things his father had never done with him.

He didn't think about him often these days, his father. He had Daphne to thank for that. Before they'd met, Simon had been obsessed with revenge. He'd wanted so badly to hurt his father, to make him suffer the way he had suffered as a boy, with all the pain and anguish of knowing he had been rejected and found wanting.

It hadn't mattered that his father was dead. Simon had thirsted for vengeance all the same, and it had taken love, first with Daphne and then with his children, to banish that ghost. He'd finally realized that he was free when Daphne had given him a bundle of letters from his father that had been entrusted into her care. He hadn't wanted to burn them; he hadn't wanted to rip them to shreds.

He hadn't particularly wanted to read them, either.

He'd looked down at the stack of envelopes, tied neatly with a red and gold ribbon, and realized that he felt nothing. Not anger, not sorrow, not even regret. It had been the greatest victory he could have imagined.

He wasn't sure how long the letters had sat in Daphne's desk.

He knew she'd put them in her bottom drawer, and every now and then he'd taken a peek to see if they were still there.

But eventually even that had tapered off. He hadn't forgotten about the letters—every now and then something would happen that would spring them to mind—but he'd forgotten about them with such constancy. And they had probably been absent from his mind for months when he opened his bottom desk drawer and saw that Daphne had moved them there.

That had been twenty years ago.

And although he still lacked the urge to burn or shred, he'd also never felt the need to open them.

Until now.

Well, no.

Maybe?

He looked at them again, still tied in that bow. *Did* he want to open them? Could there be anything in his father's letters that might be of help to Colin and Penelope as they guided Georgie through what might be a difficult childhood?

No. It was impossible. His father had been a hard man, unfeeling and unforgiving. He'd been so obsessed with his heritage and title that he'd turned his back on his only child. There could be nothing—nothing—that he might have written that could help Georgie.

Simon picked up the letters. The papers were dry. They smelled old.

The fire in the grate felt new. Hot, and bright, and redemptive. He stared at the flames until his vision blurred, just sat there for endless minutes, clutching his father's final words to him. They had not spoken for over five years when his father died. If there was anything the old duke had wanted to say to him, it would be here.

"Simon?"

He looked up slowly, barely able to pull himself from his daze. Daphne was standing in the doorway, her hand resting lightly on the edge of the door. She was dressed in her favorite pale blue dressing gown. She'd had it for years; every time he asked if she wanted to replace it, she refused. Some things were best soft and comfortable.

"Are you coming to bed?" she asked.

He nodded, coming to his feet. "Soon. I was just—" He cleared his throat, because the truth was—he wasn't sure what he'd been doing. He wasn't even sure what he'd been thinking. "How are you feeling?" he asked her.

"Better. It's always better in the evening." She took a few steps forward. "I had a bit of toast, and even some jam, and I—" She stopped, the only movement in her face the quick blink of her eyes. She was staring at the letters. He hadn't realized he was still holding them when he stood.

"Are you going to read them?" she asked quietly.

"I thought . . . perhaps . . ." He swallowed. "I don't know."

"But why now?"

"Colin told me about Georgie. I thought there might be something in here." He moved his hand slightly, holding the stack of letters just a little bit higher. "Something that might help him."

Daphne's lips parted, but several seconds passed before she was able to speak. "I think you might be one of the kindest, most generous men I have ever known."

He looked at her in confusion.

"I know you don't want to read those," she said.

"I really don't care—"

"No, you do," she interrupted gently. "Not enough to destroy them, but they still mean something to you."

"I hardly ever think about them," he said. It was the truth.

"I know." She reached out and took his hand, her thumb moving lightly over his knuckles. "But just because you let go of your father, it doesn't mean he never mattered."

He didn't speak. He didn't know what to say.

"I'm not surprised that if you do finally decide to read them, it will be to help someone else."

He swallowed, then grasped her hand like a lifeline.

"Do you want me to open them?"

He nodded, wordlessly handing her the stack.

Daphne moved to a nearby chair and sat, tugging at the ribbon until the bow fell loose. "Are these in order?" she asked.

"I don't know," he admitted. He sat back down behind his desk. It was far enough away that he couldn't see the pages.

She gave an acknowledging nod, then carefully broke the seal on the first envelope. Her eyes moved along the lines—or at least he thought they did. The light was too dim to see her expression clearly, but he had seen her reading letters enough times to know exactly what she must look like.

"He had terrible penmanship," Daphne murmured.

"Did he?" Now that he thought about it, Simon wasn't sure he'd ever seen his father's handwriting. He must have done, at some point. But it wasn't anything he recalled.

He waited a bit longer, trying not to hold his breath as she turned the page.

"He didn't write on the back," she said with some surprise.

"He wouldn't," Simon said. "He would never do anything that smacked of economization."

She looked up, her brows arched.

"The Duke of Hastings does not need to economize," Simon said dryly.

"Really?" She turned to the next page, murmuring, "I shall have to remember that the next time I go to the dressmaker."

He smiled. He loved that she could make him smile at such a moment.

After another few moments, she refolded the papers and looked up. She paused briefly, perhaps in case he wanted to say anything, and then when he did not, said, "It's rather dull, actually."

"Dull?" He wasn't sure what he had been expecting, but not this.

Daphne gave a little shrug. "It's about the harvest, and an improvement to the east wing of the house, and several tenants he suspects of cheating him." She pressed her lips together disapprovingly. "They weren't, of course. It is Mr. Miller and Mr. Bethum. They would never cheat anyone."

Simon blinked. He'd thought his father's letters might include an apology. Or if not that, then more accusations of inadequacy. It had never occurred to him that his father might have simply sent him an accounting of the estate.

"Your father was a very suspicious man," Daphne muttered.

"Oh, yes."

"Shall I read the next?"

"Please do."

She did, and it was much the same, except this time it was about a bridge that needed repairing and a window that had not been made to his specifications.

And on it went. Rents, accounts, repairs, complaints . . . There was the occasional overture, but nothing more personal than *I am considering hosting a shooting party next month, do let me know if you are interested in attending.* It was astounding. His father had not only denied his existence when he'd thought him a stuttering idiot, he'd managed to deny his own denial once Simon was speaking clearly and up to snuff. He acted as if it had never happened, as if he had never wished his own son were dead.

"Good God," Simon said, because *some*thing had to be said.

Daphne looked up. "Hmmm?"

"Nothing," he muttered.

"It's the last one," she said, holding the letter up.

He sighed.

"Do you want me to read it?"

"Of course," he said sarcastically. "It might be about rents. Or accounts."

"Or a bad harvest," Daphne quipped, obviously trying not to smile.

"Or that," he replied.

"Rents," she said once she'd finished reading. "And accounts."

"The harvest?"

She smiled slightly. "It was good that season."

Simon closed his eyes for a moment, as a strange tension eased from his body.

"It's odd," Daphne said. "I wonder why he never mailed these to you."

"What do you mean?"

"Well, he didn't. Don't you recall? He held on to all of them, then gave them to Lord Middlethorpe before he died."

"I suppose it was because I was out of the country. He wouldn't have known where to send them."

"Oh yes, of course." She frowned. "Still, I find it interesting that he would take the time to write you letters with no hope of sending them to you. If I were going to write letters to someone I couldn't send them to, it would be because I had something to say, something meaningful that I would want them to know, even after I was gone."

"One of the many ways in which you are unlike my father," Simon said.

She smiled ruefully. "Well, yes. I suppose." She stood, setting the letters down on a small table. "Shall we go to bed?"

He nodded and walked to her side. But before he took her arm, he reached down, scooped up the letters, and tossed them into the fire. Daphne let out a little gasp as she turned in time to see them blacken and shrivel.

"There's nothing worth saving," he said. He leaned down and kissed her, once on the nose and then once on the mouth. "Let's go to bed."

"What are you going to tell Colin and Penelope?" she asked as they walked arm in arm toward the stairs.

"About Georgie? The same thing I told them this afternoon." He kissed her again, this time on her brow. "Just love him. That's all they can do. If he talks, he talks. If he doesn't, he doesn't. But either way, it will all be fine, as long as they just love him."

"You, Simon Arthur Fitzranulph Basset, are a very good father."

He tried not to puff with pride. "You forgot the Henry."

"What?"

"Simon Arthur *Henry* Fitzranulph Basset."

She pfffted that. "You have too many names."

"But not too many children." He stopped walking and tugged her toward him until they were face to face. He rested one hand lightly on her abdomen. "Do you think we can do it all once more?"

She nodded. "As long as I have you."

"No," he said softly. "As long as I have *you*."

# BRIDGERTON

# THE VISCOUNT WHO LOVED ME

*For Little Goose Twist,*

*who kept me company throughout the writing of this book.*

*I can't wait to meet you!*

*And also for Paul,*

*even though he is allergic to musicals.*

# *Prologue*

Anthony Bridgerton had always known he would die young.

Oh, not as a child. Young Anthony had never had cause to ponder his own mortality. His early years had been a young boy's perfection, right from the very day of his birth.

It was true that Anthony was the heir to an ancient and wealthy viscountcy, but unlike most other aristocratic couples, Lord and Lady Bridgerton were very much in love, and they saw their son's birth not as the arrival of an heir, but rather that of a child.

And so there were no parties, no fêtes, no celebration other than that of mother and father staring in wonderment at their new son.

The Bridgertons were young parents—Edmund barely twenty and Violet just eighteen—but they were sensible and they were strong, and they loved their son with a fierceness and devotion that was rarely seen in their social circles. Much to her own mother's horror, Violet insisted upon nursing the boy herself, and Edmund never subscribed to the prevailing attitude that fathers should neither see nor hear their children. He took the infant on long hikes across the fields of Kent, spoke to him of philosophy and poetry before he could possibly understand the words, and told him a bedtime story every night.

Because the viscount and viscountess were so young and so very much in love, it came as no surprise to anyone when, just two years after Anthony's birth, he was joined by a younger brother, christened Benedict. Edmund immediately adjusted his daily routine to take two sons on his hikes, and he spent a week holed up in the stables, working with his leatherworker to devise a special pack that would hold Anthony on his back while he held the baby Benedict in his arms.

They walked across fields and streams, and he told them of wondrous things, of perfect flowers and clear blue skies, of knights in shining armor and damsels in distress. Violet used to laugh when they returned all windblown and sunkissed, and Edmund would say, "See? Here is our damsel in distress. Clearly we must save her." And Anthony would throw himself into his mother's arms, giggling as he swore he'd protect her from the fire-breathing dragon they'd seen just *two miles down the road* in the village.

"Two miles down the road in the village?" Violet would breathe, keeping her voice carefully laden with horror. "Heaven above, what would I do without three strong men to protect me?"

"Benedict's a baby," Anthony would reply.

"But he'll grow up," she'd always say, tousling his hair, "just as you did. And just as you still will."

Edmund always treated his children with equal affection and devotion, but late at night, when Anthony cradled the Bridgerton pocket watch to his chest (given to him on his eighth birthday by his father, who had received it on his eighth birthday from *his* father), he liked to think that his relationship with his father was just a little bit special. Not because Edmund loved him best; by that point the Bridgerton siblings numbered four (Colin and Daphne had arrived fairly close together) and Anthony knew very well that all the children were well loved.

No, Anthony liked to think that his relationship with his father was special simply because he'd known him the longest. After all, no matter how long Benedict had known their father, Anthony would always have two years on him. And six on Colin. And as for Daphne, well, besides the fact that she was a girl (the horror!), she'd known Father a full eight years less than he had and, he liked to remind himself, always would.

Edmund Bridgerton was, quite simply, the very center of Anthony's world. He was tall, his shoulders were broad, and he could ride a horse as if he'd been born in the saddle. He always knew the answers to arithmetic questions (even when the tutor didn't), he saw no reason why his sons should not have a tree house (and then he went and built it himself), and his laugh was the sort that warmed a body from the inside out.

Edmund taught Anthony how to ride. He taught Anthony how to shoot. He taught him to swim. He took him off to Eton himself, rather than sending him in a carriage with servants, as most of Anthony's future friends arrived, and when he saw Anthony glancing nervously about the school that would become his new home, he had a heart-to-heart talk with his eldest son, assuring him that everything would be all right.

And it was. Anthony knew it would be. His father, after all, never lied.

Anthony loved his mother. Hell, he'd probably bite off his own arm if it meant keeping her safe and well. But growing up, everything he did, every accomplishment, every goal, every single hope and dream—it was all for his father.

And then one day, everything changed. It was funny, he reflected later, how one's life could alter in an instant, how one minute everything could be a certain way, and the next it's simply . . . not.

It happened when Anthony was eighteen, home for the summer

and preparing for his first year at Oxford. He was to belong to All Souls College, as his father had before him, and his life was as bright and dazzling as any eighteen-year-old had a right to enjoy. He had discovered women, and perhaps more splendidly, they had discovered him. His parents were still happily reproducing, having added Eloise, Francesca, and Gregory to the family, and Anthony did his best not to roll his eyes when he passed his mother in the hall—pregnant with her *eighth* child! It was all a bit unseemly, in Anthony's opinion, having children at their age, but he kept his opinions to himself.

Who was he to doubt Edmund's wisdom? Maybe he, too, would want more children at the advanced age of thirty-eight.

When Anthony found out, it was late afternoon. He was returning from a long and bruising ride with Benedict and had just pushed through the front door of Aubrey Hall, the ancestral home of the Bridgertons, when he saw his ten-year-old-sister sitting on the floor. Benedict was still in the stables, having lost some silly bet with Anthony, the terms of which required him to rub down both horses.

Anthony stopped short when he saw Daphne. It was odd enough that his sister was sitting in the middle of the floor in the main hall. It was even more odd that she was crying.

Daphne never cried.

"Daff," he said hesitantly, too young to know what to do with a crying female and wondering if he'd ever learn, "what—"

But before he could finish his question, Daphne lifted her head, and the shattering heartbreak in her large brown eyes cut through him like a knife. He stumbled back a step, knowing something was wrong, terribly wrong.

"He's dead," Daphne whispered. "Papa is dead."

For a moment Anthony was sure he'd misheard. His father

couldn't be dead. Other people died young, like Uncle Hugo, but Uncle Hugo had been small and frail. Well, at least smaller and frailer than Edmund.

"You're wrong," he told Daphne. "You must be wrong."

She shook her head. "Eloise told me. He was . . . it was . . ."

Anthony knew he shouldn't shake his sister while she sobbed, but he couldn't help himself. "It was *what*, Daphne?"

"A bee," she whispered. "He was stung by a bee."

For a moment Anthony could do nothing but stare at her. Finally, his voice hoarse and barely recognizable, he said, "A man doesn't die from a bee sting, Daphne."

She said nothing, just sat there on the floor, her throat working convulsively as she tried to control her tears.

"He's been stung before," Anthony added, his voice rising in volume. "I was with him. We were both stung. We came across a nest. I was stung on the shoulder." Unbidden, his hand rose to touch the spot where he'd been stung so many years before. In a whisper he added, "He on his arm."

Daphne just stared at him with an eerily blank expression.

"He was fine," Anthony insisted. He could hear the panic in his voice and knew he was frightening his sister, but he was powerless to control it. "A man can't die from a bee sting!"

Daphne shook her head, her dark eyes suddenly looking about a hundred years old. "It was a bee," she said in a hollow voice. "Eloise saw it. One minute he was just standing there, and the next he was . . . he was . . ."

Anthony felt something very strange building within him, as if his muscles were about to jump through his skin. "The next he was *what*, Daphne?"

"Gone." She looked bewildered by the word, as bewildered as he felt.

Anthony left Daphne sitting in the hall and took the stairs three at a time up to his parents' bedchamber. Surely his father wasn't dead. A man couldn't die from a bee sting. It was impossible. Utterly mad. Edmund Bridgerton was young, he was strong. He was tall, his shoulders were broad, his muscles were powerful, and by God, no insignificant honeybee could have felled him.

But when Anthony reached the upstairs hall, he could tell by the utter and complete silence of the dozen or so hovering servants that the situation was grim.

And their pitying faces . . . for the rest of his life he'd be haunted by those pitying faces.

He'd thought he'd have to push his way into his parents' room, but the servants parted as if they were drops in the Red Sea, and when Anthony pushed open the door, he knew.

His mother was sitting on the edge of the bed, not weeping, not even making a sound, just holding his father's hand as she rocked slowly back and forth.

His father was still. Still as . . .

Anthony didn't even want to think the word.

"Mama?" he choked out. He hadn't called her that for years; she'd been "Mother" since he'd left for Eton.

She turned, slowly, as if hearing his voice through a long, long tunnel.

"What happened?" he whispered.

She shook her head, her eyes hopelessly far away. "I don't know," she said. Her lips remained parted by an inch or so, as if she'd meant to say something more but then forgotten to do it.

Anthony took a step forward, his movements awkward and jerky.

"He's gone," Violet finally whispered. "He's gone and I . . . oh,

God, I . . ." She placed a hand on her belly, full and round with child. "I told him—oh, Anthony, I told him—"

She looked as if she might shatter from the inside out. Anthony choked back the tears that were burning his eyes and stinging his throat and moved to her side. "It's all right, Mama," he said.

But he knew it wasn't all right.

"I told him this had to be our last," she gasped, sobbing onto his shoulder. "I told him I couldn't carry another, and we'd have to be careful, and . . . Oh, God, Anthony, what I'd do to have him here and give him another child. I don't understand. I just don't understand. . . ."

Anthony held her while she cried. He said nothing; it seemed useless to try to make any words fit the devastation in his heart.

He didn't understand, either.

The doctors came later that evening and pronounced themselves baffled. They'd heard of such things before, but never in one so young and strong. He was so vital, so powerful; nobody could have known. It was true that the viscount's younger brother Hugo had died quite suddenly the year before, but such things did not necessarily run in families, and besides, even though Hugo had died by himself out-of-doors, no one had noticed a bee sting on his skin.

Then again, nobody had looked.

Nobody could have known, the doctors kept saying, over and over until Anthony wanted to strangle them all. Eventually he got them out of the house, and he put his mother to bed. They had to move her into a spare bedroom; she grew agitated at the thought of sleeping in the bed she'd shared for so many years with Edmund. Anthony managed to send his six siblings to bed as well, telling them that they'd all talk in the morning, that everything would be well, and he would take care of them as their father would have wanted.

Then he walked into the room where his father's body still lay and looked at him. He looked at him and looked at him, staring at him for hours, barely blinking.

And when he left the room, he left with a new vision of his own life, and new knowledge about his own mortality.

Edmund Bridgerton had died at the age of thirty-eight. And Anthony simply couldn't imagine ever surpassing his father in any way, even in years.

# Chapter 1

*The topic of rakes has, of course, been previously discussed in this column, and This Author has come to the conclusion that there are rakes, and there are Rakes.*

*Anthony Bridgerton is a Rake.*

*A rake (lower-case) is youthful and immature. He flaunts his exploits, behaves with utmost idiocy, and thinks himself dangerous to women.*

*A Rake (upper-case)* knows *he is dangerous to women.*

*He doesn't flaunt his exploits because he doesn't need to. He knows he will be whispered about by men and women alike, and in fact, he'd rather they didn't whisper about him at all. He knows who he is and what he has done; further recountings are, to him, redundant.*

*He doesn't behave like an idiot for the simple reason that he isn't an idiot (any moreso than must be expected among all members of the male gender). He has little patience for the foibles of society, and quite frankly, most of the time This Author cannot say she blames him.*

*And if that doesn't describe Viscount Bridgerton—surely*

*this season's most eligible bachelor—to perfection, This Author shall retire Her quill immediately. The only question is: Will 1814 be the season he finally succumbs to the exquisite bliss of matrimony?*

*This Author Thinks . . .*

*Not.*

LADY WHISTLEDOWN'S SOCIETY PAPERS,
20 APRIL 1814

"Please don't tell me," Kate Sheffield said to the room at large, "that she is writing about Viscount Bridgerton again."

Her half-sister Edwina, younger by almost four years, looked up from behind the single-sheet newspaper. "How could you tell?"

"You're giggling like a madwoman."

Edwina giggled, shaking the blue damask sofa on which they both sat.

"See?" Kate said, giving her a little poke in the arm. "You always giggle when she writes about some reprehensible rogue." But Kate grinned. There was little she liked better than teasing her sister. In a good-natured manner, of course.

Mary Sheffield, Edwina's mother, and Kate's stepmother for nearly eighteen years, glanced up from her embroidery and pushed her spectacles farther up the bridge of her nose. "What are you two laughing about?"

"Kate's in a snit because Lady Whistledown is writing about that rakish viscount again," Edwina explained.

"I'm not in a snit," Kate said, even though no one was listening.

"Bridgerton?" Mary asked absently.

Edwina nodded. "Yes."

"She always writes about him."

"I think she just likes writing about rakes," Edwina commented.

"Of course she likes writing about rakes," Kate retorted. "If she wrote about boring people, no one would buy her newspaper."

"That's not true," Edwina replied. "Just last week she wrote about us, and heaven knows we're not the most interesting people in London."

Kate smiled at her sister's naïveté. Kate and Mary might not be the most interesting people in London, but Edwina, with her buttery-colored hair and startlingly pale blue eyes, had already been named the Incomparable of 1814. Kate, on the other hand, with her plain brown hair and eyes, was usually referred to as "the Incomparable's older sister."

She supposed there were worse monikers. At least no one had yet begun to call her "the Incomparable's spinster sister." Which was a great deal closer to the truth than any of the Sheffields cared to admit. At twenty (nearly twenty-one, if one was going to be scrupulously honest about it), Kate was a bit long in the tooth to be enjoying her first season in London.

But there hadn't really been any other choice. The Sheffields hadn't been wealthy even when Kate's father had been alive, and since he'd passed on five years earlier, they'd been forced to economize even further. They certainly weren't ready for the poorhouse, but they had to mind every penny and watch every pound.

With their straitened finances, the Sheffields could manage the funds for only one trip to London. Renting a house—and a carriage—and hiring the bare minimum of servants for the season cost money. More money than they could afford to spend twice. As it was, they'd had to save for five solid years to be able to afford this trip to London. And if the girls weren't successful on the Marriage Mart . . . well, no one was going to clap them into debtor's prison, but they would have to look forward to a quiet life of genteel poverty at some charmingly small cottage in Somerset.

And so the two girls were forced to make their debuts in the same year. It had been decided that the most logical time would be when Edwina was just seventeen and Kate almost twenty-one. Mary would have liked to have waited until Edwina was eighteen, and a bit more mature, but that would have made Kate nearly twenty-two, and heavens, but who would marry her then?

Kate smiled wryly. She hadn't even wanted a season. She'd known from the outset that she wasn't the sort who would capture the attention of the *ton*. She wasn't pretty enough to overcome her lack of dowry, and she'd never learned to simper and mince and walk delicately, and do all those things other girls seemed to know how to do in the cradle. Even Edwina, who didn't have a devious bone in her body, somehow knew how to stand and walk and sigh so that men came to blows just for the honor of helping her cross the street.

Kate, on the other hand, always stood with her shoulders straight and tall, couldn't sit still if her life depended upon it, and walked as if she were in a race—and why not? she always wondered. If one was going somewhere, what could possibly be the point in not getting there quickly?

As for her current season in London, she didn't even like the city very much. Oh, she was having a good enough time, and she'd met quite a few nice people, but a London season seemed a horrible waste of money to a girl who would have been perfectly content to remain in the country and find some sensible man to marry there.

But Mary would have none of that. "When I married your father," she'd said, "I vowed to love you and bring you up with all the care and affection I'd give to a child of my own blood."

Kate had managed to get in a single, "But—" before Mary carried on with, "I have a responsibility to your poor mother, God rest her soul, and part of that responsibility is to see you married off happily and securely."

"I could be happy and secure in the country," Kate had replied.

Mary had countered, "There are more men from which to choose in London."

After which Edwina had joined in, insisting that she would be utterly miserable without her, and since Kate never could bear to see her sister unhappy, her fate had been sealed.

And so here she was—sitting in a somewhat faded drawing room in a rented house in a section of London that was almost fashionable, and . . .

She looked about mischievously.

. . . and she was about to snatch a newspaper from her sister's grasp.

"Kate!" Edwina squealed, her eyes bugging out at the tiny triangle of newsprint that remained between her right thumb and forefinger. "I wasn't done yet!"

"You've been reading it forever," Kate said with a cheeky grin. "Besides, I want to see what she has to say about Viscount Bridgerton today."

Edwina's eyes, which were usually compared to peaceful Scottish lochs, glinted devilishly. "You're *awfully* interested in the viscount, Kate. Is there something you're not telling us?"

"Don't be silly. I don't even know the man. And if I did, I would probably run in the opposite direction. He is exactly the sort of man the two of us should avoid at all costs. He could probably seduce an iceberg."

"Kate!" Mary exclaimed.

Kate grimaced. She'd forgotten her stepmother was listening. "Well, it's true," she added. "I've heard he's had more mistresses than I've had birthdays."

Mary looked at her for a few seconds, as if trying to decide whether or not she wanted to respond, and then finally she said, "Not that this is an appropriate topic for your ears, but many men have."

"Oh." Kate flushed. There was little less appealing than being decisively contradicted while one was trying to make a grand point. "Well, then, he's had twice as many. Whatever the case, he's far more promiscuous than most men, and not the sort Edwina ought to allow to court her."

"*You* are enjoying a season as well," Mary reminded her.

Kate shot Mary the most sarcastic of glances. They all knew that if the viscount chose to court a Sheffield, it would not be Kate.

"I don't think there is anything in there that's going to alter your opinion," Edwina said with a shrug as she leaned toward Kate to get a better view of the newspaper. "She doesn't say very much about *him*, actually. It's more of a treatise on the topic of rakes."

Kate's eyes swept over the typeset words. "Hmmph," she said, her favorite expression of disdain. "I'll wager she's correct. He probably won't come up to scratch this year."

"You always think Lady Whistledown is correct," Mary murmured with a smile.

"She usually is," Kate replied. "You must admit, for a gossip columnist, she displays remarkable good sense. She has certainly been correct in her assessment of all the people I have met thus far in London."

"You should make your own judgments, Kate," Mary said lightly. "It is beneath you to base your opinions on a gossip column."

Kate knew her stepmother was right, but she didn't want to admit it, and so she just let out another "Hmmph" and turned back to the paper in her hands.

*Whistledown* was, without a doubt, the most interesting reading material in all London. Kate wasn't entirely certain when the gossip column had begun—sometime the previous year, she'd heard—but one thing was certain. Whoever Lady Whistledown was (and no one *really* knew who she was), she was a well-connected member of the *ton.* She had to be. No interloper could ever uncover all the gossip she printed in her columns every Monday, Wednesday, and Friday.

Lady Whistledown always had all the latest *on-dits*, and unlike other columnists, she wasn't hesitant about using people's full names. Having decided last week, for example, that Kate didn't look good in yellow, she wrote, clear as day: "The color yellow makes the dark-haired Miss Katharine Sheffield look like a singed daffodil."

Kate hadn't minded the insult. She'd heard it said on more than one occasion that one could not consider oneself "arrived" until one had been insulted by Lady Whistledown. Even Edwina, who was a huge social success by anyone's measure, had been jealous that Kate had been singled out for an insult.

And even though Kate didn't particularly want to be in London for a season, she figured that if she had to participate in the social whirl, she might as well not be a complete and utter failure. If getting insulted in a gossip column was to be her only sign of success, well then, so be it. Kate would take her triumphs where she may.

Now when Penelope Featherington bragged about being likened to an overripe citrus fruit in her tangerine satin, Kate could wave her arm and sigh with great drama, "Yes, well, I am a singed daffodil."

"Someday," Mary announced out of the blue, giving her spectacles yet another push with her index finger, "someone is going to discover that woman's true identity, and then she's going to be in trouble."

Edwina looked at her mother with interest. "Do you really think someone will ferret her out? She has managed to keep her secret for over a year now."

"Nothing that big can stay a secret forever," Mary replied. She jabbed her embroidery with her needle, pulling a long strand of yellow thread through the fabric. "Mark my words. It's all going to come out sooner or later, and when it does, a scandal the likes of which you have never seen is going to erupt all over town."

"Well, if I knew who she was," Kate announced, flipping the single-sheet newspaper over to page two, "I'd probably make her my best friend. She's fiendishly entertaining. And no matter what anyone says, she's almost always right."

Just then, Newton, Kate's somewhat overweight corgi, trotted into the room.

"Isn't that dog supposed to stay outside?" Mary asked. Then she yelped, "Kate!" as the dog angled over to her feet and panted as if waiting for a kiss.

"Newton, come here this minute," Kate ordered.

The dog gazed longingly at Mary, then waddled over to Kate, hopped up onto the sofa, and laid his front paws across her lap.

"He's covering you with fur," Edwina said.

Kate shrugged as she stroked his thick, caramel-colored coat. "I don't mind."

Edwina sighed, but she reached out and gave Newton a quick pat, anyway. "What else does she say?" she asked, leaning forward with interest. "I never did get to see page two."

Kate smiled at her sister's sarcasm. "Not much. A little something about the Duke and Duchess of Hastings, who apparently arrived in town earlier this week, a list of the food at Lady Danbury's ball, which she proclaimed 'surprisingly delicious,' and a rather unfortunate description of Mrs. Featherington's gown Monday last."

Edwina frowned. "She does seem to pick on the Featheringtons quite a bit."

"And no wonder," Mary said, setting down her embroidery as she stood up. "That woman wouldn't know how to pick out a dress color for her girls if a rainbow wrapped itself right around her neck."

"Mother!" Edwina exclaimed.

Kate clapped a hand over her mouth, trying not to laugh. Mary rarely made such opinionated pronouncements, but when she did, they were always marvelous.

"Well, it's true. She keeps dressing her youngest in tangerine. Anyone can see that poor girl needs a blue or a mint green."

"You dressed me in yellow," Kate reminded her.

"And I'm sorry I did. That will teach me to listen to a shopgirl. I should never have doubted my own judgment. We'll simply have to have that one cut down for Edwina."

Since Edwina was a full head shorter than Kate, and several shades more delicate, this would not be a problem.

"When you do," Kate said, turning to her sister, "make sure you eliminate the ruffle on the sleeve. It's dreadfully distracting. *And* it itches. I had half a mind to rip it off right there at the Ashbourne ball."

Mary rolled her eyes. "I am both surprised and thankful that you saw fit to restrain yourself."

"I am surprised but not thankful," Edwina said with a mischievous smile. "Just think of the fun Lady Whistledown would have had with *that*."

"Ah, yes," Kate said, returning her grin. "I can see it now. 'The singed daffodil rips off her petals.' "

"I am going upstairs," Mary announced, shaking her head at her daughters' antics. "Do try not to forget that we have a party to attend this evening. You girls may want to get a bit of rest before we go out. It's sure to be another late night for us."

Kate and Edwina nodded and murmured promises to that effect as Mary gathered her embroidery and left the room. As soon as she was gone, Edwina turned to Kate and asked, "Have you decided what you're going to wear tonight?"

"The green gauze, I think. I should wear white, I know, but I fear it does not suit me."

"If you don't wear white," Edwina said loyally, "then neither shall I. I shall wear my blue muslin."

Kate nodded her approval as she glanced back at the newspaper in her hand, trying to balance Newton, who had flipped over onto his back and was angling to have his belly rubbed. "Just last week Mr. Berbrooke said you are an angel in blue. On account of it matching your eyes so well."

Edwina blinked in surprise. "Mr. Berbrooke said that? To you?"

Kate looked back up. "Of course. All of your beaux try to pass on their compliments through me."

"They do? Whyever?"

Kate smiled slowly and indulgently. "Well, now, Edwina, it might have something to do with the time you announced to the entire audience at the Smythe-Smith musicale that you could never marry without your sister's approval."

Edwina's cheeks turned just the slightest bit pink. "It wasn't the entire audience," she mumbled.

"It might as well have been. The news traveled faster than fire on rooftops. I wasn't even in the room at the time and it only took two minutes for me to hear about it."

Edwina crossed her arms and let out a "Hmmph" that made her sound rather like her older sister. "Well, it's true, and I don't care who knows it. I know I'm expected to make a grand and brilliant match, but I don't have to marry someone who will ill treat me. Anyone with the fortitude to actually impress *you* would have to be up to snuff."

"Am I so difficult to impress, then?"

The two sisters looked at each other, then answered in unison, "Yes."

But as Kate laughed along with Edwina, a niggling sense of guilt rose within her. All three Sheffields knew that it would be Edwina who would snag a nobleman or marry into a fortune. It would be Edwina who would ensure that her family would not have to live out their lives in genteel poverty. Edwina was a beauty, while Kate was . . .

Kate was Kate.

Kate didn't mind. Edwina's beauty was simply a fact of life. There were certain truths Kate had long since come to accept. Kate would never learn to waltz without trying to take the lead; she'd always be afraid of electrical storms, no matter how often she told herself she was being silly; and no matter what she wore, no matter how she dressed her hair or pinched her cheeks, she'd never be as pretty as Edwina.

Besides, Kate wasn't certain that she'd like all the attention Edwina received. Nor, she was coming to realize, would she relish the responsibility of having to marry well to provide for her mother and sister.

"Edwina," Kate said softly, her eyes growing serious, "you don't have to marry anyone you don't like. You know that."

Edwina nodded, suddenly looking as if she might cry.

"If you decide there isn't a single gentleman in London who is good enough for you, then so be it. We shall simply go back to

Somerset and enjoy our own company. There's no one I like better, anyway."

"Nor I," Edwina whispered.

"And if you do find a man who sweeps you off your feet, then Mary and I shall be delighted. You should not worry about leaving us, either. We shall get on fine with each other for company."

"You might find someone to marry as well," Edwina pointed out.

Kate felt her lips twist into a small smile. "I might," she allowed, knowing that it probably wasn't true. She didn't want to remain a spinster her entire life, but she doubted she would find a husband here in London. "Perhaps one of your lovesick suitors will turn to me once he realizes you are unattainable," she teased.

Edwina swatted her with a pillow. "Don't be silly."

"But I'm not!" Kate protested. And she wasn't. Quite frankly, this seemed to her the most likely avenue by which she might actually find a husband in town.

"Do you know what sort of man I'd like to marry?" Edwina asked, her eyes turning dreamy.

Kate shook her head.

"A scholar."

"A *scholar*?"

"A scholar," Edwina said firmly.

Kate cleared her throat. "I'm not certain you'll find many of those in town for the season."

"I know." Edwina let out a little sigh. "But the truth is—and you know this even if I am not supposed to let on in public—I'm really rather bookish. I'd much rather spend my day in a library than gadding about in Hyde Park. I think I should enjoy life with a man who enjoyed scholarly pursuits as well."

"Right. Hmmm . . ." Kate's mind worked frantically. Edwina wasn't likely to find a scholar back in Somerset, either. "You know,

Edwina, it might be difficult to find you a true scholar outside the university towns. You might have to settle for a man who likes to read and learn as you do."

"That would be all right," Edwina said happily. "I'd be quite content with an amateur scholar."

Kate breathed a sigh of relief. Surely they could find someone in London who liked to read.

"And do you know what?" Edwina added. "You truly cannot tell a book by its cover. All sorts of people are amateur scholars. Why, even that Viscount Bridgerton Lady Whistledown keeps talking about might be a scholar at heart."

"Bite your tongue, Edwina. You are not to have anything to do with Viscount Bridgerton. Everyone knows he is the worst sort of rake. In fact, he's the worst rake, period. In all London. In the entire country!"

"I know, I was just using him as an example. Besides, he's not likely to choose a bride this year, anyway. Lady Whistledown said so, and you yourself said that she is almost always right."

Kate patted her sister on the arm. "Don't worry. We will find you a suitable husband. But *not*—not not not not not Viscount Bridgerton!"

At that very moment, the subject of their discussion was relaxing at White's with two of his three younger brothers, enjoying a late afternoon drink.

Anthony Bridgerton leaned back in his leather chair, regarded his scotch with a thoughtful expression as he swirled it about, and then announced, "I'm thinking about getting married."

Benedict Bridgerton, who had been indulging in a habit his mother detested—tipping his chair drunkenly on the back two legs—fell over.

Colin Bridgerton started to choke.

Luckily for Colin, Benedict regained his seat with enough time to smack him soundly on the back, sending a green olive sailing across the table.

It narrowly missed Anthony's ear.

Anthony let the indignity pass without comment. He was all too aware that his sudden declaration had come as a bit of a surprise.

Well, perhaps more than a bit. "Complete," "total," and "utter" were words that came to mind.

Anthony knew that he did not fit the image of a man who had settling down on his mind. He'd spent the last decade as the worst sort of rake, taking pleasure where he may. For as he well knew, life was short and certainly meant to be enjoyed. Oh, he'd had a certain code of honor. He never dallied with well-bred young women. Anyone who might have any right to demand marriage was strictly off-limits.

With four younger sisters of his own, Anthony had a healthy degree of respect for the good reputations of gently bred women. He'd already nearly fought a duel for one of his sisters, all over a slight to her honor. And as for the other three . . . he freely admitted that he broke out in a cold sweat at the mere thought of their getting involved with a man who bore a reputation like his.

No, he certainly wasn't about to despoil some other gentleman's younger sister.

But as for the other sort of women—the widows and actresses who knew what they wanted and what they were getting into—he'd enjoyed their company and enjoyed it well. Since the day he left Oxford and headed west to London, he'd not been without a mistress.

Sometimes, he thought wryly, he'd not been without two.

He'd ridden in nearly every horse race society had to offer, he'd boxed at Gentleman Jackson's, and he'd won more card games than he could count. (He'd lost a few, too, but he disregarded those.) He'd spent the decade of his twenties in a mindful pursuit of pleasure, tempered only by his overwhelming sense of responsibility to his family.

Edmund Bridgerton's death had been both sudden and unexpected; he'd not had a chance to make any final requests of his eldest son before he perished. But if he had, Anthony was certain that he would have asked him to care for his mother and siblings with the same diligence and affection Edmund had displayed.

And so in between Anthony's rounds of parties and horse races, he'd sent his brothers to Eton and Oxford, gone to a mind-numbing number of piano recitals given by his sisters (no easy feat; three out of four of them were tone deaf), and kept a close and watchful eye on the family finances. With seven brothers and sisters, he saw it as his duty to make sure there was enough money to secure all of their futures.

As he grew closer to thirty, he'd realized that he was spending more and more time tending to his heritage and family and less and less in his old pursuit of decadence and pleasure. And he'd realized that he liked it that way. He still kept a mistress, but never more than one at a time, and he discovered that he no longer felt the need to enter every horse race or stay late at a party just to win that last hand of cards.

His reputation, of course, stayed with him. He didn't mind that, actually. There were certain benefits to being thought England's most reprehensible rake. He was nearly universally feared, for example.

That was always a good thing.

But now it was time for marriage. He ought to settle down, have a son. He had a title to pass on, after all. He did feel a rather sharp twinge of regret—and perhaps a touch of guilt as well—over the fact that it was unlikely that he'd live to see his son into adulthood. But what could he do? He was the firstborn Bridgerton of a firstborn Bridgerton of a firstborn Bridgerton eight times over. He had a dynastic responsibility to be fruitful and multiply.

Besides, he took some comfort in knowing that he'd leave three able and caring brothers behind. They'd see to it that his son was brought up with the love and honor that every Bridgerton enjoyed. His sisters would coddle the boy, and his mother might spoil him . . .

Anthony actually smiled a bit as he thought of his large and often boisterous family. His son would not need a father to be well loved.

And whatever children he sired—well, they probably wouldn't remember him after he was gone. They'd be young, unformed. It had not escaped Anthony's notice that of all the Bridgerton children, he, the eldest, was the one most deeply affected by their father's death.

Anthony downed another sip of his scotch and straightened his shoulders, pushing such unpleasant ruminations from his mind. He needed to focus on the matter at hand, namely, the pursuit of a wife.

Being a discerning and somewhat organized man, he'd made a mental list of requirements for the position. First, she ought to be reasonably attractive. She needn't be a raving beauty (although that would be nice), but if he was going to have to bed her, he figured a bit of attraction ought to make the job more pleasant.

Second, she couldn't be stupid. This, Anthony mused, might be the most difficult of his requirements to fill. He was not universally impressed by the mental prowess of London debutantes. The last time he'd made the mistake of engaging a young chit fresh out of the schoolroom in conversation, she'd been unable to discuss anything other than food (she'd had a plate of strawberries in her hand at the time) and the weather (and she hadn't even gotten *that* right; when Anthony had asked if she thought the weather was going to turn inclement, she'd replied, "I'm sure I don't know. I've never been to Clement.")

He might be able to avoid conversation with a wife who was less than brilliant, but he did *not* want stupid children.

Third—and this was the most important—she couldn't be anyone with whom he might actually fall in love.

Under no circumstances would this rule be broken.

He wasn't a complete cynic; he knew that true love existed. Anyone who'd ever been in the same room with his parents knew that true love existed.

But love was a complication he wished to avoid. He had no desire for his life to be visited by that particular miracle.

And since Anthony was used to getting what he wanted, he had no doubt that he would find an attractive, intelligent woman with whom he would never fall in love. And what was the problem with that? Chances were he wouldn't have found the love of his life even if he had been looking for her. Most men didn't.

"Good God, Anthony, what has you frowning so? Not that olive. I saw it clearly and it didn't even touch you."

Benedict's voice broke him out of his reverie, and Anthony blinked a few times before answering, "Nothing. Nothing at all."

He hadn't, of course, shared his thoughts about his own mortality with anyone else, even his brothers. It was not the sort of thing one wanted to advertise. Hell, if someone had come up to him and said the same thing, he probably would have laughed him right out the door.

But no one else could understand the depth of the bond he'd

felt with his father. And no one could possibly understand the way Anthony felt it in his bones, how he simply knew that he could not live longer than his father had done. Edmund had been everything to him. He'd always aspired to be as great a man as his father, knowing that that was unlikely, yet trying all the same. To actually achieve more than Edmund had—in any way—that was nothing short of impossible.

Anthony's father was, quite simply, the greatest man he'd ever known, possibly the greatest man who'd ever lived. To think that he might be more than that seemed conceited in the extreme.

Something had happened to him the night his father had died, when he'd remained in his parents' bedroom with the body, just sitting there for hours, watching his father and trying desperately to remember every moment they'd shared. It would be so easy to forget the little things—how Edmund would squeeze Anthony's upper arm when he needed encouragement. Or how he could recite from memory Balthazar's entire "Sigh No More" song from *Much Ado About Nothing*, not because he thought it particularly meaningful but just because he liked it.

And when Anthony finally emerged from the room, the first streaks of dawn pinking the sky, he somehow knew that his days were numbered, and numbered in the same way Edmund's had been.

"Spit it out," Benedict said, breaking into his thoughts once again. "I won't offer you a penny for your thoughts, since I know they can't possibly be worth that much, but what are you thinking about?"

Anthony suddenly sat up straighter, determined to force his attention back to the matter at hand. After all, he had a bride to choose, and that was surely serious business. "Who is considered the diamond of this season?" he asked.

His brothers paused for a moment to think on this, and then Colin said, "Edwina Sheffield. Surely you've seen her. Rather petite, with blond hair and blue eyes. You can usually spot her by the sheeplike crowd of lovesick suitors following her about."

Anthony ignored his brother's attempts at sarcastic humor. "Has she a brain?"

Colin blinked, as if the question of a woman with a brain were one that had never occurred to him. "Yes, I rather think she does. I once heard her discussing mythology with Middlethorpe, and it sounded as if she had the right of it."

"Good," Anthony said, letting his glass of scotch hit the table with a thunk. "Then I'll marry her."

# Chapter 2

*At the Hartside ball Wednesday night, Viscount Bridgerton was seen dancing with more than one eligible young lady. This behavior can only be termed "startling" as Bridgerton normally avoids proper young misses with a perseverance that would be impressive were it not so utterly frustrating to all marriage-minded Mamas.*

*Can it be that the viscount read This Author's most recent column and, in that perverse manner all males of the species seem to endorse, decided to prove This Author wrong?*

*It may seem that This Author is ascribing to herself far more importance than She actually wields, but men have certainly made decisions based on far, far less.*

LADY WHISTLEDOWN'S SOCIETY PAPERS,
22 APRIL 1814

By eleven o'clock that evening, all of Kate's fears had been realized.

Anthony Bridgerton had asked Edwina to dance.

Even worse, Edwina had accepted.

Even worse, Mary was gazing at the couple as if she'd like to reserve a church that minute.

"Will you stop that?" Kate hissed, poking her stepmother in the ribs.

"Stop what?"

"Looking at them like that!"

Mary blinked. "Like what?"

"Like you're planning the wedding breakfast."

"Oh." Mary's cheeks turned pink. A guilty sort of pink.

"Mary!"

"Well, I might have been," Mary admitted. "And what's wrong with that, I might ask? He'd be a superb catch for Edwina."

"Were you listening this afternoon in the drawing room? It's bad enough that Edwina has any number of rakes and rogues sniffing about her. You cannot imagine the amount of time it has taken me to sort the good suitors from the bad. But Bridgerton!" Kate shuddered. "He's quite possibly the worst rake in all London. You cannot want her to marry a man like him."

"Don't you presume to tell me what I can and cannot do, Katharine Grace Sheffield," Mary said sharply, stiffening her spine until she'd straightened to her full height—which was still a full head shorter than Kate. "I am still your mother. Well, your stepmother. And that counts for something."

Kate immediately felt like a worm. Mary was all she'd ever known as a mother, and she'd never, not even once, made Kate feel any less her daughter than Edwina was. She'd tucked Kate into bed at night, told her stories, kissed her, hugged her, helped her through the awkward years between childhood and adulthood. The only thing she had not done was ask Kate to call her "Mother."

"It counts," Kate said in a quiet voice, letting her gaze fall shamefully down to her feet. "It counts for a lot. And you *are* my mother. In every way that matters."

Mary stared at her for a long moment, then started to blink rather furiously. "Oh, dear," she choked out, reaching into her reticule for a handkerchief. "Now you've gone and turned me into a watering pot."

"I'm sorry," Kate murmured. "Oh, here, turn around so no one sees you. There you are."

Mary pulled out a white square of linen and dabbed at her eyes, the exact same blue as Edwina's. "I do love you, Kate. You know that, don't you?"

"Of course!" Kate exclaimed, shocked that Mary would even ask. "And you know . . . you know that I . . ."

"I know." Mary patted her arm. "Of course I know. It's just that when you agree to be mother to a child you haven't borne, your responsibility is twice as great. You must work even harder to ensure that child's happiness and welfare."

"Oh, Mary, I do love you. And I love Edwina."

At the mention of Edwina's name, they both turned and looked out across the ballroom at her, dancing prettily with the viscount. As usual, Edwina was a vision of petite loveliness. Her blond hair was swept atop her head, a few stray curls left to frame her face, and her form was the epitome of grace as she moved through the steps of the dance.

The viscount, Kate noted with irritation, was blindingly handsome. Dressed in stark black and white, he eschewed the garish colors that had become popular among the more foppish members of the *ton*. He was tall, stood straight and proud, and had thick chestnut hair that tended to fall forward over his brow.

He was, on the surface at least, everything man was meant to be.

"They make a handsome couple, don't they?" Mary murmured.

Kate bit her tongue. She actually bit her tongue.

"He's a trifle tall for her, but I don't see that as an insurmountable obstacle, do you?"

Kate clasped her hands together and let her nails bite into her skin. It said a great deal about the strength of her grip that she could feel them all the way through her kid gloves.

Mary smiled. A rather sly smile, Kate thought. She gave her stepmother a suspicious look.

"He dances well, don't you think?" Mary asked.

"He is not going to marry Edwina!" Kate burst out.

Mary's smile slid straight into a grin. "I was wondering how long you'd manage to hold your silence."

"Far longer than was my natural inclination," Kate retorted, practically biting each word.

"Yes, that much was clear."

"Mary, you know he is not the sort of man we want for Edwina."

Mary cocked her head slightly to the side and raised her brows. "I believe the question ought to be whether he is the sort of man *Edwina* wants for Edwina."

"He's not that, either!" Kate replied heatedly. "Just this afternoon she told me that she wanted to marry a scholar. A scholar!" She jerked her head toward the dark-haired cretin dancing with her sister. "Does he look like a scholar to you?"

"No, but then again, you don't look particularly like an accomplished watercolorist, and yet I know that you are." Mary smirked a bit, which needled Kate to no end, and waited for her reply.

"I'll allow," Kate said through clenched teeth, "that one ought not judge a person merely on his outer appearance, but surely you must agree. From all that we have heard of him, he does not seem the sort to spend his afternoons bent over musty books in a library."

"Perhaps not," Mary mused, "but I had a lovely chat with his mother earlier this evening."

"His mother?" Kate fought to follow the conversation. "What has that to do with anything?"

Mary shrugged. "I find it difficult to believe that such a gracious and intelligent lady could have raised anything but the finest of gentlemen, regardless of his reputation."

"But Mary—"

"When you are a mother," she said loftily, "you will understand what I mean."

"But—"

"Have I told you," Mary said, the purposeful tone of her voice indicating that she'd meant to interrupt, "how lovely you look in that green gauze? I'm so glad we chose it."

Kate looked dumbly down at her dress, wondering why on earth Mary had changed the subject so suddenly.

"The color suits you well. Lady Whistledown shall not be calling you a singed blade of grass in Friday's column!"

Kate stared at Mary in dismay. Perhaps her stepmother had become overheated. It *was* crowded in the ballroom, and the air had grown thick.

Then she felt Mary's finger jabbing her directly below her left shoulder blade, and she knew something else was afoot entirely.

"Mr. Bridgerton!" Mary suddenly exclaimed, sounding as gleeful as a young girl.

Horrified, Kate jerked her head up to see a startlingly handsome man approach them. A startlingly handsome man who looked startlingly like the viscount currently dancing with her sister.

She swallowed. It was either that or let her jaw hang open.

"Mr. Bridgerton!" Mary said again. "How nice to see you. This is my daughter Katharine."

He took her limp, gloved hand and brushed an airy kiss across her knuckles. So airy, in fact, that Kate rather suspected he hadn't kissed her at all.

"Miss Sheffield," he murmured.

"Kate," Mary continued, "this is Mr. Colin Bridgerton. I met him earlier this evening while I was talking with his mother, Lady Bridgerton." She turned to Colin and beamed. "Such a lovely lady."

He grinned back. "We think so."

Mary tittered. Tittered! Kate thought she might gag.

"Kate," Mary said again, "Mr. Bridgerton is brother to the viscount. Who is dancing with Edwina," she added unnecessarily.

"I gathered," Kate replied.

Colin Bridgerton shot her a sideways glance, and she knew instantly that he had not missed the vague sarcasm in her tone.

"It is a pleasure to meet you, Miss Sheffield," he said politely. "I do hope you will favor me with one of your dances this evening."

"I— Of course." She cleared her throat. "I would be honored."

"Kate," Mary said, nudging her softly, "show him your dance card."

"Oh! Yes, of course." Kate fumbled for her dance card, which was tied prettily to her wrist with a green ribbon. That she had to fumble for anything actually tied to her body was a bit alarming, but Kate decided to blame her lack of composure on the sudden and unexpected appearance of a heretofore unknown Bridgerton brother.

That, and the unfortunate fact that even under the best of circumstances she was never the most graceful girl in the room.

Colin filled his name in for one of the dances later that evening, then asked if she might like to walk with him to the lemonade table.

"Go, go," Mary said, before Kate could reply. "Don't worry about me. I'll be just fine without you."

"I can bring you back a glass," Kate offered, trying to figure out if it was possible to glare at her stepmother without Mr. Bridgerton noticing.

"Not necessary. I really should get back to my position with all the other chaperones and mamas." Mary whipped her head around frantically until she spied a familiar face. "Oh, look, there is Mrs. Featherington. I must be off. Portia! Portia!"

Kate watched her stepmother's rapidly retreating form for a moment before turning back to Mr. Bridgerton. "I think," she said dryly, "that she doesn't want any lemonade."

A sparkle of humor glinted in his emerald green eyes. "Either that or she's planning to run all the way to Spain to pick the lemons herself."

Despite herself, Kate laughed. She didn't want to like Mr. Colin Bridgerton. She didn't much want to like any Bridgerton after all she'd read about the viscount in the newspaper. But she allowed that it probably wasn't fair to judge a man based on his brother's misdeeds, so she forced herself to relax a bit.

"And are you thirsty," she asked, "or were you merely being polite?"

"I am always polite," he said with a wicked grin, "but I am thirsty as well."

Kate took one look at that grin, lethally combined with those devastating green eyes, and nearly groaned. "You are a rake as well," she said with a sigh.

Colin choked—on what, she did not know, but he choked nonetheless. "I beg your pardon?"

Kate's face flushed as she realized with horror that she'd spoken aloud. "No, it is I who should beg your pardon. Please forgive me. That was unforgivably rude."

"No, no," he said quickly, looking terribly interested and not a little bit amused, "do continue."

Kate swallowed. There was really no way to get out of it now. "I was merely—" She cleared her throat. "If I might be frank . . ."

He nodded, his sly grin telling her that he could not imagine her being anything *but* frank.

Kate cleared her throat yet again. Really, this was getting ridiculous. She was starting to sound as if she'd swallowed a toad. "It had occurred to me that you might be rather like your brother, that is all."

"My brother?"

"The viscount," she said, thinking it must be obvious.

"I have three brothers," he explained.

"Oh." Now she felt stupid. "I'm sorry."

"I'm sorry, too," he said with great feeling. "Most of the time they're a dreadful nuisance."

Kate had to cough to cover up her small gasp of surprise.

"But at least you were not comparing me to Gregory," he said with a dramatic sigh of relief. He shot her a cheeky, sideways look. "He's thirteen."

Kate caught the smile in his eyes and realized he'd been bamming her all along. This was not a man who wished his brothers off to perdition. "You're rather devoted to your family, aren't you?" she asked.

His eyes, which had been laughing throughout the conversation, turned dead serious without even a blink. "Utterly."

"As am I," Kate said pointedly.

"And that means?"

"It means," she said, knowing she should hold her tongue but speaking anyway, "that I will not allow anyone to break my sister's heart."

Colin remained silent for a moment, slowly turning his head to watch his brother and Edwina, who were just then finishing up their dance. "I see," he murmured.

"Do you?"

"Oh, indeed." They arrived at the lemonade table, and he reached out and took two glasses, handing one to her. She'd already had three glasses of lemonade that evening, a fact of which she was sure Mary had been aware before she'd insisted Kate have some more. But it was hot in the ballroom—it was always hot in ballrooms—and she was thirsty again.

Colin took a leisurely sip, watching her over the rim of his glass, then said, "My brother has it in his mind to settle down this year."

Two could play at this game, Kate thought. She took a sip of her lemonade—slowly—before speaking. "Is that so?"

"I would certainly be in a position to know."

"He is reputed to be quite a rake."

Colin looked at her assessingly. "That is true."

"It is difficult to imagine so notorious a rogue settling down with one woman and finding happiness in marriage."

"You seem to have given such a scenario a great deal of thought, Miss Sheffield."

She leveled a frank stare directly at his face. "Your brother is not the first man of questionable character to court my sister, Mr. Bridgerton. And I assure you, I do not take my sister's happiness lightly."

"Surely any girl would find happiness in marriage to a wealthy and titled gentleman. Isn't that what a season in London is all about?"

"Perhaps," Kate allowed, "but I'm afraid that line of thinking does not address the true problem at hand."

"Which is?"

"Which is that a husband can break a heart with far greater intensity than a mere suitor." She smiled—a small, knowing sort of smile—then added, "Don't you think?"

"Having never been married, I am certainly not in a position to speculate."

"Shame, shame, Mr. Bridgerton. That was the worst sort of evasion."

"Was it? I rather thought it might be the best. I am clearly losing my touch."

"That, I fear, will never be a worry." Kate finished the rest of her lemonade. It was a small glass; Lady Hartside, their hostess, was notoriously stingy.

"You are far too generous," he said.

She smiled, a real smile this time. "I am rarely accused of that, Mr. Bridgerton."

He laughed. Right out loud in the middle of the ballroom. Kate realized with discomfort that they were suddenly the object of numerous curious stares.

"You," he said, still sounding most heartily amused, "must meet my brother."

"The viscount?" she asked with disbelief.

"Well, you might enjoy Gregory's company as well," he allowed, "but as I said, he is only thirteen and likely to put a frog on your chair."

"And the viscount?"

"Is not likely to put a frog on your chair," he said with an utterly straight face.

How Kate managed not to laugh she would never know. Keeping her lips completely straight and serious, she replied, "I see. He has a great deal to recommend him, then."

Colin grinned. "He's not such a bad sort."

"I am much relieved. I shall begin planning the wedding breakfast immediately."

Colin's mouth fell open. "I didn't mean— You shouldn't— That is to say, such a move would be premature—"

Kate took pity on him and said, "I was joking."

His face flushed slightly. "Of course."

"Now, if you'll excuse me, I must make my farewell."

He raised a brow. "Not leaving so early, are you, Miss Sheffield?"

"Not at all." But she wasn't about to tell him she had to go relieve herself. Four glasses of lemonade tended to do that to a body. "I promised a friend I would meet her for a moment."

"It has been a pleasure." He executed a smart bow. "May I see you to your destination?"

"No, thank you. I shall be quite all right on my own." And with a smile over her shoulder, she made her retreat from the ballroom.

Colin Bridgerton watched her go with a thoughtful expression, then made his way to his older brother, who was leaning against a wall, arms crossed in an almost belligerent manner.

"Anthony!" he called out, slapping his brother on the back. "How was your dance with the lovely Miss Sheffield?"

"She'll do," was Anthony's terse reply. They both knew what that meant.

"Really?" Colin's lips twitched ever so slightly. "You should meet the sister, then."

"I beg your pardon?"

"Her sister," Colin repeated, starting to laugh. "You simply must meet her sister."

Twenty minutes later, Anthony was confident he'd gotten the whole story on Edwina Sheffield from Colin. And it seemed that the road to Edwina's heart and hand in marriage lay squarely through her sister.

Edwina Sheffield apparently would not marry without the approval of her older sister. According to Colin, this was common knowledge, and had been for at least a week, ever since Edwina had made an announcement to this effect at the annual Smythe-Smith musicale. The Bridgerton brothers had all missed this momentous statement, as they avoided Smythe-Smith musicales like the plague (as did anyone with any affection for Bach, Mozart, or music in any form).

Edwina's older sister, one Katharine Sheffield, more commonly known as Kate, was also making her debut this year, even though she was reputed to be at least one and twenty. Such timing led Anthony to believe that the Sheffields must be among the less wealthy ranks of the *ton*, a fact which suited him nicely. He had no need of a bride with a great dowry, and a bride without one might have more need of *him*.

Anthony believed in using all of his advantages.

Unlike Edwina, the elder Miss Sheffield had not immediately taken the *ton* by storm. According to Colin, she was generally well liked, but she lacked Edwina's dazzling beauty. She was tall where Edwina was tiny, and dark where Edwina was fair. She also lacked Edwina's dazzling grace. Again, according to Colin (who, though recently arrived in London for the season, was a veritable font of knowledge and gossip), more than one gentleman had reported sore feet after a dance with Katharine Sheffield.

The entire situation seemed a bit absurd to Anthony. After all, who had ever heard of a girl requiring her sister's approval for a husband? A father, yes, a brother, or even a mother, but a sister? It was unfathomable. And furthermore, it seemed odd that Edwina would look to Katharine for guidance when Katharine clearly did not know what she was about in matters of the *ton*.

But Anthony didn't particularly feel like searching out another suitable candidate to court, so he conveniently decided this simply meant that family was important to Edwina. And since family was all-important to him, this was one more indication that she would make an excellent choice as a wife.

So now it appeared that all he had to do was charm the sister. And how difficult could that be?

"You'll have no trouble winning her over," Colin predicted, a confident smile lighting his face. "No trouble at all. A shy, aging spinster? She's probably never received attentions from such a man as you. She'll never know what hit her."

"I don't want her to fall in love with me," Anthony retorted. "I just want her to recommend me to her sister."

"You can't fail," Colin said. "You simply can't fail. Trust me, I spent a few minutes in conversation with her earlier this evening, and she could not say enough about you."

"Good." Anthony pushed himself up off the wall and gazed out with an air of determination. "Now, where is she? I need you to introduce us."

Colin scanned the room for a minute or so, then said, "Ah, there she is. She's coming this way, as a matter of fact. What a marvelous coincidence."

Anthony was coming to believe that nothing within five yards of his younger brother was ever a coincidence, but he followed his gaze nonetheless. "Which one is she?"

"In the green," Colin said, motioning toward her with a barely perceptible nod of his chin.

She was not at all what he'd expected, Anthony realized as he watched her pick her way through the crowds. She was certainly no ape-leading amazon; it was only when compared to Edwina, who barely touched five feet, that she would appear so tall. In fact, Miss Katharine Sheffield was quite pleasant-looking, with thick, medium brown hair and dark eyes. Her skin was pale, her lips pink, and she held herself with an air of confidence he could not help but find attractive.

She would certainly never be considered a diamond of the first water like her sister, but Anthony didn't see why she shouldn't be able to find a husband of her own. Perhaps after he married Edwina he'd provide a dowry for her. It seemed the very least a man could do.

Beside him, Colin strode forward, pushing through the crowd. "Miss Sheffield! Miss Sheffield!"

Anthony swept along in Colin's wake, mentally preparing himself to charm Edwina's older sister. An underappreciated spinster, was she? He'd have her eating out of his hand in no time.

"Miss Sheffield," Colin was saying, "what a delight to see you again."

She looked a bit perplexed, and Anthony didn't blame her. Colin was making it sound as if they'd bumped into each other accidentally, when they all knew he'd trampled at least a half dozen people to reach her side.

"And it's lovely to see you again as well, sir," she replied wryly. "And so unexpectedly soon after our last encounter."

Anthony smiled to himself. She had a sharper wit than he'd been led to believe.

Colin grinned winningly, and Anthony had the distinct and unsettling impression that his brother was up to something. "I can't explain why," Colin said to Miss Sheffield, "but it suddenly seemed imperative that I introduce you to my brother."

She looked abruptly to Colin's right and stiffened as her gaze settled on Anthony. In fact, she rather looked as if she'd just swallowed an antidote.

This, Anthony thought, was odd.

"How kind of you," Miss Sheffield murmured—between her teeth.

"Miss Sheffield," Colin continued brightly, motioning to Anthony, "my brother Anthony, Viscount Bridgerton. Anthony, Miss Katharine Sheffield. I believe you made the acquaintance of her sister earlier this evening."

"Indeed," Anthony said, becoming aware of an overwhelming desire—no, *need*—to strangle his brother.

Miss Sheffield bobbed a quick, awkward curtsy. "Lord Bridgerton," she said, "it is an honor to make your acquaintance."

Colin made a noise that sounded suspiciously like a snort. Or maybe a laugh. Or maybe both.

And Anthony suddenly *knew*. One look at his brother's face should have given it all away. This was no shy, retiring, underappreciated spinster. And whatever she had said to Colin earlier that evening, it had contained no compliments about Anthony.

Fratricide was legal in England, wasn't it? If not, it damn well should have been.

Anthony belatedly realized that Miss Sheffield had held out her hand to him, as was only polite. He took it and brushed a light kiss across her gloved knuckles. "Miss Sheffield," he murmured unthinkingly, "you are as lovely as your sister."

If she had seemed uncomfortable before, her bearing now turned downright hostile. And Anthony realized with a mental slap that he'd said *exactly* the wrong thing. Of course he should not have compared her to her sister. It was the one compliment she could never have believed.

"And you, Lord Bridgerton," she replied in a tone that could have frozen champagne, "are almost as handsome as your brother."

Colin snorted again, only this time it sounded as if he were being strangled.

"Are you all right?" Miss Sheffield asked.

"He's fine," Anthony barked.

She ignored him, keeping her attention on Colin. "Are you certain?"

Colin nodded furiously. "Tickle in my throat."

"Or perhaps a guilty conscience?" Anthony suggested.

Colin turned deliberately from his brother to Kate. "I think I might need another glass of lemonade," he gasped.

"Or maybe," said Anthony, "something stronger. Hemlock, perhaps?"

Miss Sheffield clapped a hand over her mouth, presumably to stifle a burst of horrified laughter.

"Lemonade will do just fine," Colin returned smoothly.

"Would you like me to fetch you a glass?" she asked. Anthony noticed that she'd already stepped out with one foot, looking for any excuse to flee.

Colin shook his head. "No, no, I'm quite capable. But I do believe I had reserved this next dance with you, Miss Sheffield."

"I shall not hold you to it," she said with a wave of her hand.

"Oh, but I could not live with myself were I to leave you unattended," he replied.

Anthony could see Miss Sheffield growing worried at the devilish gleam in Colin's eye. He took a rather uncharitable pleasure in this. His reaction was, he knew, a touch out of proportion. But something about this Miss Katharine Sheffield sparked his temper and made him positively *itch* to do battle with her.

And win. That much went without saying.

"Anthony," Colin said, sounding so deucedly innocent and earnest that it was all Anthony could do not to kill him on the spot, "you're not engaged for this dance, are you?"

Anthony said nothing, just glared at him.

"Good. Then you will dance with Miss Sheffield."

"I'm sure that's not necessary," the woman in question blurted out.

Anthony glared at his brother, then for good measure at Miss Sheffield, who was looking at him as if he'd just despoiled ten virgins in her presence.

"Oh, but it is," Colin said with great drama, ignoring the optical daggers being hurled across their little threesome. "I could never dream of abandoning a young lady in her hour of need. How"—he shuddered—"ungentlemanly."

Anthony thought seriously about pursuing some ungentlemanly behavior himself. Perhaps planting his fist in Colin's face.

"I assure you," Miss Sheffield said quickly, "that being left to my own devices would be far preferable to dan—"

Enough, Anthony thought savagely, was really enough. His own brother had already played him for a fool; he was not going to stand idly by while he was insulted by Edwina's sharp-tongued spinster sister. He laid a heavy hand on Miss Sheffield's arm and said, "Allow me to prevent you from making a grievous mistake, Miss Sheffield."

She stiffened. How, he did not know; her back was already ramrod straight. "I beg your pardon," she said.

"I believe," he said smoothly, "that you were about to say something you would soon regret."

"No," she said, sounding deliberately thoughtful, "I don't think regrets were in my future."

"They will be," he said ominously. And then he grabbed her arm and practically dragged her onto the ballroom floor.

# Chapter 3

*Viscount Bridgerton was also seen dancing with Miss Katharine Sheffield, elder sister to the fair Edwina. This can only mean one thing, as it has not escaped the notice of This Author that the elder Miss Sheffield has been in much demand on the dance floor ever since the younger Miss Sheffield made her bizarre and unprecedented announcement at the Smythe-Smith musicale last week.*

*Whoever heard of a girl needing her sister's permission to choose a husband?*

*And perhaps more importantly, whoever decided that the words "Smythe-Smith" and "musicale" might be used in the same sentence? This Author has attended one of these gatherings in the past, and heard nothing that might ethically be termed "music."*

LADY WHISTLEDOWN'S SOCIETY PAPERS,
22 APRIL 1814

There was really nothing she could do, Kate realized with dismay. He was a viscount, and she was a mere nobody from Somerset, and they were both in the middle of a crowded ballroom. It didn't matter if she'd disliked him on sight. She *had* to dance with him.

"There is no need to drag me," she hissed.

He made a great show of loosening his grip.

Kate ground her teeth together and swore to herself that this man would never take her sister as his bride. His manner was too cold, too superior. He was, she thought a touch unfairly, too handsome as well, with velvety brown eyes that matched his hair to perfection. He was tall, certainly over six feet, although probably not by more than an inch, and his lips, while classically beautiful (Kate had studied enough art to regard herself qualified to make such a judgment) were tight at the corners, as if he did not know how to smile.

"Now then," he said, once their feet began to move in the familiar steps, "suppose you tell me why you hate me."

Kate trod on his foot. Lord, he was direct. "I beg your pardon?"

"There is no need to maim me, Miss Sheffield."

"It was an accident, I assure you." And it *was*, even if she didn't really mind this particular example of her lack of grace.

"Why," he mused, "do I find I have difficulty believing you?"

Honesty, Kate quickly decided, would be her best strategy. If he could be direct, well then, so could she. "Probably," she answered with a wicked smile, "because you know that had it occurred to me to step on your foot on purpose, I would have done so."

He threw back his head and laughed. It was not the reaction she'd been either expecting or hoping for. Come to think of it, she had no idea what sort of reaction she'd been hoping for, but this *certainly* wasn't what she'd been expecting.

"Will you stop, my lord?" she whispered urgently. "People are starting to stare."

"People started to stare two minutes ago," he returned. "It's not often a man such as I dances with a woman such as you."

As barbs went, this one was well aimed, but sadly for him, also incorrect. "Not true," she replied jauntily. "You are certainly not the first of Edwina's besotted idiots to attempt to gain her favor through me."

He grinned. "Not suitors, but idiots?"

She caught his gaze with hers and was surprised to find true mirth in his eyes. "Surely you're not going to hand me such a delicious piece of bait as that, my lord?"

"And yet you did not take it," he mused.

Kate looked down to see if there was some way she might discreetly step on his foot again.

"I have very thick boots, Miss Sheffield," he said.

Her head snapped back up in surprise.

One corner of his mouth curved up in a mockery of a smile. "And quick eyes as well."

"Apparently so. I shall have to watch my step around you, to be sure."

"My goodness," he drawled, "was that a compliment? I might expire from the shock of it."

"If you'd like to consider that a compliment, I give you leave to do so," she said airily. "You're not likely to receive many more."

"You wound me, Miss Sheffield."

"Does that mean that your skin is not as thick as your boots?"

"Oh, not nearly."

She felt herself laugh before she realized she was amused. "That I find difficult to believe."

He waited for her smile to melt away, then said, "You did not answer my question. Why do you hate me?"

A rush of air slipped through Kate's lips. She hadn't expected him to repeat the question. Or at least she'd hoped that he would not. "I do not hate you, my lord," she replied, choosing her words with great care. "I do not even know you."

"Knowing is rarely a prerequisite for hating," he said softly, his eyes settling on hers with lethal steadiness. "Come now, Miss Sheffield, you don't seem a coward to me. Answer the question."

Kate held silent for a full minute. It was true, she had not been predisposed to like the man. She *certainly* wasn't about to give her blessing to his courtship of Edwina. She didn't believe for one second that reformed rakes made the best husbands. She wasn't even sure that a rake could be properly reformed in the first place.

But he might have been able to overcome her preconceptions. He could have been charming and sincere and straightforward, and been able to convince her that the stories about him in *Whistledown* were an exaggeration, that he was not the worst rogue London had seen since the turn of the century. He might have convinced her that he held to a code of honor, that he was a man of principles and honesty . . .

If he hadn't gone and compared her to Edwina.

For nothing could have been more obvious a lie. She knew she wasn't an antidote; her face and form were pleasing enough. But there was simply no way she could be compared to Edwina in this measure and emerge as her equal. Edwina was truly a diamond of the first water, and Kate could never be more than average and unremarkable.

And if this man was saying otherwise, then he had some ulterior motive, because it was obvious he wasn't blind.

He could have offered her any other empty compliment and she would have accepted it as a gentleman's polite conversation. She might have even been flattered if his words had struck anywhere close to the truth. But to compare her to Edwina . . .

Kate adored her sister. She truly did. And she knew better than anyone that Edwina's heart was as beautiful and radiant as her face. She didn't like to think herself jealous, but still . . . somehow the comparison stung right to the core.

"I do not hate you," she finally replied. Her eyes were trained on his chin, but she had no patience for cowardice, especially within herself, so she forced herself to meet his gaze when she added, "But I find I cannot like you."

Something in his eyes told her that he appreciated her stark honesty. "And why is that?" he asked softly.

"May I be frank?"

His lips twitched. "Please do."

"You are dancing with me right now because you wish to court my sister. This does not bother me," she hastened to assure him. "I am well used to receiving attentions from Edwina's suitors."

Her mind was clearly not on her feet. Anthony pulled his foot out of the way of hers before she could injure him again. He noticed with interest that she was back to referring to them as suitors rather than idiots. "Please continue," he murmured.

"You are not the sort of man I would wish my sister to marry," she said simply. Her manner was direct, and her intelligent brown eyes never left his. "You are a rake. You are a rogue. You are, in fact, notorious for being both. I would not allow my sister within ten feet of you."

"And yet," he said with a wicked little smile, "I waltzed with her earlier this evening."

"An act which shall not be repeated, I can assure you."

"And is it your place to decide Edwina's fate?"

"Edwina trusts my judgment," she said primly.

"I see," he said in what he hoped was his most mysterious manner. "That is very interesting. I thought Edwina was an adult."

"Edwina is but seventeen years old!"

"And you are so ancient at, what, twenty years of age?"

"Twenty-one," she bit off.

"Ah, that makes you a veritable expert on men, and husbands in particular. Especially since you have been married yourself, yes?"

"You know I am unwed," she ground out.

Anthony stifled the urge to smile. Good Lord, but it was *fun* baiting the elder Miss Sheffield. "I think," he said, keeping his words slow and deliberate, "that you have found it relatively easy to manage most of the men who have come knocking on your sister's door. Is that true?"

She kept her stony silence.

"Is it?"

Finally she gave him one curt nod.

"I thought so," he murmured. "You seem the sort who would."

She glared at him with such intensity that it was all he could do to keep from laughing. If he weren't dancing, he probably would have stroked his chin in an affectation of deep thought. But since his hands were otherwise engaged, he had to settle for a ponderous tilt of his head, combined with an arch raise of his eyebrows. "But I also think," he added, "that you made a grave mistake when you thought to manage *me*."

Kate's lips were set in a grim, straight line, but she managed to say, "I do not seek to manage you, Lord Bridgerton. I only seek to keep you away from my sister."

"Which just goes to show, Miss Sheffield, how very little you know of men. At least of the rakish, roguish variety." He leaned in closer, letting his hot breath brush against her cheek.

She shivered. He'd known she'd shiver.

He smiled wickedly. "There is very little we relish more than a challenge."

The music drew to a close, leaving them standing in the middle of the ballroom floor, facing one another. Anthony took her arm, but before he led her back to the perimeter of the room, he put his lips very close to her ear and whispered, "And you, Miss Sheffield, have issued to me a most delicious challenge."

Kate stepped on his foot. Hard. Enough to make him let out a small, decidedly unrakish, unroguish squeak.

When he glared at her, though, she just shrugged and said, "It was my only defense."

His eyes darkened. "You, Miss Sheffield, are a menace."

"And you, Lord Bridgerton, need thicker boots."

His grasp tightened on her arm. "Before I return you to the sanctuary of the chaperones and spinsters, there is one thing we need to make clear."

Kate held her breath. She did not like the hard tone of his voice.

"I am going to court your sister. And should I decide that she will make a suitable Lady Bridgerton, I will make her my wife."

Kate whipped her head up to face him, fire flashing in her eyes. "And I suppose, then, that you think it is *your* place to decide Edwina's fate. Do not forget, my lord, that even if you decide she will make a *suitable*"—she sneered the word—"Lady Bridgerton, she might choose otherwise."

He looked down at her with the confidence of a male who is never crossed. "Should I decide to ask Edwina, she will not say no."

"Are you trying to tell me that no woman has ever been able to resist you?"

He did not answer, just raised one supercilious brow and let her draw her own conclusions.

Kate wrenched her arm free and strode back to her stepmother, shaking with fury, resentment, and not a little bit of fear.

Because she had an awful feeling that he did not lie. And if he really did turn out to be irresistible . . .

Kate shuddered. She and Edwina were going to be in big, big trouble.

The next afternoon was like any following a major ball. The Sheffields' drawing room was filled to bursting with flower bouquets, each one accompanied by a crisp white card bearing the name, "Edwina Sheffield."

A simple "Miss Sheffield" would have sufficed, Kate thought with a grimace, but she supposed one couldn't really fault Edwina's suitors for wanting to make certain the flowers went to the correct Miss Sheffield.

Not that *anyone* was likely to make a mistake on that measure. Floral arrangements generally went to Edwina. In fact, there was nothing general about it; every bouquet that had arrived at the Sheffield residence in the last month had gone to Edwina.

Kate liked to think she had the last laugh, however. Most of the flowers made Edwina sneeze, so they tended to end up in Kate's chamber, anyway.

"You beautiful thing," she said, lovingly fingering a fine orchid. "I think you belong right on my bedstand. And you"—she leaned forward and sniffed at a bouquet of perfect white roses—"you will look smashing on my dressing table."

"Do you always talk to flowers?"

Kate whirled around at the sound of a deep male voice. Good heavens, it was Lord Bridgerton, looking sinfully handsome in a blue morning coat. What the devil was *he* doing here?

No sense in not asking.

"What the dev—" She caught herself just in time. She would not let this man reduce her to cursing aloud, no matter how often she did it in her head. "What are *you* doing here?"

He raised a brow as he adjusted the huge bouquet of flowers he had tucked under his arm. Pink roses, she noted. Perfect buds. They were lovely. Simple and elegant. Exactly the sort of thing she'd choose for herself.

"I believe it's customary for suitors to call upon young women, yes?" he murmured. "Or did I misplace my etiquette book?"

"I meant," Kate growled, "how did you get in? No one alerted me to your arrival."

He cocked his head toward the hall. "The usual manner. I knocked on your front door."

Kate's look of irritation at his sarcasm did not prevent him from continuing with, "Amazingly enough, your butler answered. Then I gave him my card, he took a look at it, and showed me to the drawing room. Much as I'd like to claim some sort of devious, underhanded subterfuge," he continued, maintaining a rather impressively supercilious tone, "it was actually quite aboveboard and straightforward."

"Infernal butler," Kate muttered. "He's supposed to see if we're 'at home' before showing you in."

"Maybe he had previous instructions that you would be 'at home' for me under any circumstances."

She bristled. "I gave him no such instructions."

"No," Lord Bridgerton said with a chuckle, "I wouldn't have thought so."

"And I know Edwina didn't."

He smiled. "Perhaps your mother?"

Of course. "Mary," she groaned, a world of accusation in the single word.

"You call her by her given name?" he asked politely.

She nodded. "She's actually my stepmother. Although she's really all I know. She married my father when I was but three. I don't know why I still call her Mary." She gave her head a little shake as her shoulders lifted into a perplexed shrug. "I just do."

His brown eyes remained fixed on her face, and she realized she'd just let this man—her nemesis, really—into a small corner of her life. She felt the words "I'm sorry" bubbling on her tongue—a reflexive reaction, she supposed, for having spoken too freely. But she didn't want to apologize to this man for anything, so instead she just said, "Edwina is out, I'm afraid, so your visit was for nothing."

"Oh, I don't know about that," he replied. He grasped the bouquet of flowers—which had been tucked under his right arm—with his other hand, and as he brought it forward Kate saw that it was not one massive bouquet, but three smaller ones.

"This," he said, putting one of the bouquets down on a side table, "is for Edwina. And this"—he did the same with the second—"is for your mother."

He was left with a single bouquet. Kate stood frozen with shock, unable to take her eyes off the perfect pink blooms. She knew what he had to be about, that the only reason he'd included her in the gesture was to impress Edwina, but blast it, no one had ever brought her flowers before, and she hadn't known until that very moment how badly she'd wanted someone to do so.

"These," he said finally, holding out the final arrangement of pink roses, "are for you."

"Thank you," she said hesitantly, taking them into her arms. "They're lovely." She leaned down to sniff them, sighing with pleasure at the thick scent. Glancing back up, she added, "It was very thoughtful of you to think of Mary and me."

He nodded graciously. "It was my pleasure. I must confess, a suitor for my sister's hand once did the same for my mother, and I don't believe I've ever seen her more delighted."

"Your mother or your sister?"

He smiled at her pert question. "Both."

"And what happened to this suitor?" Kate asked.

Anthony's grin turned devilish in the extreme. "He married my sister."

"Hmmph. Don't think history is likely to repeat itself. But—" Kate coughed, not particularly wanting to be honest with him but quite incapable of doing anything otherwise. "But the flowers are truly lovely, and—and it was a lovely gesture on your part." She swallowed. This wasn't easy for her. "And I do appreciate them."

He leaned forward slightly, his dark eyes positively melting. "A kind sentence," he mused. "And directed at me, no less. There now, that wasn't so difficult, was it?"

Kate went from bending lovingly over the flowers to standing uncomfortably straight in an instant. "You do seem to have a knack for saying the *exact* wrong thing."

"Only where you're concerned, my dear Miss Sheffield. Other women, I assure you, hang on my every word."

"So I've read," she muttered.

His eyes lit up. "Is that where you've developed your opinions of me? Of course! The estimable Lady Whistledown. I should have known. Lud, I'd like to strangle the woman."

"I find her rather intelligent and quite on the mark," Kate said primly.

"You would," he returned.

"Lord Bridgerton," Kate ground out, "I'm sure you did not come calling to insult me. May I leave a message for Edwina for you?"

"I think not. I don't particularly trust that it would reach her unadulterated."

That was really too much. "I would *never* stoop to interfering with another person's correspondence," Kate somehow managed to say. Her entire body was shaking with rage, and if she'd been a less controlled sort of woman, her hands would surely have been wrapped around his throat. "How dare you imply otherwise."

"When all is said and done, Miss Sheffield," he said with annoying calmness, "I really don't know you very well. What I do know consists of your fervent avowals that I will never find myself within ten feet of your sister's saintly presence. You tell me, would *you* feel confident to leave a note if you were me?"

"If you are attempting to gain my sister's favor through me," Kate replied icily, "you are not doing a very good job of it."

"I'm aware of that," he said. "I really shouldn't provoke you. It's not very well done of me, is it? But I'm afraid I just can't help myself." He grinned roguishly and held up his hands in a helpless manner. "What can I say? You do something to me, Miss Sheffield."

His smile, Kate realized with dismay, was truly a force to be reckoned with. She suddenly felt faint. A seat . . . yes, what she needed to do was sit down. "Please, have a seat," she said, waving at the blue damask sofa as she scrambled across the room to a chair. She didn't particularly want him to linger, but she couldn't very well sit without offering him a seat as well, and her legs were starting to feel *awfully* wobbly.

If the viscount thought oddly of her sudden burst of politeness, he did not say anything. Instead he removed a long black case off the sofa and placed it on a table, then sat down in its place. "Is that a musical instrument?" he queried, motioning to the case.

Kate nodded. "A flute."

"Do you play?"

She shook her head, then cocked her head slightly and nodded. "I'm trying to learn. I took it up just this year."

He nodded in reply, and that, apparently, was to be the end of the subject, because he then politely asked, "When do you expect Edwina to return?"

"Not for at least an hour, I should think. Mr. Berbrooke took her out for a ride in his curricle."

"Nigel Berbrooke?" He practically choked on the name.

"Yes, why?"

"The man has more hair than wit. A great deal more."

"But he's going bald," she couldn't resist pointing out.

He grimaced. "And if that doesn't prove my point, I don't know what will."

Kate had reached much the same conclusion about Mr. Berbrooke's intelligence (or lack thereof), but she said, "Isn't it considered bad form to insult one's fellow suitors?"

Anthony let out a little snort. "It wasn't an insult. It was the truth. He courted my sister last year. Or tried to. Daphne did her best to discourage him. He's a nice enough fellow, I'll grant you that, but not someone you'd want building you a boat were you stranded on a desert island."

Kate had a strange and unwelcome image of the viscount stranded on a desert island, clothes in tatters, skin kissed by the sun. It left her feeling uncomfortably warm.

Anthony cocked his head, regarding her with a quizzical gaze. "I say, Miss Sheffield, are you feeling all right?"

"Fine!" she practically barked. "Never better. You were saying?"

"You look a bit flushed." He leaned in, watching her closely. She really didn't look well.

Kate fanned herself. "It's a bit hot in here, don't you think?"

Anthony shook his head slowly. "Not at all."

She gazed longingly out the door. "I wonder where Mary is."

"Are you expecting her?"

"It's unlike her to leave me unchaperoned for so long," she explained.

Unchaperoned? The ramifications were frightening. Anthony had a sudden vision of being trapped into marriage with Miss Sheffield the elder, and it made him break out in a cold sweat. Kate was so unlike any debutante he'd ever met that he'd quite forgotten that they even needed a chaperone. "Perhaps she's not aware I'm here," he said quickly.

"Yes, that must be it." She sprang to her feet and crossed the room to the bellpull. Giving it a firm yank, she said, "I'll just ring for someone to alert her. I'm sure she won't want to miss you."

"Good. Perhaps she can keep us company while we wait for your sister to return."

Kate froze halfway back to her chair. "You're planning to wait for Edwina?"

He shrugged, enjoying her discomfort. "I have no other plans for the afternoon."

"But she might be hours!"

"An hour at most, I'm sure, and besides—" He cut himself off, noting the arrival of a maid in the doorway.

"You rang, miss?" the maid queried.

"Yes, thank you, Annie," Kate replied. "Would you please inform Mrs. Sheffield that we have a guest?"

The maid bobbed a curtsy and departed.

"I'm sure Mary will be down at any moment," Kate said, quite unable to stop tapping her foot. "Any minute now. I'm sure of it."

He just smiled in that annoying manner, looking terribly relaxed and comfortable on the sofa.

An awkward silence fell across the room. Kate offered him a tight smile. He just raised a brow in return.

"I'm sure she'll be here—"

"Any minute now," he finished for her, sounding heartily amused.

She sank back into her chair, trying not to grimace. She probably didn't succeed.

Just then a small commotion broke out in the hall—a few decidedly canine barks, followed by a high-pitched shriek of, "Newton! Newton! Stop that at once!"

"Newton?" the viscount queried.

"My dog," Kate explained, sighing as she rose to her feet. "He doesn't—"

"NEWTON!"

"—get along with Mary very well, I'm afraid." Kate moved to the door. "Mary? Mary?"

Anthony rose when Kate did, wincing as the dog let out three more earsplitting barks, which were immediately followed by another terrified shriek from Mary. "What is he," he muttered, "a mastiff?" It had to be a mastiff. Miss Sheffield the elder seemed exactly the sort to keep a man-eating mastiff at her beck and call.

"No," Kate said, rushing out into the hall as Mary let out another shriek. "He's a—"

But Anthony missed her words. It didn't matter much, anyway, because one second later, in trotted the most benign-looking corgi he'd ever seen, with thick caramel-colored fur and a belly that almost dragged on the ground.

Anthony froze with surprise. *This* was the fearsome creature from the hall? "Good day, dog," he said firmly.

The dog stopped in its tracks, sat right down, and . . .

Smiled?

# Chapter 4

*This Author was, sadly, unable to determine all the details, but there was a considerable to-do Thursday last near The Serpentine in Hyde Park involving Viscount Bridgerton, Mr. Nigel Berbrooke, both the Misses Sheffield, and an unnamed dog of indeterminate breed.*

*This Author was not an eyewitness, but all accounts seem to indicate that the unnamed dog emerged the victor.*

*Lady Whistledown's Society Papers,*
25 April 1814

Kate stumbled back into the drawing room, knocking arms with Mary as they both squeezed through the doorway at the same time. Newton was seated happily in the middle of the room, shedding on the blue-and-white rug as he grinned up at the viscount.

"I think he likes you," Mary said, somewhat accusingly.

"He likes you, too, Mary," Kate said. "The problem is that *you* don't like *him*."

"I'd like him better if he didn't try to accost me every time I come through the hall."

"I thought you said Mrs. Sheffield and the dog didn't get along," Lord Bridgerton said.

"They don't," Kate replied. "Well, they do. Well, they don't *and* they do."

"That clears things up immeasurably," he murmured.

Kate ignored his quiet sarcasm. "Newton adores Mary," she explained, "but Mary doesn't adore Newton."

"I'd adore him a bit more," Mary interrupted, "if he'd adore me a bit less."

"*So*," Kate continued determinedly, "poor Newton regards Mary as something of a challenge. So when he sees her . . ." She shrugged helplessly. "Well, I'm afraid he simply adores her *more*."

As if on cue, the dog caught sight of Mary and bounded straight over to her feet.

"Kate!" Mary exclaimed.

Kate rushed to her stepmother's side, just as Newton rose on his hind legs and planted his front paws just above Mary's knees. "Newton, down!" she scolded. "Bad dog. Bad dog."

The dog sat back down with a little whine.

"Kate," Mary said in an extremely no-nonsense voice, "that dog *must* be taken for a walk. Now."

"I had been planning to when the viscount arrived," Kate replied, motioning to the man across the room. Really, it was remarkable the number of things she could blame on the insufferable man if she put her mind to it.

"Oh!" Mary yelped. "I beg your pardon, my lord. How rude of me not to greet you."

"It is of no concern," he said smoothly. "You were a bit preoccupied upon your arrival."

"Yes," Mary grumbled, "that beastly dog. . . . Oh, but where are my manners? May we offer you tea? Something to eat? It is so kind of you to call upon us."

"No, thank you. I've just been enjoying your daughter's invigorating company while I await Miss Edwina's arrival."

"Ah, yes," Mary answered. "Edwina's off with Mr. Berbrooke, I believe. Isn't that so, Kate?"

Kate nodded stonily, not sure she liked being called "invigorating."

"Do you know Mr. Berbrooke, Lord Bridgerton?" Mary asked.

"Ah, yes," he said, with what Kate thought was fairly surprising reticence. "Yes, I do."

"I wasn't sure if I should have allowed Edwina to go off with him for a ride. Those curricles are terribly difficult to drive, aren't they?"

"I believe that Mr. Berbrooke has a steady hand with his horses," Anthony replied.

"Oh, good," Mary replied, letting out a much-relieved sigh. "You have surely set my mind at rest."

Newton let out a staccato bark, simply to remind everyone of his presence.

"I had better find his lead and take him for a walk," Kate said hurriedly. She certainly could use a bit of fresh air. And it would be nice to finally escape the viscount's fiendish company. "If you'll excuse me . . ."

"But wait, Kate!" Mary called out. "You cannot leave Lord Bridgerton here with me. I'm sure I'll bore him to tears."

Kate slowly turned around, dreading Mary's next words.

"You could never bore me, Mrs. Sheffield," the viscount said, debonair rake that he was.

"Oh, but I could," she assured him. "You've never been trapped in conversation with me for an hour. Which is about how long it will be before Edwina returns."

Kate stared at her stepmother, her jaw actually hanging open with shock. What on earth did Mary think she was doing?

"Why don't you go with Kate to take Newton for a walk?" Mary suggested.

"Oh, but I could never ask Lord Bridgerton to accompany me on a *chore*," Kate said quickly. "It would be beyond rudeness, and after all, he is our esteemed guest."

"Don't be silly," Mary answered, before the viscount could get even half of a word in. "I'm sure he wouldn't look upon it as a chore. Would you, my lord?"

"Of course not," he murmured, looking utterly sincere. But really, what else could he say?

"There. That settles it," Mary said, sounding inordinately pleased with herself. "And who knows? You may stumble across Edwina in your travels. Wouldn't that be convenient?"

"Indeed," Kate said under her breath. It would be lovely to be rid of the viscount, but the last thing she wanted to do was deliver Edwina into his clutches. Her sister was still young and impressionable. What if she couldn't resist one of his smiles? Or his glib tongue?

Even Kate was willing to admit that Lord Bridgerton exuded considerable charm, and she didn't even like the man! Edwina, with her less suspicious nature, would surely be overwhelmed.

She turned to the viscount. "You shouldn't feel you must accompany me while I walk Newton, my lord."

"I'd be delighted," he said with a wicked smile, and Kate had the distinct impression he was agreeing to go for the sole purpose of vexing her. "Besides," he continued, "as your mother said, we might see Edwina, and wouldn't that be a delightful coincidence?"

"Delightful," Kate returned flatly. "Just delightful."

"Excellent!" Mary said, clapping her hands together with joy. "I saw Newton's lead on the hall table. Here, I'll go and get it for you."

Anthony watched Mary leave, then turned to Kate and said, "That was very neatly done."

"I'll say," Kate muttered.

"Do you suppose," he whispered, leaning toward her, "that her matchmaking is directed toward Edwina or you?"

"Me?" Kate all but croaked. "Surely you jest."

Anthony rubbed his chin thoughtfully, gazing at the doorway through which Mary had just exited. "I'm not certain," he mused, "but—" He closed his mouth upon hearing Mary's footsteps drawing back near.

"Here you are," Mary said, holding the lead out to Kate. Newton barked enthusiastically and drew back as if preparing to lunge at Mary—undoubtedly to shower her with all sorts of unpalatable love—but Kate kept a firm hold on his collar.

"Here," Mary quickly amended, handing the lead instead to Anthony. "Why don't you give this to Kate? I'd rather not get too close."

Newton barked and gazed longingly at Mary, who inched farther away.

"You," Anthony said forcefully to the dog. "Sit down and be quiet."

Much to Kate's surprise, Newton obeyed, settling his plump bottom onto the rug with almost comical alacrity.

"There," Anthony said, sounding rather pleased with himself. He held out the lead toward Kate. "Shall you do the honors or shall I?"

"Oh, go right ahead," she replied. "You seem to have such an affinity for canines."

"Clearly," he shot back, keeping his voice low so that Mary could not hear, "they are not so very different from women. Both breeds hang on my every word."

Kate stepped on his hand as he knelt to fasten the lead to Newton's collar. "Oops," she said, rather insincerely. "I'm so sorry."

"Your tender solicitude quite unmans me," he returned, standing back up. "I might break into tears."

Mary's head bobbed back and forth between Kate and Anthony. She couldn't hear what they were saying but was clearly fascinated. "Is something wrong?" she queried.

"Not at all," Anthony replied, just as Kate gave a firm, "No."

"Good," Mary said briskly. "Then I'll see you to the door." At Newton's enthusiastic bark, she added, "Then again, maybe not. I don't really want to get within ten feet of that dog. But I'll wave you off."

"What would I do," Kate said to Mary as she passed her, "without you to wave me off?"

Mary smiled slyly. "I surely don't know, Kate. I surely don't know."

Which left Kate with a queasy feeling in her stomach and a vague suspicion that Lord Bridgerton might have been correct. Maybe Mary was playing matchmaker with more than just Edwina this time around.

It was a horrifying thought.

With Mary standing in the hall, Kate and Anthony exited out the doorway and headed west on Milner Street. "I usually stay to the smaller streets and make my way up to Brompton Road," Kate explained, thinking that he might not be very familiar with this area of town, "then take that to Hyde Park. But we can walk straight up Sloane Street, if you prefer."

"Whatever you wish," he demurred. "I shall follow your direction."

"Very well," Kate replied, marching determinedly up Milner Street toward Lenox Gardens. Maybe if she kept her eyes ahead of her and moved briskly, he'd be discouraged from conversation. Her daily walks with Newton were supposed to be her time for personal reflection. She did not appreciate having to drag him along.

Her strategy worked quite well for several minutes. They walked in silence all the way to the corner of Hans Crescent and Brompton Road, and then he quite suddenly said, "My brother played us for fools last night."

That stopped her in her tracks. "I beg your pardon?"

"Do you know what he told me about you before he introduced us?"

Kate stumbled a step before shaking her head, no. Newton hadn't stopped in *his* tracks, and he was tugging on the lead like mad.

"He told me you couldn't say enough about me."

"Wellll," Kate stalled, "if one doesn't want to put too fine a point on it, that's not entirely untrue."

"He implied," Anthony added, "that you could not say enough *good* about me."

She shouldn't have smiled. "*That's* not true."

He probably shouldn't have smiled, either, but Kate was glad he did. "I didn't think so," he replied.

They turned up Brompton Road toward Knightsbridge and Hyde Park, and Kate asked, "Why would he do such a thing?"

Anthony shot her a sideways look. "You don't have a brother, do you?"

"No, just Edwina, I'm afraid, and she's decidedly female."

"He did it," Anthony explained, "purely to torture me."

"A noble pursuit," Kate said under her breath.

"I heard that."

"I rather thought you would," she added.

"And I expect," he continued, "that he wanted to torture you as well."

"Me?" she exclaimed. "Whyever? What could I possibly have done to him?"

"You might have provoked him ever so slightly by denigrating his beloved brother," he suggested.

Her brows arched. "Beloved?"

"Much-admired?" he tried.

She shook her head. "That one doesn't wash, either."

Anthony grinned. Miss Sheffield the elder, for all her annoyingly managing ways, did have an admirable wit. They'd reached Knightsbridge, so he took her arm as they crossed over the thoroughfare and took one of the smaller pathways that led to South Carriage Road within Hyde Park. Newton, clearly a country dog at heart, picked up his pace considerably as they entered greener surroundings, although it would be difficult to imagine the portly canine moving with anything that might correctly be termed speed.

Still, the dog seemed rather jolly and certainly interested in every flower, small animal, or passerby that crossed their path. The spring air was crisp, but the sun was warm, and the sky was a surprisingly clear blue after so many typical London days of rain. And while the woman on his arm was not the woman he planned to take to wife, nor, in fact, was she a woman he planned to take to anything, Anthony felt a rather easy sense of contentment wash over him.

"Shall we cross over to Rotten Row?" he asked Kate.

"Hmmm?" was her distracted reply. She had her face tipped up to the sun and was basking in its warmth. And for one extremely disconcerting moment, Anthony felt a sharp stab of . . . *something*.

Something? He gave his head a little shake. It couldn't possibly be desire. Not for this woman.

"Did you say something?" she murmured.

He cleared his throat and took a deep breath, hoping it would clear his head. Instead, he simply got an intoxicating whiff of her scent, which was an odd combination of exotic lilies and sensible soap. "You seem to be enjoying the sun," he said.

She smiled, turning to face him with a clear-eyed gaze. "I know that's not what you said, but yes, I am. It's been so dreadfully rainy of late."

"I thought young ladies were not supposed to let sun on their faces," he teased.

She shrugged, looking only the slightest bit sheepish as she replied, "They're not. That is to say, we're not. But it does feel heavenly." She let out a little sigh, and a look of longing crossed her face, so intense that Anthony almost ached for her. "I do wish I could remove my bonnet," she said wistfully.

Anthony nodded his agreement, feeling much the same way about his hat. "You could probably push it back just a bit without anyone noticing," he suggested.

"Do you think?" Her entire face lit up at the prospect, and that strange stab of *something* pierced his gut again.

"Of course," he murmured, reaching up to adjust the rim of the bonnet. It was one of those bizarre confections women seemed to favor, all ribbons and lace, and tied in such a way that no reasonable man could ever make sense of it. "Here, just hold still for a moment. I'll fix it."

Kate held still, just as he'd gently ordered, but when his fingers accidentally brushed the skin on her temple she stopped breathing as well. He was so very close, and there was something very odd about it. She could feel the heat of his body, and smell the clean, soapy scent of him.

And it sent a prickle of awareness straight through her.

She hated him, or at least she heartily disliked and disapproved of him, and yet she had the most absurd inclination to lean forward slightly, until the space between their bodies was squeezed into nothingness, and . . .

She swallowed and forced herself to draw back. Good God, what had come over her?

"Hold for a moment," he said. "I haven't finished."

Kate reached up with frantic fingers to adjust her bonnet. "I'm sure it's just fine. You needn't—you needn't worry yourself."

"Can you feel the sun any better?" he asked.

She nodded, even though she was so distracted she wasn't even sure if it was true. "Yes, thank you. It's lovely. I— Oh!"

Newton let out a loud stream of barks and yanked on the lead. Hard.

"Newton!" she called out, jerking forward with the lead. But the dog already had something in his sights—Kate had no idea what—and was bounding enthusiastically forward, pulling her along until she was stumbling over her feet, her entire body pulled into a diagonal line, with her shoulder decidedly in front of the rest of her. "Newton!" she called out again, rather helplessly. "Newton! Stop!"

Anthony watched with amusement as the dog barreled forward, moving with more speed than he would have ever guessed its short, pudgy legs could have managed. Kate was making a valiant attempt to keep her grip on the lead, but Newton was now barking like mad, and running with equal vigor.

"Miss Sheffield, allow me to take the lead," he boomed, striding forward to aid her. It wasn't the most glamorous manner in which to play the hero, but anything would do when one was trying to impress the sister of one's future bride.

But just as Anthony caught up with her, Newton gave the lead a vicious tug, and it went flying from her grasp. Kate let out a shriek and dashed forward, but the dog was off and running, the lead snaking along the grass behind him.

Anthony didn't know whether to laugh or groan. Newton clearly did not intend to be caught.

Kate froze for a moment, one hand clasped over her mouth. Then her eyes caught Anthony's, and he had the worst sort of feeling that he knew what she intended to do.

"Miss Sheffield," he said quickly, "I'm sure—"

But she was off and running, hollering, "Newton!" with a decided lack of decorum. Anthony let out a weary sigh and began running after her. He couldn't very well let her chase the dog on her own and still presume to call himself a gentleman.

She had a bit of a head start on him, though, and when he caught up with her around the corner, she'd stopped. She was breathing hard, her hands on her hips as she scanned her surroundings.

"Where'd he go?" Anthony asked, trying to forget that there was something rather arousing about a woman who was panting.

"I don't know." She paused to catch her breath. "I think he's chasing a rabbit."

"Oh, now, well, *that* will make it easy to catch him," he said. "Since rabbits always stick to the well-trod paths."

She scowled at his sarcasm. "What are we to do?"

Anthony had half a mind to answer, "Go home and get a *real* dog," but she looked so worried he bit his tongue. Actually, upon closer inspection she looked more irritated than worried, but there was definitely a bit of worry in the mix.

So instead he said, "I propose we wait until we hear someone shriek. Any minute now he's bound to dash right across some young lady's feet and scare her out of her very wits."

"Do you think?" She didn't look convinced. "Because he's not the scariest dog to look at. He thinks he is, and it's really quite sweet, actually, but the truth is, he's—"

"Eeeeeeeeeeeeeeaaaaaaaaaahhhhhk!"

"I believe we have our answer," Anthony said dryly, and he took off in the direction of the anonymous lady's scream.

Kate hurried after him, cutting right across the grass toward Rotten Row. The viscount was running in front of her, and all she could think was that he must really want to marry Edwina, because despite the fact that he was clearly a splendid athlete, he looked most undignified dashing through the park after a rotund corgi. Even worse, they were going to have to run right across Rotten Row, the *ton*'s favorite spot for riding and driving.

*Everyone* was going to see them. A less determined man would have given up ages ago.

Kate kept running on after them, but she was losing ground. She hadn't spent much time in breeches, but she was fairly certain it was easier to run in them than in skirts. Especially when one was out in public and could not hitch them up above one's ankles.

She tore across Rotten Row, refusing to make eye contact with any of the fashionable ladies and gentlemen out with their horses. There was always the chance she wouldn't be recognized as the hoydenish miss racing through the park as if someone had set fire to her shoes. Not much of a chance, but a chance nonetheless.

When she reached the grass again, she stumbled for a second and had to pause to take a few deep breaths. Then horror dawned. They were almost to The Serpentine.

Oh, *no*.

There was little Newton liked better than to jump in a lake. And the sun was just warm enough that it might look tempting, especially if one happened to be a creature covered with thick, heavy fur, a creature who'd been running at breakneck speed for five minutes. Well, breakneck for an overweight corgi.

Which was still, Kate noted with some interest, fast enough to keep a six-foot-tall viscount at bay.

Kate hitched up her skirts an inch or so—hang the onlookers, she couldn't afford to be fussy right now—and took off running again. There was no way she'd catch up with Newton, but maybe she could catch up with Lord Bridgerton before he killed Newton.

Murder *had* to be on his mind by now. The man would have to be a saint not to want to murder the dog.

And if one percent of what had been written about him in *Whistledown* was true, he was no saint.

Kate gulped. "Lord Bridgerton!" she called out, intending to tell him to call off the hunt. She'd simply have to wait for Newton to exhaust himself. With four-inch-tall legs, that had to come sooner rather than later. "Lord Bridgerton! We can just—"

Kate stumbled in her tracks. Was that Edwina over there by The Serpentine? She squinted. It *was* Edwina, standing gracefully with her hands clasped in front of her. And it appeared that the hapless Mr. Berbrooke was making some sort of repair to his curricle.

Newton stopped short for one moment, spying Edwina at the same moment Kate did, and abruptly changed his course, barking joyfully as he ran toward his beloved.

"Lord Bridgerton!" Kate called out again. "See, look! There's—"

Anthony turned around at the sound of her voice, then followed her pointed finger toward Edwina. So that was why the damned dog spun on its heel and made a ninety-degree change of course. Anthony had nearly slipped on the mud and fallen on his bum trying to maneuver such a sharp turn.

He was going to kill that dog.

No, he was going to kill Kate Sheffield.

No, maybe—

Anthony's gleeful thoughts of vengeance were broken by Edwina's sudden shriek of, "Newton!"

Anthony liked to think of himself as a man of decisive action, but when he saw that dog launch himself in the air and hurtle himself toward Edwina, he was quite simply frozen with shock. Shakespeare himself could not have devised a more appropriate ending to this farce, and it was all playing out right before Anthony's eyes as if at half speed.

And there was nothing he could do about it.

The dog was going to hit Edwina straight in the chest. Edwina was going to topple backward.

Straight into The Serpentine.

"Nooooooo!" he yelled, charging forward even though he knew all attempts at heroics on his part were utterly useless.

Splash!

"Dear God!" Berbrooke exclaimed. "She's all wet!"

"Well, don't just stand there," Anthony snapped, reaching the scene of the accident and charging forward into the waters. "Do something to help!"

Berbrooke clearly did not quite understand what that meant, because he just stood there, bug-eyed, as Anthony reached down, grasped Edwina's hand, and hauled her to her feet.

"Are you all right?" he asked gruffly.

She nodded, sputtering and sneezing too hard to answer.

"Miss Sheffield," he roared, seeing Kate skid to a halt on the banks. "No, not you," he added, when he felt Edwina jerk to attention at his side. "Your sister."

"Kate?" she asked, blinking the filthy water from her eyes. "Where's Kate?"

"Dry as a bone on the embankment," he muttered, followed by a holler in Kate's direction of, "Rein in your bloody dog!"

Newton had cheerfully splashed back out of The Serpentine and was now sitting on the grass, his tongue hanging happily out of his mouth. Kate scurried to his side and grabbed the lead. Anthony noticed that she had no pithy comeback to his roared order. Good, he thought viciously. He wouldn't have thought the bloody woman would have had the sense to keep her mouth shut.

He turned back to Edwina, who, astoundingly, still managed to look lovely even while dripping with pond water. "Let me get you out of here," he said gruffly, and before she had a chance to react, he scooped her into his arms and carried her to dry ground.

"I've never seen anything like that," Berbrooke said, shaking his head.

Anthony made no reply. He didn't think he'd be able to speak without tossing the idiot into the water. What was he thinking, just standing there while Edwina was submerged by that pathetic excuse for a dog?

"Edwina?" Kate asked, walking forward as far as Newton's lead would allow. "Are you all right?"

"I think you've done enough," Anthony bit out, advancing upon her until they were barely a foot apart.

"Me?" she gasped.

"Look at her," he snapped, thrusting a pointed finger in Edwina's direction even while his full attention was focused on Kate. "Just look at her!"

"But it was an accident!"

"I'm really fine!" Edwina called out, sounding a little panicked by the level of anger simmering between her sister and the viscount. "Cold, but fine!"

"See?" Kate returned, swallowing convulsively as she took in the disheveled sight of her sister. "It was an accident."

He merely crossed his arms and arched a brow.

"You don't believe me," she breathed. "I can't believe you don't believe me."

Anthony said nothing. It was inconceivable to him that Kate Sheffield, for all her wit and intelligence, could *not* be jealous of her sister. And even if there was nothing she could have done to prevent this mishap, surely she must be taking a bit of pleasure in the fact that she was dry and comfortable while Edwina looked like a drowned rat. An attractive rat, to be sure, but certainly a drowned one.

But Kate clearly wasn't done with the conversation. "Aside from the fact," she scorned, "that I would never ever do anything to harm Edwina, how do you propose I managed this amazing feat?" She clapped her free hand to her cheek in an expression of mock discovery. "Oh, yes, I know the secret language of the corgis. I ordered the dog to yank the lead from my hand and then, since I have the second sight, I knew that Edwina was standing right here by The Serpentine, so then I said to the dog—through our powerful mind-to-mind connection, since he was much too far away to hear my voice at this point—to change his direction, head for Edwina, and topple her into the lake."

"Sarcasm doesn't become you, Miss Sheffield."

"*Nothing* becomes you, Lord Bridgerton."

Anthony leaned forward, his chin jutting out in a most menacing manner. "Women should not keep pets if they cannot control them."

"And men should not take women with pets for a walk in the park if they cannot control either," she shot back.

Anthony could actually feel the tips of his ears turning red with barely leashed rage. "You, madam, are a menace to society."

She opened her mouth as if to return the insult, but instead she just offered him an almost frighteningly devious smile and turned to the dog and said, "Shake, Newton."

Newton looked up at her finger, pointed right at Anthony, and obediently trotted a few steps closer to him before allowing himself a full-body shake, spraying pond water everywhere.

Anthony went for her throat. "I . . . am . . . going . . . to . . . KILL YOU!" he roared.

Kate ducked nimbly out of the way, dashing over to Edwina's side. "Now, now, Lord Bridgerton," she taunted, seeking safety behind her sister's dripping form. "It would not do to lose your temper in front of the fair Edwina."

"Kate?" Edwina whispered urgently. "What is going on? Why are you being so mean to him?"

"Why is he being so mean to *me*?" Kate hissed back.

"I say," Mr. Berbrooke suddenly said, "that dog got me wet."

"He got all of us wet," Kate replied. Including her. But it had been worth it. Oh, it had been worth it to see the look of surprise and rage on that pompous aristocrat's face.

"You!" Anthony roared, jabbing a furious finger at Kate. "Be quiet."

Kate held her silence. She wasn't foolhardy enough to provoke him any further. He looked as if his head might explode at any moment. And he'd certainly lost whatever claim to dignity he'd had at the beginning of the day. His right sleeve was dripping wet from when he'd hauled Edwina out of the water, his boots looked to be ruined forever, and the rest of him was spotted with water, thanks to Newton's expert shaking prowess.

"I'll tell you what we're going to do," he continued in a low, deadly voice.

"What I need to do," Mr. Berbrooke said jovially, clearly unaware that Lord Bridgerton was likely to murder the first person who opened their mouth, "is finish repairing this curricle. Then I can take Miss Sheffield home." He pointed at Edwina, just in case anyone didn't understand to which Miss Sheffield he referred.

"Mr. Berbrooke," Anthony ground out, "do you know how to fix a curricle?"

Mr. Berbrooke blinked a few times.

"Do you even know what is *wrong* with your curricle?"

Berbrooke's mouth opened and closed a few more times, and then he said, "I have a few ideas. Shouldn't take terribly long to figure out which is the actual problem."

Kate stared at Anthony, fascinated by the vein leaping in his throat. She had never before seen a man so clearly pushed to his limit. Feeling not a little apprehensive at the impending explosion, she took a prudent half step behind Edwina.

She didn't like to think herself a coward, but self-preservation was another matter entirely.

But the viscount somehow managed to keep himself under control, and his voice was terrifyingly even as he said, "This is what we're going to do."

Three pairs of eyes widened in expectation.

"I am going to walk over there"—he pointed at a lady and gentleman about twenty yards away who were trying not to stare but not succeeding—"and ask Montrose if I might borrow his carriage for a few minutes."

"I say," Berbrooke said, craning his neck, "is that Geoffrey Montrose? Haven't seen him for an age."

A second vein started leaping, this time on Lord Bridgerton's temple. Kate grasped Edwina's hand for moral support and held tight.

But Bridgerton, to his credit, ignored Berbrooke's exceedingly inappropriate interjection and continued with, "Since he will say yes—"

"Are you sure?" Kate blurted out.

Somehow his brown eyes resembled icicles. "Am I sure of what?" he bit off.

"Nothing," she mumbled, ready to kick herself. "Please continue."

"As I was saying, since as a friend and a gentleman"—he glared at Kate—"he will say yes, I will take Miss Sheffield home and then *I* will return home and have one of my men return Montrose's curricle."

No one bothered to ask which Miss Sheffield he was talking about.

"What about Kate?" Edwina inquired. After all, the curricle could only seat two.

Kate gave her hand a squeeze. Dear, sweet Edwina.

Anthony looked straight at Edwina. "Mr. Berbrooke will escort your sister home."

"But I can't," Berbrooke said. "Got to finish with the curricle, you know."

"Where do you live?" Anthony snapped.

Berbrooke blinked with surprise but gave his address.

"I will stop by your house and fetch a servant to wait with your conveyance while you escort Miss Sheffield to her home. Is that clear?" He paused and looked at everyone—including the dog—with a rather hard expression. Except for Edwina, of course, who was the only person present who had not lit a fuse directly under his temper.

"Is that clear?" he repeated.

Everyone nodded, and his plan was set into motion. Minutes later, Kate found herself watching Lord Bridgerton and Edwina ride off into the horizon—the very two people she had vowed should never even be in the same room together.

Even worse, she was left alone with Mr. Berbrooke and Newton.

And it took only two minutes to discern that of the two, Newton was the finer conversationalist.

# Chapter 5

*It has come to This Author's attention that Miss Katharine Sheffield took offense at the labeling of her beloved pet, "an unnamed dog of indeterminate breed."*

*This Author is, to be sure, prostrate with shame at this grievous and egregious error and begs of you, dear reader, to accept this abject apology and pay attention to the first ever correction in the history of this column.*

*Miss Katharine Sheffield's dog is a corgi. It is called Newton, although it is difficult to imagine that England's great inventor and physicist would have appreciated being immortalized in the form of a short, fat canine with poor manners.*

LADY WHISTLEDOWN'S SOCIETY PAPERS,
27 APRIL 1814

By that evening, it had become apparent that Edwina had not come through her (albeit brief) ordeal unscathed. Her nose turned red, her eyes began to water, and it was apparent to anyone who glimpsed her puffy face for even a second that, while not seriously ill, she'd caught a bad cold.

But even while Edwina was tucked into bed with a hot water

bottle between her feet and a therapeutic potion brewed up by the cook in a mug on her bedside table, Kate was determined to have a conversation with her.

"What did he say to you on the ride home?" Kate demanded, perching on the edge of her sister's bed.

"Who?" Edwina replied, sniffing fearfully at the remedy. "Look at this," she said, holding it forward. "It's giving off fumes."

"The viscount," Kate ground out. "Who else would have spoken to you on the ride home? And don't be a ninny. It's not giving off fumes. That's just steam."

"Oh." Edwina took another sniff and pulled a face. "It doesn't smell like steam."

"It's *steam*," Kate ground out, gripping the mattress until her knuckles hurt. "What did he *say*?"

"Lord Bridgerton?" Edwina asked blithely. "Oh, just the usual sort of things. You know what I mean. Polite conversation and all that."

"He made polite conversation while you were dripping wet?" Kate asked doubtfully.

Edwina took a hesitant sip, then nearly gagged. "What is *in* this?"

Kate leaned over and sniffed at the contents. "It smells a bit like licorice. And I think I see a raisin at the bottom." But as she sniffed, she thought she heard rain pattering against the glass of the window, and so she sat back up. "Is it raining?"

"I don't know," Edwina said. "It might be. It was rather cloudy when the sun set earlier." She gave the glass one more dubious look, then set it back on the table. "If I drink that, I *know* it will make me sicker," she stated.

"But what else did he say?" Kate persisted, getting up to check out the window. She pushed the curtain aside and peered out. It was raining, but only lightly, and it was too early to tell whether the precipitation would be accompanied by any thunder or lightning.

"Who, the viscount?"

Kate thought herself a saint for not shaking her sister senseless. "Yes, the viscount."

Edwina shrugged, clearly not as interested in the conversation as Kate. "Not much. He asked for my welfare, of course. Which was only reasonable, considering that I had just been dunked in The Serpentine. Which, I might add, was perfectly wretched. Aside from being cold, the water was most certainly not clean."

Kate cleared her throat and sat back down, preparing to ask a most scandalous question, but one which, in her opinion, simply had to be asked. Trying to keep her voice devoid of the complete and total fascination that was coursing through her veins, she asked, "Did he make any untoward advances?"

Edwina lurched back, her eyes growing round with shock. "Of course not!" she exclaimed. "He was a perfect gentleman. Really, I don't see what has you so excited. It wasn't a very interesting conversation. I can't even remember half of what was said."

Kate just stared at her sister, unable to fathom that she could have been trapped in conversation with that odious rake for a good ten minutes and it *didn't* make an indelible impression on her. Much to her own everlasting dismay, every single awful word he'd said to her was etched permanently on her brain.

"By the way," Edwina added, "how was your time with Mr. Berbrooke? It took you nearly an hour to return."

Kate shuddered visibly.

"That bad?"

"I'm sure he will make some woman a good husband," Kate said. "Just not one with a brain."

Edwina let out a little giggle. "Oh, Kate, you are awful."

Kate sighed. "I know. I know. That was terribly cruel of me. The poor man hasn't an unkind bone in his body. It's just that—"

"He hasn't an intelligent bone, either," Edwina finished.

Kate raised her brows. It was most unlike Edwina to make such a judgmental comment.

"I know," Edwina said with a sheepish smile. "Now I am the unkind one. I really shouldn't have said a word, but truly, I thought I would perish on our curricle ride."

Kate straightened with concern. "Was he a dangerous driver?"

"Not at all. It was his conversation."

"Boring?"

Edwina nodded, her blue eyes slightly bewildered. "He was so hard to follow it was almost fascinating to try to figure out how his mind works." She let out a stream of coughs, then added, "But it made my brain hurt."

"So he's not to be your perfect scholar-husband?" Kate said with an indulgent smile.

Edwina coughed some more. "I'm afraid not."

"Maybe you should try a bit more of that brew," Kate suggested, motioning to the lonely mug sitting on Edwina's bedside table. "Cook swears by it."

Edwina shook her head violently. "It tastes like death."

Kate waited a few moments, then had to ask, "Did the viscount say anything about me?"

"You?"

"No, some other me," Kate practically snapped. "Of course *me*. How many other people may I correctly refer to as 'me'?"

"No need to get upset about it."

"I'm not upset—"

"But actually, no, he didn't mention you."

Kate suddenly felt upset.

"He had a lot to say about Newton, though."

Kate's lips parted with dismay. It was never flattering to be passed over for a dog.

"I assured him that Newton is truly the perfect pet, and that I was not at all angry with him, but he was rather charmingly upset on my behalf."

"How charming," Kate muttered.

Edwina grabbed a handkerchief and blew her nose. "I say, Kate, you're rather interested in the viscount."

"I did spend practically the entire afternoon trapped in conversation with him," Kate replied, as if that ought to explain everything.

"Good. Then you've had a chance to see how polite and charming he can be. He's very wealthy, too." Edwina let out a loud sniffle, then fumbled around for a fresh handkerchief. "And while I don't think that one can choose a husband based entirely on finances, given our lack of funds, I would be remiss not to consider it, don't you think?"

"Well . . ." Kate hedged, knowing that Edwina was absolutely correct but not wanting to say anything that might be construed as approval of Lord Bridgerton.

Edwina brought the handkerchief to her face and gave her nose a rather unfeminine blow. "I think we should add him to our list," she said, snuffling over the words.

"Our list," Kate echoed, her voice strangled.

"Yes, of possible matches. I think he and I would suit very well."

"But I thought you wanted a scholar!"

"I did. I do. But you yourself pointed out the unlikelihood of my finding a true scholar. Lord Bridgerton seems intelligent enough. I'll just have to devise a way to discover if he likes to read."

"I'd be surprised if that boor *can* read," Kate muttered.

"Kate Sheffield!" Edwina exclaimed with a laugh. "Did you just say what I think you said?"

"No," Kate said baldly, because of course the viscount could read. But he was just so awful in every other way.

"You did," Edwina accused. "You are the *worst*, Kate." She smiled. "But you do make me laugh."

A low rumble of distant thunder echoed in the night, and Kate forced a smile on her face, trying not to flinch. She was usually all right when the thunder and lightning were far away. It was only when they came one on top of each other, and both seemingly on top of her, that she felt as if she were about to burst from her skin.

"Edwina," Kate said, needing to have this discussion with her sister but also needing to say something that would take her mind off the approaching storm, "you must put the viscount from your mind. He is absolutely not the sort of husband who would make you happy. Aside from the fact that he is the worst sort of rake and would probably flaunt a dozen mistresses in your face—"

At Edwina's frown, Kate cut off the rest of her sentence and decided to expand upon this point. "He would!" she said with great drama. "Haven't you been reading *Whistledown*? Or listening to anything any of the other young ladies' mamas have to say? The ones who have been on the social circuit for several years and know what's what. They *all* say he is a terrible rake. That his only saving grace is how nicely he treats his family."

"Well, that would be a mark in his favor," Edwina pointed out. "Since a wife would be family, yes?"

Kate nearly groaned. "A wife isn't the same as a blood relative. Men who would never dream of uttering a cross word in front of their mothers trample all over their wives' feelings every day."

"And how would you know this?" Edwina demanded.

Kate's mouth fell open. She couldn't remember the last time

Edwina had questioned her judgment on an important matter, and unfortunately, the only answer she could think of on such short notice was, "I just do."

Which, even she had to admit, really didn't pass muster.

"Edwina," she said in a placating voice, deciding to steer the topic in a different direction, "aside from all that, I don't think you would even like the viscount if you got to know him."

"He seemed pleasant enough while driving me home."

"But he was on his best behavior!" Kate persisted. "Of course he'd seem nice. He wants you to fall in love with him."

Edwina blinked. "So you think it was all an act."

"Exactly!" Kate exclaimed, pouncing on the concept. "Edwina, between last night and this afternoon, I spent several hours in his company, and I can assure you, he was *not* on his best behavior with me."

Edwina gasped with horror and maybe a little titillation. "Did he kiss you?" she breathed.

"No!" Kate howled. "Of course not! Where on earth would you get that idea?"

"You said he wasn't on his best behavior."

"What I meant," Kate ground out, "was that he wasn't polite. Nor was he very nice. In fact, he was insufferably arrogant and dreadfully rude and insulting."

"That's interesting," Edwina murmured.

"It wasn't the least bit interesting. It was horrible!"

"No, that's not what I meant," Edwina said, thoughtfully scratching her chin. "It's very odd that he would have behaved rudely to you. He must have heard that I shall be looking to your judgment when I choose a husband. One would think he'd go out of his way to be nice to you. Why," she mused, "would he behave the churl?"

Kate's face colored a dull red—thankfully not so noticeable in the candlelight—as she muttered, "He said he couldn't help himself."

Edwina's mouth fell open, and for one second she sat utterly frozen, as if suspended in time. Then she fell back onto her pillows, hooting with laughter. "Oh, Kate!" she gasped. "That is splendid! Oh, what a tangle. Oh, I love it!"

Kate glared at her. "It's not funny."

Edwina wiped at her eyes. "It might be the funniest thing I've heard all month. All year! Oh, my goodness." She let out a short stream of coughs, brought on by her laughing fit. "Oh, Kate, I do believe you might have cleared out my nose."

"Edwina, that's disgusting."

Edwina brought her handkerchief to her face and blew her nose. "But true," she said triumphantly.

"It won't last," Kate muttered. "You'll be sick as a dog by morning."

"You're probably right," Edwina agreed, "but oh, what fun. He said he couldn't help himself? Oh, Kate, that is just rich."

"There is no need to dwell on it," Kate grumbled.

"Do you know, but he might be the very first gentleman we've met all season you haven't been able to manage."

Kate's lips twisted into a grimace. The viscount had used the same word, and they were both correct. She'd indeed spent the season managing men—managing them for Edwina. And she suddenly wasn't so sure she liked this role of mother hen she'd been thrust into.

Or maybe she'd thrust herself into it.

Edwina saw the play of emotion on her sister's face and immediately turned apologetic. "Oh, dear," she murmured. "I'm sorry, Kate. I didn't mean to tease."

Kate arched a brow.

"Oh, very well, I did mean to tease, but never to actually hurt your feelings. I had no idea Lord Bridgerton had upset you so."

"Edwina, I just don't like the man. And I don't think you should even consider marrying him. I don't care how ardently or how persistently he pursues you. He will not make a good husband."

Edwina was silent for a moment, her magnificent eyes utterly sober. Then she said, "Well, if you say so, it must be true. I have certainly never been steered wrong by your judgment before. And, as you said, you have spent more time in his company than have I, so you would know better."

Kate let out a long and ill-disguised sigh of relief. "Good," she said firmly. "And when you are feeling more the thing, we shall look among your current suitors for a better match."

"And maybe you could look for a husband, too," Edwina suggested.

"Of course I'm always looking," Kate insisted. "What would be the point of a London season if I weren't looking?"

Edwina looked dubious. "I don't think you *are* looking, Kate. I think that all you do is interview possibilities for me. And there is no reason you shouldn't find a husband as well. You need a family of your own. I certainly can't imagine anyone more suited to be a mother than you."

Kate bit her lip, not wanting to respond directly to Edwina's point. Because behind those lovely blue eyes and perfect face, Edwina was quite the most perceptive person she knew. And Edwina was right. Kate hadn't been looking for a husband. But why should she? No one was considering her for marriage, either.

She sighed, glancing toward the window. The storm seemed to have passed without striking her area of London. She supposed she ought to be thankful for small favors.

"Why don't we see about you first," Kate finally said, "since I think we both agree that you are more likely to receive a proposal before I do, and then we'll think about my prospects?"

Edwina shrugged, and Kate knew that her deliberate silence meant that she did not agree.

"Very well," Kate said, rising to her feet. "I'll leave you to your rest. I'm sure you'll need it."

Edwina coughed as a reply.

"And drink that remedy!" Kate said with a laugh, heading out the door.

As she shut the door behind her, she heard Edwina mutter, "I'd rather die."

Four days later, Edwina was dutifully drinking Cook's remedy, although not without considerable grumbling and complaint. Her health had improved, but only to the point where she was *almost* better. She was still stuck in bed, still coughing, and very irritable.

Mary had declared that Edwina could not attend any social functions until Tuesday at the earliest. Kate had taken that to mean that they all would receive a respite (because really, what was the point of attending a ball without Edwina?), but after Kate spent a blessedly uneventful Friday, Saturday, and Sunday with nothing to do but read and take Newton for walks, Mary suddenly declared that the two of them would attend Lady Bridgerton's musicale Monday evening, and—

(Kate tried to interject a vehement argument about why this was not a good idea at this point.)

—that was *final*.

Kate gave in fairly quickly. There was really no point in arguing any further, especially since Mary turned on her heel and walked away directly after uttering the word, "final."

Kate did have certain standards, and they included not arguing with closed doors.

And so Monday evening she found herself dressed in ice blue silk, fan in hand, as she and Mary rolled through the streets of London in their inexpensive carriage, on their way to Bridgerton House in Grosvenor Square.

"Everyone will be very surprised to see us without Edwina," Kate said, her left hand fiddling with the black gauze of her cloak.

"You are looking for a husband as well," Mary replied.

Kate held silent for a moment. She couldn't very well argue that point, since, after all, it was supposed to be true.

"And stop crumpling your cloak," Mary added. "It will be wrinkled all evening."

Kate's hand went limp. She then tapped the right one rhythmically against the seat for several seconds, until Mary blurted out, "Good heavens, Kate, can't you sit still?"

"You know I can't," Kate said.

Mary just sighed.

After another long silence, punctuated only by the tapping of her foot, Kate added, "Edwina will be lonely without us."

Mary didn't even bother to look at her as she answered, "Edwina has a novel to read. The latest by that Austen woman. She won't even notice we're gone."

That much was also true. Edwina probably wouldn't notice if her bed caught on fire while she was reading a book.

So Kate said, "The music will probably be dreadful. After that Smythe-Smith affair . . ."

"The Smythe-Smith musicale was performed by the Smythe-Smith daughters," Mary replied, her voice starting to hold an edge of impatience. "Lady Bridgerton has hired a professional opera singer, visiting from Italy. We are honored simply to receive an invitation."

Kate knew without a doubt that the invitation was for Edwina; she and Mary were surely included only out of politeness. But Mary's teeth were beginning to clench together, and so Kate vowed to hold her tongue for the remainder of the ride.

Which wouldn't be so difficult, after all, as they were presently rolling up in front of Bridgerton House.

Kate's mouth dropped open as she looked out the window. "It's huge," she said dumbly.

"Isn't it?" Mary replied, gathering her things together. "I understand that Lord Bridgerton doesn't live there. Even though it belongs to him, he remains in his bachelor's lodgings so that his mother and siblings may reside at Bridgerton House. Isn't that thoughtful of him?"

*Thoughtful* and *Lord Bridgerton* were not two expressions Kate would have thought to use in the same sentence, but she nodded nonetheless, too awed by the size and grace of the stone building to make an intelligent comment.

The carriage rolled to a halt, and Mary and Kate were helped down by one of the Bridgerton footmen, who rushed to open the door. A butler took their invitation and admitted them, taking their wraps and pointing them toward the music room, which was just at the end of the hall.

Kate had been inside enough grand London homes not to publicly gape at the obvious wealth and beauty of the furnishings, but even she was impressed by the interiors, decorated with elegance and restraint in the Adam style. Even the ceilings were works of art—done up in pale shades of sage and blue, the colors separated by white plasterwork so intricate it almost appeared to be a more solid form of lace.

The music room was just as lovely, the walls painted a friendly shade of lemon yellow. Rows of chairs had been set up for attendees, and Kate quickly steered her stepmother toward the back. Truly, there could be no reason why she'd want to put herself in a noticeable position. Lord Bridgerton was sure to be in attendance—if all the tales about his devotion to his family were true—and if Kate was lucky, maybe he wouldn't even notice her presence.

Quite to the contrary, Anthony knew exactly when Kate stepped out of her carriage and entered his family home. He had been in his study, having a solitary drink before heading down to his mother's annual musicale. In a bid for privacy, he'd chosen not to live at Bridgerton House while still a bachelor, but he did keep his study here. His position as head of the Bridgerton family carried with it serious responsibilities, and Anthony generally found it easier to attend to these responsibilities while in close proximity to the rest of his family.

The study's windows looked out over Grosvenor Square, however, and so he had been amusing himself watching the carriages arrive and the guests alight. When Kate Sheffield had stepped down, she'd looked up at the facade of Bridgerton House, tipping her face up in much the same manner she'd done while enjoying the warmth of the sun in Hyde Park. The light from the sconces on either side of the front door had filtered onto her skin, bathing her with a flickering glow.

And Anthony's breath was sucked right out of him.

His glass tumbler landed on the wide windowsill with a heavy thunk. This was getting ridiculous. He wasn't self-delusional enough to mistake the tightening of his muscles as anything other than desire.

Bloody hell. He didn't even like the woman. She was too bossy, too opinionated, too quick to jump to conclusions. She wasn't even beautiful—at least not compared to quite a few of the ladies flitting about London for the season, her sister most especially included.

Kate's face was a touch too long, her chin a hair too pointed, her eyes a shade too big. Everything about her was too *some*thing. Even her mouth, which vexed him to no end with its endless stream of insults and opinions, was too full. It was a rare event when she actually had it closed and was treating him to a moment of blessed silence, but if he happened to look at her in that split second (for surely she could not be silent for much longer than that) all he saw were her lips, full and pouty, and—provided that she kept them shut and didn't actually speak—eminently kissable.

Kissable?

Anthony shuddered. The thought of kissing Kate Sheffield was terrifying. In fact, the mere fact that he'd even *thought* of it ought to be enough to have him locked up in an asylum.

And yet . . .

Anthony collapsed in a chair.

And yet he'd dreamed about her.

It had happened after the fiasco at The Serpentine. He'd been so furious with her he could barely speak. It was a wonder he'd managed to say anything at all to Edwina during the short ride back to her house. Polite conversation was all he'd been able to get out—mindless words so familiar they tripped from his tongue as if by rote.

A blessing indeed, since his mind most definitely had not been where it should be: on Edwina, his future wife.

Oh, she hadn't agreed to marry him. He hadn't even asked. But she fit his requirements for a wife in every possible way; he'd already decided that she would be the one to whom he would finally propose marriage. She was beautiful, intelligent, and even-tempered. Attractive without making his blood rush. They would spend enjoyable years together, but he'd never fall in love with her.

She was exactly what he needed.

And yet . . .

Anthony reached for his drink and downed the rest of its contents in one gasping gulp.

And yet he'd dreamed about her sister.

He tried not to remember. He tried not to remember the details of the dream—the heat and the sweat of it—but he'd only had this one drink this evening, certainly not enough to impair his memory. And although he'd had no intention of having more than this one drink, the concept of sliding into mindless oblivion was starting to sound appealing.

Anything would be appealing if it meant he wouldn't remember.

But he didn't feel like drinking. He'd not overimbibed in years. It seemed such the young man's game, not at all attractive as one neared thirty. Besides, even if he did decide to seek temporary amnesia in a bottle, it wouldn't come fast enough to make the memory of *her* go away.

Memory? Ha. It wasn't even a real memory. Just a dream, he reminded himself. Just a dream.

He'd fallen asleep quickly upon returning home that evening. He'd stripped naked and soaked in a hot bath for nearly an hour, trying to remove the chill from his bones. He hadn't been completely submerged in The Serpentine as had Edwina, but his legs had been soaked, as had one of his sleeves, and Newton's strategic shake had guaranteed that not one inch of his body remained warm during the windy ride home in the borrowed curricle.

After his bath he'd crawled into bed, not particularly caring that it was still light outside, and would be for a good hour yet. He was exhausted, and he'd had every intention of falling into a deep, dreamless sleep, not to be awakened until the first streaks of dawn touched the morning.

But sometime in the night, his body had grown restless and hungry. And his treacherous mind had filled with the most awful of images. He'd watched it as if floating near the ceiling, and yet he felt everything—his body, naked, moving over a lithe female form; his hands stroking and squeezing warm flesh. The delectable tangle of arms and legs, the musky scent of two bodies in love—it had all been there, hot and vivid in his mind.

And then he'd shifted. Just the tiniest bit, perhaps to kiss the faceless woman's ear. Except as he moved to the side, she was no longer faceless. First appeared a thick lock of dark brown hair, softly curling and tickling at his shoulder. Then he moved even farther . . .

And he saw her.

Kate Sheffield.

He'd awakened in an instant, sitting bolt upright in bed and shaking from the horror of it. It had been the most vivid erotic dream he'd ever experienced.

And his worst nightmare.

He'd felt frantically around the sheets with one of his hands, terrified that he'd find the proof of his passion. God help him if he'd actually ejaculated while dreaming of quite the most awful woman of his acquaintance.

Thankfully, his sheets were clean, and so, with beating heart and heavy breath, he'd lain back against his pillows, his movements slow and careful, as if that would somehow prevent a recurrence of the dream.

He'd stared at the ceiling for hours, first conjugating Latin verbs, then counting to a thousand, all in an attempt to keep his brain on anything but Kate Sheffield.

And amazingly, he'd exorcised her image from his brain and fallen asleep.

But now she was back. Here. In his home.

It was a terrifying thought.

And where the hell was Edwina? Why hadn't she accompanied her mother and sister?

The first strains of a string quartet drifted under his door, discordant and jumbled, no doubt the warm-up of the musicians his mother had hired to accompany Maria Rosso, the latest soprano to take London by storm.

Anthony certainly hadn't told his mother, but he and Maria had enjoyed a pleasant interlude the last time she'd been in town. Maybe he ought to consider renewing their friendship. If the sultry Italian beauty didn't cure what ailed him, nothing would.

Anthony stood and straightened his shoulders, aware that he probably looked as if he were girding himself for battle. Hell, that's how he *felt*. Maybe, if he was lucky, he'd be able to avoid Kate Sheffield entirely. He couldn't imagine she'd go out of her way to engage him in conversation. She'd made it abundantly clear that she held him in just as much esteem as he did her.

Yes, that's exactly what he would do. Avoid her. How difficult could that be?

# *Chapter 6*

*Lady Bridgerton's musicale proved to be a decidedly musical affair (not, This Author assures you, always the norm for musicales). The guest performer was none other than Maria Rosso, the Italian soprano who made her debut in London two years ago and has returned after a brief stint on the Vienna stage.*

*With thick, sable hair and flashing dark eyes, Miss Rosso proved as lovely in form as she did in voice, and more than one (indeed, more than a dozen) of society's so-called gentlemen found it difficult indeed to remove their eyes from her person, even after the performance had concluded.*

LADY WHISTLEDOWN'S SOCIETY PAPERS,
27 APRIL 1814

Kate knew the minute he walked in the room.

She tried to tell herself it had nothing to do with a heightened awareness of the man. He was excruciatingly handsome; that was fact, not opinion. She couldn't imagine that every woman didn't notice him immediately.

He arrived late. Not very—the soprano couldn't have been more than a dozen bars into her piece. But late enough so that he tried to be quiet as he slipped into a chair toward the front near his family. Kate remained motionless in her position at the back, fairly certain that he didn't see her as he settled in for the performance. He didn't look her way, and besides, several candles had been snuffed, leaving the room bathed in a dim, romantic glow. The shadows surely obscured her face.

Kate tried to keep her eyes on Miss Rosso throughout the performance. Kate's disposition was not improved, however, by the fact that the singer could not take her eyes off of Lord Bridgerton. At first Kate had thought she must be imagining Miss Rosso's fascination with the viscount, but by the time the soprano was halfway done, there could be no doubt. Maria Rosso was issuing the viscount a sultry invitation with her eyes.

Why this bothered Kate so much, she didn't know. After all, it was just another piece of proof that he was every bit the licentious rake she'd always known him to be. She should have felt smug. She should have felt vindicated.

Instead, all she felt was disappointment. It was a heavy, uncomfortable feeling around her heart, one that left her slumping slightly in her chair.

When the performance was done, she couldn't help but notice that the soprano, after graciously accepting her applause, walked brazenly up to the viscount and offered him one of those seductive smiles—the sort Kate would never learn to do if she had a dozen opera singers trying to teach her. There was no mistaking what the singer meant by that smile.

Good heavens, the man didn't even need to chase women. They practically dropped at his feet.

It was disgusting. Really, truly disgusting.

And yet Kate couldn't stop watching.

Lord Bridgerton offered the opera singer a mysterious half-smile of his own. Then he reached out and actually tucked an errant lock of her raven hair behind her ear.

Kate shivered.

Now he was leaning forward, whispering something in her ear. Kate felt her own ears straining in their direction, even though it was quite obviously impossible for her to hear a thing from so far away.

But still, was it truly a crime to be ravenously curious? And—

Good heavens, did he just kiss her neck? Surely he wouldn't do that in his mother's home. Well, she supposed Bridgerton House was technically *his* home, but his mother lived here, as did many of his siblings. Truly, the man should know better than that. A little decorum in the company of his family would not be remiss.

"Kate? Kate?"

It may have been a small kiss, just a feather-light brush of his lips against the opera singer's skin, but it was still a kiss.

"Kate!"

"Right! Yes?" Kate nearly jumped half a foot as she whirled around to face Mary, who was watching her with a decidedly irritated expression.

"Stop watching the viscount," Mary hissed.

"I wasn't—well, all right, I was, but did you see him?" Kate whispered urgently. "He's shameless."

She looked back over at him. He was still flirting with Maria Rosso, and he obviously didn't care who saw them.

Mary's lips pursed into a tight line before she said, "I'm sure his behavior isn't any of our business."

"Of course it's our business. He wants to marry Edwina."

"We don't know that for sure."

Kate thought back over her conversations with Lord Bridgerton. "I'd say it's a very, very good bet."

"Well, stop watching him. I'm certain he wants nothing to do with you after that fiasco in Hyde Park. And besides, there are any number of eligible gentlemen here. You'd do well to stop thinking of Edwina all the time and start looking around for yourself."

Kate felt her shoulders sag. The mere thought of trying to attract a suitor was exhausting. They were all interested in Edwina, anyway. And even though she wanted nothing to do with the viscount, it still stung when Mary said she was *certain* he wanted nothing to do with *her*.

Mary grasped her arm with a grip that brooked no protest. "Come now, Kate," she said quietly. "Let us go forward to greet our hostess."

Kate swallowed. Lady Bridgerton? She had to meet Lady Bridgerton? The viscount's mother? It was hard enough to believe that a creature such as he even *had* a mother.

But manners were manners, and no matter how much Kate would have liked to slip out into the hall and depart, she knew she must thank her hostess for staging such a lovely performance.

And it had been lovely. Much as Kate was loath to admit it, especially while the woman in question was hanging all over the viscount, Maria Rosso did possess the voice of an angel.

With Mary's arm firmly guiding her, Kate reached the front of the room and waited her turn to meet the viscountess. She seemed a lovely woman, with fair hair and light eyes, and rather petite to have mothered such large sons. The late viscount must have been a tall man, Kate decided.

Finally they reached the front of the small crowd, and the viscountess grasped Mary's hand. "Mrs. Sheffield," she said warmly, "what a delight to see you again. I so enjoyed our meeting at the Hartside ball last week. I am very glad you decided to accept my invitation."

"We would not dream of spending the evening anywhere else," Mary replied. "And may I present my daughter?" She motioned to Kate, who stepped forward and bobbed a dutiful curtsy.

"It is a pleasure to meet you, Miss Sheffield," Lady Bridgerton said.

"And I am likewise honored," Kate replied.

Lady Bridgerton motioned to a young lady at her side. "And this is my daughter, Eloise."

Kate smiled warmly at the girl, who looked to be about the same age as Edwina. Eloise Bridgerton had the exact same color hair as her older brothers, and her face was lit by a friendly, wide smile. Kate liked her instantly.

"How do you do, Miss Bridgerton," Kate said. "Is this your first season?"

Eloise nodded. "I'm not officially out until next year, but my mother has been allowing me to attend functions here at Bridgerton House."

"How lucky for you," Kate replied. "I should have loved to have attended a few parties last year. Everything was so new when I arrived in London this spring. The mind boggles at the simple attempt to remember everyone's name."

Eloise grinned. "Actually, my sister Daphne came out two years ago, and she always described everyone and everything to me in such detail, I feel as if I already recognize almost everyone."

"Daphne is your eldest daughter?" Mary asked Lady Bridgerton.

The viscountess nodded. "She married the Duke of Hastings last year."

Mary smiled. "You must have been delighted."

"Indeed. He is a duke, but more importantly, he is a good man and loves my daughter. I only hope the rest of my children make such excellent matches." Lady Bridgerton cocked her head slightly to the side and turned back to Kate. "I understand, Miss Sheffield, that your sister was not able to attend this evening."

Kate fought a groan. Clearly Lady Bridgerton was already pairing up Anthony and Edwina for a walk down the aisle. "I'm afraid she caught a chill last week."

"Nothing serious, I hope?" the viscountess said to Mary, in a rather mother-to-mother sort of tone.

"No, not at all," Mary replied. "In fact, she is nearly back to sorts. But I thought she should have one more day of recuperation before venturing out. It would not do for her to suffer a relapse."

"No, of course not." Lady Bridgerton paused, then smiled. "Well, that is too bad. I was so looking forward to meeting her. Edwina is her name, yes?"

Kate and Mary both nodded.

"I've heard she is lovely." But even as Lady Bridgerton said the words, she was glancing at her son—who was flirting madly with the Italian opera singer—and frowning.

Kate felt something very uneasy in her stomach. According to recent issues of *Whistledown*, Lady Bridgerton was on a mission to get her son married off. And while the viscount didn't seem the sort of man to bend to his mother's will (or anyone's, for that matter), Kate had a feeling that Lady Bridgerton would be able to exert quite a bit of pressure if she so chose.

After a few more moments of polite chatter, Mary and Kate left Lady Bridgerton to greet the rest of her guests. They were soon accosted by Mrs. Featherington, who, as the mother of three unmarried young women herself, always had a lot to say to Mary on a wide variety of topics. But as the stout woman bore down on them, her eyes were focused firmly on Kate.

Kate immediately began to assess possible escape routes.

"Kate!" Mrs. Featherington boomed. She had long since declared herself on a first-name basis with the Sheffields. "What a surprise to see you here."

"And why is that, Mrs. Featherington?" Kate asked, puzzled.

"Surely you read *Whistledown* this morning."

Kate smiled weakly. It was either that or wince. "Oh, you mean that little incident involving my dog?"

Mrs. Featherington's brows rose a good half inch. "From what I hear, it was more than a 'little incident.' "

"It was of little consequence," Kate said firmly, although truth be told, she was finding it difficult not to growl at the meddlesome woman. "And I must say I resent Lady Whistledown referring to Newton as a dog of indeterminate breed. I'll have you know he is a full-blooded corgi."

"It was truly of no matter," Mary said, finally coming to Kate's defense. "I'm surprised it even warranted a mention in the column."

Kate offered Mrs. Featherington her blandest smile, fully aware that both she and Mary were lying through their teeth. Dunking Edwina (and nearly dunking Lord Bridgerton) in The Serpentine was not an incident of "little consequence," but if Lady Whistledown hadn't seen fit to report the full details, Kate certainly wasn't about to fill the gap.

Mrs. Featherington opened her mouth, a sharp intake of breath telling Kate that she was preparing to launch into a lengthy monologue on the topic of the importance of good deportment (or good manners, or good breeding, or good whatever the day's topic was), so Kate quickly blurted out, "May I fetch you two some lemonade?"

The two matrons said yes and thanked her, and Kate slipped away. Once she returned, however, she smiled innocently and said, "But I have only two hands, so now I must return for a glass for myself."

And with that, she took her leave.

She stopped briefly at the lemonade table, just in case Mary was looking, then darted out of the room and into the hall, where she sank onto a cushioned bench about ten yards from the music room, eager to get a bit of air. Lady Bridgerton had left the music room's French doors open to the small garden at the back of the house, but it was such a crush that the air was stifling, even with the slight breeze from outside.

She remained where she sat for several minutes, more than pleased that the other guests had not chosen to spill out into the hall. But then she heard one particular voice rise slightly above the low rumble of the crowd, followed by decidedly musical laughter, and Kate realized with horror that Lord Bridgerton and his would-be mistress were leaving the music room and entering the hall.

"Oh, no," she groaned, trying to keep her voice to herself. The last thing she wanted was for the viscount to stumble across her sitting alone in the hall. She knew she was by herself by choice, but he'd probably think she'd fled the gathering because she was a social failure and all the *ton* shared his opinion of her—that she was an impertinent, unattractive menace to society.

Menace to society? Kate's teeth clamped together. It would take a long, long time before she'd forgive him *that* insult.

But still, she was tired, and she didn't feel like facing him just then, so she hitched up her skirts by a few inches to save her from tripping and ducked into the doorway next to her bench. With any luck, he and his paramour would walk on by, and she could scoot back into the music room, no one being the wiser.

Kate looked around quickly as she shut the door. There was a lighted lantern on a desk, and as her eyes adjusted to the dimness, she realized she was in some sort of office. The walls were lined with books, although not enough for this to be the Bridgertons' library, and the room was dominated by a massive oak desk.

Papers lay on top in neat piles, and a quill and inkpot still sat on the blotter.

Clearly this office was not just for show. Someone actually worked here.

Kate wandered toward the desk, her curiosity getting the better of her, and idly ran her fingers along the wooden rim. The air still smelled faintly of ink, and maybe the slightest hint of pipe smoke.

All in all, she decided, it was a lovely room. Comfortable and practical. A person could spend hours here in lazy contemplation.

But just as Kate leaned back against the desk, savoring her quiet solitude, she heard an *awful* sound.

The click of a doorknob.

With a frantic gasp, she dove under the desk, squeezing herself into the empty cube of space and thanking the heavens that the desk was completely solid, rather than the sort that rested on four spindly legs.

Barely breathing, she listened.

"But I had heard this would be the year we would finally see the notorious Lord Bridgerton fall into the parson's mousetrap," came a lilting feminine voice.

Kate bit her lip. It was a lilting feminine voice with an *Italian* accent.

"And where did you hear that?" came the unmistakable voice of the viscount, followed by another awful click of the doorknob.

Kate shut her eyes in agony. She was trapped in the office with a pair of lovers. Life simply could not get any worse than this.

Well, she could be discovered. *That* would be worse. Funny how that didn't make her feel much better about her present predicament, though.

"It is all over town, my lord," Maria replied. "Everyone is saying you have decided to settle down and choose a bride."

There was a silence, but Kate could swear she could *hear* him shrug.

Some footsteps, most probably drawing the lovers closer together, then Bridgerton murmured, "It is probably past time."

"You are breaking my heart, did you know that?"

Kate thought she might gag.

"Now, now, my sweet signorina"—the sound of lips on skin—"we both know that your heart is impervious to any of my machinations."

Next came a rustling sound, which Kate took to be Maria pulling coyly away, followed by, "But I am not inclined for a dalliance, my lord. I do not look for marriage, of course—that would be most foolish. But when I next choose a protector, it shall be for, shall we say, the long term."

Footsteps. Perhaps Bridgerton was closing the distance between them again?

His voice was low and husky as he said, "I fail to see the problem."

"Your wife may see a problem."

Bridgerton chuckled. "The only reason to give up one's mistress is if one happens to love one's wife. And as I do not intend to choose a wife with whom I might fall in love, I see no reason to deny myself the pleasures of a lovely woman like you."

*And you want to marry Edwina?* It was all Kate could do not to scream. Truly, if she weren't squatting like a frog with her hands wrapped around her ankles, she probably would have emerged like a Fury and tried to murder the man.

Then followed a few unintelligible sounds, which Kate dearly prayed were not the prelude to something considerably more intimate. After a moment, though, the viscount's voice emerged clearly. "Would you care for something to drink?"

Maria murmured her assent, and Bridgerton's forceful stride echoed along the floor, growing closer and closer, until . . .

Oh, *no.*

Kate spied the decanter, sitting on the windowsill, directly opposite her hiding spot under the desk. If he just kept his face to the window as he poured, she might escape detection, but if he turned so much as halfway . . .

She froze. Utterly froze. Completely stopped breathing.

Eyes wide and unblinking (could eyelids make a sound?) she watched with utter and complete horror as Bridgerton came into view, his athletic frame displayed to surprising benefit from her vantage point on the floor.

The tumblers clinked slightly together as he set them down, then he pulled the stopper from the decanter and poured two fingers of amber liquid into each glass.

*Don't turn around. Don't turn around.*

"Is everything all right?" Maria called out.

"Perfect," Bridgerton answered, although he sounded vaguely distracted. He lifted the glasses, humming slightly to himself as his body slowly began to turn.

*Keep walking. Keep walking.* If he walked away from her while he turned, he'd go back to Maria and she'd be safe. But if he turned, and *then* walked, Kate was as good as dead.

And she had no doubt that he *would* kill her. Frankly, she was surprised he hadn't made an attempt last week at The Serpentine.

Slowly, he turned. And turned. And didn't walk.

And Kate tried to think of all the reasons why dying at the age of twenty-one was really not such a bad thing.

Anthony knew quite well why he'd brought Maria Rosso back to his study. Surely no warm-blooded man could be immune to her charms. Her body was lush, her voice was intoxicating, and he knew from experience that her touch was equally potent.

But even as he took in that silky sable hair and those full, pouting lips, even as his muscles tightened at the memory of other full, pouting parts of her body, he knew that he was using her.

He felt no guilt that he would be using her for his own pleasure. In that regard, she was using him as well. And she at least would be compensated for it, whereas he would be out several jewels, a quarterly allowance, and the rent on a fashionable townhouse in a fashionable (but not too fashionable) part of town.

No, if he felt uneasy, if he felt frustrated, if he felt like he wanted to put his damned fist through a brick wall, it was because he was using Maria to banish the nightmare that was Kate Sheffield from his mind. He never wanted to wake up hard and tortured again, knowing that Kate Sheffield was the cause. He wanted to drown himself in another woman until the very memory of the dream dissolved and faded into nothingness.

Because God knew he was never going to act on that particular erotic fantasy. He didn't even *like* Kate Sheffield. The thought of bedding her made him break out in a cold sweat, even as it swirled a ripple of desire right through his gut.

No, the only way that dream was going to come true was if he were delirious with fever . . . and maybe she'd have to be delirious as well . . . and perhaps they would both have to be stranded on a desert isle, or sentenced to be executed in the morning, or . . .

Anthony shuddered. It simply wasn't going to happen.

But bloody hell, the woman must have bewitched him. There could be no other explanation for the dream—no, make that a nightmare—and besides that, even now he could swear that he could *smell* her. It was that maddening combination of lilies and soap, that beguiling scent that had washed over him while they were out in Hyde Park last week.

Here he was, pouring a glass of the finest whiskey for Maria Rosso, one of the few women of his acquaintance who knew how to appreciate both a fine whiskey and the devilish intoxication that followed, and all he could smell was the damned scent of Kate Sheffield. He knew she was in the house—and he was half ready to kill his mother for that—but this was ridiculous.

"Is everything all right?" Maria called out.

"Perfect," Anthony said, his voice sounding tight to his ears. He began to hum, something he'd always done to relax himself.

He turned and started to take a step forward. Maria was waiting for him, after all.

But there was that damned scent again. Lilies. He could swear it was lilies. And soap. The lilies were intriguing, but the soap made sense. A practical sort of woman like Kate Sheffield would scrub herself clean with soap.

His foot hesitated in midair, and his step forward proved to be a small one instead of his usual long stride. He couldn't quite escape the smell, and he kept turning, his nose instinctively twisting his eyes toward where he knew there couldn't be lilies, and yet the scent was, impossibly, there.

And then he saw her.

Under his desk.

It was impossible.

Surely this was a nightmare. Surely if he closed his eyes and opened them again, she'd be gone.

He blinked. She was still there.

Kate Sheffield, the most maddening, irritating, diabolical woman in all England, was crouching like a frog under his desk.

It was a wonder he didn't drop the whiskey.

Their eyes met, and he saw hers widen with panic and fright. Good, he thought savagely. She *should* be frightened. He was going to tan her bloody hide until her hide was bloody well bloody.

What the *hell* was she doing here? Wasn't dousing him with the filthy water of The Serpentine enough for her bloodthirsty spirit? Wasn't she satisfied with her attempts to stymie his courtship of her sister? Did she need to spy on him as well?

"Maria," he said smoothly, moving forward toward the desk until he was stepping on Kate's hand. He didn't step hard, but he heard her squeak.

This gave him immense satisfaction.

"Maria," he repeated, "I have suddenly remembered an urgent matter of business that must be dealt with immediately."

"This very night?" she asked, sounding quite dubious.

"I'm afraid so. Euf!"

Maria blinked. "Did you just grunt?"

"No," Anthony lied, trying not to choke on the word. Kate had removed her glove and wrapped her hand around his knee, digging her nails straight through his breeches and into his skin. Hard.

At least he hoped it was her nails. It could have been her teeth.

"Are you sure there is nothing amiss?" Maria inquired.

"Nothing . . . at"—whatever body part Kate was sinking into his leg sank a little farther—"all!" The last word came out as more of a howl, and he kicked his foot forward, connecting with something he had a sneaking suspicion was her stomach.

Normally, Anthony would die before striking a woman, but this truly seemed to be an exceptional case. In fact, he took not a little bit of pleasure in kicking her while she was down.

She was biting his leg, after all.

"Allow me to walk you to the door," he said to Maria, shaking Kate off his ankle.

But Maria's eyes were curious, and she took a few steps forward. "Anthony, is there an animal under your desk?"

Anthony let out a bark of laughter. "You could say that."

Kate's fist came down on his foot.

"Is it a dog?"

Anthony seriously considered answering in the affirmative, but even he was not that cruel. Kate obviously appreciated his uncharacteristic tact, because she let go of his leg.

Anthony took advantage of his release to quickly step out from behind the desk. "Would I be unforgivably rude," he asked, striding to Maria's side and taking her arm, "if I merely walked you to the door and not back to the music room?"

She laughed, a low, sultry sound that should have seduced him. "I am a grown woman, my lord. I believe I can manage the short distance."

"Forgive me?"

She stepped through the door he held open for her. "I suspect there isn't a woman alive who could deny you forgiveness for that smile."

"You are a rare woman, Maria Rosso."

She laughed again. "But not, apparently, rare enough."

She floated out, and Anthony shut the door with a decisive click. Then, some devil on his shoulder surely prodding him, he turned the key in the lock and pocketed it.

"You," he boomed, eliminating the distance to the desk in four long strides. "Show yourself."

When Kate didn't scramble out quickly enough, he reached down, clamped his hand around her upper arm, and hauled her to her feet.

"Explain yourself," he hissed.

Kate's legs nearly buckled as the blood rushed back to her knees, which had been bent for nearly a quarter of an hour. "It was an accident," she said, grabbing on to the edge of the desk for support.

"Funny how those words seem to emerge from your mouth with startling frequency."

"It's true!" she protested. "I was sitting in the hall, and—" She gulped. He had stepped forward and was now very, very close. "I was sitting in the hall," she said again, her voice sounding crackly and hoarse, "and I heard you coming. I was just trying to avoid you."

"And so you invaded my private office?"

"I didn't know it was your office. I—" Kate sucked in her breath. He'd moved even closer, his crisp, wide lapels now only inches from the bodice of her dress. She knew his proximity was deliberate, that he sought to intimidate rather than seduce, but that didn't do anything to quell the frantic beating of her heart.

"I think perhaps you did know that this was my office," he murmured, letting his forefinger trail down the side of her cheek. "Perhaps you did not seek to avoid me at all."

Kate swallowed convulsively, long past the point of trying to maintain her composure.

"Mmmm?" His finger slid along the line of her jaw. "What do you say to that?"

Kate's lips parted, but she couldn't have uttered a word if her life had depended on it. He wore no gloves—he must have removed them during his tryst with Maria—and the touch of his skin against hers was so powerful it seemed to control her body. She breathed when he paused, stopped when he moved. She had no doubt that her heart was beating in time to his pulse.

"Maybe," he whispered, so close now that his breath kissed her lips, "you desired something else altogether."

Kate tried to shake her head, but her muscles refused to obey.

"Are you sure?"

This time, her head betrayed her and gave a little shake.

He smiled, and they both knew he had won.

# Chapter 7

*Also in attendance at Lady Bridgerton's musicale: Mrs. Featherington and the three elder Featherington daughters (Prudence, Philippa, and Penelope, none of whom wore colors beneficial to their complexions); Mr. Nigel Berbrooke (who, as usual, had much to say, although no one save Philippa Featherington seemed interested); and, of course, Mrs. Sheffield and Miss Katharine Sheffield.*

*This Author assumes that the Sheffields' invitation had also included Miss Edwina Sheffield, but she was not present. Lord Bridgerton seemed in fine spirits despite the younger Miss Sheffield's absence, but alas, his mother appeared disappointed.*

*But then again, Lady Bridgerton's matchmaking tendencies are legendary, and surely she must be at loose ends now that her daughter has married the Duke of Hastings.*

LADY WHISTLEDOWN'S SOCIETY PAPERS,
27 APRIL 1814

Anthony knew he had to be insane.

There could be no other explanation. He'd meant to scare her, terrify her, make her understand that she could never hope to meddle in his affairs and win, and instead . . .

He kissed her.

Intimidation had been his intention, and so he'd moved closer and closer until she, an innocent, could only be cowed by his presence. She wouldn't know what it was like to have a man so near that the heat of his body seeped through her clothes, so close that she couldn't tell where his breath ended and hers began.

She wouldn't recognize the first prickles of desire, nor would she understand that slow, swirling heat in the core of her being.

And that slow, swirling heat was there. He could see it in her face.

But she, a complete innocent, would never comprehend what he could see with one look of his experienced eyes. All she would know was that he was looming over her, that he was stronger, more powerful, and that she had made a dreadful mistake by invading his private sanctuary.

He was going to stop right there and leave her bothered and breathless. But when there was barely an inch between them, the pull grew too strong. Her scent was too beguiling, the sound of her breath too arousing. The prickles of desire he'd meant to spark within her suddenly ignited within *him*, sending a warm claw of need to the very tips of his toes. And the finger he'd been trailing along her cheek—just to torture her, he told himself—suddenly became a hand that cupped the back of her head as his lips took hers in an explosion of anger and desire.

She gasped against his mouth, and he took advantage of her parted lips by sliding his tongue between them. She was stiff in his arms, but it seemed more to do with surprise than anything else, and so Anthony pressed his suit further by allowing one of his hands to slide down her back and cup the gentle curve of her derriere.

"This is madness," he whispered against her ear. But he made no move to let her go.

Her reply was an incoherent, confused moan, and her body

became slightly more pliant in his arms, allowing him to mold her even closer to his form. He knew he should stop, knew he damned well shouldn't have started, but his blood was racing with need, and she felt so . . . so . . .

So *good.*

He groaned, his lips leaving hers to taste the slightly salty skin of her neck. There was something about her that suited him like no woman ever had before, as if his body had discovered something his mind utterly refused to consider.

Something about her was . . . right.

She felt right. She smelled right. She tasted right. And he knew that if he stripped off all of her clothes and took her there on the carpet on the floor of his study, she would fit underneath him, fit around him—just right.

It occurred to Anthony that when she wasn't arguing with him, Kate Sheffield might bloody well be the finest woman in England.

Her arms, which had been imprisoned in his embrace, slowly edged up, until her hands were hesitantly resting on his back. And then her lips moved. It was a tiny thing, actually, a movement barely felt on the thin skin of his forehead, but she was definitely kissing him back.

A low, triumphant growl emerged from Anthony's mouth as he moved his mouth back to hers, kissing her fiercely, daring her to continue what she'd begun. "Oh, Kate," he moaned, nudging her back until she was leaning against the edge of the desk. "God, you taste so good."

"Bridgerton?" Her voice was tremulous, the word more of a question than anything else.

"Don't say anything," he whispered. "Whatever you do, don't say anything."

"But—"

"Not a word," he interrupted, pressing a finger to her lips. The last thing he wanted was for her to ruin this perfectly good moment by opening her mouth and arguing.

"But I—" She planted her hands on his chest and wrenched herself away, leaving him off balance and panting.

Anthony let out a curse, and not a mild one.

Kate scurried away, not all the way across the room, but over to a tall wingback chair, far enough away so that she was not in arms' reach. She gripped the stiff back of the chair, then darted around it, thinking that it might be a good idea to have a nice solid piece of furniture between them.

The viscount didn't look to be in the best of tempers.

"Why did you do that?" she said, her voice so low it was almost a whisper.

He shrugged, suddenly looking a little less angry and a little more uncaring. "Because I wanted to."

Kate just gaped at him for a moment, unable to believe that he could have such a simple answer to what was, despite its simple phrasing, such a complicated question. Finally, she blurted out, "But you can't have."

He smiled. Slowly. "But I did."

"But you don't like me!"

"True," he allowed.

"And I don't like you."

"So you've been telling me," he said smoothly. "I'll have to take your word for it, since it wasn't particularly apparent a few seconds ago."

Kate felt her cheeks flush with shame. She had responded to his wicked kiss, and she hated herself for it, almost as much as she hated him for initiating the intimacy.

But he didn't have to taunt her. That was the act of a cad. She gripped the back of the chair until her knuckles turned white, no longer certain if she was using it as a defense against Bridgerton or as a means to stop herself from lunging forward to strangle him.

"I am not going to let you marry Edwina," she said in a very low voice.

"No," he murmured, moving slowly forward until he was just on the other side of the chair. "I didn't think you were."

Her chin lifted a notch. "And *I* am certainly not going to marry you."

He planted his hands on the armrests and leaned forward until his face was only a few inches from hers. "I don't recall asking."

Kate lurched backward. "But you just kissed me!"

He laughed. "If I offered marriage to every woman I'd kissed, I'd have been thrown into jail for bigamy long ago."

Kate could feel herself begin to shake, and she held on to the back of the chair for dear life. "You, sir," she nearly spat out, "have no honor."

His eyes blazed and one of his hands shot out to grip her chin. He held her that way for several seconds, forcing her to meet his gaze. "That," he said in a deadly voice, "is not true, and were you a man, I'd call you out for it."

Kate remained still for what seemed like a very long time, her eyes locked on his, the skin on her cheek burning where his powerful fingers held her motionless. Finally she did the one thing she'd sworn she would never do with this man.

She begged.

"Please," she whispered, "let me go."

He did, his hand releasing her with a startling abruptness. "My apologies," he said, sounding the slightest bit . . . surprised?

No, that was impossible. Nothing could surprise this man.

"I didn't mean to hurt you," he added softly.

"Didn't you?"

He gave his head a small shake. "No. To scare you, perhaps. But not to hurt you."

Kate stepped backward on shaky legs. "You're nothing but a rake," she said, wishing her voice had emerged with a bit more disdain and a bit less quavering.

"I know," he said with a shrug, the intense fire in his eyes draining down to light amusement. "It's in my nature."

Kate took another step back. She didn't have the energy to try to keep up with his abrupt changes of mood. "I'm leaving now."

"Go," he said affably, waving toward the door.

"You can't stop me."

He smiled. "I wouldn't dream of it."

She began to edge away, walking slowly backward, afraid that if she took her eyes off him for one second he might pounce. "I'm leaving now," she said again, unnecessarily.

But when her hand was an inch away from the doorknob, he said, "I suppose I'll see you next time I call upon Edwina."

Kate went white. Not that she could actually see her face, of course, but for the first time in her life, she actually felt the blood drain from her skin. "You said you were going to leave her alone," she said accusingly.

"No," he replied, leaning rather insolently against the side of the chair, "I said that I didn't think you were likely to 'let' me marry her. Which doesn't really signify, as I have no plans to let you manage my life."

Kate suddenly felt as if a cannonball were lodged in her throat. "But you can't possibly want to marry her after you—after I—"

He took a few steps toward her, his movements slow and sleek like a cat. "After you kissed me?"

"I didn't—" But the words burned the back of her throat, because they were so obviously a lie. She had not initiated the kiss, but she had, in the end, participated in it.

"Oh, come now, Miss Sheffield," he said, standing up straight and crossing his arms. "Let's not go down that road. We don't like each other, that much is true, but I do respect you in an odd, perverted sort of way, and I know you're not a liar."

She said nothing. Really, what could she say? How did one respond to a statement that contained the words "respect" *and* "perverted"?

"You kissed me back," he said with a small, satisfied smile. "Not with any great enthusiasm, I'll admit, but that would be just a matter of time."

She shook her head, unable to believe what she was hearing. "How can you talk of such things not even a minute after declaring your intention to court my sister?"

"This does put a bit of a crimp in my plans, that is true," he commented, his voice light and thoughtful, as if he were considering the purchase of a new horse, or perhaps deciding which neckcloth to wear.

Maybe it was his casual posture, maybe it was the way he stroked his chin as if pretending to give the matter some thought. But something ignited a fuse inside of Kate, and without even thinking, she launched forward, all the furies of the world collecting in her soul as she threw herself against him, pounding his chest with her fists. "You will never marry her!" she cried out. "Never! Do you hear me?"

He raised one arm to ward off a blow to his face. "I'd have to be deaf not to." Then he expertly captured her wrists, holding her arms immobile while her body heaved and shook with rage.

"I won't let you make her unhappy. I won't let you ruin her life," she said, the words choking in her throat. "She is everything that is good and honorable and pure. And she deserves better than you."

Anthony watched her closely, his eyes trained on her face, somehow rendered beautiful by the force of her anger. Her cheeks were high with color, her eyes shone with tears she was fighting hard to keep off her face, and he was beginning to feel like he might be the worst sort of cad.

"Why, Miss Sheffield," he said softly, "I do believe you truly love your sister."

"Of course I love her!" she burst out. "Why do you think I have gone to such efforts to keep her away from *you*? Did you think I did it for amusement? Because I can assure you, my lord, I can think of many things more amusing than being held captive in your study."

Abruptly, he let go of her wrists.

"I should think," she said with a sniffle, rubbing her reddened, abused flesh, "that my love for Edwina would be the one thing about me you could understand with perfect clarity. You, who are supposedly so devoted to your own family."

Anthony said nothing, just watched her, and wondered if perhaps there was a great deal more to this woman than he'd originally estimated.

"If you were Edwina's brother," Kate said with deadly accuracy, "would you allow her to marry a man like you?"

He did not speak for a very long moment, long enough so that the silence rang awkwardly in his own ears. Finally he said, "That is beside the point."

To her credit, she did not smile. She did not crow, nor did she taunt. When she spoke, her words were quiet and true. "I believe I have my answer." Then she turned on her heel and began to walk away.

"My sister," he said, loudly enough to halt her progress toward the door, "married the Duke of Hastings. Are you familiar with his reputation?"

She paused, but she did not turn around. "He is reputed to be quite devoted to his wife."

Anthony chuckled. "Then you are not familiar with his reputation. At least not as it was before he married."

Kate turned slowly around. "If you are attempting to convince me that reformed rakes make the best husbands, you will meet with no success. It was in this very room, not fifteen minutes ago, that you told Miss Rosso that you saw no reason to give up a mistress for a wife."

"I believe I said that was the case only if one does not love one's wife."

A funny little sound emerged from her nose—not quite a snort, but more than a breath, and it was abundantly clear, in that moment at least, that she had no respect for him. With a sharp amusement in her eyes, she asked, "And do you love my sister, Lord Bridgerton?"

"Of course not," he replied. "And I would never insult your intelligence by saying otherwise. *But,*" he said loudly, warding off the interruption he knew was sure to come, "I have known your sister but a week. I have no reason to believe that I would not come to love her were we to spend many years in holy matrimony."

She crossed her arms. "Why is it that I cannot believe a word out of your mouth?"

He shrugged. "I'm sure I do not know." But he did know. The very reason he'd selected Edwina for his wife was that he knew he'd never come to love her. He liked her, he respected her, and he was confident that she'd make an excellent mother to his heirs, but he'd never love her. The spark simply was not there.

She shook her head, disappointment in her eyes. Disappointment that somehow made him feel less of a man. "I hadn't thought you a liar, either," she said softly. "A rake and a rogue, and perhaps a whole host of other things, but not a liar."

Anthony felt her words like blows. Something unpleasant squeezed around his heart—something that made him want to lash out, to hurt her, or at least to show her she hadn't the power to hurt him. "Oh, Miss Sheffield," he called out, his voice a rather cruel drawl, "you won't get far without *this*."

Before she had a chance to react, he reached into his pocket, pulled out the key to the study, and tossed it in her direction, deliberately aiming it at her feet. Given no warning, her reflexes were not sharp, and when she thrust out her hands to catch the key, she missed it entirely. Her hands made a hollow clapping sound as they connected, followed by the dull thud of the key hitting the carpet.

She stood there for a moment, staring at the key, and he could tell the instant she realized he had not intended for her to catch it. She remained utterly still, and then she brought her eyes to his. They were blazing with hatred, and something worse.

Disdain.

Anthony felt as if he'd been punched in the gut. He fought the most ridiculous impulse to leap forward and grab the key from the carpet, to get down on one knee and hand it to her, to apologize for his conduct and beg her forgiveness.

But he would do none of those things. He did not want to mend this breach; he did not want her favorable opinion.

Because that elusive spark—the one so noticeably absent with her sister, whom he intended to marry—crackled and burned so strongly it seemed the room ought to be as light as day.

And nothing could have terrified him more.

Kate remained motionless for far longer than he would have thought, obviously loath to kneel before him, even if it was to gather up the key that would provide her with the escape she so obviously desired.

Anthony just forced a smile, lowering his gaze to the floor and then back up to her face. "Don't you want to leave, Miss Sheffield?" he said, too smoothly.

He watched as her chin trembled, as her throat worked a convulsive swallow. And then, abruptly, she crouched down and scooped up the key. "You will never marry my sister," she vowed, her low, intense voice sending chills to his very bones. "Never."

And then, with a decisive click of the lock, she was gone.

Two days later, Kate was still furious. It didn't help that the afternoon following the musicale, a large bouquet of flowers had arrived for Edwina, the card reading, "With my wishes for a speedy recovery. Last night was dull indeed without your shining presence. —Bridgerton."

Mary had ooohed and aahed over the note—so poetic, she'd sighed, so lovely, so obviously the words of a man truly smitten. But Kate had known the truth. The note was more of an insult toward her than it was a compliment toward Edwina.

Dull indeed, she fumed, eyeing that note—enshrined now on a table in the sitting room—and wondering how she might make it look an accident if it somehow found itself torn into pieces. She might not know very much about matters of the heart and the affairs of men and women, but she'd bet her life that whatever the viscount had been feeling that night in the study, it had not been boredom.

He hadn't, however, come to call. Kate couldn't imagine why, since taking Edwina out for a drive would be an even bigger slap in the face than the note had been. In her most fanciful moments, she liked to flatter herself that he hadn't stopped by because he was afraid to face her, but she knew that was patently untrue.

That man wasn't afraid of anyone. Least of all, a plain, aging spinster he'd probably kissed out of a mix of curiosity, anger, and pity.

Kate crossed over to a window and gazed out over Milner Street; not the most picturesque view in London, but at least it stopped her from staring at the note. It was the pity that truly ate at her. She prayed that whatever had gone into that kiss, the curiosity and the anger had outweighed the pity.

She didn't think she could bear it if he pitied her.

But Kate didn't have very long to obsess over the kiss and what it might and might not have meant, because that afternoon—the afternoon after the flowers—arrived an invitation far more unsettling than anything Lord Bridgerton might have issued himself. The Sheffields' presence, it seemed, was desired at a country house party being rather spontaneously hosted in one week's time by Lady Bridgerton.

The mother of the devil himself.

And there was no way that Kate could possibly get out of going. Nothing short of an earthquake combined with a hurricane combined with a tornado—none of which were likely to occur in Great Britain, although Kate was still holding out hope for the hurricane, as long as there was no thunder or lightning involved—would prevent Mary from showing up on the Bridgertons' bucolic doorstep with Edwina in tow. And Mary certainly wasn't going to allow Kate to remain alone in London, left to her own devices. Not to mention that there was no way Kate was going to allow Edwina to go without her.

The viscount had no scruples. He'd probably kiss Edwina just as he'd kissed Kate, and Kate couldn't imagine that Edwina would have the fortitude to resist such an advance. She'd probably think it beyond romantic and fall in love with him on the spot.

Even Kate had had difficulty keeping her head when his lips had been on hers. For one blissful moment, she'd forgotten everything. She'd known nothing but an exquisite sensation of being cherished and wanted—no, *needed*—and it had been heady stuff, indeed.

Almost enough to make a lady forget that the man doing the kissing was a worthless cad.

Almost . . . but not quite.

# Chapter 8

*As any regular reader of this column knows, there are two sects in London who shall forever remain in the utmost opposition: Ambitious Mamas and Determined Bachelors.*

*The Ambitious Mama has daughters of marriageable age. The Determined Bachelor does not want a wife. The crux of the conflict should be obvious to those with half a brain, or, in other words, approximately fifty percent of This Author's readership.*

*This Author has not yet seen a guest list for Lady Bridgerton's country house party, but informed sources indicate that nearly every eligible young lady of marriageable age will be gathering in Kent next week.*

*This surprises no one. Lady Bridgerton has never made a secret of her desire to see her sons favorably married. This sentiment has made her a favorite among the Ambitious Mama set, who despairingly view the Bridgerton brothers as the worst sort of Determined Bachelors.*

*If one is to trust the betting books, then at least one of the Bridgerton brothers shall be witness to wedding bells before the year is through.*

*As much as it pains This Author to agree with the betting*

*books (they are written by men, and thus inherently flawed), This Author must concur in the prediction.*

*Lady Bridgerton will soon have her daughter-in-law. But who she will be—and to which brother she shall find herself married—ah, Gentle Reader, that is still anyone's guess.*

*Lady Whistledown's Society Papers,*
*29 April 1814*

One week later, Anthony was in Kent—in his private suite of offices, to be precise—awaiting the start of his mother's country house party.

He'd seen the guest list. There could be no doubt that his mother had decided to host this party for one reason and one reason only: to get one of her sons married off, preferably him. Aubrey Hall, the ancestral seat of the Bridgertons, would be filled to the brim with eligible young ladies, each lovelier and more empty-headed than the last. To keep numbers even, Lady Bridgerton had had to invite a number of gentlemen, to be sure, but none were as wealthy or well connected as her own sons, save for the few who were married.

His mother, Anthony thought ruefully, had never been known for her subtlety. At least not when the well-being (*her* definition of well-being, that is) of her children was concerned.

He had not been surprised to see that an invitation had been extended to the Misses Sheffield. His mother had mentioned—several times—how much she liked Mrs. Sheffield. And he had been forced to listen to his mother's "Good Parents Make Good Children" theory too many times not to know what *that* meant.

He'd actually felt a resigned sort of satisfaction upon the sight of Edwina's name on the list. He was eager to propose to her and be done with it. He did feel a measure of uneasiness over what had happened with Kate, but there seemed little to be done now unless he wanted to go to the trouble of finding another prospective bride.

Which he did not. Once Anthony made a decision—in this case to finally get married—he saw no reason in courting delays. Procrastination was for those with a bit more time to live out their lives. Anthony might have avoided the parson's mousetrap for nearly a decade, but now that he'd decided it was time for a bride, there seemed little sense in tarrying.

Marry, procreate, and die. Such was the life of a noble Englishman, even one whose father and uncle had not dropped unexpectedly dead at the ages of thirty-eight and thirty-four, respectively.

Clearly, all he could do at this point was to avoid Kate Sheffield. An apology would probably also be in order. It wouldn't be easy, since the last thing he wanted to do was humble himself to that woman, but the whispers of his conscience had risen to a dull roar, and he knew she deserved the words, "I'm sorry."

She probably deserved more, but Anthony was unwilling to contemplate what that might be.

Not to mention that unless he went and spoke to her, she was likely to block a union between him and Edwina to her dying breath.

Now was clearly the time to take action. If there ever was a romantic spot for a proposal of marriage, Aubrey Hall was it. Built in the early 1700s of warm yellow stone, it sat comfortably on a wide green lawn, surrounded by sixty acres of parkland, a full ten of which were flowering gardens. Later in the summer the roses would be out, but now the grounds were carpeted with grape hyacinths and the brilliant tulips his mother had had imported from Holland.

Anthony gazed across the room and out the window, where ancient elms rose majestically around the house. They shaded the drive and, he liked to think, made the hall seem a bit more like it was a part of nature and a bit less like the typical country homes of the aristocracy—man-made monuments to wealth, position, and power. There were several ponds, a creek, and countless hills and hollows, each one with its own special memories of childhood.

And his father.

Anthony closed his eyes and exhaled. He loved coming home to Aubrey Hall, but the familiar sights and smells brought his father to mind with a clarity so vivid it was almost painful. Even now, nearly twelve years after Edmund Bridgerton's death, Anthony still expected to see him come bounding around the corner, the smallest of the Bridgerton children screaming with delight as he rode on his father's shoulders.

The image made Anthony grin. The child on the shoulders might be a boy or a girl; Edmund had never discriminated between his children when it came to horseplay. But no matter who held the coveted spot at the top of the world, they would surely be chased after by a nurse, insisting that they stop this nonsense at once, and that a child's place was in the nursery and certainly *not* on her father's shoulders.

"Oh, Father," Anthony whispered, looking up at the portrait of Edmund that hung over the fireplace, "how on earth will I ever live up to your achievements?"

And surely that had to have been Edmund Bridgerton's greatest achievement—presiding over a family filled with love and laughter and everything that was so often absent from aristocratic life.

Anthony turned away from his father's portrait and crossed over to the window, watching the coaches pull up the drive. The afternoon had brought a steady stream of arrivals, and every conveyance seemed to carry yet another fresh-faced young lady, her eyes alight with happiness at having been gifted with an invitation to the Bridgerton house party.

Lady Bridgerton didn't often elect to fill her country home with guests. When she did, it was always the event of the season.

Although, truth be told, none of the Bridgertons spent much time at Aubrey Hall any longer. Anthony suspected that his mother suffered the same malady he did—memories of Edmund around every corner. The younger children had few memories of the place, having been raised primarily in London. They certainly didn't recall the long hikes across fields, or the fishing, or the treehouse.

Hyacinth, who was now just eleven, had never even been held in her father's arms. Anthony had tried to fill the gap as best as he could, but he knew he was a very pale comparison.

With a weary sigh, Anthony leaned heavily against the window frame, trying to decide whether or not he wanted to pour himself a drink. He was staring out over the lawn, his eyes focusing on absolutely nothing, when a carriage decidedly shabbier than the rest rolled down the drive. Not that there was anything shoddy about it; it was obviously well made and sturdy. But it lacked the gilded crests that graced the other carriages, and it seemed to bump along a tiny bit more than the rest, as if it weren't quite well sprung enough for comfort.

This would be the Sheffields, Anthony realized. Everyone else on the guest list was in possession of a respectable fortune. Only the Sheffields would have had to hire a carriage for the season.

Sure enough, when one of the Bridgerton footmen, dressed in stylish powder-blue livery, leaped forward to open the door, out stepped Edwina Sheffield, looking a veritable vision in a pale yellow traveling dress and matching bonnet. Anthony was not close enough to see her face clearly, but it was easy enough to imagine.

Her cheeks would be soft and pink, and her exquisite eyes would mirror the cloudless sky.

The next to emerge was Mrs. Sheffield. It was only when she took her place next to Edwina that he realized how closely they resembled one another. Both were charmingly graceful and petite, and as they spoke, he could see that they held themselves in the same manner. The tilt of the head was identical, as were their posture and stance.

Edwina would not outgrow her beauty. This would clearly be a good attribute in a wife, although—Anthony threw a rueful glance at his father's portrait—he wasn't likely to be around to watch her age.

Finally, Kate stepped down.

And Anthony realized he'd been holding his breath.

She didn't move like the two other Sheffield women. They had been dainty, leaning on the footman, putting their hands in his with a graceful arch of the wrist.

Kate, on the other hand, practically hopped right down. She took the footman's proffered arm, but she certainly didn't appear to need his assistance. As soon as her feet touched the ground, she stood tall and lifted her face to gaze at the facade of Aubrey Hall. Everything about her was direct and straightforward, and Anthony had no doubt that if he were close enough to gaze into her eyes, he would find them utterly forthright.

Once she saw him, however, they would fill with disdain, and perhaps a touch of hatred as well.

Which was really all he deserved. A gentleman did not treat a lady as he had Kate Sheffield and expect her continued good favor.

Kate turned to her mother and sister and said something, causing Edwina to laugh and Mary to smile indulgently. Anthony realized he hadn't had much opportunity to watch the three of them interact before. They were a true family, comfortable in each other's presence, and there was a warmth one sensed in their faces when they conversed. It was especially fascinating since he knew that Mary and Kate were not blood relatives.

There were some bonds, he was coming to realize, that were stronger than those of blood. These were not bonds he had room for in his life.

Which was why, when he married, the face behind the veil would have to be Edwina Sheffield's.

Kate had expected to be impressed by Aubrey Hall. She had not expected to be enchanted.

The house was smaller than she'd expected. Oh, it was still far, far larger than anything she'd ever had the honor to call home, but the country manor was not a hulking behemoth rising out of the landscape like a misplaced medieval castle.

Rather, Aubrey Hall seemed almost cozy. It seemed a bizarre word to use to describe a house with surely fifty rooms, but its fanciful turrets and crenellations almost made it seem like something out of a fairy story, especially with the late afternoon sun giving the yellow stone an almost reddish glow. There was nothing austere or imposing about Aubrey Hall, and Kate liked it immediately.

"Isn't it lovely?" Edwina whispered.

Kate nodded. "Lovely enough to make a week spent in the company of that awful man almost bearable."

Edwina laughed and Mary scolded, but even Mary could not resist an indulgent smile. But she did say, casting an eye to the footman, who had gone around the back of the coach to unload their luggage, "You should not say such things, Kate. One never knows who is listening, and it is unbecoming to speak thusly about our host."

"Have no fear, he didn't hear me," Kate replied. "And besides,

I thought Lady Bridgerton was our hostess. She *did* issue the invitation."

"The viscount owns the house," Mary returned.

"Very well," Kate acceded, motioning to Aubrey Hall with a dramatic wave of her arm. "The moment I enter those hallowed halls, I shall be nothing but sweetness and light."

Edwina snorted. "That will certainly be a sight to behold."

Mary shot Kate a knowing look. " 'Sweetness and light' applies to the gardens as well," she said.

Kate just smiled. "Truly, Mary, I shall be on my best behavior. I promise."

"Just do your best to avoid the viscount."

"I will," Kate promised. *As long as he does his best to avoid Edwina.*

A footman appeared at their side, his arm sweeping toward the hall in a splendid arc. "If you will step inside," he said, "Lady Bridgerton is eager to greet her guests."

The three Sheffields immediately turned and made their way to the front door. As they mounted the shallow steps, however, Edwina turned to Kate with a mischievous grin and whispered, "Sweetness and light begins here, sister mine."

"If we weren't in public," Kate returned, her voice equally hushed, "I might have to hit you."

Lady Bridgerton was in the main hall when they stepped inside, and Kate could see the ribboned hems of walking dresses disappearing up the stairs as the previous carriage's occupants made their way to their rooms.

"Mrs. Sheffield!" Lady Bridgerton called out, crossing over toward them. "How lovely to see you. And Miss Sheffield," she added, turning to Kate, "I am so glad you were able to join us."

"It was kind of you to invite us," Kate replied. "And it is truly a pleasure to escape the city for a week."

Lady Bridgerton smiled. "You are a country girl at heart, then?"

"I'm afraid so. London is exciting, and always worth a visit, but I do prefer the green fields and fresh air of the countryside."

"My son is much the same way," Lady Bridgerton said. "Oh, he spends his time in the city, but a mother knows the truth."

"The viscount?" Kate asked doubtfully. He seemed such the consummate rake, and everyone knew a rake's natural habitat was the city.

"Yes, Anthony. We lived here almost exclusively when he was a child. We went to London during the season, of course, since I do love to attend parties and balls, but never for more than a few weeks. It was only after my husband passed away that we moved our primary residence to town."

"I'm sorry for your loss," Kate murmured.

The viscountess turned to her with a wistful expression in her blue eyes. "That is very sweet of you. He has been gone for many years, but I do still miss him each and every day."

Kate felt a lump forming in her throat. She remembered how well Mary and her father had loved each other, and she knew that she was in the presence of another woman who had experienced true love. And suddenly she felt so very sad. Because Mary had lost her husband and the viscountess had lost hers as well, and . . .

And maybe most of all because she would probably never know the bliss of true love herself.

"But we're becoming so maudlin," Lady Bridgerton suddenly said, smiling a little too brightly as she turned back to Mary, "and here I haven't even met your other daughter."

"Have you not?" Mary asked, her brow furrowing. "I suppose that must be true. Edwina was not able to attend your musicale."

"I have, of course, seen you from afar," Lady Bridgerton said to Edwina, bestowing upon her a dazzling smile.

Mary made the introductions, and Kate could not help but notice the appraising manner in which Lady Bridgerton regarded Edwina. There could be no doubt about it. She'd decided Edwina would make an excellent addition to her family.

After a few more moments of chitchat, Lady Bridgerton offered them tea while their bags were being delivered to their rooms, but they declined, as Mary was tired and wanted to lie down.

"As you wish," Lady Bridgerton said, signaling to a housemaid. "I shall have Rose show you to your rooms. Dinner is at eight. Is there anything else I may do for you before you retire?"

Mary and Edwina both shook their heads no, and Kate started to follow suit, but at the last minute she blurted out, "Actually, if I might ask you a question."

Lady Bridgerton smiled warmly. "Of course."

"I noticed when we arrived that you have extensive flower gardens. Might I explore them?"

"Then you are a gardener as well?" Lady Bridgerton inquired.

"Not a very good one," Kate admitted, "but I do admire the hand of an expert."

The viscountess blushed. "I should be honored if you explored the gardens. They are my pride and joy. I don't have much a hand in them now, but when Edmund was al—" She stopped and cleared her throat. "That is to say, when I spent more time here, I was always up to my elbows in dirt. It used to drive my mother positively mad."

"And the gardener, too, I imagine," Kate said.

Lady Bridgerton's smile erupted into laughter. "Oh, indeed! He was a terrible sort. Always saying that the only thing women knew about flowers was how to accept them as a gift. But he had the greenest thumb you could ever imagine, so I learned to put up with him."

"And he learned to put up with you?"

Lady Bridgerton smiled wickedly. "No, he never did, actually. But I didn't let that stop me."

Kate grinned, instinctively warming to the older woman.

"But don't let me keep you any longer," Lady Bridgerton said. "Let Rose take you up and get you settled in. And Miss Sheffield," she said to Kate, "if you like, I should be happy to give you a tour of the gardens later in the week. I'm afraid I'm too busy greeting guests right now, but I would be delighted to make time for you at a later date."

"I would like that, thank you," Kate said, and then she and Mary and Edwina followed the maid up the stairs.

Anthony emerged from his position behind his ever-so-slightly ajar door and strode down the hall toward his mother. "Was that the Sheffields I saw you greeting?" he asked, even though he knew very well it was. But his offices were too far down the hall for him to have heard anything the quartet of women had actually said, so he decided that a brief interrogation was in order.

"Indeed it was," Violet replied. "Such a lovely family, don't you think?"

Anthony just grunted.

"I'm so glad I invited them."

Anthony said nothing, although he considered grunting again.

"They were a last-minute addition to the guest list."

"I didn't realize," he murmured.

Violet nodded. "I had to scrounge up three more gentlemen from the village to even the numbers."

"So we may expect the vicar at supper this eve?"

"And his brother, who is visiting for a spell, and his son."

"Isn't young John only sixteen?"

Violet shrugged. "I was desperate."

Anthony pondered this. His mother was indeed desperate to have the Sheffields join the house party if it meant inviting a spotty-faced sixteen-year-old to supper. Not that she wouldn't have invited him for a family meal; when not formally entertaining, the Bridgertons broke with accepted standards and had all the children eat in the dining room, regardless of age. Indeed, the first time Anthony had gone to visit a friend, he'd been shocked that he was expected to take his meals in the nursery.

But still, a house party was a house party, and even Violet Bridgerton did not allow children at the table.

"I understand you've made the acquaintance of both Sheffield girls," Violet said.

Anthony nodded.

"I find them both delightful myself," she continued. "They haven't much in the way of fortune, but I've always maintained that when choosing a spouse, fortune is not as important as character, provided, of course, that one isn't in desperate straits."

"Which I," Anthony drawled, "as I am sure you are about to point out, am not."

Violet sniffed and shot him a haughty look. "I should not be so quick to mock me, my son. I merely point out the truth. You should be down on your hands and knees thanking your maker every day that you don't *have* to marry an heiress. Most men don't have the luxury of free will when it comes to marriage, you know."

Anthony just smiled. "I should be thanking my maker? Or my mother?"

"You are a beast."

He clucked her gently under the chin. "A beast you raised."

"And it wasn't an easy task," she muttered. "I can assure you of that."

He leaned forward and dropped a kiss on her cheek. "Have fun greeting your guests, Mother."

She scowled at him, but her heart clearly wasn't in it. "Where are you going?" she asked as he started to move away.

"For a walk."

"Really?"

He turned around, a bit bewildered over her interest. "Yes, really. Is there a problem with that?"

"Not at all," she replied. "Just that you haven't taken a walk—for the simple sake of taking a walk—in ages."

"I haven't been in the country in ages," he commented.

"True," she conceded. "In that case, you should really head out to the flower gardens. The early species are just beginning to bloom, and it's simply spectacular. Like nothing you can ever see in London."

Anthony nodded. "I shall see you for supper."

Violet beamed and waved him off, watching as he disappeared back into his offices, which wrapped around the corner of Aubrey Hall and had French doors leading out to the side lawn.

Her eldest son's interest in the Sheffields was most intriguing. Now, if she could only figure out which Sheffield he was interested in. . . .

About a quarter of an hour later, Anthony was out strolling through his mother's flower gardens, enjoying the contradiction of the warm sun and the cool breeze, when he heard the light sound of a second set of footsteps on a nearby path. This piqued his curiosity. The guests were all settling in their rooms, and it was the gardener's day off. Frankly, he'd been anticipating solitude.

He turned toward the direction of the footfall, moving silently until he reached the end of his path. He looked to the right, then to the left, and then he saw . . .

*Her.*

Why, he wondered, was he surprised?

Kate Sheffield, dressed in a pale lavender frock, blending in charmingly with the irises and grape hyacinths. She was standing beside a decorative wooden arch, which, later in the year, would be covered with climbing pink and white roses.

He watched her for a moment as she trailed her fingers along some fuzzy plant he could never remember the name of, then bent down to sniff at a Dutch tulip.

"They don't have a scent," he called out, slowly making his way toward her.

She straightened immediately, her entire body reacting before she'd turned to see him. He could tell she'd recognized his voice, which left him feeling rather oddly satisfied.

As he approached her side, he motioned to the brilliant red bloom and said, "They're lovely and somewhat rare in an English garden, but alas, with no perfume."

She waited longer to reply than he would have expected, then she said, "I've never seen a tulip before."

Something about that made him smile. "Never?"

"Well, not in the ground," she explained. "Edwina has received many bouquets, and the bulb flowers are quite the rage this time of year. But I've never actually seen one growing."

"They are my mother's favorite," Anthony said, reaching down and plucking one. "That and hyacinths, of course."

She smiled curiously. "Of course?" she echoed.

"My youngest sister is named Hyacinth," he said, handing her the flower. "Or didn't you know that?"

She shook her head. "I didn't."

"I see," he murmured. "We are quite famously named in alphabetical order, from Anthony right down to Hyacinth. But then, perhaps I know a great deal more about you than you know of me."

Kate's eyes widened in surprise at his enigmatic statement, but all she said was, "That may very well be true."

Anthony quirked a brow. "I'm shocked, Miss Sheffield. I had donned all my armor and was expecting you to return with, 'I know quite enough.' "

Kate tried not to make a face at his imitation of her voice. But her expression was wry in the extreme as she said, "I promised Mary I would be on my best behavior."

Anthony let out a loud hoot of laughter.

"Strangely enough," Kate muttered, "Edwina had a similar reaction."

He leaned one hand against the arch, carefully avoiding the thorns on the climbing rose vine. "I find myself insanely curious as to what constitutes good behavior."

She shrugged and fiddled with the tulip in her hand. "I expect I shall figure that out as I go along."

"But you're not supposed to argue with your host, correct?"

Kate shot him an arch look. "There was some debate over whether or not you qualify as our host, my lord. After all, the invitation was issued by your mother."

"True," he acceded, "but I do own the house."

"Yes," she muttered, "Mary said as much."

He grinned. "This is killing you, isn't it?"

"Being nice to you?"

He nodded.

"It's not the easiest thing I've ever done."

His expression changed slightly, as if he might be done teasing her. As if he might have something entirely different on his mind. "But it's not the hardest thing, either, now, is it?" he murmured.

"I don't like you, my lord," she blurted out.

"No," he said with an amused smile. "I didn't think you did."

Kate started to feel very strange, much like she had in his study, right before he'd kissed her. Her throat suddenly felt a bit tight, and her palms grew very warm. And her insides—well, there was really nothing to describe the tense, prickly feeling that tightened through her abdomen. Instinctively, and perhaps out of self-preservation, she took a step back.

He looked amused, as if he knew exactly what she was thinking.

She fiddled with the flower some more, then blurted out, "You shouldn't have picked this."

"You should have a tulip," he said matter-of-factly. "It isn't right that Edwina receives all the flowers."

Kate's stomach, already tense and prickly, did a little flip. "Nonetheless," she managed to say, "your gardener will surely not appreciate the mutilation of his work."

He smiled devilishly. "He'll blame one of my younger siblings."

She couldn't help but smile. "I *should* think less of you for such a ploy," she said.

"But you don't?"

She shook her head. "But then again, it's not as if my opinion of you could sink very much lower."

"Ouch." He shook a finger at her. "I thought you were supposed to be on your best behavior."

Kate looked around. "It doesn't count if there is no one nearby to hear me, right?"

"*I* can hear you."

"*You* certainly don't count."

His head dipped a little closer in her direction. "I should think I was the *only* one who did."

Kate said nothing, not wanting even to meet his eyes. Whenever she allowed herself one glimpse into those velvety depths, her stomach started flipping anew.

"Miss Sheffield?" he murmured.

She looked up. Big mistake. Her stomach flipped again.

"Why did you seek me out?" she asked.

Anthony pushed off the wooden post and stood straight. "I didn't, actually. I was just as surprised to see you as you were me." Although, he thought acerbically, he shouldn't have been. He should have realized his mother was up to something the moment she actually suggested where he take his walk.

But could she possibly be steering him to the *wrong* Miss Sheffield? Surely she wouldn't choose Kate over Edwina as a prospective daughter-in-law.

"But now that I have found you," he said, "I did have something I wanted to say."

"Something you haven't already said?" she quipped. "I can't imagine."

He ignored her jibe. "I wanted to apologize."

That got her attention. Her lips parted with shock, and her eyes grew round. "I beg your pardon?" she said. Anthony thought her voice sounded rather like a frog.

"I owe you an apology for my behavior the other night," he said. "I treated you most rudely."

"You're apologizing for the kiss?" she asked, still looking rather dazed.

The kiss? He hadn't even considered apologizing for the kiss. He'd never apologized for a kiss, never before kissed someone for whom an apology might be necessary. He'd actually been thinking more of the unpleasant things he'd said to her after the kiss. "Er, yes," he lied, "the kiss. And for what I said, as well."

"I see," she murmured. "I didn't think rakes apologized."

His hand flexed, then made a tight fist. It was damned annoying, this habit of hers always to jump to conclusions about him. "This rake does," he said in clipped tones.

She took a deep breath, then let it out in a long, steady exhale. "Then I accept your apology."

"Excellent," he said, offering his most winning smile. "May I escort you back to the house?"

She nodded. "But don't think this means that I will suddenly change my mind about you and Edwina."

"I would never dream of considering you so easily swayed," he said, quite honestly.

She turned to him, her eyes startlingly direct, even for her. "The fact remains that you kissed me," she said bluntly.

"And you kissed me," he could not resist returning.

Her cheeks turned a delightful shade of pink. "The fact remains," she repeated determinedly, "that it happened. And should you marry Edwina—regardless of your reputation, which I do not consider inconsequential—"

"No," he murmured, interrupting her with velvet soft tones, "I didn't think you would."

She glared at him. "Regardless of your reputation, *it* would always be between us. Once something happens, you can't take it away."

The devil in Anthony nearly compelled him to drawl the word, "It?" forcing her to repeat the words, "The kiss," but instead he took pity on her and let it go. Besides, she had a good point. The kiss would always be between them. Even now, with her cheeks pinkened by embarrassment and her lips pursed with irritation, he found himself wondering how she'd feel if he pulled her into his arms, how she'd taste if he traced the outline of her lips with his tongue.

Would she smell like the garden? Or would that maddening scent of lilies and soap still cling to her skin?

Would she melt into his embrace? Or would she push him away and run for the house?

There was only one way to find out, and doing so would ruin his chances with Edwina forever.

But as Kate had pointed out, maybe marrying Edwina would bring with it far too many complications. It would not do to be lusting after one's sister-in-law, after all.

Maybe the time had come to search out a new bride, tedious though the prospect may be.

Maybe the time was right to kiss Kate Sheffield again, here in the perfect beauty of Aubrey Hall's gardens, with the flowers grazing their legs and the smell of lilac hanging in the air.

Maybe . . .

Maybe . . .

# Chapter 9

*Men are contrary creatures. Their heads and their hearts are never in agreement. And as women know all too well, their actions are usually governed by a different aspect altogether.*

LADY WHISTLEDOWN'S SOCIETY PAPERS,
29 APRIL 1814

Or maybe not.

Just as Anthony was plotting the best course to her lips, he heard the perfectly awful sound of his younger brother's voice.

"Anthony!" Colin shouted out. "There you are."

Miss Sheffield, blissfully unaware of how close she'd come to having been kissed utterly senseless, turned to watch Colin approach.

"One of these days," Anthony muttered, "I'm going to have to kill him."

Kate turned back. "Did you say something, my lord?"

Anthony ignored her. It was probably his best option, since *not* ignoring her tended to leave him rather desperately lusting after her, which was, as he well knew, a short, straight road to utter disaster.

In all truth, he probably should have thanked Colin for his untimely interruption. A few more seconds, and he would have kissed Kate Sheffield, which would have been the greatest mistake of his life.

One kiss with Kate could probably be excused, especially considering how far she'd provoked him the other night in his study. But two . . . well, two would have required any man of honor to withdraw his courtship of Edwina Sheffield.

And Anthony wasn't quite ready to give up on the concept of honor.

He couldn't believe how close he'd come to tossing aside his plan to marry Edwina. What was he thinking? She was the perfect bride for his purposes. It was only when her meddlesome sister was around that his brain grew confused.

"Anthony," Colin said again as he drew near, "and Miss Sheffield." He eyed them curiously; he well knew they didn't get along. "What a surprise."

"I was just exploring your mother's gardens," Kate said, "and I stumbled upon your brother."

Anthony gave a single nod of agreement.

"Daphne and Simon are here," Colin said.

Anthony turned to Kate and explained, "My sister and her husband."

"The duke?" she inquired politely.

"The very one," he grumbled.

Colin laughed at his brother's pique. "He was opposed to the marriage," he said to Kate. "It kills him that they're happy."

"Oh, for the love of—" Anthony snapped, catching himself just before he blasphemed in front of Kate. "I'm very happy that my sister is happy," he ground out, not sounding particularly happy. "It's simply that I should have had one more opportunity to beat the tar out of that bas—bounder before they embarked on 'happily ever after.'"

Kate choked on a laugh. "I see," she said, fairly certain that she had *not* kept the straight face she'd been aiming for.

Colin shot her a grin before turning back to his brother. "Daff suggested a game of Pall Mall. What do you say? We haven't played for ages. And, if we set off soon, we can escape the milksop misses Mother has invited for us." He turned back to Kate with the sort of grin that could win forgiveness for anything. "Present company excluded, of course."

"Of course," she murmured.

Colin leaned forward, his green eyes flashing with mischief. "*No one* would make the mistake of calling you a milksop miss," he added.

"Is that a compliment?" she asked acerbically.

"Without a doubt."

"Then I shall accept it with grace and good favor."

Colin laughed and said to Anthony, "I like her."

Anthony didn't look amused.

"Have you ever played Pall Mall, Miss Sheffield?" Colin asked.

"I'm afraid not. I'm not even sure what it is."

"It's a lawn game. Brilliant fun. More popular in France than it is here, although they call it *Paille Maille*."

"How does one play?" Kate asked.

"We set out wickets on a course," Colin explained, "then hit wooden balls through them with mallets."

"That sounds simple enough," she mused.

"Not," he said with a laugh, "when you're playing with the Bridgertons."

"And what does *that* mean?"

"It means," Anthony cut in, "that we've never seen the need to set out a regulation course. Colin sets out the wickets over tree roots—"

"And you aimed yours toward the lake," Colin interrupted. "We never did find the red ball after Daphne sank it."

Kate knew she shouldn't be committing herself to an afternoon in the company of Viscount Bridgerton, but dash it all, Pall Mall sounded fun. "Might there be room for one more player?" she inquired. "Since we've already excluded me from the ranks of the milksops?"

"Of course!" Colin said. "I suspect you'll fit right in with the rest of us schemers and cheaters."

"Coming from you," Kate said with a laugh, "I *know* that was a compliment."

"Oh, for certain. Honor and honesty has its time and place, but *not* in a game of Pall Mall."

"And," Anthony cut in, a smug expression on his face, "we shall have to invite your sister as well."

"Edwina?" Kate choked out. Drat. She'd just played right into his hand. She'd been doing her best to keep the two of them apart, and now she'd practically arranged an afternoon out. There was no way she could exclude Edwina after all but inviting herself into the game.

"Do you have another sister?" he asked mildly.

She just scowled at him. "She might not wish to play. I think she was resting in her room."

"I'll instruct the maid to knock very lightly on her door," Anthony said, obviously lying.

"Excellent!" Colin said brightly. "We shall be evenly matched. Three men and three women."

"Does one play on teams?" Kate asked.

"No," he replied, "but my mother has always been adamant that one must be evenly matched in all things. She'll be quite disturbed if we go out in odd numbers."

Kate couldn't imagine the lovely and gracious woman she'd chatted with just an hour earlier getting upset over a game of Pall Mall, but she figured it wasn't her place to comment.

"I'll see to fetching Miss Sheffield," Anthony murmured, looking insufferably smug. "Colin, why don't you see *this* Miss Sheffield down to the field and I'll meet you there in half an hour?"

Kate opened her mouth to protest the arrangements that would leave Edwina alone in the viscount's company, even for so short a time as a walk down to the field, but in the end she remained silent. There was no reasonable excuse she could give to prevent it, and she knew it.

Anthony caught her fishlike spluttering and quirked one corner of his mouth in the most obnoxious manner before he said, "I'm pleased to see you agree with me, Miss Sheffield."

She just grumbled. If she'd formed words, they wouldn't have been polite ones.

"Excellent," Colin said. "We'll see you then."

And then he looped his arm through hers and led her away, leaving Anthony smirking behind them.

Colin and Kate walked about a quarter of a mile from the house to a somewhat uneven clearing bordered on one side by a lake.

"Home of the prodigal red ball, I presume?" Kate queried, motioning to the water.

Colin laughed and nodded. "It's a pity, because we used to have equipment enough for eight players; Mother had insisted on our purchasing a set that could accommodate all of her children."

Kate wasn't certain whether to smile or frown. "Yours is a very close family, isn't it?"

"The best," Colin said simply, walking over to a nearby shed.

Kate trailed after him, tapping her hand idly against her thigh. "Do you know what time it is?" she called out.

He paused, pulled out his pocket watch, and flipped it open. "Ten minutes past three."

"Thank you," Kate replied, making a mental note of it. They'd probably left Anthony at five to three, and he'd promised to deliver Edwina to the Pall Mall field within thirty minutes, so they should be down at twenty-five past the hour.

Half three at the very latest. Kate was willing to be generous and allow for unavoidable delays. If the viscount had Edwina down by half three, she wouldn't quibble.

Colin resumed his trek to the shed, Kate watching with interest as he wrenched open the door. "It sounds rusty," she commented.

"It's been a while since we've been out here to play," he said.

"Really? If I had a house like Aubrey Hall, I would never go to London."

Colin turned around, his hand still on the half-open door to the shed. "You're a lot like Anthony, did you know that?"

Kate gasped. "Surely you're joking."

He shook his head, a strange little smile on his lips. "Perhaps it's because you're both the eldest. The Lord knows I'm thankful every day I wasn't born in Anthony's shoes."

"What do you mean?"

Colin shrugged. "I simply wouldn't want his responsibilities, that's all. The title, the family, the fortune—it's a great deal to fit on one man's shoulders."

Kate didn't particularly want to hear how well the viscount had assumed the responsibilities of his title; she didn't want to hear anything that might change her opinion of him, although she had to confess that she'd been impressed by the apparent sincerity of his apology earlier that afternoon. "What has this to do with Aubrey Hall?" she inquired.

Colin stared at her blankly for a moment, as if he'd forgotten that the conversation had started with her innocent comment about how lovely his country home was. "Nothing, I suppose," he said finally. "And everything as well. Anthony loves it here."

"But he spends all his time in London," Kate said. "Doesn't he?"

"I know." Colin shrugged. "Odd, isn't it?"

Kate had no reply, so she just watched as he pulled the door to the shed all the way open. "Here we are," he said, pulling out a wheeled cart that had been specially constructed to fit eight mallets and wooden balls. "A bit musty, but none the worse for the wear."

"Except for the loss of the red ball," Kate said with a smile.

"I blame that entirely on Daphne," Colin replied. "I blame everything on Daphne. It makes my life much easier."

"I heard that!"

Kate turned to see an attractive young couple approaching. The man was devastatingly handsome, with dark, dark hair and light, light eyes. The woman could only be a Bridgerton, with the same chestnut hair as both Anthony and Colin. Not to mention the same bone structure and smile. Kate had heard that all the Bridgertons looked rather alike, but she'd never fully believed it until now.

"Daff!" Colin called out. "You're just in time to help us put out the wickets."

She gave him an arch smile. "You didn't think I'd let you set up the course yourself, do you?" She turned to her husband. "I don't trust him as far as I can throw him."

"Don't listen to her," Colin said to Kate. "She's very strong. I'd wager she could toss me clear into the lake."

Daphne rolled her eyes and turned to Kate. "Since I'm sure my miserable brother won't do the honors, I'll introduce myself. I am Daphne, Duchess of Hastings, and this is my husband Simon."

Kate bobbed a quick curtsy. "Your grace," she murmured, then turned to the duke and said again, "Your grace."

Colin waved his hand toward her as he bent down to retrieve the wickets from the Pall Mall cart. "This is Miss Sheffield."

Daphne looked confused. "I just passed by Anthony at the house. I thought he said he was on his way to fetch Miss Sheffield."

"My sister," Kate explained. "Edwina. I am Katharine. Kate to my friends."

"Well, if you are brave enough to play Pall Mall with the Bridgertons, I definitely want you as my friend," Daphne said with a wide smile. "Therefore you must call me Daphne. And my husband Simon. Simon?"

"Oh, of course," he said, and Kate had the distinct impression that he would have said the same had she just declared the sky orange. Not that he wasn't listening to her, just that it was clear he adored her to distraction.

This, Kate thought, was what she wanted for Edwina.

"Let me take half of those," Daphne said, reaching for the wickets in her brother's hand. "Miss Sheffield and I . . . that is, Kate and I"—she flashed Kate a friendly grin—"will set up three of them, and you and Simon can do the rest."

Before Kate could even venture an opinion, Daphne had taken her by the arm and was leading her toward the lake.

"We have to make absolutely certain that Anthony loses his ball in the water," Daphne muttered. "I have never forgiven him for last time. I thought Benedict and Colin were going to die laughing. And Anthony was the worst. He just stood there smirking. Smirking!" She turned to Kate with a most beleaguered expression. "No one smirks quite like my eldest brother."

"I know," Kate muttered under her breath.

Thankfully, the duchess hadn't heard her. "If I could have killed him, I vow I would have."

"What will happen once all your balls are lost in the lake?" Kate couldn't resist asking. "I haven't played with you lot yet, but you do seem rather competitive, and it seems . . ."

"That it would be inevitable?" Daphne finished for her. She grinned. "You're probably right. We have no sense of sportsmanship when it comes to Pall Mall. When a Bridgerton picks up a mallet, we become the worst sorts of cheaters and liars. Truly, the game is less about winning than making sure the other players lose."

Kate fought for words. "It sounds . . ."

"Awful?" Daphne grinned. "It's not. You'll never have more fun, I guarantee it. But at the rate we're going, the entire set will end up in the lake ere long. I suppose we'll have to send to France for another set." She jammed a wicket into the ground. "It seems a waste, I know, but worth it to humiliate my brothers."

Kate tried not to laugh, but she didn't succeed.

"Do you have any brothers, Miss Sheffield?" Daphne asked.

Since the duchess had forgotten to use her given name, Kate deemed it best to revert to formal manners. "None, your grace," she replied. "Edwina is my only sibling."

Daphne shaded her eyes with her hand and scanned the area for a devilish wicket location. When she spied one—sitting right atop a tree root—she marched away, leaving Kate no choice but to follow.

"Four brothers," Daphne said, shoving the wicket into the ground, "provide quite a marvelous education."

"The things you must have learned," Kate said, quite impressed. "Can you give a man a black eye? Knock him to the ground?"

Daphne grinned wickedly. "Ask my husband."

"Ask me what?" the duke called out from where he and Colin were placing a wicket on a tree root on the opposite side of the tree.

"Nothing," the duchess called out innocently. "I've also learned," she whispered to Kate, "when it's best just to keep one's mouth shut. Men are much easier to manage once you understand a few basic facts about their nature."

"Which are?" Kate prompted.

Daphne leaned forward and whispered behind her cupped hand, "They're not as smart as we are, they're not as intuitive as we are, and they certainly don't need to know about fifty percent of what we do." She looked around. "He didn't hear that, did he?"

Simon stepped out from behind the tree. "Every word."

Kate choked on a laugh as Daphne jumped a foot. "But it's true," Daphne said archly.

Simon crossed his arms. "I'll let you think so." He turned to Kate. "I've learned a thing or two about women over the years."

"Really?" Kate asked, fascinated.

He nodded and leaned in, as if imparting a grave state secret. "They're much easier to manage if one allows them to believe that they are smarter and more intuitive than men. And," he added with a superior glance at his wife, "our lives are much more peaceful if we pretend that we're only aware of about fifty percent of what they do."

Colin approached, swinging a mallet in a low arc. "Are they having a spat?" he asked Kate.

"A discussion," Daphne corrected.

"God save me from such discussions," Colin muttered. "Let's choose colors."

Kate followed him back to the Pall Mall set, her fingers drumming against her thigh. "Do you have the time?" she asked him.

Colin pulled out his pocket watch. "A bit after half three, why?"

"I just thought that Edwina and the viscount would be down by now, that's all," she said, trying not to look too concerned.

Colin shrugged. "They should be." Then, completely oblivious to her distress, he motioned to the Pall Mall set. "Here. You're the guest. You choose first. What color do you want?"

Without giving it much thought, Kate reached in and grabbed a mallet. It was only when it was in her hand that she realized it was black.

"The mallet of death," Colin said approvingly. "I knew she'd make a fine player."

"Leave the pink one for Anthony," Daphne said, reaching for the green mallet.

The duke pulled the orange mallet out of the set, turning to Kate as he said, "You are my witness that I had nothing to do with Bridgerton's pink mallet, yes?"

Kate smiled wickedly. "I noticed that *you* didn't choose the pink mallet."

"Of course not," he returned, his grin even more devious than hers. "My wife had already chosen it for him. I could not gainsay her, now, could I?"

"Yellow for me," Colin said, "and blue for Miss Edwina, don't you think?"

"Oh, yes," Kate replied. "Edwina loves blue."

The foursome stared down at the two mallets left: pink and purple.

"He's not going to like either one," Daphne said.

Colin nodded. "But he'll like pink even less." And with that, he picked up the purple mallet and tossed it into the shed, then reached down and sent the purple ball in after it.

"I say," the duke said, "where *is* Anthony?"

"That's a very good question," Kate muttered, tapping her hand against her thigh.

"I suppose you'll want to know what time it is," Colin said slyly.

Kate flushed. She'd already asked him to check his pocket watch twice. "I'm fine, thank you," she answered, lacking a witty retort.

"Very well. It's just that I've learned that once you start moving your hand like that—"

Kate's hand froze.

"—you're usually about ready to ask me what time it is."

"You've learned quite a lot about me in the past hour," Kate said dryly.

He grinned. "I'm an observant fellow."

"Obviously," she muttered.

"But in case you wanted to know, it's a quarter of an hour before four."

"They're past due," Kate said.

Colin leaned forward and whispered, "I highly doubt that my brother is ravishing your sister."

Kate lurched back. "Mr. Bridgerton!"

"What are you two talking about?" Daphne asked.

Colin grinned. "Miss Sheffield is worried that Anthony is compromising the other Miss Sheffield."

"Colin!" Daphne exclaimed. "That isn't the least bit funny."

"And certainly not true," Kate protested. Well, almost not true. She didn't think the viscount was compromising Edwina, but he was probably doing his very best to charm her silly. And *that* was dangerous in and of itself.

Kate pondered the mallet in her hand and tried to figure out how she might bring it down upon the viscount's head and make it look like an accident.

The mallet of death, indeed.

---

Anthony checked the clock on the mantel in his study. Almost half three. They were going to be late.

He grinned. Oh, well, nothing to do about it.

Normally he was a stickler for punctuality, but when tardiness resulted in the torture of Kate Sheffield, he didn't much mind a late arrival.

And Kate Sheffield was surely writhing in agony by now, horrified at the thought of her precious younger sister in his evil clutches.

Anthony looked down at his evil clutches—hands, he reminded himself, hands—and grinned anew. He hadn't had this much fun in ages, and all he was doing was loitering about his office, picturing Kate Sheffield with her jaw clenched together, steam pouring from her ears.

It was a highly entertaining image.

Not, of course, that this was even his fault. He would have left right on time if he hadn't had to wait for Edwina. She'd sent word down with the maid that she would join him in ten minutes. That was twenty minutes ago. He couldn't help it if she was late.

Anthony had a sudden image of the rest of his life—waiting for Edwina. Was she the sort who was chronically late? That might grow vexing after a while.

As if on cue, he heard the patter of footsteps in the hall, and when he looked up, Edwina's exquisite form was framed by the doorway.

She was, he thought dispassionately, a vision. Utterly lovely in every way. Her face was perfection, her posture the epitome of grace, and her eyes were the most radiant shade of blue, so vivid that one could not help but be surprised by their hue every time she blinked.

Anthony waited for some sort of reaction to rise up within him. Surely no man could be immune to her beauty.

Nothing. Not even the slightest urge to kiss her. It almost seemed a crime against nature.

But maybe this was a good thing. After all, he didn't want a wife with whom he'd fall in love. Desire would have been nice, but desire could be dangerous. Desire certainly had a greater chance of sliding into love than did disinterest.

"I'm terribly sorry I'm late, my lord," Edwina said prettily.

"It was no trouble whatsoever," he replied, feeling a bit brightened by his recent set of rationalizations. She'd still work just fine as a bride. No need to look elsewhere. "But we should be on our way. The others will have the course set up already."

He took her arm and they strolled out of the house. He remarked on the weather. She remarked on the weather. He remarked on the previous day's weather. She agreed with whatever he'd said (he couldn't even remember, one minute later).

After exhausting all possible weather-related topics, they fell into silence, and then finally, after a full three minutes of neither of them having anything to say, Edwina blurted out, "What did you study at university?"

Anthony looked at her oddly. He couldn't remember ever being asked such a question by a young lady. "Oh, the usual," he replied.

"But what," she ground out, looking most uncharacteristically impatient, "is the usual?"

"History, mostly. A bit of literature."

"Oh." She pondered that for a moment. "I love to read."

"Do you?" He eyed her with renewed interest. He wouldn't have taken her for a bluestocking. "What do you like to read?"

She seemed to relax as she answered the question. "Novels if I'm feeling fanciful. Philosophy if I'm in the mood for self-improvement."

"Philosophy, eh?" Anthony queried. "Never could stomach the stuff myself."

Edwina let out one of her charmingly musical laughs. "Kate is the same way. She is forever telling me that she knows perfectly well how to live her life and doesn't need a dead man to give her instructions."

Anthony thought about his experiences reading Aristotle, Bentham, and Descartes at university. Then he thought about his experiences *avoiding* reading Aristotle, Bentham, and Descartes at university. "I think," he murmured, "that I would have to agree with your sister."

Edwina grinned. "*You*, agree with Kate? I feel I should find a notebook and record the moment. Surely this must be a first."

He gave her a sideways, assessing sort of glance. "You're more impertinent than you let on, aren't you?"

"Not half as much as Kate."

"*That* was never in doubt."

He heard Edwina let out a little giggle, and when he looked over at her, she appeared to be trying her hardest to maintain a straight face. They rounded the final corner to the field, and as they came over the rise, they saw the rest of the Pall Mall party waiting for them, idly swinging their mallets to and fro as they waited.

"Oh, bloody hell," Anthony swore, completely forgetting that he was in the company of the woman he planned to make his wife. "She's got the mallet of death."

# Chapter 10

*The country house party is a very dangerous event. Married persons often find themselves enjoying the company of one other than one's spouse, and unmarried persons often return to town as rather hastily engaged persons.*

*Indeed, the most surprising betrothals are announced on the heels of these spells of rustication.*

*LADY WHISTLEDOWN'S SOCIETY PAPERS*, 2 MAY 1814

"You certainly took your time getting here," Colin remarked as soon as Anthony and Edwina reached the group. "Here, we're ready to go. Edwina, you're blue." He handed her a mallet. "Anthony, you're pink."

"I'm pink and *she*"—he jabbed a finger toward Kate—"gets to have the mallet of death?"

"I gave her first pick," Colin said. "She is our guest, after all."

"Anthony is usually black," Daphne explained. "In fact, he gave the mallet its name."

"You shouldn't have to be pink," Edwina said to Anthony. "It doesn't suit you at all. Here"—she held out her mallet—"why don't we trade?"

"Don't be silly," Colin interjected. "We specifically decided that you must be blue. To match your eyes."

Kate thought she heard Anthony groan.

"I will be pink," Anthony announced, grabbing the offending mallet rather forcefully from Colin's hand, "and I will still win. Let's begin, shall we?"

As soon as the necessary introductions were made between the duke and duchess and Edwina, they all plopped their wooden balls down near the starting point and prepared to play.

"Shall we play youngest to oldest?" Colin suggested, with a gallant bow in Edwina's direction.

She shook her head. "I should rather go last, so that I might have a chance to observe the play of those more experienced than I."

"A wise woman," Colin murmured. "Then we shall play oldest to youngest. Anthony, I believe you're the most ancient among us."

"Sorry, brother dear, but Hastings has a few months on me."

"Why," Edwina whispered in Kate's ear, "do I get the feeling I am intruding upon a family spat?"

"I think the Bridgertons take Pall Mall very seriously," Kate whispered back. The three Bridgerton siblings had assumed bulldog faces, and they all appeared rather single-mindedly determined to win.

"Eh eh eh!" Colin scolded, waving a finger at them. "No collusion allowed."

"We wouldn't even begin to know where to collude," Kate commented, "as no one has seen fit to even explain to us the rules of play."

"Just follow along," Daphne said briskly. "You'll figure it out as you go."

"I think," Kate whispered to Edwina, "that the object is to sink your opponents' balls into the lake."

"Really?"

"No. But I think that's how the Bridgertons see it."

"You're still whispering!" Colin called out without sparing a glance in their direction. Then, to the duke, he barked, "Hastings, hit the bloody ball. We haven't all day."

"Colin," Daphne cut in, "don't curse. There are ladies present."

"You don't count."

"There are two ladies present who are not me," she ground out.

Colin blinked, then turned to the Sheffield sisters. "Do you mind?"

"Not at all," Kate replied, utterly fascinated. Edwina just shook her head.

"Good." Colin turned back to the duke. "Hastings, get moving."

The duke nudged his ball a bit forward from the rest of the pile. "You do realize," he said to no one in particular, "that I have never played Pall Mall before?"

"Just give the ball a good whack in that direction, darling," Daphne said, pointing to the first wicket.

"Isn't that the last wicket?" Anthony asked.

"It's the first."

"It *ought* to be the last."

Daphne's jaw jutted out. "I set up the course, and it's the first."

"I think this might get bloody," Edwina whispered to Kate.

The duke turned to Anthony and flashed him a false smile. "I believe I'll take Daphne's word for it."

"She did set up the course," Kate cut in.

Anthony, Colin, Simon, and Daphne all looked at her in shock, as if they couldn't quite believe she'd had the nerve to enter the conversation.

"Well, she did," Kate said.

Daphne looped her arm through hers. "I do believe I adore you, Kate Sheffield," she announced.

"God help me," Anthony muttered.

The duke drew back his mallet, let fly, and soon the orange ball was hurtling along the lawn.

"Well done, Simon!" Daphne cried out.

Colin turned and looked at his sister with disdain. "One never cheers one's opponents in Pall Mall," he said archly.

"He's never played before," she said. "He's not likely to win."

"Doesn't matter."

Daphne turned to Kate and Edwina and explained, "Bad sportsmanship is a requirement in Bridgerton Pall Mall, I'm afraid."

"I'd gathered," Kate said dryly.

"My turn," Anthony barked. He gave the pink ball a disdainful glance, then gave it a good whack. It sailed splendidly over the grass, only to slam into a tree and drop like a stone to the ground.

"Brilliant!" Colin exclaimed, getting ready to take his turn.

Anthony muttered a few things under his breath, none of which were suitable for gentle ears.

Colin sent the yellow ball toward the first wicket, then stepped aside to let Kate try her hand.

"Might I have a practice swing?" she inquired.

"No." It was a rather loud no, coming, as it did, from three mouths.

"Very well," she grumbled. "Stand back, all of you. I won't be held responsible if I injure anyone on the first try." She drew back on her mallet with all her might and slammed it into the ball. It sailed through the air in a rather impressive arc, then smacked into the same tree that had foiled Anthony and plopped on the ground right next to his ball.

"Oh, dear," Daphne said, setting her aim by drawing back on her mallet a few times without actually hitting the ball.

"Why 'oh, dear'?" Kate asked worriedly, not reassured by the duchess's faintly pitying smile.

"You'll see." Daphne took her turn, then marched off in the direction of her ball.

Kate looked over at Anthony. He looked very, very pleased with the current state of affairs.

"What are you going to do to me?" she asked.

He leaned forward devilishly. "What am I *not* going to do to you might be a more appropriate question."

"I believe it's my turn," Edwina said, stepping up to the starting point. She gave her ball an anemic hit, then groaned when it traveled only a third as far as the rest.

"Put a bit more muscle into it next time," Anthony said before stalking over to his ball.

"Right," Edwina muttered at his back. "I never would have figured that out."

"Hastings!" Anthony yelled. "It's your turn."

While the duke tapped his ball toward the next wicket, Anthony leaned against the tree with crossed arms, his ridiculous pink mallet hanging from one hand, and waited for Kate.

"Oh, Miss Sheffield," he finally called out. "Play of the game dictates that one follow one's ball!"

He watched her tromp over to his side. "There," she grumbled. "Now what?"

"You really ought to treat me with more respect," he said, offering her a slow, sly smile.

"After you tarried with Edwina?" she shot back. "What I ought to do is have you drawn and quartered."

"Such a bloodthirsty wench," he mused. "You'll do well at Pall Mall . . . eventually."

He watched, utterly entertained, as her face grew red, then white. "What do you mean?" she asked.

"For the love of God, Anthony," Colin yelled. "Take your bloody turn."

Anthony looked down to where the wooden balls sat kissing on the grass, hers black, his appallingly pink. "Right," he murmured. "Wouldn't want to keep dear, sweet Colin waiting." And with that, he put his foot atop his ball, drew back his mallet—

"What are you doing?" Kate shrieked.

—and let fly. His ball remained firmly in place under his boot. Hers went sailing down the hill for what seemed like miles.

"You fiend," she growled.

"All's fair in love and war," he quipped.

"I am going to *kill* you."

"You can try," he taunted, "but you'll have to catch up with me first."

Kate pondered the mallet of death, then pondered his foot.

"Don't even think about it," he warned.

"It's so very, very tempting," she growled.

He leaned forward menacingly. "We have witnesses."

"And that is the only thing saving your life right now."

He merely smiled. "I believe your ball is down the hill, Miss Sheffield. I'm sure we'll see you in a half hour or so, when you catch up."

Just then Daphne marched by, following her ball, which had sailed unnoticed past their feet. "That was why I said 'oh, dear,'" she said—rather unnecessarily, in Kate's opinion.

"You'll pay for this," Kate hissed at Anthony.

His smirk said more than words ever could.

And then she marched down the hill, letting out a loud and extremely unladylike curse when she realized her ball was lodged under a hedge.

---

Half an hour later Kate was still two wickets behind the next-to-last player. Anthony was winning, which irked her to no end. The only saving grace was that she was so far behind she couldn't see his gloating face.

Then as she was twiddling her thumbs and waiting for her turn (there was precious little else to do while waiting for her turn, as no other players were remotely near her), she heard Anthony let out an aggrieved shout.

This immediately got her attention.

Beaming with anticipation at his possible demise, she looked eagerly about until she saw the pink ball hurtling along the grass, straight at her.

"Urp!" Kate gurgled, jumping up and darting quickly to the side before she lost a toe.

Looking back up, she saw Colin leaping into the air, his mallet swinging wildly above him, as he cried out exultantly, "Woo-hoo!"

Anthony looked as if he might disembowel his brother on the spot.

Kate would have done a little victory dance herself—if she couldn't win, the next best thing was knowing that *he* wouldn't—except now it seemed that he'd be stuck back with her for a few turns. And while her solitude wasn't terribly entertaining, it was better than having to make conversation with *him*.

Still, it was difficult not to look just a little bit smug when he came tromping over toward her, scowling as if a thundercloud had just lodged itself in his brain.

"Bad luck there, my lord," Kate murmured.

He glared at her.

She sighed—just for effect, of course. "I'm sure you'll still manage to place second or third."

He leaned forward menacingly and made a sound suspiciously like a growl.

"Miss Sheffield!" came Colin's impatient holler from up the hill. "It's your turn!"

"So it is," Kate said, analyzing her possible shots. She could aim for the next wicket or she could attempt to sabotage Anthony even further. Unfortunately, his ball wasn't touching hers, so she couldn't attempt the foot-on-the-ball maneuver he'd used on her earlier in the game. Which was probably for the best. With her luck, she'd end up missing the ball entirely and instead breaking her foot.

"Decisions, decisions," she murmured.

Anthony crossed his arms. "The only way you're going to ruin my game is to ruin yours as well."

"True," she acceded. If she wanted to send him into oblivion, she'd have to send herself there as well, since she'd have to hit hers with all she was worth just to get his to move. And since she couldn't hold hers in place, heaven only knew where she'd end up.

"But," she said, looking up at him and smiling innocently, "I really have no chance of winning the game, anyway."

"You could come in second or third," he tried.

She shook her head. "Unlikely, don't you think? I'm so far behind as it is, and we are nearing the end of play."

"You don't want to do this, Miss Sheffield," he warned.

"Oh," she said with great feeling, "I *do*. I really, really do." And then, with quite the most evil grin her lips had ever formed, she drew back her mallet and smacked her ball with every ounce of every single emotion within her. It knocked into his with stunning force, sending it hurtling even farther down the hill.

Farther . . .

Farther . . .

Right into the lake.

Openmouthed with delight, Kate just stared for a moment as the pink ball sank into the lake. Then something rose up within her, some strange and primitive emotion, and before she knew what she was about, she was jumping about like a crazy woman, yelling, "Yes! Yes! I win!"

"You don't win," Anthony snapped.

"Oh, it *feels* like I've won," she reveled.

Colin and Daphne, who had come dashing down the hill, skidded to a halt before them. "Well done, Miss Sheffield!" Colin exclaimed. "I knew you were worthy of the mallet of death."

"Brilliant," Daphne agreed. "Absolutely brilliant."

Anthony, of course, had no choice but to cross his arms and scowl mightily.

Colin gave her a congenial pat on the back. "Are you certain you're not a Bridgerton in disguise? You have truly lived up to the spirit of the game."

"I couldn't have done it without you," Kate said graciously. "If you hadn't hit his ball down the hill . . ."

"I had been hoping you would pick up the reins of his destruction," Colin said.

The duke finally approached, Edwina at his side. "A rather stunning conclusion to the game," he commented.

"It's not over yet," Daphne said.

Her husband gave her a faintly amused glance. "To continue the play now seems rather anticlimactic, don't you think?"

Surprisingly, even Colin agreed. "I certainly can't imagine anything topping it."

Kate beamed.

The duke glanced up at the sky. "Furthermore, it's starting to cloud over. I want to get Daphne in before it starts to rain. Delicate condition and all, you know."

Kate looked in surprise at Daphne, who had started to blush. She didn't look the least bit pregnant.

"Very well," Colin said. "I move we end the game and declare Miss Sheffield the winner."

"I was two wickets behind the rest of you," Kate demurred.

"Nevertheless," Colin said, "any true aficionado of Bridgerton Pall Mall understands that sending Anthony into the lake is far more important than actually sending one's ball through all the wickets. Which makes you our winner, Miss Sheffield." He looked about, then straight at Anthony. "Does anyone disagree?"

No one did, although Anthony looked close to violence.

"Excellent," Colin said. "In that case, Miss Sheffield is our winner, and Anthony, *you* are our loser."

A strange, muffled sound burst from Kate's mouth, half laugh and half choke.

"Well, someone has to lose," Colin said with a grin. "It's tradition."

"It's true," Daphne agreed. "We're a bloodthirsty lot, but we do like to follow tradition."

"You're all mad in the head is what you are," the duke said affably. "And on that note, Daphne and I must bid you farewell. I do want to get her inside before it begins to rain. I trust no one will mind if we leave without helping to clear the course?"

No one minded, of course, and soon the duke and duchess were on their way back to Aubrey Hall.

Edwina, who had kept silent throughout the exchange (although she had been looking at the various Bridgertons as if they'd recently escaped from an asylum), suddenly cleared her throat. "Do you think we should try to retrieve the ball?" she asked, squinting down the hill toward the lake.

The rest of the party just stared at the calm waters as if they'd never considered such a bizarre notion.

"It's not as if it landed in the middle," she added. "It just rolled in. It's probably right by the edge."

Colin scratched his head. Anthony continued to glower.

"Surely you don't want to lose another ball," Edwina persisted. When no one had a reply, she threw down her mallet and threw up arms, saying, "Fine! I'll get the silly old ball."

That certainly roused the men from their stupor, and they jumped to help her.

"Don't be silly, Miss Sheffield," Colin said gallantly as he started to walk down the hill, "I'll get it."

"For the love of Christ," Anthony muttered. "I'll get the bloody ball." He strode down the hill, quickly overtaking his brother. For all his ire, he couldn't really blame Kate for her actions. He would have done the very same thing, although he would have hit the ball with enough force to sink hers in the middle of the lake.

Still, it was damned humiliating to be bested by a female, especially *her*.

He reached the edge of the lake and peered in. The pink ball was so brightly colored that it ought to show through the water, provided it had settled at a shallow enough level.

"Do you see it?" Colin asked, coming to a halt beside him.

Anthony shook his head. "It's a stupid color, anyway. No one ever wanted to be pink."

Colin nodded his agreement.

"Even the purple was better," Anthony continued, moving a few steps to the right so that he could inspect another stretch of shoreline. He looked up suddenly, glaring at his brother. "What the hell happened to the purple mallet, anyway?"

Colin shrugged. "I'm sure I have no idea."

"And I'm sure," Anthony muttered, "that it will miraculously reappear in the Pall Mall set tomorrow evening."

"You might very well be right," Colin said brightly, moving a bit past Anthony, keeping his eyes on the water the whole way. "Perhaps even this afternoon, if we're lucky."

"One of these days," Anthony said matter-of-factly, "I'm going to kill you."

"Of that I have no doubt." Colin scanned the water, then suddenly pointed with his index finger. "I say! There it is."

Sure enough, the pink ball sat in the shallow water, about two feet out from the edge of the lake. It looked to be only a foot or so deep. Anthony swore under his breath. He was going to have to take off his boots and wade in. It seemed Kate Sheffield was forever forcing him to take off his boots and wade into bodies of water.

No, he thought wearily, he hadn't had time to remove his boots when he'd charged into The Serpentine to save Edwina. The leather had been completely ruined. His valet had nearly fainted from the horror of it.

With a groan he sat on a rock to pull off his footwear. To save Edwina he supposed it was worth a pair of good boots. To save a stupid pink Pall Mall ball—frankly, it didn't even seem worth getting his feet wet.

"You seem to have this well in hand," Colin said, "so I'm going to go help Miss Sheffield pull up the wickets."

Anthony just shook his head in resignation and waded in.

"Is it cold?" came a feminine voice.

Good God, it was *her*. He turned around. Kate Sheffield was standing on the shore.

"I thought you were pulling up wickets," he said, somewhat testily.

"That's Edwina."

"Too bloody many Miss Sheffields," he muttered under his breath. There ought to be a law against letting sisters come out in the same season.

"I beg your pardon?" she asked, cocking her head to the side.

"I said it's freezing," he lied.

"Oh. I'm sorry."

That got his attention. "No, you're not," he finally said.

"Well, no," she admitted. "Not for your losing, anyway. But I didn't intend for you to freeze your toes off."

Anthony was suddenly gripped by the most insane desire to see her toes. It was a horrible thought. He had no business lusting after this woman. He didn't even like her.

He sighed. That wasn't true. He supposed he did like her in an odd, paradoxical sort of way. And he thought, strangely enough, she might be beginning to like him in much the same manner.

"You would have done the same thing if you were me," she called out.

He said nothing, just continued his slow wade.

"You would have!" she insisted.

He leaned down and scooped up the ball, getting his sleeve wet in the process. Damn. "I know," he replied.

"Oh," she said, sounding surprised, as if she hadn't expected him to admit it.

He waded back out, thankful that the ground by the shore was firmly packed, so that dirt didn't stick to his feet.

"Here," she said, holding out what looked like a blanket. "It was in the shed. I stopped by on my way down. I thought you might need something to dry your feet."

Anthony opened his mouth, but oddly enough, no sound emerged. Finally, he managed, "Thank you," and took the blanket from her hands.

"I'm not such a terrible person, you know," she said with a smile.

"Neither am I."

"Perhaps," she allowed, "but you shouldn't have tarried so long with Edwina. I know you did it just to vex me."

He lifted a brow as he sat on the rock so he could dry his feet, dropping the ball onto the ground next to him. "Don't you think it's possible that my delay had anything to do with my wanting to spend time with the woman I'm considering making my wife?"

She colored slightly, but then muttered, "This has to be the most self-centered thing I've ever said, but no, I think you just wanted to vex me."

She was right, of course, but he wasn't going to tell her so. "As it happens," he said, "Edwina was delayed. Why, I do not know. I deemed it impolite to seek her out in her room and demand that she hurry along, so I waited in my study until she was ready."

There was a long moment of silence, then she said, "Thank you for telling me that."

He smiled wryly. "I'm not such a terrible person, you know."

She sighed. "I know."

Something about her resigned expression made him grin. "But maybe a little terrible?" he teased.

She brightened, their return to levity obviously making her much more comfortable with the conversation. "Oh, for certain."

"Good. I'd hate to be boring."

Kate smiled, watching him as he pulled on his stockings and boots. She reached down and picked up the pink ball. "I'd better carry this back to the shed."

"In case I'm overcome by an uncontrollable urge to toss it back in the lake?"

She nodded. "Something like that."

"Very well." He stood. "I'll take the blanket, then."

"A fair trade." She turned to walk up the hill, then spied Colin and Edwina disappearing into the distance. "Oh!"

Anthony turned quickly around. "What is it? Oh, I see. It seems your sister and my brother have decided to head back without us."

Kate scowled at their errant siblings, then shrugged in resignation as she started trudging up the hill. "I suppose I can tolerate your company for a few more minutes if you can tolerate mine."

He didn't say anything, which surprised her. It seemed just the sort of comment to which he'd have a witty and perhaps even cutting comeback. She looked up at him, then drew back slightly in surprise. He was staring at her in the *oddest* manner . . .

"Is—is everything all right, my lord?" she asked hesitantly.

He nodded. "Fine." But he sounded rather distracted.

The rest of the trip to the shed was met with silence. Kate set the pink ball in its spot in the Pall Mall cart, noting that Colin and Edwina had cleared the course and put everything neatly away, including the errant purple mallet and ball. She stole a glance at Anthony and had to smile. It was obvious from his beleaguered frown that he'd noticed as well.

"The blanket goes in here, my lord," she said with a hidden grin, stepping out of his way.

Anthony shrugged. "I'll bring it up to the house. It probably needs a good cleaning."

She nodded in agreement, and they shut the door and were off.

# *Chapter 11*

*There is nothing like a spot of competition to bring out the worst in a man—or the best in a woman.*

LADY WHISTLEDOWN'S SOCIETY PAPERS, 4 MAY 1814

Anthony whistled as they ambled up the path to the house, stealing glances at Kate when she wasn't looking. She really was quite an attractive woman in her own right. He didn't know why this always surprised him, but it did. His memory of her never quite lived up to the enchanting reality of her face. She was always in motion, always smiling or frowning or pursing her lips. She'd never master the placid, serene expression to which young ladies were meant to aspire.

He'd fallen into the same trap as had the rest of society—of thinking of her only in terms of her younger sister. And Edwina was so stunning, so amazingly, startlingly beautiful that anyone near to her couldn't help but fade into the background. It was, Anthony allowed, difficult to look at anyone else when Edwina was in the room.

And yet . . .

He frowned. And yet he'd barely spared Edwina a glance through the entire Pall Mall game. This might have been understandable simply because it was Bridgerton Pall Mall, and it brought out the worst in anyone named Bridgerton; hell, he probably wouldn't have spared a glance for the Prince Regent if he'd deigned to join the game.

But that explanation wouldn't wash, for his mind was filled with other images. Kate bending over her mallet, her face tense with concentration. Kate giggling as someone missed a shot. Kate cheering on Edwina when her ball rolled through the wicket—a very un-Bridgerton-like trait, that. And, of course, Kate smiling wickedly in that last second before she'd sent his ball flying into the lake.

Clearly, even if he hadn't been able to spare a glance for Edwina, he'd been sparing plenty for Kate.

That ought to have been disturbing.

He glanced back over at her again. This time her face was tilted slightly toward the sky, and she was frowning.

"Is something wrong?" he inquired politely.

She shook her head. "Just wondering if it's going to rain."

He looked up. "Not anytime soon, I imagine."

She nodded slowly in agreement. "I hate the rain."

Something about the expression on her face—rather reminiscent of a frustrated three-year-old—made him laugh. "You live in the wrong country, then, Miss Sheffield."

She turned to him with a sheepish smile. "I don't mind a gentle rain. It's just when it grows violent that I don't like it."

"I've always rather enjoyed thunderstorms," he murmured.

She shot him a startled look but didn't say anything, then returned her gaze to the pebbles at her feet. She was kicking one along the path as they walked, occasionally breaking her stride or stepping to the side just so she could give it a kick and keep it flying ahead of her. There was something charming about it, something rather sweet about the way her booted foot peeked out from under the hem of her dress at such regular intervals and connected with the pebble.

Anthony watched her curiously, forgetting to pull his eyes off her face when she looked back up.

"Do you think—*Why* are you looking at me like that?" she asked.

"Do I think what?" he returned, deliberately ignoring the second part of her question.

Her lips settled into a peevish line. Anthony felt his own quivering, wanting to smile with amusement.

"Are you laughing at me?" she asked suspiciously.

He shook his head.

Her feet ground to a halt. "I think you are."

"I assure you," he said, sounding even to himself as if he wanted to laugh, "that I am not laughing at you."

"You're lying."

"I'm not—" He had to stop. If he spoke any further he knew he'd explode with laughter. And the strangest thing was—he hadn't a clue why.

"Oh, for heaven's sake," she muttered. "What is the problem?"

Anthony sank against the trunk of a nearby elm, his entire body shaking with barely contained mirth.

Kate planted her hands on her hips, the expression in her eyes a little bit curious, a little bit furious. "What's so funny?"

He finally gave in to the laughter and barely managed to lift his shoulders into a shrug. "I don't know," he gasped. "The expression on your face . . . it's . . ."

He noticed that she smiled. He loved that she smiled.

"The expression on your face is not exactly unamusing yourself, my lord," she remarked.

"Oh, I'm sure." He took a few deep breaths and then, when he was satisfied that he had regained control, straightened. He caught sight of her face, still vaguely suspicious, and suddenly he realized that he had to know what she thought of him.

It couldn't wait until the next day. It couldn't wait until that evening.

He wasn't sure how it had come about, but her good opinion meant a great deal to him. Of course he needed her approval in his much-neglected suit of Edwina, but there was more to it than that. She'd insulted him, she'd nearly dunked him in The Serpentine, she'd humiliated him at Pall Mall, and yet he craved her good opinion.

Anthony couldn't remember the last time someone's regard had meant so much, and frankly, it was humbling.

"I think you owe me a boon," he said, pushing off the tree and standing straight. His mind was whirring. He needed to be clever about this. He had to know what she thought. And yet, he didn't want her knowing how much it meant to him. Not until he understood *why* it meant so much to him.

"I beg your pardon?"

"A boon. For the Pall Mall game."

She let out a ladylike snort as she leaned against the tree and crossed her arms. "If anyone owes anyone else a boon, then you owe one to me. I did win, after all."

"Ah, but I was the one humiliated."

"True," she acceded.

"You would not be yourself," he said in an extremely dry voice, "if you resisted the urge to agree."

Kate gave him a demure glance. "A lady should be honest in all things."

When she raised her eyes to his face, one corner of his mouth was curved into a rather knowing smile. "I was hoping you'd say that," he murmured.

Kate felt immediately uneasy. "And why is that?"

"Because my boon, Miss Sheffield, is to ask you a question—any question of my choosing—and you must answer with the utmost honesty." He planted one hand against the tree trunk, rather close to her face, and leaned forward. Kate suddenly felt trapped, even though it would be easy enough to dart away.

With a touch of dismay—and a shiver of excitement—she realized that she felt trapped by his eyes, which were burning rather dark and hot into hers.

"Do you think you can do that, Miss Sheffield?" he murmured.

"Wh-what is your question?" she asked, not realizing that she was whispering until she heard her voice, breathy and crackling like the wind.

He cocked his head slightly to the side. "Now, remember, you have to answer honestly."

She nodded. Or at least she thought she nodded. She *meant* to nod. In all truth, she wasn't entirely convinced of her ability to move.

He leaned forward, not so much that she could feel his breath, but close enough to make her shiver. "Here, Miss Sheffield, is my question."

Her lips parted.

"Do you"—he moved closer—"still"—and another inch—"hate me?"

Kate swallowed convulsively. Whatever she'd been expecting him to ask, it hadn't been this. She licked her lips, preparing to speak, even though she had no idea what she'd say, but not a sound emerged.

His lips curved into a slow, masculine smile. "I'll take that as a no."

And then, with an abruptness that left her head spinning, he pushed off the tree and said briskly, "Well, then, I do believe it's time we went inside and prepared for the evening, don't you?"

Kate sagged against the tree, completely devoid of energy.

"You wish to remain outside for a few moments?" He planted his hands on his hips and looked up at the sky, his demeanor pragmatic and efficient—one hundred and eighty degrees changed from the slow, lazy seducer he'd been just ten seconds earlier. "You might as well. It doesn't look like it's going to rain, after all. At least not in the next few hours."

She just stared at him. Either he'd lost his mind or she'd forgotten how to talk. Or maybe both.

"Very well. I've always admired a woman who appreciates fresh air. I shall see you at supper, then?"

She nodded. She was surprised she even managed that.

"Excellent." He reached out and took her hand, dropping a searing kiss on the inside of her wrist, upon the single band of bare flesh that peeked out between her glove and the hem of her sleeve. "Until tonight, Miss Sheffield."

And then he strode off, leaving her with the oddest feeling that something rather important had just taken place.

But for the life of her, she had no idea what.

At half seven that night, Kate considered falling dreadfully ill. At quarter to eight, she'd refined her goal to an apoplectic fit. But at five minutes to the hour, as the dinner bell sounded, alerting guests that it was time to assemble in the drawing room, she squared her shoulders and walked into the hall outside her bedroom door to meet Mary.

She refused to be a coward.

She *wasn't* a coward.

And she could make it through the evening. Besides, she told herself, she wasn't likely to be seated anywhere near Lord Bridgerton. He was a viscount and the man of the house, and would therefore be at the head of the table. As the daughter of a baron's second son, she held little rank compared to the other guests, and would most certainly be seated so far down the table that she wouldn't even be able to see him without developing a crick in her neck.

Edwina, who was sharing a room with Kate, had already gone to Mary's chamber to help her choose a necklace, and so Kate found herself alone in the hall. She supposed she could enter Mary's room and wait for the two of them there, but she didn't feel terribly conversational, and Edwina had already noticed her odd, reflective mood. The last thing Kate needed was a round of "Whatever can be wrong's" from Mary.

And the truth was—Kate didn't even *know* what was wrong. All she knew was that that afternoon, something had changed between her and the viscount. Something was different, and she freely admitted (to herself, at least) that it frightened her.

Which was normal, right? People always feared what they didn't understand.

And Kate *definitely* didn't understand the viscount.

But just as she was beginning to truly enjoy her solitude, the door across the hall opened, and out walked another young lady. Kate recognized her instantly as Penelope Featherington, the youngest of the three famed Featherington sisters—well, the three who were out in society. Kate had heard that there was a fourth still in the schoolroom.

Unfortunately for the Featherington sisters, they were famed for their lack of success on the marriage mart. Prudence and Philippa had been out for three years now, without a single proposal between the two of them. Penelope was in the midst of her second season and could usually be found at social functions trying to avoid her mother and sisters, who were universally regarded as ninnies.

Kate had always liked Penelope. The two had formed a bond ever since they'd both been skewered by Lady Whistledown for wearing gowns of an unflattering color.

Kate noted with a sad sigh that Penelope's current gown of lemon yellow silk made the poor girl look hopelessly sallow. And if that weren't bad enough, it had been cut with far too many frills and flounces. Penelope wasn't a tall girl, and the gown positively overwhelmed her.

It was a pity, because she might be quite attractive if someone could convince her mother to stay away from the modiste and let Penelope choose her own clothing. She had a rather pleasing face, with the pale, pale skin of a redhead, except that her hair was truly more auburn than red, and if one really wanted to put a fine point on it, more brownish red than auburn.

Whatever you called it, Kate thought with dismay, it didn't go with lemon yellow.

"Kate!" Penelope called out, after closing her door behind her. "What a surprise. I didn't realize you were attending."

Kate nodded. "I think we might have been issued a late invitation. We met Lady Bridgerton only just last week."

"Well, I know I just said I was surprised, but I'm actually not surprised. Lord Bridgerton has been paying much attention to your sister."

Kate flushed. "Er, yes," she stammered. "He has."

"That is what the gossips say, at least," Penelope continued. "But then again, one can't always trust the gossips."

"I have rarely known Lady Whistledown to be incorrect," Kate said.

Penelope just shrugged and then looked down at her gown with disgust. "She certainly is never incorrect about *me*."

"Oh, don't be silly," Kate said quickly, but they both knew she was just being polite.

Penelope gave her head a weary shake. "My mother is convinced that yellow is a *happy* color and that a *happy* girl will snare a husband."

"Oh, dear," Kate said, snorting a giggle.

"What she doesn't grasp," Penelope continued wryly, "is that such a *happy* shade of yellow makes me look rather *un*happy and positively repels the gentlemen."

"Have you suggested green?" Kate inquired. "I think you'd be smashing in green."

Penelope shook her head. "She doesn't like green. Says it's melancholy."

"Green?" Kate asked with disbelief.

"I don't even try to understand her."

Kate, who was wearing green, held up her sleeve near Penelope's face, blocking the yellow as best as she could. "Your whole face lights up," she said.

"Don't tell me that. It will only make the yellow more painful."

Kate offered her a sympathetic smile. "I would loan you one of mine, but I'm afraid it would drag on the floor."

Penelope waved away her offer. "That's very kind of you, but I'm resigned to my fate. At least it's better than last year."

Kate raised a brow.

"Oh, that's right. You weren't out last year." Penelope winced. "I weighed nearly two stone more than I do now."

"Two stone?" Kate echoed. She couldn't believe it.

Penelope nodded and made a face. "Baby fat. I begged Mama not to force me to come out until I turned eighteen, but she thought a head start might be good for me."

Kate only had to take one look at Penelope's face to know that it hadn't been good for her. She felt a certain kinship with this girl, even though Penelope was nearly three years younger. Both of them knew the singular feeling of not being the most popular girl in the room, knew the exact expression you put on your face when you weren't asked to dance but you wanted to look as if you didn't care.

"I say," Penelope said, "why don't the two of us go down to supper together? It seems your family and mine are both delayed."

Kate wasn't in much of a rush to reach the drawing room and the inevitable company of Lord Bridgerton, but waiting for Mary and Edwina would delay the torture by only a few minutes, so she decided she might as well head down with Penelope.

They both poked their heads into their respective mother's room, informed them of the change in plans, and linked arms, heading down the hall.

When they reached the drawing room, much of the company was already in attendance, milling about and chatting as they waited for the rest of the guests to come down. Kate, who had never attended a country house party before, noted with surprise that nearly everyone seemed more relaxed and a bit more animated than they did in London. It must be the fresh air, she thought with a smile. Or perhaps distance relaxed the strict rules of the capital. Whatever the case, she decided she preferred this atmosphere to that of a London dinner party.

She could see Lord Bridgerton across the room. Or rather she supposed she could sense him. As soon as she spotted him standing over by the fireplace, she'd kept her gaze scrupulously averted.

But she could feel him nonetheless. She knew she had to be crazy, but she'd swear she knew when he tilted his head, and heard him when he spoke and when he laughed.

And she definitely knew when his eyes were on her back. Her neck felt as if it were about to go up in flames.

"I didn't realize Lady Bridgerton had invited so many people," Penelope said.

Careful to keep her eyes away from the fireplace, Kate did a sweep of the room to see who was there.

"Oh, no," Penelope half whispered, half moaned. "Cressida Cowper is here."

Kate discreetly followed Penelope's gaze. If Edwina had any competition for the role of 1814's reigning beauty, it was Cressida Cowper. Tall, slender, with honeyblond hair and sparkling green eyes, Cressida was almost never without a small bevy of admirers. But where Edwina was kind and generous, Cressida was, in Kate's estimation, a self-centered, ill-mannered witch who took her joy in the torment of others.

"She hates me," Penelope whispered.

"She hates everyone," Kate replied.

"No, she *really* hates me."

"Whyever?" Kate turned to her friend with curious eyes. "What could you possibly have done to her?"

"I bumped into her last year and caused her to spill punch all over herself *and* the Duke of Ashbourne."

"That's all?"

Penelope rolled her eyes. "It was enough for Cressida. She's convinced he would have proposed if she hadn't appeared clumsy."

Kate let out a snort that didn't even pretend to be ladylike. "Ashbourne isn't about to get hitched anytime soon. Everyone knows that. He's nearly as bad a rake as Bridgerton."

"Who is most probably going to get married this year," Penelope reminded her. "If the gossips are correct."

"Bah," Kate scoffed. "Lady Whistledown herself wrote that she doesn't think he'll marry this year."

"That was *weeks* ago," Penelope replied with a dismissive wave of her hand. "Lady Whistledown changes her mind all the time. Besides, it's obvious to everyone that the viscount is courting your sister."

Kate bit her tongue before she muttered, "Don't remind me."

But her wince of pain was drowned out by Penelope's hoarse whisper of, "Oh, *no*. She's coming this way."

Kate gave her arm a reassuring squeeze. "Don't worry about her. She's no better than you."

Penelope shot her a sarcastic look. "I *know* that. But that doesn't make her any less unpleasant. And she always goes out of her way to make sure that I *have* to deal with her."

"Kate. Penelope," Cressida trilled, drawing up alongside them, giving her shiny hair an affected shake. "What a surprise to see you here."

"And why is that?" Kate asked.

Cressida blinked, obviously surprised that Kate had even questioned her pronouncement. "Well," she said slowly, "I suppose it is not such a surprise to see *you* here, as your sister is very much in demand, and we all know that you must go where she goes, but Penelope's presence . . ." She shrugged daintily. "Well, who am I to judge? Lady Bridgerton is a most kindhearted woman."

The comment was so rude that Kate could not help but gape. And while she was staring at Cressida, open-mouthed with shock, Cressida went in for the kill.

"That's a lovely gown, Penelope," she said, her smile so sweet that Kate would swear she could taste sugar in the air. "I do love yellow," she added, smoothing down the pale yellow fabric of her own gown. "It takes a very special complexion to wear it, don't you think?"

Kate ground her teeth together. Naturally Cressida looked brilliant in her gown. Cressida would look brilliant in a sackcloth.

Cressida smiled again, this time reminding Kate of a serpent, then turned slightly to motion to someone across the room. "Oh, Grimston, Grimston! Come over here for a moment."

Kate looked over her shoulder to see Basil Grimston approaching and just barely managed to stifle a groan. Grimston was the perfect male counterpart to Cressida—rude, supercilious, and self-important. Why a lovely lady like Viscountess Bridgerton had invited him, she'd never know. Probably to even up the numbers with so many young ladies invited.

Grimston slithered over and lifted one corner of his mouth in a mockery of a smile. "Your servant," he said to Cressida after sparing Kate and Penelope a fleeting, disdainful glance.

"Don't you think dear Penelope looks fetching in that gown?" Cressida said. "Yellow truly must be the color of the season."

Grimston did a slow, insulting perusal of Penelope, from the top of her head to the tips of her feet and back. He barely moved his head, letting his eyes travel up and down her frame. Kate fought a spasm of revulsion so strong it nearly brought on a wave of nausea. More than anything, she wanted to throw her arms around Penelope and give the poor girl a hug. But such attention would only single her out further as someone who was weak and easily bullied.

When Grimston was finally done with his rude inspection, he turned to Cressida and shrugged, as if he couldn't think of anything complimentary to say.

"Don't you have somewhere else to be?" Kate blurted out.

Cressida looked shocked. "Why, Miss Sheffield, I can hardly

countenance your impertinence. Mr. Grimston and I were merely admiring Penelope's appearance. That shade of yellow does so much for her complexion. And it is so nice to see her looking so well after last year."

"Indeed," Grimston drawled, his oily tone making Kate feel positively unclean.

Kate could feel Penelope shaking next to her. She hoped it was with anger, not with pain.

"I can't imagine what you mean," Kate said in icy tones.

"Why, surely you know," Grimston said, his eyes glittering with delight. He leaned forward and then said in a whisper that was louder than his usual voice, loud enough so that a great many people could hear, "She was *fat*."

Kate opened her mouth to give a scathing retort, but before she could make a sound, Cressida added, "It was such a pity, because there were so many more men in town last year. Of course most of us still never lack for a dance partner, but I do feel for poor Penelope when I see her sitting with the dowagers."

"The dowagers," Penelope ground out, "are often the only people in the room with a modicum of intelligence."

Kate wanted to jump up and cheer.

Cressida made a breathy little "Oh" sound, as if she had any right to be offended. "Still, one cannot help but . . . Oh! Lord Bridgerton!"

Kate moved to the side to allow the viscount into their small circle, noticing with disgust that Cressida's entire demeanor changed. Her eyelids began to flutter and her mouth made a pretty little cupid's bow.

It was so appalling Kate forgot to be self-conscious around the viscount.

Bridgerton shot Cressida a hard look but did not say anything.

Instead, he turned quite deliberately to Kate and Penelope and murmured their names in greeting.

Kate nearly gasped with glee. He'd given Cressida Cowper the cut direct!

"Miss Sheffield," he said smoothly, "I hope you will excuse us as I escort Miss Featherington in to dinner."

"But you can't escort her in!" Cressida blurted out.

Bridgerton gave her an icy stare. "I'm sorry," he said in a voice that said he was anything but. "Had I included you in the conversation?"

Cressida shrank back, obviously mortified by her outburst. Still, it was beyond irregular for him to escort Penelope. As the man of the house, it was his duty to escort the highest-ranking woman. Kate wasn't sure who that happened to be this evening, but it certainly wasn't Penelope, whose father had been a mere mister.

Bridgerton offered Penelope his arm, turning his back on Cressida in the process. "I do hate a bully, don't you?" he murmured.

Kate clapped her hand over her mouth, but she couldn't stifle her giggle. Bridgerton offered her a small, secret smile over Penelope's head, and in that moment Kate had the oddest feeling that she understood this man completely.

But even stranger—suddenly she wasn't so certain that he was the soulless, reprehensible rake she'd taken such comfort in believing him.

"Did you see that?"

Kate, who, along with the rest of the assembled company, had been staring openmouthed as Bridgerton led Penelope from the room, his head bent to hers as if she were the most fascinating woman ever to walk the earth, turned to see Edwina standing next to her.

"I saw the whole thing," Kate said in a dazed voice. "I heard the whole thing."

"What happened?"

"He was . . . he was . . ." Kate stumbled over her words, unsure of how to describe what exactly he'd done. And then she said something she'd never thought possible: "He was a hero."

# Chapter 12

*A man with charm is an entertaining thing, and a man with looks is, of course, a sight to behold, but a man with honor—ah, he is the one, dear reader, to which the young ladies should flock.*

*Lady Whistledown's Society Papers*, 2 May 1814

Later that night, after supper was done and the men went off to drink their port before rejoining the ladies with superior expressions on their faces, as if they had just talked about something weightier than which horse was likely to win the Royal Ascot; after the assembled company had played a sometime tedious and sometime hilarious round of charades; after Lady Bridgerton had cleared her throat and discreetly suggested that it might be time to turn in; after the ladies had taken their candles and headed off to bed; after the gentlemen had presumably followed . . .

Kate couldn't sleep.

Clearly, it was to be one of those stare-at-the-cracks-in-the-ceiling sort of nights. Except that there were no cracks in the ceiling at Aubrey Hall. And the moon wasn't even out, so there wasn't any light filtering through the curtains, which meant that even if there were cracks, she wouldn't be able to see them, and . . .

Kate groaned as she pushed back her covers and rose to her feet. One of these days she was going to have to learn how to force her brain to stop racing in eight different directions at once. She'd already lain in bed for nearly an hour, staring up into the dark, inky night, shutting her eyes every now and then and trying to will herself to sleep.

It wasn't working.

She couldn't stop thinking about the expression on Penelope Featherington's face when the viscount had swooped in to her rescue. Her own expression, Kate was sure, must have been somewhat similar—a bit stunned, a little delighted, and a lot as if she were about to melt onto the floor at that very minute.

Bridgerton had been *that* magnificent.

Kate had spent the entire day either watching or interacting with the Bridgertons. And one thing had become clear: Everything that had been said about Anthony and his devotion to his family—it was all true.

And while she wasn't quite ready to relinquish her opinion that he was a rake and a rogue, she was starting to realize that he might be all that and something else as well.

Something good.

Something that, if she were trying to be utterly objective about the matter, which she admitted was difficult to do, really ought not disqualify him as a potential husband for Edwina.

Oh, why why why did he have to go and be *nice*? Why couldn't he have just stayed the suave but shallow libertine it had been so easy to believe him? Now he was something else altogether, someone she feared she might actually come to care for.

Kate felt her face flush, even in the dark. She had to stop thinking about Anthony Bridgerton. At this rate she wasn't going to get any sleep for a week.

Maybe if she had something to read. She'd seen a rather large and extensive library earlier that evening; surely the Bridgertons had some tome in there that would be guaranteed to put her to sleep.

She pulled on her robe and tiptoed to the door, careful not to wake Edwina. Not that that would have been an easy task. Edwina had always slept like the dead. According to Mary, she'd even slept through the night as a baby—from the very first day of her birth.

Kate slid her feet into a pair of slippers, then moved quietly into the hall, careful to look this way and that before shutting the door behind her. This was her first country house visit, but she'd heard a thing or two about these sorts of gatherings, and the last thing she wanted to do was run into someone on his way to a bedroom not his own.

If someone was carrying on with someone not his spouse, Kate decided, she didn't want to know about it.

A single lantern lit the hall, giving the dark air a dim, flickering glow. Kate had grabbed a candle on her way out, so she walked over and flipped the lid of the lantern to light her wick. Once the flame was steady, she started toward the stairs, making sure to pause at every corner and check carefully for passersby.

A few minutes later she found herself in the library. It wasn't large by *ton* standards, but the walls were covered floor to ceiling with bookcases. Kate pushed the door until it was almost closed—if someone was up and about, she didn't want to alert them to her presence by letting the door click shut—and made her way to the nearest bookcase, peering at the titles.

"Hmmm," she murmured to herself, pulling out a book and

looking at the front cover, "botany." She did love gardening, but somehow a textbook on the subject didn't sound terribly exciting. Should she seek out a novel, which would capture her imagination, or should she go for a dry text, which would be more likely to put her to sleep?

Kate replaced the book and moved over to the next bookcase, setting her candle down on a nearby table. It appeared to be the philosophy section. "Definitely not," she muttered, sliding her candle along the table as she moved one bookcase to the right. Botany might put her to sleep, but philosophy was likely to leave her in a stupor for days.

She moved the candle a bit to the right, leaning forward to peer at the next set of books, when a bright and completely unexpected flash of lightning lit up the room.

A short, staccato scream burst forth from her lungs, and she jumped backward, bumping her behind against the table. *Not now*, she silently pleaded, *not here.*

But as her mind formed the word, "here," the entire room exploded with a dull boom of thunder.

And then it was dark again, leaving Kate shaking, her fingers gripping the table so hard that her joints locked. She hated this. Oh, how she hated this. She hated the noise and the streaks of light, and the crackling tension in the air, but most of all she hated what it made her feel.

So terrified that eventually she couldn't feel anything at all.

It had been this way all her life, or at least as long as she could remember. When she'd been small, her father or Mary had comforted her whenever it had stormed. Kate had many memories of one of them sitting on the edge of her bed, holding her hand and whispering soothing words as thunder and lightning crashed around her. But as she grew older, she managed to convince people that she was over her affliction. Oh, everyone knew that she still hated storms. But she'd managed to keep the extent of her terror to herself.

It seemed the worst sort of weakness—one with no apparent cause, and unfortunately, one with no clear cure.

She didn't hear any rain against the windows; maybe the storm wouldn't be so bad. Maybe it had started far away and was moving even farther. Maybe it was—

Another flash illuminated the room, squeezing out a second scream from Kate's lungs. And this time the thunder had arrived even closer to the lightning, indicating that the storm was pulling closer.

Kate felt herself sink to the floor.

It was too loud. Too loud, and too bright, and too—

BOOM!

Kate huddled under the table, her legs folded up, her arms about her knees, waiting in terror for the next round.

And then the rain began.

It was a bit past midnight, and all the guests (who were keeping somewhat to country hours) had gone to bed, but Anthony was still in his study, tapping his fingers against the edge of his desk in time with the rain beating against his window. Every now and then a bolt of lightning lit up the room in a flash of brilliance, and each clap of thunder was so loud and unexpected, he jumped in his chair.

God, he loved thunderstorms.

Hard to tell why. Maybe it was just the proof of nature's power over man. Maybe it was the sheer energy of the light and sound that pounded around him. Whatever the case, it made him feel alive.

He hadn't been particularly tired when his mother had suggested they all turn in, and so it had seemed silly not to use these few moments of solitude to go over the Aubrey Hall books his steward had left out for him. The Lord knew his mother would have his every minute crammed with activities involving eligible young women on the morrow.

But after an hour or so of painstaking checking, the dry tip of a quill tapping against each number in the ledger as he added and subtracted, multiplied and occasionally divided, his eyelids began to droop.

It had been a long day, he allowed, closing the ledger but leaving a piece of paper sticking out to mark his place. He'd spent much of the morning visiting tenants and inspecting buildings. One family needed a door repaired. Another was having trouble harvesting their crops and paying their rent, due to the father's broken leg. Anthony had heard and settled disputes, admired new babies, and even helped to fix a leaky roof. It was all part of being a landowner, and he enjoyed it, but it was tiring.

The Pall Mall game had been an enjoyable interlude, but once back at the house, he'd been thrust into the role of host for his mother's party. Which had been almost as exhausting as the tenant visits. Eloise was barely seventeen and clearly had needed someone to watch over her, that bitchy Cowper girl had been tormenting poor Penelope Featherington, and someone had had to do something about that, and . . .

And then there was Kate Sheffield.

The bane of his existence.

And the object of his desires.

All at once.

What a muddle. He was supposed to be courting her sister, for God's sake. Edwina. The belle of the season. Lovely beyond compare. Sweet and generous and even-tempered.

And instead he couldn't stop thinking about Kate. Kate, who, much as she infuriated him, couldn't help but command his respect. How could he not admire one who clung so steadfastly to her convictions? And Anthony had to admit that the crux of her convictions—devotion to family—was the one principle he held above all else.

With a yawn, Anthony got up from behind his desk and stretched his arms. It was definitely time for bed. With any luck, he'd fall asleep the moment his head hit the pillow. The last thing he wanted was to find himself staring at the ceiling, thinking of Kate.

And of all the things he wanted to do *to* Kate.

Anthony picked up a candle and headed out into the empty hall. There was something peaceful and intriguing about a quiet house. Even with the rain beating against the walls, he could hear every click of his boots against the floor—heel, toe, heel, toe. And except for when the lightning streaked through the sky, his candle provided the only illumination in the hall. He rather enjoyed waving the flame this way and that, watching the play of shadows against the walls and furniture. It was a rather odd feeling of control, but—

One of his brows rose up in question. The library door was a few inches ajar, and he could see a pale strip of candlelight shining from within.

He was fairly certain no one else was up. And there certainly wasn't a sound coming from the library. Someone must have gone in for a book and left a candle burning. Anthony frowned. It was a damned irresponsible thing to do. Fire could devastate a house faster than anything else, even in the middle of a rainstorm, and the library—filled to the brim with books—was the ideal place to spark a flame.

He pushed the door open and entered the room. One entire wall of the library was taken up by tall windows, so the sound of the rain was much louder here than it had been in the hall. A crack of thunder shook the floor, then, practically on top of that, a flash of lightning split the night.

The electricity of the moment made him grin, and he crossed over to where the offending candle had been left burning. He leaned over, blew it out, and then . . .

He heard something.

It was the sound of breath. Panicked, labored, with the slightest touch of a whimper.

Anthony looked purposefully around the room. "Is someone here?" he called out. But he could see no one.

Then he heard it again. From below.

Holding his own candle steady, he crouched down to peer under the table.

And his breath was sucked right out of his body.

"My God," he gasped. "Kate."

She was curled up into a ball, her arms wrapped around her bent legs so tightly it looked as if she were about to shatter. Her head was bent down, her eye sockets resting on her knees, and her entire body was shaking with fast, intense tremors.

Anthony's blood ran to ice. He'd never seen someone shake like that.

"Kate?" he said again, setting his candle down on the floor as he moved closer. He couldn't tell if she could hear him. She seemed to have retreated into herself, desperate to escape something. Was it the storm? She'd said she hated the rain, but this went far deeper. Anthony knew that most people didn't thrive on electrical storms as he did, but he'd never heard of someone being reduced to this.

She looked as if she'd break into a million brittle pieces if he so much as touched her.

Thunder shook the room, and her body flinched with such torment that Anthony felt it in his gut. "Oh, Kate," he whispered. It broke his heart to see her thus. With a careful and steady hand, he reached out to her. He still wasn't sure if she'd even registered his presence; startling her might be like waking a sleepwalker.

Gently he set his hand on her upper arm and gave it the tiniest of squeezes. "I'm here, Kate," he murmured. "Everything will be all right."

Lightning tore through the night, flashing the room with a sharp burst of light, and she squeezed herself into an even tighter ball, if that was possible. It occurred to him that she was trying to shield her eyes by keeping her face to her knees.

He moved closer and took one of her hands in his. Her skin was like ice, her fingers stiff from terror. It was difficult to pry her arm from around her legs, but eventually he was able to bring her hand to his mouth, and he pressed his lips against her skin, trying to warm her.

"I'm here, Kate," he repeated, not really sure what else to say. "I'm here. It will be all right."

Eventually he managed to scoot himself under the table so that he was sitting beside her on the floor, with his arm around her trembling shoulders. She seemed to relax slightly at his touch, which left him with the oddest feeling—almost a sense of pride that he had been the one to be able to help her. That, and a bone-deep feeling of relief, because it was killing him to see her in such torment.

He whispered soothing words in her ear and softly caressed her shoulder, trying to comfort her with his mere presence. And slowly—very, slowly; he had no idea how many minutes he sat under that table with her—he could feel her muscles begin to unwind. Her skin lost that awful clammy feeling, and her breathing, while still rushed, no longer sounded quite so panicked.

Finally, when he felt she might be ready, he touched two fingers to the underside of her chin, using the softest pressure imaginable to lift her face so that he could see her eyes. "Look at me, Kate," he whispered, his voice gentle but suffused with authority. "If you just look at me, you will know that you are safe."

The tiny muscles around her eyes quivered for a good fifteen seconds before her lids finally fluttered. She was trying to open her eyes, but they were resisting. Anthony had little experience with this sort of terror, but it seemed to make sense to him that her eyes just wouldn't want to open, that they simply wouldn't want to see whatever it was that so frightened her.

After several more seconds of fluttering, she finally managed to open her eyes all the way and met his gaze.

Anthony felt as if he'd been punched in the gut.

If eyes were truly the windows to the soul, something had shattered within Kate Sheffield that night. She looked haunted, hunted, and utterly lost and bewildered.

"I don't remember," she whispered, her voice barely audible.

He took her hand, which he'd never relinquished his hold on, and brought it to his lips again. He pressed a gentle, almost paternal kiss on her palm. "You don't remember what?"

She shook her head. "I don't know."

"Do you remember coming to the library?"

She nodded.

"Do you remember the storm?"

She closed her eyes for a moment, as if the act of keeping them open had required more energy than she possessed. "It's still storming."

Anthony nodded. That was true. The rain was still beating against the windows with just as much ferocity as before, but it had been several minutes since the last bout of thunder and lightning.

She looked at him with desperate eyes. "I can't . . . I don't . . ."

Anthony squeezed her hand. "You don't have to say anything."

He felt her body shudder and relax, then heard her whisper, "Thank you."

"Do you want me to talk to you?" he asked.

She shut her eyes—not as tightly as before—and nodded.

He smiled, even though he knew she could not see it. But maybe she could sense it. Maybe she'd be able to hear his smile in his voice. "Let's see," he mused, "what can I tell you about?"

"Tell me about the house," she whispered.

"This house?" he asked in surprise.

She nodded.

"Very well," he replied, feeling rather absurdly pleased that she was interested in the one pile of stone and mortar that meant so much to him. "I grew up here, you know."

"Your mother told me."

Anthony felt a spark of something warm and powerful in his chest as she spoke. He'd told her she didn't have to say anything, and she'd been quite obviously thankful for that, but now she was actually taking part in the conversation. Surely that had to mean she was beginning to feel better. If she'd open her eyes—if they weren't sitting under a table—it might seem almost normal.

And it was stunning how much he wanted to be the one to make her feel better.

"Shall I tell you about the time my brother drowned my sister's favorite doll?" he asked.

She shook her head, then flinched when the wind picked up, causing the rain to beat against the windows with new ferocity. But she steeled her chin and said, "Tell me something about you."

"All right," Anthony said slowly, trying to ignore the vague, uncomfortable feeling that spread in his chest. It was so much easier to tell a tale of his many siblings than to talk about himself.

"Tell me about your father."

He froze. "My father?"

She smiled, but he was too shocked by her request to notice. "You must have had one," she said.

Anthony's throat began to feel very tight. He didn't often talk about his father, not even with his family. He'd told himself that it was because it was so much water under the bridge; Edmund had been dead for over ten years. But the truth was that some things simply hurt too much.

And there were some wounds that didn't heal, not even in ten years.

"He—he was a great man," he said softly. "A great father. I loved him very much."

Kate turned to look at him, the first time she'd met his gaze since he'd lifted her chin with his fingers many minutes earlier. "Your mother speaks of him with great affection. That was why I asked."

"We all loved him," he said simply, turning his head and staring out across the room. His eyes focused on the leg of a chair, but he didn't really see it. He didn't see anything but the memories in his mind. "He was the finest father a boy could ever want."

"When did he die?"

"Eleven years ago. In the summer. When I was eighteen. Right before I left for Oxford."

"That's a difficult time for a man to lose his father," she murmured.

He turned sharply to look at her. "Any time is a difficult time for a man to lose his father."

"Of course," she quickly agreed, "but some times are worse than others, I think. And surely it must be different for boys and girls. My father passed on five years ago, and I miss him terribly, but I don't think it's the same."

He didn't have to voice his question. It was there in his eyes.

"My father was wonderful," Kate explained, her eyes warming as she reminisced. "Kind and gentle, but stern when he needed to be. But a boy's father—well, he has to teach his son how to be a man. And to lose a father at eighteen, when you're just learning what all that means . . ." She let out a long exhale. "It's probably presumptuous for me even to discuss it, as I'm not a man and therefore couldn't possibly put myself in your shoes, but I think . . ." She paused, pursing her lips as she considered her words. "Well, I just think it would be very difficult."

"My brothers were sixteen, twelve, and two," Anthony said softly.

"I would imagine it was difficult for them as well," she replied, "although your youngest brother probably doesn't remember him."

Anthony shook his head.

Kate smiled wistfully. "I don't remember my mother, either. It's an odd thing."

"How old were you when she died?"

"It was on my third birthday. My father married Mary only a few months later. He didn't observe the proper mourning period, and it shocked some of the neighbors, but he thought I needed a mother more than he needed to follow etiquette."

For the first time, Anthony wondered what would have happened if it had been his mother who had died young, leaving his father with a house full of children, several of them infants and toddlers. Edmund wouldn't have had an easy time of it. None of them would have.

Not that it had been easy for Violet. But at least she'd had Anthony, who'd been able to step in and try to act the role of surrogate father to his younger siblings. If Violet had died, the Bridgertons would have been left completely without a maternal figure. After all, Daphne—the eldest of the Bridgerton daughters—had been only ten at Edmund's death. And Anthony was certain that his father would not have remarried.

No matter how his father would have wanted a mother for his children, he would not have been able to take another wife.

"How did your mother die?" Anthony asked, surprised by the depth of his curiosity.

"Influenza. Or at least that's what they thought. It could have been any sort of lung fever." She rested her chin on her hand. "It was very quick, I'm told. My father said I fell ill as well, although mine was a mild case."

Anthony thought about the son he hoped to sire, the very reason he had finally decided to marry. "Do you miss a parent you never knew?" he whispered.

Kate considered his question for some time. His voice had held a hoarse urgency that told her there was something critical about her reply. Why, she couldn't imagine, but something about her childhood clearly rang a chord within his heart.

"Yes," she finally answered, "but not in the way you would think. You can't really miss her, because you didn't know her, but there's still a hole in your life—a big empty spot, and you know who was supposed to fit there, but you can't remember her, and you don't know what she was like, and so you don't know *how* she would have filled that hole." Her lips curved into a sad sort of smile. "Does this make any sense?"

Anthony nodded. "It makes a great deal of sense."

"I think losing a parent once you know and love them is harder," Kate added. "And I know, because I've lost both."

"I'm sorry," he said quietly.

"It's all right," she assured him. "That old adage—time heals all wounds—it's really true."

He stared at her intently, and she could tell from his expression that he didn't agree.

"It really is more difficult when you're older. You're blessed because you had the chance to know them, but the pain of the loss is more intense."

"It was as if I'd lost an arm," Anthony whispered.

She nodded soberly, somehow knowing that he hadn't spoken of his sorrow to many people. She licked nervously at her lips, which had gone quite dry. Funny how that happened. All the rain in the world pounding outside, and here she was, parched as a bone.

"Perhaps it was better for me, then," Kate said softly, "losing my mother so young. And Mary has been wonderful. She loves me as a daughter. In fact—" She broke off, startled by the sudden wetness in her eyes. When she finally found her voice again, it was an emotional whisper. "In fact, she has never once treated me differently than she has Edwina. I—I don't think I could have loved my own mother any better."

Anthony's eyes burned into hers. "I'm so glad," he said, his voice low and intense.

Kate swallowed. "She's so funny about it sometimes. She visits my mother's grave, just to tell her how I'm doing. It's very sweet, actually. When I was small, I would go with her, to tell my mother how Mary was doing."

Anthony smiled. "And was your report favorable?"

"Always."

They sat in companionable silence for a moment, both staring at the candle flame, watching the wax drip down the taper to the candlestick. When the fourth drop of wax rolled down the candle, sliding along the column until it hardened in place, Kate turned to Anthony and said, "I'm sure I sound insufferably optimistic, but I think there must be some master plan in life."

He turned to her and quirked a brow.

"Everything really does work out in the end," she explained. "I lost my mother, but I gained Mary. And a sister I love dearly. And—"

A flash of lightning lit the room. Kate bit her lip, trying to force slow and even breaths through her nose. The thunder would come, but she'd be ready for it, and—

The room shook with noise, and she was able to keep her eyes open.

She let out a long exhale and allowed herself a proud smile. That hadn't been so difficult. It certainly hadn't been *fun*, but it hadn't been impossible. It might have been Anthony's comforting presence next to her, or simply that the storm was moving away, but she'd made it through without her heart jumping through her skin.

"Are you all right?" Anthony asked.

She looked over at him, and something inside of her melted at the concerned look on his face. Whatever he'd done in the past, however they'd argued and fought, in this moment he truly cared about her.

"Yes," she said, hearing surprise in her voice even though she hadn't intended it. "Yes, I think I am."

He gave her hand a squeeze. "How long have you been like this?"

"Tonight? Or in my life?"

"Both."

"Tonight since the first clap of thunder. I get quite nervous when it begins to rain, but as long as there is no thunder and lightning, I'm all right. It's not the rain, actually, which upsets me, but just the fear that it might grow into something more." She swallowed, licking her dry lips before she continued. "To answer your other query, I can't remember a time I wasn't terrified by storms. It's simply a part of me. It's quite foolish, I know—"

"It's not foolish," he interjected.

"You're very sweet to think so," she said with a sheepish half-smile, "but you're wrong. Nothing could be more foolish than to fear something with no reason."

"Sometimes . . ." Anthony said in a halting voice, "sometimes there are reasons for our fears that we can't quite explain. Sometimes it's just something we feel in our bones, something we know to be true, but would sound foolish to anyone else."

Kate stared at him intently, watching his dark eyes in the flickering candlelight, and catching her breath at the flash of pain she saw in the brief second before he looked away. And she knew—with every fiber of her being—that he wasn't speaking of intangibles. He was talking about his own fears, something very specific that haunted him every minute of every day.

Something she knew she did not have the right to ask him about. But she wished—oh, how she wished—that when he was ready to face his fears, she could be the one to help him.

But that wasn't to be. He would marry someone else, maybe even Edwina, and only his wife would have the right to talk to him about such personal matters.

"I think I might be ready to go upstairs," she said. Suddenly it was too hard to be in his presence, too painful to know that he would belong to someone else.

His lips quirked into a boyish smile. "Are you saying I might finally crawl out from under this table?"

"Oh, goodness!" She clapped one of her hands to her cheek in a sheepish expression. "I'm so sorry. I stopped noticing where we were sitting ages ago, I'm afraid. What a ninny you must think me."

He shook his head, still smiling. "Never a ninny, Kate. Even when I thought you the most insufferable female creature on the planet, I had no doubts about your intelligence."

Kate, who had been in the process of scooting out from under the table, paused. "I just don't know if I should feel complimented or insulted by that statement."

"Probably both," he admitted, "but for friendship's sake, let's decide upon complimented."

She turned to look at him, aware that she presented an awkward picture on her hands and knees, but the moment seemed too important to delay. "Then we are friends?" she whispered.

He nodded as he stood. "Hard to believe, but I think we are."

Kate smiled as she took his helping hand and rose to her feet. "I'm glad. You're—you're really not the devil I'd originally thought you."

One of his brows lifted, and his face suddenly took on a very wicked expression.

"Well, maybe you are," she amended, thinking he probably was every bit the rake and rogue that society had painted him. "But maybe you're also a rather nice person as well."

"Nice seems so bland," he mused.

"*Nice*," she said emphatically, "is nice. And given what I used to think of you, you ought to be delighted by the compliment."

He laughed. "One thing about you, Kate Sheffield, is that you are never boring."

"Boring is so bland," she quipped.

He smiled—a true grin, not that ironic curve he used at society functions, but the real thing. Kate's throat suddenly felt very tight.

"I'm afraid I cannot walk you back to your room," he said. "If someone should come across us at this hour . . ."

Kate nodded. They'd forged an unlikely friendship, but she didn't want to get trapped into marriage with him, right? And it went without saying that *he* didn't want to marry *her*.

He motioned to her. "And especially with you dressed like that. . . ."

Kate looked down and gasped, yanking her robe more tightly around her. She'd completely forgotten that she wasn't properly dressed. Her nightclothes certainly weren't risqué or revealing, especially with her thick robe, but they *were* nightclothes.

"Will you be all right?" he asked softly. "It's still raining."

Kate stopped and listened to the rain, which had softened to a gentle patter against the windows. "I think the storm is over."

He nodded and peered out into the hall. "It's empty," he said.

"I should go."

He stepped aside to let her pass.

She moved forward, but when she reached the doorway she stopped and turned around. "Lord Bridgerton?"

"Anthony," he said. "You should call me Anthony. I believe I've already called you Kate."

"You did?"

"When I found you." He waved a hand. "I don't think you heard anything I said."

"You're probably right." She smiled hesitantly. "Anthony." His name sounded strange on her tongue.

He leaned forward slightly, an odd, almost devilish light in his eyes. "Kate," he said in return.

"I just wanted to say thank you," she said. "For helping me tonight. I—" She cleared her throat. "It would have been a great deal more difficult without you."

"I didn't do anything," he said gruffly.

"No, you did everything." And then, before she'd be tempted to stay, she hurried down the hall and up the stairs.

# *Chapter 13*

*There is little to report in London with so many people away in Kent at the Bridgerton house party. This Author can only imagine all the gossip that will soon reach town. There will be a scandal, yes? There is always a scandal at a house party.*

*LADY WHISTLEDOWN'S SOCIETY PAPERS*, 4 MAY 1814

The following morning was the sort that usually follows a violent storm—bright and clear, but with a fine, damp mist that settled cold and refreshing on the skin.

Anthony was oblivious to the weather, having spent most of the night staring into the darkness and seeing nothing but Kate's face. He'd finally fallen asleep as the first streaks of dawn fingered across the sky. By the time he woke, it was well past noon, but he did not feel rested. His body was suffused with a strange combination of exhaustion and nervous energy. His eyes felt heavy and dull in their sockets, and yet his fingers kept drumming the bed, inching toward the edge as if they alone could pull him out and to his feet.

Finally, when his stomach growled so loudly that he could swear he saw the plaster on the ceiling shake, he staggered upright and pulled on his robe. With a wide, loud yawn, he moved to the window, not because he was looking for anyone or anything in particular, but simply because the view was better than anything else in his room.

And yet in the quarter second before he looked down and gazed upon the grounds, he somehow knew what he would see.

Kate. Walking slowly across the lawn, far more slowly than he'd ever seen her walk before. Usually, she walked as if in a race.

She was much too far away for him to see her face—just a sliver of her profile, the curve of her cheek. And yet he could not take his eyes off of her. There was so much magic in her form—a strange grace in the way her arm swung as she walked, an artistry in the posture of her shoulders.

She was walking toward the garden, he realized.

And he knew he had to join her.

The weather remained in its contradictory state for most of the day, dividing the house party neatly in half, between those who insisted the bright sunshine beckoned outdoor play, and those who eschewed the wet grass and damp air for the warmer, drier clime of the drawing room.

Kate was firmly in the former group, although she was not in the mood for company. Her mind was in far too reflective a mood to make polite conversation with people she barely knew, and so she stole away once again to Lady Bridgerton's spectacular gardens and found herself a quiet spot on a bench near the rose arbor. The stone was cold and just a little bit damp beneath her bottom, but she hadn't slept particularly well the night before, and she was tired, and it was better than standing.

And it was, she realized with a sigh, just about the only place where she might be left to her own company. If she remained in the house, she'd surely be roped into joining the group of ladies chatting in the drawing room while they wrote correspondence to friends and family, or worse, she'd be stuck with the coterie who'd retired to the orangery to pursue their embroidery.

As for the outdoor enthusiasts, they'd also broken into two groups. One had hied off to the village to shop and see whatever sights there were to be found, and the other was taking a constitutional walk to the lake. As Kate had no interest in shopping (and she was already quite familiar with the lake) she'd eschewed their company as well.

Hence, her solitude in the garden.

She sat for several minutes, just staring off into space, her eyes focusing somewhat blindly on the tightly furled bud of a nearby rose. It was nice to be alone, where she didn't have to cover her mouth or stifle the loud sleepy noises she made when she yawned. Nice to be alone, where no one was going to comment on the dark circles beneath her eyes or her uncommon quietude and lack of conversation.

Nice to be alone, where she could sit and attempt to sort through her muddle of thoughts about the viscount. It was a daunting task, and one she'd rather put off, but it had to be done.

But there really wasn't all that much to sort out. Because everything she had learned in the past few days pointed her conscience in one, singular direction. And she knew that she could no longer oppose Bridgerton's courtship of Edwina.

In the past few days he'd proven himself sensitive, caring, and principled. Even, she thought with a glimmer of a smile as she recalled the light in Penelope Featherington's eyes when he'd saved her from the verbal talons of Cressida Cowper, heroic.

He was devoted to family.

He had used his social position and power not to lord over others but simply to spare another person insult.

He had helped her through one of her phobic attacks with a grace and sensitivity that, now that she could view it with a clear head, stunned her.

He might have been a rake and a rogue—he might still *be* a rake and a rogue—but clearly his behavior to those ends did not define the man. And the only objection Kate had to his marrying Edwina was . . .

She swallowed painfully. There was a lump the size of a cannonball in her throat.

Because deep in her heart, she wanted him for herself.

But that was selfish, and Kate had spent her life trying to be unselfish, and she knew she could never ask Edwina not to marry Anthony for such a reason. If Edwina knew that Kate was even the tiniest bit infatuated with the viscount, she would put an end to his courtship at once. And what purpose would that serve? Anthony would just find some other beautiful, eligible woman to pursue. There were plenty to choose from in London.

It wasn't as if he were going to ask *her* instead, so what would she have to gain by preventing a match between him and Edwina?

Nothing except the agony of having to see him married to her sister. And that would fade in time, wouldn't it? It had to; she herself had just said the night before that time truly did heal all wounds. Besides, it would probably hurt just as much to see him married to some other lady; the only difference would be that she would not have to see him at holidays and christenings and the like.

Kate let out a sigh. A long, sad, weary sigh that stole every breath from her lungs and left her shoulders sagging, her posture drooping.

Her heart aching.

And then a voice filled her ears. *His* voice, low and smooth, like a warm swirl around her. "My goodness, you sound serious."

Kate stood so suddenly that the backs of her legs knocked into the edge of the stone bench, setting her off balance and causing her to stumble. "My lord," she blurted out.

His lips curved with the barest hint of a smile. "I thought I might find you here."

Her eyes widened at the realization that he'd deliberately sought her out. Her heart started beating faster as well, but at least that was something she could keep hidden from him.

He glanced briefly down to the stone bench, signaling that she should feel free to resume her seat. "Actually, I saw you from my window. I wanted to make certain that you were feeling better," he said quietly.

Kate sat down, disappointment rising in her throat. He was merely being polite. Of *course* he was merely being polite. Silly of her to dream—even for a moment—that there might be something more. He was, she'd finally realized, a nice person, and any nice person would want to make sure that she was feeling better after what had transpired the night before.

"I am," she replied. "Very much. Thank you."

If he thought anything of her broken, staccato sentences, he did not make any discernible reaction of it. "I'm glad," he said as he sat beside her. "I worried about you for much of the night."

Her heart, which had already been pounding much too quickly, skipped a beat. "You did?"

"Of course. How could I not?"

Kate swallowed. There it was, that infernal politeness again. Oh, she didn't doubt that his interest and concern were real and true. It just hurt that they were prompted by his natural kindness of spirit, not any special feeling for her.

Not that she had expected anything different. But she'd found it impossible not to hope, anyway.

"I'm sorry to have bothered you so late at night," she said quietly, mostly because she thought she should. In truth, she was desperately glad that he'd been there.

"Don't be silly," he said, straightening slightly and fixing upon her a rather stern sort of look. "I hate to think of you all alone during a storm. I'm glad I was there to comfort you."

"I'm usually alone during storms," she admitted.

Anthony frowned. "Your family does not offer you comfort during storms?"

She looked a little sheepish as she said, "They do not know that I still fear them."

He nodded slowly. "I see. There are times—" Anthony paused to clear his throat, a diversionary tactic he frequently employed when he wasn't quite certain what it was he wanted to say. "I think you would gain comfort by seeking the aid of your mother and sister, but I know—" He cleared his throat again. He knew well the singularly strange sensation of loving one's family to distraction, and yet not feeling quite able to share one's deepest and most intractable fears. It brought on an uncanny sense of isolation, of being remarkably alone in a loud and loving crowd.

"I know," he said again, his voice purposely even and subdued, "that it can often be most difficult to share one's fears with those one most deeply loves."

Her brown eyes, wise and warm and undeniably perceptive, focused on his. For one split moment he had the bizarre thought that she somehow knew everything about him, every last detail from the moment of his birth to his certainty of his own death. It seemed, in that second, with her face tipped up toward his and her lips slightly parted, that she, more than anyone else who would ever walk this earth, truly *knew* him.

It was thrilling.

But more than that, it was terrifying.

"You're a very wise man," she whispered.

It took him a moment to remember what they'd been talking about. Ah yes, fears. He knew fears. He tried to laugh off her compliment. "Most of the time I'm a very foolish man."

She shook her head. "No. I think you've hit the nail squarely on its proverbial head. Of course I would not tell Mary and Edwina. I do not want to trouble them." She chewed on her lip for a moment—a funny little movement with her teeth that he found oddly seductive.

"Of course," she added, "if I am to be true to myself, I must confess that my motives are not entirely unselfish. Surely, an equal part of my reluctance lies in my desire not to be seen as weak."

"That's not such a terrible sin," he murmured.

"Not as far as sins go, I suppose," Kate said with a smile. "But I would hazard a guess that it is one from which you, too, suffer."

He didn't say anything, just nodded his assent.

"We all have our roles to play in life," she continued, "and mine has always been to be strong and sensible. Cringing under a table during an electrical storm is neither."

"Your sister," he said quietly, "is probably a great deal stronger than you think."

Her eyes flew to his face. Was he trying to tell her that he'd fallen in love with Edwina? He'd complimented her sister's grace and beauty before, but never had he referred to her inner person.

Kate's eyes searched his for as long as she dared, but she found nothing that revealed his true feelings. "I did not mean to imply that she wasn't," she finally replied. "But I am her older sister. I have always had to be strong for her. Whereas she has only had to be strong for herself." She brought her eyes back up to his, only to find that he was staring at her with an odd intensity, almost as if he could see past her skin and into her very soul. "You are the oldest as well," she said. "I'm sure you know what I mean."

He nodded, and his eyes looked amused and resigned at the same time. "Exactly."

She gave him an answering smile, the kind that passed between people who know similar experiences and trials. And as she felt herself growing more at ease next to him, almost as if she could sink into his side and bury herself against the warmth of his body, she knew that she could put off her task no longer.

She had to tell him that she'd withdrawn her opposition to his match with Edwina. It wasn't fair to anyone to keep it to herself, just because she wanted to keep *him* to herself, if only for a few perfect moments right here in the gardens.

She took a deep breath, straightened her shoulders, and turned to him.

He looked at her expectantly. It was obvious, after all, that she had something to say.

Kate's lips parted. But nothing came out.

"Yes?" he asked, looking rather amused.

"My lord," she blurted out.

"Anthony," he corrected gently.

"Anthony," she repeated, wondering why the use of his given name made this all the more difficult. "I did need to speak with you about something."

He smiled. "I'd gathered."

Her eyes became inexplicably fastened on her right foot, which was tracing half-moons on the packed dirt of the path. "It's . . . um . . . it's about Edwina."

Anthony's brows rose and he followed her gaze to her foot, which had left half-moons behind and was now drawing squiggly lines. "Is something amiss with your sister?" he inquired gently.

She shook her head, looking back up. "Not at all. I believe she's in the drawing room, writing a letter to our cousin in Somerset. Ladies like to do that, you know."

He blinked. "Do what?"

"Write letters. I'm not a very good correspondent myself," she said, her words coming forth in an oddly rushed fashion, "as I rarely have the patience to sit still at a desk long enough to write an entire letter. Not to mention that my penmanship is abysmal. But most ladies spend a goodly portion of every day drafting letters."

He tried not to smile. "You wanted to warn me that your sister likes to write letters?"

"No, of course not," she mumbled. "It's just that you asked if she was all right, and I said of course, and I told you where she was, and then we were entirely off the topic, and—"

He laid his hand across hers, effectively cutting her off. "What is it you needed to tell me, Kate?"

He watched with interest as she steeled her shoulders and clenched her jaw. She looked as if she were preparing for a hideous task. Then, in one big rush of a sentence, she said, "I just wanted you to know that I have withdrawn my objections to your suit of Edwina."

His chest suddenly felt a bit hollow. "I . . . see," he said, not because he did see, just because he had to say something.

"I admit to a strong prejudice against you," she continued quickly, "but I have come to know you since my arrival at Aubrey Hall, and in all conscience, I could not allow you to go on thinking that I would stand in your way. It would—it would not be right of me."

Anthony just stared at her, completely at a loss. There was, he realized dimly, something a bit deflating about her willingness to marry him off to her sister, since he'd spent the better part of the last two days fighting the urge to kiss her rather senseless.

On the other hand, wasn't this what he wanted? Edwina would make the perfect wife.

Kate would not.

Edwina fit all the criteria he'd laid out when he'd finally decided it was time to wed.

Kate did not.

And he certainly couldn't dally with Kate if he meant to marry Edwina.

She was giving him what he wanted—*exactly*, he reminded himself, what he wanted; with her sister's blessing, Edwina would marry him next week if he so desired.

Then why the devil did he want to grab her by the shoulders and shake and shake and shake until she took back every bloody little annoying word?

It was that spark. That damnable spark that never seemed to dim between them. That awful prickle of awareness that burned every time she entered a room, or took a breath, or pointed a toe. That sinking feeling that he could, if he let himself, love her.

Which was the one thing he feared most.

Perhaps the only thing he feared at all.

It was ironic, but death was the one thing he wasn't afraid of. Death wasn't frightening to a man alone. The great beyond held no terror when one had managed to avoid attachments here on earth.

Love was truly a spectacular, sacred thing. Anthony knew that. He'd seen it every day of his childhood, every time his parents had shared a glance or touched hands.

But love was the enemy of the dying man. It was the only thing that could make the rest of his years intolerable—to taste bliss and know that it would all be snatched away. And that was probably why, when Anthony finally reacted to her words, he didn't yank her to him and kiss her until she was gasping, and he didn't press his lips to her ear and burn his breath against her skin, making sure she understood that he was on fire for her, and not her sister.

Never her sister.

Instead, he just looked at her impassively, his eyes far, far steadier than his heart, and said, "I am much relieved," all the while having the strangest feeling that he wasn't really there, but rather watching the entire scene—nothing more than a farce, really—from outside of his body, all the while wondering what the hell was going on.

She smiled weakly and said, "I thought you might feel that way."

"Kate, I—"

She'd never know what he meant to say. In all truth, *he* wasn't even sure what he intended to say. He hadn't even realized that he was going to speak until her name passed over his lips.

But his words would remain forever unspoken, because at that moment, he heard it.

A low buzz. A whine, really. It was the sort of sound most people found mildly annoying.

Nothing, to Anthony, could have been more terrifying.

"Don't move," he whispered, his voice harsh with fear.

Kate's eyes narrowed, and of course she moved, trying to twist about. "What are you talking about? What is wrong?"

"Just don't move," he repeated.

Her eyes slid to the left, then her chin followed by a quarter of an inch or so. "Oh, it's just a bee!" Her face broke out in a relieved grin, and she lifted her hand to swat it away. "For goodness' sake, Anthony, don't do that again. You had me scared for a moment."

Anthony's hand shot out and grasped her wrist with painful force. "I said don't move," he hissed.

"Anthony," she said, laughing, "it's a *bee*."

He held her immobile, his grasp hard and painful, his eyes never leaving the loathsome creature, watching as it buzzed purposefully around her head. He was paralyzed by fear, and fury, and something else he couldn't quite put his finger on.

It wasn't as if he hadn't come into contact with bees in the eleven years since his father's death. One couldn't reside in England, after all, and expect to avoid them altogether.

Until now, in fact, he'd forced himself to flirt with them in an odd, fatalistic manner. He'd always suspected that he might be doomed to follow in his father's footsteps in all respects. If he was going to be brought down by a humble insect, by God he'd do it standing firm and holding his ground. He was going to die sooner or . . . well, sooner, and he wasn't going to run from some bloody bug. And so when one flew by, he laughed, he mocked, he cursed, and he swatted it away with his hand, daring it to retaliate.

And he'd never been stung.

But seeing one fly so dangerously close to Kate, brushing by her hair, landing on the lacy sleeve of her dress—it was terrifying, almost hypnotizing. His mind raced ahead, and he saw the tiny monster sink its stinger into her soft flesh, he saw her gasping for air, sinking to the ground.

He saw her here at Aubrey Hall, laid out on the same bed that had served as his father's first coffin.

"Just be quiet," he whispered. "We're going to stand—*slowly*. Then we're going to walk away."

"Anthony," she said, her eyes crinkling in an impatiently confused manner, "what is *wrong* with you?"

He tugged on her hand, trying to force her to rise, but she resisted. "It's a *bee*," she said in an exasperated voice. "Stop acting so strangely. For heaven's sake, it's not going to kill me."

Her words hung heavy in the air, almost like solid objects, ready to crash to the ground and shatter them both. Then, finally, when Anthony felt his throat relax enough to speak, he said in a low, intense voice, "It might."

Kate froze, not because she meant to follow his orders, but because something in his aspect, something in his eyes, frightened her to the bone. He looked changed, possessed by some unknown demon. "Anthony," she said in what she hoped was an even, authoritative voice, "let go of my wrist this instant."

She pulled, but he did not relent, and the bee kept buzzing relentlessly about her.

"Anthony!" she exclaimed. "Stop this right—"

The rest of her sentence was lost as she somehow managed to yank her hand from his crushing grasp. The sudden freedom left her off balance, and her arm flailed up and about, the inside of her elbow knocking into the bee, which let out a loud, angry buzz as the force of the blow sent it hurtling through space, smashing right into the strip of bare skin above the lace-edged bodice of her afternoon dress.

"Oh, for the love of— Ow!" Kate let out a howl as the bee, no doubt infuriated by its abuse, sank its stinger into her flesh. "Oh, damn," she swore, completely past any pretensions toward proper language. It was just a bee sting, of course, and nothing she hadn't suffered several times before, but bloody hell, it *hurt*.

"Oh, bother," she grumbled, pulling her chin against her chest so she could look down and get the best view of the red welt rising right along the edge of her bodice. "Now I'll have to go inside for a poultice, and it'll get all over my dress." With a disdainful sniff, she brushed the dead carcass of the bee from her skirt, muttering,

"Well, at least he's dead, the vexing thing. It's probably the only justice in the—"

That was when she looked up and spied Anthony's face. He'd gone white. Not pale, not even bloodless, but white. "Oh, my God," he whispered, and the oddest thing was that his lips didn't even move. "Oh, my God."

"Anthony?" she asked, leaning forward and momentarily forgetting about the painful sting on her chest. "Anthony, what is wrong?"

Whatever trance he was in suddenly snapped, and he leaped forward, roughly grabbing one of her shoulders with one hand while his other grappled with the bodice of her gown, pulling it down to better expose her wound.

"My lord!" Kate shrieked. "Stop!"

He said nothing, but his breath was ragged and fast as he pinned her against the back of the bench, still holding her dress down, not low enough to expose her, but certainly lower than decency allowed.

"Anthony!" she tried, hoping that the use of his given name might get his attention. She didn't know this man; he wasn't the one who had sat at her side just two minutes earlier. He was crazed, frantic, and completely heedless of her protestations.

"Will you shut up?" he hissed, never once looking up at her. His eyes were focused on the red, swollen circle of flesh on her chest, and with trembling hands he plucked the stinger from her skin.

"Anthony, I'm fine!" she insisted. "You must—"

She gasped. He'd moved one of his hands slightly as he used the other to yank a handkerchief from his pocket, and it now rather indelicately cupped her entire breast.

"Anthony, what are you doing?" She grabbed at his hand, trying to remove it from her person, but his strength was beyond her.

He pinned her even more firmly against the back of the bench, his hand nearly pressing her breast flat. "Be still!" he barked, and then he took the handkerchief and began to press against the swollen sting.

"What are you doing?" she asked, still trying to scoot away.

He didn't look up. "Expressing the venom."

"*Is* there venom?"

"There must be," he muttered. "There has to be. Something is killing you."

Her mouth fell open. "Something is *killing me*? Are you mad? Nothing is killing me. It's a bee sting."

But he ignored her, too focused on his self-appointed task of treating her wound.

"Anthony," she said in a placating voice, trying to reason with him. "I appreciate your concern, but I've been stung by bees at least a half dozen times, and I—"

"He'd been stung before, too," he interrupted.

Something about his voice sent a shiver down her spine. "Who?" she whispered.

He pressed more firmly against the raised hive, dabbing the handkerchief against the clear liquid that oozed out. "My father," he said flatly, "and it killed him."

She couldn't quite believe it. "A bee?"

"Yes, a bee," he snapped. "Haven't you been listening?"

"Anthony, a little bee cannot kill a man."

He actually paused in his ministrations for a brief second to glance up at her. His eyes were hard, haunted. "I assure you that it can," he bit off.

Kate couldn't quite believe that his words were true, but she also didn't think he was lying, and so she held still for a moment, recognizing that he needed to treat her bee sting far more than she needed to scoot away from his attentions.

"It's still swollen," he muttered, pressing harder with the handkerchief. "I don't think I got it all out."

"I'm sure I'll be fine," she said gently, her ire with him turning into an almost maternal concern. His brow was wrinkled with concentration, and his movements still carried an air of frantic energy. He was petrified, she realized, scared that she would drop dead right there on the garden bench, felled by a tiny little bee.

It seemed unfathomable, and yet it was true.

He shook his head. "It's not good enough," he said hoarsely. "I have to get it all out."

"Anthony, I— What are you *doing*?"

He'd tipped her chin back and his head was closing the distance between them, almost as if he meant to kiss her.

"I'm going to have to suck the venom out," he said grimly. "Just hold still."

"Anthony!" she shrieked. "You can't—" She gasped, completely unable to finish her sentence once she felt his lips settling on her skin, applying a gentle, yet inexorable pressure, pulling her into his mouth. Kate didn't know how to respond, didn't know whether to push him away or pull him toward her.

But in the end she just froze. Because when she lifted her head and looked over his shoulder, she saw a group of three women staring at them with equal expressions of shock.

Mary.

Lady Bridgerton.

And Mrs. Featherington, arguably the *ton*'s biggest gossip.

And Kate knew, beyond a shadow of a doubt, that her life would never be the same.

# *Chapter 14*

*And indeed, if a scandal does erupt at Lady Bridgerton's party, those of us who remain in London may be assured that any and all titillating news shall reach our tender ears with all possible haste. With so many notorious gossips in attendance, we are all but guaranteed a full and detailed report.*

*Lady Whistledown's Society Papers*, 4 May 1814

For a split second, everyone remained frozen as if in a tableau. Kate stared at the three matrons in shock. They stared back at her in utter horror.

And Anthony kept trying to suck the venom from Kate's bee sting, completely oblivious to the fact that they had an audience.

Of the quintet, Kate found her voice—and her strength—first, shoving with all her might against Anthony's shoulder as she let out an impassioned cry of, "Stop!"

Caught off guard, he proved surprisingly easy to dislodge, and he landed on his bum on the ground, his eyes still burning with determination to save her from what he perceived as her deathly fate.

"Anthony?" Lady Bridgerton gasped, her voice quavering on her son's name, as if she couldn't quite believe what she was seeing.

He twisted around. "Mother?"

"Anthony, what were you doing?"

"She was stung by a bee," he said grimly.

"I'm fine," Kate insisted, then yanked up her dress. "I told him I was fine, but he wouldn't listen to me."

Lady Bridgerton's eyes misted over with understanding. "I see," she said in a small, sad voice, and Anthony knew that she did see. She was, perhaps, the only person who *could* see.

"Kate," Mary finally said, choking on her words, "he had his lips on your . . . on your—"

"On her breast," Mrs. Featherington said helpfully, folding her arms over her ample bosom. A disapproving frown crossed her face, but it was clear that she was enjoying herself immensely.

"He did not!" Kate exclaimed, struggling to her feet, which wasn't the easiest task, since Anthony had landed on one of them when she'd shoved him off the bench. "I was stung right here!" With a frantic finger, she pointed at the round red welt that was still rising on the thin skin covering her collarbone.

The three older ladies stared at her bee sting, their skin assuming identical blushes of faint crimson.

"It's not anywhere near my breast!" Kate protested, too horrified by the direction of the conversation to remember to feel embarrassed at her rather anatomical language.

"It isn't *far*," Mrs. Featherington pointed out.

"Will someone shut her up?" Anthony snapped.

"Well!" Mrs. Featherington huffed. "I never!"

"No," Anthony replied. "You *always*."

"What does he mean by that?" Mrs. Featherington demanded, poking Lady Bridgerton in the arm. When the viscountess did not respond, she turned to Mary and repeated the question.

But Mary had eyes only for her daughter. "Kate," she ordered, "come here this instant."

Dutifully, Kate moved to Mary's side.

"Well?" Mrs. Featherington asked. "What are we going to do?"

Four sets of eyes turned on her in disbelief.

" 'We'?" Kate questioned faintly.

"I fail to see how *you* have any say in the matter," Anthony bit off.

Mrs. Featherington just let out a loud, disdainful, and rather nasal sniff. "You have to marry the chit," she announced.

"What?" The word was ripped from Kate's throat. "You must be mad."

"I must be the only sensible one in the garden is what I must be," Mrs. Featherington said officiously. "Lud, girl, he had his mouth on your bubbies, and we all saw it."

"He did not!" Kate moaned. "I was stung by a bee. A bee!"

"Portia," Lady Bridgerton interjected, "I hardly think there is need for such graphic language."

"There's little use for delicacy now," Mrs. Featherington replied. "It's going to make a tidy piece of gossip no matter how you describe it. The *ton*'s most fervent bachelor, brought down by a bee. I must say, my lord, it's not how I imagined it."

"There is not going to be any gossip," Anthony growled, advancing on her with a menacing air, "because no one is going to say a word. I will not see Miss Sheffield's reputation besmirched in any way."

Mrs. Featherington's eyes bugged out with disbelief. "You think you can keep something like this quiet?"

"*I'm* not going to say anything, and I rather doubt that Miss Sheffield will, either," he said, planting his hands on his hips as he glared down at her. It was the sort of stare that brought grown men to their knees, but Mrs. Featherington was either impervious or simply stupid, so he continued with, "Which leaves our respective mothers, who would seem to have a vested interest in protecting our reputations. Which then leaves you, Mrs. Featherington, as the only member of our cozy little group who might prove herself a gossipy, loudmouthed fishwife over this."

Mrs. Featherington turned a dull red. "Anyone could have seen from the house," she said bitterly, clearly loath to lose such a prime piece of gossip. She'd be fêted for a month as the only eyewitness to such a scandal. The only eyewitness who'd talk, that is.

Lady Bridgerton glanced up at the house, her face going pale. "She's right, Anthony," she said. "You were in full view of the guest wing."

"It was a bee," Kate practically wailed. "Just a bee! Surely we can't be forced to marry because of a bee!"

Her outburst was met with silence. She looked from Mary to Lady Bridgerton, both of whom were gazing at her with expressions hovering between concern, kindness, and pity. Then she looked at Anthony, whose expression was hard, closed, and utterly unreadable.

Kate closed her eyes in misery. This wasn't how it was supposed to happen. Even as she had told him he might marry her sister, she'd secretly wished he could be hers, but not like this.

Oh, dear Lord, not like this. Not so he'd feel trapped. Not so he'd spend the rest of his life looking at her and wishing she were someone else.

"Anthony?" she whispered. Maybe if he spoke to her, maybe if he just looked at her she might glean some clue as to what he was thinking.

"We will marry next week," he stated. His voice was firm and clear, but otherwise devoid of emotion.

"Oh, good!" Lady Bridgerton said with great relief, clapping her hands together. "Mrs. Sheffield and I will begin preparations immediately."

"Anthony," Kate whispered again, this time with more urgency, "are you certain?" She grabbed his arm and tried to pull him away from the matrons. She gained only a few inches, but at least now they weren't facing them.

He gazed at her with implacable eyes. "We will marry," he said simply, his voice that of the consummate aristocrat, brooking no protest and expecting to be obeyed. "There is nothing else to do."

"But you don't want to marry me," she said.

This caused him to raise a brow. "And do you want to marry me?"

She said nothing. There was nothing she could say, not if she wanted to maintain even a shred of pride.

"I suspect we shall suit well enough," he continued, his expression softening slightly. "We've become friends of a sort, after all. That's more than most men and women have at the beginning of a union."

"You can't want this," she persisted. "You wanted to marry Edwina. What are you going to say to Edwina?"

He crossed his arms. "I never made any promises to Edwina. And I imagine we'll simply tell her we fell in love."

Kate felt her eyes rolling of their own volition. "She'll never believe *that*."

He shrugged. "Then tell her the truth. Tell her you were stung by a bee, and I was trying to aid you, and we were caught in a compromising position. Tell her whatever you want. She's your sister."

Kate sank back down onto the stone bench, sighing. "No one is going to believe you wanted to marry me," she said. "Everyone will think you were trapped."

Anthony shot a pointed glare at the three women, who were still staring at them with interest. At his, "Would you mind?" both his and Kate's mothers stepped back several feet and turned around to afford them more privacy. When Mrs. Featherington did not follow immediately, Violet reached forward and nearly pulled her arm out of the socket.

Sitting down next to Kate, he said, "There is little we can do to prevent people from talking, especially with Portia Featherington as a witness. I don't trust that woman to keep her mouth shut any longer than it takes her to return to the house." He leaned back and propped his left ankle on his right knee. "So we might as well make the best of it. I have to get married this year—"

"Why?"

"Why what?"

"Why do you have to get married this year?"

He paused for a moment. There wasn't really an answer to that question. So he said, "Because I decided I would, and that's a good enough reason for me. As for you, you have to get married eventually—"

She interrupted him again with, "To be honest, I rather assumed I wouldn't."

Anthony felt his muscles tense, and it took him several seconds to realize that what he was feeling was rage. "You planned to live your life as a spinster?"

She nodded, her eyes innocent and frank at the same time. "It seemed a definite possibility, yes."

Anthony held himself still for several seconds, thinking he might like to murder all those men and women who had compared her to Edwina and found her lacking. Kate truly had no idea that she might be attractive and desirable in her own right.

When Mrs. Featherington had announced that they must marry, his initial reaction had been the same as Kate's—utter horror. Not to mention a rather pricked sense of pride. No man liked to be forced into marriage, and it was particularly galling to be forced by a *bee.*

But as he stood there, watching Kate howl in protest (not, he thought, the most flattering of reactions, but he supposed she was allowed her pride as well), a strange sense of satisfaction washed over him.

He wanted her.

He wanted her desperately.

He wouldn't, in a million years, have allowed himself to choose her as a wife. She was far, far too dangerous to his peace of mind.

But fate had intervened, and now that it looked like he *had* to marry her . . . well, there didn't seem much use in putting up a big fuss. There were worse fates than finding oneself married to an intelligent, entertaining woman whom one happened to lust after around the clock.

All he had to do was make certain he didn't actually fall in love with her. Which shouldn't prove impossible, right? The Lord knew she drove him crazy half the time with her incessant arguing. He could have a pleasant marriage with Kate. He'd enjoy her friendship and enjoy her body and keep it at that. It didn't have to go any deeper.

And he couldn't have asked for a better woman to serve as mother to his sons after he was gone. That was certainly worth a great deal.

"This will work," he said with great authority. "You'll see."

She looked doubtful, but she nodded. Of course, there was little else she could do. She'd just been caught by the biggest gossip in London with a man's mouth on her chest. If he hadn't offered to marry her, she'd have been ruined forever.

And if she'd refused to marry him . . . well, then she'd be branded a fallen woman *and* an idiot.

Anthony suddenly stood. "Mother!" he barked, leaving Kate on the bench as he strode over to her. "My fiancée and I desire a bit of privacy here in the garden."

"Of course," Lady Bridgerton murmured.

"Do you think that's wise?" Mrs. Featherington asked.

Anthony leaned forward, placed his mouth very close to his mother's ear, and whispered, "If you do not remove her from my presence within the next ten seconds, I shall murder her on the spot."

Lady Bridgerton choked on a laugh, nodded, and managed to say, "Of course."

In under a minute, Anthony and Kate were alone in the garden.

He turned to face her; she'd stood and taken a few steps toward him. "I think," he murmured, slipping his arm through hers, "that we ought to consider moving out of sight of the house."

His steps were long and purposeful, and she stumbled to keep up with him until she found her stride. "My lord," she asked, hurrying along, "do you think this is wise?"

"You sound like Mrs. Featherington," he pointed out, not breaking his pace, even for a second.

"Heaven forbid," Kate muttered, "but the question still stands."

"Yes, I do think it's very wise," he replied, pulling her into a gazebo. Its walls were partially open to the air, but it was surrounded by lilac bushes and afforded them considerable privacy.

"But—"

He smiled. Slowly. "Did you know you argue too much?"

"You brought me here to tell me *that*?"

"No," he drawled, "I brought you here to do *this*."

And then, before she had a chance to utter a word, before she even had a chance to draw breath, his mouth swooped down and captured hers in a hungry, searing kiss. His lips were voracious, taking everything she had to give and then demanding even more. The fire that glowed within her burned and crackled even hotter than what he'd stoked that night in his study, hotter by a tenfold.

She was melting. Dear God, she was melting, and she wanted so much more.

"You shouldn't do this to me," he whispered against her mouth. "You shouldn't. Everything about you is absolutely wrong. And yet . . ."

Kate gasped as his hands stole around to her backside and pressed her harshly against his arousal.

"Do you see?" he said raggedly, his lips moving along her cheek. "Do you feel?" He chuckled hoarsely, an odd mocking sound. "Do you even understand?" He squeezed mercilessly, then nibbled the tender skin of her ear. "Of course you don't."

Kate felt herself sliding into him. Her skin was starting to burn, and her traitorous arms stole up and around his neck. He was stoking a fire in her, something she could not even begin to control. She'd been possessed by some primitive urge, something hot and molten which needed nothing so much as the touch of his skin against hers.

She wanted him. Oh, how she wanted him. She shouldn't want him, shouldn't desire this man who was marrying her for all the wrong reasons.

And yet she wanted him with a desperation that left her breathless.

It was wrong, so very wrong. She had grave doubts about this marriage, and she knew she ought to maintain a clear head. She kept trying to remind herself of that, but it didn't stop her lips from parting to allow his entry, nor her own tongue from shyly flicking out to taste the corner of his mouth.

And the desire pooling in her belly—and surely that was what this strange, prickly, swirling feeling had to be—it just kept getting stronger and stronger.

"Am I a terrible person?" she whispered, more for her ears than for his. "Does this mean I am fallen?"

But he heard her, and his voice was hot and moist on the skin of her cheek.

"*No.*"

He moved to her ear and made her listen more closely.

"*No.*"

He traveled to her lips and forced her to swallow the word.

"*No.*"

Kate felt her head fall back. His voice was low and seductive, and it almost made her feel like she'd been born for this moment.

"You're perfect," he whispered, his large hands moving urgently over her body, one settling on her waist and the other moving up toward the gentle swell of her breast. "Right here, right now, in this moment, in this garden, you're perfect."

Kate found something unsettling about his words, as if he were trying to tell her—and perhaps himself as well—that she might not be perfect tomorrow, and perhaps even less so the next day. But his lips and hands were persuasive, and she forced the unpleasant thoughts from her head, instead reveling in the heady bliss of the moment.

She felt beautiful. She felt . . . perfect. And right there, right then, she couldn't help but adore the man who made her feel that way.

Anthony slid the hand at her waist to the small of her back, supporting her as his other hand found her breast and squeezed her flesh through the thin muslin of her dress. His fingers seemed beyond his control, tight and spasmodic, gripping her as if he were falling off a cliff and had finally found purchase. Her nipple was hard and tight against his palm, even through the fabric of her dress, and it took everything in him, every last ounce of restraint, not to reach around to the back of her frock and slowly pull each button from its prison.

He could see it all in his mind, even as his lips met hers in another searing kiss. Her dress would slip from her shoulders, the muslin doing a tantalizing slide along her skin until her breasts were bared. He could picture those in his mind, too, and he somehow knew they, too, would be perfect. He'd cup one, lifting the nipple to the sun, and slowly, ever so slowly, he'd bend his head toward her until he could just barely touch her with his tongue.

She'd moan, and he'd tease her some more, holding her tightly so that she couldn't wriggle away. And then, just when her head dropped back and she was gasping, he'd replace his tongue with his lips and suckle her until she screamed.

Dear God, he wanted that so badly he thought he might explode.

But this wasn't the time or the place. It wasn't that he felt a need to wait for his marriage vows. As far as he was concerned, he'd declared himself in public, and she was his. But he wasn't going to tumble her in his mother's garden gazebo. He had more pride—and more respect for her—than that.

With great reluctance, he slowly tore himself away from her, letting his hands rest on her slim shoulders and straightening his arms to keep himself far enough away so that he wouldn't be tempted to continue where he'd left off.

And the temptation was there. He made the mistake of looking at her face, and in that moment he would have sworn that Kate Sheffield was every bit as beautiful as her sister.

Hers was a different sort of attraction. Her lips were fuller, less in fashion but infinitely more kissable. Her lashes—how had he not noticed before how long they were? When she blinked they seemed to rest on her cheeks like a carpet. And when her skin was tinged with the pinks of desire, she glowed. Anthony knew he was being fanciful, but when he gazed upon her face, he could not help thinking of the new dawn, of that exact moment when the sun was creeping over the horizon, painting the sky with its subtle palette of peaches and pinks.

They stood that way for a full minute, both catching their breath, until Anthony finally let his arms drop, and they each took a step back. Kate lifted a hand to her mouth, her fore, middle, and ring fingers just barely touching her lips. "We shouldn't have done that," she whispered.

He leaned back against one of the gazebo posts, looked extremely satisfied with his lot. "Why not? We're betrothed."

"We're not," she admitted. "Not really."

He quirked a brow.

"No agreements have been made," Kate explained hastily. "Or papers signed. And I have no dowry. You should know that I have no dowry."

This caused him to smile. "Are you trying to get rid of me?"

"Of course not!" She fidgeted slightly, shifting her weight from foot to foot.

He took a step toward her. "Surely you're not trying to provide me with a reason to be rid of *you*?"

Kate flushed. "N-no," she lied, even though that was exactly what she had been doing. It was, of course, the utmost stupidity on her part. If he backed out of this marriage, she'd be ruined forever, not just in London, but also in her little village in Somerset. News of a fallen woman always traveled fast.

But it was never easy to be the second choice, and a part of her almost wanted him to confirm all of her suspicions—that he didn't want her as his bride, that he'd much prefer Edwina, that he was only marrying her because he had to. It would hurt dreadfully, but if he would just say it, she would know, and knowing—even if the knowledge was bitter—was always better than not knowing.

At least then she would know exactly where she stood. As it was, she felt as if her feet were planted firmly in quicksand.

"Let us make one thing clear," Anthony said, capturing her attention with his decisive tone. His eyes caught hers, burning with such intensity that she could not look away. "I said I was going to marry you. I am a man of my word. Any further speculation on the subject would be highly insulting."

Kate nodded. But she couldn't help thinking: *Be careful what you wish for . . . be careful what you wish for.*

She'd just agreed to marry the very man with whom she feared she was falling in love. And all she could wonder was: *Does he think of Edwina when he kisses me?*

*Be careful what you wish for*, her mind thundered.

*You just might get it.*

# *Chapter 15*

*Once again, This Author has been proven correct. Country house parties do result in the most surprising of betrothals.*

*Yes indeed, dear reader, you are surely reading it here first: Viscount Bridgerton is to marry Miss Katharine Sheffield. Not Miss Edwina, as gossips had speculated, but Miss Katharine.*

*As to how the betrothal came about, details have been surprisingly difficult to obtain. This Author has it on the best authority that the new couple was caught in a compromising position, and that Mrs. Featherington was a witness, but Mrs. F has been uncharacteristically close-lipped about the entire affair. Given that lady's propensity for gossip, This Author can only assume that the viscount (never known for lacking a spine) threatened bodily injury upon Mrs. F should she even breathe a syllable.*

LADY WHISTLEDOWN'S SOCIETY PAPERS,
11 MAY 1814

Kate soon realized that notoriety did not agree with her.

The remaining two days in Kent had been bad enough; once Anthony had announced their engagement at supper following their somewhat precipitous betrothal, she had scarcely a chance to breathe between all the congratulations, questions, and innuendos that were being tossed her way by Lady Bridgerton's guests.

The only time she felt truly at ease was when, a few hours after Anthony's announcement, she finally had a chance to talk privately with Edwina, who'd thrown her arms around her sister and declared herself "thrilled," "overjoyed," and "not even one tiny bit surprised."

Kate had expressed *her* surprise that Edwina was not surprised, but Edwina had just shrugged and said, "It was obvious to me that he was smitten. I do not know why no one else saw it."

Which had left Kate rather puzzled, since she'd been fairly certain that Anthony had had his matrimonial sights set on Edwina.

Once Kate returned to London, the speculation was even worse. Every single member of the *ton*, it seemed, found it imperative to stop by the Sheffields' small rented home on Milner Street to call on the future viscountess. Most managed to infuse their congratulations with a healthy dose of unflattering implication. No one believed it possible that the viscount might actually *want* to marry Kate, and no one seemed to realize how rude it was to say as much to her face.

"My goodness, you were lucky," said Lady Cowper, the mother of the infamous Cressida Cowper, who, for her part, did not say two words to Kate, just sulked in the corner and glared daggers in her direction.

"I had no *idea* he was interested in you," gushed Miss Gertrude Knight, with a facial expression that clearly said she still didn't believe it, and perhaps even hoped that the betrothal might still prove to be a sham, announcement in the *London Times* notwithstanding.

And from Lady Danbury, who'd never been known to mince

words: "Don't know how you trapped him, but it must have been a neat trick. There are a few gels out there who wouldn't mind taking lessons from you, mark my words."

Kate just smiled (or tried to, at least; she suspected that her attempts at gracious and friendly response were not always convincing) and nodded, and murmured, "I am a fortunate girl," whenever Mary poked her in the side.

As for Anthony, the lucky man had been able to avoid the harsh scrutiny she'd been forced to endure. He had told her he needed to remain at Aubrey Hall to take care of a few estate details before the wedding, which had been set for the following Saturday, only nine days after the incident in the garden. Mary had worried that such hastiness would lead to "talk," but Lady Bridgerton had rather pragmatically explained that there would be "talk" no matter what, and that Kate would be less subject to unflattering innuendo once she had the protection of Anthony's name.

Kate suspected that the viscountess—who had gained a certain reputation for her single-minded desire to see her adult children married off—simply wanted to get Anthony in front of the bishop before he had the chance to change his mind.

Kate found herself in agreement with Lady Bridgerton. As nervous as she was about the wedding and the marriage to follow, she'd never been the sort to put things off. Once she made a decision—or, in this case, had one made for her—she saw no reason for delay. And as for the "talk," a hasty wedding might increase its volume, but Kate suspected that the sooner she and Anthony were married, the sooner it would die down, and the sooner she might hope to return to the normal obscurity of her own life.

Of course, her life would not be her own for much longer. She was going to have to get used to that.

Not that it felt like her own even now. Her days were a whirlwind of activity, with Lady Bridgerton dragging her from shop to shop, spending an enormous amount of Anthony's money for her trousseau. Kate had quickly learned that resistance was useless; when Lady Bridgerton—or Violet, as she had now been instructed to call her—made up her mind, heaven help the fool who got in her way. Mary and Edwina had accompanied them on a few of the outings, but they had quickly declared themselves exhausted by Violet's indefatigable energy and gone off to Gunter's for a flavored ice.

Finally, a mere two days before the wedding, Kate received a note from Anthony, asking her to be at home at four that afternoon so that he might pay her a call. Kate was a little nervous at seeing him again; somehow everything seemed different—more formal—in town. Nonetheless, she seized upon the opportunity to avoid another afternoon on Oxford Street, at the dressmaker, and the milliner, and the glovemaker, and to whomever else Violet had it in mind to drag her.

And so, while Mary and Edwina were out running errands—Kate had conveniently forgotten to mention that the viscount was expected—she sat down in the drawing room, Newton sleeping contentedly at her feet, and waited.

Anthony had spent most of the week thinking. Not surprisingly, all of his thoughts were of Kate and their upcoming union.

He'd been worried that he could, if he let himself, love her. The key, it seemed, was simply not to let himself. And the more he thought about it, the more convinced he was that this would not pose a problem. He was a man, after all, and well in control of his actions and emotions. He was no fool; he knew that love existed. But he also believed in the power of the mind, and perhaps even more importantly, the power of the will. Frankly, he saw no reason why love should be an involuntary thing.

If he didn't want to fall in love, then by damn, he wasn't going to. It was as simple as that. It *had* to be as simple as that. If it weren't, then he wasn't much of a man, was he?

He would, however, have to have a talk with Kate on this measure prior to the wedding. There were certain things about their marriage that needed to be made clear. Not rules, exactly, but . . . *understandings*. Yes, that was a good word for it.

Kate needed to understand exactly what she could expect from him, and what he expected in return. Theirs was not a love match. And it wasn't going to grow into one. That simply was not an option. He didn't think she had any delusions on that measure, but just in case, he wanted to make it clear now, before any misunderstandings had the chance to grow into full-fledged disasters.

It was best to lay everything out on the proverbial table so that neither party would be unpleasantly surprised later on. Surely Kate would agree. She was a practical girl. She'd want to know where she stood. She wasn't the sort who liked to be kept guessing.

At precisely two minutes before four, Anthony rapped twice on the Sheffields' front door, trying to ignore the half dozen members of the *ton* who just *happened* to be strolling along Milner Street that afternoon. They were, he thought with a grimace, a bit far from their usual haunts.

But he wasn't surprised. He might be recently returned to London, but he was well aware that his betrothal was the current scandal *du jour*. *Whistledown* was delivered all the way in Kent, after all.

The butler opened the door quickly and ushered him in, showing him to the nearby drawing room. Kate was waiting on the sofa, her hair swept up into a neat something-or-other (Anthony never could remember the names of all those coiffures the ladies seemed to favor) and topped with a ridiculous little cap of some sort that he supposed was meant to match the white trim on her pale blue afternoon dress.

The cap, he decided, would be the first thing to go once they were married. She had lovely hair, long and lustrous and thick. He knew that good manners dictated that she wear bonnets when she was out and about, but really, it seemed a crime to cover it up in the comfort of her own home.

Before he could open his mouth, however, even in greeting, she motioned to a silver tea service on the table in front of her and said, "I took the liberty of ordering tea. There's a slight chill in the air and I thought you might like some. If you don't, I'd be happy to ring for something else."

There hadn't been a chill in the air, at least not one that Anthony had detected, but he nonetheless said, "That would be lovely, thank you."

Kate nodded and picked up the pot to pour. She tipped it about an inch, then righted it, frowning as she said, "I don't even know how you take your tea."

Anthony felt one corner of his mouth tipping up slightly. "Milk. No sugar."

She nodded, setting the pot down in favor of the milk. "It seems a thing a wife should know."

He sat down in a chair that sat at a right angle to the sofa. "And now you do."

She took a deep breath and then let it go. "Now I do," she murmured.

Anthony cleared his throat as he watched her pour. She wasn't wearing gloves, and he found he liked to watch her hands as she worked. Her fingers were long and slender, and they were incredibly graceful, which surprised him, considering how many times she'd trod on his toes while dancing.

Of course some of those missteps had been done on purpose, but not, he suspected, as many as she would have liked to have him believe.

"Here you are," she murmured, holding out his tea. "Be careful, it's hot. I've never been one for lukewarm tea."

No, he thought with a smile, she wouldn't be. Kate wasn't the sort to do anything in half measures. It was one of the things he liked best about her.

"My lord?" she said politely, moving the tea a few inches farther in his direction.

Anthony grasped the saucer, allowing his gloved fingers to brush against her bare ones. He kept his eyes on her face, noticing the faint pink stain of blush that touched her cheeks.

For some reason that pleased him.

"Did you have something specific you wanted to ask me, my lord?" she asked, once her hand was safely away from his and her fingers wrapped around the handle of her own teacup.

"It's Anthony, as I'm sure you recall, and I can't call upon my fiancée merely for the pleasure of her company?"

She gave him a shrewd look over the rim of her cup. "Of course you can," she replied, "but I don't think you are."

He raised a brow at her impertinence. "As it happens, you're right."

She murmured something. He didn't quite catch it, but he had a sneaking suspicion it had been, "I usually am."

"I thought we ought to discuss our marriage," he said.

"I beg your pardon?"

He leaned back in his chair. "We're both practical people. I think we'll find ourselves more at ease once we understand what we can expect from one another."

"Of—of course."

"Good." He set his teacup down in the saucer, then set both down on the table in front of him. "I'm glad you feel that way."

Kate nodded slowly but didn't say anything, instead choosing to keep her eyes trained on his face as he cleared his throat. He looked as if he were preparing for a parliamentary speech.

"We did not get off to the most favorable of starts," he said, scowling slightly when she nodded her agreement, "but I feel—and I hope that you do as well—that we have since reached a friendship of sorts."

She nodded again, thinking that she might make it all the way through the conversation doing nothing but nodding.

"Friendship between the husband and the wife is of the utmost importance," he continued, "even more important, in my opinion, than love."

This time she didn't nod.

"Our marriage will be one based on mutual friendship and respect," he pontificated, "and I for one could not be more pleased."

"Respect," Kate echoed, mostly because he was looking at her expectantly.

"I will do my best to be a good husband to you," he said. "And, provided that you do not bar me from your bed, I shall be faithful to both you and our vows."

"That's rather enlightened of you," she murmured. He was saying nothing she did not expect, and yet she found it somewhat needling all the same.

His eyes narrowed. "I hope you're taking me seriously, Kate."

"Oh, very much so."

"Good." But he gave her a funny look, and she wasn't sure if he believed her. "In return," he added, "I expect that you will not behave in any manner that will sully my family's name."

Kate felt her spine stiffen. "I would not dream of it."

"I didn't think you would. That is one of the reasons I am so pleased with this marriage. You will make an excellent viscountess."

It was meant as a compliment, Kate knew, but still it felt a bit hollow, and maybe a touch condescending. She'd much rather have been told that she'd make an excellent wife.

"We shall have friendship," he announced, "and we shall have mutual respect, and children—intelligent children, thank God, since you are quite the most intelligent woman of my acquaintance."

That made up for his condescension, but Kate had barely time to smile at his compliment before he added, "But you should not expect love. This marriage will not be about love."

An awful lump rose in Kate's throat, and she found herself nodding yet again, except this time every movement of her neck somehow brought pain to her heart.

"There are certain things I cannot give you," Anthony said, "and love, I'm afraid, is one of them."

"I see."

"Do you?"

"Of course," she practically snapped. "You could not make it any plainer if you wrote it on my arm."

"I had never planned to marry for love," he said.

"That is not what you told me when you were courting Edwina."

"When I was courting Edwina," he returned, "I was trying to impress *you*."

Her eyes narrowed. "You are not impressing me now."

He let out a long breath. "Kate, I did not come here to argue. I merely thought it best if we were honest with one another before the wedding on Saturday morning."

"Of course," she sighed, forcing herself to nod. His intention hadn't been to insult her, and she shouldn't have overreacted. She knew him well enough now to know that he was merely acting out of concern. He knew he would never love her; better to make that clear in the beginning.

But still it hurt. She didn't know if she loved him, but she was fairly certain she *could* love him, and deathly afraid that after a few weeks of marriage, she *would* love him.

And it would be so nice if he could just love her back.

"It is best that we understand each other now," he said softly.

Kate just kept nodding. A body in motion tended to remain in motion, and she was afraid that if she stopped, she might do something really stupid, like cry.

He reached across the table and took her hand, which made her flinch. "I didn't want you to enter this marriage with any delusions," he said. "I didn't think you'd want that."

"Of course not, my lord," she said.

He frowned. "I thought I told you to call me Anthony."

"You did," she said, "my lord."

He withdrew his hand. Kate watched as he returned it to his own lap, feeling strangely bereft.

"Before I go," he said, "I have something for you." Without taking his eyes off of her face, he reached into his pocket and pulled out a small jeweler's box. "I must apologize for being so delayed in presenting you with a betrothal ring," he murmured, handing it to her.

Kate smoothed her fingers over the blue velvet covering before flipping the box open. Inside lay a rather simple gold ring, adorned by a single round-cut diamond.

"It's a Bridgerton heirloom," he said. "There are several betrothal rings in the collection, but I thought you'd like this one best. The others were rather heavy and fussy."

"It's beautiful," Kate said, quite unable to take her eyes off of it.

He reached out and took the box from her. "May I?" he murmured, plucking the ring from its velvet nest.

She held out her hand, cursing at herself when she realized she was trembling—not a great deal, but surely enough for him to notice. He didn't say a word, though, just steadied her hand with his as he used the other to slip the ring on her finger.

"Looks rather nice, don't you think?" he asked, still holding the tips of her fingers with his.

Kate nodded, unable to take her eyes off of it. She'd never been one for rings; this would be the first she wore with any regularity. It felt strange on her finger, heavy and cold and very, very solid. It somehow made everything that had happened in the past week seem more real. More final. It occurred to her as she was staring at the ring that she'd been half expecting a bolt of lightning to come down from heaven and stop the proceedings before they actually said their vows.

Anthony moved closer, then brought her newly adorned fingers to his lips. "Perhaps we should seal the bargain with a kiss?" he murmured.

"I'm not sure. . . ."

He pulled her onto his lap and grinned devilishly. "I am."

But as Kate tumbled onto him, she accidentally kicked Newton, who let out a loud, whiny bark, obviously distressed at having his nap so rudely interrupted.

Anthony raised a brow and peered over Kate at Newton. "I didn't even see him here."

"He was taking a nap," Kate explained. "He's a very sound sleeper."

But once awake, Newton refused to be left out of the action, and with a slightly more awake bark, he leaped up onto the chair, landing on Kate's lap.

"Newton!" she squealed.

"Oh, for the love of—" But Anthony's mutterings were cut short by a big, sloppy kiss from Newton.

"I think he likes you," Kate said, so amused by Anthony's disgusted expression that she forgot to be self-conscious about her position on his lap.

"Dog," Anthony ordered, "get down on the floor this instant."

Newton hung his head and whined.

"Now!"

Letting out a big sigh, Newton turned about and plopped down onto the floor.

"My goodness," Kate said, peering down at the dog, who was now moping under the table, his snout lying sorrowfully on the carpet, "I'm impressed."

"It's all in the tone of voice," Anthony said archly, snaking a viselike arm around her waist so that she could not get up.

Kate looked at his arm, then looked at his face, her brows arching in question. "Why," she mused, "do I get the impression you find that tone of voice effective on women as well?"

He shrugged and leaned toward her with a heavy-lidded smile. "It usually is," he murmured.

"Not this one." Kate planted her hands on the arms of the chair and tried to wrench herself up.

But he was far too strong. "Especially this one," he said, his voice dropping to an impossibly low purr. With his free hand, he cupped her chin and turned her face to his. His lips were soft but demanding, and he explored her mouth with a thoroughness that left her breathless.

His mouth moved along the line of her jaw to her neck, pausing only to whisper, "Where is your mother?"

"Out," Kate gasped.

His teeth tugged at the edge of her bodice. "For how long?"

"I don't know." She let out a little squeal as his tongue dipped below the muslin and traced an erotic line on her skin. "Good heavens, Anthony, what are you doing?"

"How long?" he repeated.

"An hour. Maybe two."

Anthony glanced up to make sure he'd shut the door when he had entered earlier. "Maybe two?" he murmured, smiling against her skin. "Really?"

"M-maybe just one."

He hooked a finger under the edge of her bodice up near her shoulder, making sure to catch the edge of her chemise as well. "One," he said, "is still quite splendid." Then, pausing only to bring his mouth to hers so that she could not utter any protest, he swiftly pulled her dress down, taking the chemise along with it.

He felt her gasp into his mouth, but he just deepened the kiss as he palmed the round fullness of her breast. She was perfect under his fingers, soft and pert, filling his hand as if she'd been made for him.

When he felt the last of her resistance melt away, he moved his kiss to her ear, nibbling softly on her lobe. "Do you like this?" he whispered, squeezing gently with his hand.

She nodded jerkily.

"Mmmm, good," he murmured, letting his tongue do a slow sweep of her ear. "It would make things very difficult if you did not."

"H-how?"

He fought the bubble of mirth that was rising in his throat. This absolutely wasn't the time to laugh, but she was so damned innocent. He'd never made love to a woman like her before; he was finding it surprisingly delightful. "Let's just say," he said, "that I like it very much."

"Oh." She offered him the most tentative of smiles.

"There's more, you know," he whispered, letting his breath caress her ear.

"I'm sure there must be," she replied, her voice mere breath.

"You are?" he asked teasingly, squeezing her again.

"I'm not so green that I think one can make a baby from what we've been doing."

"I'd be happy to show you the rest," he murmured.

"Not—Oh!"

He'd squeezed again, this time allowing his fingers to tickle her skin. He loved that she couldn't think when he touched her breasts. "You were saying?" he prompted, nibbling on her neck.

"I—I was?"

He nodded, the faint stubble of his beard brushing her throat. "I'm sure you were. But then again, perhaps I'd rather not hear. You'd begun with the word 'not.' Surely," he added with a flick of his tongue against the underside of her chin, "not a word that belongs between us at a time like this. But"—his tongue moved down the line of her throat to the hollow above her collarbone—"I digress."

"You—you do?"

He nodded. "I believe I was trying to determine what pleases you, as all good husbands should do."

She said nothing, but her breathing quickened.

He smiled against her skin. "What, for example, about this?" He flattened his hand so that he was no longer cupping her, instead just letting his palm graze lightly over her nipple.

"Anthony!" she choked out.

"Good," he said, moving to her neck, nudging her chin up so that she was more open to him. "I'm glad we're back to Anthony. 'My lord' is so formal, don't you think? Far too formal for *this*."

And then he did what he'd been fantasizing about for weeks. He lowered his head to her breast and took her into his mouth, tasting, suckling, teasing, reveling in each gasp he heard spill forth from her lips, each spasm of desire he felt shivering across her body.

He loved that she reacted this way, thrilled that he did this to her. "So good," he murmured, his breath hot and moist against her skin. "You taste so damn good."

"Anthony," she said, her voice hoarse, "Are you sure—"

He put a finger to her lips without even lifting his face to look at her. "I have no idea what you're asking, but whatever it is"—he moved his attention to her other breast—"I'm sure."

She made a soft little moaning sound, the sort that came from the very bottom of one's throat. Her body arched under his ministrations, and with renewed fervor, he teased her nipple, grazing it gently between his teeth.

"Oh, my—oh, Anthony!"

He ran his tongue around the aureole. She was perfect, simply perfect. He loved the sound of her voice, hoarse and broken with desire, and his body tingled at the thought of their wedding night, of her cries of passion and need. She'd be an inferno beneath him, and he relished the prospect of making her explode.

He pulled away so that he could see her face. She was flushed and her eyes were dazed and dilated. Her hair was starting to come undone from that hideous cap.

"This," he said, plucking it from her head, "has got to go."

"My lord!"

"Promise me you'll never wear it again."

She twisted in her seat—on his lap, actually, which did little to help the rather urgent state of his groin—to look over the edge of the chair. "I'll do no such thing," she retorted. "I quite like that cap."

"You can't possibly," he said in all seriousness.

"I can and— Newton!"

Anthony followed her line of vision and broke out into loud laughter, shaking the both of them in their seats. Newton was happily munching away on Kate's cap. "Good dog!" he said on a laugh.

"I would make you buy me another," Kate muttered, yanking her dress back up, "except that you've already spent a fortune on me this week."

This amused him. "I have?" he inquired mildly.

She nodded. "I've been shopping with your mother."

"Ah. Good. I'm sure she didn't let you pick out anything like *that*." He motioned toward the now mangled cap in Newton's mouth.

When he looked back at her, her mouth was twisted into a fetchingly disgruntled line. He couldn't help but smile. She was so easy to read. His mother hadn't let her buy such an unattractive cap, and it was killing her that she couldn't offer a retort to his last statement.

He sighed rather contentedly. Life with Kate wasn't going to be dull.

But it was getting late, and he should probably be going. Kate had said her mother wasn't expected for at least an hour, but Anthony knew better than to trust the female sense of time. Kate could be wrong, or her mother could have changed her mind, or any number of things might have happened, and even though he and Kate were due to be married in just two days, it didn't seem particularly prudent to get caught in the drawing room in such a compromising position.

With great reluctance—sitting in the chair with Kate and doing nothing but hold her was surprisingly satisfying—he stood, lifting her in his arms as he did so, and then set her back in the chair.

"This has been a delightful interlude," he murmured, leaning down to drop a kiss on her forehead. "But I fear your mother's early return. I shall see you Saturday morning?"

She blinked. "Saturday?"

"A superstition of my mother's," he said with a sheepish smile. "She thinks it's bad luck for the bride and groom to see one another the day before the wedding."

"Oh." She rose to her feet, self-consciously smoothing her dress and hair. "And do you believe it as well?"

"Not at all," he said with a snort.

She nodded. "It's very sweet of you to indulge your mother, then."

Anthony paused for a moment, well aware that most men of his reputation did not want to appear tied to apron strings. But this was Kate, and he knew that she valued devotion to family as much as he did, so he finally said, "There is little I would not do to keep my mother content."

She smiled shyly. "It is one of the things I like best about you."

He made some sort of gesture designed to change the subject, but she interrupted with, "No, it's true. You're far more caring a person than you'd like people to believe."

Since he wasn't going to be able to win the argument with her—and there was little point in contradicting a woman when she was being complimentary—he put a finger to his lips and said, "Shhh. Don't tell anyone." And then, with one last kiss to her hand and a murmured, "Adieu," he made his way out the door and outside.

Once on his horse and on his way back to his small townhouse across town, he allowed himself to assess the visit. It went well, he thought. Kate had seemed to understand the limits he had set upon their marriage, and she'd reacted to his lovemaking with a desire that was sweet and fierce at the same time.

All in all, he thought with a satisfied smile, the future looked bright. His marriage would be a success. As for his previous concerns—well, it was clear he had nothing to worry about.

---

Kate was worried. Anthony had been practically tripping over himself to make certain that she understood that he would never love her. And he certainly didn't seem to want her love in return.

Then he'd gone and kissed her as if there were no tomorrow, as if she were the most beautiful woman on earth. She'd be the first to admit that she had little experience with men and their desires, but he'd certainly seemed to desire her.

Or was he simply wishing she was someone else? She was not his first choice for a wife. She'd do well to remember that fact.

And even if she did fall in love with him—well, she'd simply have to keep it to herself. There was really nothing else to do.

# Chapter 16

*It has come to This Author's attention that the wedding of Lord Bridgerton and Miss Sheffield is to be a small, intimate, and private affair.*

*In other words, This Author is not invited.*

*But have no fear, dear reader, This Author is at her most resourceful at times such as these, and promises to uncover the details of the ceremony, both the interesting and the banal.*

*The wedding of London's most eligible bachelor is surely something which must be reported in This Author's humble column, don't you agree?*

LADY WHISTLEDOWN'S SOCIETY PAPERS,
13 MAY 1814

The night before the wedding, Kate was sitting on her bed in her favorite dressing gown, looking dazedly at the multitude of trunks strewn across the floor. Her every belonging was packed away, neatly folded or stored, ready for transport to her new home.

Even Newton had been prepared for the journey. He'd been bathed and dried, a new collar had been affixed to his neck, and his favorite toys were loaded into a small satchel that now sat in the front hall, right next to the delicately carved wooden chest Kate had had since she was a baby. The chest was filled with Kate's childhood toys and treasures, and she'd found tremendous comfort in their presence here in London. It was silly and sentimental, but to Kate it made her upcoming transition a little less scary. Bringing her things—funny little items that meant nothing to anyone but her—to Anthony's home made it seem more like it would truly be her home as well.

Mary, who always seemed to understand what Kate needed before she understood it herself, had sent word to friends back in Somerset as soon as Kate had become betrothed, asking them to ship the chest to London in time for the wedding.

Kate stood and wandered about the room, stopping to run her fingers across a nightgown that was folded and laid upon a table, awaiting transfer to the last of her trunks. It was one that Lady Bridgerton—Violet, she had to start thinking of her as Violet—had picked out, modest in cut but sheer in fabric. Kate had been mortified throughout the entire visit to the lingerie maker. This was her betrothed's mother, after all, selecting items for the wedding night!

As Kate picked up the gown and set it carefully in a trunk, she heard a knock at the door. She called out her greeting, and Edwina poked her head in. She, too, was dressed for bed, her pale hair pulled back into a sloppy bun at the nape of her neck.

"I thought you might like some hot milk," Edwina said.

Kate smiled gratefully. "That sounds heavenly."

Edwina reached down and picked up the ceramic mug she'd set on the floor. "Can't hold two mugs and twist the doorknob at the same time," she explained with a smile. Once inside, she kicked the door shut and handed one of the mugs to Kate. Eyes trained on Kate, Edwina asked without preamble, "Are you scared?"

Kate took a gingerly sip, checking the temperature before gulping it down. It was hot but not scalding, and it somehow comforted her. She'd been drinking hot milk since childhood, and the taste and feel of it always made her feel warm and secure.

"Not scared precisely," she finally replied, sitting down on the edge of her bed, "but nervous. Definitely nervous."

"Well, of course you're nervous," Edwina said, her free hand waving animatedly through the air. "Only an idiot wouldn't be nervous. Your whole life is going to change. Everything! Even your name. You'll be a married woman. A viscountess. After tomorrow, you will not be the same woman, Kate, and after tomorrow *night*—"

"That's enough, Edwina," Kate interrupted.

"But—"

"You are *not* doing anything to ease my mind."

"Oh." Edwina offered her a sheepish smile. "Sorry."

"It's all right," Kate assured her.

Edwina managed to hold her tongue for about four seconds before she asked, "Has Mother been in to speak with you?"

"Not yet."

"She must, don't you think? Tomorrow is your wedding day, and I'm sure there are all sorts of things one needs to know." Edwina took a big gulp of her milk, leaving a rather incongruous white mustache on her upper lip, then perched on the edge of the bed across from Kate. "I know there are all sorts of things *I* don't know. And unless you've been up to something I don't know about, I don't see how *you* could know them, either."

Kate wondered if it would be impolite to muzzle her sister with some of the lingerie Lady Bridgerton had picked out. There seemed to be some rather nice poetic justice in such a maneuver.

"Kate?" Edwina asked, blinking curiously. "Kate? Why are you looking at me so strangely?"

Kate gazed at the lingerie longingly. "You don't want to know."

"Hmmph. Well, I—"

Edwina's mutterings were cut short by a soft knock at the door. "That'll be Mother," Edwina said with a wicked grin. "I can't wait."

Kate rolled her eyes at Edwina as she rose to open the door. Sure enough, Mary was standing in the hall, holding two steaming mugs. "I thought you might like some hot milk," she said with a weak smile.

Kate lifted her mug in response. "Edwina had the same notion."

"What is Edwina doing here?" Mary asked, entering the room.

"Since when do I need a reason to talk with my sister?" Edwina asked with a snort.

Mary shot her a peevish look before turning her attention back to Kate. "Hmmm," she mused. "We do seem to have a surfeit of hot milk."

"This one's gone lukewarm, anyway," Kate said, setting her mug down on one of the already-closed-up trunks and replacing it with the warmer one in Mary's hand. "Edwina can take the other one down to the kitchen when she leaves."

"Beg pardon?" Edwina asked, vaguely distracted. "Oh, of course. I'm happy to help." But she didn't rise to her feet. In fact, she didn't even twitch, save for the back and forth of her head as she looked from Mary to Kate and back again.

"I need to speak with Kate," Mary said.

Edwina nodded enthusiastically.

"Alone."

Edwina blinked. "I have to leave?"

Mary nodded and held out the lukewarm mug.

"Now?"

Mary nodded again.

Edwina looked stricken, then her expression melted into a wary smile. "You're joking, right? I may stay, right?"

"Wrong," Mary replied.

Edwina turned pleading eyes to Kate.

"Don't look to me," Kate said with a barely suppressed smile. "It's her decision. She'll be doing the talking, after all. I'll just be listening."

"And asking questions," Edwina pointed out. "And I have questions, too." She turned to her mother. "Lots of questions."

"I'm sure you do," Mary said, "and I'll be happy to answer them all the night before you get married."

Edwina groaned her way upright. "This isn't fair," she grumbled, snatching the mug out of Mary's hand.

"Life isn't fair," Mary said with a grin.

"I'll say," Edwina muttered, dragging her feet as she crossed the room.

"And no listening at the door!" Mary called out.

"I wouldn't dream of it," Edwina drawled. "Not that you'd talk loudly enough for me to hear a thing, anyway."

Mary sighed as Edwina stepped out into the hall and shut the door, her movements punctuated by a constant stream of unintelligible grumbles. "We shall have to whisper," she said to Kate.

Kate nodded, but she did feel enough loyalty toward her sister to say, "She *might* not be eavesdropping."

The look Mary gave her was dubious in the extreme. "Do you want to swing the door open to find out?"

Kate grinned despite herself. "Point taken."

Mary sat down in the spot Edwina had just vacated and gave Kate a rather direct look. "I'm sure you know why I'm here."

Kate nodded.

Mary took a sip of her milk and was silent for a long moment before she said, "When I married—for the first time, not to your father—I knew nothing of what to expect in the marriage bed. It was not—" She closed her eyes briefly, and for a moment she looked to be in pain. "My lack of knowledge made it all the more difficult," she finally said, the slowness of her carefully chosen words telling Kate that "difficult" was probably a euphemism.

"I see," Kate murmured.

Mary looked up sharply. "No, you don't see. And I hope you never do. But that is beside the point. I always swore that no daughter of mine would enter into marriage ignorant of what occurs between a husband and wife."

"I'm already aware of the basics of the maneuver," Kate admitted.

Clearly surprised, Mary asked, "You are?"

Kate nodded. "It can't be very much different from animals."

Mary shook her head, her lips pursed into a slightly amused smile. "No, it's not."

Kate pondered how best to phrase her next question. From what she'd seen on her neighbor's farm back in Somerset, the act of procreation didn't look terribly enjoyable at all. But when Anthony kissed her, she felt as if she were losing her mind. And when he kissed her twice, she wasn't even sure if she wanted it back! Her entire body tingled, and she suspected that if their recent encounters had occurred in more suitable locales, she would have let him have his way with her with nary a protest.

But then there was that awful screaming mare at the farm. . . . Frankly, the various pieces of the puzzle didn't seem to reconcile.

Finally, after much clearing of her throat, she said, "It doesn't look very pleasant."

Mary closed her eyes again, her face taking on that same look as before—as if she were remembering something she'd rather keep tucked away in the darkest recesses of her mind. When she opened her eyes again, she said, "A woman's enjoyment depends entirely on her husband."

"And a man's?"

"The act of love," Mary said, blushing, "can and should be a pleasant experience for both man and woman. But—" She coughed and took a sip of her milk. "I would be remiss if I did not tell you that a woman does not always find pleasure in the act."

"But a man does?"

Mary nodded.

"That doesn't seem fair."

Mary's smile was wry. "I believe I just told Edwina that life wasn't always fair."

Kate frowned, staring down into her milk. "Well, this *really* doesn't seem fair."

"This doesn't mean," Mary hastened to add, "that the experience is necessarily distasteful to the woman. And I'm certain it won't be distasteful to you. I assumed the viscount has kissed you?"

Kate nodded without looking up.

When Mary spoke, Kate could hear the smile in her voice. "I'll assume from your blush," Mary said, "that you enjoyed it."

Kate nodded again, her cheeks now burning.

"If you enjoyed his kiss," Mary said, "then I am certain you won't be upset by his further attentions. I'm sure that he will be gentle and attentive with you."

"Gentle" didn't quite capture the essence of Anthony's kisses, but Kate didn't think that was the sort of thing one was meant to share with one's mother. Truly, the entire conversation was embarrassing enough as it was.

"Men and women are very different," Mary continued, as if that weren't completely obvious, "and a man—even one who is faithful to his wife, which I'm sure the viscount will be to you—can find his pleasure with almost any woman."

This was disturbing, and not what Kate had wanted to hear. "And a woman?" she had prompted.

"It is different for a woman. I have heard that wicked women find their pleasure like a man, in the arms of any who will satisfy, but I do not believe it. I think that a woman must care for her husband in order to enjoy the marriage bed."

Kate was silent for a moment. "You did not love your first husband, did you?"

Mary shook her head. "It makes all the difference, sweet one. That, and a husband's regard for his wife. But I have seen the viscount in your company. I realize that your match was sudden and unexpected, but he treats you with care and respect. You will have nothing to fear, I'm sure of it. The viscount will treat you well."

And with that, Mary kissed Kate upon the forehead and bade her good night, picking up both empty milk mugs as she left the room. Kate sat on her bed, staring sightlessly at the wall for several minutes.

Mary was wrong. Kate was sure of it. She had much to fear.

She hated that she was not Anthony's first choice for a wife, but she was practical, and she was pragmatic, and she knew that certain things in life simply had to be accepted as fact. But she'd been consoling herself with the memory of the desire she had felt—and she thought Anthony had felt—when she was in his arms.

Now it seemed that this desire wasn't even necessarily for her, but rather some primitive urge that every man felt for every woman.

And Kate would never know if, when Anthony snuffed the candles and took her to bed, he closed his eyes . . .

And pictured another woman's face.

---

The wedding, which was held in the drawing room of Bridgerton House, was a small, private affair. Well, as small as one could expect with the entire Bridgerton family in attendance, from Anthony all the way down to little eleven-year-old Hyacinth, who'd taken her role as flower girl *very* seriously. When her brother Gregory, aged thirteen, had tried to tip her basket of rose petals, she'd walloped him in the chin, delaying the ceremony by a good ten minutes but interjecting a much-needed note of levity and laughter.

Well, for everyone except Gregory, who'd been quite put out by the entire episode and certainly *wasn't* laughing, even though he was, as Hyacinth was quick to point out to anyone who would listen (and her voice was loud enough so that one didn't really have the option of *not* listening), the one who'd started it.

Kate had seen it all from her vantage point in the hall, where she'd been peeking through a crack in the door. It had made her smile, which was much appreciated, since her knees had been knocking for over an hour. She could only thank her lucky stars that Lady Bridgerton had not insisted upon a large, grand affair. Kate, who'd never thought of herself as a nervous sort of person before, would probably have passed out from fright.

Indeed, Violet had mentioned the possibility of a huge wedding as a method by which to combat the rumors that were circulating about Kate, Anthony, and their rather sudden engagement. Mrs. Featherington was, true to her word, remaining mostly silent on the details of the matter, but she'd let enough innuendo slip that *everyone* knew that the betrothal had not come about in the usual matter.

As a result, *everyone* was talking, and Kate knew it was only a matter of time before Mrs. Featherington could no longer restrain herself and everyone learned the true story of her downfall at the hands—or rather, the stinger—of a bee.

But in the end Violet had decided that a quick marriage was best, and since one couldn't throw together a grand party in one week, the guest list had been limited to family. Kate was attended by Edwina, Anthony by his brother Benedict, and in due course they were man and wife.

It was strange, Kate thought later that afternoon as she stared at the gold band that had joined the diamond on her left hand, how quickly one's life could change. The ceremony had been brief, rushing by in a crazy blur, and yet her life was forever altered. Edwina had been correct. Everything was different. She was a married woman now, a viscountess.

*Lady Bridgerton.*

She chewed on her lower lip. It sounded like someone else. How long would it take before someone said, "Lady Bridgerton," and she actually thought they were talking to *her*, and not Anthony's mother?

She was a wife now, with a wife's responsibilities.

It terrified her.

Now that the wedding was done, Kate reflected upon Mary's words from the previous night and knew that she was right. In many respects, she was the luckiest woman alive. Anthony would treat her well. He would treat any woman well. And that was the problem.

And now she was in a carriage, traveling the short distance between Bridgerton House, where the reception had been held, and Anthony's private residence, which she supposed could no longer be referred to as "bachelor's lodgings."

She stole a glance at her new husband. He was facing straight ahead, his face oddly serious.

"Do you plan to move into Bridgerton House now that you are married?" she inquired quietly.

Anthony started, almost as if he'd forgotten she was there.

"Yes," he replied, turning to face her, "although not for several months. I thought we could do with a bit of privacy at the start of our marriage, don't you think?"

"Of course," Kate murmured. She looked down at her hands, which were fidgeting in her lap. She tried to still them, but it was impossible. It was a wonder she had not burst out of her gloves.

Anthony followed the line of her gaze and placed one of his large hands over both of hers. She went still instantly.

"Are you nervous?" he inquired.

"Did you think I wouldn't be?" she replied, trying to keep her voice dry and ironic.

He smiled in response. "There is nothing to fear."

Kate nearly burst out in jittery laughter. It seemed she was destined to hear that platitude over and over again. "Perhaps," she allowed, "but still much about which to be nervous."

His smile broadened. "Touché, my dear wife."

Kate swallowed convulsively. It was strange to be someone's wife, especially strange to be this man's wife. "And are *you* nervous?" she countered.

He leaned in toward her, his dark eyes hot and heavy with the promise of things to come. "Oh, desperately," he murmured. He closed the rest of the distance between them, his lips finding the sensitive hollow of her ear. "My heart is pounding," he whispered.

Kate's body seemed to stiffen and melt at the same time. And then she blurted out, "I think we should wait."

He nibbled on her ear. "Wait for what?"

She tried to wiggle away. He didn't understand. If he'd understood, he'd be furious, and he didn't seem particularly upset.

Yet.

"F-for the marriage," she stammered.

That seemed to amuse him, and he playfully wiggled the rings that now rested on her gloved fingers. "It's a bit late for that, don't you think?"

"For the wedding night," she clarified.

He drew back, his dark brows flattening into a straight, and perhaps a little bit angry, line. "No," he said simply. But he did not move to embrace her again.

Kate tried to think of words that would make him understand, but it wasn't easy; she wasn't so sure that she understood herself. And she was rather certain that he would not believe her if she told him that she'd not intended to make this request; it had just burst forth from within her, born of a panic she hadn't even known was there until that very moment.

"I'm not asking for forever," she said, hating the tremor that shook her words. "Just a week."

This caught his attention, and one of his brows rose in ironic query. "And what, pray tell, do you hope to gain by a week?"

"I don't know," she answered quite honestly.

His eyes focused onto hers, hard, hot, and sardonic. "You're going to have to do better than that," he said.

Kate didn't want to look at him, didn't want the intimacy he forced upon her when she was caught in his dark gaze. It was easy to hide her feelings when she could keep her focus on his chin or his shoulder, but when she had to look straight into his eyes . . .

She was afraid he could see into her very soul.

"This has been a week of a great many changes in my life," she began, wishing she knew where she was going with the statement.

"For me as well," he interjected softly.

"Not so much for you," she returned. "The intimacies of marriage are nothing new to you."

One corner of his mouth quirked into a lopsided, slightly arrogant smile. "I assure you, my lady, that I have never before been married."

"That's not what I meant, and you know it."

He did not contradict her.

"I simply would like a bit of time to prepare," she said, primly folding her hands in her lap. But she couldn't keep her thumbs still, and they twiddled anxiously, giving proof to the state of her nerves.

Anthony stared at her for a long moment, then leaned back, propping his left ankle rather casually on his right knee. "Very well," he allowed.

"Really?" She straightened with surprise. She had not expected him to capitulate with such ease.

"Provided . . ." he continued.

She slumped. She should have known that there would be a contingency.

". . . that you edify me on one point."

She gulped. "And what would that be, my lord?"

He leaned forward, the very devil in his eyes. "How, precisely, do you plan to prepare?"

Kate glanced out the window, then swore under her breath when she realized they weren't even to Anthony's street. There would be no escaping his question; she was stuck in the carriage for at least another five minutes. "We-e-e-e-ll," she stalled, "I'm sure I don't understand what you mean."

He chuckled. "I'm sure you don't, either."

Kate scowled at him. There was nothing worse than being the butt of someone else's joke, and it seemed especially inappropriate when one happened to be a bride on her wedding day. "Now you're having fun with me," she accused.

"No," he said with what could only have been called a leer, "I'd *like* to have fun with you. There's quite a difference."

"I wish you wouldn't talk like that," she grumbled. "You know I don't understand."

His eyes focused on her lips as his tongue darted out to wet his own. "You would," he murmured, "if you'd simply give in to the inevitable and forget your silly request."

"I don't enjoy being condescended to," Kate said stiffly.

His eyes flashed. "And I don't like being denied my rights," he returned, his voice cold and his face a harsh rendition of aristocratic power.

"I'm not denying you anything," she insisted.

"Oh, really?" His drawl lacked all humor.

"I'm just asking for a reprieve. A brief, temporary, *brief*"—she repeated the word, just in case his brain was too dulled by single-minded male pride to have understood her the first time—"reprieve. Surely you would not deny me such a simple request."

"Of the two of us," he said, his voice clipped, "I don't think I'm the one doing the denying."

He was right, drat the man, and she had no idea what else to say. She knew she hadn't a leg to stand on with her spur-of-the-moment request; he had every right to toss her over his shoulder, drag her off to bed, and lock her in the room for a week if he so desired.

She was acting foolishly, a prisoner of her own insecurities—insecurities she hadn't even known she possessed until she'd met Anthony.

All her life, she'd been the one who'd received the second glance, the second greeting, the second kiss on the hand. As the elder daughter, it should have been her due to be addressed before her younger sister, but Edwina's beauty was so stunning, the pure and perfect blue of her eyes so startling, that people simply forgot themselves in her presence.

Introductions to Kate were usually met with an embarrassed,

"Of course," and a polite murmured greeting while their eyes slid back to Edwina's pure and shining face.

Kate had never minded it much. If Edwina had been spoiled or bad-tempered it might have been difficult, and in all truth, most of the men she'd met were shallow and silly, and she hadn't much cared if they only took the time to acknowledge her after her sister.

Until now.

She wanted Anthony's eyes to light up when *she* entered the room. She wanted him to scan a crowd until he saw *her* face. She didn't need him to love her—or at least that's what she was telling herself—but she desperately wanted to be first in his affections, first in his desires.

And she had an awful, terrible feeling that all this meant she was falling in love.

Falling in love with one's husband—who would have thought it could be such a disaster?

"I see you have no response," Anthony said quietly.

The carriage rolled to a halt, thankfully sparing her from having to make a reply. But when a liveried footman rushed forward and attempted to open the door, Anthony yanked it back shut, never once taking his eyes off of her face.

"How, my lady?" he repeated.

"How . . ." she echoed. She'd quite forgotten what he was asking.

"How," he said yet again, his voice hard as ice but hot as flame, "do you plan to prepare for your wedding night?"

"I—I had not considered," Kate replied.

"I thought not." He let go of the door handle, and the door swung open, revealing the faces of two footmen who were obviously trying very hard not to look curious. Kate remained silent as Anthony helped her down and led her into the house.

His household staff was assembled in the small entry hall, and Kate murmured her greetings as each member was introduced to her by the butler and housekeeper. The staff wasn't very extensive, as the house was small by *ton* standards, but the introductions took a good twenty minutes.

Twenty minutes which, unfortunately, did little to calm her nerves. By the time he placed his hand at the small of her back and guided her toward the stairs, her heart was racing, and for the first time in her life, she thought she might actually pass out.

It wasn't that she feared the marriage bed.

It wasn't even that she feared not pleasing her husband. Even an innocent virgin such as herself could tell that his actions and reactions when they kissed were proof enough of his desire. He would show her what to do; of that she had no doubt.

What she feared . . .

What she feared . . .

She caught her throat closing, choking, and she brought her fist to her mouth, biting on the knuckle to steady her stomach, as if that might actually do something to help the awful churning that had her in knots.

"My God," Anthony whispered as they reached the landing. "You're terrified."

"No," she lied.

He took her by the shoulders and twisted her to face him, staring deeply into her eyes. Cursing under his breath, he grabbed her hand and pulled her into his bedroom, muttering, "We need privacy."

When they reached his chamber—a richly appointed, masculine room exquisitely decorated in shades of burgundy and gold—he planted his hands on his hips and demanded, "Didn't your mother tell you about . . . ah . . . about . . ."

Kate would have laughed at his flailings if she hadn't been so nervous. "Of course," she said quickly. "Mary explained everything."

"Then what the hell is the problem?" He cursed again, then apologized. "I beg your pardon," he said stiffly. "That certainly is not the way to set you at ease."

"I can't say," she whispered, her eyes sliding to the floor, focusing on the intricate pattern of the carpet until they swam with tears.

A strange, horrible choking noise emerged from Anthony's throat. "Kate?" he asked hoarsely. "Did someone . . . has a man . . . ever forced unwelcome attentions on you?"

She looked up, and the concern and terror on his face nearly made her heart melt. "No!" she cried out. "It isn't that. Oh, don't look that way, I can't bear it."

"*I* can't bear it," Anthony whispered, closing the distance between them as he took her hand and raised it to his lips. "You must tell me," he said, his voice oddly choked. "Do you fear me? Do I repulse you?"

Kate shook her head frantically, unable to believe that he could possibly think any woman would find him repulsive.

"Tell me," he whispered, his lips pressing against her ear. "Tell me how to make it right. For I don't think I can grant you your reprieve." He molded his body against hers, his strong arms holding her close as he groaned, "I can't wait a week, Kate. I simply cannot do it."

"I . . ." Kate made the mistake of looking up into his eyes, and she forgot everything she'd meant to say. He was staring at her with a burning intensity that forged a fire in the very center of her being, leaving her breathless, hungry, and desperate for something she did not quite understand.

And she knew that she could not make him wait. If she looked into her own soul, and looked with honesty and without delusion, she was forced to admit that she did not wish to wait, either.

For what could be the point? Maybe he would never love her. Maybe his desire would never be focused as single-mindedly on her as hers was for him.

But she could pretend. And when he held her in his arms and pressed his lips to her skin, it was so, so easy to pretend.

"Anthony," she whispered, his name a benediction, a plea, a prayer all in one.

"Anything," he replied raggedly, dropping to his knees before her, his lips trailing a hot path along her skin as his fingers frantically worked to release her from her gown. "Ask me anything," he groaned. "Anything in my power, I give to you."

Kate felt her head fall back, felt the last of her resistance melting away. "Just love me," she whispered. "Just love me."

His only answer was a low growl of need.

# Chapter 17

*The deed is done! Miss Sheffield is now Katharine, Viscountess Bridgerton.*

*This Author extends the very best of wishes to the happy couple. Sensible and honorable people are surely scarce among the ton, and it's certainly gratifying to see two of this rare breed joined in marriage.*

LADY WHISTLEDOWN'S SOCIETY PAPERS,
16 MAY 1814

Until that moment, Anthony had not even realized just how badly he'd needed for her to say yes, to admit to her need. He clutched her to him, his cheek pressing against the gentle curve of her belly. Even in her wedding gown she smelled of lilies and soap, that maddening scent that had haunted him for weeks.

"I need you," he growled, not sure if his words were getting lost in the layers of silk that still kept her from him. "I need you now."

He rose to his feet and lifted her in his arms, taking remarkably few steps to reach the large four-poster bed that dominated his bedroom. He'd never taken a woman there before, always preferring to conduct his liaisons elsewhere, and suddenly he was absurdly glad of that fact.

Kate was different, special, his wife. He wanted no other memories to intrude upon this or any night.

He laid her down on the mattress, his eyes never leaving her charmingly disheveled form as he methodically stripped off his clothing. First his gloves, one by one, then his coat, already rumpled by his ardor.

He caught her eyes, dark and large and filled with wonder, and he smiled, slowly and with satisfaction. "You've never seen a naked man before, have you?" he murmured.

She shook her head.

"Good." He leaned forward and plucked one of her slippers from her foot. "You'll never see another."

He moved to the buttons of his shirt, slowly slipping each from its buttonhole, his desire increased tenfold when he saw her tongue dart out to wet her lips.

She wanted him. He knew enough of women to be positive of that. And by the time this night was through, she wouldn't be able to live without him.

That *he* might not be able to live without *her* was something he refused to consider. What smoldered in the bedroom and what whispered in his heart were two different things. He could keep them separate. He *would* keep them separate.

He might not wish to love his wife, but that did not mean they could not enjoy each other thoroughly in bed.

His hands slid to the top button of his trousers and unfastened it, but stopped there. She was still fully clothed, and still fully an innocent. She wasn't yet ready to see the proof of his desire.

He climbed onto the bed and, like a feral cat, crawled toward her, inching closer and closer until her elbows, which had been propping her up, slid out from under her and she was flat on her back, staring up at him, her breath coming fast and shallow through her parted lips.

There was nothing, he decided, more breathtaking than Kate's face when flushed with desire. Her hair, dark and silky and thick, was already pulling free of the pins and fasteners that had held her elaborate wedding day coiffure in place. Her lips, always a bit too full for conventional beauty, had taken on a dusky pink color in the slanted light of the late afternoon. And her skin—never had it seemed so flawless, so luminescent. A pale blush tinted her cheeks, denying her the bloodless complexion that the fashionable ladies always seemed to desire, but Anthony found the color enchanting. She was real, human, and trembling with desire. He couldn't have wished for more.

With a reverent hand, he stroked her cheek with the backs of his fingers, then slid them down her neck to the tender skin that peeked above the edge of her bodice. Her gown was fastened by a maddening row of buttons at the back, but he'd already undone nearly a third of them, and it was now loose enough to slide the silken fabric over her breasts.

If anything, they looked even more beautiful than they had two days earlier. Her nipples were rosy pink, cresting breasts that he knew fit his hands to perfection. "No chemise?" he murmured appreciatively, running his finger along the prominent line of her collarbone.

She shook her head, her voice breathy as she answered, "The cut of the gown didn't allow it."

One side of his mouth lifted into a very male smile. "Remind me to send a bonus to your modiste."

His hand moved ever lower, and he cupped one of her breasts, squeezing it softly, feeling a groan of desire rise up within him as he heard a similar moan escape her lips.

"So lovely," he murmured, lifting his hand and letting his eyes caress her. It had never occurred to him that there could be such pleasure from the simple act of gazing at a woman. Lovemaking had always been about touch and taste; for the first time sight was equally seductive.

She was so perfect, so utterly beautiful to him, and he felt a rather strange and primitive sense of satisfaction that most men were blind to her beauty. It was as if a certain side of her were visible only to him. He loved that her charms were hidden to the rest of the world.

It made her seem more *his*.

Suddenly eager to be touched as he was touching, he lifted one of her hands, still wrapped in a long satin glove, and brought it to his chest. He could feel the heat of her skin even through the fabric, but it wasn't enough. "I want to feel you," he whispered, then removed the two rings that rested on her fourth finger. He laid them in the hollow between her breasts, a space made shallow by her supine position.

Kate gasped and shivered at the touch of the cold metal against her skin, then watched with breathless fascination as Anthony went to work on her glove, tugging gently at each finger until it was loose, then sliding the length of it down her arm and over her hand. The rush of satin was like an endless kiss, raising goose bumps over her entire body.

Then, with a tenderness that nearly brought tears to her eyes, he replaced the rings on her finger, one by one, stopping only to kiss the sensitive palm of her hand in between.

"Give me your other hand," he gently ordered.

She did, and he repeated the same exquisite torture, tugging and sliding the satin along her skin. But this time, when he was through, he brought her pinkie finger to his mouth, then drew it between his lips and sucked, swirling his tongue around the tip.

Kate felt an answering tug of desire pulling through her arm, shivering through her chest, snaking through her until it pooled, hot and mysterious, between her legs. He was awakening something within her, something dark and maybe just a little bit dangerous, something that had lain dormant for years, just waiting for a single kiss from this man.

Her entire life had been preparation for this very moment, and she didn't even know what to expect next.

His tongue slid down the inner length of her finger, then traced the lines on her palm. "Such lovely hands," he murmured, nibbling on the fleshy part of her thumb as his fingers entwined with hers. "Strong, and yet so graceful and delicate."

"You're talking nonsense," Kate said self-consciously. "My hands—"

But he silenced her with a finger to her lips. "Shhh," he admonished. "Haven't you learned that you should never ever contradict your husband when he is admiring your form?"

Kate shivered with delight.

"For example," he continued, the very devil in his voice, "if I want to spend an hour examining the inside of your wrist"—with lightning-quick movements, his teeth grazed the delicate thin skin on the inside of her wrist—"it is certainly my prerogative, don't you think?"

Kate had no response, and he chuckled, the sound low and warm in her ears.

"And don't think I won't," he warned, using the pad of his finger to trace the blue veins that pulsed under her skin. "I may decide to spend *two* hours examining your wrist."

Kate watched with fascination as his fingers, touching her so softly that she tingled from the contact, made their way to the inside of her elbow, then stopped to twirl circles on her skin.

"I can't imagine," he said softly, "that I could spend two hours examining your wrist and *not* find it lovely." His hand made the jump to her torso, and he used his palm to lightly graze the tip of her puckered breast. "I should be most aggrieved were you to disagree."

He leaned down and captured her lips in a brief, yet searing kiss. Lifting his head just an inch, he murmured, "It is a wife's place to agree with her husband in all things, hmmm?"

His words were so absurd that Kate finally managed to find her voice. "If," she said with an amused smile, "his opinions are agreeable, my lord."

One of his brows arched imperiously. "Are you arguing with me, my lady? And on my wedding night, no less."

"It's my wedding night, too," she pointed out.

He made a clucking noise and shook his head. "I may have to punish you," he said. "But how? By touching?" His hand skimmed over one breast, then the next. "Or not touching?"

He lifted his hands from her skin, but he leaned down, and through pursed lips, blew a soft stream of air over her nipple.

"Touching," Kate gasped, arching off the bed. "Definitely touching."

"You think?" He smiled, slowly like a cat. "I never thought I'd say this, but not touching has its appeal."

Kate stared up at him. He loomed over her on his hands and knees like some primitive hunter coming in for the final kill. He looked feral, triumphant, and powerfully possessive. His thick chestnut hair fell over his forehead, giving him an oddly boyish air, but his eyes burned and gleamed with a very adult desire.

He wanted her. It was thrilling. He might be a man, and thus able to find his satisfaction with any woman, but right now, in this moment, he wanted her. Kate was sure of it.

And it made her feel like the most beautiful woman alive.

Emboldened by the knowledge of his desire, she reached up and cupped one hand around the back of his head, drawing him down until his lips were just a whisper away from hers. "Kiss me," she ordered, surprised by the imperiousness of her voice. "Kiss me now."

He smiled in vague disbelief, but his words, in that last second before their lips met, were, "Anything you wish, Lady Bridgerton. Anything you wish."

And then it all seemed to happen at once. His lips were on hers, teasing and devouring, while his hands were lifting her up into a seated position. His fingers worked nimbly at the buttons of her gown, and she could feel the cool brush of the air on her skin as the fabric slipped down, inch by inch, exposing her rib cage, then her navel, and then . . .

And then his hands slid beneath her hips, and he was lifting her up, yanking the dress out from underneath her. Kate gasped at the intimacy of it. She was clad only in her unmentionables, stockings, and garters. She'd never felt so exposed in her life, and yet she thrilled in every moment, every sweep of his eyes over her body.

"Lift your leg," Anthony ordered softly.

She did, and with a slowness that was exquisite and agonizing at the same time, he rolled one of her silk stockings down to her toes. The other soon followed, and then her drawers came next, and before she knew it she was nude, completely bared before him.

His hand skimmed softly over her stomach, then he said, "I think I'm a little overdressed, don't you?"

Kate's eyes widened as he left the bed and stripped off the rest of his clothing. His body was perfection, his chest finely muscled, his arms and legs powerful, and his—

"Oh, my God," she gasped.

He grinned. "I'll take that as a compliment."

Kate swallowed convulsively. No wonder those animals on her neighbor's farm hadn't looked as if they were enjoying the act of procreation. At least not the female ones. Surely this wasn't going to work.

But she didn't want to seem naive and foolish, so she didn't say anything, just gulped and tried to smile.

Anthony caught the flash of terror in her eyes and smiled gently. "Trust me," he murmured, sliding onto the bed beside her. His hands settled on the curve of her hip as he nuzzled her neck. "Just trust me."

He felt her nod, and he propped himself up on one of his elbows, using his free hand to idly trace circles and swirls on her abdomen, moving lower and lower, until he brushed the edge of the dark thatch of hair nestling between her legs.

Her muscles quivered, and he heard a rush of indrawn breath pass over her lips. "Shhhh," he said soothingly, leaning down to distract her with a kiss. The last time he'd lain with a virgin he'd been one himself, and he was relying on instinct to guide him with Kate. He wanted this, her first time, to be perfect. Or if not perfect, then at least damn good.

While his lips and tongue explored her mouth, his hand dipped ever lower, until he reached the moist heat of her womanhood. She gasped again, but he was relentless, teasing and tickling, delighting in each of her squirms and moans.

"What are you doing?" she whispered against his lips.

He gave her a lopsided grin, as one of his fingers slid inside. "Making you feel really, really good?"

She moaned, which pleased him. If she'd managed intelligible speech he would have known he wasn't doing his job correctly.

He moved over her, nudging her legs farther apart with one of his thighs, and letting out a moan of his own as his manhood settled against her hip. Even there, she felt perfect, and he was nearly bursting at the thought of sinking within her.

He was trying to hold his control, trying to make sure that he remained slow and gentle, but his need was getting stronger and stronger, and his own breath was growing fast and ragged.

She was ready for him, or at least as ready as she was going to be. He knew that this first time would bring her pain, but he prayed it wouldn't last more than a moment.

He fitted himself against her opening, using his arms to brace his body a few inches above hers. He whispered her name, and her dark eyes, hazed by passion, focused on his.

"I'm going to make you mine now," he said, inching forward as he spoke. Her body tightened spasmodically around him; the feeling was so exquisite he had to grit his teeth against it. It would be so, so easy to lose himself in the moment, to plunge forward and seek only his own pleasure.

"Tell me if it hurts," he whispered hoarsely, allowing himself to move forward only by tiny increments. She was certainly aroused, but she was very small, and he knew he needed to give her time to adjust to his intimate invasion.

She nodded.

He froze, barely able to comprehend the stab of pain in his chest. "It hurts?"

She shook her head. "No, I only meant I'll tell you if it does. It doesn't hurt, but it feels so very . . . odd."

Anthony fought a smile and he leaned down to kiss the tip of her nose. "I don't know that I've ever been called odd while making love to a woman before."

For a moment it looked as if she were afraid that she'd insulted him, then her mouth quivered into a small smile. "Perhaps," she said softly, "you've been making love to the wrong women."

"Perhaps so," he replied, moving forward yet another inch.

"May I tell you a secret?" she asked.

He nudged farther. "Of course," he murmured.

"When I first saw you . . . tonight, I mean . . ."

"In all my glory?" he teased, lifting his brows into an arrogant arch.

She shot him a rather enchanting scowl. "I didn't think this could possibly work."

He moved forward. He was close, so close to embedding himself fully within her. "May I tell *you* a secret?" he returned.

"Of course."

"Your secret"—one more little thrust and he was resting against her maidenhead—"wasn't very much of a secret."

Her brows drew together in question.

He grinned. "It was written all over your face."

She scowled again, and it made him want to explode in laughter. "But now," he said, keeping a scrupulously straight face, "I have a question for you."

She gazed at him in response, clearly waiting for him to elucidate further.

He leaned down, brushed his lips against her ear, and whispered, "What do you think now?"

For a moment she didn't respond in any way, then he felt her start in surprise when she finally figured out what he was asking. "Are we done?" she asked in clear disbelief.

This time he did burst out in laughter. "Far from it, my dear wife," he gasped, wiping his eyes with one hand as he tried to hold himself up with the other. "Far, far from it." His eyes growing serious, he added, "This is where it might hurt a little, Kate. But I promise you, the pain will never be repeated."

She nodded, but he could feel her body tense up, which he knew would only make it worse. "Shhh," he crooned. "Relax."

She nodded, her eyes shut. "I am relaxed."

He was glad she couldn't see him smile. "You are most definitely *not* relaxed."

Her eyes flew open. "Yes, I am."

"I can't believe this," Anthony said, as if there were someone else in the room to hear him. "She's arguing with me on our wedding night."

"I'm—"

He cut her off with a finger to her lips. "Are you ticklish?"

"Am I *ticklish*?"

He nodded. "Ticklish."

Her eyes narrowed suspiciously. "Why?"

"That sounds like a yes to me," he said with a grin.

"Not at— Oooohhh!" She let out a squeal as one of his hands found a particularly sensitive spot under her arm. "Anthony, stop!" she gasped, squirming desperately beneath him. "I can't bear it! I—"

He plunged forward.

"Oh," she breathed. "Oh, my."

He groaned, barely able to believe just how good it felt to be buried completely within her. "Oh, my, indeed."

"We're not done now, are we?"

He shook his head slowly as his body began to move in an ancient rhythm. "Not even close," he murmured.

His mouth took hers as one of his hands snaked up to caress her breast. She was utter perfection beneath him, her hips rising to meet his, moving tentatively at first, then with a vigor that matched her rising passion.

"Oh, God, Kate," he moaned, his ability to form flowery sentences completely lost in the primitive heat of the moment. "You're so good. So good."

Her breath was coming faster and faster, and each little wispy gasp inflamed his passion even more. He wanted to possess her, to own her, to hold her beneath him and never let her go. And with each thrust it was getting more difficult to put her needs before his. His mind screamed that this was her first time and he had to have a care for her, but his body demanded release.

With a ragged groan, he forced himself to stop thrusting and catch his breath. "Kate?" he said, barely recognizing his own voice. It sounded hoarse, detached, desperate.

Her eyes, which had been closed as her head tossed from side to side, flew open. "Don't stop," she gasped, "please don't stop. I'm so close to something . . . I don't know what."

"Oh, God," he groaned, plunging back in to the hilt, throwing his head back as his spine arched. "You're so beautiful, so unbelievably— Kate?"

She'd stiffened beneath him, and not in climax.

He froze. "What's wrong?" he whispered.

He saw a brief flash of pain—the emotional sort, not the physical—flash across her face before she hid it and whispered, "Nothing."

"That's not true," he said in a low voice. His arms were straining from holding himself above her, but he barely noticed. Every fiber of his being was focused on her face, which was shuttered and pained, despite her obvious attempts to hide it.

"You called me beautiful," she whispered.

For a good ten seconds he just stared at her. For the life of him, he couldn't understand how that was a bad thing. But then again, he'd never professed to understand the female mind. He thought he should simply reaffirm the statement, that she *was* beautiful, and what the hell was the problem, but a little voice inside warned him that this was one of *those* moments, and no matter what he said, it would be the wrong thing, so he decided to tread very, very carefully, and he just murmured her name, which he had a feeling might be the only word guaranteed not to get him into trouble.

"I'm not beautiful," she whispered, her eyes meeting his. She looked shattered and broken, but before he could contradict her, she asked, "Who were you picturing?"

He blinked. "I beg your pardon?"

"Who do you think of when you make love to me?"

Anthony felt as if he'd been punched in the gut. The breath whooshed from his body. "Kate," he said slowly. "Kate, you're mad, you're—"

"I know a man doesn't have to feel desire for a woman to find pleasure with her," she cried out.

"You think I don't desire you?" he choked out. God in heaven, he was ready to explode right now within her and he hadn't even moved for the last thirty seconds.

Her lower lip trembled between her teeth, and a muscle spasmed in her neck. "Do you—do you think of Edwina?"

Anthony froze. "How could I *possibly* confuse the two of you?"

Kate felt her face crumple, felt hot tears stinging at her eyes. She didn't want to cry in front of him, oh, God, especially not now, but it hurt, it hurt so much, and—

His hand grasped her cheeks with stunning speed, forcing her to look up at him.

"Listen to me," he said, his voice even and intense, "and listen well, because I'm only going to say this once. I desire you. I burn for you. I can't sleep at night for wanting you. Even when I didn't *like* you, I lusted for you. It's the most maddening, beguiling, damnable thing, but there it is. And if I hear one more word of nonsense from your lips, I'm going to have to tie you to the bloody bed and have my way with you a hundred different ways, until you finally get it through your silly skull that you are the most beautiful and desirable woman in England, and if everyone else doesn't see that, then they're all bloody fools."

Kate wouldn't have thought it possible for her mouth to fall open while she was lying down, but somehow it did.

One of his brows arched into what had to be the most arrogant expression ever to grace a face. "Is that understood?"

She just stared at him, not quite able to form a response.

He leaned down until his nose was a mere inch from hers. "Is that understood?"

She nodded.

"Good," he grunted, and then, before she had a moment even to catch her breath, his lips were devouring hers in a kiss so fierce she was clutching the bed just to keep from screaming. His hips ground into hers, frenzied in their power, thrusting, rotating, stroking her until she was certain she must be on fire.

She clutched at him, not certain whether she was trying to bind him to her or tear him away. "I can't do this," she moaned, certain she would shatter. Her muscles were stiff, tense, and it was getting hard to breathe.

But if he'd heard her, he didn't care. His face was a harsh mask of concentration, sweat beading on his brow.

"Anthony," she gasped, "I can—"

One of his hands slipped between them and touched her intimately, and she screamed. He slammed forward one last time, and her world simply fell apart. She was stiff, then shaking, then she thought she must be falling. She couldn't breathe, couldn't even gasp. Her throat had to be closing, and her head fell back as her hands grabbed at the mattress with a ferocity she'd never have believed she possessed.

He went utterly still above her, his mouth open in a silent scream, and then he collapsed, the weight of him pressing her farther into the mattress.

"Oh, my God," he gasped, his body now shaking. "Never . . . it's never . . . so good . . . it's never been so good."

Kate, who'd had a few seconds longer to recover, smiled as she smoothed his hair. A wicked thought came to her, a perfectly wonderful wicked thought. "Anthony?" she murmured.

How he lifted his head she would never know, because it looked like it took a Herculean effort just to open his eyes and grunt his response.

She smiled, slowly, and with a womanly seductiveness she'd learned just that evening. Letting one of her fingers trail down the angular edge of his jaw, she whispered, "Are we done yet?"

For a second he made no response, then his lips broke into a smile far more devilish than she could ever have imagined. "For now," he murmured huskily, rolling onto his side and pulling her along with him. "But only for now."

# Chapter 18

*Although gossip still surrounds the hasty marriage of Lord and Lady Bridgerton (formerly Miss Katharine Sheffield, for those of you who have been in hibernation for these past few weeks), This Author is of the firm opinion that theirs was a love match. Viscount Bridgerton does not escort his wife to every society function (but then again, what husband does?), but when he is present, This Author cannot fail to note that he always seems to be murmuring something in his lady's ear, and that something always seems to make her smile and blush.*

*Furthermore, he always dances with her one more time than is considered de rigueur. Considering how many husbands don't like to dance with their wives at all, this is romantic stuff, indeed.*

LADY WHISTLEDOWN'S SOCIETY PAPERS,
10 JUNE 1814

The next few weeks flew by in a delirious rush. After a brief stay in the country at Aubrey Hall, the newlyweds returned to London, where the season was in full swing. Kate had hoped to use her afternoons to resume her flute lessons, but she quickly discovered that she was in great demand, and her days were filled with social calls, shopping excursions with her family, and the occasional ride in the park. Her evenings were a whirlwind of balls and parties.

But her nights were for Anthony alone.

Marriage, she decided, agreed with her. She saw less of Anthony than she would have liked, but she understood and accepted that he was a very busy man. His many concerns, both in Parliament and on his estates, took up a great deal of his time. But when he returned home at night and met her in the bedroom (no separate bedchambers for Lord and Lady Bridgerton!) he was marvelously attentive, asking about her day, telling her of his, and making love to her until the wee hours of the night.

He'd even taken the time to listen to her practice her flute. She'd managed to hire a musician to come and tutor her two mornings a week. Considering the (not very expert) level of play which Kate had achieved, Anthony's willingness to sit through an entire thirty minutes of rehearsal could only be interpreted as a sign of great affection.

Of course, it did not escape her notice that he'd never repeated the gesture.

Hers was a fine existence, a far better marriage than most women of her station could expect. If her husband did not love her, if he would never love her, then at least he did a good job of making her feel cared for and appreciated. And for now Kate was able to content herself with that.

And if he seemed distant during the day, well, he certainly wasn't distant at night.

The rest of society, however, and Edwina in particular, had gotten it into their heads that Lord and Lady Bridgerton's marriage was a love match. Edwina had taken to visiting in the afternoons, and this day was no exception. She and Kate were sitting in the drawing room, sipping tea and nibbling on biscuits, enjoying a rare moment of privacy now that Kate had bidden farewell to her daily swarm of visitors.

Everyone, it seemed, wanted to see how the new viscountess was getting along, and Kate's drawing room was almost never empty in the afternoon.

Newton had hopped up onto the sofa beside Edwina, and she was idly stroking his fur as she said, "Everyone is talking about you today."

Kate didn't even pause as she lifted her tea to her lips and took a sip. "Everyone is always talking about me," she said with a shrug. "They'll soon find another topic."

"Not," Edwina replied, "as long as your husband keeps looking at you the way he did last night."

Kate felt her cheeks grow warm. "He did nothing out of the ordinary," she murmured.

"Kate, he was positively smoldering!" Edwina shifted her position as Newton shifted his, letting her know with a little whine that he wanted his belly rubbed. "I personally saw him push Lord Haveridge out of the way in his haste to reach your side."

"We arrived separately," Kate explained, although her heart was filling with a secret—and most probably foolish—joy. "I'm sure he just had something he needed to tell me."

Edwina looked dubious. "And did he?"

"Did he what?"

"*Tell* you something," Edwina said with palpable exasperation. "You just said you were sure he just had something he needed to tell you. If that were the case, wouldn't he have told you whatever it was? And then you'd *know* he had something to tell you, right?"

Kate blinked. "Edwina, you're making me dizzy."

Edwina's lips smooshed together in a disgruntled frown. "You never tell me anything."

"Edwina, there's nothing to tell!" Kate reached forward, grabbed a biscuit, and took a large, extremely uncouth bite so that her mouth would be too full to speak. What was she supposed to say to her sister—that before they'd even wed, her husband had informed her in a most matter-of-fact and straightforward manner that he would never love her?

That would make for charming conversation over tea and biscuits.

"Well," Edwina finally announced, after watching Kate chew for an improbable full minute, "I actually had another reason for coming here today. I have something I wish to tell you."

Kate swallowed gratefully. "Really?"

Edwina nodded, then blushed.

"What is it?" Kate implored, sipping at her tea. Her mouth was awfully dry after all that chewing.

"I think I'm in love."

Kate nearly spit out her tea. "With whom?"

"Mr. Bagwell."

Try as she might, Kate could not for the life of her recall who Mr. Bagwell was.

"He's a scholar," Edwina said with a dreamy sigh. "I met him at Lady Bridgerton's country house party."

"I don't recall meeting him," Kate said, her brow knitting into thoughtful lines.

"You were rather busy throughout the visit," Edwina replied in an ironic voice. "Getting yourself betrothed and all that."

Kate pulled the sort of face one could only display with a sibling. "Just tell me about Mr. Bagwell."

Edwina's eyes grew warm and bright. "He's a second son, I'm

afraid, so he cannot expect much in the way of income. But now that you've married so well, I needn't worry about that."

Kate felt an unexpected welling of tears in her eyes. She hadn't realized just how pressured Edwina must have felt earlier that season. She and Mary had been careful to assure Edwina that she might marry anyone she liked, but they had all known exactly where their finances stood, and they had certainly all been guilty of making jokes about how it was just as easy to fall in love with a wealthy man as it was with a poor one.

It only took one look at Edwina's face to realize that a huge burden had been lifted from her shoulders.

"I'm glad you've found someone who suits you," Kate murmured.

"Oh, he does. I know that we shall not have much in the way of money, but truly, I don't need silks and jewels." Her eyes fell on the glittering diamond on Kate's hand. "Not that I think you do, of course!" she quickly interjected, her face growing red. "Just that—"

"Just that it's nice not to have to worry about supporting your sister and mother," Kate finished for her in a gentle voice.

Edwina let out a huge sigh. "Exactly."

Kate reached across the table and took her sister's hands in hers. "You certainly needn't worry about me, and I'm sure that Anthony and I will always be able to provide for Mary, should she ever need assistance."

Edwina's lips curved into a wobbly smile.

"As for you," Kate added, "I think it's high time you were able to think only of yourself for a change. To make a decision based on what *you* desire, not what you think others need."

Edwina pulled one of her hands free to brush back a tear. "I really like him," she whispered.

"Then I am certain I will like him as well," Kate said firmly. "When may I meet him?"

"He is in Oxford for the next fortnight, I'm afraid. He has prior commitments which I should not want him to break on my account."

"Of course not," Kate murmured. "You wouldn't want to marry the sort of gentleman who does not honor his commitments."

Edwina nodded in agreement. "I received a letter from him this morning, though, and he says he will come down to London at the end of the month and hopes that he might call on me."

Kate smiled wickedly. "He's already sending you letters?"

Edwina nodded and blushed. "Several per week," she admitted.

"And what is his area of study?"

"Archaeology. He's quite brilliant. He has been to Greece. Twice!"

Kate hadn't thought that her sister—already renowned throughout the land for her beauty—could possibly grow any lovelier, but when Edwina spoke of her Mr. Bagwell, her face shone with a radiance that was nothing short of heart-stopping.

"I cannot wait to meet him," Kate announced. "We must have an informal dinner party with him as our guest of honor."

"That would be wonderful."

"And perhaps the three of us might go for a ride in the park ahead of time so that we might become better acquainted. Now that I am an old married lady, I qualify as a suitable chaperone." Kate let out a little laugh. "Isn't that funny?"

A very amused, very male voice sounded from the doorway: "Isn't what funny?"

"Anthony!" Kate exclaimed, surprised to see her husband in the middle of the day. He always seemed to have appointments and meetings that kept him from their home. "How delightful to see you."

He smiled slightly as he nodded toward Edwina in greeting. "I found myself with an unexpected block of free time."

"Would you care to join us for tea?"

"I'll join you," he murmured as he crossed the room and picked up a crystal decanter that sat on a mahogany side table, "but I believe I'll have a brandy instead."

Kate watched as he poured himself a drink, then swirled it absently in his hand. It was at times like these that she found it so difficult to keep her heart out of her eyes. He was so handsome in the late afternoon. She wasn't sure why; maybe it was the faint hint of stubble on his cheeks or the fact that his hair was always slightly mussed from whatever it was he did all day. Or maybe it was simply that she didn't often get to see him this time of day; she'd once read a poem that said the unexpected moment was always sweeter.

As Kate gazed upon her husband, she rather thought that poet might be right.

"So," Anthony said after taking a sip of his drink, "what have you two ladies been discussing?"

Kate looked to her sister for permission to share her news, and when Edwina nodded, she said, "Edwina has met a gentleman she fancies."

"Really?" Anthony asked, sounding interested in a strangely paternal sort of manner. He perched on the arm of Kate's chair, a relaxed, overstuffed piece of furniture that was not at all in fashion but well loved nonetheless in the Bridgerton household for its uncommon comfort. "I should like to meet him," he added.

"You should?" Edwina echoed, blinking like an owl. "You would?"

"Of course. In fact, I insist upon it." When neither lady commented, he scowled a bit and added, "I am the head of the family, after all. That's what we do."

Edwina's lips parted with surprise. "I—I hadn't realized you felt a responsibility toward me."

Anthony looked at her as if she'd gone momentarily insane. "You're Kate's sister," he said, as if that should explain everything.

Edwina's blank expression remained fixed on her face for another second, and then it melted into a rather radiant delight. "I have always wondered what it would be like to have a brother," she said.

"I hope I pass muster," Anthony grunted, not entirely comfortable with the sudden outpouring of emotion.

She beamed at him. "Brilliantly. I vow I do not understand why Eloise complains so much."

Kate turned to Anthony and explained, "Edwina and your sister have become fast friends since our marriage."

"God help us," he muttered. "And what, may I ask, could Eloise possibly have to complain about?"

Edwina smiled innocently. "Oh, nothing, really. Just that you can, at times, be a touch overprotective."

"That's ridiculous," he scoffed.

Kate choked on her tea. She was quite certain that by the time their daughters were of marriageable age, Anthony would have converted to Catholicism just so that he could lock them in a convent with twelve-foot walls!

Anthony glanced at her with narrowed eyes. "What are you laughing about?"

Kate quickly patted her mouth with a napkin, mumbling, "Nothing," under the folds of the cloth.

"Hmmmph."

"Eloise says that you were quite the bear when Daphne was being courted by Simon," Edwina said.

"Oh, did she?"

Edwina nodded. "She says the two of you dueled!"

"Eloise talks too much," Anthony grumbled.

Edwina nodded happily. "She always knows everything. Everything! Even more than Lady Whistledown."

Anthony turned to Kate with an expression that was one part beleaguered and one part pure irony. "Remind me to buy a muzzle for my sister," he said drolly. "And one for your sister as well."

Edwina let out a musical laugh. "I never dreamed a brother would be as much fun to tease as a sister. I'm so glad you decided to marry him, Kate."

"I didn't have much choice in the matter," Kate said with a dry smile, "but I'm rather pleased with the way things turned out myself."

Edwina stood, waking up Newton, who had fallen into blissful sleep next to her on the sofa. He let out an affronted whine and toddled to the floor, where he promptly curled up under a table.

Edwina watched the dog and chuckled before saying, "I should be going. No, don't see me out," she added when both Kate and Anthony stood to escort her to the front door. "I can make my own way."

"Nonsense," Kate said, linking her arm in Edwina's. "Anthony, I shall be right back."

"I shall be counting the seconds," he murmured, and then, as he took another sip of his drink, the two ladies left the room, followed by Newton, who was now barking enthusiastically, presumably guessing that someone was going to take him for a walk.

Once the two sisters were gone, he settled into the comfortable chair so recently vacated by Kate. It was still warm from her body, and he rather fancied that he could smell her scent in the fabric. More soap than lilies this time, he thought with a careful sniff. Perhaps the lilies were a perfume, something she added at night.

He wasn't entirely sure why he'd returned home this afternoon;

he certainly hadn't intended to. Contrary to what he'd been telling Kate, his many meetings and responsibilities did not require him to be away from the house all the day long; quite a few of his appointments could easily have been scheduled at home. And while he was indeed a busy man—he'd never subscribed to the indolent lifestyle of so many of the *ton*—he'd spent many a recent afternoon at White's, reading the paper and playing cards with his friends.

He'd thought it best. It was important to keep a certain distance from one's wife. Life—or at least *his* life—was meant to be compartmentalized, and a wife fit rather neatly in the sections he'd mentally labeled "society affairs" and "bed."

But when he'd reached White's that afternoon, there was no one there with whom he felt a particular urge to converse. He'd skimmed through the paper, but there was very little of interest in the most recent edition. And as he sat by the window, trying to enjoy his own company (but finding it pathetically lacking), he'd been struck by the most ridiculous urge to return home and see what Kate was up to.

One afternoon couldn't hurt. He wasn't likely to fall in love with his wife for having spent one afternoon in her presence. Not that he thought there was a danger of his falling in love with her at all, he reminded himself sternly. He'd been married nearly a month now and he'd managed to keep his life blessedly free of such entanglements. There was no reason to think that he could not maintain the status quo indefinitely.

Feeling rather satisfied with himself, he took another sip of his brandy, looking up when he heard Kate reenter the room.

"I do think Edwina might be in love," she said, her entire face lit up with a radiant smile.

Anthony felt his body tighten in response. It was rather ridiculous, actually, how he reacted to her smiles. Happened all the time, and it was a damned nuisance.

Well, most of the time it was a nuisance. He didn't mind it much when he was able to follow it with a nudge and a trip to the bedroom.

But Kate's mind was obviously not lodged as firmly in the gutter as his, since she chose to sit in the chair opposite him, even though there was plenty of room in his chair, provided they didn't mind squeezing next to each other. Even the chair kitty-corner to his would have been better; at least then he could have yanked her up and hauled her onto his lap. If he tried that maneuver where she was seated across the table, he'd have to drag her through the middle of the tea service.

Anthony narrowed his eyes as he assessed the situation, trying to guess exactly how much tea would spill on the rug, and then how much it would cost to replace the rug, and then whether he really cared about such a piddling amount of money, anyway . . .

"Anthony? Are you listening to me?"

He looked up. Kate was resting her arms on her knees as she leaned forward to talk with him. She looked very intent and just a little bit irritated.

"Were you?" she persisted.

He blinked.

"Listening to me?" she ground out.

"Oh." He grinned. "No."

She rolled her eyes but didn't bother to scold him any further than that. "I was saying that we should have Edwina and her young man over for dinner one night. To see if we think they suit. I have never before seen her so interested in a gentleman, and I do so want her to be happy."

Anthony reached for a biscuit. He was hungry, and he'd pretty much given up on the prospect of getting his wife into his lap. On the other hand, if he managed to clear off the cups and saucers, yanking her across the table might not have such messy consequences . . .

He surreptitiously pushed the tray bearing the tea service to the side. "Hmmm?" he grunted, chewing on the biscuit. "Oh, yes, of course. Edwina should be happy."

Kate eyed him suspiciously. "Are you certain you don't want some tea with that biscuit? I'm not a great aficionado of brandy, but I would imagine that tea would taste better with shortbread."

Actually, Anthony thought, the brandy did quite well with shortbread, but it certainly couldn't hurt to empty out the teapot a bit, just in case he toppled it over. "Capital idea," he said, grabbing a teacup and thrusting it toward her. "Tea's just the thing. Can't imagine why I didn't think of it earlier."

"I can't imagine, either," she murmured acerbically—if one could murmur in an acerbic manner, and after hearing Kate's low sarcasm, Anthony rather thought one could.

But he just gave her a jovial smile as he reached out and took his teacup from her outstretched hand. "Thank you," he said, checking to see that she'd added milk. She had, which didn't surprise him; she was very good at remembering such details.

"Is it still hot enough?" Kate asked politely.

Anthony drained the cup. "Perfect," he replied, letting out a satisfied exhale. "Might I trouble you for some more?"

"You seem to be developing quite a taste for tea," she said dryly.

Anthony eyed the teapot, wondering how much was left and whether he'd be able to finish it off without being attacked by an urgent need to relieve himself. "You should have some more, too," he suggested. "You look a bit parched."

Her eyebrows shot up. "Is that so?"

He nodded, then worried he might have laid it on a little too thick. "Just a bit, of course," he said.

"Of course."

"Is there enough tea left for me to have another cup?" he asked, as nonchalantly as he could manage.

"If there isn't, I'm sure I could have Cook brew another pot."

"Oh, no, I'm sure that won't be necessary," he exclaimed, probably a little too loudly. "I'll just take whatever is left."

Kate tipped the pot until the last dregs of tea swirled in his cup. She added a dollop of milk, then handed it back to him in silence, although her arched eyebrows spoke volumes.

As he sipped at his tea—his belly was a little too full to gulp it down as quickly as the last cup—Kate cleared her throat and asked, "Do you know Edwina's young man?"

"I don't even know who he *is*."

"Oh. I'm sorry. I must have forgotten to mention his name. It's Mr. Bagwell. I don't know his Christian name, but Edwina said he's a second son, if that's helpful. She met him at your mother's party."

Anthony shook his head. "Never heard of him. He's probably one of the poor chaps my mother invited to even out the numbers. My mother invited a bloody lot of women. She always does, hoping that one of us might actually fall in love, but then she has to find a pack of unremarkable men to even up the numbers."

"Unremarkable?" Kate echoed.

"So that the women don't fall in love with them instead of us," he replied, his grin rather lopsided.

"She's rather desperate to marry the lot of you off, isn't she?"

"All I know," Anthony said with a shrug, "is that my mother invited so many eligible women last time that she had to go down to the vicar's and beg his sixteen-year-old son to come up for supper."

Kate winced. "I think I met him."

"Yes, he's painfully shy, poor fellow. The vicar told me he had hives for a week after ending up seated next to Cressida Cowper at supper."

"Well, that would give anyone hives."

Anthony grinned. "I knew you had a mean streak in you."

"I'm not being mean!" Kate protested. But her smile was sly. "It was nothing more than the truth."

"Don't defend yourself on my account." He finished the tea; it was bitterly strong from having sat in the pot for so long, but the milk made it almost palatable. Setting the cup down, he added, "Your mean streak is one of the things I like best about you."

"Goodness," she muttered, "I should hate to know what you like least."

Anthony just waved a dismissive hand in the air. "But getting back to your sister and her Mr. Bugwell—"

"Bagwell."

"Pity."

"Anthony!"

He ignored her. "I've actually been thinking I ought to provide Edwina with a dowry."

The irony of the gesture was not lost on him. Back when he'd intended to wed Edwina, he'd planned to provide a dowry for *Kate*.

He peeked over at Kate to see her reaction.

He hadn't, of course, made the offer just to gain her good favor, but he wasn't so noble that he couldn't admit to himself that he'd been hoping for a little more than the stunned silence she was displaying.

Then he realized she was near tears.

"Kate?" he asked, not certain whether to be delighted or worried.

She wiped her nose rather inelegantly with the back of her

hand. "That's the nicest thing anyone has ever done for me," she sniffled.

"I actually did it for Edwina," he mumbled, never comfortable with weepy females. But inside, she was making him feel about eight feet tall.

"Oh, Anthony!" she practically wailed. And then, much to his extreme surprise, she jumped to her feet and leaped across the table and into his arms, the heavy hem of her afternoon dress sweeping three teacups, two saucers, and a spoon onto the floor.

"You are so sweet," she said, wiping at her eyes as she landed rather solidly in his lap. "The nicest man in London."

"Well, I don't know about that," he returned, sliding his arm around her waist. "The most dangerous, perhaps, or handsome—"

"Nicest," she interrupted firmly, tucking her head into the crook of his neck. "Definitely the nicest."

"If you insist," he murmured, not at all unhappy with the recent turn of events.

"It's a good thing we finished that tea," Kate said, eyeing the cups on the floor. "It would have made a dreadful mess."

"Oh, indeed." He smiled to himself as he pulled her closer. There was something warm and comfortable about holding Kate. Her legs were dangling over the arm of the chair and her back was resting against the curve of his arm. They fit together nicely, he realized. She was just the right size for a man of his proportions.

There were a lot of things about her that were just right. It was the sort of realization that usually terrified him, but at that moment he was so damned *happy* just sitting here with her in his lap that he simply refused to think about the future.

"You are so good to me," she murmured.

Anthony thought of all the times he'd purposely stayed away, all the times he'd left her to her own devices, but he pushed away the guilt. If he was forcing a distance between them, it was for her own good. He didn't want her to fall in love with him. It would make it that much harder for her when he died.

And if he fell in love with her . . .

He didn't even want to think about how much harder it would be for him.

"Do we have any plans for this evening?" he whispered in her ear.

She nodded; the motion caused her hair to tickle his cheek. "A ball," she said. "At Lady Mottram's."

Anthony couldn't resist the soft silkiness of her hair, and he threaded two fingers through it, letting it slide across his hand and wrap around his wrist. "Do you know what I think?" he murmured.

He heard her smile as she asked, "What?"

"I think I've never cared that much for Lady Mottram. And do you know what else I think?"

Now he heard her trying not to giggle. "What?"

"I think we should go upstairs."

"You do?" she asked, clearly feigning ignorance.

"Oh, indded. This very minute, as a matter of fact."

She wiggled her bottom, the minx, ascertaining for herself just how quickly he needed to go upstairs. "I see," she murmured gravely.

He pinched her hip lightly. "I rather thought you *felt*."

"Well, that, too," she admitted. "It was quite enlightening."

"I'm sure it was," he muttered. Then, with a very wicked smile, he nudged her chin until they were nose to nose. "Do you know what *else* I think?" he said huskily.

Her eyes widened. "I'm sure I can't imagine."

"I think," he said, one of his hands creeping under her dress and slithering up her leg, "that if we don't go upstairs this instant, I might be content to remain right here."

"Here?" she squeaked.

His hand found the edge of her stockings. "Here," he affirmed.

"Now?"

His fingers tickled her soft thatch of hair, then sank into the very core of her womanhood. She was soft and wet and felt like heaven. "Oh, most definitely now," he said.

"Here?"

He nibbled on her lips. "Didn't I already answer that question?"

And if she had any further questions, she didn't voice them for the next hour.

Or maybe it was just that he was trying his damnedest to rob her of speech.

And if a man could judge from the little squeals and mewls that slipped from her mouth, he was doing a ripping good job.

# Chapter 19

*Lady Mottram's annual ball was a crush, as always, but society watchers could not fail to note that Lord and Lady Bridgerton did not make an appearance. Lady Mottram insists that they had promised to attend, and This Author can only speculate as to what kept the newlyweds at home . . .*

LADY WHISTLEDOWN'S SOCIETY PAPERS,
13 JUNE 1814

Much later that night, Anthony was lying on his side in bed, cradling his wife, who had snuggled her back up to his front and was presently sleeping soundly.

Which was fortunate, he realized, because it had started to rain.

He tried to nudge the covers up over her exposed ear so that she would not hear the drops beating against the windows, but she was as fidgety in sleep as she was when awake, and he could not manage to pull the coverlet much above the level of her neck before she shook it off.

He couldn't yet tell whether the storm would grow electrical in nature, but the force of the rain had increased, and the wind had picked up until it howled through the night, rattling the tree branches against the side of the house.

Kate was growing a little more restless at his side, and he made shhhh-ing sounds as he smoothed her hair with his hand. The storm hadn't woken her up, but it had definitely intruded upon her slumber. She had begun to mumble in her sleep, tossing and turning until she was curled on her opposite side, facing him.

"What happened to make you hate the rain so?" he whispered, tucking one dark lock of hair behind her ear. But he did not judge her for her terrors; he knew well the frustration of unfounded fears and premonitions. His certainty of his own impending death, for example, had haunted him since the moment he'd picked up his father's limp hand and laid it gently on his unmoving chest.

It wasn't something he could explain, or even something he could understand. It was just something he *knew*.

He'd never feared death, though, not really. The knowledge of it had been a part of him for so long that he merely accepted it, just as other men accepted the other truths that made up the cycle of life. Spring followed winter, and summer after that. For him, death was much the same way.

Until now. He'd been trying to deny it, trying to shut the niggling notion from his mind, but death was beginning to show a frightening face.

His marriage to Kate had sent his life down an alternate path, no matter how much he tried to convince himself that he could restrict their marriage to nothing but friendship and sex.

He cared about her. He cared about her far too much. He craved her company when they were apart, and he dreamed about her at night, even as he held her in his arms.

He wasn't ready to call it love, but it terrified him all the same.

And whatever it was that burned between them, he didn't want it to end.

Which was, of course, the cruelest irony of all.

Anthony closed his eyes as he let out a weary and nervous exhale, wondering what the hell he was going to do about the complication that lay beside him in the bed. But even while his eyes were shut, he saw the flash of lightning that lit up the night, turning the black of the inside of his eyelids into a bloody red-orange.

Opening his eyes, he saw that they'd left the drapes partway open when they'd retired to bed earlier in the evening. He'd have to shut those; they'd help to keep the lightning from illuminating the room.

But when he shifted his weight and tried to nudge his way out from under the covers, Kate grabbed his arm, her fingers pressing frantically into his muscles.

"Shhhh, now, it's all right," he whispered, "I'm only going to close the drapes."

But she did not let go, and the whimper that escaped her lips when a clap of thunder shook the night nearly broke his heart.

A pale sliver of moonlight filtered through the window, just enough to illuminate the tense, drawn lines of her face. Anthony peered down to assure himself that she was still sleeping, then pried her hands from his arm and got up to close the drapes. He suspected that the flashes of lightning would still sneak into the room, though, so when he was done with the drapes, he lit a lone candle and set it on his nightstand. It didn't give off enough light to wake her up—at least he hoped it wouldn't—but at the same time it saved the room from utter blackness.

And there was nothing quite so startling as a streak of lightning cutting through utter blackness.

He crawled back into bed and regarded Kate. She was still sleeping, but not peacefully. She'd curled into a semi-fetal position and her breathing was labored. The lightning didn't seem to bother her much, but every time the room shook with thunder she flinched.

He took her hand and smoothed her hair, and for several minutes he simply lay with her, trying to soothe her as she slept. But the storm was increasing in intensity, with the thunder and lightning practically coming on top of each other. Kate was growing more restless by the second, and then, as a particularly loud clap of thunder exploded in the air, her eyes flew open, her face a mask of utter panic.

"Kate?" Anthony whispered.

She sat up, scrambling back until her spine was pressed against the solid headboard of the bed. She looked like a statue of terror, her body stiff and frozen into place. Her eyes were still open, barely blinking, and though she did not move her head, they flicked frantically back and forth, scanning the entire room, but not seeing anything.

"Oh, Kate," he whispered. This was far, far worse than what she'd been through that night in the library at Aubrey Hall. And he could feel the force of her pain slicing right through his heart.

No one should feel terror like this. And especially not his wife.

Moving slowly, so as not to startle her, he made his way to her side, then carefully laid an arm over her shoulders. She was shaking, but she did not push him away.

"Are you even going to remember any of this in the morning?" he whispered.

She made no response, but then, he hadn't expected her to.

"There, there," he said gently, trying to remember the soothing nonsense words his mother used whenever one of her children was upset. "It's all right now. You'll be fine."

Her tremors seemed to slow a bit, but she was still very clearly disturbed, and when the next clap of thunder shook the room, her entire body flinched, and she buried her face in the crook of her neck.

"No," she moaned, "no, no."

"Kate?" Anthony blinked several times, then gazed at her intently. She sounded different, not awake but more lucid, if that was possible.

"No, no."

And she sounded very . . .

"No, no, don't go."

. . . *young.*

"Kate?" He held her tightly, unsure of what to do. Should he wake her? Her eyes might be open, but she was clearly asleep and dreaming. Part of him longed to break her of her nightmare, but once she woke, she'd still be in the same place—in bed in the middle of a horrible electrical storm. Would she even feel any better?

Or should he let her sleep? Perhaps if she rode out the nightmare he might actually gain some idea as to what had caused her terror.

"Kate?" he whispered, as if she herself might actually give him a clue as to how to proceed.

"No," she moaned, growing more agitated by the second. "Nooooo."

Anthony pressed his lips to her temple, trying to soothe her with his presence.

"No, please. . . ." She started to sob, her body racked with huge gasps of air as her tears drenched his shoulder. "No, oh, no . . . *Mama*!"

Anthony stiffened. He knew that Kate always referred to her stepmother as Mary. Could she actually be speaking of her true mother, the woman who had given her life and then died so many years ago?

But as he pondered that question, Kate's entire body stiffened and she let out a shrill, high-pitched scream.

The scream of a very young girl.

In an instant, she turned about, and then she leaped into his arms, grabbing at him, clutching his shoulders with a terrifying desperation. "No, Mama," she wailed, her entire body heaving from the exertion of her cries. "No, you can't go! Oh, Mama Mama Mama Mama Mama Mama . . ."

If Anthony hadn't had his back to the headboard, she would have knocked him over, the force of her fervor was that strong.

"Kate?" he blurted out, surprised by the slight note of panic in his voice. "Kate? It's all right. You're all right. You're fine. Nobody is going anywhere. Do you hear me? No one."

But her words had melted away, and all that was left was the low sound of a weeping that came from deep in her soul. Anthony held her, and then when she'd calmed a bit, he eased her down until she was lying on her side again, and then he held her some more, until she drifted back into sleep.

Which, he noticed ironically, was right about the time the last of the thunder and lightning split the room.

When Kate woke the following morning, she was surprised to see her husband sitting up in bed, staring down at her with the oddest look . . . a combination of concern, and curiosity, and maybe even the barest hint of pity. He didn't say anything when her eyes opened, even though she could see that he was watching her face intently. She waited, to see what he would do, and then finally she just said, somewhat hesitantly, "You look tired."

"I didn't sleep well," he admitted.

"You didn't?"

He shook his head. "It rained."

"It did?"

He nodded. "And thundered."

She swallowed nervously. "And lightninged as well, I suppose."

"It did," he said, nodding again. "It was quite a storm."

There was something very profound in the way he was speaking in short, concise sentences, something that raised the hair on the back of her neck. "H-how fortunate that I missed it, then," she said. "You know I don't do well with strong storms."

"I know," he said simply.

But there was a wealth of meaning behind those two short words, and Kate felt her heartbeat speed up slightly. "Anthony," she asked, not certain she wanted to know the answer, "what happened last night?"

"You had a nightmare."

She closed her eyes for a second. "I didn't think I had those any longer."

"I didn't realize you'd ever suffered from nightmares."

Kate let out a long exhale and sat up, pulling the covers along with her and tucking them under her arms. "When I was small. Whenever it stormed, I'm told. I don't know for a fact; I never remembered anything. I thought I'd—" She had to stop for a moment; her throat felt like it was closing up, and her words seemed to choke her.

He reached out and took her hand. It was a simple gesture, but somehow it touched her heart far more than any words would have done. "Kate?" he asked quietly. "Are you all right?"

She nodded. "I thought I'd stopped, that's all."

He didn't say anything for a moment, and the room was so quiet that Kate was sure she could hear both of their heartbeats. Finally, she heard the slight rush of indrawn breath across Anthony's lips, and he asked, "Did you know that you speak in your sleep?"

She hadn't been facing him, but at that comment, her head jerked quite suddenly to the right, her eyes colliding with his. "I do?"

"You did last night."

Her fingers clutched the coverlet. "What did I say?"

He hesitated, but when his words emerged, they were steady and even. "You called out to your mother."

"Mary?" she whispered.

He shook his head. "I don't think so. I've never heard you call Mary anything but Mary; last night you were crying for 'Mama.' You sounded . . ." He paused and took a slightly ragged breath. "You sounded quite young."

Kate licked her lips, then chewed on the bottom one. "I don't know what to tell you," she finally said, afraid to press into the deepest recesses of her memory. "I have no idea why I'd be calling out to my mother."

"I think," he said gently, "that you should ask Mary."

Kate gave her head a quick and immediate shake. "I didn't even know Mary when my mother died. Neither did my father. She couldn't know why I was calling out to her."

"Your father might have told her something," he said, lifting her hand to his lips and giving it a reassuring kiss.

Kate let her eyes drop to her lap. She wanted to understand why she was so afraid of the storms, but prying into one's deepest fears was almost as terrifying as the fear itself. What if she discovered something she didn't want to know? What if—

"I'll go with you," Anthony said, breaking into her thoughts.

And somehow that made everything all right.

Kate looked to him and nodded, tears in her eyes. "Thank you," she whispered. "Thank you so much."

---

Later that day, the two of them walked up the steps to Mary's small townhouse. The butler showed them into the drawing room, and Kate sat on the familiar blue sofa while Anthony walked over to the window, leaning on the sill as he peered out.

"See something interesting?" she asked.

He shook his head, smiling sheepishly as he turned to face her. "I just like looking out windows, that's all."

Kate thought there was something awfully sweet about that, although she couldn't really put her finger on what. Every day seemed to reveal some new little quirk to his character, some uniquely endearing habit that bound them ever closer. She *liked* knowing strange little things about him, like how he always doubled up his pillow before going to sleep, or that he detested orange marmalade but adored the lemon.

"You look rather introspective."

Kate jerked to attention. Anthony was staring at her quizzically. "You drifted off," he said with an amused expression, "and you had the dreamiest smile on your face."

She shook her head, blushed, and mumbled, "It was nothing."

His answering snort was dubious, and as he walked over to the sofa, he said, "I'd give a hundred pounds for those thoughts."

Kate was saved from having to comment by Mary's entrance. "Kate!" Mary exclaimed. "What a lovely surprise. And Lord Bridgerton, how nice to see you both."

"You really should call me Anthony," he said somewhat gruffly.

Mary smiled as he took her hand in greeting. "I shall endeavor to remember to do so," she said. She sat across from Kate, then waited for Anthony to take his place on the sofa before saying, "Edwina is out, I'm afraid. Her Mr. Bagwell came rather unexpectedly down to town. They've gone for a walk in the park."

"We should lend them Newton," Anthony said affably. "A more capable chaperone I cannot imagine."

"We actually came to see you, Mary," Kate said.

Kate's voice held an uncommon note of seriousness, and Mary responded instantly. "What is it?" she asked, her eyes flicking back and forth from Kate to Anthony. "Is everything all right?"

Kate nodded, swallowing as she searched for the right words. Funny how she'd been rehearsing what to ask all morning, and now she was speechless. But then she felt Anthony's hand on hers, the weight and the warmth of it strangely comforting, and she looked up and said to Mary, "I'd like to ask you about my mother."

Mary looked a little startled, but she said, "Of course. But you know that I did not know her personally. I only know what your father told me of her."

Kate nodded. "I know. And you might not have the answers to any of my questions, but I don't know who else to ask."

Mary shifted in her seat, her hands clasped primly in her lap. But Kate noticed that her knuckles had gone white.

"Very well," Mary said. "What is it you wish to learn? You know that I will tell you anything I know."

Kate nodded again and swallowed, her mouth having gone dry. "How did she die, Mary?"

Mary blinked, then sagged slightly, perhaps with relief. "But you know that already. It was influenza. Or some sort of lung fever. The doctors were never certain."

"I know, but . . ." Kate looked to Anthony, who gave her a reassuring nod. She took a deep breath and plunged on. "I'm still afraid of storms, Mary. I want to know why. I don't want to be afraid any longer."

Mary's lips parted, but she was silent for many seconds as she stared at her stepdaughter. Her skin slowly paled, taking on an odd, translucent hue, and her eyes grew haunted. "I didn't realize," she whispered. "I didn't know you still—"

"I hid it well," Kate said softly.

Mary reached up and touched her temple, her hands shaking. "If I'd known, I'd have . . ." Her fingers moved to her forehead, smoothing over worry lines as she fought for words. "Well, I don't know what I'd have done. Told you, I suppose."

Kate's heart stopped. "Told me what?"

Mary let out a long breath, both of her hands at her face now, pressing against the upper edge of her eye sockets. She looked as if she had a terrible headache, the weight of the world pounding against her skull, from the inside out.

"I just want you to know," she said in a choked voice, "that I didn't tell you because I thought you didn't remember. And if you didn't remember, well, it didn't seem right to *make* you remember."

She looked up, and there were tears streaking her face. "But obviously you do," she whispered, "or you wouldn't be so afraid. Oh, Kate. I'm so sorry."

"I am sure there is nothing for you to be sorry about," Anthony said softly.

Mary looked at him, her eyes momentarily startled, as if she'd forgotten he was in the room. "Oh, but there is," she said sadly. "I didn't know that Kate was still suffering from her fears. I should have known. It's the sort of thing a mother should sense. I may not have given her life, but I have tried to be a true mother to her—"

"You have," Kate said fervently. "The very best."

Mary turned back to her, holding her silence for a few seconds before saying, in an oddly detached voice, "You were three when your mother died. It was your birthday, actually."

Kate nodded, mesmerized.

"When I married your father I made three vows. There was the vow I made to him, before God and witnesses, to be his wife. But in my heart I made two other vows. One was to you, Kate. I took one look at you, so lost and forlorn with those huge brown eyes—and they were sad, oh, they were so sad, eyes no child should have—and I vowed that I would love you as my own, and raise you with everything I had within me."

She paused to wipe her eyes, gratefully accepting the handkerchief that Anthony handed to her. When she continued, her voice was barely a whisper. "The other vow was to your mother. I visited her grave, you know."

Kate's nod was accompanied by a wistful smile. "I know. I went with you on several occasions."

Mary shook her head. "No. I mean before I married your father. I knelt there, and that was when I made my third vow. She had been a good mother to you; everyone said so, and any fool could see that you missed her with everything in your heart. So I promised her all the same things I promised you, to be a good mother, to love and cherish you as if you were of my own flesh." She lifted her head, and her eyes were utterly clear and direct when she said, "And I'd like to think that I brought her some peace. I don't think any mother can die in peace leaving behind a child so young."

"Oh, Mary," Kate whispered.

Mary looked at her and smiled sadly, then turned to Anthony. "And that, my lord, is why I am sorry. I should have known, should have seen that she suffered."

"But Mary," Kate protested, "I didn't want you to see. I hid in my room, under my bed, in the closet. Anything to keep it from you."

"But why, sweetling?"

Kate sniffed back a tear. "I don't know. I didn't want to worry you, I suppose. Or maybe I was afraid of appearing weak."

"You've always tried to be so strong," Mary whispered. "Even when you were a tiny thing."

Anthony took Kate's hand, but he looked at Mary. "She is strong. And so are you."

Mary gazed at Kate's face for a long minute, her eyes nostalgic and sad, and then, in a low, even voice, she said, "When your mother died, it was . . . I wasn't there, but when I married your father, he told the story to me. He knew that I loved you already, and he thought it might help me to understand you a bit better.

"Your mother's death was very quick. According to your father, she fell ill on a Thursday and died on a Tuesday. And it rained the whole time. It was one of those awful storms that never ends, just beats the ground mercilessly until the rivers flood and the roads become impassable.

"He said that he was sure she would turnabout if only the rain would stop. It was silly, he knew, but every night he'd go to bed praying for the sun to peek out from the clouds. Praying for anything that might give him a little hope."

"Oh, Papa," Kate whispered, the words slipping unbidden from her lips.

"You were confined to the house, of course, which apparently rankled you to no end." Mary looked up and smiled at Kate, the sort of smile that spoke of years of memories. "You've always loved to be outdoors. Your father told me that your mother used to bring your cradle outside and rock you in the fresh air."

"I didn't know that," Kate whispered.

Mary nodded, then continued with her story. "You didn't realize your mother was ill right away. They kept you from her, fearing contagion. But eventually you must have sensed that something was wrong. Children always do.

"The night she died the rain had grown worse, and I'm told the thunder and lightning were as terrifying as anyone had ever seen." She paused, then tilted her head slightly to the side as she asked, "Do you remember the old gnarled tree in the back garden—the one you and Edwina always used to scramble on?"

"The one that was split in two?" Kate whispered.

Mary nodded. "It happened that night. Your father said it was the most terrifying sound he'd ever heard. The thunder and lightning were coming on top of each other, and a bolt split the tree at the exact moment that the thunder shook the earth.

"I suppose you couldn't sleep," she continued. "I remember that storm, even though I lived in the next county. I don't know how anyone could have slept through it. Your father was with your mother. She was dying, and everyone knew it, and in their grief they'd forgotten about you. They'd been so careful to keep you out, but on that night, their attention was elsewhere.

"Your father told me that he was sitting by your mother's side, trying to hold her hand as she passed. It wasn't a gentle death, I'm afraid. Lung disease often isn't." Mary looked up. "My mother died the same way. I know. The end wasn't peaceful. She was gasping for breath, suffocating before my very eyes."

Mary swallowed convulsively, then trained her eyes on Kate's. "I can only assume," she whispered, "that you witnessed the same thing."

Anthony's hand tightened on Kate's.

"But where I was five and twenty at my mother's death," Mary said, "you were but three. It's not the sort of thing a child should see. They tried to make you leave, but you would not go. You bit and clawed and screamed and screamed and screamed, and then—"

Mary stopped, choking on her words. She lifted the handkerchief Anthony had given her to her face, and several moments passed before she was able to continue.

"Your mother was near death," she said, her voice so low it was nearly a whisper. "And just as they found someone strong enough to remove such a wild child, a flash of lightning pierced the room. Your father said—"

Mary stopped and swallowed. "Your father told me that what happened next was the most eerie and awful moment he'd ever experienced. The lightning—it lit the room up as bright as day. And the flash wasn't over in an instant, as it should be; it almost seemed to hang in the air. He looked at you, and you were frozen. I'll never forget the way he described it. He said it was as if you were a little statue."

Anthony jerked.

"What is it?" Kate asked, turning to him.

He shook his head disbelievingly. "That's how you looked last night," he said. "Exactly how you looked. I thought those very words."

"I . . ." Kate looked from Anthony to Mary. But she didn't know what to say.

Anthony gave her hand another squeeze as he turned to Mary and urged, "Please, go on."

She nodded once. "Your eyes were fixed on your mother, and so your father turned to see what had horrified you so, and that's when he . . . when he saw . . ."

Kate gently disengaged her hand from Anthony's grasp and got up to sit beside Mary, pulling an ottoman down next to her chair. She took one of Mary's hands in both of her own. "It's all right, Mary," she murmured. "You can tell me. I need to know."

Mary nodded. "It was the moment of her death. She sat upright. Your father said she hadn't lifted her body from the pillows for days, and yet she sat bolt upright. He said she was stiff, her head thrown back, and her mouth was open as if she were screaming, but she couldn't make a sound. And then the thunder came, and you must have thought the sound came from her mouth, because you screamed like nothing anyone had ever heard and came running forward, jumping onto the bed and throwing your arms around her.

"They tried to pry you off, but you just wouldn't let go. You kept screaming and screaming and calling her name, and then there was a terrible crash. Glass shattering. A bolt of lightning severed a branch from a tree, and it crashed right through the window. There was glass everywhere, and wind, and rain, and thunder, and more lightning, and through the whole thing you didn't stop screaming. Even after she was dead and had fallen back onto the pillows, your little arms were still clutched around her neck, and you screamed and sobbed and begged for her to wake up, and not to leave.

"And you just wouldn't let go," Mary whispered. "Finally they had to wait until you wore yourself out and fell asleep."

The room was hung with silence for a full minute, and then Kate finally whispered, "I didn't know. I didn't know that I'd witnessed that."

"Your father said you wouldn't speak of it," Mary said. "Not that you could, right away. You slept for hours and hours, and then when you woke up, it was clear that you'd caught your mother's illness. Not with the same gravity; your life was never in danger. But you were ill, and not in any state to talk about your mother's death. And when you were well, you *wouldn't* talk about it. Your father tried, but he said that every time he mentioned it, you shook your head and clamped your hands over your ears. And eventually he stopped trying."

Mary gave Kate an intent gaze. "He said you seemed happier when he stopped trying. He did what he thought was best."

"I know," Kate whispered. "And at the time, it probably *was* best. But now I needed to know." She turned to Anthony, not for reassurance exactly, but for some sort of validation, and she repeated, "I needed to know."

"How do you feel now?" he asked, his words soft and direct.

She thought about that for a moment. "I don't know. Good, I think. A little lighter." And then, without even realizing what she was doing, she smiled. It was a hesitant, slow thing, but nonetheless a smile. She turned to Anthony with astonished eyes. "I feel as if a huge weight has been lifted from my shoulders."

"Do you remember now?" Mary asked.

Kate shook her head. "But I still feel better. I can't explain it, really. It's good to know, even if I can't remember."

Mary made a choked sort of sound and then she was out of her chair and next to Kate on the ottoman, embracing her with all her might. And they both were crying, the odd, energetic sort of sobs that were mixed with laughter. There were tears, but they were happy tears, and when Kate finally pulled away and looked at Anthony, she saw that he, too, was wiping at the corner of his eye.

He pulled his hand away, of course, and assumed a dignified mien, but she'd seen him. And in that moment, she knew she loved him. With every thought, every emotion, every piece of her being, she loved him.

And if he never loved her back—well, she didn't want to think about that. Not now, not in this profound moment.

Probably not ever.

# Chapter 20

*Has anyone besides This Author noticed that Miss Edwina Sheffield has been very distracted of late? Rumor has it that she has lost her heart, although no one seems to know the identity of the lucky gentleman.*

*Judging from Miss Sheffield's behavior at parties, however, This Author feels it is safe to assume that the mystery gentleman is not someone currently residing here in London. Miss Sheffield has shown no marked interest in any one gentleman, and indeed, even sat out the dancing at Lady Mottram's ball Friday last.*

*Could her suitor be someone she met in the country last month? This Author will have to do a bit of sleuthing to uncover the truth.*

*LADY WHISTLEDOWN'S SOCIETY PAPERS,*
13 JUNE 1814

"Do you know what I think?" Kate asked, as she sat at her vanity table later that night, brushing her hair.

Anthony was standing by the window, one hand leaning against the frame as he gazed out. "Mmmm?" was his reply, mostly because he was too distracted by his own thoughts to formulate a more coherent word.

"I think," she continued in a cheery voice, "that next time it storms, I'm going to be just fine."

He turned slowly around. "Really?" he asked.

She nodded. "I don't know why I think that. A gut feeling, I suppose."

"Gut feelings," he said, in a voice that sounded strange and flat even to his own ears, "are often the most accurate."

"I feel the strangest sense of optimism," she said, waving her silver-backed hairbrush in the air as she spoke. "All my life, I've had this awful thing hanging over my head. I didn't tell you—I never told anyone—but every time it stormed, and I fell to pieces, I thought . . . well, I didn't just *think*, I somehow *knew* . . ."

"What, Kate?" he asked, dreading the answer without even having a clue why.

"Somehow," she said thoughtfully, "as I shook and sobbed, I just knew that I was going to die. I knew it. There was just no way I could feel that awful and live to see the next day." Her head cocked slightly to the side, and her face took on a vaguely strained expression, as if she weren't sure how to say what she needed to say.

But Anthony understood all the same. And it made his blood run to ice.

"I'm sure you'll think it's the silliest thing imaginable," she said, her shoulders rising and falling in a sheepish shrug. "You're so rational, so levelheaded and practical. I don't think you could understand something like this."

*If she only knew*. Anthony rubbed at his eyes, feeling strangely drunk. He staggered to a chair, hoping she wouldn't notice how off balance he was, and sat down.

Luckily, her attention had returned to the various bottles and trinkets on her vanity table. Or maybe she was just too embarrassed to look at him, thinking he'd scoff at her irrational fears.

"Whenever the storm passed," she continued, talking down at her table, "I knew how foolish I'd been and how ridiculous the notion was. After all, I'd endured thunderstorms before, and none had ever killed me. But knowing that in my rational mind never seemed to help. Do you know what I mean?"

Anthony tried to nod. He wasn't sure if he actually did.

"When it rained," she said, "nothing really existed except for the storm. And, of course, my fear. Then the sun would come out, and I'd realize again how silly I'd been, but the next time it stormed, it was just like before. And once again, I knew I would die. I just knew it."

Anthony felt sick. His body felt strange, not his own. He couldn't have said anything if he'd tried.

"In fact," she said, raising her head to look at him, "the only time I felt I might actually live to see the next day was in the library at Aubrey Hall." She stood and walked to his side, resting her cheek on his lap as she knelt before him. "With you," she whispered.

He lifted his hand to stroke her hair. The motion was more out of reflex than anything else. He certainly wasn't conscious of his actions.

He'd had no idea that Kate had any sense of her own mortality. Most people didn't. It was something that had lent Anthony an odd sense of isolation through the years, as if he understood some basic, awful truth that eluded the rest of society.

And while Kate's sense of doom wasn't the same as his—hers was fleeting, brought on by a temporary burst of wind and rain and electricity, whereas his was with him always, and would be until the day he died—she, unlike him, had beaten it.

Kate had fought her demons and she had won.

And Anthony was so damned jealous.

It was not a noble reaction; he knew that. And, caring for her as he did, he was thrilled and relieved and overjoyed and every good and pure emotion imaginable that she had beaten the terrors that came with the storms, but he was still jealous. So goddamned jealous.

Kate had won.

Whereas he, who had acknowledged his demons but refused to fear them, was now petrified with terror. And all because the one thing he swore would never happen had come to pass.

He had fallen in love with his wife.

He had fallen in love with his wife, and now the thought of dying, of leaving her, of knowing that their moments together would form a short poem and not a long and lusty novel—it was more than he could bear.

And he didn't know where to set the blame. He wanted to point his finger at his father, for dying young and leaving him as the bearer of this awful curse. He wanted to rail at Kate, for coming into his life and making him fear his own end. Hell, he would have blamed a stranger on the street if he'd thought there'd be any use to it.

But the truth was, there was no one to blame, not even himself. It would make him feel so much better if he could point his finger at someone—anyone—and say, "This is *your* fault." It was juvenile, he knew, this need to assign blame, but everyone had a right to childish emotions from time to time, didn't they?

"I'm so happy," Kate murmured, her head still resting on his lap.

And Anthony wanted to be happy, too. He wanted so damned much for everything to be uncomplicated, for happiness just to be happiness and nothing more. He wanted to rejoice in her recent victories without any thought to his own worries. He wanted to lose himself in the moment, to forget about the future, to hold her in his arms and . . .

In one abrupt, unpremeditated movement, he hauled them both to their feet.

"Anthony?" Kate queried, blinking in surprise.

In answer, he kissed her. His lips met hers in an explosion of passion and need that blurred the mind until he could be ruled by body alone. He didn't want to think, he didn't want to be *able* to think. All he wanted was this very moment.

And he wanted this moment to last forever.

He swept his wife into his arms and stalked to the bed, depositing her on the mattress half a second before his body came down to cover hers. She was stunning beneath him, soft and strong, and consumed by the same fire that raged within his own body. She might not understand what had prompted his sudden need, but she felt it and shared it all the same.

Kate had already dressed for bed, and her nightrobe fell open easily under his experienced fingers. He had to touch her, to feel her, to assure himself that she was there beneath him and he was there to make love to her. She was wearing a silky little confection of ice blue that tied at the shoulders and hugged her curves. It was the sort of gown designed to reduce men to liquid fire, and Anthony was no exception.

There was something desperately erotic about the feel of her warm skin through the silk, and his hands roamed over her body relentlessly, touching, squeezing, doing anything he could to bind her to him.

If he could have drawn her within him, he would have done it and kept her there forever.

"Anthony," Kate gasped, in that brief moment when he removed his mouth from hers, "are you all right?"

"I want you," he grunted, bunching her gown up around the tops of her legs. "I want you now."

Her eyes widened with shock and excitement, and he sat up, straddling her, his weight on his knees so as not to crush her. "You are so beautiful," he whispered. "So unbelievably gorgeous."

Kate glowed at his words, and her hands went up to his face, smoothing her fingers over his faintly stubbled cheeks. He caught one of her hands and turned his face into it, kissing her palm as her other hand trailed down the muscled cords of his neck.

His fingers found the delicate straps at her shoulders, tied into loose bow-tie loops. It took the barest of tugs to release the knots, but once the silky fabric slid over her breasts, Anthony lost all semblance of patience, and he yanked at the garment until it pooled at her feet, leaving her completely and utterly naked under his gaze.

With a ragged groan he tore at his shirt, buttons flying as he pulled it off, and it took mere seconds to divest himself of his trousers. And then, when there was finally nothing in the bed but glorious skin, he covered her again, one muscular thigh nudging her legs apart.

"I can't wait," he said hoarsely. "I can't make this good for you."

Kate let out a fevered groan as she grabbed him by the hips, steering him toward her entrance. "It *is* good for me," she gasped. "And I don't want you to wait."

And at that point, words ceased. Anthony let out a primitive, guttural cry as he plunged into her, burying himself fully with one long and powerful stroke. Kate's eyes flew wide open, and her mouth formed a little *Oh* of surprise at the shock of his swift invasion. But she'd been ready for him—more than ready for him. Something about the relentless pace of his lovemaking had stirred a passion deep within her, until she needed him with a desperation that left her breathless.

They weren't delicate, and they weren't gentle. They were hot, and sweaty, and needy, and they held on to each other as if they could make time last forever by sheer force of will. When they climaxed, it was fiery and it was simultaneous, both their bodies arching as their cries of release mingled in the night.

But when they were done, curled in each other's arms as they fought for control over their labored breath, Kate closed her eyes in bliss and surrendered to an overwhelming lassitude.

Anthony did not.

He stared at her as she drifted off, then watched her as she slumbered. He watched the way her eyes sometimes moved under her sleepy eyelids. He measured the pace of her breathing by counting the gentle rise and fall of her chest. He listened for each sigh, each mumble.

There were certain memories a man wanted to sear on his brain, and this was one of them.

But just when he was sure that she was totally and completely asleep, she made a funny, warm sort of noise as she snuggled more deeply into his embrace, and her eyelids fluttered slowly open.

"You're still awake," she murmured, her voice scratchy and mellow with sleep.

He nodded, wondering if he was holding her too tightly. He didn't want to let go. He never wanted to let go.

"You should sleep," she said.

He nodded again, but he couldn't seem to make his eyes close.

She yawned. "This is nice."

He kissed her forehead, making an "Mmmm" sound of agreement.

She arched her neck and kissed him back, full on the lips, then settled into her pillow. "I hope we'll be like this always," she murmured, yawning yet again as sleep overtook her. "Always and forever."

Anthony froze.

*Always.*

She couldn't know what that word meant to him. Five years? Six? Maybe seven or eight.

*Forever.*

That was a word that had no meaning, something he simply couldn't comprehend.

Suddenly he couldn't breathe.

The coverlet felt like a brick wall atop him, and the air grew thick.

He had to get out of there. He had to go. He had to—

He vaulted from the bed, and then, stumbling and choking, he reached for his clothes, tossed so recklessly to the floor, and started thrusting his limbs into the appropriate holes.

"Anthony?"

His head jerked up. Kate was pushing herself upright in the bed, yawning. Even in the dim light, he could see that her eyes were confused. And hurt.

"Are you all right?" she asked.

He gave her one curt nod.

"Then why are you trying to put your leg into the armhole of your shirt?"

He looked down and bit off a curse he'd never before even considered uttering in front of a female. With yet another choice expletive, he balled the offending piece of linen into a wrinkled mess and threw it on the floor, pausing for barely a second before yanking his trousers on.

"Where are you going?" Kate asked anxiously.

"I have to go out," he grunted.

"Now?"

He didn't answer because he didn't know how to answer.

"Anthony?" She stepped out of bed and reached for him, but a split second before her hand touched his cheek he flinched, stumbling backward until his back hit the bedpost. He saw the hurt on her face, the pain of his rejection, but he knew that if she touched him in tenderness, he'd be lost.

"Damn it all," he bit off. "Where the hell are my shirts?"

"In your dressing room," she said nervously. "Where they always are."

He stalked off in search of a fresh shirt, unable to bear the sound of her voice. No matter what she said, he kept hearing *always* and *forever.*

And it was killing him.

When he emerged from his dressing room, coat and shoes on their proper places on his body, Kate was on her feet, pacing the floor and anxiously fidgeting with the wide blue sash on her dressing gown.

"I have to go," he said tonelessly.

She didn't make a sound, which was what he'd thought he wanted, but instead he just found himself standing there, waiting for her to speak, unable to move until she did.

"When will you be back?" she finally asked.

"Tomorrow."

"That's . . . good."

He nodded. "I can't be here," he blurted out. "I have to go."

She swallowed convulsively. "Yes," she said, her voice achingly small, "you've said as much."

And then, without a backward glance and without a clue as to where he was going, he left.

Kate walked slowly to the bed and stared at it. Somehow it seemed wrong to climb in alone, to pull the covers around her and make a little huddle of one. She thought she should cry, but no tears pricked her eyes. So finally she moved to the window, pushed aside the drapes, and stared out, surprising herself with a soft prayer for a storm.

Anthony was gone, and while she was certain he'd return in body, she was not so confident about his spirit. And she realized that she needed something—she needed the storm—to prove to herself that she could be strong, by herself and for herself.

She didn't want to be alone, but she might not have a choice in that matter. Anthony seemed determined to maintain a distance. There were demons within him—demons she feared he would never choose to face in her presence.

But if she was destined to be alone, even with a husband at her side, then by God she'd be alone and strong.

Weakness, she thought as she let her forehead rest against the smooth, cool glass of her window, never got anyone anywhere.

Anthony had no recollection of his off-balance stumble through the house, but somehow he found himself tripping down the front steps, made slippery by the light fog that hung in the air. He crossed the street, not having a clue where he was going, only knowing that he needed to be *away*. But when he reached the opposite pavement, some devil within him forced his eyes upward toward his bedroom window.

*He shouldn't have seen her* was his rather inane thought. She should have been in bed or the drapes should have been pulled or he should have been halfway to his club by now.

But he did see her and the dull ache in his chest grew sharper, more viciously unrelenting. His heart felt as if it had been sliced wide open—and he had the most unsettling sensation that the hand wielding the knife had been his own.

He watched her for a minute—or maybe it was an hour. He

didn't think she saw him; nothing in her posture gave any indication that she was aware of his presence. She was too far away for him to see her face, but he rather thought her eyes were closed.

*Probably hoping it doesn't storm*, he thought, glancing up at the murky sky. She'd most likely be out of luck. The mist and fog were already coalescing into drops of moisture on his skin, and it seemed only a quick transition to out-and-out rain.

He knew he should leave, but some invisible cord kept him rooted to the spot. Even after she'd left her position at the window, he remained in place, staring up at the house. The pull back inside was nearly impossible to deny. He wanted to run back into the house, fall to his knees before her, and beg her forgiveness. He wanted to sweep her into his arms and make love to her until the first streaks of dawn touched the sky. But he knew he couldn't do any of those things.

Or maybe it was that he *shouldn't*. He just didn't know anymore.

And so, after standing frozen in place for nearly an hour, after the rain came, after the wind blew gusts of chilly air down the street, Anthony finally left.

He left, not feeling the cold, not feeling the rain, which had begun to fall with surprising force.

He left, not feeling anything.

# Chapter 21

*It has been whispered that Lord and Lady Bridgerton were forced to marry, but even if that is true, This Author refuses to believe that theirs is anything but a love match.*

LADY WHISTLEDOWN'S SOCIETY PAPERS,
15 JUNE 1814

It was strange, Kate thought as she looked at the morning repast laid upon the side table in the small dining room, how one could feel utterly famished and at the same time have no appetite. Her stomach was rumbling and churning, demanding food now, and yet everything—from the eggs to the scones to the kippers to the roast pork—looked awful.

With a dejected sigh, she reached for a solitary triangle of toast and sank into her chair with a cup of tea.

Anthony had not come home last night.

Kate took a nibble of the toast and forced it down. She'd been hoping that he might at least make an appearance in time for breakfast. She'd delayed the meal as long as she could—it was already nearly eleven in the morning and she usually ate at nine—but her husband was still absent.

"Lady Bridgerton?"

Kate looked up and blinked. A footman was standing before her bearing a small cream-colored envelope.

"This arrived for you a few minutes ago," he said.

Kate murmured her thanks and reached for the envelope, which had been secured with a neat dollop of pale pink sealing wax. Bringing it closer to her eyes, she made out the initials *EOB*. One of Anthony's relations? The E would be Eloise, of course, since all of the Bridgertons had been named in alphabetical order.

Kate carefully broke the seal and slipped out the contents—a single piece of paper, neatly folded in half.

*Kate—*

*Anthony is here. He looks a wreck. It is, of course,* none *of my business, but I thought you might like to know.*

*Eloise*

Kate stared at the note a few seconds longer, then shoved her chair back and stood. It was time she paid a call upon Bridgerton House.

Much to Kate's surprise, when she knocked at Bridgerton House, the door was swung open not by the butler but by Eloise, who immediately said, "That was fast!"

Kate looked around the hall, half expecting another Bridgerton sibling or two to jump out at her. "Were you waiting for me?"

Eloise nodded. "And you don't have to knock at the door, you know. Bridgerton House belongs to Anthony, after all. And you *are* his wife."

Kate smiled weakly. She didn't feel much like a wife this morning.

"I hope you don't think me a hopeless meddler," Eloise continued, linking her arm through Kate's and guiding her down the hall, "but Anthony does look awful, and I had a sneaking suspicion you didn't know he was here."

"Why would you think that?" Kate couldn't help asking.

"Well," Eloise said, "he didn't go to any great pains to tell any of *us* that he was here."

Kate eyed her sister-in-law suspiciously. "Meaning?"

Eloise had the grace to blush a faint pink. "Meaning, ah, that the only reason I know he's here is that I was spying upon him. I don't think my mother even knows he's in residence."

Kate felt her eyelids blink in rapid succession. "You've been spying upon us?"

"No, of course not. But I happened to be up and about rather early this morning, and I heard someone come in, and so I went to investigate and I saw light coming from under the door in his study."

"How, then, do you know he looks awful?"

Eloise shrugged. "I figured he'd have to emerge eventually to eat or relieve himself, so I waited on the steps for an hour or so—"

"Or so?" Kate echoed.

"Or three," Eloise admitted. "It's really not that long when one is interested in one's subject, and besides, I had a book with me to while away the time."

Kate shook her head in reluctant admiration. "What time did he come in last night?"

"Around four or so."

"What were you doing up so late?"

Eloise shrugged again. "I couldn't sleep. I often can't. I'd gone down to get a book to read from the library. Finally, at around seven—well, I suppose it was a bit before seven, so it wasn't quite three hours I waited—"

Kate began to feel dizzy.

"—he emerged. He didn't head in the direction of the breakfast room, so I can only assume it was for other reasons. After a minute or two, he reemerged and headed back into his study. Where," Eloise finished with a flourish, "he has been ever since."

Kate stared at her for a good ten seconds. "Have you ever considered offering your services to the War Department?"

Eloise grinned, a smile so like Anthony's Kate almost cried. "As a spy?" she asked.

Kate nodded.

"I'd be brilliant, don't you think?"

"Superb."

Eloise gave Kate a spontaneous hug. "I'm so glad you married my brother. Now go and see what is wrong."

Kate nodded, straightened her shoulders, and took a step toward Anthony's study. Turning around, she pointed a finger at Eloise and said, "You will not be listening at the door."

"I wouldn't dream of it," Eloise replied.

"I mean it, Eloise!"

Eloise sighed. "It's time I went up to bed, anyway. I could use a nap after staying up all night."

Kate waited until the younger girl had disappeared up the stairs, then made her way to Anthony's study door. She put her hand on the knob, whispering, "Don't be locked," as she gave it a twist. To her extreme relief, it turned, and the door swung open.

"Anthony?" she called out. Her voice was soft and hesitant, and she found she didn't like the sound of it. She wasn't used to being soft and hesitant.

There was no reply, so Kate stepped farther into the room. The drapes were tightly closed, and the heavy velvet admitted little light. Kate scanned the room until her eyes fell on the figure of her husband, slouched over his desk, sound asleep.

Kate walked quietly across the room to the windows and pulled the drapes partway open. She didn't want to blind Anthony when he woke up, but at the same time, she wasn't going to conduct such an important conversation in the dark. Then she walked back over to his desk and gently shook his shoulder.

"Anthony?" she whispered. "Anthony?"

His reply was closer to a snore than anything else.

Frowning impatiently, she shook a little harder. "Anthony?" she said softly. "Anthon—"

"Yibbledeedad—!" He came awake in one sudden movement, an incoherent rush of speech bursting forth as his torso snapped upright.

Kate watched as he blinked himself into coherency, then focused on her. "Kate," he said, his voice hoarse and husky with sleep and something else—maybe alcohol. "What are you doing here?"

"What are *you* doing here?" she countered. "The last time I checked, we lived nearly a mile away."

"I didn't want to disturb you," he mumbled.

Kate didn't believe that for one second, but she decided not to argue the point. Instead, she opted for the direct approach and asked, "Why did you leave last night?"

A long stretch of silence was followed by a weary, tired sigh, and Anthony finally said, "It's complicated."

Kate fought the urge to cross her arms. "I'm an intelligent woman," she said in a purposefully even voice. "I'm generally able to grasp complex concepts."

Anthony didn't look pleased by her sarcasm. "I don't want to go into this now."

"When *do* you want to go into it?"

"Go home, Kate," he said softly.

"Do you plan to come with me?"

Anthony let out a little groan as he raked a hand through his hair. Christ, she was like a dog with a bone. His head was pounding, his mouth tasted like wool, all he really wanted to do was splash some water on his face and clean his teeth, and here his wife would not stop *interrogating him*. . . .

"Anthony?" she persisted.

That was *enough*. He stood so suddenly that his chair tipped back and slammed into the floor with a resounding crash. "You will cease your questions this instant," he bit off.

Her mouth settled into a flat, angry line. But her eyes. . . .

Anthony swallowed against the acidic taste of guilt that flooded his mouth.

Because her eyes were awash with pain.

And the anguish in his own heart grew tenfold.

He wasn't ready. Not yet. He didn't know what to do with her. He didn't know what to do with himself. All his life—or at least since his father had died—he'd known that certain things were true, that certain things *had* to be true. And now Kate had gone and turned his world upside down.

He hadn't wanted to love her. Hell, he hadn't wanted to love anyone. It was the one thing—the only thing—that could make him fear his own mortality. And what about Kate? He'd promised to love and protect her. How could he do that, all the while knowing he would leave her? He certainly couldn't tell her of his odd convictions. Aside from the fact that she'd probably think he was crazy, all it would do was subject her to the same pain and fear that racked him. Better to let her live in blissful ignorance.

Or was it even better if she didn't love him at all?

Anthony just didn't know the answer. And he needed more time. And he couldn't think with her standing there before him, those pain-filled eyes raking his face. And—

"Go," he choked out. "Just go."

"No," she said with a quiet determination that made him love her all the more. "Not until you tell me what is bothering you."

He strode out from behind his desk and took her arm. "I can't be with you right now," he said hoarsely, his eyes avoiding hers. "Tomorrow. I'll see you tomorrow. Or the next day."

"Anthony—"

"I need time to think."

"About *what*?" she cried out.

"Don't make this any harder than—"

"How could it possibly get any harder?" she demanded. "I don't even know what you're talking about."

"I just need a few days," he said, feeling like an echo. Just a few days to think. To figure out what he was going to do, how he was going to live his life.

But she twisted around until she was facing him, and then her hand was on his cheek, touching him with a tenderness that made his heart ache. "Anthony," she whispered, "please . . ."

He couldn't form a word, couldn't make a sound.

Her hand slipped to the back of his head, and then she was drawing him closer . . . closer . . . and he couldn't help himself. He wanted her so damned badly, wanted to feel her body pressed against his, to taste the faint salt of her skin. He wanted to smell her, to touch her, to hear the rasp of her breath in his ear.

Her lips touched his, soft and seeking, and her tongue tickled the corner of her mouth. It would be so easy to lose himself in her, to sink down to the carpet and . . .

"No!" The word was ripped from his throat, and by God, he'd had no idea it was there until it burst forth.

"No," he said again, pushing her away. "Not now."

"But—"

He didn't deserve her. Not right now. Not yet. Not until he understood how he was meant to live out the rest of his life. And if it meant he had to deny himself the one thing that might bring him salvation, so be it.

"Go," he ordered, his voice sounding a bit more harsh than he'd intended. "Go now. I'll see you later."

And this time, she did go.

She went, without looking back.

And Anthony, who'd only just learned what it was to love, learned what it was to die inside.

By the following morning, Anthony was drunk. By afternoon, he was hungover.

His head was pounding, his ears were ringing, and his brothers, who had been surprised to discover him in such a state at their club, were talking *far* too loudly.

Anthony put his hands over his ears and groaned. *Everyone* was talking far too loudly.

"Kate boot you out of the house?" Colin asked, grabbing a walnut from a large pewter dish in the middle of their table and splitting it open with a viciously loud crack.

Anthony lifted his head just far enough to glare at him.

Benedict watched his brother with raised brows and the vaguest hint of a smirk. "She definitely booted him out," he said to Colin. "Hand me one of those walnuts, will you?"

Colin tossed one across the table. "Do you want the crackers as well?"

Benedict shook his head and grinned as he held up a fat, leather-bound book. "Much more satisfying to smash them."

"Don't," Anthony bit out, his hand shooting out to grab the book, "even think about it."

"Ears a bit sensitive this afternoon, are they?"

If Anthony had had a pistol, he would have shot them both, hang the noise.

"If I might offer you a piece of advice?" Colin said, munching on his walnut.

"You might not," Anthony replied. He looked up. Colin was chewing with his mouth open. As this had been strictly forbidden while growing up in their household, Anthony could only deduce that Colin was displaying such poor manners only to make more noise. "Close your damned mouth," he muttered.

Colin swallowed, smacked his lips, and took a sip of his tea to wash it all down. "Whatever you did, apologize for it. I know you, and I'm getting to know Kate, and knowing what I know—"

"What the hell is he talking about?" Anthony grumbled.

"I think," Benedict said, leaning back in his chair, "that he's telling you you're an ass."

"Just so!" Colin exclaimed.

Anthony just shook his head wearily. "It's more complicated than you think."

"It always is," Benedict said, with sincerity so false it almost managed to sound sincere.

"When you two idiots find women gullible enough to actually marry you," Anthony snapped, "then you may presume to offer me advice. But until then . . . *shut up.*"

Colin looked at Benedict. "Think he's angry?"

Benedict quirked a brow. "That or drunk."

Colin shook his head. "No, not drunk. Not anymore, at least. He's clearly hungover."

"Which would explain," Benedict said with a philosophical nod, "why he's so angry."

Anthony spread one hand over his face and pressed hard against his temples with his thumb and middle finger. "God above," he muttered. "What would it take to get you two to leave me alone?"

"Go home, Anthony," Benedict said, his voice surprisingly gentle.

Anthony closed his eyes and let out a long breath. There was nothing he wanted to do more, but he wasn't sure what to say to Kate, and more importantly, he had no idea how he'd feel once he got there.

"Yes," Colin agreed. "Just go home and tell her that you love her. What could be more simple?"

And suddenly it *was* simple. He had to tell Kate that he loved her. Now. This very day. He had to make sure she *knew*, and he vowed to spend every last minute of his miserably short life proving it to her.

It was too late to change the destiny of his heart. He'd tried not to fall in love, and he'd failed. Since he wasn't likely to fall back *out* of love, he might as well make the best of the situation. He was going to be haunted by the premonition of his own death whether or not Kate knew of his love for her. Wouldn't he be happier during these last few years if he spent them loving her openly and honestly?

He was fairly certain she'd fallen in love with him as well; surely she'd be glad to hear that he felt the same way. And when a man loved a woman, truly loved her from the depths of her soul to the tips of her toes, wasn't it his God-given duty to try to make her happy?

He wouldn't tell her of his premonitions, though. What would be the point? He might suffer the knowledge that their time together would be cut short, but why should she? Better she be struck by sharp and sudden pain at his death than suffer the anticipation of it beforehand.

He was going to die. Everyone died, he reminded himself. He was just going to have to do it sooner rather than later. But by God, he was going to enjoy his last years with every breath of his being. It might have been more convenient not to have fallen in love, but now that he had, he wasn't going to hide from it.

It was simple. His world was Kate. If he denied that, he might as well stop breathing right now.

"I have to go," he blurted out, standing up so suddenly that his thighs hit the edge of the table, sending walnut shell shards skittering across the tabletop.

"I thought you might," Colin murmured.

Benedict just smiled and said, "Go."

His brothers, Anthony realized, were a bit smarter than they let on.

"We'll speak to you in a week or so?" Colin asked.

Anthony had to grin. He and his brothers had met at their club every day for the past fortnight. Colin's oh-so-innocent query could only imply one thing—that it was obvious that Anthony had completely lost his heart to his wife and planned to spend at least the next seven days proving it to her. And that the family he was creating had grown as important as the one he'd been born into.

"Two weeks," Anthony replied, yanking on his coat. "Maybe three."

His brothers just grinned.

But when Anthony pushed through the door of his home, slightly out of breath from taking the front steps three at a time, he discovered that Kate was not in.

"Where did she go?" he asked the butler. Stupidly, he'd never once considered that she might not be at home.

"Out for a ride in the park," the butler replied, "with her sister and a Mr. Bagwell."

"Edwina's suitor," Anthony muttered to himself. Damn. He supposed he ought to be happy for his sister-in-law, but the timing was bloody annoying. He'd just made a life-altering decision regarding his wife; it would have been nice if she'd been home.

"Her *creature* went as well," the butler said with a shudder. He'd never been able to tolerate what he considered the corgi's invasion into his home.

"She took Newton, eh?" Anthony murmured.

"I imagine they'll be back within an hour or two."

Anthony tapped his booted toe against the marble floor. He didn't want to wait an hour. Hell, he didn't want to wait even a minute. "I'll find them myself," he said impatiently. "It can't be that difficult."

The butler nodded and motioned through the open doorway to the small carriage in which Anthony had ridden home. "Will you be needing another carriage?"

Anthony gave his head a single shake. "I'll go on horseback. It'll be quicker."

"Very well." The butler bent into a small bow. "I'll have a mount brought 'round."

Anthony watched the butler make his slow and sedate way toward the rear of the house for about two seconds before impatience set in. "I'll take care of it myself," he barked.

And the next thing he knew, he was dashing out of the house.

Anthony was in jaunty spirits by the time he reached Hyde Park. He was eager to find his wife, to hold her in his arms and watch her face as he told her he loved her. He prayed that she would offer words returning the sentiment. He thought she would; he'd seen her heart in her eyes on more than one occasion. Perhaps she was just waiting for him to say something first. He couldn't blame her if that was the case; he'd made a rather big fuss about how theirs would *not* be a love match right before their wedding.

What an idiot he'd been.

Once he entered the park, he made the decision to turn his mount and head over to Rotten Row. The busy path seemed the most likely destination for the threesome; Kate certainly would have no reason to encourage a more private route.

He nudged his horse into as fast a trot as he could safely manage within the confines of the park, trying to ignore the calls and waves of greeting that were directed his way by other riders and pedestrians.

Then, just when he thought he'd made it through without delay, he heard an aged, female, and very imperious voice call out his name.

"Bridgerton! I say, Bridgerton! Stop at once. I'm speaking to you!"

He groaned as he turned about. Lady Danbury, the dragon of the *ton*. There was simply no way he could ignore her. He had no idea how old she was. Sixty? Seventy? Whatever her age, she was a force of nature, and *no one* ignored her.

"Lady Danbury," he said, trying not to sound resigned as he reined in his mount. "How nice to see you."

"Good gad, boy," she barked, "you sound as if you've just taken an antidote. Perk up!"

Anthony smiled weakly.

"Where's your wife?"

"I'm looking for her right now," he replied, "or at least I *was*."

Lady Danbury was far too sharp to miss his pointed hint, so he could only deduce that she ignored him apurpose when she said, "I like your wife."

"I like her, too."

"Never could understand why you were so set on courting her sister. Nice gel, but clearly not for you." She rolled her eyes and let out an indignant huff. "The world would be a much happier place if people would just listen to me before they up and got married," she added. "I could have the entire Marriage Mart matched up in a week."

"I'm sure you could."

Her eyes narrowed. "Are you patronizing me?"

"I wouldn't dream of it," Anthony said with complete honesty.

"Good. You always seemed like the sensible sort. I . . ." Her mouth fell open. "What the devil is that?"

Anthony followed Lady Danbury's horrified gaze until his eyes fell on an open-topped carriage careening out of control as it rounded a corner on two wheels. It was still too far to see the faces of the occupants, but then he heard a shriek, and then the terrified bark of a dog.

Anthony's blood froze in his veins.

His wife was in that carriage.

With nary a word to Lady Danbury, he kicked his horse into motion and galloped full speed ahead. He wasn't sure what he'd do once he reached the carriage. Maybe he'd grab the reins from the hapless driver. Maybe he'd be able to pull someone to safety. But he knew that he could not sit still and watch while the vehicle crashed before his eyes.

And yet that was exactly what happened.

Anthony was halfway to the drunken carriage when it veered off the path and ran up over a large rock, upsetting the balance and sending it tumbling onto its side.

And Anthony could only watch in horror as his wife died before his eyes.

# Chapter 22

*Contrary to popular opinion, This Author is aware that she is viewed as something of a cynic.*

*But that, dear reader, could not be further from the truth. This Author likes nothing better than a happy ending. And if that makes her a romantic fool, so be it.*

LADY WHISTLEDOWN'S SOCIETY PAPERS,
15 JUNE 1814

By the time Anthony reached the overturned carriage, Edwina had managed to crawl from the wreckage and was clawing at a mangled piece of wood, trying to open a hole on the other side of the carriage. The sleeve of her dress was torn, and the hem was ragged and dirty, but she seemed not to notice as she tugged frantically at the door. Newton was jumping and squirming at her feet, his barks sharp and frenzied.

"What happened?" Anthony asked, his voice curt and panicked as he leapt from his horse.

"I don't know," Edwina gasped, wiping at the streaky tears that ran down her face. "Mr. Bagwell's not such an experienced driver, I think, and then Newton got loose, and then I don't know *what* happened. One minute we were rolling along, and the next—"

"Where is Bagwell?"

She motioned to the other side of the carriage. "He was thrown. He hit his head. But he'll be all right. But Kate . . ."

"What about Kate?" Anthony dropped to his knees as he tried to peer into the wreckage. The entire carriage had overturned, smashing the right side of the vehicle as it had rolled. "Where is she?"

Edwina swallowed convulsively, and her voice barely rose above a whisper as she said, "I think she's trapped beneath the carriage."

In that moment Anthony tasted death. It was bitter in his throat, metallic and hard. It scraped his flesh like a knife, choking and squeezing, pulling the air from his very lungs.

Anthony yanked viciously at the wreckage, trying to open a wider hole. It wasn't as bad as it had looked during the crash, but that did little to calm his racing heart. "Kate!" he yelled, trying to sound calm and unworried. "Kate, can you hear me?"

The only sound he heard in reply, however, was the frantic whinny of the horses. Damn. He'd have to get them unharnessed and loose before they panicked and started trying to drag the debris. "Edwina?" Anthony called sharply, looking over his shoulder.

She hurried over, wringing her hands. "Yes?"

"Do you know how to unharness the horses?"

She nodded. "I'm not very fast, but I can do it."

Anthony flicked his head toward the onlookers who were hurrying over. "See if you can find someone to help you."

She nodded again and quickly got to work.

"Kate?" Anthony yelled again. He couldn't see anyone; a dislodged bench was blocking the opening. "Can you hear me?"

Still no response.

"Try the other side," came Edwina's frantic voice. "The opening isn't as crushed."

Anthony jumped to his feet and ran around the back of the carriage to the other side. The door had already come off its hinges, leaving a hole just large enough for him to stuff his upper body into. "Kate?" he called out, trying not to notice the sharp sound of panic in his voice. Every breath from his lips seemed overloud, reverberating in the tight space, reminding him that he wasn't hearing the same sounds from Kate.

And then, as he carefully moved a seat cushion that had turned sideways, he saw her. She was terrifyingly still, but her head didn't appear to be stuck in an unnatural position, and he didn't see any blood.

That had to be a good sign. He didn't know much of medicine, but he held on to that thought like a miracle.

"You can't die, Kate," he said as his terrified fingers yanked away at the wreckage, desperate to open the hole until it was wide enough to pull her through. "Do you hear me? *You can't die!*"

A jagged piece of wood sliced open the back of his hand, but Anthony didn't notice the blood running over his skin as he pulled on another broken beam. "You had better be breathing," he warned, his voice shaking and precariously close to a sob. "This wasn't supposed to be you. It was never supposed to be you. It isn't your time. Do you understand me?"

He tore away another broken piece of wood and reached through the newly widened hole to grasp her hand. His fingers found her pulse, which seemed steady enough to him, but it was still impossible to tell if she was bleeding, or had broken her back, or had hit her head, or had . . .

His heart shuddered. There were so many ways to die. If a bee could bring down a man in his prime, surely a carriage accident could steal the life of one small woman.

Anthony grabbed the last piece of wood that stood in his way and heaved, but it didn't budge. "Don't do this to me," he muttered. "Not now. It isn't her time. Do you hear me? It isn't her time!" He felt something wet on his cheeks and dimly realized that it was tears. "It was supposed to be me," he said, choking on the words. "It was always supposed to be me."

And then, just as he was preparing to give that last piece of wood another desperate yank, Kate's fingers tightened like a claw around his wrist. His eyes flew to her face, just in time to see her eyes open wide and clear, with nary a blink.

"What the devil," she asked, sounding quite lucid and utterly awake, "are you talking about?"

Relief flooded his chest so quickly it was almost painful. "Are you all right?" he asked, his voice wobbling on every syllable.

She grimaced, then said, "I'll be fine."

Anthony paused for the barest of seconds as he considered her choice of words. "But are you fine right now?"

She let out a little cough, and he fancied he could hear her wince with pain. "I did something to my leg," she admitted. "But I don't think I'm bleeding."

"Are you faint? Dizzy? Weak?"

She shook her head. "Just in pain. What are you doing here?"

He smiled through his tears. "I came to find you."

"You did?" she whispered.

He nodded. "I came to— That is to say, I realized . . ." He swallowed convulsively. He'd never dreamed that the day would come when he'd say these words to a woman, and they'd grown so big in his heart he could barely squeeze them out. "I love you, Kate," he said chokingly. "It took me a while to figure it out, but I do, and I had to tell you. Today."

Her lips wobbled into a shaky smile as she motioned to the rest of her body with her chin. "You've bloody good timing."

Amazingly, he found himself grinning in return. "Almost makes you glad I waited so long, eh? If I'd told you last week, I wouldn't have followed you out to the park today."

She stuck out her tongue, which, considering the circumstances, made him love her even more. "Just get me out," she said.

"Then you'll tell me you love me?" he teased.

She smiled, wistful and warm, and nodded.

It was, of course, as good as a declaration, and even though he was crawling through the wreckage of an overturned carriage, even though Kate was *stuck* in the cursed carriage, with what might very well be a broken leg, he was suddenly consumed with an overwhelming sense of contentment and peace.

And he realized he hadn't felt that way for nearly twelve years, not since that fateful afternoon when he'd walked into his parents' bedroom and seen his father laid out on the bed, cold and still.

"I'm going to pull you through now," he said, sliding his arms beneath her back. "It'll hurt your leg, I'm afraid, but it can't be avoided."

"My leg already hurts," she said, smiling bravely. "I just want to get out."

Anthony gave her a single, serious nod, then curved his hands around her side and began to pull. "How is that?" he asked, his heart stopping every time he saw her wince with pain.

"Fine," she gasped, but he could tell she was merely putting up a brave front.

"I'm going to have to turn you," he said, eyeing a broken and jagged piece of wood that stuck down from above. It was going to be difficult to maneuver her around it. He couldn't care less if he tore her clothing—hell, he'd buy her a hundred new dresses if she'd only promise never again to step into a carriage if it was being driven by anyone other than himself. But he couldn't bear the thought of scratching even an inch of her skin. She'd been through enough already. She didn't need more.

"I need to pull you out headfirst," he told her. "Do you think you can wiggle yourself around? Just enough so I can grasp under your arms."

She nodded, gritting her teeth as she painstakingly turned herself inch by inch, lifting herself up on her hands as she scooted her hips around clockwise.

"There you are," Anthony said encouragingly. "Now I'm going to—"

"Just do it," Kate ground out. "You don't need to explain."

"Very well," he replied, inching backward until his knees found purchase on the grass. On a mental count of three, he gritted his teeth and began to pull her out.

And stopped a second later, as Kate let out an earsplitting scream. If he hadn't been so convinced that he'd die within the next nine years, he would have sworn she'd just taken ten off his life.

"Are you all right?" he asked urgently.

"I'm fine," she insisted. But she was breathing hard, puffing through pursed lips, and her face was tense with pain.

"What happened?" came a voice from just outside the carriage. It was Edwina, done with the horses and sounding frantic. "I heard Kate scream."

"Edwina?" Kate asked, twisting her neck as she tried to see out. "Are you all right?" She yanked on Anthony's sleeve. "Is Edwina all right? Is she hurt? Does she need a doctor?"

"Edwina's fine," he replied. "*You* need a doctor."

"And Mr. Bagwell?"

"How's Bagwell?" Anthony asked Edwina, his voice curt as he concentrated on maneuvering Kate around the debris.

"A bump on his head, but he's back on his feet."

"It's nothing. Can I help?" came a worried male voice.

Anthony had a feeling that the accident had been as much Newton's fault as Bagwell's, but still, the young man had been in control of the reins, and Anthony wasn't inclined to feel charitable toward him just now. "I'll let you know," he said curtly, before turning back to Kate and saying, "Bagwell's fine."

"I can't believe I forgot to ask after them."

"I'm sure your lapse will be pardoned, given the circumstances," Anthony said, edging farther back until he was nearly entirely out of the carriage. Kate was now positioned at the opening, and it would take only one more—rather long and almost certainly painful—tug to get her out.

"Edwina? Edwina?" Kate was calling out. "Are you sure you're not injured?"

Edwina jammed her face into the opening. "I'm fine," she said reassuringly. "Mr. Bagwell was thrown clear, and I was able to—"

Anthony elbowed her out of the way. "Grit your teeth, Kate," he ordered.

"What? I—*Aaaaaaaargh*!"

With one single tug, he freed her completely from the wreckage, both of them landing on the ground, both of them breathing hard. But where Anthony's hyperventilation was from exertion, Kate's was obviously from intense pain.

"Good God!" Edwina nearly yelled. "Look at her leg!"

Anthony glanced over at Kate and felt his stomach drop down clear to his toes. Her lower leg was crooked and bent, and more than obviously broken. He swallowed convulsively, trying not to let his concern show. Legs could be set, but he'd also heard of men who'd lost limbs due to infection and bad medical care.

"What's wrong with my leg?" Kate asked. "It hurts, but—Oh, my God!"

"Best not to look," Anthony said, trying to tip her chin in the other direction.

Her breathing, which was already rapid from trying to control the pain, grew erratic and panicked. "Oh, my God," she gasped. "It hurts. Didn't realize how much it hurt until I saw—"

"Don't look," Anthony ordered.

"Oh, my God. Oh, my God."

"Kate?" Edwina asked in a concerned voice, leaning in. "Are you all right?"

"Look at my leg!" Kate nearly shrieked. "Does it look all right?"

"I was actually speaking of your face. You look a bit green."

But Kate couldn't reply. She was hyperventilating too hard. And then, with Anthony, Edwina, Mr. Bagwell, and Newton all staring down at her, her eyes rolled back in her head, and she fainted.

Three hours later, Kate was installed in her bed, certainly not comfortable but at least in a bit less pain thanks to the laudanum Anthony had forced down her throat the minute they'd gotten home. Her leg had been expertly set by the three surgeons Anthony had summoned (not, as all three surgeons had pointed out, that more than one was needed to set a bone, but Anthony had crossed his arms implacably and stared them all down until they'd shut up), and a physician had stopped by to leave several prescriptions that he swore would hasten the bone-knitting process.

Anthony had fussed over her like a mother hen, second-guessing every move from every doctor until one of them had actually had the audacity to ask him when he'd received his license from the Royal College of Physicians.

Anthony had not been amused.

But after much haranguing, Kate's leg was set and splinted, and she was told to look forward to at least a month of confinement in bed.

"Look forward?" she groaned to Anthony once the last of the surgeons had gone. "How can I look forward to that?"

"You'll be able to catch up on your reading," he suggested.

She let out an impatient exhale through her nose; it was hard to breathe through her mouth while clenching her teeth. "I wasn't aware I was behind on my reading."

If he'd been tempted to laugh, he did a good job of hiding it. "Perhaps you could take up needlework," he suggested.

She just glared at him. As if the prospect of needlework were going to make her feel better.

He sat gingerly on the edge of her bed and patted the back of her hand. "I'll keep you company," he said with an encouraging smile. "I'd already decided to cut back on the time I spent at my club."

Kate sighed. She was tired and cranky and in pain, and she was taking it out on her husband, which really wasn't fair. She turned her hand over so that their palms met and then entwined her fingers through his. "I love you, you know," she said softly.

He squeezed her hands and nodded, the warmth of his eyes on hers saying more than words ever could.

"You told me not to," Kate said.

"I was an ass."

She didn't argue; a quirk of his lips told her that he noticed her lack of contradiction. After a moment of silence, she said, "You were saying some odd things in the park."

Anthony's hand remained in hers, but his body pulled back slightly. "I don't know what you mean," he replied.

"I think you do," she said softly.

Anthony closed his eyes for a moment, then stood, his fingers trailing through her grasp until finally they were no longer touching at all. For so many years he'd been careful to keep his odd convictions to himself. It seemed best. Either people would believe him and then worry or they wouldn't and then think him insane.

Neither option was particularly appealing.

But now, in the heat of one terrified moment, he'd blurted it out to his wife. He couldn't even remember exactly what he'd said. But it had been enough to make her curious. And Kate wasn't the sort to let go of a curiosity. He could practice all the avoidance he wanted, but eventually she'd get it out of him. A more stubborn woman had never been born.

He walked to the window and leaned against the sill, gazing blankly in front of him as if he could actually see the streetscape through the heavy burgundy drapes that had long since been pulled shut. "There is something you should know about me," he whispered.

She didn't say anything, but he knew she'd heard. Maybe it was the sound of her changing her position in bed, maybe it was the sheer electricity in the air. But somehow he knew.

He turned around. It would have been easier to speak his words to the curtains, but she deserved better from him. She was sitting up in bed, her leg propped up on pillows, her eyes wide and filled with a heartbreaking mix of curiosity and concern.

"I don't know how to tell you this without sounding ridiculous," he said.

"Sometimes the easiest way is just to say it," she murmured. She patted an empty spot on the bed. "Do you want to sit beside me?"

He shook his head. Proximity would only make it that much more difficult. "Something happened to me when my father died," he said.

"You were very close to him, weren't you?"

He nodded. "Closer than I'd ever been to anyone, until I met you."

Her eyes glistened. "What happened?"

"It was very unexpected," he said. His voice was flat, as if he were recounting an obscure news item and not the single most disturbing event of his life. "A bee, I told you."

She nodded.

"Who would have thought a bee could kill a man?" Anthony said with a caustic laugh. "It would have been funny if it weren't so tragic."

She didn't say anything, just looked at him with a sympathy that made his heart break.

"I stayed with him throughout the night," he continued, turning slightly so that he would not have to look into her eyes. "He was dead, of course, but I needed a little more time. I just sat beside him and watched his face." Another short burst of angry laughter escaped his lips. "God, what a fool I was. I think I half expected him to open his eyes at any moment."

"I don't think that's foolish," Kate said softly. "I've seen death, too. It's hard to believe that someone is gone when he looks so normal and at peace."

"I don't know when it happened," Anthony said, "but by morning I was sure."

"That he was dead?" she asked.

"No," he said roughly, "that I would be, too."

He waited for her to comment, he waited for her to cry, to do anything, but she just sat there staring at him with no perceptible change of expression, until finally he had to say, "I'm not as great a man as my father was."

"He might choose to disagree," she said quietly.

"Well, he's not here to do that, is he?" Anthony snapped.

Again, she said nothing. Again, he felt like a heel.

He cursed under his breath and pressed his fingers against his temples. His head was starting to throb. He was starting to feel dizzy, and he realized that he couldn't remember the last time he'd eaten. "It's my judgment to make," he said in a low voice. "You didn't know him."

He sagged against a wall with a long, weary exhale, and said, "Just let me tell you. Don't talk, don't interrupt, don't judge. It's hard enough to get it out as it is. Can you do that for me?"

She nodded.

Anthony took a shaky breath. "My father was the greatest man I've ever known. Not a day goes by when I don't realize that I'm not living up to his standards. I knew that he was everything to which I could aspire. I might not ever match his greatness, but if I could come close I'd be satisfied. That's all I ever wanted. Just to come close."

He looked at Kate. He wasn't sure why. Maybe for reassurance, maybe for sympathy. Maybe just to see her face.

"If there was one thing I knew," he whispered, somehow finding the courage to keep his eyes focused on hers, "it was that I would never surpass him. Not even in years."

"What are you trying to tell me?" she whispered.

He shrugged helplessly. "I know it makes no sense. I know I can offer no rational explanation. But since that night when I sat with my father's dead body, I knew I couldn't possibly live any longer than he had."

"I see," she said quietly.

"Do you?" And then, as if a dam had burst, the words poured forth. It all gushed out of him—why he'd been so dead set against marrying for love, the jealousy he'd felt when he'd realized that she'd managed to fight her demons and win.

He watched as she brought one of her hands to her mouth and bit the end of her thumb. He'd seen her do that before, he realized—whenever she was disturbed or deep in thought.

"How old was your father when he died?" she asked.

"Thirty-eight."

"How old are you now?"

He looked at her curiously; she knew his age. But he said it anyway. "Twenty-nine."

"So by your estimation, we have nine years left."

"At most."

"And you truly believe this."

He nodded.

She pursed her lips and let out a long breath through her nose. Finally, after what felt like an endless silence, she looked back up at him with clear, direct eyes, and said, "Well, you're wrong."

Oddly enough, the straightforward tone of her voice was rather reassuring. Anthony even felt one corner of his mouth lift up in the palest of smiles. "You think I'm unaware of how ludicrous it all sounds?"

"I don't think it sounds ludicrous at all. It sounds like a perfectly normal reaction, actually, especially considering how much you adored your father." She lifted her shoulders in a rather self-aware shrug as her head tipped to the side. "But it's still wrong."

Anthony didn't say anything.

"Your father's death was an accident," Kate said. "An accident. A terrible, horrible twist of fate that no one could have predicted."

Anthony shrugged fatalistically. "I'll probably go the same way."

"Oh, for the love of—" Kate managed to bite her tongue a split second before she blasphemed. "Anthony, I could die tomorrow as well. I could have died today when that carriage rolled on top of me."

He paled. "Don't ever remind me of that."

"My mother died when she was my age," Kate reminded him harshly. "Did you ever think of that? By your laws, I should be dead by my next birthday."

"Don't be—"

"Silly?" she finished for him.

Silence reigned for a full minute.

Finally, Anthony said, his voice barely above a whisper, "I don't know if I can get past this."

"You don't have to get past it," Kate said. She caught her lower lip, which had begun to tremble, between her teeth, and then laid her hand on an empty spot on the bed. "Could you come over here so I can hold your hand?"

Anthony responded instantly; the warmth of her touch flooded him, seeping through his body until it caressed his very soul. And in that moment he realized that this was about more than love. This woman made him a better person. He'd been good and strong and kind before, but with her at his side, he was something more.

And together they could do anything.

It almost made him think that forty might not be such an impossible dream.

"You don't have to get past it," she said again, her words blowing softly between them. "To be honest, I don't see how you *could* get completely past it until you turn thirty-nine. But what you *can* do"—she gave his hand a squeeze, and Anthony somehow felt even stronger than he had just moments before—"is refuse to allow it to rule your life."

"I realized that this morning," he whispered, "when I knew I had to tell you I loved you. But somehow now—now I *know* it."

She nodded, and he saw that her eyes were filling with tears. "You have to live each hour as if it's your last," she said, "and each day as if you were immortal. When my father grew ill, he had so many regrets. There were so many things he wished he'd done, he told me. He'd always assumed he had more time. That's something I've always carried with me. Why on earth do you think I decided to attempt the flute at such an advanced age? Everyone told me I was too old, that to be truly good at it I had to have started as a child. But that's not the point, really. I don't need to be truly good. I just need to enjoy it for myself. And I need to know I tried."

Anthony smiled. She was a terrible flutist. Even Newton couldn't bear to listen.

"But the opposite is true as well," Kate added softly. "You can't shun new challenges or hide yourself from love just because you think you might not be here to carry your dreams to completion. In the end, you'll have just as many regrets as did my father."

"I didn't want to love you," Anthony whispered. "It was the one thing I feared above all. I'd grown rather used to my rather odd little outlook on life. Almost comfortable, actually. But love—" His voice caught; the choking sound seemed unmanly, it made him vulnerable. But he didn't care, because this was Kate.

And it didn't matter if she saw his deepest fears, because he knew she'd love him no matter what. It was a sublimely freeing feeling.

"I've seen true love," he continued. "I wasn't the cynical jade society made me out to be. I knew love existed. My mother—my father—" He stopped, sucking in a ragged breath. This was the hardest thing he'd ever done. And yet he knew the words had to be said. He knew, no matter how difficult it was to get them out, that in the end, his heart would soar.

"I was so sure that it was the one thing that could make this . . . this . . . I don't really know what to call it—this knowledge of my own mortality . . ." He raked his hand through his hair, fighting for words. "Love was the only thing that was going to make that unbearable. How could I love someone, truly and deeply, knowing that it was doomed?"

"But it's not doomed," Kate said, squeezing his hand.

"I know. I fell in love with you, and then I knew. Even if I am right, even if I'm fated to live only as long as my father did before me, I'm not doomed." He leaned forward and brushed a feather-light kiss on her lips. "I have you," he whispered, "and I'm not going to waste a single moment we have together."

Kate's lips spread into a smile. "What does that mean?"

"It means that love isn't about being afraid that it will all be snatched away. Love's about finding the one person who makes your heart complete, who makes you a better person than you ever dreamed you could be. It's about looking in the eyes of your wife and knowing, all the way to your bones, that she's simply the best person you've ever known."

"Oh, Anthony," Kate whispered, tears streaming down her cheeks. "That's how I feel about you."

"When I thought you'd died—"

"Don't say it," she choked out. "You don't have to relive that."

"No," he said. "I do. I have to tell you. It was the first time—even after all these years of expecting my own death—that I truly knew what it meant to die. Because with you gone . . . there was nothing left for me to live for. I don't know how my mother did it."

"She had her children," Kate said. "She couldn't leave you."

"I know," he whispered, "but the pain she must have endured . . ."

"I think the human heart must be stronger than we could ever imagine."

Anthony stared at her for a long moment, his eyes locking with hers until he felt they must be one person. Then, with a shaking hand, he cupped the back of her head and leaned down to kiss her. His lips worshiped hers, offering her every ounce of love and devotion and reverence and prayer that he felt in his soul.

"I love you, Kate," he whispered, his lips brushing the words against her mouth. "I love you so much."

She nodded, unable to make a sound.

"And right now I wish . . . I wish . . ."

And then the strangest thing happened. Laughter bubbled up inside of him. He was overtaken by the pure joy of the moment, and it was all he could do not to pick her up and twirl her grandly through the air.

"Anthony?" she asked, sounding equal parts confused and amused.

"Do you know what else love means?" he murmured, planting his hands on either side of her body and letting his nose rest against hers.

She shook her head. "I couldn't possibly even hazard a guess."

"It means," he grumbled, "that I'm finding this broken leg of yours a damned nuisance."

"Not half so much as I, my lord," she said, casting a rueful glance at her splinted leg.

Anthony frowned. "No vigorous exercise for two months, eh?"

"At least."

He grinned, and in that moment he looked every inch the rake she'd once accused him of being. "Clearly," he murmured, "I shall have to be very, very gentle."

"Tonight?" she croaked.

He shook his head. "Even I haven't the talent to express myself with *that* light a touch."

Kate giggled. She couldn't help herself. She loved this man and he loved her and whether he knew it or not, they were going to grow very, very old together. It was enough to make a girl—even a girl with a broken leg—positively giddy.

"Are you laughing at me?" he queried, one of his brows arching arrogantly as he slid his body into place next to her.

"I wouldn't dream of it."

"Good. Because I have some very important things to tell you."

"Really?"

He nodded gravely. "I may not be able to show you how much I love you this eve, but I can tell you."

"I should never tire of hearing it," she murmured.

"Good. Because when I'm done telling you, I'm going to tell you how I'd like to *show* you."

"Anthony!" she squeaked.

"I think I'd start with your earlobe," he mused. "Yes, definitely the earlobe. I'd kiss it, and then nibble it, and then . . ."

Kate gasped. And then she squirmed. And then she fell in love with him all over again.

And as he whispered sweet nothings in her ear, she had the strangest sensation, almost as if she could see her entire future laid out before her. Each day was richer and fuller than the last, and every day she was falling, falling, falling . . .

Was it possible to fall in love with the same man over and over again, every single day?

Kate sighed as she settled into the pillows, letting his wicked words wash over her.

By God, she was going to try.

# *Epilogue*

*Lord Bridgerton celebrated his birthday—This Author believes that it was his thirty-ninth—at home with his family.*

*This Author was not invited.*

*Nonetheless, details of the fête have reached This Author's always attentive ears, and it sounds to have been a most amusing party. The day began with a short concert: Lord Bridgerton on the trumpet and Lady Bridgerton on the flute. Mrs. Bagwell (Lady Bridgerton's sister) apparently offered to mediate on the pianoforte, but her offer was refused.*

*According to the dowager viscountess, a more discordant concert has never been performed, and we are told that eventually young Miles Bridgerton stood atop his chair and begged his parents to cease.*

*We are also told that no one scolded the boy for his rudeness, but rather just heaved huge sighs of relief when Lord and Lady Bridgerton laid down their instruments.*

*Lady Whistledown's Society Papers,*
17 September 1823

"She must have a spy in the family," Anthony said to Kate, shaking his head.

Kate laughed as she brushed her hair, readying herself for bed. "She didn't realize that today is your birthday, not yesterday."

"A trifling matter," he grumbled. "She must have a spy. There's no other explanation."

"She did get everything else right," Kate couldn't help noting. "I tell you, I've always admired that woman."

"We weren't that bad," Anthony protested.

"We were dreadful." She set the brush down and walked to his side. "We're always dreadful. But at least we try."

Anthony wound his arms around his wife's waist and settled his chin on the top of her head. There was little that brought him more peace than simply holding her in his arms. He didn't know how any man survived without a woman to love.

"It's almost midnight," Kate murmured. "Your birthday is almost over."

Anthony nodded. Thirty-nine. He'd never thought he'd see the day.

No, that wasn't true. Since the moment he'd let Kate into his heart, his fears had been slowly melting away. But still, it was nice to be thirty-nine. Settling. He'd spent a goodly portion of the day in his study, staring up at his father's portrait. And he'd found himself talking. For hours on end, he'd talked to his father. He told him of his three children, of his siblings' marriages and their children. He told him of his mother, and how she'd recently taken up painting with oils, and that she was actually quite good. And he told him of Kate, and how she'd freed his soul, and how he loved her so damn much.

It was, Anthony realized, what his father had always wanted or him.

The clock on the mantel began to chime, and neither Anthony nor Kate spoke until the twelfth bell rang.

"That's it, then," Kate whispered.

He nodded. "Let's go to bed."

She moved away, and he could see that she was smiling. "That's how you want to celebrate?"

He took her hand and raised it to his lips. "I can think of no better way. Can you?"

Kate shook her head, then giggled as she ran for the bed. "Did you read what else she wrote in her column?"

"That Whistledown woman?"

She nodded.

Anthony planted his hands on either side of his wife and leered down at her. "Was it about us?"

Kate shook her head.

"Then I don't care."

"It was about Colin."

Anthony let out a little sigh. "She does seem to write about Colin a great deal."

"Maybe she has a *tendre* for him," Kate suggested.

"Lady Whistledown?" Anthony rolled his eyes. "That old biddy?"

"She might not be old."

Anthony snorted derisively. "She's a wrinkled old crone and you know it."

"I don't know," Kate said, scooting out of his grasp and crawling under the covers. "I think she might be young."

"And *I* think," Anthony announced, "that I don't much want to talk about Lady Whistledown just now."

Kate smiled. "You don't?"

He slid into place next to her, his fingers settling around the curve of her hip. "I have much better things to do."

"You do?"

"Much." His lips found her ear. "Much, much, *much* better."

And in a small, elegantly furnished chamber, not so very far from Bridgerton House, a woman—no longer in the first blush of youth, but certainly not wrinkled and old—sat at her desk with a quill and a pot of ink and pulled out a piece of paper.

Stretching her neck from side to side, she set her quill to paper and wrote:

*Lady Whistledown's Society Papers, 19 September, 1823 Ah, Gentle Reader, it has come to This Author's attention . . .*

# Author's Note

Anthony's reaction to his father's untimely death is a very common one, especially among men. (To a much lesser degree, women whose mothers die young react in a similar fashion.) Men whose fathers die at a very young age are very often gripped by a certainty that they, too, will suffer the same fate. Such men usually know their fears are irrational, but it is nearly impossible to get past these fears until one has reached (and passed) the age of one's father's death.

Since my readers are almost exclusively women, and Anthony's issue is such (to use a very modern phrase) a "guy thing," I worried that you might not be able to relate to his problem. As a writer of romance, I constantly find myself walking a fine line between making my heroes utterly and completely heroic, and making them real. With Anthony, I hope I struck a balance. It's easy to scowl at a book and grumble, "Get over it already!" but the truth is, for most men, it's not so easy to "get over" the sudden and premature loss of a beloved father.

Sharp-eyed readers will note that the bee sting that killed Edmund Bridgerton was actually the second sting he'd received in his life. This is medically accurate; bee sting allergies generally don't manifest themselves until the second sting. Since Anthony has only been stung once in his life, it's impossible to know whether or not he's allergic. As the author of this book, however, I'd like to think I have a certain creative control over the medical conditions of my characters, so I've decided that Anthony has no allergies of any kind, and furthermore will live to the ripe old age of 92.

My very best wishes,

*Dear Reader,*

*Have you ever wondered what happened to your favorite characters after you closed the final page? Wanted just a little bit more of a favorite novel? I have, and if the questions from my readers are any indication, I'm not the only one. So after countless requests from Bridgerton fans, I decided to try something a little different, and I wrote a "2nd Epilogue" for each of the novels. These are the stories that come* after *the stories.*

*At first, the Bridgerton 2nd Epilogues were available exclusively online; later they were published (along with a novella about Violet Bridgerton) in a collection called* The Bridgertons: Happily Ever After. *Now, for the first time, each 2nd Epilogue is being included with the novel it follows. I hope you enjoy Anthony and Kate as they continue their journey.*

*Warmly,*
*Julia Quinn*

# The Viscount Who Loved Me: The 2nd Epilogue

*Two days prior . . .*

Kate stomped across the lawn, glancing over her shoulder to make sure that her husband was not following her. Fifteen years of marriage had taught her a thing or two, and she knew that he would be watching her every move.

But she was clever. And she was determined. And she knew that for a pound, Anthony's valet could feign the most marvelous sartorial disaster. Something involving jam on the iron, or perhaps an infestation in the wardrobe—spiders, mice, it really didn't matter which—Kate was more than happy to leave the details up to the valet as long as Anthony was suitably distracted long enough for her to make her escape.

"It is mine, all mine," she chortled, in much the same tones she'd used during the previous month's Bridgerton family production of *Macbeth*. Her eldest son had casted the roles; she had been named First Witch.

Kate had pretended not to notice when Anthony had rewarded him with a new horse.

He'd pay now. His shirts would be stained pink with raspberry jam, and she—

She was smiling so hard she was laughing.

"Mine mine mine *miiiiiiiiiiine*," she sang, wrenching open the door to the shed on the last syllable, which just so happened to be the deep, serious note of Beethoven's Fifth.

"Mine mine mine *miiiiiiiiiine*."

She would have it. It was hers. She could practically taste it. She would have tasted it, even, if this would somehow have bonded it to her side. She had no taste for wood, of course, but this was no ordinary implement of destruction. This was . . .

The mallet of death.

"Mine mine mine *mine* mine mine mine *mine* mine mine mine *miiiiiiiiiine*," she continued, moving into the hoppy little section that followed the familiar refrain.

She could barely contain herself as she tossed a blanket aside. The Pall Mall set would be resting in the corner, as it always was, and in just a moment—

"Looking for this?"

Kate whirled around. There was Anthony, standing in the doorway, smiling diabolically as he spun the black Pall Mall mallet in his hands.

His shirt was blindingly white.

"You . . . You . . ."

One of his brows lifted dangerously. "You never were terribly skilled at vocabulary retrieval when crossed."

"How did you . . . How did you . . ."

He leaned forward, his eyes narrowing. "I paid him *five* pounds."

"You gave Milton five pounds?" Good Lord, that was practically his annual salary.

"It's a deuced sight cheaper than replacing all of my shirts," he said with a scowl. "Raspberry jam. Really. Have you no thought toward economies?"

Kate stared longingly at the mallet.

"Game's in three days," Anthony said with a pleased sigh, "and I have already won."

Kate didn't contradict him. The other Bridgertons might think the annual Pall Mall rematch began and ended in a day, but she and Anthony knew better.

She'd beaten him to the mallet for three years running. She was damned if he was going to get the better of her this time.

"Give up now, dear wife," Anthony taunted. "Admit defeat, and we shall all be happier."

Kate sighed softly, almost as if she acquiesced.

Anthony's eyes narrowed.

Kate idly touched her fingers to the neckline of her frock.

Anthony's eyes widened.

"It's hot in here, don't you think?" she asked, her voice soft, and sweet, and terribly breathless.

"You little minx," he murmured.

She slid the fabric from her shoulders. She wasn't wearing anything underneath.

"No buttons?" he whispered.

She shook her head. She wasn't stupid. Even the best laid plans could find their way awry. One always had to dress for the occasion. There was still a slight chill in the air, and she felt her nipples tighten into insulted little buds.

Kate shivered, then tried to hide it with a breathy pant, as if she were desperately aroused.

Which she might have been, had she not been single-mindedly

focused on trying *not* to focus on the mallet in her husband's hand.

Not to mention the chill.

"Lovely," Anthony murmured, reaching out and stroking the side of her breast.

Kate made a mewling sound. He could never resist that.

Anthony smiled slowly, then moved his hand forward, until he could roll her nipple between his fingers.

Kate let out a gasp, and her eyes flew to his. He looked—not calculating exactly, but still, very much in control. And it occurred to her—he knew precisely what *she* could never resist.

"Ah, wife," he murmured, cupping her breast from the bottom, and lifting it higher until it sat plump in his hand.

He smiled.

Kate stopped breathing.

He bent forward and took the bud in his mouth.

*"Oh!"* She wasn't faking anything now.

He repeated his torture on the other side.

Then he stepped back.

Back.

Kate stood still, panting.

"Ah, to have a painting of this," he said. "I would hang it in my office."

Kate's mouth fell open.

He held up the mallet in triumph. "Goodbye, dear wife." He exited the shed, then poked his head back 'round the corner. "Try not to catch a chill. You'd hate to miss the rematch, wouldn't you?"

He was lucky, Kate later reflected, that she hadn't thought to grab one of the Pall Mall balls when she'd been rummaging for the set. Although on second thought, his head was probably far too hard for her to have made a dent.

*One day prior*

There were few moments, Anthony decided, quite so delicious as the utter and complete besting of one's wife. It depended upon the wife, of course, but as he had chosen to wed a woman of superb intellect and wit, his moments, he was sure, were more delicious than most.

He savored this over tea in his office, sighing with pleasure as he gazed upon the black mallet, which lay across his desk like a prized trophy. It looked gorgeous, gleaming in the morning light—or at least gleaming where it wasn't scuffed and battered from decades of rough play.

No matter. Anthony loved every last dent and scratch. Perhaps it was childish, infantile even, but he *adored* it.

Mostly he adored that he had it in his possession, but he was still rather fond of it. When he was able to forget that he had brilliantly snatched it from under Kate's nose, he actually recalled that it marked something else—

The day he'd fallen in love.

Not that he'd realized it at the time. Nor had Kate, he imagined, but he was certain that that was the day they had been fated to be together—the day of the infamous Pall Mall match.

She left him with the pink mallet. She had sent his ball into the lake.

God, what a woman.

It had been a most excellent fifteen years.

He smiled contentedly, then let his gaze drop to the black mallet again. Every year they replayed the match. All of the original players—Anthony, Kate, his brother Colin, his sister Daphne and her husband Simon, and Kate's sister Edwina—they all trooped dutifully to Aubrey Hall each spring and took up their places on the ever-shifting course. Some agreed to attend with zeal and some with mere amusement, but they were all there, every year.

And this year—

Anthony chortled with glee. He had the mallet and Kate did not.

Life was good. Life was very very good.

"Kaaaaaaaaaaate!"

Kate looked up from her book.

"Kaaaaaaaaaaate!"

She tried to gauge his distance. After fifteen years of hearing her name bellowed in much the same fashion, she'd become quite proficient at calculating the time between the first roar and her husband's appearance.

It was not as straightforward a calculation as it might seem. There was her location to consider—was she upstairs or down, visible from the doorway, et cetera, et cetera.

Then one had to add in the children. Were they at home? Possibly in his way? They would slow him down, certainly, perhaps even by a full minute, and—

*"You!"*

Kate blinked with surprise. Anthony was in the doorway, panting with exertion and glaring at her with a surprising degree of venom.

"Where is it?" he demanded.

Well, perhaps not so surprising.

She blinked impassively. "Would you like to sit down?" she inquired. "You look somewhat overexerted."

"Kate . . ."

"You're not as young as you used to be," she said with a sigh.

"Kate . . ." The volume was rising.

"I can ring for tea," she said sweetly.

"It was locked," he growled. "My office was locked."

"Was it?" she murmured.

"I have the only key."

"Do you?"

His eyes widened. "What have you done?"

She flipped a page, even though she wasn't looking at the print. "When?"

"What do you mean, when?"

"I mean . . ." She paused, because this was not a moment to let pass without proper internal celebration. "When? This morning? Or last month?"

It took him a moment. No more than a second or two, but it was just long enough for Kate to watch his expression slide from confusion to suspicion to outrage.

It was glorious. Enchanting. Delicious. She'd have cackled with it, but that would only encourage another month of double-double-toil-and-trouble jokes, and she'd only just got him to cease.

"You made a key to my office?"

"I am your wife," she said, glancing at her fingernails. "There should be no secrets between us, don't you think?"

"You made a key?"

"You wouldn't wish for me to keep secrets, would you?"

His fingers gripped the door frame until his knuckles turned white. "Stop looking like you're enjoying this," he ground out.

"Ah, but that would be a lie, and it's a sin to lie to one's husband."

Strange choking sounds began to emanate from his throat.

Kate smiled. "Didn't I pledge honesty at some point?"

"That was *obedience*," he growled.

"Obedience? Surely not."

"Where is it?"

She shrugged. "Not telling."

"Kate!"

She slid into a singsong. "Not *tellllllllling*."

"Woman . . ." He moved forward. Dangerously.

Kate swallowed. There was a small, rather tiny actually but nonetheless very real chance that she might have gone just a wee bit too far.

"I will tie you to the bed," he warned.

"Yeeeessss," she said, acknowledging his point as she gauged the distance to the door. "But I might not *mind* it precisely."

His eyes flared, not quite with desire—he was still too focused on the Pall Mall mallet for that—but she rather thought she saw a flash of . . . *interest* there.

"Tie you up, you say," he murmured, moving forward, "and you'd like it, eh?"

Kate caught his meaning and gasped. "You wouldn't!"

"Oh, I would."

He was aiming for a repeat performance. He was going to tie her up and *leave* her there while he searched for the mallet.

Not if she had anything to say about it.

Kate scrambled over the arm of her chair and then scooted behind it. Always good to have a physical barrier in situations like these.

"Oh, Kaaaaate," he taunted, moving toward her.

"It's mine," she declared. "It was mine fifteen years ago, and it's still mine."

"It was mine before it was yours."

"But you married me!"

"And this makes it yours?"

She said nothing, just locked her eyes with his. She was breathless, panting, caught up in the rush of the moment.

And then, fast as lightning, he jumped forward, reaching over the chair, catching hold of her shoulder for a brief moment before she squirmed away.

"You will never find it," she practically shrieked, scooting behind the sofa.

"Don't think you'll escape now," he warned, doing a sideways sort of maneuver that put him between her and the door.

She eyed the window.

"The fall would kill you," he said.

"Oh, for the love of God," came a voice from the doorway.

Kate and Anthony turned. Anthony's brother Colin was standing there, regarding them both with an air of disgust.

"Colin," Anthony said tightly. "How nice to see you."

Colin merely quirked a brow. "I suppose you're looking for *this*."

Kate gasped. He was holding the black mallet. "How did you—"

Colin stroked the blunt, cylindrical end almost lovingly. "I can only speak for myself, of course," he said with a happy sigh, "but as far as I'm concerned, I've already won."

*Game day*

"I fail to comprehend," Anthony's sister Daphne remarked, "why you get to set up the course."

"Because I bloody well own the lawn," he bit off. He held his hand up to shield his eyes from the sun as he inspected his work. He'd done a brilliant job this time, if he did say so himself. It was diabolical.

Pure genius.

"Any chance you might be capable of refraining from profanity in the company of ladies?" This, from Daphne's husband, Simon, the Duke of Hastings.

"She's no lady," Anthony grumbled. "She's my sister."

"She's *my* wife."

Anthony smirked. "She was my sister first."

Simon turned to Kate, who was tapping her mallet—green, which she'd declared herself happy with, but Anthony knew better—against the grass.

"How," he asked, "do you tolerate him?"

She shrugged. "It's a talent few possess."

Colin stepped up, clutching the black mallet like the Holy Grail. "Shall we begin?" he asked grandly.

Simon's lips parted with surprise. "The mallet of death?"

"I'm very clever," Colin confirmed.

"He bribed the housemaid," Kate grumbled.

"You bribed my valet," Anthony pointed out.

"So did you!"

"I bribed no one," Simon said, to no one in particular.

Daphne patted his arm condescendingly. "You were not born to this family."

"Neither was she," he returned, motioning to Kate.

Daphne pondered that. "She is an aberration," she finally concluded.

"An aberration?" Kate demanded.

"It's the highest of compliments," Daphne informed her. She paused, then added, "In this context." She then turned to Colin. "How much?"

"How much what?"

"How much did you give the housemaid?"

He shrugged. "Ten pounds."

"Ten *pounds*?" Daphne nearly shrieked.

"Are you mad?" Anthony demanded.

"You gave the valet five," Kate reminded him.

"I hope it wasn't one of the *good* housemaids," Anthony grumbled, "for she'll surely quit by the day's end with that sort of money in her pocket."

"All of the housemaids are good," Kate said, with some irritation.

"Ten pounds," Daphne repeated, shaking her head. "I'm going to tell your wife."

"Go ahead," Colin said indifferently as he nodded toward the hill sloping down to the Pall Mall course. "She's right there."

Daphne looked up. "Penelope's here?"

"Penelope's here?" Anthony barked. "Why?"

"She's my wife," Colin returned.

"She's never attended before."

"She wanted to see me win," Colin shot back, rewarding his brother with a sickly stretch of a smile.

Anthony resisted the urge to throttle him. Barely. "And how do you know you're going to win?"

Colin waved the black mallet before him. "I already have."

"Good day, all," Penelope said, ambling down to the gathering.

"No cheering," Anthony warned her.

Penelope blinked in confusion. "I beg your pardon?"

"And under no circumstances," he continued, because really, someone had to make sure the game retained some integrity, "may you come within ten paces of your husband."

Penelope looked at Colin, bobbed her head nine times as she estimated the steps between them, and took a step back.

"There will be no cheating," Anthony warned.

"At least no *new* types of cheating," Simon added. "Previously established cheating techniques are permissible."

"May I speak with my husband during the course of play?" Penelope inquired mildly.

"No!" A resounding chorus, three voices strong.

"You'll notice," Simon said to her, "that I made no objection."

"As I said," Daphne said, brushing by him on her way to inspect a wicket, "you were not born of this family."

"Where is Edwina?" Colin asked briskly, squinting up toward the house.

"She'll be down shortly," Kate replied. "She was finishing breakfast."

"She is delaying the play."

Kate turned to Daphne. "My sister does not share our devotion to the game."

"She thinks we're all mad?" Daphne asked.

"Quite."

"Well, she is sweet to come down every year," Daphne said.

"It's tradition," Anthony barked. He'd managed to get hold of the orange mallet and was swinging it against an imaginary ball, narrowing his eyes as he rehearsed his aim.

"He hasn't been practicing the course, has he?" Colin demanded.

"How could he?" Simon asked. "He only just set it up this morning. We all watched him."

Colin ignored him and turned to Kate. "Has he made any strange nocturnal disappearances recently?"

She gaped at him. "You think he's been sneaking out to play Pall Mall by the light of the moon?"

"I wouldn't put it past him," Colin grumbled.

"Neither would I," Kate replied, "but I assure you, he has been sleeping in his own bed."

"It's not a matter of *beds*," Colin informed her. "It's a matter of competition."

"This can't be an appropriate conversation in front of a lady," Simon said, but it was clear he was enjoying himself.

Anthony shot Colin an irritated look, then sent one in Simon's direction for good measure. The conversation was growing ludicrous, and it was well past time they began the match. "Where *is* Edwina?" he demanded.

"I see her coming down the hill," Kate replied.

He looked up to see Edwina Bagwell, Kate's younger sister, trudging down the slope. She'd never been much for outdoor pursuits, and he could well imagine her sighing and rolling her eyes.

"Pink for me this year," Daphne declared, plucking one of the remaining mallets from the stack. "I am feeling feminine and delicate." She gave her brothers an arch look. "Deceptively so."

Simon reached behind her and selected the yellow mallet. "Blue for Edwina, of course."

"Edwina always gets blue," Kate said to Penelope.

"Why?"

Kate paused. "I don't know."

"What about purple?" Penelope asked.

"Oh, we never use *that*."

"Why?"

Kate paused again. "I don't know."

"Tradition," Anthony put in.

"Then why do the rest of you switch colors every year?" Penelope persisted.

Anthony turned to his brother. "Does she always ask so many questions?"

"Always."

He turned back to Penelope and said, "We like it this way."

"I'm here!" Edwina called out cheerfully as she approached the rest of the players. "Oh, blue again. How thoughtful." She picked up her equipment, then turned to Anthony. "Shall we play?"

He gave a nod, then turned to Simon. "You're first, Hastings."

"As always," he murmured, and he dropped his ball into the starting position. "Stand back," he warned, even though no one was within swinging distance. He drew his mallet back and then brought it forward with a magnificent crack. The ball went sailing across the lawn, straight and true, landing mere yards from the next wicket.

"Oh, well-done!" Penelope cheered, clapping her hands.

"I said no cheering," Anthony grumbled. Couldn't anyone follow instructions these days?

"Even for Simon?" Penelope returned. "I thought it was just Colin."

Anthony set his ball down carefully. "It's distracting."

"As if the rest of us aren't distracting," Colin commented. "Cheer away, darling."

But she held silent as Anthony took aim. His swing was even more powerful than the duke's, and his ball rolled even farther.

"Hmmm, bad luck there," Kate said.

Anthony turned on her suspiciously. "What do you mean? It was a brilliant swing."

"Well, yes, but—"

"Out of my way," Colin ordered, marching to the starting position.

Anthony locked eyes with his wife. "What do you *mean*?"

"Nothing," she said offhandedly, "just that it's a trifle muddy right there."

"Muddy?" Anthony looked toward his ball, then back to his wife, then back to the ball. "It hasn't rained for days."

"Hmmm, no."

He looked back to his wife. His maddening, diabolical, and soon-to-be-locked-in-a-dungeon wife. "How did it get muddy?"

"Well, perhaps not *muddy* . . ."

"Not muddy," he repeated, with far more patience than she deserved.

"Puddle-ish might be more appropriate."

Words failed him.

"Puddly?" She scrunched her face a touch. "How does one make an adjective out of a puddle?"

He took a step in her direction. She darted behind Daphne.

"What is happening?" Daphne asked, twisting about.

Kate poked her head out and smiled triumphantly. "I do believe he's going to kill me."

"With so many witnesses?" Simon asked.

"How," Anthony demanded, "did a puddle form in the midst of the driest spring of my recollection?"

Kate shot him another one of her annoying grins. "I spilled my tea."

"An entire puddle's worth?"

She shrugged. "I was cold."

"Cold."

"And thirsty."

"And apparently clumsy, as well," Simon put in.

Anthony glared at him.

"Well, if you are going to kill her," Simon said, "would you mind waiting until my wife is out from between you?" He turned to Kate. "How did you know where to put the puddle?"

"He's very predictable," she replied.

Anthony stretched out his fingers and measured her throat.

"Every year," she said, smiling straight at him. "You always put the first wicket in the same place, and you always hit the ball precisely the same way."

Colin chose that moment to return. "Your play, Kate."

She darted out from behind Daphne and scooted toward the

starting pole. "All's fair, dear husband," she called out gaily. And then she bent forward, aimed, and sent the green ball flying.

Straight into the puddle.

Anthony sighed happily. There was justice in this world, after all.

Thirty minutes later Kate was waiting by her ball near the third wicket.

"Pity about the mud," Colin said, strolling past.

She glared at him.

Daphne passed by a moment later. "You've a bit in . . ." She motioned to her hair. "Yes, there," she added, when Kate brushed furiously against her temple. "Although there is a bit more, well . . ." She cleared her throat. "Er, everywhere."

Kate glared at her.

Simon stepped up to join them. Good God, did everyone need to pass by the third wicket on their way to the sixth?

"You've a bit of mud," he said helpfully.

Kate's fingers wrapped more tightly around her mallet. His head was so very, very close.

"But at least it's mixed with tea," he added.

"What has that to do with anything?" Daphne asked.

"I'm not certain," Kate heard him say as he and Daphne took their leave toward wicket number five, "but it seemed as if I ought to say *some*thing."

Kate counted to ten in her head, and then sure enough, Edwina happened across her, Penelope trailing three steps behind. The pair had become something of a team, with Edwina doing all the swinging and Penelope consulting on strategy.

"Oh, Kate," Edwina said with a pitying sigh.

"Don't say it," Kate growled.

"You did make the puddle," Edwina pointed out.

"Whose sister *are* you?" Kate demanded.

Edwina gave her an arch smile. "Sisterly devotion does not obscure my sense of fair play."

"This is Pall Mall. There *is* no fair play."

"Apparently not," Penelope remarked.

"Ten paces," Kate warned.

"From Colin, not from you," Penelope returned. "Although I do believe I shall remain at least a mallet's length away at all times."

"Shall we go?" Edwina inquired. She turned to Kate. "We just finished with the fourth wicket."

"And you needed to take the long way 'round?" Kate muttered.

"It seemed only sporting to pay you a visit," Edwina demurred.

She and Penelope turned to walk away, and then Kate blurted it out. She couldn't help herself:

"Where is Anthony?"

Edwina and Penelope turned. "Do you really want to know?" Penelope asked.

Kate forced herself to nod.

"On the last wicket, I'm afraid," Penelope replied.

"Before or after?" Kate ground out.

"I beg your pardon?"

"Is he before the wicket or after it?" she repeated impatiently. And then, when Penelope did not answer instantly she added, "Has he gone through the bloody thing yet?"

Penelope blinked with surprise. "Er, no. He has about two more strokes, I should think. Perhaps three."

Kate watched them depart through narrowed eyes. She wasn't going to win—there was no chance of that now. But if she couldn't win, then by God, neither would Anthony. He deserved no glory this day, not after tripping her and sending her tumbling into the mud puddle.

Oh, he'd claimed it was an accident, but Kate found it highly suspicious that his ball had gone spluttering out of the puddle at the exact moment she'd stepped forward to reach her own ball. She'd had to do a little hop to avoid it and was congratulating herself on her near miss when Anthony had swung around with a patently false "I say, are you all right?"

His mallet had swung with him, conveniently at ankle level. Kate had not been able to outhop that one, and she'd gone flying into the mud.

Face down.

And then Anthony had had the gall to offer her a handkerchief.

She was going to kill him.

Kill.

Kill kill kill.

But first she was going to make sure he didn't win.

Anthony was smiling broadly—whistling, even—as he waited his turn. It was taking a ridiculously long amount of time to get back 'round to him, what with Kate so far behind that someone had to dash back to let her know when it was her turn, not to mention Edwina, who never seemed to understand the virtue of speedy play. It had been bad enough the last fourteen years, with her ambling along as if she had all day, but now she had Penelope, who would not allow her to hit the ball without her analysis and advice.

But for once, Anthony didn't mind. He was in the lead, so far so that no one could possibly catch up. And just to make his victory all the sweeter, Kate was in last place.

So far so that she could not hope to overtake anyone.

It almost made up for the fact that Colin had snatched the mallet of death.

He turned toward the last wicket. He needed one stroke to get his ball at the ready, and one more to push it through. After that, he needed only to steer it to the final pole and end the game with a tap.

Child's play.

He glanced back over his shoulder. He could see Daphne standing by the old oak tree. She was at the crest of a hill, and thus could see down where he could not.

"Whose turn is it?" he called out.

She craned her neck as she watched the others playing down the hill. "Colin's, I believe," she said, twisting back around, "which means Kate is next."

He smiled at that.

He'd set the course up a little differently this year, in something of a circular fashion. The players had to follow a twisting pattern, which meant that as the crow flew, he was actually closer to Kate than he was to the others. In fact, he need only move about ten yards to the south, and he'd be able to watch her as she pushed on toward the fourth wicket.

Or was it merely the third?

Either way, he wasn't going to miss it.

So, with a grin on his face, he jogged over. Should he call out? It would irritate her more if he called out.

But that would be cruel. And on the other hand—

CRACK!

Anthony looked up from his ponderings just in time to see the green ball hurtling in his direction.

What the devil?

Kate let out a triumphant cackle, picked up her skirts, and began running over.

"What in God's name are you doing?" Anthony demanded. "The

fourth wicket is *that* way." He jabbed his finger in the appropriate direction even though he knew she knew where it was.

"I'm only on the third wicket," she said archly, "and anyway, I've given up on winning. It's hopeless at this point, don't you think?"

Anthony looked at her, then he looked at his ball, resting peacefully near the last wicket.

Then he looked at her again.

"Oh no you don't," he growled.

She smiled slowly.

Deviously.

Like a witch.

"Watch me," she said.

Just then Colin came dashing over the rise. "Your turn, Anthony!"

"How is that possible?" he demanded. "Kate just went, so there is Daphne, Edwina, and Simon between."

"We went very quickly," Simon said, striding forward. "We certainly don't want to miss *this*."

"Oh, for God's sake," he muttered, watching as the rest of them hurried near. He stalked over to his ball, narrowing his eyes as he prepared his aim.

"Be careful of the tree root!" Penelope called out.

Anthony grit his teeth.

"It wasn't cheering," she said, her face magnificently bland. "Surely a warning doesn't qualify as cheer—"

"Shut *up*," Anthony ground out.

"We all have our place in this game," she said, lips twitching.

Anthony turned around. "Colin!" he barked. "If you don't wish to find yourself a widower, kindly muzzle your wife."

Colin walked over to Penelope. "I love you," he said, kissing her on the cheek.

"And I—"

"Stop it!" Anthony exploded. When all eyes turned to him, he added, rather in a grunt, "I'm trying to concentrate."

Kate danced in a little closer.

"Get away from me, woman."

"I just want to *see*," she said. "I've hardly had the chance to *see* anything this game, being so far behind the entire time."

He narrowed his eyes. "I *might* be responsible for the mud, and please note my emphasis on the word *might*, which does not imply any sort of confirmation on my part."

He paused, quite pointedly ignoring the rest of the gathering, all of whom were gaping at him.

"However," he continued, "I fail to see how your position in last place is *my* responsibility."

"The mud made my hands slippery," she ground out. "I could not properly grip the mallet."

Off to the side, Colin winced. "Weak, I'm afraid, Kate. I'll have to grant this point to Anthony, much as it pains me."

"Fine," she said, after tossing Colin a withering glare. "It's no one's fault but my own. However."

And then she said nothing.

"Er, however what?" Edwina finally inquired.

Kate could have been a queen with her scepter as she stood there, all covered with mud. "However," she continued regally, "I don't have to like it. And this being Pall Mall, and we being Bridgertons, I don't have to play fair."

Anthony shook his head and bent back down to make his aim.

"She has a point this time," Colin said, irritating sod that he was. "Good sportsmanship has never been valued highly in this game."

"Be quiet," Anthony grunted.

"In fact," Colin continued, "one could make the argument that—"

"I said be quiet."

"—the opposite is true, and that *bad* sportsmanship—"

"Shut *up*, Colin."

"—is in fact to be lauded, and—"

Anthony decided to give up and take a swing. At this rate they'd be standing there until Michaelmas. Colin was never going to stop talking, not when he thought he had a chance of irritating his brother.

Anthony forced himself to hear nothing but the wind. Or at least he tried.

He aimed.

He drew back.

Crack!

Not too hard, not too hard.

The ball rolled forward, unfortunately not quite far enough. He was not going to make it through the last wicket on his next try. At least not without intervention divine enough to send his ball around a fist-sized stone.

"Colin, you're next," Daphne said, but he was already dashing back to his ball. He gave it a haphazard tap, then yelled out, "Kate!"

She stepped forward, blinking as she assessed the lay of the land. Her ball was about a foot away from his. The stone, however, was on the other side, meaning that if she attempted to sabotage him, she couldn't send him very far—surely the stone would stop the ball.

"An interesting dilemma," Anthony murmured.

Kate circled around the balls. "It would be a romantic gesture," she mused, "if I allowed you to win."

"Oh, it's not a question of your *allowing*," he taunted.

"Wrong answer," she said, and she aimed.

Anthony narrowed his eyes. What was she doing?

Kate hit the ball with a fair bit of force, aiming not squarely at his ball but at the left side. Her ball slammed into his, sending it spiraling off to the right. Because of the angle, she couldn't send it as far as she might have with a direct shot, but she did manage to get it right to the top of the hill.

Right to the top.

Right to the top.

And then down it.

Kate let out a whoop of delight that would not have been out of place on a battlefield.

"You'll pay," Anthony said.

She was too busy jumping up and down to pay him any attention.

"Who do you suppose will win now?" Penelope asked.

"Do you know," Anthony said quietly, "I don't care." And then he walked over to the green ball and took aim.

"Hold up, it's not your turn!" Edwina called out.

"And it's not your ball," Penelope added.

"Is that so?" he murmured, and then let fly, smashing his mallet into Kate's ball and sending it hurtling across the lawn, down the shallower slope, and into the lake.

Kate let out a huff of outrage. "That wasn't very sporting of you!"

He gave her a maddening grin. "All's fair and all that, wife."

"You will fish it out," she retorted.

"You're the one who needs a bath."

Daphne let out a chuckle, and then said, "I think it must be my turn. Shall we continue?"

She departed, Simon, Edwina, and Penelope in her wake.

"Colin!" Daphne barked.

"Oh, very well," he grumbled, and he trailed along after.

Kate looked up at her husband, her lips beginning to twitch. "Well," she said, scratching at a spot on her ear that was particularly caked with mud, "I suppose that's the end of the match for us."

"I'd say."

"Brilliant job this year."

"You as well," he added, smiling down at her. "The puddle was inspired."

"I thought so," she said, with no modesty whatsoever. "And, well, about the mud . . ."

"It was not *quite* on purpose," he murmured.

"I should have done the same," she allowed.

"Yes, I know."

"I am filthy," she said, looking down at herself.

"The lake's right there," he said.

"It's so cold."

"A bath, then?"

She smiled seductively. "You'll join me?"

"But of course."

He held out his arm and together they began to stroll back toward the house.

"Should we have told them we forfeit?" Kate asked.

"No."

"Colin's going to try to steal the black mallet, you know."

He looked at her with interest. "You think he'll attempt to remove it from Aubrey Hall?"

"Wouldn't you?"

"Absolutely," he replied, with great emphasis. "We shall have to join forces."